The Shapes of Fiction

Open and Closed

The Shapes of Fiction
Open and Closed

Beverly Gross
Queens College, The City University of New York

Richard Giannone
Fordham University

HOLT, RINEHART AND WINSTON, INC.
New York Chicago San Francisco
Atlanta Dallas Montreal Toronto

Library of Congress Catalog Card Number: 70–127096
SBN: 03–081389–1
Printed in the United States of America
1 2 3 4 40 9 8 7 6 5 4 3 2 1

Preface

The classical idea of narrative form is that a story has a beginning, a middle, and an end. This is a useful description for some works, but not for all. Much of modern fiction—indeed the fiction that is most distinctly "modern"—does not come to any resolving end. Does this mean that it lacks form?

The aim of *The Shapes of Fiction: Open and Closed* is to help the reader deal with the question of what form is and what it does. Most of the stories in this collection are departures from the classical idea of form. Their departures offer a way into the problem of form under conditions of apparent formlessness.

The term *open* denotes a work's irresolution, connotes its provocativeness. Open stories do not provide easy answers. They puzzle and leave the reader dangling. Our aim is to help the reader value the complexity that these stories proclaim. The collection favors modern fiction because that is where the concept of openness emerges most fully. Our intention, though, is not to divide fiction into experiment and tradition. For finally, an understanding of form permits the reader to view classical models of the past—closed forms—with a new sensitivity.

One word about arrangement. The stories are in alphabetical order. Our thought was that any systematic arrangement would have led to arbitrary classifications, which is what the spirit of this book is most decidedly working against.

New York City
October 1970

BEVERLY GROSS
RICHARD GIANNONE

Contents

The Shapes of Fiction

Open and Closed

Introduction

I laughed uneasily; everything was wide open again; I was back in the game!

John Barth *The Floating Opera*

I Plot

Mickey Spillane has said that the only reason people listen to a joke or read a story is to find out how it ends. Spillane's comparison of stories and jokes is revealing, for a whole esthetic of fiction is implied in it: but a limiting esthetic, and, for this reason, deadening.

A joke (at least of the narrative kind) is a sequence of events leading to a punch line. How a joke ends is of course its point. What happens along the way is only important in preparing for the final event and final effect—a laugh if the joke works.

[I] A hobo is brought before a judge.
[II] "You have been arrested for vagrancy eight times," the judge tells him. "That will be ten days or ten dollars."
[III] "I'll take the ten dollars."

There is no doubt about the ending of this "story." The punch line caps everything that has come before. There is nothing equivocal about this ending: we do not wonder what will happen next; we are not left with anything to be explained or explored. The ending settles, makes final, closes off the whole. It is total, satisfying, immediate, and clear.

Here is another story that works pretty much the same way, although it is very different in impact and intent. It is Jesus' parable about the prodigal son.

> [I] "A certain man had two sons: and the younger of them said to his father, 'Father, give me the portion of goods that falleth to me.' And he divided unto them his living. And not many days after the younger son gathered all together, and took his journey into a far country, and there wasted his substance with riotous living. And when he had spent all, there arose a mighty famine in that land; and he began to be in want. And he went and joined himself to a citizen of that country; and he sent him into his fields to feed swine. And he would fain have filled his belly with the husks that the swine did eat: and no man gave unto him.
>
> [II] "And when he came to himself, he said, 'How many hired servants of my father's have bread enough and to spare, and I perish with hunger! I will arise and go to my father, and will say unto him, Father, I have sinned against heaven, and before thee, and am no more worthy to be called thy son: make me as one of thy hired servants.'
>
> "And he arose, and came to his father. But when he was yet a great way off, his father saw him, and had compassion, and ran, and fell on his neck, and kissed him. And the son said unto him, 'Father, I have sinned against heaven, and in thy sight, and am no more worthy to be called thy son.'
>
> [III] "But the father said to his servants, 'Bring forth the best robe, and put it on him; and put a ring on his hand, and shoes on his feet: and bring hither the fatted calf, and kill it; and let us eat, and be merry: for this my son was dead, and is alive again; he was lost, and is found.' And they began to be merry.
>
> "Now his elder son was in the field: and as he came and drew nigh to the house, he heard music and dancing. And he called one of the servants, and asked what these things meant. And he said unto him, 'Thy brother is come; and thy father hath killed the fatted calf, because he hath received him safe and sound.' And he was angry, and would not go in: therefore came his father out, and entreated him. And he answering said to his father, 'Lo, these many years do I serve thee, neither transgressed I at any time thy commandment: and yet thou never gavest me a kid, that I might make merry with my friends: but as soon as this thy son was come, which hath devoured thy living with harlots, thou hast killed for him the fatted calf.'
>
> "And he said unto him, 'Son, thou art ever with me, and all that I have is thine. It was meet that we should make merry, and be glad: for this brother was dead, and is alive again; and was lost, and is found.' "
>
> Luke 15:11–32

The parable, like the joke, has a specific purpose: a lesson, though, instead of a laugh. The lesson is furnished in the father's response to his two sons at the end. He forgives his prodigal son, rejoices at his return, and rewards him. The lesson reaches greater amplitude in the father's response to his elder son's jealousy: why should such lavish attention, even favoritism, be bestowed on this apparently unworthy brother? The answer is the ultimate message of the story. Salvation is not just a matter of simple justice—the good getting their just reward. The elder brother's steady virtue insures his salvation. But this story is really about redemption: how the contrition of sinners brings them back to grace. No matter how fallen one may be, if he returns to his father (that is, Father) he will be embraced and saved.

It is a simple story, but with momentous theological implications. The action says it all. And the contour of its action is virtually the same as the joke's. The three parts of the joke that we have labeled [I], [II], and [III] are like the three parts of the parable that we have similarly labeled. The first part, [I], is the *exposition*: the characters and their initial situation are introduced. [II] is the *complication*: difficulties develop and are compounded until a crisis is reached. [III] is the *resolution*: the impending crisis is settled. In the joke, of course, the resolution does not really "solve" the problem of the hobo as the parable's resolution does for the prodigal son. The hobo's triumph is only temporary; no doubt if one were to imagine the story continued one would see him in pretty bad shape. The point however is that one does not need or want to project the story any further: this is all the ending that the materials of this particular story warrant. The hobo is really too anonymous for us to be concerned about what happens to him next. All the potential interest that this story contains is fulfilled and realized by the time it is over.

"What happens next?" is a proper question to ask at any point in stages I and II of either story; as the stories advance the question gains greater urgency. But the resolution satisfies us into no longer needing to ask "what happens next?" The success of both endings and of the stories as a whole depends on the irrelevance of that question at the end. Continuation would not enhance anything, would make the stories less meaningful, less powerful. Imagine the tedium of a recital of the judge's exasperation, the hobo's imprisonment, his remorse, his release, his return to society. . . . This of course is the art of the shaggy-dog story, the supreme form of the antijoke. The parable, too, can go no further without drifting into pointlessness. What happens to the two sons later is a peripheral question unrelated to the dramatic energies and moral scope of the story we have read. That story has reached completion: its drama is resolved; its meaning, proclaimed. To continue would reduce it to the sporadic creepings of a soap opera.

Plot is what we call narrative structure: the final shape assumed by the relationship of the parts. Both plots are pretty rudimentary, the joke's more so than the parable's. Yet theirs is basically the same plot structure (exposition, complication, resolution) found in many plays, stories, and novels with a much more complex organization. Sophocles' *Oedipus Rex* is the classical example of such a play. Jane Austen's *Pride and Prejudice* is an example of such a novel. The whole structure of these works is designed to bring the developing action to a final resolution. The ending of these works is the end for which their plot exists.

And with all due respect to Mickey Spillane, it is questionable whether we read these works *only* to find out how they end. If so, there would be little point in rereading them—as little point as in hearing a joke repeated. And here is where Spillane has shown us false. This is exactly why stories are *not* like jokes. There is something rich and satisfying about the narrative works that we like; we read, *and reread,* them for many things more than the curiosity they may evoke in us. A great work of fiction carries with it much more than the narrative equivalent to a punch line.

There is another problem with Spillane's contention. Some stories do not have "endings"—at least not in the sense that Spillane insists upon. Some stories end without resolution: their development is not hinged upon a well-defined and unified line of action; they leave us dangling with nagging doubts about what will happen next, perhaps even with doubts about what has happened, and doubts about what it all means. By Spillane's standards, these cannot be very good stories; perhaps they are not stories at all.

This book is a collection of fictional works that risk that indictment. The development of many of these stories is not carried through a beginning, a middle, and an end; their conflicts and tensions are not always brought to a final settlement and equilibrium. These stories invite readers to do some rethinking about narrative art, literary form, and above all their own responses.

II "Revelation"

As we read, many of our questions about meaning and form must be held in abeyance until the ending has been reached. Some endings pointedly work against our expectations by failing to tie together the preceding events. Such endings complicate and disturb. Flannery O'Connor's "Revelation," included in this collection, is a good example; especially so because the story's title suggests a final clarification —nothing less than a revelation—which the ending does not offer.

The story concerns Ruby Turpin, who, not being either "white-trash or a nigger or ugly," thinks of herself as a "good woman." The way she arrives at this self-estimate characterizes her moral responses. She transforms accidents of her nature into virtues, and accidents of other peoples' natures into vices. White is right. Money talks. Ruby Turpin has neatly categorized the intricate variety of human nature. At the bottom of the scale are most blacks; then come white-trash, homeowners, home-and-land owners, and at the top, those with big money and big houses. She calls it God's scheme and worships it. Mrs. Turpin modestly places herself and her husband Claud next to the top class as good home-and-land people.

Her nice place in God's scheme is a source of endless gratitude, which she expresses by reminding others that they are either trash or nigger or ugly. The story begins in a physician's waiting room, where Mrs. Turpin finds fresh reasons to be grateful for being good, white, and beautiful. Her strategy for insult on this occasion is to address a respectable-looking lady so that others, whom she will not stoop to acknowledge, can hear her judge them. Her stunt fails. She literally gets the book thrown at her. Angered by Mrs. Turpin's naked malice, a patient called Mary Grace, a Wellesley student, flings a book at Mrs. Turpin, then chokes her. After jumping her, Mary Grace whispers with demonic pleasure: "Go back to hell where you came from, you old wart hog."

In the last scene of the story Mrs. Turpin is back on her farm, the pride of which is an elevated concrete pig-parlor that is hosed daily to keep the pigs clean. Ruby Turpin does not recover easily from the incident in the doctor's office. The angry cut made by the book above Mrs. Turpin's left eye hurts less than does the burning caused by Mary Grace's words. The words burn Mrs. Turpin's inner eye, the eye through which she sees herself. The portrait of "a respectable, hard-working, church-going woman" as a pig blinds her with wrath. "How am I a hog and me both? How am I saved and from hell too?" Like Job, who also suffered undue pain, she asks God, "Why me?" God's unresponsiveness sharpens her anger. Finally, while hosing down her pig-parlor, she receives the light. She has a vision:

> . . . a vast horde of souls were rumbling toward heaven. There were whole companies of white-trash, clean for the first time in their lives, and bands of black niggers in white robes, and battalions of freaks and lunatics shouting and clapping and leaping like frogs. And bringing up the end of the procession was a tribe of people whom she recognized at once as those who, like herself and Claud, had always had a little of everything and the God-given wit to use it right. She leaned forward to observe them closer.

> They were marching behind the others with great dignity, accountable as they had always been for good order and common sense and respectable behavior. They alone were on key. Yet she could see by their shocked and altered faces that even their virtues were being burned away. She lowered her hands and gripped the rail of the hog pen, her eyes small but fixed unblinkingly on what lay ahead. In a moment the vision faded but she remained where she was, immobile.
>
> At length she got down and turned off the faucet and made her slow way on the darkening path to the house. In the woods around her the invisible cricket choruses had struck up, but what she heard were the voices of the souls climbing upward into the starry field and shouting hallelujah.

This is where the story ends, with an apocalyptic vision of the End.

It is a puzzling end. Our first impression is necessarily a sense of incompleteness. For the story's action has not really gone anywhere; there has been no significant development; nothing much has "happened"; there has been no "tying together"; nothing seems resolved. We are left at the end with only a vision to interpret.

Does the story end? The answer to this fundamental and truly legitimate question is what *The Shapes of Fiction* is about. The answer depends on what one means by *story*, what one means by *end*. The question gives rise to at least three distinct meanings for the word *story*:

a)	*story as object:*	the printed thing before us, the words covering ten or so pages
b)	*story as action:*	the events that can be related in a "plot summary" (what we mean when we say, "Tell me the story of *Bonnie and Clyde*")
c)	*story as formal entity:*	a work of art with its own internal order, unity, and wholeness

The word *end* has a separate meaning for each of these contexts:

a)	*end as over:*	when the words stop, that is the end of the story
b)	*end as resolution:*	when the dramatic conflicts are settled and the action reaches its resolution
c)	*end as fulfillment:*	the completion of the story as an artistic structure

The question of ending that "Revelation" raises is essentially a matter of context (c). That it ends (a), without ending (b), invites us to consider whether it may still achieve completion (c).

To recognize not only how a story like "Revelation" may be complete (c), but also why it does not end in resolution (b), is to understand what is really developing in this story. Why is it not resolved? The first possibility is that Flannery O'Connor may be an incompetent or a tease, in which case we do not have to go any further. But suppose we assume for the time being that she as a literary artist is doing something deliberate for a specific purpose and effect. We may then discover artistic justification for what would seem to be so flagrant a violation of the Spillane Principle of narrative art. This is not a supposition to be rejected automatically or, what may be worse, to be automatically conceded. It is a supposition to be tentatively granted and explored. Such a procedure is the only way to approach an unfamiliar form; and to follow it is the best advice we can offer you in reading and thinking about the stories in this volume.

So, then, even if its ending does not resolve an action, are there ways in which "Revelation" is fulfilled and completed by it?

For Ruby Turpin the imaginary spectacle at the end is simply another, more irritating put-down in a day of put-downs. She asks God how she could be simultaneously saved, as her faith guarantees her, and a creature from hell, as His message through Mary Grace said she was. The answer that she receives in the vision is nothing more than a revised version of her own absurd dream of "a top and bottom." She expected a reassurance and is angered because it is withheld. White-trash appear clean, blacks sport white robes, freaks and lunatics are beautiful. Ruby's pecking order is turned topsy-turvy, with the respectable virtues she prizes exposed as sins.

The procession should have shaken up Ruby, brought on a moral correction, made her see herself for what she is. Instead she feels only indignation, which shows the depth of her intractability. Ruby reacts to divine justice as though it were a breach of etiquette. If a glimpse beyond the grave does not budge her, what will? She sees but she does not see. Ruby goes nowhere. In dramatic terms the story is a demonstration of the moral paralysis brought about by Ruby's refusal to see. She remains "immobile" after the vision. Her "little black eyes," which had sized up the waiting room, are at the end "small but fixed unblinkingly on what lay ahead." She is locked into her own moral gaze. Scrutinizing the world through those unreflective black eyes, she will go on twisting fortuities and moral maxims to square with her view.

For the reader the ending means something very different from

Ruby's apprehension. All along the reader is invited to see what Ruby does not. The first sentence starts the procedure with the name Turpin, which tells us something about Ruby that she will never know or accept if shown. *Turpis* in Latin means base and foul (we have the word turpitude), and "Turpin" precisely locates Ruby on a larger moral scale than that she has devised. Ruby's self-inflation invites us mentally to correct her distortions. The ironic manner in which this story is told stylistically encourages the reader to make these corrections. The story amounts to a series of disclosures that the reader assists in the making of. The Doomsday extravaganza, with the conventional people stalking in a madhouse dignity, culminates the series. At that point the reader recognizes most fully the limitations of Ruby's mind. She does not see that the vision repudiates her moral scale by revising it. She misses its message just as she misses its comedy. The revelation has too much truth for her categorizing spirit. So it is that the story has no resolution. Ruby's way of thinking is the path to stupid self-congratulation; the mocking of it suggests a way to wisdom.

The ending is as much a critique of the neat resolution as it is a parody of Ruby's "top and bottom." It does not set the issues straight. In its obvious failure to do so, there is an ironic mockery of all such setting straight. Ruby thinks of redemption as a detachable state that finishes life on earth. Flannery O'Connor ends the story by having life and afterlife define each other. Ruby's glimpse into infinity throws us back to actuality, which in turn comments on the question of divine justice.

The revelation of "Revelation" is that human destiny remains secret. Heaven deepens the mystery of earth, and earth does the same thing for heaven. Understanding is a process, not a product or system as Ruby Turpin assumes. And that is the form of "Revelation": the act of the mind coming to tentative terms with complexity. That is the way to wisdom. The story is much more the reader's than Ruby's, for it is his awareness that is deepened, not hers. He is offered the key to salvation and grace by participating in and coming to recognize the inadequacy of her way of pursuing these divine sanctions. Because Ruby refuses every opportunity for experience, she does not change.

The story presents two kinds of faith. Ruby's kind proceeds dogmatically. The other kind is the way of wisdom. It is a discovery of the complex relation between ultimate realities and actualities. This faith is embodied in the form of the story, in the act of the mind seeking to know. Where Ruby has answers for questions before they arise, the reader, who participates in the story by discovering its formal movement, learns to perceive, not to solve or to impose. One approach (Ruby's) makes man a judge, the other (the reader's) makes him an observer. The revelation at the end tests the value of these two kinds of faith. The watchful observer can recognize the interaction between heaven and earth. The form of the story is an affirmation of the very issue, grace and salvation, that the ending does not settle.

III Open Form

What we have been discussing so far is two kinds of narrative form: open and closed. Closed form achieves its unity and wholeness through resolution; the parable of the prodigal son exemplifies closed form. Open form, exemplified by "Revelation," achieves its unity and wholeness through a more complex kind of synthesis, describable only in terms of the individual story at hand. It follows from the organic nature of open form that there will be countless open structures. Such diversity makes it accurate to speak about open forms, not something called *the* open form. There are no models, no paradigm. There are, though, a number of characteristics present in varying degrees among fictional works that allow us to call them open. A few points to consider are these:

1 Openness and closure are only relative terms

No narrative is completely open, none completely closed. Any story contains elements of both openness and closure. To say that a story is closed is to say that it attains a high degree of finality by seeing its central character through to some fairly well-settled fate, that its dramatic and thematic issues are pretty well solved. But it is obvious that not all problems can be solved, not all questions can be answered, not all conflicts and issues can be settled. We include O. Henry's "The Last Leaf" in this book as a story with a particularly high degree of closure, so high, in fact, that the story seems a mock exercise. But even here there are elements of openness. This anthology is weighted toward stories that exhibit openness to a striking extent, but there are elements of closure, sometimes quite pronounced, in these stories as well.

2 Openness is a descriptive term bearing on a variety of conditions

A story may be open in one or more of several ways. Unresolved action, unsettled meaning, ambiguous authorial intent—these are the basic possibilities of openness. Stories may be open in one, two, or all three of these aspects.

Most of our discussion so far has been about *dramatic* openness and closure (that is, plot resolution). But a story whose plot achieves a high degree of dramatic finality and settlement may still remain thematically open—complex, bewildering, and controversial in its implications. There is nothing more final than death, yet the death of the central character in Kafka's "A Hunger Artist," rather than resolving the story, opens up new complexities about his supposed martyrdom to art. At the end of Melville's story "Bartleby the Scrivener," when the narrator offers what he regards as a full explanation of the unfathomable behavior of the clerk, Bartleby, the reader is struck with the inadequacy of all explanations. The death of Prince Hamlet does not close the issues of Shakespeare's play: three centuries of drama criticism testify to that.

3 Openness is a statement about a work's total form, not just its ending

Open fiction is quite commonly called "open-ended," an indication of how important the end of a story is in defining its form. The end is where openness is most fully to be seen, but openness is not purely a matter of endings. A story does not suddenly become open-ended because its concluding lines fail to provide a resolution. If this were so, an open story theoretically could be transformed into a closed one by a revision or expansion of its conclusion. It is not the final lines of a story that establish its openness but the story's total development, which the ending only culminates. To put this another way, the plot of an open-ended story is not to be considered as a dramatic action with a beginning and a middle but no end. The traditional Aristotelian concept of plot does not hold for most of these stories. Each is doing something different, forging out its own form. (A striking example, Donald Barthelme's "Robert Kennedy Saved from Drowning," is a collage of seemingly insignificant moments in which no line of action is initiated at all.)

4 Openness produces a variety of effects, is used for a variety of purposes

Why are stories open? Why do they run the risk of disappointing the reader, who, as Mickey Spillane claims, is only reading in order to find out how things end? The answer can only depend on the individual story. Nevertheless, openness contains several expressive possibilities in and of itself.

Open form makes particular use of the provocative effects that may be afforded by assertions of disequilibrium, disharmony, and disturbance at precisely the point at which the narrative forces of a closed structure would usually be moving toward a final equilibrium, harmony, and quietude. An ending that refuses to interpret a story's meaning provides, instead, an implicit insight into the meaning of that meaning. An ending that refuses to round off a story's action may often redefine what we had thought that action was. The absence of finality can often be the most appropriate and meaningful culmination to a story's development. Indeterminacy can be a story's most expressive fulfillment and completion.

It is a natural thing to tend to rely on familiar expectations. As moviegoers, we expect that the man with the moustache and the dark stetson is the villain. As readers, we expect beginnings, middles, and ends to narratives. Writers who do not deal this way are aware of our expectations. By violating our expectations, they are quite deliberately saying something through form.

5 Openness and closure are descriptive terms, not value judgments; openness is not automatically a good or bad thing in itself

Despite Spillane's contention, closure is not better (that is, more artistic, more effective) than openness. And although we are presenting you with a collection of open stories, we would hardly want to make the opposite claim.

IV Form

The concept of form is basic to human doing and thinking. The diversified ways the word *form* operates in our language are a trustworthy sign of that importance. *Form* serves not only as the source of a large, necessary family of words (like *inform, format, formality*) but also as both primary parts of speech, noun and verb; and it belongs to vocabularies ranging from the colloquial to the philosophical. Form means shape (from the Latin *forma*). All of its derivations go back to this root meaning. Shaping is what man is all about, physically and spiritually. Hand, mind, and heart all shape. Form describes how we express ourselves by giving shape to ideas, feelings, and things. We need shapes. They are one way of defining and refining experience, one way of relating to the world.

Some use the term judgmentally. For them form is a positive quality that signifies the opposite of formlessness. Others make no such distinction and apply the term more generously as a description of that which gives a thing coherence. In this view everything has form. The rival notions of form parallel a common way of talking about style. One can say that something either has style or lacks it; or one can say that everything has a style that can be good or bad, fit or unfit.

Buying clothes with a fixed notion of style might work, but approaching a work of art with a fixed notion of form will not. It amounts to kicking boulders. One gets nowhere. One begins with a dichotomy, form and formlessness, and one ends with two sets of works justifying one's prejudices. And like kicking boulders, the habit harms. A conception of form with particular features invariably draws its standard from existing models that cannot accommodate newer works. The production of art is not like the production of a jello mold. Art thrives on innovation, dies of repetition. The best art renovates preceding models and in this sense carries with it an implicit attack on formal traditions. The artist's job is to find new patterns of experience. His discovery marks his achievement and constitutes our difficulty. Breakthroughs—political, scientific, intellectual, as well as artistic—invariably meet resistance, sometimes hostility, before they are accepted. They threaten prior securities. Witness Freud, Marx, SDS, Joyce, rock, explicit sexuality in movies. We cope with the unfamiliar by squaring it against the familiar, just as the artist casts the new out of the old. In doing so, we must guard against defending ignorances by staying too close to what we know. If we cling to the known, it will bind. Bind, give us false confidence, desensitize us to novelty, and check our moral growth. The harm lies in deprivation.

Art is only accessible when we regard form as *descriptive* rather than *prescriptive*. If we react to newness with a conviction of what form ought to be, we beg the important question of what is before us. This recognition permits us to proceed with a work more sympathetically and more precisely. We will be inclined to yield to the specialness of the work rather than to our expectations.

If there is no predetermined standard for form, how do we judge it? How do we come to terms with the dynamic organizing principle of a work? The standard for the success of artistic form is fulfillment, that capacity to piece together the shifting references and rhythms of a work in a way that they serve, in the case of literary fiction, its narrative content and purpose. The best place to begin is the ending. That is where the success of a story's form is most fully to be realized.

Openness has become dominant in twentieth-century fiction because it is a formal reflection of the spirit of our times. The shattering of ethical and metaphysical certainties, our contentions with futilities, the sense that life is not a progress toward some grand finale—these are the facts that we live with; this is what the artist writes about.

Fiction is not the opposite of truth: it is a way of rendering truth. And form is not the opposite of content: it is the shape of content.

The history of fiction is the history of ways achieved, duplicated, discarded, revised. Openness expresses an attitude toward experience that distrusts ends because they connote rational or discernible relations that we have come to find either facile or false or both. Doubt is hope turned inside out. Like a person who does not say good-bye, openness looks forward to new beginnings as life brings them, to a lifetime of personal change in a turning world.

The Nightingale

Hans Christian Andersen

In China, you must know, the Emperor is a Chinaman, and all whom he has about him are Chinamen too. It happened a good many years ago, but that's just why it's worthwhile to hear the story, before it is forgotten. The Emperor's palace was the most splendid in the world; it was made entirely of porcelain, very costly, but so delicate and brittle that one had to take care how one touched it. In the garden were to be seen the most wonderful flowers, and to the costliest of them silver bells were tied, which sounded, so that nobody should pass by without noticing the flowers. Yes, everything in the Emperor's garden was admirably arranged. And it extended so far, that the gardener himself did not know where the end was. If a man went on and on, he came into a glorious forest with high trees and deep lakes. The wood extended straight down to the sea, which was blue and deep; great ships could sail to and fro beneath the branches of the trees; and in the trees lived a nightingale, which sang so splendidly that even the poor Fisherman, who had many other things to do, stopped still and listened, when he had gone out at night to throw out his nets, and heard the Nightingale.

"How beautiful that is!" he said; but he was obliged to attend to his property, and thus forgot the bird. But when in the next night the bird sang again, and the Fisherman heard it, he exclaimed again, "How beautiful that is!"

From all the countries of the world travellers came to the city of the Emperor and admired it, and the palace, and the garden, but when they heard the Nightingale, they said, "That is the best of all!"

And the travellers told of it when they came home; and the learned men wrote many books about the town, the palace, and the garden. But they did not forget the Nightingale; that was placed highest of all; and those who were poets wrote most magnificent poems about the Nightingale in the wood by the deep lake.

The books went through all the world, and a few of them once came to the Emperor. He sat in his golden chair, and read, and read: every moment he nodded his head, for it pleased him to peruse the masterly descriptions of the city, the palace, and the garden. "But the Nightingale is the best of all!"—it stood written there.

"What's that?" exclaimed the Emperor. "I don't know the Nightingale at all! Is there such a bird in my empire, and even in my garden? I've never heard of that. To think that I should have to learn such a thing for the first time from books!"

And hereupon he called his Cavalier. This Cavalier was so grand that if any one lower in rank than himself dared to speak to him, or to ask him any question, he answered nothing but "P!"—and that meant nothing.

"There is said to be a wonderful bird here called a Nightingale!" said the Emperor. "They say it is the best thing in all my great empire. Why have I never heard anything about it?"

"I have never heard him named," replied the Cavalier. "He has never been introduced at court."

"I command that he shall appear this evening, and sing before me," said the Emperor. "All the world knows what I possess, and I do not know it myself!"

"I have never heard him mentioned," said the Cavalier. "I will seek for him. I will find him."

But where was he to be found? The Cavalier ran up and down all the staircases, through halls and passages, but no one among all those whom he met had heard talk of the Nightingale. And the Cavalier ran back to the Emperor, and said that it must be a fable invented by the writers of books.

"Your Imperial Majesty cannot believe how much is written that is fiction, besides something that they call the black art."

"But the book in which I read this," said the Emperor, "was sent to me by the high and mighty Emperor of Japan, and therefore it cannot be a falsehood. I will hear the Nightingale! It must be here this evening! It has my imperial favor; and if it does not come, all the court shall be trampled upon after the court has supped!"

"Tsing-pe!" said the Cavalier; and again he ran up and down all the staircases, and through all the halls and corridors; and half the court ran with him, for the courtiers did not like being trampled upon.

Then there was a great inquiry after the wonderful Nightingale, which all the world knew excepting the people at court.

At last they met with a poor little girl in the kitchen, who said,—

"The Nightingale? I know it well: yes, it can sing gloriously. Every evening I get leave to carry my poor sick mother the scraps from the table. She lives down by the strand, and when I get back and am tired, and rest in the wood, then I hear the Nightingale sing. And then the water comes into my eyes, and it is just as if my mother kissed me!"

"Little Kitchen Girl," said the Cavalier, "I will get you a place in the kitchen, with permission to see the Emperor dine, if you will lead us to the Nightingale, for it is announced for this evening."

So they all went out into the wood where the Nightingale was accustomed to sing; half the court went forth. When they were in the midst of their journey a cow began to low.

"O!" cried the court pages, "now we have it! That shows a wonderful power in so small a creature! I have certainly heard it before."

"No, those are cows lowing!" said the little Kitchen Girl. "We are a long way from the place yet."

Now the frogs began to croak in the marsh.

"Glorious!" said the Chinese Court Preacher. "Now I hear it—it sounds just like little church bells."

"No, those are frogs!" said the little Kitchen-maid. "But now I think we shall soon hear it."

And then the Nightingale began to sing.

"That is it!" exclaimed the little Girl. "Listen, listen! and yonder it sits."

And she pointed to a little gray bird up in the boughs.

"Is it possible?" cried the Cavalier. "I should never have thought it looked like that! How simple it looks! It must certainly have lost its color at seeing such grand people around."

"Little Nightingale!" called the little Kitchen-maid, quite loudly, "our gracious Emperor wishes you to sing before him."

"With the greatest pleasure!" replied the Nightingale, and began to sing most delightfully.

"It sounds just like glass bells!" said the Cavalier. "And look at its little throat, how it's working! It's wonderful that we should never have heard it before. That bird will be a great success at court."

"Shall I sing once more before the Emperor?" asked the Nightingale, for it thought the Emperor was present.

"My excellent little Nightingale," said the Cavalier, "I have great pleasure in inviting you to a court festival this evening, when you shall charm his Imperial Majesty with your beautiful singing."

"My song sounds best in the greenwood!" replied the Nightingale; still it came willingly when it heard what the Emperor wished.

The palace was festively adorned. The walls and the flooring, which were of porcelain, gleamed in the rays of thousands of golden lamps. The most glorious flowers, which could ring clearly, had been placed in the passages. There was a running to and fro, and a thorough draught, and all the bells rang so loudly that one could not hear one's self speak.

In the midst of the great hall, where the Emperor sat, a golden perch had been placed, on which the Nightingale was to sit. The whole court was there, and the little Cook-maid had got leave to stand behind the door, as she had now received the title of a real court cook. All were in full dress, and all looked at the little gray bird, to which the Emperor nodded.

And the Nightingale sang so gloriously that the tears came into the Emperor's eyes, and the tears ran down over his cheeks; and then the Nightingale sang still more sweetly, that went straight to the heart. The Emperor was so much pleased that he said the Nightingale should have his golden slipper to wear round its neck. But the Nightingale declined this with thanks, saying it had already received a sufficient reward.

"I have seen tears in the Emperor's eyes—that is the real treasure to me. An emperor's tears have a peculiar power. I am rewarded enough!" And then it sang again with a sweet, glorious voice.

"That's the most amiable coquetry I ever saw!" said the ladies who stood round about, and then they took water in their mouths to gurgle when any one spoke to them. They thought they should be nightingales too. And the lackeys and chambermaids reported that they were satisfied too; and that was saying a good deal, for they are the most difficult to please. In short, the Nightingale achieved a real success.

It was now to remain at court, to have its own cage, with liberty to go out twice every day and once at night. Twelve servants were appointed when the Nightingale went out, each of whom had a silken string fastened to the bird's leg, which they held very tight. There was really no pleasure in an excursion of that kind.

The whole city spoke of the wonderful bird, and when two people met, one said nothing but "Nightin," and the other said "gale"; and then they sighed, and understood one another. Eleven peddlers' children were named after the bird, but not one of them could sing a note.

One day the Emperor received a large parcel, on which was written "The Nightingale."

"There we have a new book about this celebrated bird," said the Emperor.

But it was not a book, but a little work of art, contained in a box, an artificial nightingale, which was to sing like a natural one, and was brilliantly ornamented with diamonds, rubies, and sapphires. So soon as the artificial bird was wound up, he could sing one of the pieces that he really sang, and then his tail moved up and down, and shone with silver and gold. Round his neck hung a little ribbon, and on that was written, "The Emperor of China's Nightingale is poor compared to that of the Emperor of Japan."

"That is capital!" said they all, and he who had brought the artificial bird immediately received the title, Imperial Head-Nightingale-Bringer.

"Now they must sing together; what a duet that will be!"

And so they had to sing together; but it did not sound very well, for the real Nightingale sang in its own way, and the artificial bird sang waltzes.

"That's not his fault," said the Play-master; "he's quite perfect, and very much in my style."

Now the artificial bird was to sing alone. He had just as much success as the real one, and then it was much handsomer to look at—it shone like bracelets and breastpins.

Three-and-thirty times over did it sing the same piece, and yet was not tired. The people would gladly have heard it again, but the Emperor said that the living Nightingale ought to sing something now. But where was it? No one had noticed that it had flown away out of the open window, back to the greenwood.

"But what is become of that?" said the Emperor.

And all the courtiers abused the Nightingale, and declared that it was a very ungrateful creature.

"We have the best bird, after all," said they.

And so the artificial bird had to sing again, and that was the thirty-fourth time that they listened to the same piece. For all that they did not know it quite by heart, for it was so very difficult. And the Play-master praised the bird particularly; yes, he declared that it was better than a nightingale, not only with regard to its plumage and the many beautiful diamonds, but inside as well.

"For you see, ladies and gentlemen, and above all, your Imperial Majesty, with a real nightingale one can never calculate what is coming, but in this artificial bird everything is settled. One can explain it; one can open it, and make people understand where the waltzes come from, how they go, and how one follows up another."

"Those are quite our own ideas," they all said.

And the speaker received permission to show the bird to the people on the next Sunday. The people were to hear it sing too, the Emperor commanded; and they did hear it, and were as much pleased as if they had all got tipsy upon tea, for that's quite the Chinese fashion; and they all said, "O!" and held up their forefingers and nodded. But the poor Fisherman, who had heard the real Nightingale, said,—

"It sounds pretty enough, and the melodies resemble each other, but there's something wanting, though I know not what!"

The real Nightingale was banished from the country and empire. The artificial bird had its place on a silken cushion close to the Emperor's bed; all the presents it had received, gold and precious stones, were ranged about it; in title it had advanced to be the High Imperial After-Dinner-Singer, and in rank, to number one on the left hand; for the Emperor considered that side the most important on which the heart is placed, and even in an emperor the heart is on the left side; and the Play-master wrote a work of five-and-twenty volumes about the artificial bird; it was very learned and very long, full of the most difficult Chinese words; but yet all the people declared that they had read it, and understood it, for fear of being considered stupid, and having their bodies trampled on.

So a whole year went by. The Emperor, the court, and all the other Chinese knew every little twitter in the artificial bird's song by heart. But just for that reason it pleased them best—they could sing with it themselves, and they did so. The street boys sang, "Tsi-tsi-tsi-glug-glug!" and the Emperor himself sang it too. Yes, that was certainly famous.

But one evening, when the artificial bird was singing its best, and the Emperor lay in bed listening to it, something inside the bird said, "Whizz!" Something cracked. "Whir-r-r!" All the wheels ran round, and then the music stopped.

The Emperor immediately sprang out of bed, and caused his body physician to be called; but what could *he* do? Then they sent for a watchmaker, and after a good deal of talking and investigation, the bird was put into something like order; but the Watchmaker said that the bird must be carefully treated, for the barrels were worn, and it would be impossible to put new ones in in such a manner that the music would go. There was a great lamentation; only once in a year was it permitted to let the bird sing, and that was almost too much. But then the Play-master made a little speech, full of heavy words, and said this was just as good as before—and so of course it was as good as before.

Now five years had gone by, and a real grief came upon the whole nation. The Chinese were really fond of their Emperor, and now he was ill, and could not, it was said, live much longer. Already a new Emperor had been chosen, and the people stood out in the street and asked the Cavalier how their old Emperor did.

"P!" said he, and shook his head.

Cold and pale lay the Emperor in his great gorgeous bed; the whole court thought him dead, and each one ran to pay homage to the new ruler. The chamberlains ran out to talk it over, and the ladies'-maids had a great coffee party. All about, in all the halls and passages, cloth had been laid down so that no footstep could be heard, and therefore it was quiet there, quite quiet. But the Emperor was not dead yet: stiff and pale he lay on the gorgeous bed with the long velvet curtains and the heavy gold tassels; high up, a window stood open, and the moon shone in upon the Emperor and the artificial bird.

The poor Emperor could scarcely breathe; it was just as if something lay upon his chest: he opened his eyes, and then he saw that it was Death who sat upon his chest, and had put on his golden crown, and held in one hand the Emperor's sword, and in the other his beautiful banner. And all around, from among the folds of the splendid velvet curtains, strange heads peered forth; a few very ugly, the rest quite lovely and mild. These were all the Emperor's bad and good deeds, that stood before him now that Death sat upon his heart.

"Do you remember this?" whispered one to the other. "Do you remember that?" and then they told him so much that the perspiration ran from his forehead.

"I did not know that!" said the Emperor. "Music! music! the great Chinese drum!" he cried, "so that I need not hear all they say!"

And they continued speaking, and Death nodded like a Chinaman to all they said.

"Music! music!" cried the Emperor. "You little precious golden bird, sing, sing! I have given you gold and costly presents; I have even hung my golden slipper around your neck—sing now, sing!"

But the bird stood still; no one was there to wind him up, and he could not sing without that; but Death continued to stare at the Emperor with his great hollow eyes, and it was quiet, fearfully quiet.

Then there sounded from the window, suddenly, the most lovely song. It was the little live Nightingale, that sat outside on a spray. It had heard of the Emperor's sad plight, and had come to sing to him of comfort and hope. And as it sang the spectres grew paler and paler; the blood ran quicker and more quickly through the Emperor's weak limbs; and even Death listened, and said,—

"Go on, little Nightingale, go on!"

"But will you give me that splendid golden sword? Will you give me that rich banner? Will you give me the Emperor's crown?"

And Death gave up each of these treasures for a song. And the Nightingale sang on and on; and it sang of the quiet church-yard where the white roses grow, where the elder-blossom smells sweet, and where the fresh grass is moistened by the tears of survivors. Then Death felt a longing to see his garden, and floated out at the window in the form of a cold, white mist.

"Thanks! thanks!" said the Emperor. "You heavenly little bird! I know you well. I banished you from my country and empire, and yet you have charmed away the evil faces from my couch, and banished Death from my heart! How can I reward you?"

"You have rewarded me!" replied the Nightingale. "I have drawn tears from your eyes, when I sang the first time—I shall never forget that. Those are the jewels that rejoice a singer's heart. But now sleep and grow fresh and strong again. I will sing you something."

And it sang, and the Emperor fell into a sweet slumber. Ah! how mild and refreshing that sleep was! The sun shone upon him through the windows, when he awoke refreshed and restored; not one of his servants had yet returned, for they all thought he was dead; only the Nightingale still sat beside him and sang.

"You must always stay with me," said the Emperor. "You shall sing as you please; and I'll break the artificial bird into a thousand pieces."

"Not so," replied the Nightingale. "It did well as long as it could; keep it as you have done till now. I cannot build my nest in the palace to dwell in it, but let me come when I feel the wish; then I will sit in the evening on the spray yonder by the window, and sing you something, so that you may be glad and thoughtful at once. I will sing of those who are happy and of those who suffer. I will sing of good and of evil that remain hidden round about you. The little singing bird flies far around, to the poor fisherman, to the peasant's roof, to every one who dwells far away from you and from your court. I love your heart more than your crown, and yet the crown has an air of sanctity about it. I will come and sing to you—but one thing you must promise me."

"Everything!" said the Emperor; and he stood there in his imperial robes, which he had put on himself, and pressed the sword which was heavy with gold to his heart.

"One thing I beg of you: tell no one that you have a little bird who tells you everything. Then it will go all the better."

And the Nightingale flew away.

The servants came in to look to their dead Emperor, and—yes, there he stood, and the Emperor said "Good morning!"

Title

John Barth

Beginning: in the middle, past the middle, nearer three-quarters done, waiting for the end. Consider how dreadful so far: passionlessness, abstraction, pro, dis. And it will get worse. Can we possibly continue?

Plot and theme: notions vitiated by this hour of the world but as yet not successfully succeeded. Conflict, complication, no climax. The worst is to come. Everything leads to nothing: future tense; past tense; present tense. Perfect. The final question is, Can nothing be made meaningful? Isn't that the final question? If not, the end is at hand. Literally, as it were. Can't stand any more of this.

I think she comes. The story of our life. This is the final test. Try to fill the blank. Only hope is to fill the blank. Efface what can't be faced or else fill the blank. With words or more words, otherwise I'll fill in the blank with this noun here in my prepositional object. Yes, she already said that. And I think. What now. Everything's been said already, over and over; I'm as sick of this as you are; there's nothing to say. Say nothing.

What's new? Nothing.

Conventional startling opener. Sorry if I'm interrupting the Progress of Literature, she said, in a tone that adjective clause suggesting good-humored irony but in fact defensively and imperfectly masking a taunt. The conflict is established though as yet unclear in detail. Standard conflict. Let's skip particulars. What do you want from me? What'll the story be this time? Same old story. Just thought I'd see if you were still around. Before. What? Quit right here. Too late. Can't we start over? What's past is past. On the contrary, what's forever past is eternally present. The future? Blank. All this is just fill in. Hang on.

Still around. In what sense? Among the gerundive. What is that supposed to mean? Did you think I meant to fill in the blank? Why should I? On the other hand, why not? What makes you think I wouldn't fill in the blank instead? Some conversation this is. Do you want to go on, or shall we end it right now? Suspense. I don't care for this either. It'll be over soon enough in any case. But it gets worse and worse. Whatever happens, the ending will be deadly. At least let's have just one real conversation. Dialogue or monologue? What has it been from the first? Don't ask me. What is there to say at this late date? Let me think; I'm trying to think. Same old story. Or. Or? Silence.

This isn't so bad. Silence. There are worse things. Name three. This, that, the other. Some choices. Who said there was a choice?

Let's try again. That's what I've been doing; I've been thinking while you've been blank. Story of Our Life. However, this may be the final complication. The ending may be violent. That's been said before. Who cares? Let the end be blank; anything's better than this.

It didn't used to be so bad. It used to be less difficult. Even enjoyable. For whom? Both of us. To do what? Complicate the conflict. I am weary of this. What, then? To complete this sentence, if I may bring up a sore subject. That never used to be a problem. Now it's impossible; we just can't manage it. You can't fill in the blank; I can't fill in the blank. Or won't. Is this what we're going to talk about, our obscene verbal problem? It'll be our last conversation. Why talk at all? Are you paying attention? I dare you to quit now! Never dare a desperate person. On with it, calmly, one sentence after another, like a recidivist. A what? A common noun. Or another common noun. Hold tight. Or a chronic forger, let's say; committed to the pen for life. Which is to say, death. The point, for pity's sake! Not yet. Forge on.

We're more than halfway through, as I remarked at the outset: youthful vigor, innocent exposition, positive rising action—all that is behind us. How sophisticated we are today. I'll ignore her, he vowed, and went on. In this dehuman, exhausted, ultimate adjective hour, when every humane value has become untenable, and not only love, decency, and beauty but even compassion and intelligibility are no more than one or two subjective complements to complete the sentence. . . .

This is a story? It's a story, he replied equably, or will be if the author can finish it. Without interruption I suppose you mean? she broke in. I can't finish anything; that is my final word. Yet it's these interruptions that make it a story. Escalate the conflict further. Please let me start over.

Once upon a time you were satisfied with incidental felicities and niceties of technique: the unexpected image, the refreshingly accurate word-choice, the memorable simile that yields deeper and subtler significances upon reflection, like a memorable simile. Somebody please stop me. Or arresting dialogue, so to speak. For example?

Why do you suppose it is, she asked, lone participial phrase of the breathless variety characteristic of dialogue attributions in nineteenth-century fiction, that literate people such as we talk like characters in a story? Even supplying the dialogue-tags, she added with wry disgust. Don't put words in her mouth. The same old story, an old-fashioned one at that. Even if I should fill in the blank with my idle pen? Nothing new about that, to make a fact out of a figure. At least it's good for something. Every story is penned in red ink, to make a figure out of a fact. This whole idea is insane.

And might therefore be got away with.

No turning back now, we've gone too far. Everything's finished. Name eight. Story, novel, literature, art, humanism, humanity, the self itself. Wait: the story's not finished. And you and I, Howard? whispered Martha, her sarcasm belied by a hesitant alarm in her glance, flickering as it were despite herself to the blank instrument in his hand. Belied indeed; put that thing away! And what does flickering modify? A person who can't verb adverb ought at least to speak correctly.

A tense moment in the evolution of the story. Do you know, declared the narrator, one has no idea, especially nowadays, how close the end may be, nor will one necessarily be aware of it when it occurs. Who can say how near this universe has come to mere cessation? Or take two people, in a story of the sort it once was possible to tell. Love affairs, literary genres, third item in exemplary series, fourth—everything blossoms and decays, does it not, from the primitive and classical through the mannered and baroque to the abstract, stylized, dehumanized, unintelligible, blank. And you and I, Rosemary? Edward. Snapped! Patience. The narrator gathers that his audience no longer cherishes him. And conversely. But little does he know of the common noun concealed for months in her you name it, under her eyelet chemise. This is a slip. The point is the same. And she fetches it out nightly as I dream, I think. That's no slip. And she regards it and sighs, a quantum grimlier each night it may be. Is this supposed to be amusing? The world might end before this sentence, or merely someone's life. And/or someone else's. I speak metaphorically. Is the sentence ended? Very nearly. No telling how long a sentence will be until one reaches the stop It sounds as if somebody intends to fill in the blank. What *is* all this nonsense about?

It may not be nonsense. Anyhow it will presently be over. As the narrator was saying, things have been kaput for some time, and while we may be pardoned our great reluctance to acknowledge it, the fact is that the bloody century for example is nearing the three-quarter mark, and the characters in this little tale, for example, are similarly past their prime, as is the drama. About played out. Then God damn it let's ring the curtain. Wait wait. We're left with the following three possibilities, at least in theory. Horseshit. Hold onto yourself, it's too soon to fill in the blank. I hope this will be a short story.

Shorter than it seems. It seems endless. Be thankful it's not a novel. The novel is predicate adjective, as is the innocent anecdote of bygone days when life made a degree of sense and subject joined to complement by copula. No longer are these things the case, as you have doubtless remarked. There was I believe some mention of possibilities, three in number. The first is rejuvenation: having become an exhausted parody of itself, perhaps a form—Of what? Of anything—may rise neoprimitively from its own ashes. A tiresome prospect. The second, more appealing I'm sure but scarcely likely at this advancèd date, is that moribund what-have-yous will be supplanted by vigorous new: the demise of the novel and short story, he went on to declare, needn't be the end of narrative art, nor need the dissolution of a used-up blank fill in the blank. The end of one road might be the beginning of another. Much good that'll do me. And you may not find the revolution as bloodless as you think, either. Shall we try it? Never dare a person who is fed up to the ears.

The final possibility is a temporary expedient, to be sure, the self-styled narrator of this so-called story went on to admit, ignoring the hostile impatience of his audience, but what is not, and every sentence completed is a step closer to the end. That is to say, every day gained is a day gone. Matter of viewpoint, I suppose. Go on. I am. Whether anyone's paying attention or not. The final possibility is to turn ultimacy, exhaustion, paralyzing self-consciousness and the adjective weight of accumulated history. . . . Go on. Go on. To turn ultimacy against itself to make something new and valid, the essence whereof would be the impossibility of making something new. What a nauseating notion. And pray how does it bear upon the analogy uppermost in everyone's mind? We've gotten this far, haven't we? Look how far we've come together. Can't we keep on to the end? I think not. Even another sentence is too many. Only if one believes the end to be a long way off; actually it might come at any moment; I'm surprised it hasn't before now. Nothing does when it's expected to.

Silence. There's a fourth possibility, I suppose. Silence. General anesthesia. Self-extinction. Silence.

Historicity and self-awareness, he asseverated, while ineluctable and even greatly to be prized, are always fatal to innocence and spontaneity. Perhaps adjective period Whether in a people, an art, a love affair, on a fourth term added not impossibly to make the third less than ultimate. In the name of suffering humanity cease this harangue. It's over. And the story? Is there a plot here? What's all this leading up to?

No climax. There's the story. Finished? Not quite. Story of our lives. The last word in fiction, in fact. I chose the first-person narrative viewpoint in order to reflect interest from the peculiarities of the technique (such as the normally unbearable self-consciousness, the abstraction, and the blank) to the nature and situation of the narrator and his companion, despite the obvious possibility that the narrator and his companion might be mistaken for the narrator and his companion. Occupational hazard. The technique is advanced, as you see, but the situation of the characters is conventionally dramatic. That being the case, may one of them, or one who may be taken for one of them, make a longish speech in the old-fashioned manner, charged with obsolete emotion? Of course.

I begin calmly, though my voice may rise as I go along. Sometimes it seems as if things could instantly be altogether different and more admirable. The times be damned, one still wants a man vigorous, confident, bold, resourceful, adjective, and adjective. One still wants a woman spirited, spacious of heart, loyal, gentle, adjective, adjective. That man and that woman are as possible as the ones in this miserable story, and a good deal realer. It's as if they live in some room of our house that we can't find the door to, though it's so close we can hear echoes of their voices. Experience has made them wise instead of bitter; knowledge has mellowed instead of souring them; in their forties and fifties, even in their sixties, they're gayer and stronger and more authentic than they were in their twenties; for the twenty-year-olds they have only affectionate sympathy. So? Why aren't the couple in this story that man and woman, so easy to imagine? God, but I am surfeited with clever irony! Ill of sickness! Parallel phrase to wrap up series! This last-resort idea, it's dead in the womb, excuse the figure. A false pregnancy, excuse the figure. God damn me though if that's entirely my fault. Acknowledge your complicity. As you see, I'm trying to do something about the present mess; hence this story. Adjective in the noun! Don't lose your composure. You tell me it's self-defeating to talk about it instead of just up and doing it; but to acknowledge what I'm doing while I'm doing it is exactly the point. Self-defeat implies a victor, and who do you suppose it is, if not blank? That's the only victory left. Right? Forward! Eyes open.

No. The only way to get out of a mirror-maze is to close your eyes and hold out your hands. And be carried away by a valiant metaphor, I suppose, like a simile.

There's only one direction to go in. Ugh. We must make something out of nothing. Impossible. Mystics do. Not only turn contradiction into paradox, but *employ* it, to go on living and working. Don't bet on it. I'm betting my cliché on it, yours too. What is that supposed to mean? On with the refutation; every denial is another breath, every word brings us closer to the end.

Very well: to write this allegedly ultimate story is a form of artistic fill in the blank, or an artistic form of same, if you like. I don't. What I mean is, same idea in other terms. The storyteller's alternatives, as far as I can see, are a series of last words, like an aging actress making one farewell appearance after another, or actual blank. And I mean literally fill in the blank. Is this a test? But the former is contemptible in itself, and the latter will certainly become so when the rest of the world shrugs its shoulders and goes on about its business. Just as people would do if adverbial clause of obvious analogical nature. The fact is, the narrator has narrated himself into a corner, a state of affairs more tsk-tsk than boo-hoo, and because his position is absurd he calls the world absurd. That some writers lack lead in their pencils does not make writing obsolete. At this point they were both smiling despite themselves. At this point they were both flashing hatred despite themselves. Every woman has a blade concealed in the neighborhood of her garters. So disarm her, so to speak, don't geld yourself. At this point they were both despite themeselves. Have we come to the point at last? Not quite. Where there's life there's hope.

There's no hope. This isn't working. But the alternative is to supply an alternative. That's no alternative. Unless I make it one. Just try; quit talking about it, quit talking, quit! Never dare a desperate man. Or woman. That's the one thing that can drive even the first part of a conventional metaphor to the second part of same. Talk, talk, talk. Yes yes, go on, I believe literature's not likely ever to manage abstraction successfully, like sculpture for example, is that a fact, what a time to bring up that subject, anticlimax, that's the point, do set forth the exquisite reason. Well, because wood and iron have a native appeal and first-order reality, whereas words are artificial to begin with, invented specifically to represent. Go on, please go on. I'm going. Don't you dare. Well, well, weld iron rods into abstract patterns, say, and you've still got real iron, but arrange words into abstract patterns and you've got nonsense. Nonsense is right. For example. On, God damn it; take linear plot, take resolution of conflict, take third direct object, all that business, they may very well be obsolete notions, indeed they are, no doubt untenable at this late date, no doubt at all, but in fact we still lead our lives by clock and calendar, for example, and though the seasons recur our mortal human time does not; we grow old and tired, we think of how things used to be or might have been and how they are now, and in fact, and in fact we get exasperated and desperate and out of expedients and out of words.

Go on. Impossible. I'm going, too late now, one more step and we're done, you and I. Suspense. The fact is, you're driving me to it, the fact is that people still lead lives, mean and bleak and brief as they are, briefer than you think, and people have characters and motives that we divine more or less inaccurately from their appearance, speech, behavior, and the rest, you aren't listening, go on then, what do you think I'm doing, people still fall in love, and out, yes, in and out, and out and in, and they please each other, and hurt each other, isn't that the truth, and they do these things in more or less conventionally dramatic fashion, unfashionable or not, go on, I'm going, and what goes on between them is still not only the most interesting but the most important thing in the bloody murderous world, pardon the adjectives. And that my dear is what writers have got to find ways to write about in this adjective adjective hour of the ditto ditto same noun as above, or their, that is to say our, accursed self-consciousness will lead them, that is to say us, to here it comes, say it straight out, I'm going to, say it in plain English for once, that's what I'm leading up to, me and my bloody anticlimactic noun, we're pushing each other to fill in the blank.

Goodbye. Is it over? Can't you read between the lines? One more step. Goodbye suspense goodbye.

Blank.

Oh God comma I abhor self-consciousness. I despise what we have come to; I loathe our loathesome loathing, our place our time our situation, our loathesome art, this ditto necessary story. The blank of our lives. It's about over. Let the *dénouement* be soon and unexpected, painless if possible, quick at least, above all soon. Now now! How in the world will it ever

Robert Kennedy Saved from Drowning

Donald Barthelme

K. at His Desk

He is neither abrupt with nor excessively kind to associates. Or he is both abrupt and kind.

The telephone is, for him, a whip, a lash, but also a conduit for soothing words, a sink into which he can hurl gallons of syrup if it comes to that.

He reads quickly, scratching brief comments ("Yes," "No") in corners of the paper. He slouches in the leather chair, looking about him with a slightly irritated air for new visitors, new difficulties. He spends his time sending and receiving messengers.

"I spend my time sending and receiving messengers," he says. "Some of these messages are important. Others are not."

Described by Secretaries

A: "Quite frankly I think he forgets a lot of things. But the things he forgets are those which are inessential. I even think he might forget deliberately, to leave his mind free. He has the ability to get rid of unimportant details. And he does."

B: "Once when I was sick, I hadn't heard from him, and I thought he had forgotten me. You know usually your boss will send flowers or something like that. I was in the hospital, and I was mighty blue. I was in a room with another girl, and *her* boss hadn't sent her anything either. Then suddenly the door opened and there he was with the biggest bunch of yellow tulips I'd ever seen in my life. And the other girl's boss was with him, and he had tulips too. They were standing there with all those tulips, smiling."

Behind the Bar

At a crowded party, he wanders behind the bar to make himself a Scotch and water. His hand is on the bottle of Scotch, his glass is waiting. The bartender, a small man in a beige uniform with gilt buttons, politely asks K. to return to the other side, the guests' side, of the bar. "You let one behind here, they all be behind here," the bartender says.

K. Reading the Newspaper

His reactions are impossible to catalogue. Often he will find a note that amuses him endlessly, some anecdote involving, say, a fireman who has propelled his apparatus at record-breaking speed to the wrong address. These small stories are clipped, carried about in a pocket, to be produced at appropriate moments for the pleasure of friends. Other manifestations please him less. An account of an earthquake in Chile, with its thousands of dead and homeless, may depress him for weeks. He memorizes the terrible statistics, quoting them everywhere and saying, with a grave look: "We must do something." Important actions often follow, sometimes within a matter of hours. (On the other hand, these two kinds of responses may be, on a given day, inexplicably reversed.)

The more trivial aspects of the daily itemization are skipped. While reading, he maintains a rapid drumming of his fingertips on the desktop. He receives twelve newspapers, but of these, only four are regarded as serious.

Attitude toward His Work

"Sometimes I can't seem to do anything. The work is there, piled up, it seems to me an insurmountable obstacle, really out of reach. I sit and look at it, wondering where to begin, how to take hold of it. Perhaps I pick up a piece of paper, try to read it but my mind is elsewhere, I am thinking of something else, I can't seem to get the gist of it, it seems meaningless, devoid of interest, not having to do with human affairs, drained of life. Then, in an hour, or even a moment, everything changes suddenly: I realize I only have to *do* it, hurl myself into the midst of it, proceed mechanically, the first thing and then the second thing, that it is simply a matter of moving from one step to the next, plowing through it. I become interested, I become excited, I work very fast, things fall into place, I am exhilarated, amazed that these things could ever have seemed dead to me."

Sleeping on the Stones of Unknown Towns (Rimbaud)

K. is walking, with that familiar slight dip of the shoulders, through the streets of a small city in France or Germany. The shop signs are in a language which alters when inspected closely, MÖBEL becoming MEUBLES for example, and the citizens mutter to themselves with dark virtuosity a mixture of languages. K. is very interested, looks closely at everything, at the shops, the goods displayed, the clothing of the people, the tempo of street life, the citizens themselves, wondering about them. What are their water needs?

"In the West, wisdom is mostly gained at lunch. At lunch, people tell you things."

The nervous eyes of the waiters.

The tall bald cook, white apron, white T-shirt, grinning through an opening in the wall.

"Why is that cook looking at me?"

Urban Transportation

"The transportation problems of our cities and their rapidly expanding suburbs are the most urgent and neglected transportation problems confronting the country. In these heavily populated and industrialized areas, people are dependent on a system of transportation that is at once complex and inadequate. Obsolete facilities and growing demands have created seemingly insoluble difficulties and present methods of dealing with these difficulties offer little prospect of relief."

K. Penetrated with Sadness

He hears something playing on someone else's radio, in another part of the building.

The music is wretchedly sad; now he can (barely) hear it, now it fades into the wall.

He turns on his own radio. There it is, on his own radio, the same music. The sound fills the room.

Karsh of Ottawa

"We sent a man to Karsh of Ottawa and told him that we admired his work very much. Especially, I don't know, the Churchill thing and, you know, the Hemingway thing, and all that. And we told him we wanted to set up a sitting for K. sometime in June, if that would be convenient for him, and he said yes, that was okay, June was okay, and where did we want to have it shot, there or in New York or where. Well, that was a problem because we didn't know exactly what K.'s schedule would be for June, it was up in the air, so we tentatively said New York around the fifteenth. And he said, that was okay, he could do that. And he wanted to know how much time he could have, and we said, well, how much time do you need? And he said he didn't know, it varied from sitter to sitter. He said some people were very restless and that made it difficult to get just the right shot. He said there was one shot in each sitting that was, you know, the key shot, the right one. He said he'd have to see, when the time came."

Dress

He is neatly dressed in a manner that does not call attention to itself. The suits are soberly cut and in dark colors. He must at all times present an aspect of freshness difficult to sustain because of frequent movements from place to place under conditions which are not always the most favorable. Thus he changes clothes frequently, especially shirts. In the course of a day he changes his shirt many times. There are always extra shirts about, in boxes.

"Which of you has the shirts?"

A Friend Comments: K.'s Aloneness

"The thing you have to realize about K. is that essentially he's absolutely alone in the world. There's this terrible loneliness which prevents people from getting too close to him. Maybe it comes from something in his childhood, I don't know. But he's very hard to get to know, and a lot of people who think they know him rather well don't really know him at all. He says something or does something that surprises you, and you realize that all along you really didn't know him at all.

"He has surprising facets. I remember once we were out in a small boat. K. of course was the captain. Some rough weather came up and we began to head back in. I began worrying about picking up a landing and I said to him that I didn't think the anchor would hold, with the wind and all. He just looked at me. Then he said: 'Of course it will hold. That's what it's for.' "

K. on Crowds

"There are exhausted crowds and vivacious crowds.

"Sometimes, standing there, I can sense whether a particular crowd is one thing or the other. Sometimes the mood of the crowd is disguised, sometimes you only find out after a quarter of an hour what sort of crowd a particular crowd is.

"And you can't speak to them in the same way. The variations have to be taken into account. You have to say something to them that is meaningful to them *in that mood.*"

Gallery-going

K. enters a large gallery on Fifty-seventh Street, in the Fuller Building. His entourage includes several ladies and gentlemen. Works by a geometricist are on show. K. looks at the immense, rather theoretical paintings.

"Well, at least we know he has a ruler."

The group dissolves in laughter. People repeat the remark to one another, laughing.

The artist, who has been standing behind a dealer, regards K. with hatred.

K. Puzzled by His Children

The children are crying. There are several children, one about four, a boy, then another boy, slightly older, and a little girl, very beautiful, wearing blue jeans, crying. There are various objects on the grass, an electric train, a picture book, a red ball, a plastic bucket, a plastic shovel.

K. frowns at the children whose distress issues from no source immediately available to the eye, which seems indeed uncaused, vacant, a general anguish. K. turns to the mother of these children who is standing nearby wearing hip-huggers which appear to be made of linked marshmallows studded with diamonds but then I am a notoriously poor observer.

"Play with them," he says.

This mother of ten quietly suggests that K. himself "play with them."

K. picks up the picture book and begins to read to the children. But the book has a German text. It has been left behind, perhaps, by some foreign visitor. Nevertheless K. perseveres.

"A ist der Affe, er isst mit der Pfote." ("A is the Ape, he eats with his Paw.")

The crying of the children continues.

A Dream

Orange trees.

Overhead, a steady stream of strange aircraft which resemble kitchen implements, bread boards, cookie sheets, colanders.

The shiny aluminum instruments are on their way to complete the bombing of Sidi-Madani.

A farm in the hills.

Matters (from an Administrative Assistant)

"A lot of matters that had been pending came to a head right about that time, moved to the front burner, things we absolutely had to take care of. And we couldn't find K. Nobody knew where he was. We had looked everywhere. He had just withdrawn, made himself unavailable. There was this one matter that was probably more pressing than all the rest put together. Really crucial. We were all standing around wondering what to do. We were getting pretty nervous because this thing was really . . . . Then K. walked in and disposed of it with a quick phone call. A quick phone call!"

Childhood of K. as Recalled by a Former Teacher

"He was a very alert boy, very bright, good at his studies, very thorough, very conscientious. But that's not unusual; that describes a good number of the boys who pass through here. It's not unusual, that is, to find these qualities which are after all the qualities that we look for and encourage in them. What *was* unusual about K. was his compassion, something very rare for a boy of that age—even if they have it, they're usually very careful not to display it for fear of seeming soft, girlish. I remember, though, that in K. this particular attribute was very marked. I would almost say that it was his strongest characteristic."

Speaking to No One but Waiters, He—

"The dandelion salad with bacon, I think."

"The *rysstafel.*"

"The poached duck."

"The black bean purée."

"The cod fritters."

K. Explains a Technique

"It's an expedient in terms of how not to destroy a situation which has been a long time gestating, or, again, how *to* break it up if it appears that the situation has changed, during the gestation period, into one whose implications are not quite what they were at the beginning. What I mean is that in this business things are constantly altering (usually for the worse) and usually you want to give the impression that you're not watching this particular situation particularly closely, that you're paying no special attention to it, until you're ready to make your move. That is, it's best to be sudden, if you can manage it. Of course you can't do that all the time. Sometimes you're just completely wiped out, cleaned out, totaled, and then the only thing to do is shrug and forget about it."

K. on His Own Role

"Sometimes it seems to me that it doesn't matter what I do, that it is enough to exist, to sit somewhere, in a garden for example, watching whatever is to be seen there, the small events. At other times, I'm aware that other people, possibly a great number of other people, could be affected by what I do or fail to do, that I have a responsibility, as we all have, to make the best possible use of whatever talents I've been given, for the common good. It is not enough to sit in that garden, however restful or pleasurable it might be. The world is full of unsolved problems, situations that demand careful, reasoned and intelligent action. In Latin America, for example."

As Entrepreneur

The original cost estimates for burying the North Sea pipeline have been exceeded by a considerable margin. Everyone wonders what he will say about this contretemps which does not fail to have its dangers for those responsible for the costly miscalculations, which are viewed in many minds as inexcusable.

He says only: "Exceptionally difficult rock conditions."

With Young People

K., walking the streets of unknown towns, finds himself among young people. Young people line these streets, narrow and curving, which are theirs, dedicated to them. They are everywhere, resting on the embankments, their guitars, small radios, long hair. They sit on the sidewalks, back to back, heads turned to stare. They stand implacably on street corners, in doorways, or lean on their elbows in windows, or squat in small groups at that place where the sidewalk meets the walls of buildings. The streets are filled with these young people who say nothing, reveal only a limited interest, refuse to declare themselves. Street after street contains them, a great number, more displayed as one turns a corner, rank upon rank stretching into the distance, drawn from the arcades, the plazas, staring.

He Discusses the French Writer, Poulet

"For Poulet, it is not enough to speak of *seizing the moment.* It is rather a question of, and I quote, 'recognizing in the instant which lives and dies, which surges out of nothingness and which ends in dream, an intensity and depth of significance which ordinarily attaches only to the whole of existence.'

"What Poulet is describing is neither an ethic nor a prescription but rather what he has discovered in the work of Marivaux. Poulet has taken up the Marivaudian canon and squeezed it with both hands to discover the essence of what may be called the Marivaudian being, what Poulet in fact calls the Marivaudian being.

"The Marivaudian being is, according to Poulet, a pastless futureless man, born anew at every instant. The instants are points which organize themselves into a line, but what is important is the instant, not the line. The Marivaudian being has in a sense no history. Nothing follows from what has gone before. He is constantly surprised. He cannot predict his own reaction to events. He is constantly being *overtaken* by events. A condition of breathlessness and dazzlement surrounds him. In consequence he exists in a certain freshness which seems, if I may say so, very desirable. This freshness Poulet, quoting Marivaux, describes very well."

K. Saved from Drowning

K. in the water. His flat black hat, his black cape, his sword are on the shore. He retains his mask. His hands beat the surface of the water which tears and rips about him. The white foam, the green depths. I throw a line, the coils leaping out over the surface of the water. He has missed it. No, it appears that he has it. His right hand (sword arm) grasps the line that I have thrown him. I am on the bank, the rope wound round my waist, braced against a rock. K. now has both hands on the line. I pull him out of the water. He stands now on the bank, gasping.

"Thank you."

Looking for Mr. Green

Saul Bellow

Whatsoever thy hand findeth to do, do it with thy might. . . .

Hard work? No, it wasn't really so hard. He wasn't used to walking and stair-climbing, but the physical difficulty of his new job was not what George Grebe felt most. He was delivering relief checks in the Negro district, and although he was a native Chicagoan this was not a part of the city he knew much about—it needed a depression to introduce him to it. No, it wasn't literally hard work, not as reckoned in foot-pounds, but yet he was beginning to feel the strain of it, to grow aware of its peculiar difficulty. He could find the streets and numbers, but the clients were not where they were supposed to be, and he felt like a hunter inexperienced in the camouflage of his game. It was an unfavorable day, too—fall, and cold, dark weather, windy. But, anyway, instead of shells in his deep trenchcoat pocket he had the cardboard of checks, punctured for the spindles of the file, the holes reminding him of the holes in player-piano paper. And he didn't look much like a hunter, either; his was a city figure entirely, belted up in this Irish conspirator's coat. He was slender without being tall, stiff in the back, his legs looking shabby in a pair of old tweed pants gone through and fringy at the cuffs. With this stiffness, he kept his head forward, so that his face was red from the sharpness of the weather; and it was an indoors sort of face with gray eyes that persisted in some kind of thought and yet seemed to avoid definiteness of conclusion. He wore sideburns that surprised you somewhat by the tough curl of the blond hair and the effect of assertion in their length. He was not so mild as he looked, nor so youthful; and nevertheless there was no effort on his part to seem what he was not. He was an educated man; he was a bachelor; he was in some ways simple; without lushing, he liked a drink; his luck had not been good. Nothing was deliberately hidden.

He felt that his luck was better than usual today. When he had reported for work that morning he had expected to be shut up in the relief office at a clerk's job, for he had been hired downtown as a clerk, and he was glad to have, instead, the freedom of the streets and welcomed, at least at first, the vigor of the cold and even the blowing of the hard wind. But on the other hand he was not getting on with the distribution of the checks. It was true that it was a city job; nobody expected you to push too hard at a city job. His supervisor, that young Mr. Raynor, had practically told him that. Still, he wanted to do well at it. For one thing, when he knew how quickly he could deliver a batch of checks, he would know also how much time he could expect to clip for himself. And then, too, the clients would be waiting for their money. That was not the most important consideration, though it certainly mattered to him. No, but he wanted to do well, simply for doing-well's sake, to acquit himself decently of a job because he so rarely had a job to do that required just this sort of energy. Of this peculiar energy he now had a superabundance; once it had started to flow, it flowed all too heavily. And, for the time being anyway, he was balked. He could not find Mr. Green.

So he stood in his big-skirted trenchcoat with a large envelope in his hand and papers showing from his pocket, wondering why people should be so hard to locate who were too feeble or sick to come to the station to collect their own checks. But Raynor had told him that tracking them down was not easy at first and had offered him some advice on how to proceed. "If you can see the postman, he's your first man to ask, and your best bet. If you can't connect with him, try the stores and tradespeople around. Then the janitor and the neighbors. But you'll find the closer you come to your man the less people will tell you. They don't want to tell you anything."

"Because I'm a stranger."

"Because you're white. We ought to have a Negro doing this, but we don't at the moment, and of course you've got to eat, too, and this is public employment. Jobs have to be made. Oh, that holds for me too. Mind you, I'm not letting myself out. I've got three years of seniority on you, that's all. And a law degree. Otherwise, you might be back of the desk and I might be going out into the field this cold day. The same dough pays us both and for the same, exact, identical reason. What's my law degree got to do with it? But you have to pass out these checks, Mr. Grebe, and it'll help if you're stubborn, so I hope you are."

"Yes, I'm fairly stubborn."

Raynor sketched hard with an eraser in the old dirt of his desk, left-handed, and said, "Sure, what else can you answer to such a question. Anyhow, the trouble you're going to have is that they don't like to give information about anybody. They think you're a plain-clothes dick or an installment collector, or summons-server or something like that. Till you've been seen around the neighborhood for a few months and people know you're only from the relief."

It was dark, ground-freezing, pre-Thanksgiving weather; the wind played hob with the smoke, rushing it down, and Grebe missed his gloves, which he had left in Raynor's office. And no one would admit knowing Green. It was past three o'clock and the postman had made his last delivery. The nearest grocer, himself a Negro, had never heard the name Tulliver Green, or said he hadn't. Grebe was inclined to think that it was true, that he had in the end convinced the man that he wanted only to deliver a check. But he wasn't sure. He needed experience in interpreting looks and signs and, even more, the will not to be put off or denied and even the force to bully if need be. If the grocer did know, he had got rid of him easily. But since most of his trade was with reliefers, why should he prevent the delivery of a check? Maybe Green, or Mrs. Green, if there was a Mrs. Green, patronized another grocer. And was there a Mrs. Green? It was one of Grebe's great handicaps that he hadn't looked at any of the case records. Raynor should have let him read files for a few hours. But he apparently saw no need for that, probably considering the job unimportant. Why prepare systematically to deliver a few checks?

But now it was time to look for the janitor. Grebe took in the building in the wind and gloom of the late November day—trampled, frost-hardened lots on one side; on the other, an automobile junk yard and then the infinite work of Elevated frames, weak-looking, gaping with rubbish fires; two sets of leaning brick porches three stories high and a flight of cement stairs to the cellar. Descending, he entered the underground passage, where he tried the doors until one opened and he found himself in the furnace room. There someone rose toward him and approached, scraping on the coal grit and bending under the canvas-jacketed pipes.

"Are you the janitor?"

"What do you want?"

"I'm looking for a man who's supposed to be living here. Green."

"What Green?"

"Oh, you maybe have more than one Green?" said Grebe with new, pleasant hope. "This is Tulliver Green."

"I don't think I c'n help you, mister. I don't know any."

"A crippled man."

The janitor stood bent before him. Could it be that he was crippled? Oh, God! what if he was. Grebe's gray eyes sought with excited difficulty to see. But no, he was only very short and stooped. A head awakened from meditation, a strong-haired beard, low, wide shoulders. A staleness of sweat and coal rose from his black shirt and the burlap sack he wore as an apron.

"Crippled how?"

Grebe thought and then answered with the light voice of unmixed candor, "I don't know. I've never seen him." This was damaging, but his only other choice was to make a lying guess, and he was not up to it. "I'm delivering checks for the relief to shut-in cases. If he weren't crippled he'd come to collect himself. That's why I said crippled. Bedridden, chair-ridden—is there anybody like that?"

This sort of frankness was one of Grebe's oldest talents, going back to childhood. But it gained him nothing here.

"No suh. I've got four buildin's same as this that I take care of. I don' know all the tenants, leave alone the tenants' tenants. The rooms turn over so fast, people movin' in and out every day. I can't tell you."

The janitor opened his grimy lips but Grebe did not hear him in the piping of the valves and the consuming pull of air to flame in the body of the furnace. He knew, however, what he had said.

"Well, all the same, thanks. Sorry I bothered you. I'll prowl around upstairs again and see if I can turn up someone who knows him."

Once more in the cold air and early darkness he made the short circle from the cellarway to the entrance crowded between the brickwork pillars and began to climb to the third floor. Pieces of plaster ground under his feet; strips of brass tape from which the carpeting had been torn away marked old boundaries at the sides. In the passage, the cold reached him worse than in the street; it touched him to the bone. The hall toilets ran like springs. He thought grimly as he heard the wind burning around the building with a sound like that of the furnace, that this was a great piece of constructed shelter. Then he struck a match in the gloom and searched for names and numbers among the writings and scribbles on the walls. He saw WHOODY-DOODY GO TO JESUS, and zigzags, caricatures, sexual scrawls, and curses. So the sealed rooms of pyramids were also decorated, and the caves of human dawn.

The information on his card was, TULLIVER GREEN—APT 3D. There were no names, however, and no numbers. His shoulders drawn up, tears of cold in his eyes, breathing vapor, he went the length of the corridor and told himself that if he had been lucky enough to have the temperament for it he would bang on one of the doors and bawl out "Tulliver Green!" until he got results. But it wasn't in him to make an uproar and he continued to burn matches, passing the light over the walls. At the rear, in a corner off the hall, he discovered a door he had not seen before and he thought it best to investigate. It sounded empty when he knocked, but a young Negress answered, hardly more than a girl. She opened only a bit, to guard the warmth of the room.

"Yes suh?"

"I'm from the district relief station on Prairie Avenue. I'm looking for a man named Tulliver Green to give him his check. Do you know him?"

No, she didn't; but he thought she had not understood anything of what he had said. She had a dream-bound, dream-blind face, very soft and black, shut off. She wore a man's jacket and pulled the ends together at her throat. Her hair was parted in three directions, at the sides and transversely, standing up at the front in a dull puff.

"Is there somebody around here who might know?"

"I jus' taken this room las' week."

He observed that she shivered, but even her shiver was somnambulistic and there was no sharp consciousness of cold in the big smooth eyes of her handsome face.

"All right, miss, thank you. Thanks," he said, and went to try another place.

Here he was admitted. He was grateful, for the room was warm. It was full of people, and they were silent as he entered—ten people, or a dozen, perhaps more, sitting on benches like a parliament. There was no light, properly speaking, but a tempered darkness that the window gave, and everyone seemed to him enormous, the men padded out in heavy work clothes and winter coats, and the women huge, too, in their sweaters, hats, and old furs. And, besides, bed and bedding, a black cooking range, a piano piled towering to the ceiling with papers, a dining-room table of the old style of prosperous Chicago. Among these people Grebe, with his cold-heightened fresh color and his smaller stature, entered like a schoolboy. Even though he was met with smiles and good will, he knew, before a single word was spoken, that all the currents ran against him and that he would make no headway. Nevertheless he began. "Does anybody here know how I can deliver a check to Mr. Tulliver Green?"

"Green?" It was the man that had let him in who answered. He was in short sleeves, in a checkered shirt, and had a queer, high head, profusely overgrown and long as a shako; the veins entered it strongly from his forehead. "I never heard mention of him. Is this where he live?"

"This is the address they gave me at the station. He's a sick man, and he'll need his check. Can't anybody tell me where to find him?"

He stood his ground and waited for a reply, his crimson wool scarf wound about his neck and drooping outside his trenchcoat, pockets weighted with the block of checks and official forms. They must have realized that he was not a college boy employed afternoons by a bill collector, trying foxily to pass for a relief clerk, recognized that he was an older man who knew himself what need was, who had had more than an average seasoning in hardship. It was evident enough if you looked at the marks under his eyes and at the sides of his mouth.

"Anybody know this sick man?"

"No suh." On all sides he saw heads shaken and smiles of denial. No one knew. And maybe it was true, he considered, standing silent in the earthen, musky human gloom of the place as the rumble continued. But he could never really be sure.

"What's the matter with this man?" said shako-head.

"I've never seen him. All I can tell you is that he can't come in person for his money. It's my first day in this district."

"Maybe they given you the wrong number?"

"I don't believe so. But where else can I ask about him?" He felt that this persistence amused them deeply, and in a way he shared their amusement that he should stand up so tenaciously to them. Though smaller, though slight, he was his own man, he retracted nothing about himself, and he looked back at them, gray-eyed, with amusement and also with a sort of courage. On the bench some man spoke in his throat, the words impossible to catch, and a woman answered with a wild, shrieking laugh, which was quickly cut off.

"Well, so nobody will tell me?"

"Ain't nobody who knows."

"At least, if he lives here, he pays rent to someone. Who manages the building?"

"Greatham Company. That's on Thirty-ninth Street."

Grebe wrote it in his pad. But, in the street again, a sheet of wind-driven paper clinging to his leg while he deliberated what direction to take next, it seemed a feeble lead to follow. Probably this Green didn't rent a flat, but a room. Sometimes there were as many as twenty people in an apartment; the real-estate agent would know only the lessee. And not even the agent could tell you who the renters were. In some places the beds were even used in shifts, watchmen or jitney drivers or short-order cooks in night joints turning out after a day's sleep and surrendering their beds to a sister, a nephew, or perhaps a stranger, just off the bus. There were large numbers of newcomers in this terrific, blight-bitten portion of the city between Cottage Grove and Ashland, wandering from house to house and room to room. When you saw them, how could you know them? They didn't carry bundles on their backs or look picturesque. You only saw a man, a Negro, walking in the street or riding in the car, like everyone else, with his thumb closed on a transfer. And therefore how were you supposed to tell? Grebe thought the Greatham agent would only laugh at his question.

But how much it would have simplified the job to be able to say that Green was old, or blind, or consumptive. An hour in the files, taking a few notes, and he needn't have been at such a disadvantage. When Raynor gave him the block of checks he asked, "How much should I know about these people?" Then Raynor had looked as though he were preparing to accuse him of trying to make the job more important than it was. He smiled, because by then they were on fine terms, but nevertheless he had been getting ready to say something like that when the confusion began in the station over Staika and her children.

Grebe had waited a long time for this job. It came to him through the pull of an old schoolmate in the Corporation Counsel's office, never a close friend, but suddenly sympathetic and interested—pleased to show, moreover, how well he had done, how strongly he was coming on even in these miserable times. Well, he was coming through strongly, along with the Democratic administration itself. Grebe had gone to see him in City Hall, and they had had a counter lunch or beers at least once a month for a year, and finally it had been possible to swing the job. He didn't mind being assigned the lowest clerical grade, nor even being a messenger, though Raynor thought he did.

This Raynor was an original sort of guy and Grebe had taken to him immediately. As was proper on the first day, Grebe had come early, but he waited long, for Raynor was late. At last he darted into his cubicle of an office as though he had just jumped from one of those hurtling huge red Indiana Avenue cars. His thin, rough face was wind-stung and he was grinning and saying something breathlessly to himself. In his hat, a small fedora, and his coat, the velvet collar a neat fit about his neck, and his silk muffler that set off the nervous twist of his chin, he swayed and turned himself in his swivel chair, feet leaving the ground; so that he pranced a little as he sat. Meanwhile he took Grebe's measure out of his eyes, eyes of an unusual vertical length and slightly sardonic. So the two men sat for a while, saying nothing, while the supervisor raised his hat from his miscombed hair and put it in his lap. His cold-darkened hands were not clean. A steel beam passed through the little makeshift room, from which machine belts once had hung. The building was an old factory.

"I'm younger than you; I hope you won't find it hard taking orders from me," said Raynor. "But I don't make them up, either. You're how old, about?"

"Thirty-five."

"And you thought you'd be inside doing paper work. But it so happens I have to send you out."

"I don't mind."

"And it's mostly a Negro load we have in this district."

"So I thought it would be."

"Fine. You'll get along. *C'est un bon boulot.* Do you know French?"

"Some."

"I thought you'd be a university man."

"Have you been in France?" said Grebe.

"No, that's the French of the Berlitz School. I've been at it for more than a year, just as I'm sure people have been, all over the world, office boys in China and braves in Tanganyika. In fact, I damn well know it. Such is the attractive power of civilization. It's overrated, but what do you want? *Que voulez-vous?* I get *Le Rire* and all the spicy papers, just like in Tanganyika. It must be mystifying, out there. But my reason is that I'm aiming at the diplomatic service. I have a cousin who's a courier, and the way he describes it is awfully attractive. He rides in the *wagon-lits* and reads books. While we— What did you do before?"

"I sold."

"Where?"

"Canned meat at Stop and Shop. In the basement."

"And before that?"

"Window shades, at Goldblatt's."

"Steady work?"

"No, Thursdays and Saturdays. I also sold shoes."

"You've been a shoe-dog too. Well. And prior to that? Here it is in your folder." He opened the record. "Saint Olaf's College, instructor in classical languages. Fellow, University of Chicago, 1926–27. I've had Latin, too. Let's trade quotations—'*Dum spiro spero.*' "

"*'Da dextram misero.'* "

"*'Alea jacta est.'* "

"*'Excelsior.'* "

Raynor shouted with laughter, and other workers came to look at him over the partition. Grebe also laughed, feeling pleased and easy. The luxury of fun on a nervous morning.

When they were done and no one was watching or listening, Raynor said rather seriously, "What made you study Latin in the first place? Was it for the priesthood?"

"No."

"Just for the hell of it? For the culture? Oh, the things people think they can pull!" He made his cry hilarious and tragic. "I ran my pants off so I could study for the bar, and I've passed the bar, so I get twelve dollars a week more than you as a bonus for having seen life straight and whole. I'll tell you, as a man of culture, that even though nothing looks to be real, and everything stands for something else, and that thing for another thing, and that thing for a still further one—there ain't any comparison between twenty-five and thirty-seven dollars a week, regardless of the last reality. Don't you think that was clear to your Greeks? They were a thoughtful people, but they didn't part with their slaves."

This was a great deal more than Grebe had looked for in his first interview with his supervisor. He was too shy to show all the astonishment he felt. He laughed a little, aroused, and brushed at the sunbeam that covered his head with its dust. "Do you think my mistake was so terrible?"

"Damn right it was terrible, and you know it now that you've had the whip of hard times laid on your back. You should have been preparing yourself for trouble. Your people must have been well off to send you to the university. Stop me, if I'm stepping on your toes. Did your mother pamper you? Did your father give in to you? Were you brought up tenderly, with permission to go and find out what were the last things that everything else stands for while everybody else labored in the fallen world of appearances?"

"Well, no, it wasn't exactly like that." Grebe smiled. *The fallen world of appearances!* no less. But now it was his turn to deliver a surprise. "We weren't rich. My father was the last genuine English butler in Chicago—"

"Are you kidding?"

"Why should I be?"

"In a livery?"

"In livery. Up on the Gold Coast."

"And he wanted you to be educated like a gentleman?"

"He did not. He sent me to the Armour Institute to study chemical engineering. But when he died I changed schools."

He stopped himself, and considered how quickly Raynor had reached him. In no time he had your valise on the table and all your stuff unpacked. And afterward, in the streets, he was still reviewing how far he might have gone, and how much he might have been led to tell if they had not been interrupted by Mrs. Staika's great noise.

But just then a young woman, one of Raynor's workers, ran into the cubicle exclaiming, "Haven't you heard all the fuss?"

"We haven't heard anything."

"It's Staika, giving out with all her might. The reporters are coming. She said she phoned the papers, and you know she did."

"But what is she up to?" said Raynor.

"She brought her wash and she's ironing it here, with our current, because the relief won't pay her electric bill. She has her ironing board set up by the admitting desk, and her kids are with her, all six. They never are in school more than once a week. She's always dragging them around with her because of her reputation."

"I don't want to miss any of this," said Raynor, jumping up. Grebe, as he followed with the secretary, said, "Who is this Staika?"

"They call her the 'Blood Mother of Federal Street.' She's a professional donor at the hospitals. I think they pay ten dollars a pint. Of course it's no joke, but she makes a very big thing out of it and she and the kids are in the papers all the time."

A small crowd, staff and clients divided by a plywood barrier, stood in the narrow space of the entrance, and Staika was shouting in a gruff, mannish voice, plunging the iron on the board and slamming it on the metal rest.

"My father and mother came in a steerage, and I was born in our house, Robey by Huron. I'm no dirty immigrant. I'm a U.S. citizen. My husband is a gassed veteran from France with lungs weaker'n paper, that hardly can he go to the toilet by himself. These six children of mine, I have to buy the shoes for their feet with my own blood. Even a lousy little white Communion necktie, that's a couple of drops of blood; a little piece of mosquito veil for my Vadja so she won't be ashamed in church for the other girls, they take my blood for it by Goldblatt. That's how I keep goin'. A fine thing if I had to depend on the relief. And there's plenty of people on the rolls—fakes! There's nothin' *they* can't get, that can go and wrap bacon at Swift and Armour any time. They're lookin' for them by the Yards. They never have to be out of work. Only they rather lay in their lousy beds and eat the public's money." She was not afraid, in a predominantly Negro station, to shout this way about Negroes.

Grebe and Raynor worked themselves forward to get a closer view of the woman. She was flaming with anger and with pleasure at herself, broad and huge, a golden-headed woman who wore a cotton cap laced with pink ribbon. She was barelegged and had on black gym shoes, her Hoover apron was open and her great breasts, not much restrained by a man's undershirt, hampered her arms as she worked at the kid's dress on the ironing board. And the children, silent and white, with a kind of locked obstinacy, in sheepskins and lumberjackets, stood behind her. She had captured the station, and the pleasure this gave her was enormous. Yet her grievances were true grievances. She was telling the truth. But she behaved like a liar. The look of her small eyes was hidden, and while she raged she also seemed to be spinning and planning.

"They send me out college case workers in silk pants to talk me out of what I got comin'. Are they better'n me? Who told them? Fire them. Let 'em go and get married, and then you won't have to cut electric from people's budget."

The chief supervisor, Mr. Ewing, couldn't silence her and he stood with folded arms at the head of his staff, bald, bald-headed, saying to his subordinates like the ex-school principal he was, "Pretty soon she'll be tired and go."

"No she won't," said Raynor to Grebe. "She'll get what she wants. She knows more about the relief even than Ewing. She's been on the rolls for years, and she always gets what she wants because she puts on a noisy show. Ewing knows it. He'll give in soon. He's only saving face. If he gets bad publicity, the Commissioner'll have him on the carpet, downtown. She's got him submerged; she'll submerge everybody in time, and that includes nations and governments."

Grebe replied with his characteristic smile, disagreeing completely. Who would take Staika's orders, and what changes could her yelling ever bring about?

No, what Grebe saw in her, the power that made people listen, was that her cry expressed the war of flesh and blood, perhaps turned a little crazy and certainly ugly, on this place and this condition. And at first, when he went out, the spirit of Staika somehow presided over the whole district for him, and it took color from her; he saw her color, in the spotty curb fires, and the fires under the El, the straight alley of flamy gloom. Later, too, when he went into a tavern for a shot of rye, the sweat of beer, association with West Side Polish streets, made him think of her again.

He wiped the corners of his mouth with his muffler, his handkerchief being inconvenient to reach for, and went out again to get on with the delivery of his checks. The air bit cold and hard and a few flakes of snow formed near him. A train struck by and left a quiver in the frames and a bristling icy hiss over the rails.

Crossing the street, he descended a flight of board steps into a basement grocery, setting off a little bell. It was a dark, long store and it caught you with its stinks of smoked meat, soap, dried peaches, and fish. There was a fire wrinkling and flapping in the little stove, and the proprietor was waiting, an Italian with a long, hollow face and stubborn bristles. He kept his hands warm under his apron.

No, he didn't know Green. You knew people but not names. The same man might not have the same name twice. The police didn't know, either, and mostly didn't care. When somebody was shot or knifed they took the body away and didn't look for the murderer. In the first place, nobody would tell them anything. So they made up a name for the coroner and called it quits. And in the second place, they didn't give a goddamn anyhow. But they couldn't get to the bottom of a thing even if they wanted to. Nobody would get to know even a tenth of what went on among these people. They stabbed and stole, they did every crime and abomination you ever heard of, men and men, women and women, parents and children, worse than the animals. They carried on their own way, and the horrors passed off like a smoke. There was never anything like it in the history of the whole world.

It was a long speech, deepening with every word in its fantasy and passion and becoming increasingly senseless and terrible: a swarm amassed by suggestion and invention, a huge, hugging, despairing knot, a human wheel of heads, legs, bellies, arms, rolling through his shop.

Grebe felt that he must interrupt him. He said sharply, "What are you talking about! All I asked was whether you knew this man."

"That isn't even the half of it. I been here six years. You probably don't want to believe this. But suppose it's true?"

"All the same," said Grebe, "there must be a way to find a person."

The Italian's close-spaced eyes had been queerly concentrated, as were his muscles, while he leaned across the counter trying to convince Grebe. Now he gave up the effort and sat down on his stool. "Oh—I suppose. Once in a while. But I been telling you, even the cops don't get anywhere."

"They're always after somebody. It's not the same thing."

"Well, keep trying if you want. I can't help you."

But he didn't keep trying. He had no more time to spend on Green. He slipped Green's check to the back of the block. The next name on the list was FIELD, WINSTON.

He found the back-yard bungalow without the least trouble; it shared a lot with another house, a few feet of yard between. Grebe knew these two-shack arrangements. They had been built in vast numbers in the days before the swamps were filled and the streets raised, and they were all the same—a boardwalk along the fence, well under street level, three or four ball-headed posts for clotheslines, greening wood, dead shingles, and a long, long flight of stairs to the rear door.

A twelve-year-old boy let him into the kitchen, and there the old man was, sitting by the table in a wheel chair.

"Oh, it's d' Government man," he said to the boy when Grebe drew out his checks. "Go bring me my box of papers." He cleared a space on the table.

"Oh, you don't have to go to all that trouble," said Grebe. But Field laid out his papers: Social Security card, relief certification, letters from the state hospital in Manteno, and a naval discharge dated San Diego, 1920.

"That's plenty," Grebe said. "Just sign."

"You got to know who I am," the old man said. "You're from the Government. It's not your check, it's a Government check and you got no business to hand it over till everything is proved."

He loved the ceremony of it, and Grebe made no more objections. Field emptied his box and finished out the circle of cards and letters.

"There's everything I done and been. Just the death certificate and they can close book on me." He said this with a certain happy pride and magnificence. Still he did not sign; he merely held the little pen upright on the golden-green corduroy of his thigh. Grebe did not hurry him. He felt the old man's hunger for conversation.

"I got to get better coal," he said. "I send my little gran'son to the yard with my order and they fill his wagon with screening. The stove ain't made for it. It fall through the grate. The order says Franklin County egg-size coal."

"I'll report it and see what can be done."

"Nothing can be done, I expect. You know and I know. There ain't no little ways to make things better, and the only big thing is money. That's the only sunbeams, money. Nothing is black where it shines, and the only place you see black is where it ain't shining. What we colored have to have is our own rich. There ain't no other way."

Grebe sat, his reddened forehead bridged levelly by his close-cut hair and his cheeks lowered in the wings of his collar—the caked fire shone hard within the isinglass-and-iron frames but the room was not comfortable—sat and listened while the old man unfolded his scheme. This was to create one Negro millionaire a month by subscription. One clever, good-hearted young fellow elected every month would sign a contract to use the money to start a business employing Negroes. This would be advertised by chain letters and word of mouth, and every Negro wage earner would contribute a dollar a month. Within five years there would be sixty millionaires.

"That'll fetch respect," he said with a throat-stopped sound that came out like a foreign syllable. "You got to take and organize all the money that gets thrown away on the policy wheel and horse race. As long as they can take it away from you, they got no respect for you. Money, that's d' sun of human kind!" Field was a Negro of mixed blood, perhaps Cherokee, or Natchez; his skin was reddish. And he sounded, speaking about a golden sun in this dark room, and looked, shaggy and slab-headed, with the mingled blood of his face and broad lips, the little pen still upright in his hand, like one of the underground kings of mythology, old judge Minos himself.

And now he accepted the check and signed. Not to soil the slip, he held it down with his knuckles. The table budged and creaked, the center of the gloomy, heathen midden of the kitchen covered with bread, meat, and cans, and the scramble of papers.

"Don't you think my scheme'd work?"

"It's worth thinking about. Something ought to be done, I agree."

"It'll work if people will do it. That's all. That's the only thing, any time. When they understand it in the same way, all of them."

"That's true," said Grebe, rising. His glance met the old man's.

"I know you got to go," he said. "Well, God bless you, boy, you ain't been sly with me. I can tell it in a minute."

He went back through the buried yard. Someone nursed a candle in a shed, where a man unloaded kindling wood from a sprawl-wheeled baby buggy and two voices carried on a high conversation. As he came up the sheltered passage he heard the hard boost of the wind in the branches and against the house fronts, and then, reaching the sidewalk, he saw the needle-eye red of cable towers in the open icy height hundreds of feet above the river and the factories—those keen points. From here, his view was obstructed all the way to the South Branch and its timber banks, and the cranes beside the water. Rebuilt after the Great Fire, this part of the city was, not fifty years later, in ruins again, factories boarded up, buildings deserted or fallen, gaps of prairie between. But it wasn't desolation that this made you feel, but rather a faltering of organization that set free a huge energy, an escaped, unattached, unregulated power from the giant raw place. Not only must people feel it but, it seemed to Grebe, they were compelled to match it. In their very bodies. He no less than others, he realized. Say that his parents had been servants in their time, whereas he was not supposed to be one. He thought that they had never done any service like this, which no one visible asked for, and probably flesh and blood could not even perform. Nor could anyone show why it should be performed; or see where the performance would lead. That did not mean that he wanted to be released from it, he realized with a grimly pensive face. On the contrary. He had something to do. To be compelled to feel this energy and yet have no task to do—that was horrible; that was suffering; he knew what that was. It was now quitting time. Six o'clock. He could go home if he liked, to his room, that is, to wash in hot water, to pour a drink, lie down on his quilt, read the paper, eat some liver paste on crackers before going out to dinner. But to think of this actually made him feel a little sick, as though he had swallowed hard air. He had six checks left, and he was determined to deliver at least one of these: Mr. Green's check.

So he started again. He had four or five dark blocks to go, past open lots, condemned houses, old foundations, closed schools, black churches, mounds, and he reflected that there must be many people alive who had once seen the neighborhood rebuilt and new. Now there was a second layer of ruins; centuries of history accomplished through human massing. Numbers had given the place forced growth; enormous numbers had also broken it down. Objects once so new, so concrete that it could have occurred to anyone they stood for other things, had crumbled. Therefore, reflected Grebe, the secret of them was out. It was that they stood for themselves by agreement, and were natural and not unnatural by agreement, and when the things themselves collapsed the agreement became visible. What was it, otherwise, that kept cities from looking peculiar? Rome, that was almost permanent, did not give rise to thoughts like these. And was it abidingly real? But in Chicago, where the cycles were so fast and the familiar died out, and again rose changed, and died again in thirty years, you saw the common agreement or covenant, and you were forced to think about appearances and realities. (He remembered Raynor and he smiled. Raynor was a clever boy.) Once you had grasped this, a great many things became intelligible. For instance, why Mr. Field should conceive such a scheme. Of course, if people were to agree to create a millionaire, a real millionaire would come into existence. And if you wanted to know how Mr. Field was inspired to think of this, why, he had within sight of his kitchen window the chart, the very bones of a successful scheme—the El with its blue and green confetti of signals. People consented to pay dimes and ride the crash-box cars, and so it was a success. Yet how absurd it looked; how little reality there was to start with. And yet Yerkes, the great financier who built it, had known that he could get people to agree to do it. Viewed as itself, what a scheme of a scheme it seemed, how close to an appearance. Then why wonder at Mr. Field's idea? He had grasped a principle. And then

Grebe remembered, too, that Mr. Yerkes had established the Yerkes Observatory and endowed it with millions. Now how did the notion come to him in his New York museum of a palace or his Aegean-bound yacht to give money to astronomers? Was he awed by the success of his bizarre enterprise and therefore ready to spend money to find out where in the universe being and seeming were identical? Yes, he wanted to know what abides; and whether flesh is Bible grass; and he offered money to be burned in the fire of suns. Okay, then, Grebe thought further, these things exist because people consent to exist with them—we have got so far—and also there is a reality which doesn't depend on consent but within which consent is a game. But what about need, the need that keeps so many vast thousands in position? You tell me that, you *private* little gentleman and *decent* soul—he used these words against himself scornfully. Why is the consent given to misery? And why so painfully ugly? Because there is *something* that is dismal and permanently ugly? Here he sighed and gave it up, and thought it was enough for the present moment that he had a real check in his pocket for a Mr. Green who must be real beyond question. If only his neighbors didn't think they had to conceal him.

This time he stopped at the second floor. He struck a match and found a door. Presently a man answered his knock and Grebe had the check ready and showed it even before he began. "Does Tulliver Green live here? I'm from the relief."

The man narrowed the opening and spoke to someone at his back.

"Does he live here?"

"Uh-uh. No."

"Or anywhere in this building? He's a sick man and he can't come for his dough." He exhibited the check in the light, which was smoky—the air smelled of charred lard—and the man held off the brim of his cap to study it.

"Uh-uh. Never seen the name."

"There's nobody around here that uses crutches?"

He seemed to think, but it was Grebe's impression that he was simply waiting for a decent interval to pass.

"No, suh. Nobody I ever see."

"I've been looking for this man all afternoon"—Grebe spoke out with sudden force—"and I'm going to have to carry this check back to the station. It seems strange not to be able to find a person to *give* him something when you're looking for him for a good reason. I suppose if I had bad news for him I'd find him quick enough."

There was a responsive motion in the other man's face. "That's right, I reckon."

"It almost doesn't do any good to have a name if you can't be found by it. It doesn't stand for anything. He might as well not have any," he went on, smiling. It was as much of a concession as he could make to his desire to laugh.

"Well, now, there's a little old knot-back man I see once in a while. He might be the one you lookin' for. Downstairs."

"Where? Right side or left? Which door?"

"I don't know which. Thin-face little knot-back with a stick."

But no one answered at any of the doors on the first floor. He went to the end of the corridor, searching by matchlight, and found only a stairless exit to the yard, a drop of about six feet. But there was a bungalow near the alley, an old house like Mr. Field's. To jump was unsafe. He ran from the front door, through the underground passage and into the yard. The place was occupied. There was a light through the curtains, upstairs. The name on the ticket under the broken, scoop-shaped mailbox was Green! He exultantly rang the bell and pressed against the locked door. Then the lock clicked faintly and a long staircase opened before him. Someone was slowly coming down—a woman. He had the impression in the weak light that she was shaping her hair as she came, making herself presentable, for he saw her arms raised. But it was for support that they were raised; she was feeling her way downward, down the wall, stumbling. Next he wondered about the pressure of her feet on the treads; she did not seem to be wearing shoes. And it was a freezing stairway. His ring had got her out of bed, perhaps, and she had forgotten to put them on. And then he saw that she was not only shoeless but naked; she was entirely naked, climbing down while she talked to herself, a heavy woman, naked and drunk. She blundered into him. The contact of her breasts, though they touched only his coat, made him go back against the door with a blind shock. See what he had tracked down, in his hunting game!

The woman was saying to herself, furious with insult, "So I cain't ——k, huh? I'll show that son-of-a-bitch kin I, cain't I."

What should he do now? Grebe asked himself. Why, he should go. He should turn away and go. He couldn't talk to this woman. He couldn't keep her standing naked in the cold. But when he tried he found himself unable to turn away.

He said, "Is this where Mr. Green lives?"

But she was still talking to herself and did not hear him.

"Is this Mr. Green's house?"

At last she turned her furious drunken glance on him. "What do you want?"

Again her eyes wandered from him; there was a dot of blood in their enraged brilliance. He wondered why she didn't feel the cold.

"I'm from the relief."

"Awright, what?"

"I've got a check for Tulliver Green."

This time she heard him and put out her hand.

"No, no, for *Mr.* Green. He's got to sign," he said. How was he going to get Green's signature tonight!

"I'll take it. He cain't."

He desperately shook his head, thinking of Mr. Field's precautions about identification. "I can't let you have it. It's for him. Are you Mrs. Green?"

"Maybe I is, and maybe I ain't. Who want to know?"

"Is he upstairs?"

"Awright. Take it up yourself, you goddamn fool."

Sure, he was a goddamn fool. Of course he could not go up because Green would probably be drunk and naked, too. And perhaps he would appear on the landing soon. He looked eagerly upward. Under the light was a high narrow brown wall. Empty! It remained empty!

"Hell with you, then!" he heard her cry. To deliver a check for coal and clothes, he was keeping her in the cold. She did not feel it, but his face was burning with frost and self-ridicule. He backed away from her.

"I'll come tomorrow, tell him."

"Ah, hell with you. Don' never come. What you doin' here in the nighttime? Don' come back." She yelled so that he saw the breadth of her tongue. She stood astride in the long cold box of the hall and held on to the banister and the wall. The bungalow itself was shaped something like a box, a clumsy, high box pointing into the freezing air with its sharp, wintry lights.

"If you are Mrs. Green, I'll give you the check," he said, changing his mind.

"Give here, then." She took it, took the pen offered with it in her left hand, and tried to sign the receipt on the wall. He looked around, almost as though to see whether his madness was being observed, and came near believing that someone was standing on a mountain of used tires in the auto-junking shop next door.

"But are you Mrs. Green?" he now thought to ask. But she was already climbing the stairs with the check, and it was too late, if he had made an error, if he was now in trouble, to undo the thing. But he wasn't going to worry about it. Though she might not be Mrs. Green, he was convinced that Mr. Green was upstairs. Whoever she was, the woman stood for Green, whom he was not to see this time. Well, you silly bastard, he said to himself, so you think you found him. So what? Maybe you really did find him—what of it? But it was important that there was a real Mr. Green whom they could not keep him from reaching because he seemed to come as an emissary from hostile appearances. And though the self-ridicule was slow to diminish, and his face still blazed with it, he had, nevertheless, a feeling of elation, too. "For after all," he said, "he *could* be found!"

To Victoria Ocampo

The Garden of Forking Paths

Jorge Luis Borges

In his *A History of the World War* (page 212), Captain Liddell Hart reports that a planned offensive by thirteen British divisions, supported by fourteen hundred artillery pieces, against the German line at Serre-Montauban, scheduled for July 24, 1916, had to be postponed until the morning of the 29th. He comments that torrential rain caused this delay—which lacked any special significance. The following deposition, dictated by, read over, and then signed by Dr. Yu Tsun, former teacher of English at the Tsingtao *Hochschule,* casts unsuspected light upon this event. The first two pages are missing.

. . . and I hung up the phone. Immediately I recollected the voice that had spoken in German. It was that of Captain Richard Madden. Madden, in Viktor Runeberg's office, meant the end of all our work and—though this seemed a secondary matter, *or should have seemed so to me*— of our lives also. His being there meant that Runeberg had been

Translated by Helen Temple and Ruthven Todd. Reprinted by permission of Grove Press, Inc.

arrested or murdered.* Before the sun set on this same day, I ran the same risk. Madden was implacable. Rather, to be more accurate, he was obliged to be implacable. An Irishman in the service of England, a man suspected of equivocal feelings if not of actual treachery, how could he fail to welcome and seize upon this extraordinary piece of luck: the discovery, capture and perhaps the deaths of two agents of Imperial Germany?

I went up to my bedroom. Absurd though the gesture was, I closed and locked the door. I threw myself down on my narrow iron bed, and waited on my back. The never changing rooftops filled the window, and the hazy six o'clock sun hung in the sky. It seemed incredible that this day, a day without warnings or omens, might be that of my implacable death. In despite of my dead father, in despite of having been a child in one of the symmetrical gardens of Hai Feng, was I to die now?

Then I reflected that all things happen, happen to one, precisely *now*. Century follows century, and things happen only in the present. There are countless men in the air, on land and at sea, and all that really happens happens to me. . . . The almost unbearable memory of Madden's long horseface put an end to these wandering thoughts.

In the midst of my hatred and terror (now that it no longer matters to me to speak of terror, now that I have outwitted Richard Madden, now that my neck hankers for the hangman's noose), I knew that the fast-moving and doubtless happy soldier did not suspect that I possessed the Secret—the name of the exact site of the new British artillery park on the Ancre. A bird streaked across the misty sky and, absently, I turned it into an airplane and then that airplane into many in the skies of France, shattering the artillery park under a rain of bombs. If only my mouth, before it should be silenced by a bullet, could shout this name in such a way that it could be heard in Germany. . . . My voice, my human voice, was weak. How could it reach the ear of the Chief? The ear of that sick and hateful man who knew nothing of Runeberg or of me except that we were in Staffordshire. A man who, sitting in his arid Berlin office, leafed infinitely through newspapers, looking in vain for news from us. I said aloud, "I must flee."

I sat up on the bed, in senseless and perfect silence, as if Madden was already peering at me. Something—perhaps merely a desire to

*A malicious and outlandish statement. In point of fact, Captain Richard Madden had been attacked by the Prussian spy Hans Rabener, alias Viktor Runeberg, who drew an automatic pistol when Madden appeared with orders for the spy's arrest. Madden, in self-defense, had inflicted wounds of which the spy later died.—*Note by the manuscript editor.*

prove my total penury to myself—made me empty out my pockets. I found just what I knew I was going to find. The American watch, the nickel-plated chain and the square coin, the key ring with the useless but compromising keys to Runeberg's office, the notebook, a letter which I decided to destroy at once (and which I did not destroy), a five shilling piece, two single shillings and some pennies, a red and blue pencil, a handkerchief—and a revolver with a single bullet. Absurdly I held it and weighed it in my hand, to give myself courage. Vaguely I thought that a pistol shot can be heard for a great distance.

In ten minutes I had developed my plan. The telephone directory gave me the name of the one person capable of passing on the information. He lived in a suburb of Fenton, less than half an hour away by train.

I am a timorous man. I can say it now, now that I have brought my incredibly risky plan to an end. It was not easy to bring about, and I know that its execution was terrible. I did not do it for Germany—no! Such a barbarous country is of no importance to me, particularly since it had degraded me by making me become a spy. Furthermore, I knew an Englishman—a modest man—who, for me, is as great as Goethe. I did not speak with him for more than an hour, but during that time, he *was* Goethe.

I carried out my plan because I felt the Chief had some fear of those of my race, of those uncountable forebears whose culmination lies in me. I wished to prove to him that a yellow man could save his armies. Besides, I had to escape the Captain. His hands and voice could, at any moment, knock and beckon at my door.

Silently, I dressed, took leave of myself in the mirror, went down the stairs, sneaked a look at the quiet street, and went out. The station was not far from my house, but I thought it more prudent to take a cab. I told myself that I thus ran less chance of being recognized. The truth is that, in the deserted street, I felt infinitely visible and vulnerable. I recall that I told the driver to stop short of the main entrance. I got out with a painful and deliberate slowness.

I was going to the village of Ashgrove, but took a ticket for a station further on. The train would leave in a few minutes, at eight-fifty. I hurried, for the next would not go until half past nine. There was almost no one on the platform. I walked through the carriages. I remember some farmers, a woman dressed in mourning, a youth deep in Tacitus' *Annals* and a wounded, happy soldier.

At last the train pulled out. A man I recognized ran furiously, but vainly, the length of the platform. It was Captain Richard Madden. Shattered, trembling, I huddled in the distant corner of the seat, as far as possible from the fearful window.

From utter terror I passed into a state of almost abject happiness. I told myself that the duel had already started and that I had won the first encounter by besting my adversary in his first attack—even if it was only for forty minutes—by an accident of fate. I argued that so small a victory prefigured a total victory. I argued that it was not so trivial, that were it not for the precious accident of the train schedule, I would be in prison or dead. I argued, with no less sophism, that my timorous happiness was proof that I was man enough to bring this adventure to a successful conclusion. From my weakness I drew strength that never left me.

I foresee that man will resign himself each day to new abominations, that soon only soldiers and bandits will be left. To them I offer this advice: *Whosoever would undertake some atrocious enterprise should act as if it were already accomplished, should impose upon himself a future as irrevocable as the past.*

Thus I proceeded, while with the eyes of a man already dead, I contemplated the fluctuations of the day which would probably be my last, and watched the diffuse coming of night.

The train crept along gently, amid ash trees. It slowed down and stopped, almost in the middle of a field. No one called the name of a station. "Ashgrove?" I asked some children on the platform. "Ashgrove," they replied. I got out.

A lamp lit the platform, but the children's faces remained in a shadow. One of them asked me: "Are you going to Dr. Stephen Albert's house?" Without waiting for my answer, another said: "The house is a good distance away but you won't get lost if you take the road to the left and bear to the left at every crossroad." I threw them a coin (my last), went down some stone steps and started along a deserted road. At a slight incline, the road ran downhill. It was a plain dirt way, and overhead the branches of trees intermingled, while a round moon hung low in the sky as if to keep me company.

For a moment I thought that Richard Madden might in some way have divined my desperate intent. At once I realized that this would be impossible. The advice about turning always to the left reminded me that such was the common formula for finding the central courtyard of certain labyrinths. I know something about labyrinths. Not for nothing am I the great-grandson of Ts'ui Pên. He was Governor of Yunnan and gave up temporal power to write a novel with more characters than there are in the *Hung Lou Mêng,* and to create a maze in which all men would lose themselves. He spent thirteen years on these oddly assorted tasks before he was assassinated by a stranger. His novel had no sense to it and nobody ever found his labyrinth.

Under the trees of England I meditated on this lost and perhaps mythical labyrinth. I imagined it untouched and perfect on the secret summit of some mountain; I imagined it drowned under rice paddies or beneath the sea; I imagined it infinite, made not only of eight-sided pavilions and of twisting paths but also of rivers, provinces and kingdoms. . . . I thought of a maze of mazes, of a sinuous, ever growing maze which would take in both past and future and would somehow involve the stars.

Lost in these imaginary illusions I forgot my destiny—that of the hunted. For an undetermined period of time I felt myself cut off from the world, an abstract spectator. The hazy and murmuring countryside, the moon, the decline of the evening, stirred within me. Going down the gently sloping road I could not feel fatigue. The evening was at once intimate and infinite.

The road kept descending and branching off, through meadows misty in the twilight. A high-pitched and almost syllabic music kept coming and going, moving with the breeze, blurred by the leaves and by distance.

I thought that a man might be an enemy of other men, of the differing moments of other men, but never an enemy of a country: not of fireflies, words, gardens, streams, or the West wind.

Meditating thus I arrived at a high, rusty iron gate. Through the railings I could see an avenue bordered with poplar trees and also a kind of summer house or pavilion. Two things dawned on me at once, the first trivial and the second almost incredible: the music came from the pavilion and that music was Chinese. That was why I had accepted it fully, without paying it any attention. I do not remember whether there was a bell, a push-button, or whether I attracted attention by clapping my hands. The stuttering sparks of the music kept on.

But from the end of the avenue, from the main house, a lantern approached; a lantern which alternately, from moment to moment, was crisscrossed or put out by the trunks of the trees; a paper lantern shaped like a drum and colored like the moon. A tall man carried it. I could not see his face for the light blinded me.

He opened the gate and spoke slowly in my language.

"I see that the worthy Hsi P'eng has troubled himself to see to relieving my solitude. No doubt you want to see the garden?"

Recognizing the name of one of our consuls, I replied, somewhat taken aback.

"The garden?"

"The garden of forking paths."

Something stirred in my memory and I said, with incomprehensible assurance:

"The garden of my ancestor, Ts'ui Pên."

"Your ancestor? Your illustrious ancestor? Come in."

The damp path zigzagged like those of my childhood. When we reached the house, we went into a library filled with books from both East and West. I recognized some large volumes bound in yellow silk —manuscripts of the Lost Encyclopedia which was edited by the Third Emperor of the Luminous Dynasty. They had never been printed. A phonograph record was spinning near a bronze phoenix. I remember also a rose-glazed jar and yet another, older by many centuries, of that blue color which our potters copied from the Persians. . . .

Stephen Albert was watching me with a smile on his face. He was, as I have said, remarkably tall. His face was deeply lined and he had gray eyes and a gray beard. There was about him something of the priest, and something of the sailor. Later, he told me he had been a missionary in Tientsin before he "had aspired to become a Sinologist."

We sat down, I upon a large, low divan, he with his back to the window and to a large circular clock. I calculated that my pursuer, Richard Madden, could not arrive in less than an hour. My irrevocable decision could wait.

"A strange destiny," said Stephen Albert, "that of Ts'ui Pên—Governor of his native province, learned in astronomy, in astrology and tireless in the interpretation of the canonical books, a chess player, a famous poet and a calligrapher. Yet he abandoned all to make a book and a labyrinth. He gave up all the pleasures of oppression, justice, of a well-stocked bed, of banquets, and even of erudition, and shut himself up in the Pavilion of the Limpid Sun for thirteen years. At his death, his heirs found only a mess of manuscripts. The family, as you doubtless know, wished to consign them to the fire, but the executor of the estate—a Taoist or a Buddhist monk—insisted on their publication."

"Those of the blood of Ts'ui Pên," I replied, "still curse the memory of that monk. Such a publication was madness. The book is a shapeless mass of contradictory rough drafts. I examined it once upon a time: the hero dies in the third chapter, while in the fourth he is alive. As for that other enterprise of Ts'ui Pên . . . his Labyrinth. . . ."

"Here is the Labyrinth," Albert said, pointing to a tall, lacquered writing cabinet.

"An ivory labyrinth?" I exclaimed. "A tiny labyrinth indeed . . . !"

"A symbolic labyrinth," he corrected me. "An invisible labyrinth of time. I, a barbarous Englishman, have been given the key to this transparent mystery. After more than a hundred years most of the details are irrecoverable, lost beyond all recall, but it isn't hard to image what must have happened. At one time, Ts'ui Pên must have said, 'I am going into seclusion to write a book,' and at another, 'I am retiring to construct a maze.' Everyone assumed these were separate activities. No one realized that the book and the labyrinth were one and the same. The Pavilion of the Limpid Sun was set in the middle of an intricate garden. This may have suggested the idea of a physical maze.

"Ts'ui Pên died. In all the vast lands which once belonged to your family, no one could find the labyrinth. The novel's confusion suggested that *it* was the labyrinth. Two circumstances showed me the direct solution to the problem. First, the curious legend that Ts'ui Pên had proposed to create an infinite maze, second, a fragment of a letter which I discovered."

Albert rose. For a few moments he turned his back to me. He opened the top drawer in the high black and gilded writing cabinet. He returned holding in his hand a piece of paper which had once been crimson but which had faded with the passage of time: it was rose colored, tenuous, quadrangular. Ts'ui Pên's calligraphy was justly famous. Eagerly, but without understanding, I read the words which a man of my own blood had written with a small brush: "I leave to various future times, but not to all, my garden of forking paths."

I handed back the sheet of paper in silence. Albert went on:

"Before I discovered this letter, I kept asking myself how a book could be infinite. I could not imagine any other than a cyclic volume, circular. A volume whose last page would be the same as the first and so have the possibility of continuing indefinitely. I recalled, too, the night in the middle of *The Thousand and One Nights* when Queen Scheherezade, through a magical mistake on the part of her copyist, started to tell the story of *The Thousand and One Nights,* with the risk of again arriving at the night upon which she will relate it, and thus on to infinity. I also imagined a Platonic hereditary work, passed on from father to son, to which each individual would add a new chapter or correct, with pious care, the work of his elders.

"These conjectures gave me amusement, but none seemed to have the remotest application to the contradictory chapters of Ts'ui Pên. At this point, I was sent from Oxford the manuscript you have just seen.

"Naturally, my attention was caught by the sentence, 'I leave to various future times, but not to all, my garden of forking paths.' I had no sooner read this, than I understood. *The Garden of Forking Paths* was the chaotic novel itself. The phrase 'to various future times, but not to all' suggested the image of bifurcating in time, not in space. Rereading the whole work confirmed this theory. In all fiction, when a man is faced with alternatives he chooses one at the expense of the others. In the almost unfathomable Ts'ui Pên, he chooses—simultaneously—all of them. He thus *creates* various futures, various times which start others that will in their turn branch out and bifurcate in other times. This is the cause of the contradictions in the novel.

"Fang, let us say, has a secret. A stranger knocks at his door. Fang makes up his mind to kill him. Naturally there are various possible outcomes. Fang can kill the intruder, the intruder can kill Fang, both can be saved, both can die and so on and so on. In Ts'ui Pên's work, all the possible solutions occur, each one being the point of departure for other bifurcations. Sometimes the pathways of this labyrinth converge. For example, you come to this house; but in other possible pasts you are my enemy; in others my friend.

"If you will put up with my atrocious pronunciation, I would like to read you a few pages of your ancestor's work."

His countenance, in the bright circle of lamplight, was certainly that of an ancient, but it shone with something unyielding, even immortal.

With slow precision, he read two versions of the same epic chapter. In the first, an army marches into battle over a desolate mountain pass. The bleak and somber aspect of the rocky landscape made the soldiers feel that life itself was of little value, and so they won the battle easily. In the second, the same army passes through a palace where a banquet is in progress. The splendor of the feast remained a memory throughout the glorious battle, and so victory followed.

With proper veneration I listened to these old tales, although perhaps with less admiration for them in themselves than for the fact that they had been thought out by one of my own blood, and that a man of a distant empire had given them back to me, in the last stage of a desperate adventure, on a Western island. I remember the final words, repeated at the end of each version like a secret command: "Thus the heroes fought, with tranquil heart and bloody sword. They were resigned to killing and to dying."

At that moment I felt within me and around me something invisible and intangible pullulating. It was not the pullulation of two divergent, parallel, and finally converging armies, but an agitation more inaccessible, more intimate, prefigured by them in some way. Stephen Albert continued:

"I do not think that your illustrious ancestor toyed idly with variations. I do not find it believable that he would waste thirteen years laboring over a never ending experiment in rhetoric. In your country the novel is an inferior genre; in Ts'ui Pên's period, it was a despised one. Ts'ui Pên was a fine novelist but he was also a man of letters who, doubtless, considered himself more than a mere novelist. The testimony of his contemporaries attests to this, and certainly the known facts of his life confirm his leanings toward the metaphysical and the mystical. Philosophical conjectures take up the greater part of his novel. I know that of all problems, none disquieted him more, and none concerned him more than the profound one of time. Now then, this is the *only* problem that does not figure in the pages of *The Garden.* He does not even use the word which means *time.* How can these voluntary omissions be explained?"

I proposed various solutions, all of them inadequate. We discussed them. Finally Stephen Albert said: "In a guessing game to which the answer is chess, which word is the only one prohibited?" I thought for a moment and then replied:

"The word is *chess.*"

"Precisely," said Albert. "*The Garden of Forking Paths* is an enormous guessing game, or parable, in which the subject is time. The rules of the game forbid the use of the word itself. To eliminate a word completely, to refer to it by means of inept phrases and obvious paraphrases, is perhaps the best way of drawing attention to it. This, then, is the tortuous method of approach preferred by the oblique Ts'ui Pên in every meandering of his interminable novel. I have gone over hundreds of manuscripts, I have corrected errors introduced by careless copyists, I have worked out the plan from this chaos, I have restored, or believe I have restored, the original. I have translated the whole work. I can state categorically that not once has the word *time* been used in the whole book.

"The explanation is obvious. *The Garden of Forking Paths* is a picture, incomplete yet not false, of the universe such as Ts'ui Pên conceived it to be. Differing from Newton and Schopenhauer, your ancestor did not think of time as absolute and uniform. He believed in an infinite series of times, in a dizzily growing, ever spreading network of diverging, converging and parallel times. This web of time —the strands of which approach one another, bifurcate, intersect or ignore each other through the centuries—embraces *every* possibility. We do not exist in most of them. In some you exist and not I, while in others I do, and you do not, and in yet others both of us exist. In this one, in which chance has favored me, you have come to my gate. In another, you, crossing the garden, have found me dead. In yet another, I say these very same words, but am an error, a phantom."

"In all of them," I enunciated, with a tremor in my voice. "I deeply appreciate and am grateful to you for the restoration of Ts'ui Pên's garden."

"Not in *all,*" he murmured with a smile. "Time is forever dividing itself toward innumerable futures and in one of them I am your enemy."

Once again I sensed the pullulation of which I have already spoken. It seemed to me that the dew-damp garden surrounding the house was infinitely saturated with invisible people. All were Albert and myself, secretive, busy and multiform in other dimensions of time. I lifted my eyes and the short nightmare disappeared. In the black and yellow garden there was only a single man, but this man was as strong as a statue and this man was walking up the path and he was Captain Richard Madden.

"The future exists now," I replied. "But I am your friend. Can I take another look at the letter?"

Albert rose from his seat. He stood up tall as he opened the top drawer of the high writing cabinet. For a moment his back was again turned to me. I had the revolver ready. I fired with the utmost care: Albert fell without a murmur, at once. I swear that his death was instantaneous, as if he had been struck by lightning.

What remains is unreal and unimportant. Madden broke in and arrested me. I have been condemned to hang. Abominably, I have yet triumphed! The secret name of the city to be attacked got through to Berlin. Yesterday it was bombed. I read the news in the same English newspapers which were trying to solve the riddle of the murder of the learned Sinologist Stephen Albert by the unknown Yu Tsun. The Chief, however, had already solved this mystery. He knew that my problem was to shout, with my feeble voice, above the tumult of war, the name of the city called Albert, and that I had no other course open to me than to kill someone of that name. He does not know, for no one can, of my infinite penitence and sickness of the heart.

Paul's Case

Willa Cather

It was Paul's afternoon to appear before the faculty of the Pittsburgh High School to account for his various misdemeanours. He had been suspended a week ago, and his father had called at the Principal's office and confessed his perplexity about his son. Paul entered the faculty room suave and smiling. His clothes were a trifle outgrown, and the tan velvet on the collar of his open overcoat was frayed and worn; but for all that there was something of the dandy about him, and he wore an opal pin in his neatly knotted black four-in-hand, and a red carnation in his buttonhole. This latter adornment the faculty somehow felt was not properly significant of the contrite spirit befitting a boy under the ban of suspension.

Paul was tall for his age and very thin, with high, cramped shoulders and a narrow chest. His eyes were remarkable for a certain hysterical brilliancy, and he continually used them in a conscious, theatrical sort of way, peculiarly offensive in a boy. The pupils were abnormally large, as though he were addicted to belladonna, but there was a glassy glitter about them which that drug does not produce.

When questioned by the Principal as to why he was there, Paul stated, politely enough, that he wanted to come back to school. This was a lie, but Paul was quite accustomed to lying; found it, indeed, indispensable for overcoming friction. His teachers were asked to state their respective charges against him, which they did with such a rancour and aggrievedness as evinced that this was not a usual case. Disorder and impertinence were among the offences named, yet each of his instructors felt that it was scarcely possible to put into words the real cause of the trouble, which lay in a sort of hysterically defiant manner of the boy's; in the contempt which they all knew he felt for them, and which he seemingly made not the least effort to conceal. Once, when he had been making a synopsis of a paragraph at the blackboard, his English teacher had stepped to his side and attempted to guide his hand. Paul had started back with a shudder and thrust his hands violently behind him. The astonished woman could scarcely have been more hurt and embarrassed had he struck at her. The insult was so involuntary and definitely personal as to be unforgettable. In one way and another, he had made all his teachers, men and women alike, conscious of the same feeling of physical aversion. In one class he habitually sat with his hand shading his eyes; in another he always looked out of the window during the recitation; in another he made a running commentary on the lecture, with humorous intent.

His teachers felt this afternoon that his whole attitude was symbolized by his shrug and his flippantly red carnation flower, and they fell upon him without mercy, his English teacher leading the pack. He stood through it smiling, his pale lips parted over his white teeth. (His lips were continually twitching, and he had a habit of raising his eyebrows that was contemptuous and irritating to the last degree.) Older boys than Paul had broken down and shed tears under that ordeal, but his set smile did not once desert him, and his only sign of discomfort was the nervous trembling of the fingers that toyed with the buttons of his overcoat, and an occasional jerking of the other hand which held his hat. Paul was always smiling, always glancing about him, seeming to feel that people might be watching him and trying to detect something. This conscious expression, since it was as far as possible from boyish mirthfulness, was usually attributed to insolence or "smartness."

As the inquisition proceeded, one of his instructors repeated an impertinent remark of the boy's, and the Principal asked him whether he thought that a courteous speech to make to a woman. Paul shrugged his shoulders slightly and his eyebrows twitched.

"I don't know," he replied. "I didn't mean to be polite or impolite, either. I guess it's a sort of way I have, of saying things regardless."

The Principal asked him whether he didn't think that a way it would be well to get rid of. Paul grinned and said he guessed so. When he was told that he could go, he bowed gracefully and went out. His bow was like a repetition of the scandalous red carnation.

His teachers were in despair, and his drawing master voiced the feeling of them all when he declared there was something about the boy which none of them understood. He added: "I don't really believe that smile of his comes altogether from insolence; there's something sort of haunted about it. The boy is not strong, for one thing. There is something wrong about the fellow."

The drawing master had come to realize that, in looking at Paul, one saw only his white teeth and the forced animation of his eyes. One warm afternoon the boy had gone to sleep at his drawing-board, and his master had noted with amazement what a white, blue-veined face it was; drawn and wrinkled like an old man's about the eyes, the lips twitching even in his sleep.

His teachers left the building dissatisfied and unhappy; humiliated to have felt so vindictive toward a mere boy, to have uttered this feeling in cutting terms, and to have set each other on, as it were, in the gruesome game of intemperate reproach. One of them remembered having seen a miserable street cat set at bay by a ring of tormentors.

As for Paul, he ran down the hill whistling the Soldiers' Chorus from *Faust,* looking wildly behind him now and then to see whether some of his teachers were not there to witness his light-heartedness. As it was now late in the afternoon and Paul was on duty that evening as usher at Carnegie Hall, he decided that he would not go home to supper.

When he reached the concert hall the doors were not yet open. It was chilly outside, and he decided to go up into the picture gallery—always deserted at this hour—where there were some of Raffelli's gay studies of Paris streets and an airy blue Venetian scene or two that always exhilarated him. He was delighted to find no one in the gallery but the old guard, who sat in the corner, a newspaper on his knee, a black patch over one eye and the other closed. Paul possessed himself of the place and walked confidently up and down, whistling under his breath. After a while he sat down before a blue Rico and lost himself. When he bethought him to look at his watch, it was after seven o'clock, and he rose with a start and ran downstairs, making a face at Augustus Caesar, peering out from the cast-room, and an evil gesture at the Venus of Milo as he passed her on the stairway.

When Paul reached the ushers' dressing-room half-a-dozen boys were there already, and he began excitedly to tumble into his uniform. It was one of the few that at all approached fitting, and Paul thought it very becoming—though he knew the tight, straight coat accentuated his narrow chest, about which he was exceedingly sensitive. He was always excited while he dressed, twanging all over to the tuning of the strings and the preliminary flourishes of the horns in the music-room; but tonight he seemed quite beside himself, and he teased and plagued the boys until, telling him that he was crazy, they put him down on the floor and sat on him.

Somewhat calmed by his suppression, Paul dashed out to the front of the house to seat the early comers. He was a model usher. Gracious and smiling he ran up and down the aisles. Nothing was too much trouble for him; he carried messages and brought programs as though it were his greatest pleasure in life, and all the people in his section thought him a charming boy, feeling that he remembered and admired them. As the house filled, he grew more and more vivacious and animated, and the colour came to his cheeks and lips. It was very much as though this were a great reception and Paul were the host. Just as the musicians came out to take their places, his English teacher arrived with checks for the seats which a prominent manufacturer had taken for the season. She betrayed some embarrassment when she handed Paul the tickets, and a *hauteur* which subsequently made her feel very foolish. Paul was startled for a moment, and had the feeling of wanting to put her out; what business had she here among all these fine people and gay colours? He looked her over and decided that she was not appropriately dressed and must be a fool to sit downstairs in such togs. The tickets had probably been sent her out of kindness, he reflected, as he put down a seat for her, and she had about as much right to sit there as he had.

When the symphony began Paul sank into one of the rear seats with a long sigh of relief, and lost himself as he had done before the Rico. It was not that symphonies, as such, meant anything in particular to Paul, but the first sigh of the instruments seemed to free some hilarious spirit within him; something that struggled there like the Genius in the bottle found by the Arab fisherman. He felt a sudden zest of life; the lights danced before his eyes and the concert hall blazed into unimaginable splendour. When the soprano soloist came on, Paul forgot even the nastiness of his teacher's being there, and gave himself up to the peculiar intoxication such personages always had for him. The soloist chanced to be a German woman, by no means in her first youth, and the mother of many children; but she wore a satin gown and a tiara, and she had that indefinable air of achievement, that world-shine upon her, which always blinded Paul to any possible defects.

After a concert was over, Paul was often irritable and wretched until he got to sleep—and tonight he was even more than usually restless. He had the feeling of not being able to let down; of its being impossible to give up this delicious excitement which was the only thing that could be called living at all. During the last number he withdrew and, after hastily changing his clothes in the dressing-room, slipped out to the side door where the singer's carriage stood. Here he began pacing rapidly up and down the walk, waiting to see her come out.

Over yonder the Schenley, in its vacant stretch, loomed big and square through the fine rain, the windows of its twelve stories glowing like those of a lighted cardboard house under a Christmas tree. All the actors and singers of any importance stayed there when they were in the city, and a number of the big manufacturers of the place lived there in the winter. Paul had often hung about the hotel, watching the people go in and out, longing to enter and leave school-masters and dull care behind him for ever.

At last the singer came out, accompanied by the conductor, who helped her into her carriage and closed the door with a cordial *auf wiedersehen*—which set Paul to wondering whether she were not an old sweetheart of his. Paul followed the carriage over to the hotel, walking so rapidly as not to be far from the entrance when the singer alighted and disappeared behind the swinging glass doors which were opened by a negro in a tall hat and a long coat. In the moment that the door was ajar, it seemed to Paul that he, too, entered. He seemed to feel himself go after her up the steps, into the warm, lighted building, into an exotic, a tropical world of shiny, glistening surfaces and basking ease. He reflected upon the mysterious dishes that were brought into the dining-room, the green bottles in buckets of ice, as he had seen them in the supper party pictures of the Sunday supplement. A quick gust of wind brought the rain down with sudden vehemence, and Paul was startled to find that he was still outside in the slush of the gravel driveway; that his boots were letting in the water and his scanty overcoat was clinging wet about him; that the lights in front of the concert hall were out, and that the rain was driving in sheets between him and the orange glow of the windows above him. There it was, what he wanted—tangibly before him, like the fairy world of a Christmas pantomime; as the rain beat in his face, Paul wondered whether he were destined always to shiver in the black night outside, looking up at it.

He turned and walked reluctantly toward the car tracks. The end had to come sometime; his father in his night-clothes at the top of the stairs, explanations that did not explain, hastily improvised fictions that were forever tripping him up, his upstairs room and its horrible yellow wallpaper, the creaking bureau with the greasy plush collar-box, and over his painted wooden bed the pictures of George Washington and John Calvin, and the framed motto, "Feed my Lambs," which had been worked in red worsted by his mother, whom Paul could not remember.

Half an hour later, Paul alighted from the Negley Avenue car and went slowly down one of the side streets off the main thoroughfare. It was a highly respectable street, where all the houses were exactly alike, and where business men of moderate means begot and reared large families of children, all of whom went to Sabbath-school and learned the shorter catechism, and were interested in arithmetic; all of whom were as exactly alike as their homes, and of a piece with the monotony in which they lived. Paul never went up Cordelia Street without a shudder of loathing. His home was next to the house of the Cumberland minister. He approached it tonight with the nerveless sense of defeat, the hopeless feeling of sinking back forever into ugliness and commonness that he had always had when he came home. The moment he turned into Cordelia Street he felt the waters close above his head. After each of these orgies of living, he experienced all the physical depression which follows a debauch; the loathing of respectable beds, of common food, of a house permeated by kitchen odours; a shuddering repulsion for the flavourless, colourless mass of everyday existence; a morbid desire for cool things and soft lights and fresh flowers.

The nearer he approached the house, the more absolutely unequal Paul felt to the sight of it all; his ugly sleeping chamber; the cold bathroom with the grimy zinc tub, the cracked mirror, the dripping spiggots; his father, at the top of the stairs, his hairy legs sticking out from his nightshirt, his feet thrust into carpet slippers. He was so much later than usual that there would certainly be inquiries and reproaches. Paul stopped short before the door. He felt that he could not be accosted by his father tonight; that he could not toss again on that miserable bed. He would not go in. He would tell his father that he had no car fare, and it was raining so hard he had gone home with one of the boys and stayed all night.

Meanwhile, he was wet and cold. He went around to the back of the house and tried one of the basement windows, found it open, raised it cautiously, and scrambled down the cellar wall to the floor. There he stood, holding his breath, terrified by the noise he had made; but the floor above him was silent, and there was no creak on the stairs. He found a soap-box, and carried it over to the soft ring of light that streamed from the furnace door, and sat down. He was horribly afraid of rats, so he did not try to sleep, but sat looking distrustfully at the dark, still terrified lest he might have awakened his father. In such reactions, after one of the experiences which made days and nights out of the dreary blanks of the calendar, when his senses were deadened, Paul's head was always singularly clear. Suppose his father had heard him getting in at the window and had come down and shot him for a burglar? Then, again, suppose his father had come down, pistol in hand, and he had cried out in time to save himself, and his father had been horrified to think how nearly he had killed him? Then, again, suppose a day should come when his father would remember that night, and wish there had been no warning cry to stay his hand? With this last supposition Paul entertained himself until daybreak.

The following Sunday was fine; the sodden November chill was broken by the last flash of autumnal summer. In the morning Paul had to go to church and Sabbath-school, as always. On seasonable Sunday afternoons the burghers of Cordelia Street usually sat out on their front "stoops," and talked to their neighbours on the next stoop, or called to those across the street in neighbourly fashion. The men sat placidly on gay cushions placed upon the steps that led down to the sidewalk, while the women, in their Sunday "waists," sat in rockers on the cramped porches, pretending to be greatly at their ease. The children played in the streets; there were so many of them that the place resembled the recreation grounds of a kindergarten. The men on the steps—all in their shirt sleeves, their vests unbuttoned—sat with their legs well apart, their stomachs comfortably protruding, and talked of the prices of things, or told anecdotes of the sagacity of their various chiefs and overlords. They occasionally looked over the multitude of squabbling children, listened affectionately to their high-pitched, nasal voices, smiling to see their own proclivities reproduced in their offspring, and interspersed their legends of the iron kings with remarks about their sons' progress at school, their grades in arithmetic, and the amounts they had saved in their toy banks.

On this last Sunday of November, Paul sat all the afternoon on the lowest step of his "stoop," staring into the street, while his sisters, in their rockers, were talking to the minister's daughters next door about how many shirt-waists they had made in the last week, and how many waffles some one had eaten at the last church supper. When the weather was warm, and his father was in a particularly jovial frame of mind, the girls made lemonade, which was always brought out in a red-glass pitcher, ornamented with forget-me-nots in blue enamel. This the girls thought very fine, and the neighbours joked about the suspicious colour of the pitcher.

Today Paul's father, on the top step, was talking to a young man who shifted a restless baby from knee to knee. He happened to be the young man who was daily held up to Paul as a model, and after whom it was his father's dearest hope that he would pattern. This young man was of a ruddy complexion, with a compressed, red mouth, and faded, near-sighted eyes, over which he wore thick spectacles, with gold bows that curved about his ears. He was clerk to one of the magnates of a great steel corporation, and was looked upon in Cordelia Street as a young man with a future. There was a story that, some five years ago —he was now barely twenty-six—he had been a trifle "dissipated," but in order to curb his appetites and save the loss of time and strength that a sowing of wild oats might have entailed, he had taken his chief's advice, oft reiterated to his employees, and at twenty-one had married the first woman whom he could persuade to share his fortunes. She happened to be an angular school-mistress, much older than he, who also wore thick glasses, and who had now borne him four children, all near-sighted, like herself.

The young man was relating how his chief, now cruising in the Mediterranean, kept in touch with all the details of the business, arranging his office hours on his yacht just as though he were at home, and "knocking off work enough to keep two stenographers busy." His father told, in turn, the plan his corporation was considering, of putting in an electric railway plant at Cairo. Paul snapped his teeth; he had an awful apprehension that they might spoil it all before he got there. Yet he rather liked to hear these legends of the iron kings, that were told and retold on Sundays and holidays; these stories of palaces in Venice, yachts on the Mediterranean, and high play at Monte Carlo appealed to his fancy, and he was interested in the triumphs of cash boys who had become famous, though he had no mind for the cash-boy stage.

After supper was over, and he had helped to dry the dishes, Paul nervously asked his father whether he could go to George's to get some help in his geometry, and still more nervously asked for car fare. This latter request he had to repeat, as his father, on principle, did not like to hear requests for money, whether much or little. He asked Paul whether he could not go to some boy who lived nearer, and told him that he ought not to leave his school work until Sunday; but he gave him the dime. He was not a poor man, but he had a worthy ambition to come up in the world. His only reason for allowing Paul to usher was that he thought a boy ought to be earning a little.

Paul bounded upstairs, scrubbed the greasy odour of the dishwater from his hands with the ill-smelling soap he hated, and then shook over his fingers a few drops of violet water from the bottle he kept hidden in his drawer. He left the house with his geometry conspicuously under his arm, and the moment he got out of Cordelia Street and boarded a downtown car, he shook off the lethargy of two deadening days, and began to live again.

The leading juvenile of the permanent stock company which played at one of the downtown theatres was an acquaintance of Paul's, and the boy had been invited to drop in at the Sunday-night rehearsals whenever he could. For more than a year Paul had spent every available moment loitering about Charley Edwards's dressing-room. He had won a place among Edwards's following not only because the young actor, who could not afford to employ a dresser, often found him useful, but because he recognized in Paul something akin to what churchmen term "vocation."

It was at the theatre and at Carnegie Hall that Paul really lived; the rest was but a sleep and a forgetting. This was Paul's fairy tale, and it had for him all the allurement of a secret love. The moment he inhaled the gassy, painty, dusty odour behind the scenes, he breathed like a prisoner set free, and felt within him the possibility of doing or saying splendid, brilliant things. The moment the cracked orchestra beat out the overture from *Martha,* or jerked at the serenade from *Rigoletto,* all stupid and ugly things slid from him, and his senses were deliciously, yet delicately fired.

Perhaps it was because, in Paul's world, the natural nearly always wore the guise of ugliness, that a certain element of artificiality seemed to him necessary in beauty. Perhaps it was because his experience of life elsewhere was so full of Sabbath-school picnics, petty economies, wholesome advice as to how to succeed in life, and the unescapable odours of cooking, that he found this existence so alluring, these smartly-clad men and women so attractive, that he was so moved by these starry apple orchards that bloomed perennially under the limelight.

It would be difficult to put it strongly enough how convincingly the stage entrance of that theatre was for Paul the actual portal of Romance. Certainly none of the company ever suspected it, least of all Charley Edwards. It was very like the old stories that used to float about London of fabulously rich Jews, who had subterranean halls, with palms, and fountains, and soft lamps, and richly apparelled women who never saw the disenchanting light of London day. So, in the midst of that smoke-palled city, enamoured of figures and grimy toil, Paul had his secret temple, his wishing-carpet, his bit of blue-and-white Mediterranean shore bathed in perpetual sunshine.

Several of Paul's teachers had a theory that his imagination had been perverted by garish fiction; but the truth was, he scarcely ever read at all. The books at home were not such as would either tempt or corrupt a youthful mind, and as for reading the novels that some of his friends urged upon him—well, he got what he wanted much more quickly from music; any sort of music, from an orchestra to a barrel organ. He needed only the spark, the indescribable thrill that made his imagination master of his senses, and he could make plots and pictures enough of his own. It was equally true that he was not stage-struck—not, at any rate, in the usual acceptation of that expression. He had no desire to become an actor, any more than he had to become a musician. He felt no necessity to do any of these things; what he wanted was to see, to be in the atmosphere, float on the wave of it, to be carried out, blue league after blue league, away from everything.

After a night behind the scenes, Paul found the schoolroom more than ever repulsive; the bare floors and naked walls; the prosy men who never wore frock coats, or violets in their buttonholes; the women with their dull gowns, shrill voices, and pitiful seriousness about prepositions that govern the dative. He could not bear to have the other pupils think, for a moment, that he took these people seriously; he must convey to them that he considered it all trivial, and was there only by way of a joke, anyway. He had autograph pictures of all the members of the stock company which he showed his classmates, telling them the most incredible stories of his familiarity with these people, of his acquaintance with the soloists who came to Carnegie Hall, his suppers with them and the flowers he sent them. When these stories lost their effect, and his audience grew listless, he would bid all the boys good-bye, announcing that he was going to travel for awhile; going to Naples, to California, to Egypt. Then, next Monday, he would slip back, conscious and nervously smiling; his sister was ill, and he would have to defer his voyage until spring.

Matters went steadily worse with Paul at school. In the itch to let his instructors know how heartily he despised them, and how thoroughly he was appreciated elsewhere, he mentioned once or twice that he had no time to fool with theorems; adding—with a twitch of the eyebrows and a touch of that nervous bravado which so perplexed them—that he was helping the people down at the stock company; they were old friends of his.

The upshot of the matter was, that the Principal went to Paul's father, and Paul was taken out of school and put to work. The manager at Carnegie Hall was told to get another usher in his stead; the doorkeeper at the theatre was warned not to admit him to the house; and Charley Edwards remorsefully promised the boy's father not to see him again.

The members of the stock company were vastly amused when some of Paul's stories reached them—especially the women. They were hard-working women, most of them supporting indolent husbands or brothers, and they laughed rather bitterly at having stirred the boy to such fervid and florid inventions. They agreed with the faculty and with his father, that Paul's was a bad case.

The east-bound train was ploughing through a January snowstorm; the dull dawn was beginning to show grey when the engine whistled a mile out of Newark. Paul started up from the seat where he had lain curled in uneasy slumber, rubbed the breath-misted window glass with his hand, and peered out. The snow was whirling in curling eddies above the white bottom lands, and the drifts lay already deep in the fields and along the fences, while here and there the long dead grass and dried weed stalks protruded black above it. Lights shone from the scattered houses, and a gang of labourers who stood beside the track waved their lanterns.

Paul had slept very little, and he felt grimy and uncomfortable. He had made the all-night journey in a day coach because he was afraid if he took a Pullman he might be seen by some Pittsburgh business man who had noticed him in Denny & Carson's office. When the whistle woke him, he clutched quickly at his breast pocket, glancing about him with an uncertain smile. But the little, clay-bespattered Italians were still sleeping, the slatternly women across the aisle were in open-mouthed oblivion, and even the crumby, crying babies were for the nonce stilled. Paul settled back to struggle with his impatience as best he could.

When he arrived at the Jersey City station, he hurried through his breakfast, manifestly ill at ease and keeping a sharp eye about him. After he reached the Twenty-third Street station, he consulted a cabman, and had himself driven to a men's furnishing establishment which was just opening for the day. He spent upward of two hours there, buying with endless reconsidering and great care. His new street suit he put on in the fitting-room; the frock coat and dress clothes he had bundled into the cab with his new shirts. Then he drove to a hatter's and a shoe house. His next errand was at Tiffany's, where he selected silver mounted brushes and a scarf-pin. He would not wait to have his silver marked, he said. Lastly, he stopped at a trunk shop on Broadway, and had his purchases packed into various travelling bags.

It was a little after one o'clock when he drove up to the Waldorf, and, after settling with the cabman, went into the office. He registered from Washington; said his mother and father had been abroad, and that he had come down to await the arrival of their steamer. He told his story plausibly and had no trouble, since he offered to pay for them in advance, in engaging his rooms; a sleeping-room, sitting-room and bath.

Not once, but a hundred times Paul had planned this entry into New York. He had gone over every detail of it with Charley Edwards, and in his scrap book at home there were pages of description about New York hotels, cut from the Sunday papers.

When he was shown to his sitting-room on the eighth floor, he saw at a glance that everything was as it should be; there was but one detail in his mental picture that the place did not realize, so he rang for the bell boy and sent him down for flowers. He moved about nervously until the boy returned, putting away his new linen and fingering it delightedly as he did so. When the flowers came, he put them hastily into water, and then tumbled into a hot bath. Presently he came out of his white bathroom, resplendent in his new silk underwear, and playing with the tassels of his red robe. The snow was whirling so fiercely outside his windows that he could scarcely see across the street; but within, the air was deliciously soft and fragrant. He put the violets and jonquils on the tabouret beside the couch, and threw himself down with a long sigh, covering himself with a Roman blanket. He was thoroughly tired; he had been in such haste, he had stood up to such a strain, covered so much ground in the last twenty-four hours, that he wanted to think how it had all come about. Lulled by the sound of the wind, the warm air, and the cool fragrance of the flowers, he sank into deep, drowsy retrospection.

It had been wonderfully simple; when they had shut him out of the theatre and concert hall, when they had taken away his bone, the whole thing was virtually determined. The rest was a mere matter of opportunity. The only thing that at all surprised him was his own courage—for he realized well enough that he had always been tormented by fear, a sort of apprehensive dread that, of late years, as the meshes of the lies he had told closed about him, had been pulling the muscles of his body tighter and tighter. Until now, he could not remember a time when he had not been dreading something. Even when he was a little boy, it was always there—behind him, or before, or on either side. There had always been the shadowed corner, the dark place into which he dared not look, but from which something seemed always to be watching him—and Paul had done things that were not pretty to watch, he knew.

But now he had a curious sense of relief, as though he had at last thrown down the gauntlet to the thing in the corner.

Yet it was but a day since he had been sulking in the traces; but yesterday afternoon that he had been sent to the bank with Denny & Carson's deposit, as usual—but this time he was instructed to leave the book to be balanced. There was above two thousand dollars in checks, and nearly a thousand in the bank notes which he had taken from the book and quietly transferred to his pocket. At the bank he had made out a new deposit slip. His nerves had been steady enough to permit of his returning to the office, where he had finished his work and asked for a full day's holiday tomorrow, Saturday, giving a perfectly reasonable pretext. The bank book, he knew, would not be returned before Monday or Tuesday, and his father would be out of town for the next week. From the time he slipped the bank notes into his pocket until he boarded the night train for New York, he had not known a moment's hesitation.

How astonishingly easy it had all been; here he was, the thing done; and this time there would be no awakening, no figure at the top of the stairs. He watched the snow flakes whirling by his window until he fell asleep.

When he awoke, it was four o'clock in the afternoon. He bounded up with a start; one of his precious days gone already! He spent nearly an hour in dressing, watching every stage of his toilet carefully in the mirror. Everything was quite perfect; he was exactly the kind of boy he had always wanted to be.

When he went downstairs, Paul took a carriage and drove up Fifth avenue toward the Park. The snow had somewhat abated; carriages and tradesmen's wagons were hurrying soundlessly to and fro in the winter twilight; boys in woollen mufflers were shovelling off the doorsteps; the avenue stages made fine spots of colour against the white street. Here and there on the corners whole flower gardens blooming behind glass windows, against which the snow flakes stuck and melted; violets, roses, carnations, lilies of the valley—somehow vastly more lovely and alluring that they blossomed thus unnaturally in the snow. The Park itself was a wonderful stage winter-piece.

When he returned, the pause of the twilight had ceased, and the tune of the streets had changed. The snow was falling faster, lights streamed from the hotels that reared their many stories fearlessly up into the storm, defying the raging Atlantic winds. A long, black stream of carriages poured down the avenue, intersected here and there by other streams, tending horizontally. There were a score of cabs about the entrance of this hotel, and his driver had to wait. Boys in livery were running in and out of the awning stretched across the sidewalk, up and down the red velvet carpet laid from the door to the street. Above, about, within it all, was the rumble and roar, the hurry and toss of thousands of human beings as hot for pleasure as himself, and on every side of him towered the glaring affirmation of the omnipotence of wealth.

The boy set his teeth and drew his shoulders together in a spasm of realization; the plot of all dramas, the text of all romances, the nerve-stuff of all sensations was whirling about him like the snow flakes. He burnt like a faggot in a tempest.

When Paul came down to dinner, the music of the orchestra floated up the elevator shaft to greet him. As he stepped into the thronged corridor, he sank back into one of the chairs against the wall to get his breath. The lights, the chatter, the perfumes, the bewildering medley of colour—he had, for a moment, the feeling of not being able to stand it. But only for a moment; these were his own people, he told himself. He went slowly about the corridors, through the writing-rooms, smoking-rooms, reception-rooms, as though he were exploring the chambers of an enchanted palace, built and peopled for him alone.

When he reached the dining-room he sat down at a table near a window. The flowers, the white linen, the many-coloured wine glasses, the gay toilettes of the women, the low popping of corks, the undulating repetitions of the *Blue Danube* from the orchestra, all flooded Paul's dream with bewildering radiance. When the roseate tinge of his champagne was added—that cold, precious, bubbling stuff that creamed and foamed in his glass—Paul wondered that there were honest men in the world at all. This was what all the world was fighting for, he reflected; this was what all the struggle was about. He doubted the reality of his past. Had he ever known a place called Cordelia Street, a place where fagged looking business men boarded the early car? Mere rivets in a machine they seemed to Paul—sickening men, with combings of children's hair always hanging to their coats, and the smell of cooking in their clothes. Cordelia Street— Ah, that belonged to another time and country! Had he not always been thus, had he not sat here night after night, from as far back as he could remember, looking pensively over just such shimmering textures, and slowly twirling the stem of a glass like this one between his thumb and middle finger? He rather thought he had.

He was not in the least abashed or lonely. He had no especial desire to meet or to know any of these people; all he demanded was the right to look on and conjecture, to watch the pageant. The mere stage properties were all he contended for. Nor was he lonely later in the evening, in his loge at the Opera. He was entirely rid of his nervous misgivings, of his forced aggressiveness, of the imperative desire to show himself different from his surroundings. He felt now that his surroundings explained him. Nobody questioned the purple; he had only to wear it passively. He had only to glance down at his dress coat to reassure himself that here it would be impossible for anyone to humiliate him.

He found it hard to leave his beautiful sitting-room to go to bed that night, and sat long watching the raging storm from his turret window. When he went to sleep, it was with the lights turned on in his bedroom; partly because of his old timidity, and partly so that, if he should wake in the night, there would be no wretched moment of doubt, no horrible suspicion of yellow wallpaper, or of Washington and Calvin above his bed.

On Sunday morning the city was practically snowbound. Paul breakfasted late, and in the afternoon he fell in with a wild San Francisco boy, a freshman at Yale, who said he had run down for a "little flyer" over Sunday. The young man offered to show Paul the night side of the town, and the two boys went off together after dinner, not returning to the hotel until seven o'clock the next morning. They had started out in the confiding warmth of a champagne friendship, but their parting in the elevator was singularly cool. The freshman pulled himself together to make his train, and Paul went to bed. He awoke at two o'clock in the afternoon, very thirsty and dizzy, and rang for ice-water, coffee, and the Pittsburgh papers.

On the part of the hotel management, Paul excited no suspicion. There was this to be said for him, that he wore his spoils with dignity and in no way made himself conspicuous. His chief greediness lay in his ears and eyes, and his excesses were not offensive ones. His dearest pleasures were the grey winter twilights in his sitting-room; his quiet enjoyment of his flowers, his clothes, his wide divan, his cigarette and his sense of power. He could not remember a time when he had felt so at peace with himself. The mere release from the necessity of petty lying, lying every day and every day, restored his self-respect. He had never lied for pleasure, even at school; but to make himself noticed and admired, to assert his difference from other Cordelia Street boys; and he felt a good deal more manly, more honest, even, now that he had no need for boastful pretensions, now that he could, as his actor friends used to say, "dress the part." It was characteristic that remorse did not occur to him. His golden days went by without a shadow, and he made each as perfect as he could.

On the eighth day after his arrival in New York, he found the whole affair exploited in the Pittsburgh papers, exploited with a wealth of detail which indicated that local news of a sensational nature was at a low ebb. The firm of Denny & Carson announced that the boy's father had refunded the full amount of his theft, and that they had no intention of prosecuting. The Cumberland minister had been interviewed, and expressed his hope of yet reclaiming the motherless lad, and Paul's Sabbath-school teacher declared that she would spare no effort to that end. The rumour had reached Pittsburgh that the boy had been seen in a New York hotel, and his father had gone East to find him and bring him home.

Paul had just come in to dress for dinner; he sank into a chair, weak in the knees, and clasped his head in his hands. It was to be worse than jail, even; the tepid waters of Cordelia Street were to close over him finally and forever. The grey monotony stretched before him in hopeless, unrelieved years; Sabbath-school, Young People's Meeting, the yellow-papered room, the damp dish-towels; it all rushed back upon him with sickening vividness. He had the old feeling that the orchestra had suddenly stopped, the sinking sensation that the play was over. The sweat broke out on his face, and he sprang to his feet, looked about him with his white, conscious smile, and winked at himself in the mirror. With something of the childish belief in miracles with which he had so often gone to class, all his lessons unlearned, Paul dressed and dashed whistling down the corridor to the elevator.

He had no sooner entered the dining-room and caught the measure of the music, than his remembrance was lightened by his old elastic power of claiming the moment, mounting with it, and finding it all sufficient. The glare and glitter about him, the mere scenic accessories had again, and for the last time, their old potency. He would show himself that he was game, he would finish the thing splendidly. He doubted, more than ever, the existence of Cordelia Street, and for the first time he drank his wine recklessly. Was he not, after all, one of these fortunate beings? Was he not still himself, and in his own place? He drummed a nervous accompaniment to the music and looked about him, telling himself over and over that it had paid.

He reflected drowsily, to the swell of the violin and the chill sweetness of his wine, that he might have done it more wisely. He might have caught an outbound steamer and been well out of their clutches before now. But the other side of the world had seemed too far away and too uncertain then; he could not have waited for it; his need had been too sharp. If he had to choose over again, he would do the same thing tomorrow. He looked affectionately about the dining-room, now gilded with a soft mist. Ah, it had paid indeed!

Paul was awakened next morning by a painful throbbing in his head and feet. He had thrown himself across the bed without undressing, and had slept with his shoes on. His limbs and hands were lead heavy, and his tongue and throat were parched. There came upon him one of those fateful attacks of clearheadedness that never occurred except when he was physically exhausted and his nerves hung loose. He lay still and closed his eyes and let the tide of realities wash over him.

His father was in New York; "Stopping at some joint or other," he told himself. The memory of successive summers on the front stoop fell upon him like a weight of black water. He had not a hundred dollars left; and he knew now, more than ever, that money was everything, the wall that stood between all he loathed and all he wanted. The thing was winding itself up; he had thought of that on his first glorious day in New York, and had even provided a way to snap the thread. It lay on his dressing-table now; he had got it out last night when he came blindly up from dinner—but the shiny metal hurt his eyes, and he disliked the look of it, anyway.

He rose and moved about with a painful effort, succumbing now and again to attacks of nausea. It was the old depression exaggerated; all the world had become Cordelia Street. Yet somehow he was not afraid of anything, was absolutely calm; perhaps because he had looked into the dark corner at last, and knew. It was bad enough, what he saw there; but somehow not so bad as his long fear of it had been. He saw everything clearly now. He had a feeling that he had made the best of it, that he had lived the sort of life he was meant to live, and for half an hour he sat staring at the revolver. But he told himself that was not the way, so he went downstairs and took a cab to the ferry.

When Paul arrived at Newark, he got off the train and took another cab, directing the driver to follow the Pennsylvania tracks out of the town. The snow lay heavy on the roadways and had drifted deep in the open fields. Only here and there the dead grass or dried weed stalks projected, singularly black, above it. Once well into the country, Paul dismissed the carriage and walked, floundering along the tracks, his mind a medley of irrelevant things. He seemed to hold in his brain an actual picture of everything he had seen that morning. He remembered every feature of both his drivers, the toothless old woman from whom he had bought the red flowers in his coat, the agent from whom he had got his ticket, and all of his fellow-passengers on the ferry. His mind, unable to cope with vital matters near at hand, worked feverishly and deftly at sorting and grouping these images. They made for him a part of the ugliness of the world, of the ache in his head, and the bitter burning on his tongue. He stooped and put a handful of snow into his mouth as he walked, but that, too, seemed hot. When he reached a little hillside, where the tracks ran through a cut some twenty feet below him, he stopped and sat down.

The carnations in his coat were drooping with the cold, he noticed; all their red glory over. It occurred to him that all the flowers he had seen in the show windows that first night must have gone the same way, long before this. It was only one splendid breath they had, in spite of their brave mockery at the winter outside the glass. It was a losing game in the end, it seemed, this revolt against the homilies by which the world is run. Paul took one of the blossoms carefully from his coat and scooped a little hole in the snow, where he covered it up. Then he dozed a while, from his weak condition, seeming insensible to the cold.

The sound of an approaching train woke him, and he started to his feet, remembering only his resolution, and afraid lest he should be too late. He stood watching the approaching locomotive, his teeth chattering, his lips drawn away from them in a frightened smile; once or twice he glanced nervously sidewise, as though he were being watched. When the right moment came, he jumped. As he fell, the folly of his haste occurred to him with merciless clearness, the vastness of what he had left undone. There flashed through his brain, clearer than ever before, the blue of Adriatic water, the yellow of Algerian sands.

He felt something strike his chest—his body was being thrown swiftly through the air, on and on, immeasurably far and fast, while his limbs gently relaxed. Then, because the picture making mechanism was crushed, the disturbing visions flashed into black, and Paul dropped back into the immense design of things.

Gooseberries

Anton Chekhov

From early morning the sky had been overcast with clouds; the day was still, cool, and wearisome, as usual on grey, dull days when the clouds hang low over the fields and it looks like rain, which never comes. Ivan Ivanich, the veterinary surgeon, and Bourkin, the schoolmaster, were tired of walking and the fields seemed endless to them. Far ahead they could just see the windmills of the village of Mirousky; to the right, stretched away to disappear behind the village, a line of hills, and they knew that it was the bank of the river; meadows, green willows, farmhouses; and from one of the hills there could be seen a field as endless, telegraph posts, and the train, looking from a distance like a crawling caterpillar, and in clear weather even the town. In the calm weather when all Nature seemed gentle and melancholy, Ivan Ivanich and Bourkin were filled with love for the fields and thought how grand and beautiful the country was.

"Last time, when we stopped in Prokufyi's shed," said Bourkin, "you were going to tell me a story."

"Yes. I wanted to tell you about my brother."

Ivan Ivanich took a deep breath and lighted his pipe before beginning his story, but just then the rain began to fall. And in about five minutes it came pelting down and showed no signs of stopping. Ivan Ivanich stopped and hesitated; the dogs, wet through, stood with their tails between their legs and looked at them mournfully.

"We ought to take shelter," said Bourkin. "Let us go to Aliokhin. It is close by."

"Very well."

They took a short cut over a stubble-field and then bore to the right, until they came to the road. Soon there appeared poplars, a garden, the red roofs of granaries; the river began to glimmer and they came to a wide road with a mill and a white bathing-shed. It was Sophino, where Aliokhin lived.

The mill was working, it drowned the sound of the rain, and the dam shook. Round the carts stood wet horses, hanging their heads, and men were walking about with their heads covered with sacks. It was wet, muddy, and unpleasant, and the river looked cold and sullen. Ivan Ivanich and Bourkin felt wet and uncomfortable through and through; their feet were tired with walking in the mud, and they walked past the dam to the barn in silence as though they were angry with each other.

In one of the barns a winnowing-machine was working, sending out clouds of dust. On the threshold stood Aliokhin himself, a man of about forty, tall and stout, with long hair, more like a professor or a painter than a farmer. He was wearing a grimy white shirt and rope belt, and pants instead of trousers; and his boots were covered with mud and straw. His nose and eyes were black with dust. He recognised Ivan Ivanich and was apparently very pleased.

"Please, gentlemen," he said, "go to the house. I'll be with you in a minute."

The house was large and two-storied. Aliokhin lived downstairs in two vaulted rooms with little windows designed for the farm-hands; the farmhouse was plain, and the place smelled of rye bread and vodka, and leather. He rarely used the reception-rooms, only when guests arrived. Ivan Ivanich and Bourkin were received by a chambermaid; such a pretty young woman that both of them stopped and exchanged glances.

"You cannot imagine how glad I am to see you, gentlemen," said Aliokhin, coming after them into the hall. "I never expected you. Pelageya," he said to the maid, "give my friends a change of clothes. And I will change, too. But I must have a bath. I haven't had one since the spring. Wouldn't you like to come to the bathing-shed? And meanwhile our things will be got ready."

Pretty Pelageya, dainty and sweet, brought towels and soap, and Aliokhin led his guests to the bathing-shed.

"Yes," he said, "it is a long time since I had a bath. My bathing-shed is all right, as you see. My father and I put it up, but somehow I have no time to bathe."

He sat down on the step and lathered his long hair and neck, and the water round him became brown.

"Yes, I see," said Ivan Ivanich heavily, looking at his head.

"It is a long time since I bathed," said Aliokhin shyly, as he soaped himself again, and the water round him became dark blue, like ink.

Ivan Ivanich came out of the shed, plunged into the water with a splash, and swam about in the rain, flapping his arms, and sending waves back, and on the waves tossed white lilies; he swam out to the middle of the pool and dived, and in a minute came up again in another place and kept on swimming and diving, trying to reach the bottom. "Ah! how delicious!" he shouted in his glee. "How delicious!" He swam to the mill, spoke to the peasants, and came back, and in the middle of the pool he lay on his back to let the rain fall on his face. Bourkin and Aliokhin were already dressed and ready to go, but he kept on swimming and diving.

"Delicious," he said. "Too delicious!"

"You've had enough," shouted Bourkin.

They went to the house. And only when the lamp was lit in the large drawing-room upstairs, and Bourkin and Ivan Ivanich, dressed in silk dressing-gowns and warm slippers, lounged in chairs, and Aliokhin himself, washed and brushed, in a new frock coat, paced up and down evidently delighting in the warmth and cleanliness and dry clothes and slippers, and pretty Pelageya, noiselessly tripping over the carpet and smiling sweetly, brought in tea and jam on a tray, only then did Ivan Ivanich begin his story, and it was as though he was being listened to not only by Bourkin and Aliokhin, but also by the old and young ladies and the officer who looked down so staidly and tranquilly from the golden frames.

"We are two brothers," he began, "I, Ivan Ivanich, and Nicholai Ivanich, two years younger. I went in for study and became a veterinary surgeon, while Nicholai was at the Exchequer Court when he was nineteen. Our father, Tchimsha-Himalaysky, was a cantonist, but he died with an officer's rank and left us his title of nobility and a small estate. After his death the estate went to pay his debts. However, we spent our childhood there in the country. We were just like peasant children, spent days and nights in the fields and the woods, minded the house, barked the lime-trees, fished, and so on. . . . And you know once a man has fished, or watched the thrushes hovering in flocks over the village in the bright, cool, autumn days, he can never really be a townsman, and to the day of his death he will be drawn to the country. My brother pined away in the Exchequer. Years passed and he sat in the same place, wrote out the same documents, and thought of one thing, how to get back to the country. And little by little his distress became a definite disorder, a fixed idea—to buy a small farm somewhere by the bank of a river or a lake.

"He was a good fellow and I loved him, but I never sympathised with the desire to shut oneself up on one's own farm. It is a common saying that a man needs only six feet of land. But surely a corpse wants that, not a man. And I hear that our intellectuals have a longing for the land and want to acquire farms. But it all comes down to the six feet of land. To leave town, and the struggle and the swim of life, and go and hide yourself in a farmhouse is not life—it is egoism, laziness; it is a kind of monasticism, but monasticism without action. A man needs, not six feet of land, not a farm, but the whole earth, all Nature, where in full liberty he can display all the properties and qualities of the free spirit.

"My brother Nicholai, sitting in his office, would dream of eating his own *schi,* with its savoury smell floating across the farmyard; and of eating out in the open air, and of sleeping in the sun, and of sitting for hours together on a seat by the gate and gazing at the fields and the forest. Books on agriculture and the hints in almanacs were his joy, his favourite spiritual food; and he liked reading newspapers, but only the advertisements of land to be sold, so many acres of arable and grass land, with a farmhouse, river, garden, mill, and mill-pond. And he would dream of garden hedges, flowers, fruit, nests, carp in the pond, don't you know, and all the rest of it. These fantasies of his used to vary according to the advertisements he found, but somehow there was always a gooseberry-bush in every one. Not a house, not a romantic spot could he imagine without its gooseberry-bush.

" 'Country life has its advantages,' he used to say. 'You sit on the veranda drinking tea and your ducklings swim on the pond, and everything smells good . . . and there are gooseberries.'

"He used to draw out a plan of his estate and always the same things were shewn on it: (*a*) farmhouse, (*b*) cottage, (*c*) vegetable garden, (*d*) gooseberry-bush. He used to live meagrely and never had enough to eat and drink, dressed God knows how, exactly like a beggar, and always saved and put his money into the bank. He was terribly stingy. It used to hurt me to see him, and I used to give him money to go away for a holiday, but he would put that away, too. Once a man gets a fixed idea, there's nothing to be done.

"Years passed; he was transferred to another province. He completed his fortieth year and was still reading advertisements in the papers and saving up his money. Then I heard he was married. Still with the same idea of buying a farmhouse with a gooseberry-bush, he married an elderly, ugly widow, not out of any feeling for her, but because she had money. With her he still lived stingily, kept her half-starved, and put the money into the bank in his own name. She had been the wife of a postmaster and was used to good living, but with her second husband she did not even have enough black bread; she pined away in her new life, and in three years or so gave up her soul to God. And my brother never for a moment thought himself to blame for her death. Money, like vodka, can play queer tricks with a man. Once in our town a merchant lay dying. Before his death he asked for some honey, and he ate all his notes and scrip with the honey so that nobody should get it. Once I was examining a herd of cattle at a station and a horse-jobber fell under the engine, and his foot was cut off. We carried him into the waiting-room, with the blood pouring down—a terrible business—and all the while he kept on asking anxiously for his foot; he had twenty-five roubles in his boot and did not want to lose them."

"Keep to your story," said Bourkin.

"After the death of his wife," Ivan Ivanich continued, after a long pause, "my brother began to look out for an estate. Of course you may search for five years, and even then buy a pig in a poke. Through an agent my brother Nicholai raised a mortgage and bought three hundred acres with a farmhouse, a cottage, and a park, but there was no orchard, no gooseberry-bush, no duck-pond; there was a river but the water in it was coffee-coloured because the estate lay between a brick-yard and a gelatine factory. But my brother Nicholai was not worried about that; he ordered twenty gooseberry-bushes and settled down to a country life.

"Last year I paid him a visit. I thought I'd go and see how things were with him. In his letters my brother called his estate Tchimbarshov Corner, or Himalayskoe. I arrived at Himalayskoe in the afternoon. It was hot. There were ditches, fences, hedges, rows of young fir-trees, trees everywhere, and there was no telling how to cross the yard or where to put your horse. I went to the house and was met by a red-haired dog, as fat as a pig. He tried to bark but felt too lazy. Out of the kitchen came the cook, barefooted, and also as fat as a pig, and said that the master was having his afternoon rest. I went in to my brother and found him sitting on his bed with his knees covered with a blanket; he looked old, stout, flabby; his cheeks, nose, and lips were pendulous. I half expected him to grunt like a pig.

"We embraced and shed a tear of joy and also of sadness to think that we had once been young, but were now both going grey and nearing death. He dressed and took me to see his estate.

" 'Well? How are you getting on?' I asked.

" 'All right, thank God. I am doing very well.'

"He was no longer the poor, tired official, but a real landowner and a person of consequence. He had got used to the place and liked it, ate a great deal, took Russian baths, was growing fat, had already gone to law with the parish and the two factories, and was much offended if the peasants did not call him 'Your Excellency.' And, like a good landowner, he looked after his soul and did good works pompously, never simply. What good works? He cured the peasants of all kinds of diseases with soda and castor-oil, and on his birthday he would have a thanksgiving service held in the middle of the village, and would treat the peasants to half a bucket of vodka, which he thought the right thing to do. Ah! Those horrible buckets of vodka. One day a greasy landowner will drag the peasants before the Zemstvo Court for trespass, and the next, if it's a holiday, he will give them a bucket of vodka, and they drink and shout Hooray! and lick his boots in their drunkenness. A change to good eating and idleness always fills a Russian with the most preposterous self-conceit. Nicholai Ivanich who, when he was in the Exchequer, was terrified to have an opinion of his own, now imagined that what he said was law. 'Education is necessary for the masses, but they are not fit for it.' 'Corporal punishment is generally harmful, but in certain cases it is useful and indispensable.'

" 'I know the people and I know how to treat them,' he would say. 'The people love me. I have only to raise my finger and they will do as I wish.'

"And all this, mark you, was said with a kindly smile of wisdom. He was constantly saying: 'We noblemen,' or 'I, as a nobleman.' Apparently he had forgotten that our grandfather was a peasant and our father a common soldier. Even our family name, Tchimsha-Himalaysky, which is really an absurd one, seemed to him full-sounding, distinguished, and very pleasing.

"But my point does not concern him so much as myself. I want to tell you what a change took place in me in those few hours while I was in his house. In the evening, while we were having tea, the cook laid a plateful of gooseberries on the table. They had not been bought, but were his own gooseberries, plucked for the first time since the bushes were planted. Nicholai Ivanich laughed with joy and for a minute or two he looked in silence at the gooseberries with tears in his eyes. He could not speak for excitement, then put one into his mouth, glanced at me in triumph, like a child at last being given its favourite toy, and said:

" 'How good they are!'

"He went on eating greedily, and saying all the while:

" 'How good they are! Do try one!'

"It was hard and sour, but, as Pushkin said, the illusion which exalts us is dearer to us than ten thousand truths. I saw a happy man, one whose dearest dream had come true, who had attained his goal in life, who had got what he wanted, and was pleased with his destiny and with himself. In my idea of human life there is always some alloy of sadness, but now at the sight of a happy man I was filled with something like despair. And at night it grew on me. A bed was made up for me in the room near my brother's and I could hear him, unable to sleep, going again and again to the plate of gooseberries. I thought: 'After all, what a lot of contented, happy people there must be! What an overwhelming power that means! I look at this life and see the arrogance and the idleness of the strong, the ignorance and bestiality of the weak, the horrible poverty everywhere, overcrowding, drunkenness, hypocrisy, falsehood. . . . Meanwhile in all the houses, all the streets, there is peace; out of fifty thousand people who live in our town there is but one to kick against it all. Think of the people who go to the market for food: during the day they eat; at night they sleep, talk nonsense, marry, grow old, piously follow their dead to the cemetery; one never sees or hears those who suffer, and all the horror of life goes on somewhere behind the scenes. Everything is quiet, peaceful, and against it all there is only the silent protest of statistics; so many go mad, so many gallons are drunk, so many children die of starvation. . . . And such a state of things is obviously what we want; apparently a happy man only feels so because the unhappy bear their burden in silence, but for which happiness would be impossible. It is a general hypnosis. Every happy man should have someone with a little hammer at his door to knock and remind him that there are unhappy people, and that, however happy he may be, life will sooner or later show its claws, and some misfortune will befall him—illness, poverty, loss, and then no one will see or hear him, just as he now neither sees nor hears others. But there is no man with a hammer, and the happy go on living, just a little fluttered with the petty cares of every day, like an aspen tree in the wind—and everything is all right.'

"That night I was able to understand how I, too, had been content and happy," Ivan Ivanich went on, getting up. "I, too, at meals or out hunting, used to lay down the law about living, and religion, and governing the masses. I, too, used to say that teaching is right, that education is necessary, but that for simple folk reading and writing is enough for the present. Freedom is a boon, I used to say, as essential as the air we breathe, but we must wait. Yes—I used to say so, but now

I ask: 'Why do we wait?' " Ivan Ivanich glanced angrily at Bourkin. "Why do we wait, I ask you? What considerations keep us fast? I am told that we cannot have everything at once, and that every idea is realised in time. But who says so? Where is the proof that it is so? You refer me to the natural order of things, to the law of cause and effect, but is there order or natural law in that I, a living, thinking creature, should stand by a ditch until it fills up, or is narrowed, when I could jump in or throw a bridge over it? Tell me, I say, why should we wait? Wait, when we have no strength to live, and yet must live and are full of the desire to live!

"I left my brother early the next morning, and from that time on I found it impossible to live in town. The peace and the quiet of it oppress me. I dare not look in at the windows, for nothing is more dreadful to see than the sight of a happy family, sitting round a table, having tea. I am an old man now and am no good for the struggle. I commenced late. I can only grieve within my soul, and fret and sulk. At night my head buzzes with the rush of my thoughts and I cannot sleep. . . . Ah! If I were young!"

Ivan Ivanich walked excitedly up and down the room and repeated:

"If I were young."

He suddenly walked up to Aliokhin and shook him first by one hand and then by the other.

"Pavel Konstantinich," he said in a voice of entreaty, "don't be satisfied, don't let yourself be lulled to sleep! While you are young, strong, wealthy, do not cease to do good! Happiness does not exist, nor should it, and if there is any meaning or purpose in life, they are not in our peddling little happiness, but in something reasonable and grand. Do good!"

Ivan Ivanich said this with a piteous supplicating smile, as though he were asking a personal favour.

Then they all three sat in different corners of the drawing-room and were silent. Ivan Ivanich's story had satisfied neither Bourkin nor Aliokhin. With the generals and ladies looking down from their gilt frames, seeming alive in the firelight, it was tedious to hear the story of a miserable official who ate gooseberries. . . . Somehow they had a longing to hear and to speak of charming people, and of women. And the mere fact of sitting in the drawing-room where everything—the lamp with its coloured shade, the chairs, and the carpet under their feet—told how the very people who now looked down at them from their frames once walked, and sat and had tea there, and the fact that pretty Pelageya was near—was much better than any story.

Aliokhin wanted very much to go to bed; he had to get up for his work very early, about two in the morning, and now his eyes were closing, but he was afraid of his guests saying something interesting without his hearing it, so he would not go. He did not trouble to think whether what Ivan Ivanich had been saying was clever or right; his guests were talking of neither groats, nor hay, nor tar, but of something which had no bearing on his life, and he liked it and wanted them to go on. . . .

"However, it's time to go to bed," said Bourkin, getting up. "I will wish you good night."

Aliokhin said good night and went downstairs, and left his guests. Each had a large room with an old wooden bed and carved ornaments; in the corner was an ivory crucifix; and their wide, cool beds, made by pretty Pelageya, smelled sweetly of clean linen.

Ivan Ivanich undressed in silence and lay down.

"God forgive me, a wicked sinner," he murmured, as he drew the clothes over his head.

A smell of burning tobacco came from his pipe which lay on the table, and Bourkin could not sleep for a long time and was worried because he could not make out where the unpleasant smell came from.

The rain beat against the windows all night long.

Heart of Darkness

Joseph Conrad

The *Nellie,* a cruising yawl, swung to her anchor without a flutter of the sails, and was at rest. The flood had made, the wind was nearly calm, and being bound down the river, the only thing for it was to come to and wait for the turn of the tide.

The sea-reach of the Thames stretched before us like the beginning of an interminable waterway. In the offing the sea and the sky were welded together without a joint, and in the luminous space the tanned sails of the barges drifting up with the tide seemed to stand still in red clusters of canvas sharply peaked, with gleams of varnished spirits. A haze rested on the low shores that ran out to sea in vanishing flatness. The air was dark above Gravesend, and farther back still seemed condensed into a mournful gloom, brooding motionless over the biggest, and the greatest, town on earth.

The Director of Companies was our captain and our host. We four affectionately watched his back as he stood in the bows looking to seaward. On the whole river there was nothing that looked half so nautical. He resembled a pilot, which to a seaman is trustworthiness personified. It was difficult to realize his work was not out there in the luminous estuary, but behind him, within the brooding gloom.

Between us there was, as I have already said somewhere, the bond of the sea. Besides holding our hearts together through long periods of separation, it had the effect of making us tolerant of each other's yarns—and even convictions. The lawyer—the best of old fellows—had, because of his many years and many virtues, the only cushion on deck, and was lying on the only rug. The accountant had brought out already a box of dominoes, and was toying architecturally with the bones. Marlow sat cross-legged right aft, leaning against the mizzen-mast. He had sunken cheeks, a yellow complexion, a straight back, an ascetic aspect, and, with his arms dropped, the palms of hands outwards, resembled an idol. The director, satisfied the anchor had good hold, made his way aft and sat down amongst us. We exchanged a few words lazily. Afterwards there was silence on board the yacht. For some reason or other we did not begin that game of dominoes. We felt meditative, and fit for nothing but placid staring. The day was ending in a serenity of still and exquisite brilliance. The water shone pacifically; the sky, without a speck, was a benign immensity of unstained light; the very mist on the Essex marshes was like a gauzy and radiant fabric, hung from the wooded rises inland, and draping the low shores in diaphanous folds. Only the gloom to the west, brooding over the upper reaches, became more somber every minute, as if angered by the approach of the sun.

And at last, in its curved and imperceptible fall, the sun sank low, and from glowing white changed to a dull red without rays and without heat, as if about to go out suddenly, stricken to death by the touch of that gloom brooding over a crowd of men.

Forthwith a change came over the waters, and the serenity became less brilliant but more profound. The old river in its broad reach rested unruffled at the decline of day, after ages of good service done to the race that peopled its banks, spread out in the tranquil dignity of a waterway leading to the uttermost ends of the earth. We looked at the venerable stream not in the vivid flush of a short day that comes and departs forever, but in the august light of abiding memories. And indeed nothing is easier for a man who has, as the phrase goes, "followed the sea" with reverence and affection, than to evoke the great spirit of the past upon the lower reaches of the Thames. The tidal current runs to and fro in its unceasing service, crowded with memories of men and ships it had borne to the rest of home or to the battles of the sea. It had known and served all the men of whom the nation is proud, from Sir Francis Drake to Sir John Franklin, knights all, titled and untitled—the great knights-errant of the sea. It had borne all the ships whose names are like jewels flashing in the night of time, from the *Golden Hind* returning with her round flanks full of treasure, to be visited by the Queen's Highness and thus pass out of the gigantic tale, to the *Erebus* and *Terror*, bound on other conquests—and that never returned. It had known the ships and the men. They had sailed from Deptford, from Greenwich, from Erith—the adventurers and the settlers; kings' ships and the ships of men on 'Change; captains, admirals, the dark "interlopers" of the Eastern trade, and the commissioned "generals" of East India fleets. Hunters for gold or pursuers of fame, they all had gone out on that stream, bearing the sword, and often the torch, messengers of the might within the land, bearers of a spark from the sacred fire. What greatness had not floated on the ebb of that river into the mystery of an unknown earth! . . . The dreams of men, the seed of commonwealths, the germs of empires.

The sun set; the dusk fell on the stream, and lights began to appear along the shore. The Chapman lighthouse, a three-legged thing erect on a mud-flat, shone strongly. Lights of ships moved in the fairway—a great stir of lights going up and going down. And farther west on the upper reaches the place of the monstrous town was still marked ominously on the sky, a brooding gloom in sunshine, a lurid glare under the stars.

"And this also," said Marlow suddenly, "has been one of the dark places of the earth."

He was the only man of us who still "followed the sea." The worse that could be said of him was that he did not represent his class. He was a seaman, but he was a wanderer, too, while most seamen lead, if one may so express it, a sedentary life. Their minds are of the stay-at-home order, and their home is always with them—the ship; and so is their country—the sea. One ship is very much like another, and the sea is always the same. In the immutability of their surroundings the foreign shores, the foreign faces, the changing immensity of life, glide past, veiled not by a sense of mystery but by a slightly disdainful ignorance; for there is nothing mysterious to a seaman unless it be the sea itself, which is the mistress of his existence and as inscrutable as destiny. For the rest, after his hours of work, a casual stroll or a casual spree on shore suffices to unfold for him the secret of a whole continent, and generally he finds the secret not worth knowing. The yarns of seamen have a direct simplicity, the whole meaning of which lies within the shell of a cracked nut. But Marlow was not typical (if his propensity to spin yarns be excepted), and to him the meaning of an episode was not inside like a kernel but outside, enveloping the tale which brought it out only as a glow brings out a haze, in the likeness of one of these misty halos that sometimes are made visible by the spectral illumination of moonshine.

His remark did not seem at all surprising. It was just like Marlow.

It was accepted in silence. No one took the trouble to grunt even; and presently he said, very slow:

"I was thinking of very old times, when the Romans first came here, nineteen hundred years ago—the other day. . . . Light came out of this river since—you say knights? Yes; but it is like a running blaze on a plain, like a flash of lightning in the clouds. We live in the flicker—may it last as long as the old earth keeps rolling! But darkness was here yesterday. Imagine the feelings of a commander of a fine—what d'ye call 'em?—trireme in the Mediterranean, ordered suddenly to the north; run overland across the Gauls in a hurry; put in charge of one of these craft the legionaries—a wonderful lot of handy men they must have been, too—used to build, apparently by the hundred, in a month or two, if we may believe what we read. Imagine him here—the very end of the world, a sea the color of lead, a sky the color of smoke, a kind of ship about as rigid as a concertina—and going up this river with stores, or orders, or what you like. Sandbanks, marshes, forests, savages—precious little to eat fit for a civilized man, nothing but Thames water to drink. No Falernian wine here, no going ashore. Here and there a military camp lost in a wilderness, like a needle in a bundle of hay—cold, fog, tempests, disease, exile, and death—death skulking in the air, in the water, in the bush. They must have been dying like flies here. Oh, yes—he did it. Did it very well, too, no doubt, and without thinking much about it either, except afterwards to brag of what he had gone through in his time, perhaps. They were men enough to face the darkness. And perhaps he was cheered by keeping his eye on a chance of promotion to the fleet at Ravenna by and by, if he had good friends in Rome and survived the awful climate. Or think of a decent young citizen in a toga—perhaps too much dice, you know—coming out here in the train of some prefect, or tax-gatherer, or trader even, to mend his fortunes. Land in a swamp, march through the woods, and in some inland post feel the savagery, the utter savagery, had closed round him—all that mysterious life of the wilderness that stirs in the forest, in the jungles, in the hearts of wild men. There's no initiation either into such mysteries. He has to live in the midst of the incomprehensible, which is also detestable. And it has a fascination, too, that goes to work upon him. The fascination of the abomination—you know, imagine the growing regrets, the longing to escape, the powerless disgust, the surrender, the hate."

He paused.

"Mind," he began again, lifting one arm from the elbow, the palm of the hand outwards, so that, with his legs folded before him, he had the pose of a Buddha preaching in European clothes and without a lotus flower—"Mind, none of us would feel exactly like this. What saves us is efficiency—the devotion to efficiency. But these chaps were not much account, really. They were no colonists; their administration was merely a squeeze, and nothing more, I suspect. They were conquerors, and for that you want only brute force—nothing to boast of, when you have it, since your strength is just an accident arising from the weakness of others. They grabbed what they could get for the sake of what was to be got. It was just robbery with violence, aggravated murder on a great scale, and men going at it blind—as is very proper for those who tackle a darkness. The conquest of the earth, which mostly means the taking it away from those who have a different complexion or slightly flatter noses than ourselves, is not a pretty thing when you look into it too much. What redeems it is the idea only. An idea at the back of it; not a sentimental pretence but an idea; and an unselfish belief in the idea—something you can set up, and bow down before, and offer a sacrifice to. . . ."

He broke off. Flames glided in the river, small green flames, red flames, white flames, pursuing, overtaking, joining, crossing each other—then separating slowly or hastily. The traffic of the great city went on in the deepening night upon the sleepless river. We looked on, waiting patiently—there was nothing else to do till the end of the flood; but it was only after a long silence, when he said, in a hesitating voice, "I suppose you fellows remember I did once turn fresh-water sailor for a bit," that we knew we were fated, before the ebb began to run, to hear about one of Marlow's inconclusive experiences.

"I don't want to bother you much with what happened to me personally," he began, showing in this remark the weakness of many tellers of tales who seem so often unaware of what their audience would best like to hear; "yet to understand the effect of it on me you ought to know how I got out there, what I saw, how I went up that river to the place where I first met the poor chap. It was the farthest point of navigation and the culminating point of my experience. It seemed somehow to throw a kind of light on everything about me—and into my thoughts. It was somber enough, too—and pitiful—not extraordinary in any way—not very clear either. No, not very clear. And yet it seemed to throw a kind of light.

"I had then, as you remember, just returned to London after a lot of Indian Ocean, Pacific, China Seas—a regular dose of the East—six years or so, and I was loafing about, hindering you fellows in your work and invading your homes, just as though I had got a heavenly mission to civilize you. It was very fine for a time, but after a bit I did get tired of resting. Then I began to look for a ship—I should think the hardest work on earth. But the ships wouldn't even look at me. And I got tired of that game, too.

"Now when I was a little chap I had a passion for maps. I would look for hours at South America, or Africa, or Australia, and lose myself in all the glories of exploration. At that time there were many blank spaces on the earth, and when I saw one that looked particularly inviting on a map (but they all look that) I would put my finger on it and say, 'When I grow up I will go there.' The North Pole was one of these places, I remember. Well, I haven't been there yet, and shall not try now. The glamor's off. Other places were scattered about the Equator, and in every sort of latitude all over the two hemispheres. I have been in some of them, and . . . well, we won't talk about that. But there was one yet—the biggest, the most blank, so to speak—that I had a hankering after.

"True, by this time it was not a blank space any more. It had got filled since my boyhood with rivers and lakes and names. It had ceased to be a blank space of delightful mystery—a white patch for a boy to dream gloriously over. It had become a place of darkness. But there was in it one river especially, a mighty big river, that you could see on the map, resembling an immense snake uncoiled, with its head in the sea, its body at rest curving afar over a vast country, and its tail lost in the depths of the land. And as I looked at the map of it in a shop window, it fascinated me as a snake would a bird—a silly little bird. Then I remembered there was a big concern, a company for trade on that river. Dash it all! I thought to myself, they can't trade without using some kind of craft on that lot of fresh water—steamboats! Why shouldn't I try to get charge of one? I went on along Fleet Street, but could not shake off the idea. The snake had charmed me.

"You understand it was a continental concern, that trading society; but I have a lot of relations living on the continent, because it's cheap and not so nasty as it looks, they say.

"I am sorry to own I began to worry them. This was already a fresh departure for me. I was not used to get things that way, you know. I always went my own road and on my own legs where I had a mind to go. I wouldn't have believed it of myself; but, then—you see—I felt somehow I must get there by hook or by crook. So I worried them. The men said 'My dear fellow,' and did nothing. Then—would you believe it?—I tried the women. I, Charlie Marlow, set the women to work—to get a job. Heavens! Well, you see, the notion drove me. I had an aunt, a dear enthusiastic soul. She wrote: 'It will be delightful. I am ready to do anything, anything for you. It is a glorious idea. I know the wife of a very high personage in the administration, and also a man who has lots of influence with,' etc., etc. She was determined to make no end of fuss to get me appointed skipper of a river steamboat, if such was my fancy.

"I got my appointment—of course; and I got it very quick. It appears the company had received news that one of their captains had been killed in a scuffle with the natives. This was my chance, and it made me the more anxious to go. It was only months and months afterwards, when I made the attempt to recover what was left of the body, that I heard the original quarrel arose from a misunderstanding about some hens. Yes, two black hens. Fresleven—that was the fellow's name, a Dane—thought himself wronged somehow in the bargain, so he went ashore and started to hammer the chief of the village with a stick. Oh, it didn't surprise me in the least to hear this, and at the same time to be told that Fresleven was the gentlest, quietest creature that ever walked on two legs. No doubt he was; but he had been a couple of years already out there engaged in the noble cause, you know, and he probably felt the need at last of asserting his self-respect in some way. Therefore he whacked the old nigger mercilessly, while a big crowd of his people watched him, thunderstruck, till some man—I was told the chief's son—in desperation at hearing the old chap yell, made a tentative jab with a spear at the white man—and of course it went quite easy between the shoulder blades. Then the whole population cleared into the forest, expecting all kinds of calamities to happen, while, on the other hand, the steamer Fresleven commanded left also in a bad panic, in charge of the engineer, I believe. Afterwards nobody seemed to trouble much about Fresleven's remains, till I got out and stepped into his shoes. I couldn't let it rest, though; but when an opportunity offered at last to meet my predecessor, the grass growing through his ribs was tall enough to hide his bones. They were all there. The supernatural being had not been touched after he fell. And the village was deserted, the huts gaped black, rotting, all askew within the fallen enclosures. A calamity had come to it, sure enough. The people had vanished. Mad terror had scattered them, men, women, and children, through the bush, and they had never returned. What became of the hens I don't know either. I should think the cause of progress got them, anyhow. However, through this glorious affair I got my appointment, before I had fairly begun to hope for it.

"I flew around like mad to get ready, and before forty-eight hours I was crossing the Channel to show myself to my employers, and sign the contract. In a very few hours I arrived in a city that always makes me think of a whited sepulcher. Prejudice no doubt. I had no difficulty in finding the company's offices. It was the biggest thing in the town, and everybody I met was full of it. They were going to run an oversea empire, and make no end of coin by trade.

"A narrow and deserted street in deep shadow, high houses, innumerable windows with venetian blinds, a dead silence, grass sprouting between the stones, imposing carriage archways right and left, immense double doors standing ponderously ajar. I slipped through one of these cracks, went up a swept and ungarnished staircase, as arid as a desert, and opened the first door I came to. Two women, one fat and the other slim, sat on straw-bottomed chairs, knitting black wool. The slim one got up and walked straight at me—still knitting with downcast eyes—and only just as I began to think of getting out of her way, as you would for a somnambulist, stood still, and looked up. Her dress was as plain as an umbrella-cover, and she turned round without a word and preceded me into a waiting room. I gave my name, and looked about. Deal table in the middle, plain chairs all round the walls, on one end a large shining map, marked with all the colors of a rainbow. There was a vast amount of red—good to see at any time, because one knows that some real work is done in there, a deuce of a lot of blue, a little green, smears of orange, and, on the East Coast, a purple patch, to show where the jolly pioneers of progress drink the jolly lager beer. However, I wasn't going into any of these. I was going into the yellow. Dead in the center. And the river was there—fascinating—deadly—like a snake. Ough! A door opened, a white-haired secretarial head, but wearing a compassionate expression, appeared, and a skinny forefinger beckoned me into the sanctuary. Its light was dim, and a heavy writing desk squatted in the middle. From behind that structure came out an impression of pale plumpness in a frock coat. The great man himself. He was five feet six, I should judge, and had his grip on the handle-end of ever so many millions. He shook hands, I fancy, murmured vaguely, was satisfied with my French. *Bon voyage.*

"In about forty-five seconds I found myself again in the waiting room with the compassionate secretary, who, full of desolation and sympathy, made me sign some document. I believe I undertook amongst other things not to disclose any trade secrets. Well, I am not going to.

"I began to feel slightly uneasy. You know I am not used to such ceremonies, and there was something ominous in the atmosphere. It was just as though I had been let into some conspiracy—I don't know—something not quite right; and I was glad to get out. In the outer room the two women knitted black wool feverishly. People were arriving, and the younger one was walking back and forth introducing them. The old one sat on her chair. Her flat cloth slippers were propped up on a foot-warmer, and a cat reposed on her lap. She wore a starched white affair on her head, had a wart on one cheek, and silver-rimmed spectacles hung on the tip of her nose. She glanced at me above the glasses. The swift and indifferent placidity of that look troubled me. Two youths with foolish and cheery countenances were being piloted over, and she threw at them the same quick glance of unconcerned wisdom. She seemed to know all about them and about me, too. An eerie feeling came over me. She seemed uncanny and fateful. Often far away there I thought of these two, guarding the door of darkness, knitting black wool as for a warm pall, one introducing, introducing continuously to the unknown, the other scrutinizing the cheery and foolish faces with unconcerned old eyes. *Ave!* Old knitter of black wool. *Morituri te salutant.* Not many of those she looked at ever saw her again—not half, by a long way.

"'There was yet a visit to the doctor. 'A simple formality,' assured me the secretary, with an air of taking an immense part in all my sorrows. Accordingly a young chap wearing his hat over the left eyebrow, some clerk I suppose—there must have been clerks in the business, though the house was as still as a house in a city of the dead—came from somewhere upstairs, and led me forth. He was shabby and careless, with inkstains on the sleeves of his jacket, and his cravat was large and billowy, under a chin shaped like the toe of an old boot. It was a little too early for the doctor, so I proposed a drink, and thereupon he developed a vein of joviality. As we sat over our vermouths he glorified the company's business, and by and by I expressed casually my surprise at him not going out there. He became very cool and collected all at once. 'I am not such a fool as I look, quoth Plato to his disciples,' he said sententiously, emptied his glass with great resolution, and we rose.

"'The old doctor felt my pulse, evidently thinking of something else the while. 'Good, good for there,' he mumbled, and then with a certain eagerness asked me whether I would let him measure my head. Rather surprised, I said 'yes,' when he produced a thing like calipers and got the dimensions back and front and every way, taking notes carefully. He was an unshaven little man in a threadbare coat like a gaberdine, with his feet in slippers, and I thought him a harmless fool. 'I always ask leave, in the interests of science, to measure the crania of those going out there,' he said. 'And when they come back, too?' I asked. 'Oh, I never see them,' he remarked; 'and, moreover, the changes take place inside, you know.' He smiled, as if at some quiet joke. 'So you are going out there. Famous. Interesting, too.' He gave me a searching glance, and made another note. 'Ever any madness in your family?' he asked, in a matter-of-fact tone. I felt very annoyed. 'Is that question in the interests of science, too?' 'It would be,' he said, without taking notice of my irritation, 'interesting for science to watch the mental changes of individuals, on the spot, but . . .' 'Are you an alienist?' I interrupted. 'Every doctor should be—a little,' answered that original, imperturbably. 'I have a little theory which you messieurs who go out there must help me to prove. This is my share in the advantages my country shall reap from the possession of such a magnificent dependency. The mere wealth I leave to others. Pardon my questions, but you are the first Englishman coming under my observation. . . .' I hastened to assure him I was not in the least typical. 'If I were,' said I, 'I wouldn't be talking like this with you.' 'What you say is rather profound, and probably erroneous,' he said, with a laugh. 'Avoid irritation more than exposure to the sun. Adieu. How do you English say, eh? Good-by. Ah! Good-by. Adieu. In the tropics one must before everything keep calm.' . . . He lifted a warning forefinger. . . . *'Du calme, du calme. Adieu.'*

"One thing more remained to do—say good-by to my excellent aunt. I found her triumphant. I had a cup of tea—the last decent cup of tea for many days—and in a room that most soothingly looked just as you would expect a lady's drawing room to look, we had a long quiet chat by the fireside. In the course of these confidences it became quite plain to me I had been represented to the wife of the high dignitary, and goodness knows to how many more people besides, as an exceptional and gifted creature—a piece of good fortune for the company—a man you don't get hold of every day. Good heavens! and I was going to take charge of a two-penny-half-penny river steamboat with a penny whistle attached! It appeared, however, I was also one of the Workers, with a capital—you know. Something like an emissary of light, something like a lower sort of apostle. There had been a lot of such rot let loose in print and talk just about that time, and the excellent woman, living right in the rush of all that humbug, got carried off her feet. She talked about 'weaning those ignorant millions from their horrid ways,' till, upon my word, she made me quite uncomfortable. I ventured to hint that the company was run for profit.

" 'You forget, dear Charlie, that the laborer is worthy of his hire,' she said, brightly. It's queer how out of touch with truth women are. They live in a world of their own, and there had never been anything like it, and never can be. It is too beautiful altogether, and if they were to set it up it would go to pieces before the first sunset. Some confounded fact we men have been living contentedly with ever since the day of creation would start up and knock the whole thing over.

"After this I got embraced, told to wear flannel, be sure to write often, and so on—and I left. In the street—I don't know why—a queer feeling came to me that I was an impostor. Odd thing that I, who used to clear out for any part of the world at twenty-four hours' notice, with less thought than most men give to the crossing of a street, had a moment—I won't say of hesitation, but of startled pause, before this commonplace affair. The best way I can explain it to you is by saying that, for a second or two, I felt as though, instead of going to the center of a continent, I were about to set off for the center of the earth.

"I left in a French steamer, and she called in every blamed port they have out there, for, as far as I could see, the sole purpose of landing soldiers and customhouse officers. I watched the coast. Watching a coast as it slips by the ship is like thinking about an enigma. There it is before you—smiling, frowning, inviting, grand, mean, insipid, or savage, and always mute with an air of whispering, Come and find out. This one was almost featureless, as if still in the making, with an aspect of monotonous grimness. The edge of a colossal jungle, so dark-green as to be almost black, fringed with white surf, ran straight, like a ruled line, far, far away along a blue sea whose glitter was blurred by a creeping mist. The sun was fierce, the land seemed to glisten and drip with steam. Here and there grayish-whitish specks showed up clustered inside the white surf, with a flag flying above them perhaps. Settlements some centuries old, and still no bigger than pinheads on the untouched expanse of their background. We pounded along, stopped, landed soldiers; went on, landed customhouse clerks to levy toll in what looked like a God-forsaken wilderness, with a tin shed and a flagpole lost in it; landed more soldiers—to take care of the customhouse clerks, presumably. Some, I heard, got drowned in the surf; but whether they did or not, nobody seemed particularly to care. They were just flung out there, and on we went. Every day the coast looked the same, as though we had not moved; but we passed various places—trading places—with names like Gran' Bassam, Little Popo; names that seemed to belong to some sordid farce acted in front of a sinister back-cloth. The idleness of a passenger, my isolation amongst all these men with whom I had no point of contact, the oily and languid sea, the uniform somberness of the coast, seemed to keep me away from the truth of things, within the toil of a mournful and senseless delusion. The voice of the surf heard now and then was a positive pleasure, like the speech of a brother. It was something natural, that had its reason, that had a meaning. Now and then a boat from the shore gave one a momentary contact with reality. It was paddled by black fellows. You could see from afar the white of their eyeballs glistening. They shouted, sang; their bodies streamed with perspiration; they had faces like grotesque masks—these chaps; but they had bone, muscle, a wild vitality, an intense energy of movement, that was as natural and true as the surf along their coast. They wanted no excuse for being there. They were a great comfort to look at. For a time I would feel I belonged still to a world of straightforward facts;

but the feeling would not last long. Something would turn up to scare it away. Once, I remember, we came upon a man-of-war anchored off the coast. There wasn't even a shed there, and she was shelling the bush. It appears the French had one of their wars going on thereabouts. Her ensign dropped limp like a rag; the muzzles of the long six-inch guns stuck out all over the low hull; the greasy, slimy swell swung her up lazily and let her down, swaying her thin masts. In the empty immensity of earth, sky, and water, there she was, incomprehensible, firing into a continent. Pop, would go one of the six-inch guns; a small flame would dart and vanish, a little white smoke would disappear, a tiny projectile would give a feeble screech—and nothing happened. Nothing could happen. There was a touch of insanity in the proceeding, a sense of lugubrious drollery in the sight; and it was not dissipated by somebody on board assuring me earnestly there was a camp of natives—he called them enemies!—hidden out of sight somewhere.

"We gave her her letters (I heard the men in that lonely ship were dying of fever at the rate of three a day) and went on. We called at some more places with farcical names, where the merry dance of death and trade goes on in a still and earthly atmosphere as of an overheated catacomb; all along the formless coast bordered by dangerous surf, as if Nature herself had tried to ward off intruders; in and out of rivers, streams of death in life, whose banks were rotting into mud, whose waters, thickened into slime, invaded the contorted mangroves, that seemed to writhe at us in the extremity of an impotent despair. Nowhere did we stop long enough to get a particularized impression, but the general sense of vague and oppressive wonder grew upon me. It was like a weary pilgrimage amongst hints for nightmares.

"It was upward of thirty days before I saw the mouth of the big river. We anchored off the seat of the government. But my work would not begin till some two hundred miles farther on. So as soon as I could I made a start for a place thirty miles higher up.

"I had my passage on a little seagoing steamer. Her captain was a Swede, and knowing me for a seaman, invited me on the bridge. He was a young man, lean, fair, and morose, with lanky hair and a shuffling gait. As we left the miserable little wharf, he tossed his head contemptuously at the shore. 'Been living there?' he asked. I said, 'Yes.' 'Fine lot these government chaps—are they not?' he went on, speaking English with great precision and considerable bitterness. 'It is funny what some people will do for a few francs a month. I wonder what becomes of that kind when it goes up country?' I said to him I expected to see that soon. 'So-o-o!' he exclaimed. He shuffled athwart, keeping one eye ahead vigilantly. 'Don't be too sure,' he continued. 'The other day I took up a man who hanged himself on the road. He was a Swede, too.' 'Hanged himself! Why, in God's name?' I cried. He kept on looking out watchfully. 'Who knows? The sun too much for him, or the country perhaps.'

"At last we opened a reach. A rocky cliff appeared, mounds of turned-up earth by the shore, houses on a hill, others with iron roofs, amongst a waste of excavations, or hanging to the declivity. A continuous noise of the rapids above hovered over this scene of inhabited devastation. A lot of people, mostly black and naked, moved about like ants. A jetty projected into the river. A blinding sunlight drowned all this at times in a sudden recrudescence of glare. 'There's your company's station,' said the Swede, pointing to three wooden barrack-like structures on the rocky slope. 'I will send your things up. Four boxes did you say? So. Farewell.'

"I came upon a boiler wallowing in the grass, then found a path leading up the hill. It turned aside for the boulders, and also for an undersized railway truck lying there on its back with its wheels in the air. One was off. The thing looked as dead as the carcass of some animal. I came upon more pieces of decaying machinery, a stack of rusty rails. To the left a clump of trees made a shady spot, where dark things seemed to stir feebly. I blinked, the path was steep. A horn tooted to the right, and I saw the black people run. A heavy and dull detonation shook the ground, a puff of smoke came out of the cliff, and that was all. No change appeared on the face of the rock. They were building a railway. The cliff was not in the way or anything; but this objectless blasting was all the work going on.

"A slight clinking behind me made me turn my head. Six black men advanced in a file, toiling up the path. They walked erect and slow, balancing small baskets full of earth on their heads, and the clink kept time with their footsteps. Black rags were wound round their loins, and the short ends behind waggled to and fro like tails. I could see every rib, the joints of their limbs were like knots in a rope; each had an iron collar on his neck, and all were connected together with a chain whose bights swung between them, rhythmically clinking. Another report from the cliff made me think suddenly of that ship of war I had seen firing into a continent. It was the same kind of ominous voice; but these men could by no stretch of imagination be called enemies. They were called criminals, and the outraged law, like the bursting shells, had come to them, an insoluble mystery from the sea. All their meager breasts panted together, the violently dilated nostrils quivered, the eyes stared stonily uphill. They passed me within six inches, without a glance, with that complete, deathlike indifference of unhappy savages. Behind this raw matter one of the reclaimed, the product of the new forces at work, strolled despondently, carrying a rifle by its middle. He had a uniform jacket with one button off, and seeing a white man on the path, hoisted his weapon to this shoulder with alacrity. This was simple prudence, white men being so much alike at a distance that he could not tell who I might be. He was speedily reassured, and with a large, white, rascally grin, and a glance at his charge, seemed to take me into partnership in his exalted trust. After all, I also was a part of the great cause of these high and just proceedings.

"Instead of going up, I turned and descended to the left. My idea was to let that chain gang get out of sight before I climbed the hill. You know I am not particularly tender; I've had to strike and to fend off. I've had to resist and to attack sometimes—that's only one way of resisting—without counting the exact cost, according to the demands of such sort of life as I had blundered into. I've seen the devil of violence, and the devil of greed, and the devil of hot desire; but, by all the stars! these were strong, lusty, red-eyed devils, that swayed and drove men—men, I tell you. But as I stood on this hillside, I foresaw that in the blinding sunshine of that land I would become acquainted with a flabby, pretending, weak-eyed devil of a rapacious and pitiless folly. How insidious he could be, too, I was only to find out several months later and a thousand miles farther. For a moment I stood appalled, as though by a warning. Finally I descended the hill, obliquely, towards the trees I had seen.

"I avoided a vast artificial hole somebody had been digging on the slope, the purpose of which I found it impossible to divine. It wasn't a quarry or a sandpit, anyhow. It was just a hole. It might have been connected with the philanthropic desire of giving the criminals something to do. I don't know. Then I nearly fell into a very narrow ravine, almost no more than a scar in the hillside. I discovered that a lot of imported drainage pipes for the settlement had been tumbled in there. There wasn't one that was not broken. It was a wanton smashup. At last I got under the trees. My purpose was to stroll into the shade for a moment; but no sooner within than it seemed to me I had stepped into the gloomy circle of some inferno. The rapids were near, and an uninterrupted, uniform, headlong, rushing noise filled the mournful stillness of the grove, where not a breath stirred, not a leaf moved, with a mysterious sound—as though the tearing pace of the launched earth had suddenly become audible.

"Black shapes crouched, lay, sat between the trees leaning against the trunks, clinging to the earth, half coming out, half effaced within the dim light, in all the attitudes of pain, abandonment, and despair. Another mine on the cliff went off, followed by a slight shudder of the soil under my feet. The work was going on. The work! And this was the place where some of the helpers had withdrawn to die.

"They were dying slowly—it was very clear. They were not enemies, they were not criminals, they were nothing earthly now, nothing but black shadows of disease and starvation, lying confusedly in the greenish gloom. Brought from all the recesses of the coast in all the legality of time contracts, lost in uncongenial surroundings, fed on unfamiliar food, they sickened, became inefficient, and were then allowed to crawl away and rest. These moribund shapes were free as air —and nearly as thin. I began to distinguish the gleam of the eyes under the trees. Then, glancing down, I saw a face near my hand. The black bones reclined at full length with one shoulder against the tree, and slowly the eyelids rose and the sunken eyes looked up at me, enormous and vacant, a kind of blind, white flicker in the depths of the orbs, which died out slowly. The man seemed young—almost a boy—but you know with them it's hard to tell. I found nothing else to do but to offer him one of my good Swede's ship's biscuits I had in my pocket. The fingers closed slowly on it and held—there was no other movement and no other glance. He had tied a bit of white worsted round his neck—Why? Where did he get it? Was it a badge—an ornament —a charm—a propitiatory act? Was there any idea at all connected with it? It looked startling round his black neck, this bit of white thread from beyond the seas.

"Near the same tree two more bundles of acute angles sat with their legs drawn up. One, with his chin propped on his knees, stared at nothing, in an intolerable and appalling manner: his brother phantom rested its forehead, as if overcome with a great weariness; and all about others were scattered in every pose of contorted collapse, as in some picture of a massacre or a pestilence. While I stood horror-struck, one of these creatures rose to his hands and knees, and went off on all fours towards the river to drink. He lapped out of his hand, then sat up in the sunlight, crossing his shins in front of him, and after a time let his wooly head fall on his breastbone.

"I didn't want any more loitering in the shade, and I made haste towards the station. When near the buildings I met a white man, in such an unexpected elegance of getup that in the first moment I took him for a sort of vision. I saw a high starched collar, white cuffs, a light alpaca jacket, snowy trousers, a clear necktie, and varnished boots. No hat. Hair parted, brushed, oiled, under a green-lined parasol held in a big white hand. He was amazing, and had a penholder behind his ear.

"I shook hands with this miracle, and I learned he was the company's chief accountant, and that all the bookkeeping was done at this station. He had come out for a moment, he said, 'to get a breath of fresh air.' The expression sounded wonderfully odd, with its suggestion of sedentary desk life. I wouldn't have mentioned the fellow to you at all, only it was from his lips that I first heard the name of the man who is so indissolubly connected with the memories of that time. Moreover, I respected the fellow. Yes; I respected his collars, his vast cuffs, his brushed hair. His appearance was certainly that of a hairdresser's dummy; but in the great demoralization of the land he kept up his appearance. That's backbone. His starched collars and got-up shirt fronts were achievements of character. He had been out nearly three years; and, later, I could not help asking him how he managed to sport such linen. He had just the faintest blush, and said modestly, 'I've been teaching one of the native women about the station. It was difficult. She had a distaste for the work.' Thus this man had truly accomplished something. And he was devoted to his books, which were in apple-pie order.

"Everything else in the station was in a muddle—heads, things, buildings. Strings of dusty niggers with splay feet arrived and departed; a stream of manufactured goods, rubbishy cottons, beads, and brass wire set into the depths of darkness, and in return came a precious trickle of ivory.

"I had to wait in the station for ten days—an eternity. I lived in a hut in the yard, but to be out of the chaos I would sometimes get into the accountant's office. It was built of horizontal planks, and so badly put together that, as he bent over his high desk, he was barred from neck to heels with narrow strips of sunlight. There was no need to open the big shutter to see. It was hot there, too; big flies buzzed fiendishly, and did not sting, but stabbed. I sat generally on the floor, while, of faultless appearance (and even slightly scented), perching on a high stool, he wrote, he wrote. Sometimes he stood up for exercise. When a truckle bed with a sick man (some invalid agent from upcountry) was put in there, he exhibited a gentle annoyance. 'The groans of this sick person,' he said, 'distract my attention. And without that it is extremely difficult to guard against clerical errors in this climate.'

"One day he remarked, without lifting his head, 'In the interior you will no doubt meet Mr. Kurtz.' On my asking who Mr. Kurtz was, he said he was a first-class agent; and seeing my disappointment at this information, he added slowly, laying down his pen, 'He is a very remarkable person.' Further questions elicited from him that Mr. Kurtz was at present in charge of a trading post, a very important one, in the true ivory-country, at 'the very bottom of there. Sends in as much ivory as all the others put together. . . .' He began to write again. The sick man was too ill to groan. The flies buzzed in a great peace.

"Suddenly there was a growing murmur of voices and a great tramping of feet. A caravan had come in. A violent babble of uncouth sounds burst out on the other side of the planks. All the carriers were speaking together, and in the midst of the uproar the lamentable voice of the chief agent was heard 'giving it up' tearfully for the twentieth time that day. . . . He rose slowly 'What a frightful row,' he said. He crossed the room gently to look at the sick man, and returning, said to me, 'He does not hear.' 'What! Dead?' I asked, startled. 'No, not yet,' he answered, with great composure. Then, alluding with a toss of the head to the tumult in the station yard, 'When one has got to make correct entries, one comes to hate those savages—hate them to the death.' He remained thoughtful for a moment. 'When you see Mr. Kurtz,' he went on, 'tell him from me that everything here'—he glanced at the desk—'is very satisfactory. I don't like to write to him —with those messengers of ours you never know who may get hold of your letter—at that Central Station.' He stared at me for a moment with his mild, bulging eyes. 'Oh, he will go far, very far,' he began again. 'He will be a somebody in the administration before long. They, above—the council in Europe, you know—mean him to be.'

"He turned to his work. The noise outside had ceased, and presently in going out I stopped at the door. In the steady buzz of flies the homeward-bound agent was lying flushed and insensible; the other, bent over his books, was making correct entries of perfectly correct transactions; and fifty feet below the doorstep I could see the still treetops of the grove of death.

"Next day I left that station at last, with a caravan of sixty men, for a two-hundred-mile tramp.

"No use telling you much about that. Paths, paths, everywhere; a stamped-in network of paths spreading over the empty land, through long grass, through burnt grass, through thickets, down and up chilly ravines, up and down stony hills ablaze with heat; and a solitude, a solitude, nobody, not a hut. The population had cleared out a long time ago. Well, if a lot of mysterious niggers armed with all kinds of fearful weapons suddenly took to traveling on the road between Deal and Gravesend, catching the yokels right and left to carry heavy loads for them, I fancy every farm and cottage thereabouts would get empty very soon. Only here the dwellings were gone, too. Still I passed through several abandoned villages. There's something pathetically childish in the ruins of grass walls. Day after day, with the stamp and shuffle of sixty pair of bare feet behind me, each pair under a sixty-lb. load. Camp, cook, sleep, strike camp, march. Now and then a carrier dead in harness, at rest in the long grass near the path, with an empty water gourd and his long staff lying by his side. A great silence around and above. Perhaps on some quiet night the tremor of far-off drums, sinking, swelling, a tremor vast, faint; a sound weird, appealing, suggestive, and wild—and perhaps with as profound a meaning as the sound of bells in a Christian country. Once a white man in an unbuttoned uniform, camping on the path with an armed escort of lank Zanzibaris, very hospitable and festive—not to say drunk. Was looking after the upkeep of the road he declared. Can't say I saw any road or any upkeep, unless the body of a middle-aged Negro, with a bullet-hole in the forehead, upon which I absolutely stumbled three miles farther on, may be considered as a permanent improvement. I had a white companion, too, not a bad chap, but rather too fleshy and with the exasperating habit of fainting on the hot hillsides, miles away from the least bit of shade and water. Annoying, you know, to hold your own coat like a parasol over a man's head while he is coming to. I couldn't help asking him once what he meant by coming there at all. 'To make money, of course. What do you think?' he said, scornfully. Then he got fever, and had to be carried in a hammock slung under a pole. As he weighed 224 pounds I had no end of rows with the carriers. They jibbed, ran away, sneaked off with their loads in the night—quite a mutiny. So, one evening, I made a speech in English with gestures, not one of which was lost to the sixty pairs of eyes before me, and the next morning I started the hammock off in front all right. An hour afterwards I came upon the whole concern wrecked in a bush—man, hammock, groans, blankets, horrors. The heavy pole had skinned his poor nose. He was very anxious for me to kill somebody, but there wasn't the shadow of a carrier near. I remembered the old doctor, 'It would be interesting for science to watch the mental changes of individuals, on the spot.' I felt I was becoming scientifically interesting. However, all that is to no purpose. On the fifteenth day I came in sight of the big river again, and hobbled into the Central Station. It was on a back water surrounded by scrub and forest, with a pretty border of smelly mud on one side, and on the three others enclosed by a crazy fence of rushes. A neglected gap was all the gate it had, and the first glance at the place was enough to let you see the flabby devil was running that show. White men with long staves in their hands appeared languidly from amongst the buildings, strolling up to take a look at me, and then retired out of sight somewhere. One of them, a stout, excitable chap with black mustaches, informed me with great volubility and many digressions, as soon as I told him who I was, that my steamer was at the bottom of the river. I was thunderstruck. What, how, why? Oh, it was 'all right.' The 'manager himself' was there. All quite correct. 'Everybody had behaved splendidly! splendidly!'—'you must,' he said in agitation, 'go and see the general manager at once. He is waiting!'

"I did not see the real significance of that wreck at once. I fancy I see it now, but I am not sure—not at all. Certainly the affair was too stupid—when I think of it—to be altogether natural. Still . . . But at the moment it presented itself simply as a confounded nuisance. The steamer was sunk. They had started two days before in a sudden hurry up the river with the manager on board, in charge of some volunteer skipper, and before they had been out three hours they tore the bottom out of her on stones, and she sank near the south bank. I asked myself what I was to do there, now my boat was lost. As a matter of fact, I had plenty to do in fishing my command out of the river. I had to set about it the very next day. That, and the repairs when I brought the pieces to the station, took some months.

"My first interview with the manager was curious. He did not ask me to sit down after my twenty-mile walk that morning. He was commonplace in complexion, in feature, in manners, and in voice. He was of middle size and of ordinary build. His eyes, of the usual blue, were perhaps remarkably cold, and he certainly could make his glance fall on one as trenchant and heavy as an axe. But even at these times the rest of his person seemed to disclaim the intention. Otherwise there was only an indefinable, faint expression of his lips, something stealthy—a smile—not a smile—I remember it, but I can't explain. It was unconscious, this smile was, though just after he had said something it got intensified for an instant. It came at the end of his speeches like a seal applied on the words to make the meaning of the commonest phrase appear absolutely inscrutable. He was a common trader, from his youth up employed in these parts—nothing more. He was obeyed, yet he inspired neither love nor fear, nor even respect. He inspired uneasiness. That was it! Uneasiness. Not a definite mistrust —just uneasiness—nothing more. You have no idea how effective such a . . . a . . . faculty can be. He had no genius for organizing, for initiative, or for order even. That was evident in such things as the deplorable state of the station. He had no learning, and no intelligence. His position had come to him—why? Perhaps because he was never ill . . . He had served three terms of three years out there. . . . Because triumphant health in the general rout of constitutions is a kind of power in itself. When he went home on leave he rioted on a large scale—pompously. Jack ashore—with a difference—in externals only. This one could gather from his casual talk. He originated nothing, he could keep the routine going—that's all. But he was great. He was great by this little thing that it was impossible to tell what could control such a man. He never gave that secret away. Perhaps there was nothing within him. Such a suspicion made one pause—for out there there were no external checks. Once when various tropical diseases had laid low almost every 'agent' in the station, he was heard to say, 'Men who come out here should have no entrails.' He sealed the utterance with that smile of his, as though it had been a door opening into a darkness he had in his keeping. You fancied you had seen things—but the seal was on. When annoyed at mealtimes by the constant quarrels of the white men about precedence, he ordered an immense round table to be made, for which a special house had to be built. This was the station's messroom. Where he sat was the first place—the rest were nowhere. One felt this to be his unalterable conviction. He was neither civil nor uncivil. He was quiet. He allowed his 'boy'—an overfed young Negro from the coast—to treat the white men, under his very eyes, with provoking insolence.

"He began to speak as soon as he saw me. I had been very long on the road. He could not wait. Had to start without me. The up-river stations had to be relieved. There had been so many delays already that he did not know who was dead and who was alive, and how they got on—and so on, and so on. He paid no attention to my explanations, and, playing with a stick of sealing wax, repeated several times that the situation was 'very grave, very grave.' There were rumors that a very important station was in jeopardy, and its chief, Mr. Kurtz, was ill. Hoped it was not true. Mr. Kurtz was . . . I felt weary and irritable. Hang Kurtz, I thought. I interrupted him by saying I had heard of Mr. Kurtz on the coast. 'Ah! So they talk of him down there,' he murmured to himself. Then he began again, assuring me Mr. Kurtz was the best agent he had, an exceptional man, of the greatest importance to the company; therefore I could understand his anxiety. He was, he said, 'very, very uneasy.' Certainly he fidgeted on his chair a good deal, exclaimed, 'Ah, Mr. Kurtz!' broke the stick of sealing wax and seemed dumfounded by the accident. Next thing he wanted to know 'how long it would take to' . . . I interrupted him again. Being hungry, you know, and kept on my feet, too, I was getting savage. 'How could I tell?' I said. 'I hadn't even seen the wreck yet—some months, no doubt.' All this talk seemed to me so futile. 'Some months,' he said. 'Well, let us say three months before we can make a start. Yes. That ought to do the affair.' I flung out of his hut (he lived all alone in a clay hut with a sort of veranda) muttering to myself my opinion of him. He was a chattering idiot. Afterwards I took it back when it was borne in upon me startlingly with what extreme nicety he had estimated the time requisite for the 'affair.'

"I went to work the next day, turning, so to speak, my back on that station. In that way only it seemed to me I could keep my hold on the redeeming facts of life. Still, one must look about sometimes; and then I saw this station, these men strolling aimlessly about in the sunshine of the yard. I asked myself sometimes what it all meant. They wandered here and there with their absurd long staves in their hands, like a lot of faithless pilgrims bewitched inside a rotten fence. The word 'ivory' rang in the air, was whispered, was sighed. You would think they were praying to it. A taint of imbecile rapacity blew through it all, like a whiff from some corpse. By Jove! I've never seen anything so unreal in my life. And outside, the silent wilderness surrounding this cleared speck on the earth struck me as something great and invincible, like evil or truth, waiting patiently for the passing away of this fantastic invasion.

"Oh, these months! Well, never mind. Various things happened. One evening a grass shed full of calico, cotton prints, beads, and I don't know what else, burst into a blaze so suddenly that you would have thought the earth had opened to let an avenging fire consume all that trash. I was smoking my pipe quietly by my dismantled steamer, and saw them all cutting capers in the light, with their arms lifted high, when the stout man with mustaches came tearing down to the river, a tin pail in his hand, assured me that everybody was 'behaving splendidly, splendidly,' dipped about a quart of water and tore back again. I noticed there was a hole in the bottom of his pail.

"I strolled up. There was no hurry. You see the thing had gone off like a box of matches. It had been hopeless from the very first. The flame had leaped high, driven everybody back, lighted up everything —and collapsed. The shed was already a heap of embers glowing fiercely. A nigger was being beaten near by. They said he had caused the fire in some way; be that as it may, he was screeching most horribly. I saw him, later, for several days, sitting in a bit of shade looking very sick and trying to recover himself: afterwards he arose and went out—and the wilderness without a sound took him into its bosom again. As I approached the glow from the dark I found myself at the back of two men, talking. I heard the name of Kurtz pronounced, then the words, 'take advantage of this unfortunate accident.' One of the men was the manager. I wished him a good evening. 'Did you ever see anything like it—eh? It is incredible,' he said, and walked off. The other man remained. He was a first-class agent, young, gentlemanly, a bit reserved, with a forked little beard and a hooked nose. He was standoffish with the other agents, and they on their side said he was the manager's spy upon them. As to me, I had hardly ever spoken to him before. We got into talk, and by and by we strolled away from the hissing ruins. Then he asked me to his room, which was in the main building of the station. He struck a match, and I perceived that this young aristocrat had not only a silver-mounted dressing case but also a whole candle all to himself. Just at that time the manager was the only man supposed to have any right to candles. Native mats covered the clay walls; a collection of spears, assagais, shields, knives was hung up in trophies. The business intrusted to this fellow was the making of bricks—so I had been informed; but there wasn't a fragment of a brick anywhere in the station, and he had been there more than a year —waiting. It seems he could not make bricks without something, I don't know what—straw maybe. Anyways, it could not be found there, and as it was not likely to be sent from Europe, it did not appear clear to me what he was waiting for. An act of special creation perhaps. However, they were all waiting—all the sixteen or twenty pilgrims of them—for something; and upon my word it did not seem an uncongenial occupation, from the way they took it, though the only thing that ever came to them was disease—as far as I could see. They beguiled the time by backbiting and intriguing against each other in a foolish kind of way. There was an air of plotting about that station, but nothing came of it, of course. It was as unreal as everything else—as the philanthropic pretense of the whole concern, as their talk, as their government, as their show of work. The only real feeling was a desire to get appointed to a trading post where ivory was to be had, so that they could earn percentages. They intrigued and slandered and hated each other only on that account, but as to effectually lifting a little finger—oh, no. By heavens! There is something after all in the world allowing one man to steal a horse while another must not look at a halter. Steal a horse straight out. Very well. He has done it. Perhaps he can ride. But there is a way of looking at a halter that would provoke the most charitable of saints into a kick.

"I had no idea why he wanted to be sociable, but as we chatted in there it suddenly occurred to me the fellow was trying to get at something—in fact, pumping me. He alluded constantly to Europe, to the people I was supposed to know there—putting leading questions as to my acquaintances in the sepulchral city, and so on. His little eyes glittered like mica discs—with curiosity—though he tried to keep up a bit of superciliousness. At first I was astonished, but very soon I became awfully curious to see what he would find out from me. I couldn't possibly imagine what I had in me to make it worth his while. It was very pretty to see how he baffled himself, for in truth my body was full only of chills, and my head had nothing in it but that wretched steamboat business. It was evident he took me for a perfectly shameless prevaricator. At last he got angry, and, to conceal a movement of furious annoyance, he yawned. I rose. Then I noticed a small sketch in oils, on a panel, representing a woman, draped and blindfolded, carrying a lighted torch. The background was somber—almost black. The movement of the woman was stately, and the effect of the torchlight on the face was sinister.

"It arrested me, and he stood by civilly, holding an empty half-pint champagne bottle (medical comforts) with the candle stuck in it. To my question he said Mr. Kurtz had painted this—in this very station more than a year ago—while waiting for means to go to his trading post. 'Tell me, pray,' said I, 'who is this Mr. Kurtz?'

" 'The chief of the Inner Station,' he answered in a short tone, looking away. 'Much obliged,' I said, laughing. 'And you are the brickmaker of the Central Station. Everyone knows that.' He was silent for a while. 'He is a prodigy,' he said at last. 'He is an emissary of pity, and science, and progress, and devil knows what else. We want,' he began to declaim suddenly, 'for the guidance of the cause intrusted to us by Europe, so to speak, higher intelligence, wide sympathies, a singleness of purpose.' 'Who says that?' I asked. 'Lots of them,' he replied. 'Some even write that; and so *he* comes here, a special being, as you ought to know.' 'Why ought I to know?' I interrupted, really surprised. He paid no attention. 'Yes. Today he is chief of the best station, next year he will be assistant manager, two years more and . . . but I daresay you know what he will be in two years' time. You are of the new gang—the gang of virtue. The same people who sent him specially also recommended you. Oh, don't say no. I've my own eyes to trust.' Light dawned upon me. My dear aunt's influential acquaintances were producing an unexpected effect upon that young man. I nearly burst into a laugh. 'Do you read the company's confidential correspondence?' I asked. He hadn't a word to say. It was great fun. 'When Mr. Kurtz,' I continued, severely, 'is general manager, you won't have the opportunity.'

"He blew the candle out suddenly, and we went outside. The moon had risen. Black figures strolled about listlessly, pouring water on the glow, whence proceeded a sound of hissing; steam ascended in the moonlight, the beaten nigger groaned somewhere. 'What a row the brute makes!' said the indefatigable man with the mustaches, appearing near us. 'Serve him right. Transgression—punishment—bang! Pitiless, pitiless. That's the only way. This will prevent all conflagrations for the future. I was just telling the manager . . .' He noticed my companion, and became crestfallen all at once. 'Not in bed yet,' he said, with a kind of servile heartiness; 'it's so natural. Ha! Danger—agitation.' He vanished. I went on to the river side, and the other followed me. I heard a scathing murmur at my ear, 'Heap of muffs—go to.' The pilgrims could be seen in knots gesticulating, discussing. Several had still their staves in their hands. I truly believe they took these sticks to bed with them. Beyond the fence the forest stood up spectrally in the moonlight, and through the dim stir, through the faint sounds of that lamentable courtyard, the silence of the land went home to one's very heart—its mystery, its greatness, the amazing reality of its concealed life. The hurt nigger moaned feebly somewhere near by, and then fetched a deep sigh that made me mend my pace away from there. I felt a hand introducing itself under my arm. 'My dear sir,' said the fellow, 'I don't want to be misunderstood, and especially by you, who will see Mr. Kurtz long before I can have that pleasure. I wouldn't like him to get a false idea of my disposition. . . .'

"I let him run on, this papier-mâché Mephistopheles, and it seemed to me that if I tried I could poke my forefinger through him, and would find nothing inside but a little loose dirt, maybe. He, don't you see, had been planning to be assistant manager by and by under the present man, and I could see that the coming of that Kurtz had upset them both not a little. He talked precipitately, and I did not try to stop him. I had my shoulders against the wreck of my steamer, hauled up on the slope like a carcass of some big river animal. The smell of mud, of primeval mud, by Jove! was in my nostrils, the high stillness of primeval forest was before my eyes; there were shiny patches on the black creek. The moon had spread over everything a thin layer of silver—over the rank grass, over the mud, upon the wall of matted vegetation standing higher than the wall of a temple, over the great river I could see through a somber gap glittering, glittering, as it flowed broadly by without a murmur. All this was great, expectant, mute, while the man jabbered about himself. I wondered whether the stillness on the face of the immensity looking at us two were meant as an appeal or as a menace. What were we who had strayed in here? Could we handle that dumb thing, or would it handle us? I felt how big, how confoundedly big, was that thing that couldn't talk, and perhaps was deaf as well. What was in there? I could see a little ivory coming out from there, and I had heard Mr. Kurtz was in there. I had heard enough about it, too—God knows! Yet somehow it didn't bring any image with it—no more than if I had been told an angel or a fiend was in there. I believed it in the same way one of you might believe there are inhabitants in the planet Mars. I knew once a Scotch sailmaker who was certain, dead sure, there were people in Mars. If you asked him for some idea how they looked and behaved, he would get shy and mutter something about 'walking on all fours.' If you as much as smiled, he would—

though a man of sixty—offer to fight you. I would not have gone so far as to fight for Kurtz, but I went for him near enough to a lie. You know I hate, detest, and can't bear a lie, not because I am straighter than the rest of us, but simply because it appalls me. There is a taint of death, a flavor of mortality in lies—which is exactly what I hate and detest in the world—what I want to forget. It makes me miserable and sick, like biting something rotten would do. Temperament, I suppose. Well, I went near enough to it by letting the young fool there believe anything he liked to imagine as to my influence in Europe. I became in an instant as much of a pretense as the rest of the bewitched pilgrims. This simply because I had a notion it somehow would be of help to that Kurtz whom at the time I did not see—you understand. He was just a word for me. I did not see the man in the name any more than you do. Do you see him? Do you see the story? Do you see anything? It seems to me I am trying to tell you a dream—making a vain attempt, because no relation of a dream can convey the dream-sensation, that commingling of absurdity, surprise, and bewilderment in a tremor of struggling revolt, that notion of being captured by the incredible which is of the very essence of dreams. . . ."

He was silent for a while.

". . . No, it is impossible; it is impossible to convey the life-sensation of any given epoch of one's existence—that which makes its truth, its meaning—its subtle and penetrating essence. It is impossible. We live, as we dream—alone. . . ."

He paused again as if reflecting, then added:

"Of course in this you fellows see more than I could then. You see me, whom you know. . . ."

It had become so pitch dark that we listeners could hardly see one another. For a long time already he, sitting apart, had been no more to us than a voice. There was not a word from anybody. The others might have been asleep, but I was awake. I listened, I listened on the watch for the sentence, for the word, that would give me the clue to the faint uneasiness inspired by this narrative that seemed to shape itself without human lips in the heavy night air of the river.

". . . Yes—I let him run on," Marlow began again, "and think what he pleased about the powers that were behind me. I did! And there was nothing behind me! There was nothing but that wretched, old, mangled steamboat I was leaning against, while he talked fluently about 'the necessity for every man to get on.' 'And when one comes out here, you conceive, it is not to gaze at the moon.' Mr. Kurtz was a 'universal genius,' but even a genius would find it easier to work with 'adequate tools—intelligent men.' He did not make bricks—why, there was a physical impossibility in the way—as I was well aware; and if he did secretarial work for the manager, it was because 'no sensible man rejects wantonly the confidence of his superiors.' Did I see it? I saw it. What more did I want? What I really wanted was rivets, by heaven! Rivets. To get on with the work—to stop the hole. Rivets I wanted. There were cases of them down at the coast—cases—piled up—burst —split! You kicked a loose rivet at every second step in that station yard on the hillside. Rivets had rolled into the grove of death. You could fill your pockets with rivets for the trouble of stooping down— and there wasn't one rivet to be found where it was wanted. We had plates that would do, but nothing to fasten them with. And every week the messenger, a lone Negro, letter bag on shoulder and staff in hand, left our station for the coast. And several times a week a coast caravan came in with trade goods—ghastly glazed calico that made you shudder only to look at it, glass beads, value about a penny a quart, confounded spotted cotton handkerchiefs. And no rivets. Three carriers could have brought all that was wanted to set that steamboat afloat.

"He was becoming confidential now, but I fancy my unresponsive attitude must have exasperated him at last, for he judged it necessary to inform me he feared neither God nor devil, let alone any mere man. I said I could see that very well, but what I wanted was a certain quantity of rivets—and rivets were what really Mr. Kurtz wanted, if he had only known it. Now letters went to the coast every week. . . . 'My dear sir,' he cried, 'I write from dictation.' I demanded rivets. There was a way—for an intelligent man. He changed his manner; became very cold, and suddenly began to talk about a hippopotamus; wondered whether sleeping on board the steamer (I stuck to my salvage night and day) I wasn't disturbed. There was an old hippo that had the bad habit of getting out on the bank and roaming at night over the station grounds. The pilgrims used to turn out in a body and empty every rifle they could lay hands on at him. Some even had sat up o' nights for him. All this energy was wasted, though. 'That animal has a charmed life,' he said; 'but you can say this only of brutes in this country. No man—you apprehend me?—no man here bears a charmed life.' He stood there for a moment in the moonlight with his delicate hooked nose set a little askew, and his mica eyes glittering without a wink, then, with a curt good night, he strode off. I could see he was disturbed and considerably puzzled, which made me feel more hopeful than I had been for days. It was a great comfort to turn from that chap to my influential friend, the battered, twisted, ruined, tinpot steamboat. I clambered on board. She rang under my feet like an empty Huntley and Palmer biscuit tin kicked along a gutter; she was nothing so solid in make, and rather less pretty in shape, but I had expended enough hard work on her to make me love her. No influential friend would have served me better. She had given me a chance to come out a bit—to find out what I could do. No, I don't like work. I had rather laze about and think of all the fine things that can be done. I don't like work—no man does—but I like what is in the work, the chance to find yourself. Your own reality—for yourself, not for others—what no other man can ever know. They can only see the mere show, and never can tell what it really means.

"I was not surprised to see somebody sitting aft, on the deck, with his legs dangling over the mud. You see I rather chummed with the few mechanics there were in that station, whom the other pilgrims naturally despised—on account of their imperfect manners, I suppose. This was the foreman—a boilermaker by trade—a good worker. He was a lank, bony, yellow-faced man, with big intense eyes. His aspect was worried, and his head was as bald as the palm of my hand; but his hair in falling seemed to have stuck to his chin, and had prospered in the new locality, for his beard hung down to his waist. He was a widower with six young children (he had left them in charge of a sister of his to come out there), and the passion of his life was pigeon flying. He was an enthusiast and a connoisseur. He would rave about pigeons. After work hours he used sometimes to come over from his hut for a talk about his children and his pigeons; at work, when he had to crawl in the mud under the bottom of the steamboat, he would tie up that beard of his in a kind of white serviette he brought for the purpose. It had loops to go over his ears. In the evening he could be seen squatted on the bank rinsing that wrapper in the creek with great care, then spreading it solemnly on a bush to dry.

"I slapped him on the back and shouted, 'We shall have rivets!' He scrambled to his feet exclaiming 'No! Rivets!' as though he couldn't believe his ears. Then in a low voice, 'You . . . eh?' I don't know why we behaved like lunatics. I put my finger to the side of my nose and nodded mysteriously. 'Good for you!' he cried, snapped his fingers above his head, lifting one foot. I tried a jig. We capered on the iron deck. A frightful clatter came out of that hulk, and the virgin forest on the other bank of the creek sent it back in a thundering roll upon the sleeping station. It must have made some of the pilgrims sit up in their hovels. A dark figure obscured the lighted doorway of the manager's hut, vanished, then a second or so after, the doorway itself vanished, too. We stopped, and the silence driven away by the stamping of our feet flowed back again from the recesses of the land. The great wall of vegetation, an exuberant and entangled mass of trunks, branches, leaves, boughs, festoons, motionless in the moonlight, was like a rioting invasion of soundless life, a rolling wave of plants, piled up, crested, ready to topple over the creek, to sweep every little man of us out of his little existence. And it moved not. A deadened burst of mighty splashes and snorts reached us from afar, as though an ichthyosaurus had been taking a bath of glitter in the great river. 'After all,' said the boilermaker in a reasonable tone, 'why shouldn't we get the rivets?' Why not, indeed! I did not know of any reason why we shouldn't. 'They'll come in three weeks,' I said, confidently.

"But they didn't. Instead of rivets there came an invasion, an infliction, a visitation. It came in sections during the next three weeks, each section headed by a donkey carrying a white man in new clothes and tan shoes, bowing from that elevation right and left to the impressed pilgrims. A quarrelsome band of footsore sulky niggers trod on the heels of the donkey; a lot of tents, campstools, tin boxes, white cases, brown bales would be shot down in the courtyard, and the air of mystery would deepen a little over the muddle of the station. Five such instalments came, with their absurd air of disorderly flight with the loot of innumerable outfit shops and provision stores, that, one would think, they were lugging, after a raid, into the wilderness for equitable division. It was an inextricable mess of things decent in themselves but that human folly made look like spoils of thieving.

"This devoted band called itself the Eldorado Exploring Expedition, and I believe they were sworn to secrecy. Their talk, however, was the talk of sordid buccaneers: it was reckless without hardihood, greedy without audacity, and cruel without courage; there was not an atom of foresight or of serious intention in the whole batch of them, and they did not seem aware these things are wanted for the work of the world. To tear treasure out of the bowels of the land was their desire, with no more moral purpose at the back of it than there is in burglars breaking into a safe. Who paid the expenses of the noble enterprise I don't know; but the uncle of our manager was leader of that lot.

"In exterior he resembled a butcher in a poor neighborhood, and his eyes had a look of sleepy cunning. He carried his fat paunch with ostentation on his short legs, and during the time his gang infested the station spoke to no one but his nephew. You could see these two roaming about all day long with their heads close together in an everlasting confab.

"I had given up worrying myself about the rivets. One's capacity for that kind of folly is more limited than you would suppose. I said Hang!—and let things slide. I had plenty of time for meditation, and now and then I would give some thought to Kurtz. I wasn't very interested in him. No. Still, I was curious to see whether this man, who had come out equipped with moral ideas of some sort, would climb to the top after all and how he would set about his work when there."

II

"One evening as I was lying flat on the deck of my steamboat, I heard voices approaching—and there were the nephew and the uncle strolling along the bank. I laid my head on my arm again, and had nearly lost myself in a doze, when somebody said in my ear, as it were: 'I am as harmless as a little child, but I don't like to be dictated to. Am I the manager—or am I not? I was ordered to send him there. It's incredible.' . . . I became aware that the two were standing on the shore alongside the forepart of the steamboat, just below my head. I did not move; it did not occur to me to move: I was sleepy. 'It *is* unpleasant,' grunted the uncle. 'He has asked the administration to be sent there,' said the other, 'with the idea of showing what he could do; and I was instructed accordingly. Look at the influence that man must have. Is it not frightful?' They both agreed it was frightful, then made several bizarre remarks: 'Make rain and fine weather—one man—the council—by the nose'—bits of absurd sentences that got the better of my drowsiness, so that I had pretty near the whole of my wits about me when the uncle said, 'The climate may do away with this difficulty for you. Is he alone there?' 'Yes,' answered the manager; 'he sent his assistant down the river with a note to me in these terms: "Clear this poor devil out of the country, and don't bother sending more of that sort. I had rather be alone than have the kind of men you can dispose of with me." It was more than a year ago. Can you imagine such impudence!' 'Anything since then?' asked the other, hoarsely. 'Ivory,' jerked the nephew; 'lots of it—prime sort—lots—most annoying, from him.' 'And with that?' questioned the heavy rumble. 'Invoice,' was the reply fired out, so to speak. Then silence. They had been talking about Kurtz.

"I was broad awake by this time, but, lying perfectly at ease, remained still, having no inducement to change my position. 'How did that ivory come all this way?' growled the elder man, who seemed very vexed. The other explained that it had come with a fleet of canoes in charge of an English half-caste clerk Kurtz had with him; that Kurtz had apparently intended to return himself, the station being by that time bare of goods and stores, but after coming three hundred miles, had suddenly decided to go back, which he started to do alone in a small dugout with four paddlers, leaving the half-caste to continue down the river with the ivory. The two fellows there seemed astounded at anybody attempting such a thing. They were at a loss for an adequate motive. As to me, I seemed to see Kurtz for the first time. It was a distinct glimpse: the dugout, four paddling savages, and the lone white man turning his back suddenly on the headquarters, on relief, on thoughts of home—perhaps; setting his face towards the depths of the wilderness, towards his empty and desolate station. I did not know the motive. Perhaps he was just simply a fine fellow who stuck to his work for its own sake. His name, you understand, had not been pronounced once. He was 'that man.' The half-caste, who, as far as I could see, had conducted a difficult trip with great prudence and pluck, was invariably alluded to as 'that scoundrel.' The 'scoundrel' had reported that the 'man' had been very ill—had recovered imperfectly. . . . The two below me moved away then a few paces, and strolled back and forth at some little distance. I heard: 'Military post—doctor —two hundred miles—quite alone now—unavoidable delays—nine months—no news—strange rumors.' They approached again, just as the manager was saying, 'No one, as far as I know, unless a species of wandering trader—a pestilential fellow, snapping ivory from the natives.' Who was it they were talking about now? I gathered in snatches that this was some man supposed to be in Kurtz's district, and of whom the manager did not approve. 'We will not be free from unfair competition till one of these fellows is hanged for an example,' he said. 'Certainly,' grunted the other; 'get him hanged! Why not? Anything—anything can be done in this country. That's what I say; nobody here, you understand, *here*, can endanger your position. And why? You stand the climate—you outlast them all. The danger is in Europe; but there before I left I took care to—' They moved off and whispered, then their voices rose again. 'The extraordinary series of delays is not my fault. I did my best.' The fat man sighed. 'Very sad.' 'And the pestiferous absurdity of his talk,' continued the other; 'he bothered me enough when he was here. "Each station should be like a beacon on the road towards better things, a center for trade of course, but also for humanizing, improving, instructing." Conceive you—that ass! And he wants to be manager! No, it's—' Here he got choked by excessive indignation, and I lifted my head the least bit. I was surprised to see how near they were—right under me. I could have spat upon their hats. They were looking on the ground, absorbed in thought. The manager was switching his leg with a slender twig; his sagacious relative lifted his head. 'You have been well since you came out this time?' he asked. The other gave a start. 'Who? I? Oh! Like a charm—like a charm. But the rest—oh, my goodness! All sick. They die so quick, too, that I haven't the time to send them out of the country—it's incredible!' 'H'm. Just so,' grunted the uncle. 'Ah! my boy, trust to this—I say, trust to this.' I saw him extend his short flipper of an arm for a gesture that took in the forest, the creek, the mud, the river—seemed to beckon with a dishonoring flourish before the sunlit face of the land a treacherous appeal to the lurking death, to the hidden evil, to the profound darkness of its heart. It was so startling that I leaped to my feet and looked back at the edge of the forest, as though I had expected an answer of some sort to that black display of confidence. You know the foolish notions that come to one sometimes. The high stillness confronted these two figures with its ominous patience, waiting for the passing away of a fantastic invasion.

"They swore aloud together—out of sheer fright, I believe—then pretending not to know anything of my existence, turned back to the station. The sun was low; and leaning forward side by side, they seemed to be tugging painfully uphill their two ridiculous shadows of unequal length, that trailed behind them slowly over the tall grass without bending a single blade.

"In a few days the Eldorado Expedition went into the patient wilderness, that closed upon it as the sea closes over a diver. Long afterwards the news came that all the donkeys were dead. I know nothing as to the fate of the less valuable animals. They, no doubt, like the rest of us, found what they deserved. I did not inquire. I was then rather excited at the prospect of meeting Kurtz very soon. When I say very soon I mean it comparatively. It was just two months from the day we left the creek when we came to the bank below Kurtz's station.

"Going up that river was like traveling back to the earliest beginnings of the world, when vegetation rioted on the earth and the big trees were kings. An empty stream, a great silence, an impenetrable forest. The air was warm, thick, heavy, sluggish. There was no joy in the brilliance of sunshine. The long stretches of the waterway ran on, deserted, into the gloom of overshadowed distances. On silvery sandbanks hippos and alligators sunned themselves side by side. The broadening waters flowed through a mob of wooded islands; you lost your way on that river as you would in a desert, and butted all day long against shoals, trying to find the channel, till you thought yourself bewitched and cut off forever from everything you had known once—somewhere—far away—in another existence perhaps. There were moments when one's past came back to one, as it will sometimes when you have not a moment to spare to yourself; but it came in the shape of an unrestful and noisy dream, remembered with wonder amongst the overwhelming realities of this strange world of plants, and water, and silence. And this stillness of life did not in the least resemble a peace. It was the stillness of an implacable force brooding over an inscrutable intention. It looked at you with a vengeful aspect. I got used to it afterwards; I did not see it any more; I had no time. I had to keep guessing at the channel; I had to discern, mostly by inspiration, the signs of hidden banks; I watched for sunken stones; I was learning to clap my teeth smartly before my heart flew out, when I shaved by a fluke some infernal sly old snag that would have ripped the life out of the tin-pot steamboat and drowned all the pilgrims; I had to keep a lookout for the signs of dead wood we could cut up in the night for next day's steaming. When you have to attend to things of that sort, to the mere incidents of the surface, the reality—the reality, I tell you —fades. The inner truth is hidden—luckily, luckily. But I felt it all the same; I felt often its mysterious stillness watching me at my monkey tricks, just as it watches you fellows performing on your respective tightropes for—what is it? a half crown a tumble—"

"Try to be civil, Marlow," growled a voice, and I knew there was at least one listener awake besides myself.

"I beg your pardon. I forgot the heartache which makes up the rest of the price. And indeed what does the price matter, if the trick be well done? You do your tricks very well. And I didn't do badly either, since I managed not to sink that steamboat on my first trip. It's a wonder to me yet. Imagine a blindfolded man set to drive a van over a bad road. I sweated and shivered over that business considerably, I can tell you. After all, for a seaman, to scrape the bottom of the thing that's supposed to float all the time under his care is the unpardonable sin. No one may know of it, but you never forget the thump—eh? A blow on the very heart. You remember it, you dream of it, you wake up at night and think of it—years after—and go hot and cold all over. I don't pretend to say that steamboat floated all the time. More than once she had to wade for a bit, with twenty cannibals splashing around and pushing. We had enlisted some of these chaps on the way for a crew. Fine fellows—cannibals—in their place. They were men one could work with, and I am grateful to them. And, after all, they did not eat each other before my face: they had brought along a provision of hippo meat which went rotten, and made the mystery of the wilderness stink in my nostrils. Phoo! I can sniff it now. I had the manager on board and three or four pilgrims with their staves—all complete. Sometimes we came upon a station close by the bank, clinging to the skirts of the unknown, and the white men rushing out of a tumble-down hovel, with great gestures of joy and surprise and welcome, seemed very strange —had the appearance of being held there captive by a spell. The word ivory would ring in the air for a while—and on we went again into the silence, along empty reaches, round the still bends, between the high walls of our winding way, reverberating in hollow claps the ponderous beat of the stern wheel. Trees, trees, millions of trees, massive, immense, running up high; and at their foot, hugging the bank against the stream, crept the little begrimed steamboat, like a sluggish beetle crawling on the floor of a lofty portico. It made you feel very small, very lost, and yet it was not altogether depressing, that feeling. After all, if you were small, the grimy beetle crawled on—which was just what you wanted it to do. Where the pilgrims imagined it crawled to I don't know. To some place where they expected to get something, I bet! For me it crawled towards Kurtz—exclusively; but when the steam pipes started leaking we crawled very slow. The reaches opened before us and closed behind, as if the forest had stepped leisurely across the water to bar the way for our return. We penetrated deeper and deeper into the heart of darkness. It was very quiet there. At night sometimes the roll of drums behind the curtain of trees would run up the river and remain sustained faintly, as if hovering in the air high over our heads, till the first break of day. Whether it meant war, peace, or prayer we could not tell. The dawns were heralded by the descent of a chill stillness; the woodcutters slept, their fires burned low; the snapping of a twig would make you start. We were wanderers on prehistoric earth, on an earth that wore the aspect of an unknown planet. We could have fancied ourselves the first of men taking possession of an accursed inheritance, to be subdued at the cost of profound anguish and of excessive toil. But suddenly, as we struggled round a bend, there would be a glimpse of rush walls, of peaked grass roofs, a burst of yells, a whirl of black limbs, a mass of hands clapping, of feet stamping, of bodies swaying, of eyes rolling, under the droop of heavy and motionless foliage. The steamer toiled along slowly on the edge of a black and incomprehensible frenzy. The prehistoric man was cursing us, praying to us, welcoming us—who could tell? We were cut off from the comprehension of our surroundings; we glided past like phantoms, wondering and secretly appalled, as sane men would be before an enthusiastic outbreak in a madhouse. We could not understand because we were too far and could not remember, because we were traveling in the night of first ages, of those ages that are gone, leaving hardly a sign—and no memories.

"The earth seemed unearthly. We are accustomed to look upon the shackled form of a conquered monster, but there—there you could look at a thing monstrous and free. It was unearthly, and the men were— No, they were not inhuman. Well, you know, that was the worst of it—this suspicion of their not being inhuman. It would come slowly to one. They howled and leaped, and spun, and made horrid faces; but what thrilled you was just the thought of their humanity—like yours—the thought of your remote kinship with this wild and passionate uproar. Ugly. Yes, it was ugly enough; but if you were man enough you would admit to yourself that there was in you just the faintest trace of a response to the terrible frankness of that noise, a dim suspicion of there being a meaning in it which you—you so remote from the night of first ages—could comprehend. And why not? The mind of man is capable of anything—because everything is in it, all the past as well as all the future. What was there after all? Joy, fear, sorrow, devotion, valor, rage—who can tell?—but truth—truth stripped of its cloak of time. Let the fool gape and shudder—the man knows, and can look on without a wink. But he must at least be as much of a man as these on the shore. He must meet that truth with his own true stuff—with his own inborn strength. Principles won't do. Acquisitions, clothes, pretty rags—rags that would fly off at the first good shake. No; you want a deliberate belief. An appeal to me in this fiendish row—is there? Very well; I hear; I admit, but I have a voice, too, and for good or evil mine is the speech that cannot be silenced. Of course, a fool, what with sheer fright and fine sentiments, is always safe. Who's that grunting? You wonder I didn't go ashore for a howl and a dance? Well, no—I didn't. Fine sentiments, you say? Fine sentiments, be hanged! I had no time. I had to mess about with white lead and strips of woolen blanket helping to put bandages on those leaky steam pipes—I tell you. I had to watch the steering, and circumvent those snags, and get the tin-pot along by hook or by crook. There was surface truth enough in these things to save a wiser man. And between whiles I had to look after the savage who was fireman. He was an improved specimen; he could fire up a vertical boiler. He was there below me, and, upon my word, to look at him was as edifying as seeing a dog in a parody of breeches and a feather hat, walking on his hind legs. A few months of training had done for that really fine chap. He squinted at the steam gauge and at the water gauge with an evident effort of intrepidity—and he had filed teeth, too, the poor devil, and the wool of his pate shaved into queer patterns, and three ornamental scars on each of his cheeks. He ought to have been clapping his hands and stamping his feet on the bank, instead of which he was hard at work, a thrall to strange witchcraft, full of improving knowledge. He was useful because he had been instructed; and what he knew was this —that should the water in that transparent thing disappear, the evil spirit inside the boiler would get angry through the greatness of his thirst, and take a terrible vengeance. So he sweated and fired up and watched the glass fearfully (with an impromptu charm, made of rags, tied to his arm, and a piece of polished bone, as big as a watch, stuck flatways through his lower lip), while the wooded banks slipped past us slowly, the short noise was left behind, the interminable miles of silence—and we crept on, towards Kurtz. But the snags were thick, the water was treacherous and shallow, the boiler seemed indeed to have a sulky devil in it, and thus neither that fireman nor I had any time to peer into our creepy thoughts.

"Some fifty miles below the Inner Station we came upon a hut of reeds, an inclined and melancholy pole, with the unrecognizable tatters of what had been a flag of some sort flying from it, and a neatly stacked wood pile. This was unexpected. We came to the bank, and on the stack of firewood found a flat piece of board with some faded pencil writing on it. When deciphered it said: 'Wood for you. Hurry up. Approach cautiously.' There was a signature, but it was illegible—not Kurtz—a much longer word. Hurry up. Where? Up the river? 'Approach cautiously.' We had not done so. But the warning could not have been meant for the place where it could be only found after approach. Something was wrong above. But what—and how much? That was the question. We commented adversely upon the imbecility of that telegraphic style. The bush around said nothing, and would not let us look very far, either. A torn curtain of red twill hung in the doorway of the hut, and flapped sadly in our faces. The dwelling was dismantled; but we could see a white man had lived there not very long ago. There remained a rude table—a plank on two posts; a heap of rubbish reposed in a dark corner, and by the door I picked up a book. It had lost its covers, and the pages had been thumbed into a state of extremely dirty softness; but the back had been lovingly stitched afresh with white cotton thread, which looked clean yet. It was an extraordinary find. Its title was, *An Inquiry into Some Points of Seamanship,* by a man Tower, Towson—some such name—Master in his Majesty's Navy. The matter looked dreary reading enough, with illustrative diagrams and repulsive tables of figures, and the copy was sixty years old. I handled this amazing antiquity with the greatest possible tenderness, lest it should dissolve in my hands. Within, Towson or Towser was inquiring earnestly into the breaking strain of ships' chains and tackle, and other such matters. Not a very enthralling book; but at the first glance you could see there a singleness of intention, an honest concern for the right way of going to work, which made these humble pages, thought out so many years ago, luminous with another than a professional light. The simple old sailor, with his talk of chains and purchases, made me forget the jungle and the pilgrims in a delicious sensation of having come upon something unmistakably real. Such a book being there was wonderful enough; but still more astounding were the notes penciled in the margin, and plainly referring to the text. I couldn't believe my eyes! They were in cipher! Yes, it looked like cipher. Fancy a man lugging with him a book of that description into this nowhere and studying it—and making notes—in cipher at that! It was an extravagant mystery.

"I had been dimly aware for some time of a worrying noise, and when I lifted my eyes I saw the wood pile was gone, and the manager, aided by all the pilgrims, was shouting at me from the river side. I slipped the book into my pocket. I assure you to leave off reading was like tearing myself away from the shelter of an old and solid friendship.

"I started the lame engine ahead. 'It must be this miserable trader—this intruder,' exclaimed the manager, looking back malevolently at the place we had left. 'He must be English,' I said. 'It will not save him from getting into trouble if he is not careful,' muttered the manager darkly. I observed with assumed innocence that no man was safe from trouble in this world.

"The current was more rapid now, the steamer seemed at her last gasp, the stern wheel flopped languidly, and I caught myself listening on tiptoe for the next beat of the boat, for in sober truth I expected the wretched thing to give up every moment. It was like watching the last flickers of a life. But still we crawled. Sometimes I would pick out a tree a little way ahead to measure our progress towards Kurtz by, but I lost it invariably before we got abreast. To keep the eyes so long on one thing was too much for human patience. The manager displayed a beautiful resignation. I fretted and fumed and took to arguing with myself whether or no I would talk openly with Kurtz; but before I could come to any conclusion it occurred to me that my speech or my silence, indeed any action of mine, would be a mere futility. What did it matter what anyone knew or ignored? What did it matter who was manager? One gets sometimes such a flash of insight. The essentials of this affair lay deep under the surface, beyond my reach, and beyond my power of meddling.

"Towards the evening of the second day we judged ourselves about eight miles from Kurtz's station. I wanted to push on; but the manager looked grave, and told me the navigation up there was so dangerous that it would be advisable, the sun being very low already, to wait where we were till next morning. Moreover, he pointed out that if the warning to approach cautiously were to be followed, we must approach in daylight—not at dusk, or in the dark. This was sensible enough. Eight miles meant nearly three hours' steaming for us, and I could also see suspicious ripples at the upper end of the reach. Nevertheless, I was annoyed beyond expression at the delay, and most unreasonably, too, since one night more could not matter much after so many months. As we had plenty of wood, and caution was the word,

I brought up in the middle of the stream. The reach was narrow, straight, with high sides like a railway cutting. The dusk came gliding into it long before the sun had set. The current ran smooth and swift, but a dumb immobility sat on the banks. The living trees, lashed together by the creepers and every living bush of the undergrowth, might have been changed into stone, even to the slenderest twig, to the lightest leaf. It was not sleep—it seemed unnatural, like a state of trance. Not the faintest sound of any kind could be heard. You looked on amazed, and began to suspect yourself of being deaf—then the night came suddenly, and struck you blind as well. About three in the morning some large fish leaped, and the loud splash made me jump as though a gun had been fired. When the sun rose there was a white fog, very warm and clammy, and more blinding than the night. It did not shift or drive; it was just there, standing all round you like something solid. At eight or nine, perhaps, it lifted as a shutter lifts. We had a glimpse of the towering multitude of trees, of the immense matted jungle, with the blazing little ball of the sun hanging over it—all perfectly still—and then the white shutter came down again, smoothly, as if sliding in greased grooves. I ordered the chain, which we had begun to heave in, to be paid out again. Before it stopped running with a muffled rattle, a cry, a very loud cry, as of infinite desolation, soared slowly in the opaque air. It ceased. A complaining clamor, modulated in savage discords, filled our ears. The sheer unexpectedness of it made my hair stir under my cap. I don't know how it struck the others: to me it seemed as though the mist itself had screamed, so suddenly, and apparently from all sides at once, did this tumultuous and mournful uproar arise. It culminated in a hurried outbreak of almost intolerably excessive shrieking, which stopped short, leaving us stiffened in a variety of silly attitudes, and obstinately listening to the nearly as appalling and excessive silence. 'Good God! What is the meaning—' stammered at my elbow one of the pilgrims, a little fat man, with sandy hair and red whiskers, who wore sidespring boots, and pink pajamas tucked into his socks. Two others remained openmouthed a whole minute, then dashed into the little cabin, to rush out incontinently and stand darting scared glances, with Winchesters at 'ready' in their hands. What we could see was just the steamer we were on, her outlines blurred as though she had been on the point of dissolving, and a misty strip of water, perhaps two feet broad, around her—and that was all. The rest of the world was nowhere, as far as our eyes and ears were concerned. Just nowhere. Gone, disappeared; swept off without leaving a whisper or a shadow behind.

"I went forward, and ordered the chain to be hauled in short, so as to be ready to trip the anchor and move the steamboat at once if necessary. 'Will they attack?' whispered an awed voice. 'We will be all butchered in this fog,' murmured another. The faces twitched with the strain, the hands trembled slightly, the eyes forgot to wink. It was very curious to see the contrast of expressions of the white men and of the black fellows of our crew, who were as much strangers to that part of the river as we, though their homes were only eight hundred miles away. The whites, of course greatly discomposed, had besides a curious look of being painfully shocked by such an outrageous row. The others had an alert, naturally interested expression; but their faces were essentially quiet, even those of the one or two who grinned as they hauled at the chain. Several exchanged short, grunting phrases, which seemed to settle the matter to their satisfaction. Their headman, a young, broad-chested black, severely draped in dark-blue fringed cloths, with fierce nostrils and his hair all done up artfully in oily ringlets, stood near me. 'Aha!' I said, just for good fellowship's sake. 'Catch 'im,' he snapped, with a bloodshot widening of his eyes and a flash of sharp teeth—'catch 'im. Give 'im to us.' 'To you, eh?' I asked; 'what would you do with them?' 'Eat 'im!' he said, curtly, and, leaning his elbow on the rail, looked out into the fog in a dignified and profoundly pensive attitude. I would no doubt have been properly horrified, had it not occurred to me that he and his chaps must be very hungry: that they must have been growing increasingly hungry for at least this month past. They had been engaged for six months (I don't think a single one of them had any clear idea of time, as we at the end of countless ages have. They still belonged to the beginnings of time —had no inherited experience to teach them as it were), and of course, as long as there was a piece of paper written over in accordance with some farcical law or other made down the river, it didn't enter anybody's head to trouble how they would live. Certainly they had brought with them some rotten hippo meat, which couldn't have lasted very long, anyway, even if the pilgrims hadn't, in the midst of a shocking hullabaloo, thrown a considerable quantity of it overboard. It looked like a high-handed proceeding; but it was really a case of legitimate self-defense. You can't breathe dead hippo waking, sleeping, and eating, and at the same time keep your precarious grip on existence. Besides that, they had given them every week three pieces of brass wire, each about nine inches long; and the theory was they were to buy their provisions with that currency in river-side villages. You can see how *that* worked. There were either no villages, or the people were hostile, or the director, who like the rest of us fed out of tins, with an occasional old he-goat thrown in, didn't want to stop the steamer for some more or less recondite reasons. So, unless they swallowed the wire itself, or made loops of it to snare the fishes with, I don't see what good their extravagant salary could be to them. I must say it was paid with a regularity worthy of a large and honorable trading company. For the rest, the only thing to eat—though it didn't look eatable in the least—I saw in their possession was a few lumps of some stuff like half-cooked dough, of a dirty lavender color, they kept wrapped in leaves, and now and then swallowed a piece of, but so small that it seemed done more for the looks of the thing than for any serious purpose of sustenance. Why in the name of all the gnawing devils of hunger they didn't go for us—they were thirty to five—and have a good tuck in for once, amazes me now when I think of it. They were big powerful men, with not much capacity to weigh the consequences, with courage, with strength, even yet, though their skins were no longer glossy and their muscles no longer hard. And I saw that something restraining, one of those human secrets that baffle probability, had come into play there. I looked at them with a swift quickening of interest—not because it occurred to me I might be eaten by them before very long, though I own to you that just then I perceived—in a new light, as it were—how unwholesome the pilgrims looked, and I hoped, yes, I positively hoped, that my aspect was not so—what shall I say?—so—unappetizing: a touch of fantastic vanity which fitted well with the dream-sensation that pervaded all my days at that time. Perhaps I had a little fever, too. One can't live with one's finger everlastingly on one's pulse. I had often 'a little fever,' or a little touch of other things—the playful paw-strokes of the wilderness, the preliminary trifling before the more serious onslaught which came in due course. Yes; I looked at them as you would on any human being, with a curiosity of their impulses, motives, capacities, weaknesses, when brought to the test of an inexorable physical necessity. Restraint! What possible restraint? Was it superstition, disgust, patience, fear—or some kind of primitive honor? No fear can stand up to hunger, no patience can wear it out, disgust simply does not exist where hunger is; and as to superstition, beliefs, and what you may call principles, they are less than chaff in a breeze. Don't you know the devilry of lingering starvation, its exasperating torment, its black thoughts, its somber and brooding ferocity? Well, I do. It takes a man all his inborn strength to fight hunger properly. It's really easier to face bereavement, dishonor, and the perdition of one's soul—than this kind of prolonged hunger. Sad, but true. And these chaps, too, had no earthly reason for any kind of scruple. Restraint! I would just as soon have expected restraint from a hyena prowling amongst the corpses of a battlefield. But there was the fact facing me—the fact dazzling, to be seen, like the foam on the depths of the sea, like a ripple on an unfathomable enigma, a mystery greater—when I thought of it—than the curious, inexplicable note of desperate grief in this savage clamor that had swept by us on the river bank, behind the blind whiteness of the fog.

"Two pilgrims were quarreling in hurried whispers as to which bank. 'Left.' 'No, no; how can you? Right, right, of course.' 'It is very serious,' said the manager's voice behind me; 'I would be desolated if anything should happen to Mr. Kurtz before we came up.' I looked at him, and had not the slightest doubt he was sincere. He was just the kind of man who would wish to preserve appearances. That was his restraint. But when he muttered something about going on at once, I did not even take the trouble to answer him. I knew, and he knew, that it was impossible. Were we to let go our hold of the bottom, we would be absolutely in the air—in space. We wouldn't be able to tell where we were going to—whether up- or down-stream, or across—till we fetched against one bank or the other, and then we wouldn't know at first which it was. Of course I made no move. I had no mind for a smashup. You couldn't imagine a more deadly place for a shipwreck. Whether drowned at once or not, we were sure to perish speedily in one way or another. 'I authorize you to take all the risks,' he said, after a short silence. 'I refuse to take any,' I said, shortly; which was just the answer he expected, though its tone might have surprised him. 'Well, I must defer to your judgment. You are captain,' he said, with marked civility. I turned my shoulder to him in sign of my appreciation, and looked into the fog. How long would it last? It was the most hopeless lookout. The approach to this Kurtz grubbing for ivory in the wretched bush was beset by as many dangers as though he had been an enchanted princess sleeping in a fabulous castle. 'Will they attack, do you think?' asked the manager, in a confidential tone.

"I did not think they would attack, for several obvious reasons. The thick fog was one. If they left the bank in their canoes they would get lost in it, as we would be if we attempted to move. Still, I had also judged the jungle of both banks quite impenetrable—and yet eyes were in it, eyes that had seen us. The riverside bushes were certainly very thick; but the undergrowth behind was evidently penetrable. However, during the short lift I had seen no canoes anywhere in the reach—certainly not abreast of the steamer. But what made the idea of attack inconceivable to me was the nature of the noise—of the cries we had heard. They had not the fierce character boding of immediate hostile intention. Unexpected, wild, and violent as they had been, they had given me an irresistible impression of sorrow. The glimpse of the steamboat had for some reason filled those savages with unrestrained grief. The danger, if any, I expounded, was from our proximity to a great human passion let loose. Even extreme grief may ultimately vent itself in violence—but more generally takes the form of apathy. . . .

"You should have seen the pilgrims stare! They had no heart to grin, or even to revile me: but I believe they thought me gone mad—with fright, maybe. I delivered a regular lecture. My dear boys, it was no good bothering. Keep a lookout? Well, you may guess I watched the fog for the signs of lifting as a cat watches a mouse; but for anything else our eyes were of no more use to us than if we had been buried miles deep in a heap of cotton-wool. It felt like it, too—choking, warm, stifling. Besides, all I said, though it sounded extravagant, was absolutely true to fact. What we afterwards alluded to as an attack was really an attempt at repulse. The action was very far from being aggressive—it was not even defensive, in the usual sense: it was undertaken under the stress of desperation, and in its essence was purely protective.

"It developed itself, I should say, two hours after the fog lifted, and its commencement was at a spot, roughly speaking, about a mile and a half below Kurtz's station. We had just floundered and flopped round a bend, when I saw an islet, a mere grassy hummock of bright green, in the middle of the stream. It was the only thing of the kind; but as we opened the reach more, I perceived it was the head of a long sandbank, or rather of a chain of shallow patches stretching down the middle of the river. They were discolored, just awash, and the whole lot was seen just under the water, exactly as a man's backbone is seen running down the middle of his back under the skin. Now, as far as I did see, I could go to the right or to the left of this. I didn't know either channel, of course. The banks looked pretty well alike, the depth appeared the same; but as I had been informed the station was on the west side, I naturally headed for the western passage.

"No sooner had we fairly entered it than I became aware it was much narrower than I had supposed. To the left of us there was the long uninterrupted shoal, and to the right a high, steep bank heavily overgrown with bushes. Above the bush the trees stood in serried ranks. The twigs overhung the current thickly, and from distance to distance a large limb of some tree projected rigidly over the stream. It was then well on in the afternoon, the face of the forest was gloomy, and a broad strip of shadow had already fallen on the water. In this shadow we steamed up—very slowly, as you may imagine. I sheered her well inshore—the water being deepest near the bank, as the sounding pole informed me.

"One of my hungry and forbearing friends was sounding in the bows just below me. This steamboat was exactly like a decked scow.

On the deck, there were two little teakwood houses, with doors and windows. The boiler was in the fore-end, and the machinery right astern. Over the whole there was a light roof, supported on stanchions. The funnel projected through that roof, and in front of the funnel a small cabin built of light planks served for a pilot house. It contained a couch, two campstools, a loaded Martini-Henry leaning in one corner, a tiny table, and the steering wheel. It had a wide door in front and a broad shutter at each side. All these were always thrown open, of course. I spent my days perched up there on the extreme fore-end of that roof, before the door. At night I slept, or tried to, on the couch. An athletic black belonging to some coast tribe, and educated by my poor predecessor, was the helmsman. He sported a pair of brass earrings, wore a blue cloth wrapper from the waist to the ankles, and thought all the world of himself. He was the most unstable kind of fool I had ever seen. He steered with no end of a swagger while you were by; but if he lost sight of you, he became instantly the prey of an abject funk, and would let that cripple of a steamboat get the upper hand of him in a minute.

"I was looking down at the sounding pole, and feeling much annoyed to see at each try a little more of it stick out of that river, when I saw my poleman give up the business suddenly, and stretch himself flat on the deck, without even taking the trouble to haul his pole in. He kept hold on it though, and it trailed in the water. At the same time the fireman, whom I could also see below me, sat down abruptly before his furnace and ducked his head. I was amazed. Then I had to look at the river mighty quick, because there was a snag in the fairway. Sticks, little sticks, were flying about—thick: they were whizzing before my nose, dropping below me, striking behind me against my pilot house. All this time the river, the shore, the woods, were very quiet—perfectly quiet. I could only hear the heavy splashing thump of the stern wheel and the patter of these things. We cleared the snag clumsily. Arrows, by Jove! We were being shot at! I stepped in quickly to close the shutter on the land side. That fool helmsman, his hands on the spokes, was lifting his knees high, stamping his feet, champing his mouth, like a reined-in horse. Confound him! And we were staggering within ten feet of the bank. I had to lean right out to swing the heavy shutter, and I saw a face amongst the leaves on the level with my own, looking at me very fierce and steady; and then suddenly, as though a veil had been removed from my eyes, I made out, deep in the tangled gloom, naked breasts, arms, legs, glaring eyes—the bush was swarming with human limbs in movement, glistening, of bronze color. The twigs shook, swayed, and rustled, the arrows flew out of them, and then the shutter came to. 'Steer her straight,' I said to the helmsman.

He held his head rigid, face forward; but his eyes rolled, he kept on, lifting and setting down his feet gently, his mouth foamed a little. 'Keep quiet!' I said in a fury. I might just as well have ordered a tree not to sway in the wind. I darted out. Below me there was a great scuffle of feet on the iron deck; confused exclamations; a voice screamed, 'Can you turn back?' I caught sight of a V-shaped ripple on the water ahead. What? Another snag! A fusillade burst out under my feet. The pilgrims had opened with their Winchesters, and were simply squirting lead into that bush. A deuce of a lot of smoke came up and drove slowly forward. I swore at it. Now I couldn't see the ripple or the snag either. I stood in the doorway, peering, and the arrows came in swarms. They might have been poisoned, but they looked as though they wouldn't kill a cat. The bush began to howl. Our woodcutters raised a warlike whoop; the report of a rifle just at my back deafened me. I glanced over my shoulder, and the pilot house was yet full of noise and smoke when I made a dash at the wheel. The fool nigger had dropped everything, to throw the shutter open and let off that Martini-Henry. He stood before the wide opening, glaring, and I yelled at him to come back, while I straightened the sudden twist out of that steamboat. There was no room to turn even if I had wanted to, the snag was somewhere very near ahead in that confounded smoke, there was no time to lose, so I just crowded her into the bank—right into the bank, where I knew the water was deep.

"We tore slowly along the overhanging bushes in a whirl of broken twigs and flying leaves. The fusillade below stopped short, as I had foreseen it would when the squirts got empty. I threw my head back to a glinting whizz that traversed the pilot house, in at one shutter-hole and out at the other. Looking past that mad helmsman, who was shaking the empty rifle and yelling at the shore, I saw vague forms of men running bent double, leaping, gliding, distinct, incomplete, evanescent. Something big appeared in the air before the shutter, the rifle went overboard, and the man stepped back swiftly, looked at me over his shoulder in an extraordinary, profound, familiar manner, and fell upon my feet. The side of his head hit the wheel twice, and the end of what appeared a long cane clattered round and knocked over a little campstool. It looked as though after wrenching that thing from somebody ashore he had lost his balance in the effort. The thin smoke had blown away, we were clear of the snag, and looking ahead I could see that in another hundred yards or so I would be free to sheer off, away from the bank; but my feet felt so very warm and wet that I had to look down. The man had rolled on his back and stared straight up at me; both his hands clutched that cane. It was the shaft of a spear that, either thrown or lunged through the opening, had caught him in the side just below the ribs; the blade had gone in out of sight, after making a frightful gash; my shoes were full; a pool of blood lay very still, gleaming dark-red under the wheel; his eyes shone with an amazing luster. The fusillade burst out again. He looked at me anxiously, gripping the spear like something precious, with an air of being afraid I would try to take it away from him. I had to make an effort to free my eyes from his gaze and attend to the steering. With one hand I felt above my head for the line of the steam whistle, and jerked out screech after screech hurriedly. The tumult of angry and warlike yells was checked instantly, and then from the depths of the woods went out such a tremulous and prolonged wail of mournful fear and utter despair as may be imagined to follow the flight of the last hope from the earth. There was a great commotion in the bush; the shower of arrows stopped, a few dropping shots rang out sharply—then silence, in which the languid beat of the stern wheel came plainly to my ears. I put the helm hard a-starboard at the moment when the pilgrim in pink pajamas, very hot and agitated, appeared in the doorway. 'The manager sends me—' he began in an official tone, and stopped short. 'Good God!' he said, glaring at the wounded man.

"We two whites stood over him, and his lustrous and inquiring glance enveloped us both. I declare it looked as though he would presently put to us some question in an understandable language; but he died without uttering a sound, without moving a limb, without twitching a muscle. Only in the very last moment, as though in response to some sign we could not see, to some whisper we could not hear, he frowned heavily, and that frown gave to his black death mask an inconceivably somber, brooding, and menacing expression. The luster of inquiring glance faded swiftly into vacant glassiness. 'Can you steer?' I asked the agent eagerly. He looked very dubious; but I made a grab at his arm, and he understood at once I meant him to steer whether or no. To tell you the truth, I was morbidly anxious to change my shoes and socks. 'He is dead,' murmured the fellow, immensely impressed. 'No doubt about it,' said I, tugging like mad at the shoelaces. 'And by the way, I suppose Mr. Kurtz is dead as well by this time.'

"For the moment that was the dominant thought. There was a sense of extreme disappointment, as though I had found out I had been striving after something altogether without a substance. I couldn't have been more disgusted if I had traveled all this way for the sole purpose of talking with Mr. Kurtz. Talking with . . . I flung one shoe overboard, and became aware that that was exactly what I had been looking forward to—a talk with Kurtz. I made the strange discovery that I had never imagined him as doing, you know, but as discoursing.

I didn't say to myself, 'Now I will never see him,' or 'Now I will never shake him by the hand,' but, 'Now I will never hear him.' The man presented himself as a voice. Not of course that I did not connect him with some sort of action. Hadn't I been told in all the tones of jealousy and admiration that he had collected, bartered, swindled, or stolen more ivory than all the other agents together? That was not the point. The point was in his being a gifted creature, and that of all his gifts the one that stood out pre-eminently, that carried with it a sense of real presence, was his ability to talk, his words—the gift of expression, the bewildering, the illuminating, the most exalted and the most contemptible, the pulsating stream of light, or the deceitful flow from the heart of an impenetrable darkness.

"The other shoe went flying unto the devil-god of that river. I thought, by Jove! it's all over. We are too late; he has vanished—the gift has vanished, by means of some spear, arrow, or club. I will never hear that chap speak after all, and my sorrow had a startling extravagance of emotion, even such as I had noticed in the howling sorrow of these savages in the bush. I couldn't have felt more of lonely desolation somehow, had I been robbed of a belief or had missed my destiny in life. . . . Why do you sigh in this beastly way, somebody? Absurd? Well, absurd. Good Lord! mustn't a man ever— Here, give me some tobacco." . . .

There was a pause of profound stillness, then a match flared, and Marlow's lean face appeared, worn, hollow, with downward folds and dropped eyelids, with an aspect of concentrated attention; and as he took vigorous draws at his pipe, it seemed to retreat and advance out of the night in the regular flicker of the tiny flame. The match went out.

"Absurd!" he cried. "This is the worst of trying to tell. . . . Here you all are, each moored with two good addresses, like a hulk with two anchors, a butcher round one corner, a policeman round another, excellent appetites, and temperature normal—you hear—normal from year's end to year's end. And you say, Absurd! Absurd be—exploded! Absurd! My dear boys, what can you expect from a man who out of sheer nervousness had just flung overboard a pair of new shoes! Now I think of it, it is amazing I did not shed tears. I am, upon the whole, proud of my fortitude. I was cut to the quick at the idea of having lost the inestimable privilege of listening to the gifted Kurtz. Of course I was wrong. The privilege was waiting for me. Oh, yes, I heard more than enough. And I was right, too. A voice. He was very little more than a voice. And I heard—him—it—this voice—other voices—all of them were so little more than voices—and the memory of that time itself lingers around me, impalpable, like a dying vibration of one immense jabber, silly, atrocious, sordid, savage, or simply mean, without any kind of sense. Voices, voices—even the girl herself —now—"

He was silent for a long time.

"I laid the ghost of his gifts at last with a lie," he began, suddenly. "Girl! What? Did I mention a girl? Oh, she is out of it—completely. They—the women I mean—are out of it—should be out of it. We must help them to stay in that beautiful world of their own, lest ours gets worse. Oh, she had to be out of it. You should have heard the disinterred body of Mr. Kurtz saying, 'My Intended.' You would have perceived directly then how completely she was out of it. And the lofty frontal bone of Mr. Kurtz! They say the hair goes on growing sometimes, but this—ah—specimen, was impressively bald. The wilderness had patted him on the head, and, behold, it was like a ball—an ivory ball; it had caressed him, and—lo!—he had withered; it had taken him, loved him, embraced him, got into his veins, consumed his flesh, and sealed his soul to its own by the inconceivable ceremonies of some devilish initiation. He was its spoiled and pampered favorite. Ivory? I should think so. Heaps of it, stacks of it. The old mud shanty was bursting with it. You would think there was not a single tusk left either above or below the ground in the whole country. 'Mostly fossil,' the manager had remarked, disparagingly. It was no more fossil than I am; but they call it fossil when it is dug up. It appears these niggers do bury the tusks sometimes—but evidently they couldn't bury this parcel deep enough to save the gifted Mr. Kurtz from his fate. We filled the steamboat with it, and had to pile a lot on the deck. Thus he could see and enjoy as long as he could see, because the appreciation of his favor had remained with him to the last. You should have heard him say, 'My ivory.' Oh yes, I heard him. 'My Intended, my ivory, my station, my river, my—' everything belonged to him. It made me hold my breath in expectation of hearing the wilderness burst into a prodigious peal of laughter that would shake the fixed stars in their places. Everything belonged to him—but that was a trifle. The thing was to know what he belonged to, how many powers of darkness claimed him for their own. That was the reflection that made you creepy all over. It was impossible—it was not good for one either—trying to imagine. He had taken a high seat amongst the devils of the land—I mean literally. You can't understand. How could you?—with solid pavement under your feet, surrounded by kind neighbors ready to cheer you or to fall on you, stepping delicately between the butcher and the policeman, in the holy terror of scandal and gallows and lunatic asylums—how can you imagine what particular region of the first ages a man's untrammeled feet may take him into by the way of solitude—utter solitude without a policeman—by the way of silence—utter silence, where no warning voice of a kind neighbor can be heard whispering of public opinion? These little things make all the great difference. When they are gone you must fall back upon your own innate strength, upon your own capacity for faithfulness. Of course you may be too much of a fool to go wrong—too dull even to know you are being assaulted by the powers of darkness. I take it, no fool ever made a bargain for his soul with the devil: the fool is too much of a fool, or the devil too much of a devil—I don't know which. Or you may be such a thunderingly exalted creature as to be altogether deaf and blind to anything but heavenly sights and sounds. Then the earth for you is only a standing place—and whether to be like this is your loss or your gain I won't pretend to say. But most of us are neither one nor the other. The earth for us is a place to live in, where we must put up with sights, with sounds, with smells, too, by Jove!—breathe dead hippo, so to speak, and not be contaminated. And there, don't you see? Your strength comes in, the faith in your ability for the digging of unostentatious holes to bury the stuff in—your power of devotion, not to yourself, but to an obscure, back-breaking business. And that's difficult enough. Mind, I am not trying to excuse or even explain—I am trying to account to myself for—for—Mr. Kurtz—for the shade of Mr. Kurtz. This initiated wraith from the back of Nowhere honored me with its amazing confidence before it vanished altogether. This was because it could speak English to me. The original Kurtz had been educated partly in England, and—as he was good enough to say himself—his sympathies were in the right place. His mother was half-English, his father was half-French. All Europe contributed to the making of Kurtz; and by and by I learned that, most appropriately, the International Society for the Suppression of Savage Customs had intrusted him with the making of a report, for its future guidance. And he had written it, too. I've seen it. I've read it. It was eloquent, vibrating with eloquence, but too high-strung, I think. Seventeen pages of close writing he had found time for! But this must have been before his—let us say—nerves, went wrong, and caused him to preside at certain midnight dances ending with unspeakable rites, which—as far as I reluctantly gathered from what I heard at various times—were offered up to him—do you understand?—to Mr. Kurtz himself. But it was a beautiful piece of writing. The opening paragraph, however, in the light of later information, strikes me now as ominous. He began with the argument that we whites, from the point of development we had arrived at, 'must necessarily appear to them [savages] in the nature of supernatural beings—we approach them with the might as of a deity,' and so on, and so on. 'By the simple exercise of our will we can exert a power for good practically unbounded,' etc., etc. From that point he soared and took me with him. The peroration was magnificent, though difficult to remember, you know. It gave me the notion of an exotic Immensity ruled by an august Benevolence. It made me tingle with enthusiasm. This was the unbounded power of eloquence —of words—of burning noble words. There were no practical hints to interrupt the magic current of phrases, unless a kind of note at the foot of the last page, scrawled evidently much later, in an unsteady hand, may be regarded as the exposition of a method. It was very simple, and at the end of that moving appeal to every altruistic sentiment it blazed at you, luminous and terrifying, like a flash of lightning in a serene sky: 'Exterminate all the brutes!' The curious part was that he had apparently forgotten all about that valuable postscriptum, because, later on, when he in a sense came to himself, he repeatedly entreated me to take good care of 'my pamphlet' (he called it), as it was sure to have in the future a good influence upon his career. I had full information about all these things, and, besides, as it turned out, I was to have the care of his memory. I've done enough for it to give me the indisputable right to lay it, if I choose, for an everlasting rest in the dust bin of progress, amongst all the sweepings and, figuratively speaking, all the dead cats of civilization. But then, you see, I can't choose. He won't be forgotten. Whatever he was, he was not common. He had the power to charm or frighten rudimentary souls into an aggravated witch dance in his honor; he could also fill the small souls of the pilgrims with bitter misgivings: he had one devoted friend at least, and he had conquered one soul in the world that was neither rudimentary nor tainted with self-seeking. No; I can't forget him, though I am not prepared to affirm the fellow was exactly worth the life we lost in getting to him. I missed my late helmsman awfully—I missed him even while his body was still lying in the pilot house. Perhaps you will think it passing strange this regret for a savage who was no more account than a grain of sand in a black Sahara. Well, don't you see, he had done something, he had steered; for months I had him at my back—a help—an instrument. It was a kind of partnership. He steered for me—I had to look after him, I worried about his deficiencies, and thus a subtle bond had been created, of which I only became aware when it was suddenly broken. And the intimate profundity of that look he gave me when he received his hurt remains to this day in my memory—like a claim of distant kinship affirmed in a supreme moment.

"Poor fool! If he had only left that shutter alone. He had no restraint, no restraint—just like Kurtz—a tree swayed by the wind. As soon as I had put on a dry pair of slippers, I dragged him out, after first jerking the spear out of his side, which operation I confess I performed with my eyes shut tight. His heels leaped together over the little doorstep; his shoulders were pressed to my breast; I hugged him from behind desperately. Oh! he was heavy, heavy; heavier than any man on earth, I should imagine. Then without more ado I tipped him overboard. The current snatched him as though he had been a wisp of grass, and I saw the body roll over twice before I lost sight of it forever. All the pilgrims and the manager were then congregated on the awning deck about the pilot house, chattering at each other like a flock of excited magpies, and there was a scandalized murmur at my heartless promptitude. What they wanted to keep that body hanging about for I can't guess. Embalm it, maybe. But I had also heard another, and a very ominous, murmur on the deck below. My friends the woodcutters were likewise scandalized, and with a better show of reason—though I admit that the reason itself was quite inadmissible. Oh, quite! I had made up my mind that if my late helmsman was to be eaten, the fishes alone should have him. He had been a very second-rate helmsman while alive, but now he was dead he might have become a first-class temptation, and possibly cause some startling trouble. Besides, I was anxious to take the wheel, the man in pink pajamas showing himself a hopeless duffer at the business.

"'This I did directly the simple funeral was over. We were going half-speed, keeping right in the middle of the stream, and I listened to the talk about me. They had given up Kurtz, they had given up the station; Kurtz was dead, and the station had been burnt—and so on—and so on. The red-haired pilgrim was beside himself with the thought that at least this poor Kurtz had been properly avenged. 'Say! We must have made a glorious slaughter of them in the bush. Eh? What do you think? Say?' He positively danced, the bloodthirsty little gingery beggar. And he had nearly fainted when he saw the wounded man! I could not help saying, 'You made a glorious lot of smoke, anyhow.' I had seen, from the way the tops of the bushes rustled and flew, that almost all the shots had gone too high. You can't hit anything unless you take aim and fire from the shoulder; but these chaps fired from the hip with their eyes shut. The retreat, I maintained—and I was right—was caused by the screeching of the steam whistle. Upon this they forgot Kurtz, and began to howl at me with indignant protests.

"'The manager stood by the wheel murmuring confidentially about the necessity of getting well away down the river before dark at all events, when I saw in the distance a clearing on the river side and the outlines of some sort of building. 'What's this?' I asked. He clapped his hands in wonder. 'That station!' he cried. I edged in at once, still going half-speed.

"'Through my glasses I saw the slope of a hill interspersed with rare trees and perfectly free from undergrowth. A long decaying building on the summit was half buried in the high grass; the large holes in the peaked roof gaped black from afar; the jungle and the woods made a background. There was no enclosure or fence of any kind; but there had been one apparently, for near the house half-a-dozen slim posts remained in a row, roughly trimmed, and with their upper ends ornamented with round carved balls. The rails, or whatever there had been between, had disappeared. Of course the forest surrounded all that. The river bank was clear, and on the water side I saw a white man under a hat like a cart wheel beckoning persistently with his whole arm. Examining the edge of the forest above and below, I was almost certain I could see movements—human forms gliding here and there. I steamed past prudently, then stopped the engines and let her drift down. The man on the shore began to shout, urging us to land. 'We have been attacked,' screamed the manager. 'I know—I know. It's all right,' yelled back the other, as cheerful as you please. 'Come along. It's all right. I am glad.'

"His aspect reminded me of something I had seen—something funny I had seen somewhere. As I maneuvered to get alongside, I was asking myself, 'What does this fellow look like?' Suddenly I got it. He looked like a harlequin. His clothes had been made of some stuff that was brown holland probably, but it was covered with patches all over, with bright patches, blue, red, and yellow—patches on the back, patches on the front, patches on elbows, on knees; colored binding around his jacket, scarlet edging at the bottom of his trousers; and the sunshine made him look extremely gay and wonderfully neat withal, because you could see how beautifully all this patching had been done. A beardless, boyish face, very fair, no features to speak of, nose peeling, little blue eyes, smiles and frowns chasing each other over that open countenance like sunshine and shadow on a wind-swept plain. 'Look out, captain!' he cried; 'there's a snag lodged in here last night.' What! Another snag? I confess I swore shamefully. I had nearly holed my cripple, to finish off that charming trip. The harlequin on the bank turned his little pug nose up to me. 'You English?' he asked, all smiles. 'Are you?' I shouted from the wheel. The smiles vanished, and he shook his head as if sorry for my disappointment. Then he brightened up. 'Never mind!' he cried, encouragingly. 'Are we in time?' I asked. 'He is up there,' he replied, with a toss of the head up the hill, and becoming gloomy all of a sudden. His face was like the autumn sky, overcast one moment and bright the next.

"When the manager, escorted by the pilgrims, all of them armed to the teeth, had gone to the house this chap came on board. 'I say, I don't like this. These natives are in the bush,' I said. He assured me earnestly it was all right. 'They are simple people,' he added; 'well, I am glad you came. It took me all my time to keep them off.' 'But you said it was all right,' I cried. 'Oh, they meant no harm,' he said; and as I stared he corrected himself, 'Not exactly.' Then vivaciously, 'My faith, your pilot house wants a clean-up!' In the next breath he advised me to keep enough steam on the boiler to blow the whistle in case of any trouble. 'One good screech will do more for you than all your rifles. They are simple people,' he repeated. He rattled away at such a rate he quite overwhelmed me. He seemed to be trying to make up for lots of silence, and actually hinted, laughing, that such was the case. 'Don't you talk with Mr. Kurtz?' I said. 'You don't talk with that man—you listen to him,' he exclaimed with severe exaltation. 'But now—' He waved his arm, and in the twinkling of an eye was in the uttermost depths of despondency. In a moment he came up again with a jump, possessed himself of both my hands, shook them continuously, while he gabbled: 'Brother sailor . . . honor . . . pleasure . . . delight . . . introduce myself . . . Russian . . . son of an arch-priest . . . Government of Tambov. . . . What? Tobacco! English tobacco; the excellent English tobacco! Now, that's brotherly. Smoke? Where's a sailor that does not smoke?'

"'The pipe soothed him, and gradually I made out he had run away from school, had gone to sea in a Russian ship; ran away again; served some time in English ships; was now reconciled with the arch-priest. He made a point of that. 'But when one is young one must see things, gather experience, ideas; enlarge the mind.' 'Here!' I interrupted. 'You can never tell! Here I met Mr. Kurtz,' he said, youthfully solemn and reproachful. I held my tongue after that. It appears he had persuaded a Dutch trading house on the coast to fit him out with stores and goods, and had started for the interior with a light heart, and no more idea of what would happen to him than a baby. He had been wandering about that river for nearly two years alone, cut off from everybody and everything. 'I am not so young as I look. I am twenty-five,' he said. 'At first old Van Shuyten would tell me to go to the devil,' he narrated with keen enjoyment; 'but I stuck to him, and talked and talked, till at last he got afraid I would talk the hind leg off his favorite dog, so he gave me some cheap things and a few guns, and told me he hoped he would never see my face again. Good old Dutchman, Van Shuyten. I've sent him one small lot of ivory a year ago, so that he can't call me a little thief when I get back. I hope he got it. And for the rest I don't care. I had some wood stacked for you. That was my old house. Did you see?'

"'I gave him Towson's book. He made as though he would kiss me, but restrained himself. 'The only book I had left, and I thought I had lost it,' he said, looking at it ecstatically. 'So many accidents happen to a man going about alone, you know. Canoes get upset sometimes—and sometimes you've got to clear out so quick when the people get angry.' He thumbed the pages. 'You made notes in Russian?' I asked. He nodded. 'I thought they were written in cipher,' I said. He laughed, then became serious. 'I had lots of trouble to keep these people off,' he said. 'Did they want to kill you?' I asked. 'Oh, no!' he cried, and checked himself. 'Why did they attack us?' I pursued. He hesitated, then said shamefacedly, 'They don't want him to go.' 'Don't they?' I said, curiously. He nodded a nod full of mystery and wisdom. 'I tell you,' he cried, 'this man has enlarged my mind.' He opened his arms wide, staring at me with his little blue eyes that were perfectly round.

III

"I looked at him, lost in astonishment. There he was before me, in motley, as though he had absconded from a troupe of mimes, enthusiastic, fabulous. His very existence was improbable, inexplicable, and altogether bewildering. He was an insoluble problem. It was inconceivable how he had existed, how he had succeeded in getting so far, how he had managed to remain—why he did not instantly disappear. 'I went a little farther,' he said, 'then still a little farther—till I had gone so far that I don't know how I'll ever get back. Never mind. Plenty time. I can manage. You take Kurtz away quick—quick—I tell you.' The glamor of youth enveloped his parti-colored rags, his destitution, his loneliness, the essential desolation of his futile wanderings. For months—for years—his life hadn't been worth a day's purchase; and there he was gallantly, thoughtlessly alive, to all appearance indestructible solely by the virtue of his few years and of his unreflecting audacity. I was seduced into something like admiration—like envy. Glamor urged him on, glamor kept him unscathed. He surely wanted nothing from the wilderness but space to breathe in and to push on through. His need was to exist, and to move onwards at the greatest possible risk, and with a maximum of privation. If the absolutely pure, uncalculating, unpractical spirit of adventure had ever ruled a human being, it ruled this bepatched youth. I almost envied him the possession of this modest and clear flame. It seemed to have consumed all thought of self so completely, that even while he was talking to you, you forgot that it was he—the man before your eyes—who had gone through these things. I did not envy him his devotion to Kurtz, though. He had not meditated over it. It came to him, and he accepted it with a sort of eager fatalism. I must say that to me it appeared about the most dangerous thing in every way he had come upon so far.

"They had come together unavoidably, like two ships becalmed near each other, and lay rubbing sides at last. I suppose Kurtz wanted an audience, because on a certain occasion, when encamped in the forest, they had talked all night, or more probably Kurtz had talked. 'We talked of everything,' he said, quite transported at the recollection. 'I forgot there was such a thing as sleep. The night did not seem to last an hour. Everything! Everything! . . . Of love, too.' 'Ah, he talked to you of love!' I said, much amused. 'It isn't what you think,' he cried, almost passionately. 'It was in general. He made me see things—things.'

"He threw his arms up. We were on deck at the time, and the headman of my woodcutters, lounging near by, turned upon him his heavy and glittering eyes. I looked around, and I don't know why, but I assure you that never, never before, did this land, this river, this jungle, the very arch of this blazing sky, appear to me so hopeless and so dark, so impenetrable to human thought, so pitiless to human weakness. 'And, ever since, you have been with him, of course?' I said.

"On the contrary. It appears their intercourse had been very much broken by various causes. He had, as he informed me proudly, managed to nurse Kurtz through two illnesses (he alluded to it as you would to some risky feat), but as a rule Kurtz wandered alone, far in the depths of the forest. 'Very often coming to this station, I had to wait days and days before he would turn up,' he said. 'Ah, it was worth waiting for!—sometimes.' 'What was he doing? Exploring or what?' I asked. 'Oh, yes, of course'; he had discovered lots of villages, a lake, too—he did not know exactly in what direction; it was dangerous to inquire too much—but mostly his expeditions had been for ivory. 'But he had no goods to trade with by that time,' I objected. 'There's a good lot of cartridges left even yet,' he answered, looking away. 'To speak plainly, he raided the country,' I said. He nodded. 'Not alone, surely!' He muttered something about the villages round that lake. 'Kurtz got the tribe to follow him, did he?' I suggested. He fidgeted a little. 'They adored him,' he said. The tone of these words was so extraordinary that I looked at him searchingly. It was curious to see his mingled eagerness and reluctance to speak of Kurtz. The man filled his life, occupied his thoughts, swayed his emotions. 'What can you expect?' he burst out; 'he came to them with thunder and lightning, you know—and they had never seen anything like it—and very terrible. He could be very terrible. You can't judge Mr. Kurtz as you would an ordinary man. No, no, no! Now—just to give you an idea—I don't mind telling you, he wanted to shoot me, too, one day—but I don't judge him.' 'Shoot you!' I cried. 'What for?' 'Well, I had a small lot of ivory the chief of that village near my house gave me. You see I used to shoot game for them. Well, he wanted it, and wouldn't hear reason. He declared he would shoot me unless I gave him the ivory and then cleared out of the country, because he could do so, and had a fancy for it, and there was nothing on earth to prevent him killing whom he jolly well pleased. And it was true, too. I gave him the ivory. What did I care! But I didn't clear out. No, no. I couldn't leave him. I had to be careful, of course, till we got friendly again for a time. He had his second illness then. Afterwards I had to keep out of the way; but I didn't mind. He was living for the most part in those villages on the lake. When he came down to the river, sometimes he would take to me, and sometimes it was better for me to be careful. This man suffered too much. He hated all this, and somehow he couldn't get away. When I had a chance I begged him to try and leave while there was time; I offered to go back with him. And he would say yes, and then he would remain; go off on another ivory hunt; disappear for weeks; forget himself amongst these people—forget himself—you know.' 'Why! he's mad,' I said. He protested indignantly. Mr. Kurtz couldn't be mad. If I had heard him talk, only two days ago, I wouldn't dare hint at such a thing. . . . I had taken up my binoculars while we talked, and was looking at the shore, sweeping the limit of the forest at each side and at the back of the house. The consciousness of there being people in that bush, so silent, so quiet—as silent and quiet as the ruined house on the hill—made me uneasy. There was no sign on the face of nature of this amazing tale that was not so much told as suggested to me in desolate exclamations, completed by shrugs, in interrupted phrases, in hints ending in deep sighs. The woods were unmoved, like a mask—heavy, like the closed door of a prison—they looked with their air of hidden knowledge, of patient expectation, of unapproachable silence. The Russian was explaining to me that it was only lately that Mr. Kurtz had come down to the river, bringing along with him all the fighting men of that lake tribe. He had been absent for several months—getting himself adored, I suppose—and had come down unexpectedly, with the intention to all appearances of making a raid either across the river or downstream. Evidently the appetite for more ivory had got the better of the—what shall I say?—less material aspirations. However he had got much worse suddenly. 'I heard he was lying helpless, and so I came up—took my chance,' said the Russian. 'Oh, he is bad, very bad.' I directed my glass to the house. There were no signs of life, but there was the ruined roof, the long mud wall peeping above the grass, with three little square window holes, no two of the same size; all this brought within reach of my hand, as it were. And then I made a brusque movement, and one of the remaining posts of that vanished fence leaped up in the field of my glass. You remember I told you I had been struck at the distance by certain attempts at ornamentation, rather remarkable in the ruinous aspect of the place. Now I had suddenly a nearer view, and its first result was to make me throw my head back as if before a blow. Then I went carefully from post to post with my glass, and I saw my mistake. These round knobs were not ornamental but symbolic; they were expressive and puzzling, striking and disturbing—food for thought and also for the vultures if there had been any looking down from the sky; but at all events for such ants as were industrious enough to ascend the pole. They would have been even more impressive, those heads on the stakes, if their faces had not been turned to the house. Only one, the first I had made out, was facing my way. I was not so shocked as you may think. The start back I had given was really nothing but a movement of surprise. I had expected to see a knob of wood there, you know. I returned deliberately to the first I had seen—and there it was, black, dried, sunken, with closed eyelids, a head that seemed to sleep at the top of that pole, and, with the shrunken dry lips showing a narrow white line of the teeth, was smiling, too, smiling continuously at some endless and jocose dream of that eternal slumber.

"I am not disclosing any trade secrets. In fact, the manager said afterwards that Mr. Kurtz's methods had ruined the district. I have no opinion on that point, but I want you clearly to understand that there was nothing exactly profitable in these heads being there. They only showed that Mr. Kurtz lacked restraint in the gratification of his various lusts, that there was something wanting in him—some small matter which, when the pressing need arose, could not be found under his magnificent eloquence. Whether he knew of this deficiency himself I can't say. I think the knowledge came to him at last—only at the very last. But the wilderness had found him out early, and had taken on him a terrible vengeance for the fantastic invasion. I think it had whispered to him things about himself which he did not know, things of which he had no conception till he took counsel with this great solitude—and the whisper had proved irresistibly fascinating. It echoed loudly within him because he was hollow at the core. . . . I put down the glass, and the head that had appeared near enough to be spoken to seemed at once to have leaped away from me into inaccessible distance.

"The admirer of Mr. Kurtz was a bit crestfallen. In a hurried, indistinct voice he began to assure me he had not dared to take these —say, symbols—down. He was not afraid of the natives; they would not stir till Mr. Kurtz gave the word. His ascendancy was extraordinary. The camps of these people surrounded the place, and the chiefs came every day to see him. They would crawl. . . . 'I don't want to know anything of the ceremonies used when approaching Mr. Kurtz,' I shouted. Curious, this feeling that came over me that such details would be more intolerable than those heads drying on the stakes under Mr. Kurtz's windows. After all, that was only a savage sight, while I seemed at one bound to have been transported into some lightless region of subtle horrors, where pure, uncomplicated savagery was a positive relief, being something that had a right to exist —obviously—in the sunshine. The young man looked at me with surprise. I suppose it did not occur to him that Mr. Kurtz was no idol of mine. He forgot I hadn't heard any of these splendid monologues on, what was it? On love, justice, conduct of life—or whatnot. If it had come to crawling before Mr. Kurtz, he crawled as much as the veriest savage of them all. I had no idea of the conditions, he said: these heads were the heads of rebels. I shocked him excessively by laughing. Rebels! What would be the next definition I was to hear? There had been enemies, criminals, workers—and these were rebels. Those rebellious heads looked very subdued to me on their sticks. 'You don't know how such a life tries a man like Kurtz,' cried Kurtz's last disciple. 'Well, and you?' I said. 'I! I! I am a simple man. I have no great thoughts. I want nothing from anybody. How can you compare me to? . . .' His feelings were too much for speech, and suddenly he broke down. 'I don't understand,' he groaned. 'I've been doing my best to keep him alive, and that's enough. I had no hand in all this. I have no abilities. There hasn't been a drop of medicine or a mouthful of invalid food for months here. He was shamefully abandoned. A man like this, with such ideas. Shamefully! Shamefully! I—I—haven't slept for the last ten nights. . . .'

"His voice lost itself in the calm of the evening. The long shadows of the forest had slipped downhill while we talked, had gone far beyond the ruined hovel, beyond the symbolic row of stakes. All this was in the gloom, while we down there were yet in the sunshine, and the stretch of the river abreast of the clearing glittered in a still and dazzling splendor, with a murky and overshadowed bend above and below. Not a living soul was seen on the shore. The bushes did not rustle.

"Suddenly round the corner of the house a group of men appeared, as though they had come up from the ground. They waded waist-deep in the grass, in a compact body, bearing an improvised stretcher in their midst. Instantly, in the emptiness of the landscape, a cry arose whose shrillness pierced the still air like a sharp arrow flying straight to the very heart of the land; and, as if by enchantment, streams of human beings—of naked human beings—with spears in their hands, with bows, with shields, with wild glances and savage movements, were poured into the clearing by the dark-faced and pensive forest. The bushes shook, the grass swayed for a time, and then everything stood still in attentive immobility.

" 'Now, if he does not say the right thing to them we are all done for,' said the Russian at my elbow. The knot of men with the stretcher had stopped, too, halfway to the steamer, as if petrified. I saw the man on the stretcher sit up, lank and with an uplifted arm, above the shoulders of the bearers. 'Let us hope that the man who can talk so well of love in general will find some particular reason to spare us this time,' I said. I resented bitterly the absurd danger of our situation, as if to be at the mercy of that atrocious phantom had been a dishonoring necessity. I could not hear a sound, but through my glasses I saw the thin arm extended commandingly, the lower jaw moving, the eyes of that apparition shining darkly far in its bony head that nodded with grotesque jerks. Kurtz—Kurtz—that means short in German—don't it? Well, the name was as true as everything else in his life—and death. He looked at least seven feet long. His covering had fallen off, and his body emerged from it pitiful and appalling as from a winding sheet. I could see the cage of his ribs all astir, the bones of his arm waving. It was as though an animated image of death carved out of old ivory had been shaking its hand with menaces at a motionless crowd of men made of dark and glittering bronze. I saw him open his mouth wide—it gave him a weirdly voracious aspect, as though he had wanted to swallow all the air, all the earth, all the men before him. A deep voice reached me faintly. He must have been shouting. He fell back suddenly. The stretcher shook as the bearers staggered forward again, and almost at the same time I noticed that the crowd of savages was vanishing without any perceptible movement of retreat, as if the forest that had ejected these beings so suddenly had drawn them in again as the breath is drawn in a long aspiration.

"Some of the pilgrims behind the stretcher carried his arms—two shotguns, a heavy rifle, and a light revolver carbine—the thunderbolts of that pitiful Jupiter. The manager bent over him murmuring as he walked beside his head. They laid him down in one of the little cabins—just a room for a bedplace and a campstool or two, you know. We had brought his belated correspondence, and a lot of torn envelopes and open letters littered his bed. His hand roamed feebly amongst these papers. I was struck by the fire of his eyes and the composed languor of his expression. It was not so much the exhaustion of disease. He did not seem in pain. This shadow looked satiated and calm, as though for the moment it had had its fill of all the emotions.

"He rustled one of the letters, and looking straight in my face said, 'I am glad.' Somebody had been writing to him about me. These special recommendations were turning up again. The volume of tone he emitted without effort, almost without the trouble of moving his lips, amazed me. A voice! a voice! It was grave, profound, vibrating, while the man did not seem capable of a whisper. However, he had enough strength in him—factitious no doubt—to very nearly make an end of us, as you shall hear directly.

"The manager appeared silently in the doorway; I stepped out at once and he drew the curtain after me. The Russian, eyed curiously by the pilgrims, was staring at the shore. I followed the direction of his glance.

"Dark human shapes could be made out in the distance, flitting indistinctly against the gloomy border of the forest, and near the river two bronze figures, leaning on tall spears, stood in the sunlight under fantastic headdresses of spotted skins, warlike and still in statuesque repose. And from right to left along the lighted shore moved a wild and gorgeous apparition of a woman.

"She walked with measured steps, draped in striped and fringed cloths, treading the earth proudly, with a slight jingle and flash of barbarous ornaments. She carried her head high; her hair was done in the shape of a helmet; she had brass leggings to the knee, brass wire gauntlets to the elbow, a crimson spot on her tawny cheek, innumerable necklaces of glass beads on her neck; bizarre things, charms, gifts of witch men, that hung about her, glittered and trembled at every step. She must have had the value of several elephant tusks upon her. She was savage and superb, wild-eyed and magnificent; there was something ominous and stately in her deliberate progress. And in the hush that had fallen suddenly upon the whole sorrowful land, the immense wilderness, the colossal body of the fecund and mysterious life seemed to look at her, pensive, as though it had been looking at the image of its own tenebrous and passionate soul.

"She came abreast of the steamer, stood still, and faced us. Her long shadow fell to the water's edge. Her face had a tragic and fierce aspect of wild sorrow and of dumb pain mingled with the fear of some struggling, half-shaped resolve. She stood looking at us without a stir, and like the wilderness itself, with an air of brooding over an inscrutable purpose. A whole minute passed, and then she made a step forward. There was a low jingle, a glint of yellow metal, a sway of fringed draperies, and she stopped as if her heart had failed her. The young fellow by my side growled. The pilgrims murmured at my back. She looked at us all as if her life had depended upon the unswerving steadiness of her glance. Suddenly she opened her bared arms and threw them up rigid above her head, as though in an uncontrollable desire to touch the sky, and at the same time the swift shadows darted out on the earth, swept around on the river, gathering the steamer into a shadowy embrace. A formidable silence hung over the scene.

"She turned away slowly, walked on, following the bank, and passed into the bushes to the left. Once only her eyes gleamed back at us in the dusk of the thickets before she disappeared.

" 'If she had offered to come aboard I really think I would have tried to shoot her,' said the man of patches, nervously. 'I had been risking my life every day for the last fortnight to keep her out of the house. She got in one day and kicked up a row about those miserable rags I picked up in the storeroom to mend my clothes with. I wasn't decent. At least it must have been that, for she talked like a fury to Kurtz for an hour, pointing at me now and then. I don't understand the dialect of this tribe. Luckily for me, I fancy Kurtz felt too ill that day to care, or there would have been mischief. I don't understand. . . . No—it's too much for me. Ah, well, it's all over now.'

"At this moment I heard Kurtz's deep voice behind the curtain: 'Save me!—save the ivory, you mean. Don't tell me. Save *me!* Why, I've had to save you. You are interrupting my plans now. Sick! Sick! Not so sick as you would like to believe. Never mind. I'll carry my ideas out yet—I will return. I'll show you what can be done. You with your little peddling notions—you are interfering with me. I will return. I . . .'

"The manager came out. He did me the honor to take me under the arm and lead me aside. 'He is very low, very low,' he said. He considered it necessary to sigh, but neglected to be consistently sorrowful. 'We have done all we could for him—haven't we? But there is no disguising the fact, Mr. Kurtz has done more harm than good to the Company. He did not see the time was not ripe for vigorous action. Cautiously, cautiously—that's my principle. We must be cautious yet. The district is closed to us for a time. Deplorable! Upon the whole, the trade will suffer. I don't deny there is a remarkable quantity of ivory —mostly fossil. We must save it, at all events—but look how precarious the position is—and why? Because the method is unsound.' 'Do you,' said I, looking at the shore, 'call it "unsound method?" ' 'Without doubt,' he exclaimed, hotly. 'Don't you?' . . .

" 'No method at all,' I murmured after a while. 'Exactly,' he exulted. 'I anticipated this. Shows a complete want of judgment. It is my duty to point it out in the proper quarter.' 'Oh,' said I, 'that fellow—what's his name?—the brickmaker, will make a readable report for you.' He appeared confounded for a moment. It seemed to me I had never breathed an atmosphere so vile, and I turned mentally to Kurtz for relief—positively for relief. 'Nevertheless I think Mr. Kurtz is a remarkable man,' I said with emphasis. He started, dropped on me a cold heavy glance, said very quietly, 'he *was,'* and turned his back on me. My hour of favor was over; I found myself lumped along with Kurtz as a partisan of methods for which the time was not ripe: I was unsound! Ah! but it was something to have at least a choice of nightmares.

"I had turned to the wilderness really, not to Mr. Kurtz, who, I was ready to admit, was as good as buried. And for a moment it seemed to me as if I also were buried in a vast grave full of unspeakable secrets. I felt an intolerable weight oppressing my breast, the smell of the damp earth, the unseen presence of victorious corruption, the darkness of an impenetrable night. . . . The Russian tapped me on the shoulder. I heard him mumbling and stammering something about 'brother seaman—couldn't conceal—knowledge of matters that would affect Mr. Kurtz's reputation.' I waited. For him evidently Mr. Kurtz was not in his grave; I suspect that for him Mr. Kurtz was one of the immortals. 'Well!' said I at last, 'speak out. As it happens, I am Mr. Kurtz's friend—in a way.'

"He stated with a good deal of formality that had we not been 'of the same profession,' he would have kept the matter to himself without regard to consequences. 'He suspected there was an active ill will towards him on the part of these white men that—' 'You are right,' I said, remembering a certain conversation I had overheard. 'The manager thinks you ought to be hanged.' He showed a concern at this intelligence which amused me at first. 'I had better get out of the way quietly,' he said, earnestly. 'I can do no more for Kurtz now, and they would soon find some excuse. What's to stop them? There's a military post three hundred miles from here.' 'Well, upon my word,' said I, 'perhaps you had better go if you have any friends amongst the savages near by.' 'Plenty,' he said. 'They are simple people—and I want nothing, you know.' He stood biting his lip, then: 'I don't want any harm to happen to these whites here, but of course I was thinking of Mr. Kurtz's reputation—but you are a brother seaman and—' 'All right,' said I, after a time. 'Mr. Kurtz's reputation is safe with me.' I did not know how truly I spoke.

"He informed me, lowering his voice, that it was Kurtz who had ordered the attack to be made on the steamer. 'He hated sometimes the idea of being taken away—and then again . . . But I don't understand these matters. I am a simple man. He thought it would scare you away—that you would give it up, thinking him dead. I could not stop him. Oh, I had an awful time of it this last month.' 'Very well,' I said. 'He is all right now.' 'Ye-e-es,' he muttered, not very convinced apparently. 'Thanks,' said I; 'I shall keep my eyes open.' 'But quiet—eh?' he urged, anxiously. 'It would be awful for his reputation if anybody here —' I promised a complete discretion with great gravity. 'I have a canoe and three black fellows waiting not very far. I am off. Could you give me a few Martini-Henry cartridges?' I could, and did, with proper secrecy. He helped himself, with a wink at me, to a handful of my tobacco. 'Between sailors—you know—good English tobacco.' At the door of the pilot house he turned round—'I say, haven't you a pair of shoes you could spare?' He raised one leg. 'Look.' The soles were tied with knotted strings sandal-wise under his bare feet. I rooted out an old pair, at which he looked with admiration before tucking it under his left arm. One of his pockets (bright red) was bulging with cartridges, from the other (dark blue) peeped 'Towson's Inquiry,' etc., etc. He seemed to think himself excellently well equipped for a renewed encounter with the wilderness. 'Ah! I'll never, never meet such a man again. You ought to have heard him recite poetry—his own, too, it was, he told me. Poetry!' He rolled his eyes at the recollection of these delights. 'Oh, he enlarged my mind!' 'Good-by,' said I. He shook hands and vanished in the night. Sometimes I ask myself whether I had ever really seen him—whether it was possible to meet such a phenomenon! . . .

"When I woke up shortly after midnight his warning came to my mind with its hint of danger that seemed, in the starred darkness, real enough to make me get up for the purpose of having a look round. On the hill a big fire burned, illuminating fitfully a crooked corner of the station house. One of the agents with a picket of a few of our blacks, armed for the purpose, was keeping guard over the ivory; but deep within the forest, red gleams that wavered, that seemed to sink and rise from the ground amongst confused columnar shapes of intense blackness, showed the exact position of the camp where Mr. Kurtz's adorers were keeping their uneasy vigil. The monotonous beating of a big drum filled the air with muffled shocks and a lingering vibration. A steady droning sound of many men chanting each to himself some weird incantation came out from the black, flat wall of the woods as the humming of bees comes out of a hive, and had a strange narcotic effect upon my half-awake senses. I believe I dozed off leaning over the rail, till an abrupt burst of yells, an overwhelming outbreak of a pent-up and mysterious frenzy, woke me up in a bewildered wonder. It was cut short all at once, and the low droning went on with an effect of audible and soothing silence. I glanced casually into the little cabin. A light was burning within, but Mr. Kurtz was not there.

"I think I would have raised an outcry if I had believed my eyes. But I didn't believe them at first—the thing seemed so impossible. The fact is I was completely unnerved by a sheer blank fright, pure abstract terror, unconnected with any distinct shape of physical danger. What made this emotion so overpowering was—how shall I define it? —the moral shock I received, as if something altogether monstrous, intolerable to thought and odious to the soul, had been thrust upon me unexpectedly. This lasted of course the merest fraction of a second, and then the usual sense of commonplace, deadly danger, the possibility of a sudden onslaught and massacre, or something of the kind, which I saw impending, was positively welcome and composing. It pacified me, in fact, so much, that I did not raise an alarm.

"There was an agent buttoned up inside an ulster and sleeping on a chair on deck within three feet of me. The yells had not awakened him; he snored very slightly; I left him to his slumbers and leaped ashore. I did not betray Mr. Kurtz—it was ordered I should never betray him—it was written I should be loyal to the nightmare of my choice. I was anxious to deal with this shadow by myself alone—and to this day I don't know why I was so jealous of sharing with anyone the peculiar blackness of that experience.

"As soon as I got on the bank I saw a trail—a broad trail through the grass. I remember the exultation with which I said to myself, 'He can't walk—he is crawling on all fours—I've got him.' The grass was wet with dew. I strode rapidly with clenched fists. I fancy I had some vague notion of falling upon him and giving him a drubbing. I don't know. I had some imbecile thoughts. The knitting old woman with the cat obtruded herself upon my memory as a most improper person to be sitting at the other end of such an affair. I saw a row of pilgrims squirting lead in the air out of Winchesters held to the hip. I thought I would never get back to the steamer, and imagined myself living alone and unarmed in the woods to an advanced age. Such silly things —you know. And I remember I confounded the beat of the drum with the beating of my heart, and was pleased at its calm regularity.

"I kept to the track though—then stopped to listen. The night was very clear; a dark blue space, sparkling with dew and starlight, in which black things stood very still. I thought I could see a kind of motion ahead of me. I was strangely cocksure of everything that night. I actually left the track and ran in a wide semicircle (I truly believe chuckling to myself) so as to get in front of that stir, of that motion I had seen—if indeed I had seen anything. I was circumventing Kurtz as though it had been a boyish game.

"I came upon him, and, if he had not heard me coming, I would have fallen over him, too, but he got up in time. He rose, unsteady, long, pale, indistinct, like a vapor exhaled by the earth, and swayed slightly, misty and silent before me; while at my back the fires loomed between the trees, and the murmur of many voices issued from the forest. I had cut him off cleverly; but when actually confronting him I seemed to come to my senses, I saw the danger in its right proportion. It was by no means over yet. Suppose he began to shout? Though he could hardly stand, there was still plenty of vigor in his voice. 'Go away—hide yourself,' he said, in that profound tone. It was very awful. I glanced back. We were within thirty yards from the nearest fire. A black figure stood up, strode on long black legs, waving long black arms, across the glow. It had horns—antelope horns, I think—on its head. Some sorcerer, some witch man, no doubt: it looked fiend-like enough. 'Do you know what you are doing?' I whispered. 'Perfectly,' he answered, raising his voice for that single word: it sounded to me far off and yet loud, like a hail through a speaking trumpet. If he makes a row we are lost, I thought to myself. This clearly was not a case for fisticuffs, even apart from the very natural aversion I had to beat that Shadow—this wandering and tormented thing. 'You will be lost,' I said—'utterly lost.' One gets sometimes such a flash of inspiration, you know. I did say the right thing, though indeed he could not have been more irretrievably lost than he was at this very moment, when the foundations of our intimacy were being laid—to endure—to endure—even to the end—even beyond.

" 'I had immense plans,' he muttered irresolutely. 'Yes,' said I; 'but if you try to shout I'll smash your head with—' There was not a stick or a stone near. 'I will throttle you for good,' I corrected myself. 'I was on the threshold of great things,' he pleaded, in a voice of longing, with a wistfulness of tone that made my blood run cold. 'And now for this stupid scoundrel—' 'Your success in Europe is assured in any case,' I affirmed, steadily. I did not want to have the throttling of him, you understand—and indeed it would have been very little use for any practical purpose. I tried to break the spell—the heavy, mute spell of the wilderness—that seemed to draw him to its pitiless breast by the awakening of forgotten and brutal instincts, by the memory of gratified and monstrous passions. This alone, I was convinced, had driven him out to the edge of the forest, to the bush, towards the gleam of fires, the throb of drums, the drone of weird incantations; this alone had beguiled his unlawful soul beyond the bounds of permitted aspirations. And, don't you see, the terror of the position was not in being knocked on the head—though I had a very lively sense of that danger, too—but in this, that I had to deal with a being to whom I could not appeal in the name of anything high or low. I had, even like the niggers, to invoke him—himself—his own exalted and incredible degradation. There was nothing either above or below him, and I knew it. He had kicked himself loose of the earth. Confound the man! he had kicked the very earth to pieces. He was alone, and I before him did not know whether I stood on the ground or floated in the air. I've been telling you what we said—repeating the phrases we pronounced—but what's the good? They were common everyday words—the familiar, vague sounds exchanged on every waking day of life. But what of that? They had behind them, to my mind, the terrific suggestiveness of words heard in dreams, of phrases spoken in nightmares. Soul! If anybody had ever struggled with a soul, I am the man. And I wasn't arguing with a lunatic either. Believe me or not, his intelligence was perfectly clear—concentrated, it is true, upon himself with horrible intensity, yet clear; and therein was my only chance—barring, of course, the killing him there and then, which wasn't so good, on account of unavoidable noise. But his soul was mad. Being alone in the wilderness, it had looked within itself, and, by heavens! I tell you, it had gone mad. I had—for my sins, I suppose—to go through the ordeal of looking into it myself. No eloquence could have been so withering to one's belief in mankind as his final burst of sincerity. He struggled with himself, too. I saw it. I heard it. I saw the inconceivable mystery of a soul that knew no restraint, no faith, and no fear, yet struggling blindly with itself. I kept my head pretty well; but when I had him at last stretched on the couch, I wiped my forehead, while my legs shook under me as though I had carried half a ton on my back down that hill. And yet I had only supported him, his bony arm clasped round my neck—and he was not much heavier than a child.

"When next day we left at noon, the crowd, of whose presence behind the curtain of trees I had been acutely conscious all the time, flowed out of the woods again, filled the clearing, covered the slope with a mass of naked, breathing, quivering, bronze bodies. I steamed up a bit, then swung downstream, and two thousand eyes followed the evolutions of the splashing, thumping, fierce river-demon beating the water with its terrible tail and breathing black smoke into the air. In front of the first rank, along the river, three men, plastered with bright red earth from head to foot, strutted to and fro restlessly. When we came abreast again, they faced the river, stamped their feet, nodded their horned heads, swayed their scarlet bodies; they shook towards the fierce river-demon a bunch of black feathers, a mangy skin with a pendent tail—something that looked like a dried gourd; they shouted periodically together strings of amazing words that resembled no sounds of human language; and the deep murmurs of the crowd, interrupted suddenly, were like the responses of some satanic litany.

"We had carried Kurtz into the pilot house: there was more air there. Lying on the couch, he stared through the open shutter. There was an eddy in the mass of human bodies, and the woman with helmeted head and tawny cheeks rushed out to the very brink of the stream. She put out her hands, shouted something, and all that wild mob took up the shout in a roaring chorus of articulated, rapid, breathless utterance.

" 'Do you understand this?' I asked.

"He kept on looking out past me with fiery, longing eyes, with a mingled expression of wistfulness and hate. He made no answer, but I saw a smile, a smile of indefinable meaning, appear on his colorless lips that a moment after twitched convulsively. 'Do I not?' he said slowly, gasping, as if the words had been torn out of him by a supernatural power.

"I pulled the string of the whistle, and I did this because I saw the pilgrims on deck getting out their rifles with an air of anticipating a jolly lark. At the sudden screech there was a movement of abject terror through that wedged mass of bodies. 'Don't! Don't you frighten them away,' cried someone on deck disconsolately. I pulled the string time after time. They broke and ran, they leaped, they crouched, they swerved, they dodged the flying terror of the sound. The three red chaps had fallen flat, face down on the shore, as though they had been shot dead. Only the barbarous and superb woman did not so much as flinch, and stretched tragically her bare arms after us over the somber and glittering river.

"And then that imbecile crowd down on the deck started their little fun, and I could see nothing more for smoke.

"The brown current ran swiftly out of the heart of darkness, bearing us down towards the sea with twice the speed of our upward progress; and Kurtz's life was running swiftly, too, ebbing, ebbing out of his heart into the sea of inexorable time. The manager was very placid, he had no vital anxieties now, he took us both in with a comprehensive and satisfied glance: the 'affair' had come off as well as could be wished. I saw the time approaching when I would be left alone of the party of 'unsound method.' The pilgrims looked upon me with disfavor. I was, so to speak numbered with the dead. It is strange how I accepted this unforeseen partnership, this choice of nightmares forced upon me in the tenebrous land invaded by these mean and greedy phantoms.

"Kurtz discoursed. A voice! a voice! It rang deep to the very last.

It survived his strength to hide in the magnificent folds of eloquence the barren darkness of his heart. Oh, he struggled! he struggled! The wastes of his weary brain were haunted by shadowy images now—images of wealth and fame revolving obsequiously round his unextinguishable gift of noble and lofty expression. My Intended, my station, my career, my ideas—these were the subjects for the occasional utterances of elevated sentiments. The shade of the original Kurtz frequented the bedside of the hollow sham, whose fate it was to be buried presently in the cold of primeval earth. But both the diabolic love and the unearthly hate of the mysteries it had penetrated fought for the possession of that soul satiated with primitive emotions, avid of lying fame, of sham distinction, of all the appearances of success and power.

"Sometimes he was contemptibly childish. He desired to have kings meet him at railway stations on his return from some ghastly Nowhere, where he intended to accomplish great things. 'You show them you have in you something that is really profitable, and then there will be no limits to the recognition of your ability,' he would say. 'Of course you must take care of the motives—right motives—always.' The long reaches that were like one and the same reach, monotonous bends that were exactly alike, slipped past the steamer with their multitude of secular trees looking patiently after this grimy fragment of another world, the forerunner of change, of conquest, of trade, of massacres, of blessings. I looked ahead—piloting. 'Close the shutter,' said Kurtz suddenly one day; 'I can't bear to look at this.' I did so. There was silence. 'Oh, but I will wring your heart yet!' he cried at the invisible wilderness.

"We broke down—as I had expected—and had to lie-up for repairs at the head of an island. This delay was the first thing that shook Kurtz's confidence. One morning he gave me a packet of papers and a photograph—the lot tied together with a shoestring. 'Keep this for me,' he said. 'This noxious fool' (meaning the manager) 'is capable of prying into my boxes when I am not looking.' In the afternoon I saw him. He was lying on his back with closed eyes, and I withdrew quietly, but I heard him mutter, 'Live rightly, die, die. . . .' I listened. There was nothing more. Was he rehearsing some speech in his sleep, or was it a fragment of a phrase from some newspaper article? He had been writing for the papers and meant to do so again, 'for the furthering of my ideas. It's a duty.'

"His was an impenetrable darkness. I looked at him as you peer down at a man who is lying at the bottom of a precipice where the sun never shines. But I had not much time to give him, because I was helping the engine driver to take to pieces the leaky cylinders, to straighten a bent connecting rod, and in other such matters. I lived in an infernal mess of rust, filings, nuts, bolts, spanners, hammers, ratchet drills—things I abominate, because I don't get on with them. I tended the little forge we fortunately had aboard; I toiled wearily in a wretched scrapheap—unless I had the shakes too bad to stand.

"One evening coming in with a candle I was startled to hear him say a little tremulously, 'I am lying here in the dark waiting for death.' The light was within a foot of his eyes. I forced myself to murmur, 'Oh, nonsense!' and stood over him as if transfixed.

"Anything approaching the change that came over his features I have never seen before, and hope never to see again. Oh, I wasn't touched. I was fascinated. It was as though a veil had been rent. I saw on that ivory face the expression of somber pride, of ruthless power, of craven terror—of an intense and hopeless despair. Did he live his life again in every detail of desire, temptation, and surrender during that supreme moment of complete knowledge? He cried in a whisper at some image, at some vision—he cried out twice, a cry that was no more than a breath: 'The horror! The horror!'

"I blew the candle out and left the cabin. The pilgrims were dining in the messroom, and I took my place opposite the manager, who lifted his eyes to give me a questioning glance, which I successfully ignored. He leaned back, serene, with that peculiar smile of his sealing the unexpressed depths of his meanness. A continuous shower of small flies streamed upon the lamp, upon the cloth, upon our hands and faces. Suddenly the manager's boy put his insolent black head in the doorway, and said in a tone of scathing contempt—

" 'Mistah Kurtz—he dead.'

"All the pilgrims rushed out to see. I remained, and went on with my dinner. I believe I was considered brutally callous. However, I did not eat much. There was a lamp in there—light, don't you know—and outside it was so beastly, beastly dark. I went no more near the remarkable man who had pronounced a judgment upon the adventures of his soul on this earth. The voice was gone. What else had been there? But I am of course aware that next day the pilgrims buried something in a muddy hole.

"And then they very nearly buried me.

"However, as you see, I did not go to join Kurtz there and then. I did not. I remained to dream the nightmare out to the end, and to show my loyalty to Kurtz once more. Destiny. My destiny! Droll thing life is—that mysterious arrangement of merciless logic for a futile purpose. The most you can hope from it is some knowledge of yourself—that comes too late—a crop of unextinguishable regrets. I have wrestled with death. It is the most unexciting contest you can imagine. It takes place in an impalpable grayness, with nothing underfoot, with nothing around, without spectators, without clamor, without glory, without the great desire of victory, without the great fear of defeat, in a sickly atmosphere of tepid skepticism, without much belief in your own right, and still less in that of your adversary. If such is the form of ultimate wisdom, then life is a greater riddle than some of us think it to be. I was within a hair's-breadth of the last opportunity for pronouncement, and I found with humiliation that probably I would have nothing to say. This is the reason why I affirm that Kurtz was a remarkable man. He had something to say. He said it. Since I had peeped over the edge myself, I understand better the meaning of his stare, that could not see the flame of the candle, but was wide enough to embrace the whole universe, piercing enough to penetrate all the hearts that beat in the darkness. He had summed up—he had judged. 'The horror!' He was a remarkable man. After all, this was the expression of some sort of belief; it had candor, it had conviction, it had a vibrating note of revolt in its whisper, it had the appalling face of a glimpsed truth—the strange commingling of desire and hate. And it is not my own extremity I remember best—a vision of grayness without form filled with physical pain, and a careless contempt for the evanescence of all things—even of this pain itself. No! It is his extremity that I seem to have lived through. True, he had made that last stride, he had stepped over the edge, while I had been permitted to draw back my hesitating foot. And perhaps in this is the whole difference; perhaps all the wisdom, and all truth, and all sincerity, are just compressed into that inappreciable moment of time in which we step over the threshold of the invisible. Perhaps! I like to think my summing-up would not have been a word of careless contempt. Better his cry—much better. It was an affirmation, a moral victory paid for by innumerable defeats, by abominable terrors, by abominable satisfactions. But it was a victory! That is why I have remained loyal to Kurtz to the last, and even beyond, when a long time after I heard once more, not his own voice, but the echo of his magnificent eloquence thrown to me from a soul as translucently pure as a cliff of crystal.

"No, they did not bury me, though there is a period of time which I remember mistily, with a shuddering wonder, like a passage through some inconceivable world that had no hope in it and no desire. I found myself back in the sepulchral city resenting the sight of people hurrying through the streets to filch a little money from each other, to devour their infamous cookery, to gulp their unwholesome beer, to dream their insignificant and silly dreams. They trespassed upon my thoughts. They were intruders whose knowledge of life was to me an irritating pretense, because I felt so sure they could not possibly know the things I knew. Their bearing, which was simply the bearing of commonplace individuals going about their business in the assurance of perfect safety, was offensive to me like the outrageous flauntings of folly in the face of a danger it is unable to comprehend. I had no particular desire to enlighten them, but I had some difficulty in restraining myself from laughing in their faces, so full of stupid importance. I daresay I was not very well at that time. I tottered about the streets—there were various affairs to settle—grinning bitterly at perfectly respectable persons. I admit my behavior was inexcusable, but then my temperature was seldom normal in these days. My dear aunt's endeavors to 'nurse up my strength' seemed altogether beside the mark. It was not my strength that wanted nursing, it was my imagination that wanted soothing. I kept the bundle of papers given me by Kurtz, not knowing exactly what to do with it. His mother had died lately, watched over, as I was told, by his Intended. A clean-shaved man, with an official manner and wearing gold-rimmed spectacles, called on me one day and made inquiries, at first circuitous, afterwards suavely pressing, about what he was pleased to denominate certain 'documents.' I was not surprised, because I had had two rows with the manager on the subject out there. I had refused to give up the smallest scrap out of that package, and I took the same attitude with the spectacled man. He became darkly menacing at last, and with much heat argued that the company had the right to every bit of information about its 'territories.' And said he, 'Mr. Kurtz's knowledge of unexplored regions must have been necessarily extensive and peculiar—owing to his great abilities and to the deplorable circumstances in which he had been placed: therefore—' I assured him Mr. Kurtz's knowledge, however extensive, did not bear upon the problems of commerce or administration. He invoked then the name of science. 'It would be an incalculable loss if,' etc., etc. I offered him the report on the 'Suppression of Savage Customs,' with the postscriptum torn off. He took it up eagerly, but ended by sniffing at it with an air of contempt. 'This is not what we had a right to expect,' he remarked. 'Expect nothing else,' I said. 'There are only private letters.' He withdrew upon some threat of legal proceedings, and I saw him no more; but another fellow, calling himself Kurtz's cousin, appeared two days later, and was anxious to hear all the details about his dear relative's last moments. Incidentally he gave me to understand that Kurtz had been essentially a great musician. 'There was the making of an immense success,' said the man, who was an organist, I believe, with lank gray hair flowing over a greasy coat collar. I had no reason to doubt his statement; and to this day I am unable to say what was Kurtz's profession, whether he ever had any—which was the greatest of his talents. I had taken him for a painter who wrote for the papers, or else for a journalist who could paint—but even the cousin (who took snuff during the interview) could not tell me what he had been—exactly. He was a universal genius—on that point I agreed with the old chap, who thereupon blew his nose noisily into a large cotton handkerchief and withdrew in senile agitation, bearing off some family letters and memoranda without importance. Ultimately a journalist anxious to know something of the fate of his 'dear colleague' turned up. This visitor informed me Kurtz's proper sphere ought to have been politics 'on the popular side.' He had furry straight eyebrows, bristly hair cropped short, an eyeglass on a broad ribbon, and, becoming expansive, confessed his opinion that Kurtz really couldn't write a bit—'but heavens! how that man could talk. He electrified large meetings. He had faith—don't you see?—he had the faith. He could get himself to believe anything—anything. He would have been a splendid leader of an extreme party.' 'What party?' I asked. 'Any party,' answered the other. 'He was an—an—extremist.' Did I not think so? I assented. Did I know, he asked, with a sudden flash of curiosity, 'what it was that had induced him to go out there?' 'Yes,' said I, and forthwith handed him the famous report for publication, if he thought fit. He glanced through it hurriedly, mumbling all the time, judged 'it would do,' and took himself off with this plunder.

"Thus I was left at last with a slim packet of letters and the girl's portrait. She struck me as beautiful—I mean she had a beautiful expression. I know that the sunlight can be made to lie, too, yet one felt that no manipulation of light and pose could have conveyed the delicate shade of truthfulness upon those features. She seemed ready to listen without mental reservation, without suspicion, without a thought for herself. I concluded I would go and give her back her portrait and those letters myself. Curiosity? Yes; and also some other feeling perhaps. All that had been Kurtz's had passed out of my hands: his soul, his body, his station, his plans, his ivory, his career. There remained only his memory and his Intended—and I wanted to give that up, too, to the past, in a way—to surrender personally all that remained of him with me to that oblivion which is the last word of our common fate. I don't defend myself. I had no clear perception of what it was I really wanted. Perhaps it was an impulse of unconscious loyalty, or the fulfillment of one of these ironic necessities that lurk in the facts of human existence. I don't know. I can't tell. But I went.

"I thought his memory was like the other memories of the dead that accumulate in every man's life—a vague impress on the brain of shadows that had fallen on it in their swift and final passage; but before the high and ponderous door, between the tall houses of a street as still and decorous as a well-kept alley in a cemetery, I had a vision of him on the stretcher, opening his mouth voraciously, as if to devour all the earth with all its mankind. He lived then before me; he lived as much as he had ever lived—a shadow insatiable of splendid appearances, of frightful realities; a shadow darker than the shadow of the night, and draped nobly in the folds of a gorgeous eloquence. The vision seemed to enter the house with me—the stretcher, the phantom-bearers, the wild crowd of obedient worshipers, the gloom of the forests, the glitter of the reach between the murky bends, the beat of the drum, regular and muffled like the beating of a heart—the heart of a conquering darkness. It was a moment of triumph for the wilderness, an invading and vengeful rush which, it seemed to me, I would have to keep back alone for the salvation of another soul. And the memory of what I had heard him say afar there, with the horned shapes stirring at my back, in the glow of fires, within the patient woods, those broken phrases came back to me, were heard again in their ominous and terrifying simplicity. I remembered his abject pleading, his abject threats, the colossal scale of his vile desires, the meanness, the torment, the tempestuous anguish of his soul. And later on I seemed to see his collected languid manner, when he said one day, 'This lot of ivory now is really mine. The company did not pay for it. I collected it myself at a very great personal risk. I am afraid they will try to claim it as theirs though. H'm. It is a difficult case. What do you think I ought to do—resist? Eh? I want no more than justice.' . . . He wanted no more than justice—no more than justice. I rang the bell before a mahogany door on the first floor, and while I waited he seemed to stare at me out of the glassy panel—stare with that wide and immense stare embracing, condemning, loathing all the universe. I seemed to hear the whispered cry, 'The horror! The horror!'

"The dusk was falling. I had to wait in a lofty drawing room with three long windows from floor to ceiling that were like three luminous and bedraped columns. The bent gilt legs and backs of the furniture shone in indistinct curves. The tall marble fireplace had a cold and monumental whiteness. A grand piano stood massively in a corner; with dark gleams on the flat surfaces like a somber and polished sarcophagus. A high door opened—closed. I rose.

"She came forward, all in black, with a pale head, floating towards me in the dusk. She was in mourning. It was more than a year since his death, more than a year since the news came; she seemed as though she would remember and mourn forever. She took both my hands in hers and murmured, 'I had heard you were coming.' I noticed she was not very young—I mean not girlish. She had a mature capacity for fidelity, for belief, for suffering. The room seemed to have grown darker, as if all the sad light of the cloudy evening had taken refuge on her forehead. This fair hair, this pale visage, this pure brow, seemed surrounded by an ashy halo from which the dark eyes looked out at me. Their glance was guileless, profound, confident, and trustful. She carried her sorrowful head as though she were proud of that sorrow, as though she would say, I—I alone know how to mourn for him as he deserves. But while we were still shaking hands, such a look of awful desolation came upon her face that I perceived she was one of those creatures that are not the playthings of Time. For her he had died only yesterday. And, by Jove! the impression was so powerful that for me, too, he seemed to have died only yesterday—nay, this very minute. I saw her and him in the same instant of time—his death and her sorrow—I saw her sorrow in the very moment of his death. Do you understand? I saw them together—I heard them together. She had said, with a deep catch of the breath, 'I have survived,' while my strained ears seemed to hear distinctly, mingled with her tone of despairing regret, the summing-up whisper of his eternal condemnation. I asked myself what I was doing there, with a sensation of panic in my heart as though I had blundered into a place of cruel and absurd mysteries not fit for a human being to behold. She motioned me to a chair. We sat down. I laid the packet gently on the little table, and she put her hand over it. . . . 'You knew him well,' she murmured, after a moment of mourning silence.

" 'Intimacy grows quickly out there,' I said. 'I knew him as well as it is possible for one man to know another.'

" 'And you admired him,' she said. 'It was impossible to know him and not to admire him. Was it?'

" 'He was a remarkable man,' I said, unsteadily. Then before the appealing fixity of her gaze, that seemed to watch for more words on my lips, I went on, 'It was impossible not to—'

" 'Love him,' she finished eagerly, silencing me into an appalled dumbness. 'How true! how true! But when you think that no one knew him so well as I! I had all his noble confidence. I knew him best.'

" 'You knew him best,' I repeated. And perhaps she did. But with every word spoken the room was growing darker, and only her forehead, smooth and white, remained illumined by the unextinguishable light of belief and love.

" 'You were his friend,' she went on. 'His friend,' she repeated, a little louder. 'You must have been, if he had given you this, and sent you to me. I feel I can speak to you—and oh! I must speak. I want you—you who have heard his last words—to know I have been worthy of him. . . . It is not pride. . . . Yes! I am proud to know I understood him better than anyone on earth—he told me so himself. And since his mother died I have had no one—no one—to—to—'

"I listened. The darkness deepened. I was not even sure whether he had given me the right bundle. I rather suspect he wanted me to take care of another batch of his papers which, after his death, I saw the manager examining under the lamp. And the girl talked, easing her pain in the certitude of my sympathy; she talked as thirsty men drink. I had heard that her engagement with Kurtz had been disapproved by her people. He wasn't rich enough or something. And indeed I don't know whether he had not been a pauper all his life. He had given me some reason to infer that it was his impatience of comparative poverty that drove him out there.

" '. . . Who was not his friend who had heard him speak once?' she was saying. 'He drew men towards him by what was best in them.' She looked at me with intensity. 'It is the gift of the great,' she went on, and the sound of her low voice seemed to have the accompaniment of all the other sounds, full of mystery, desolation, and sorrow, I had ever heard—the ripple of the river, the soughing of the trees swayed by the wind, the murmurs of the crowds, the faint ring of incomprehensible words cried from afar, the whisper of a voice speaking from beyond the threshold of an eternal darkness. 'But you have heard him! You know!' she cried.

" 'Yes, I know,' I said with something like despair in my heart, but bowing my head before the faith that was in her, before that great and saving illusion that shone with an unearthly glow in the darkness, in the triumphant darkness from which I could not have defended her—from which I could not even defend myself.

" 'What a loss to me—to us!'—she corrected herself with beautiful generosity; then added in a murmur, 'To the world.' By the last gleams of twilight I could see the glitter of her eyes, full of tears—of tears that would not fall.

" 'I have been very happy—very fortunate—very proud,' she went on. 'Too fortunate. Too happy for a little while. And now I am unhappy for—for life.'

"She stood up; her fair hair seemed to catch all the remaining light in a glimmer of gold. I rose, too.

" 'And of all this,' she went on, mournfully, 'of all his promise, and of all his greatness, of his generous mind, of his noble heart, nothing remains—nothing but a memory. You and I—'

" 'We shall always remember him,' I said, hastily.

" 'No!' she cried. 'It is impossible that all this should be lost—that such a life should be sacrificed to leave nothing—but sorrow. You know what vast plans he had. I knew of them, too—I could not perhaps understand—but others knew of them. Something must remain. His words, at least, have not died.'

" 'His words will remain,' I said.

" 'And his example,' she whispered to herself. 'Men looked up to him—his goodness shone in every act. His example—'

" 'True,' I said; 'his example, too. Yes, his example. I forgot that.'

" 'But I do not. I cannot—I cannot believe—not yet. I cannot believe that I shall never see him again, that nobody will see him again, never, never, never.'

"She put out her arms as if after a retreating figure, stretching them black and with clasped pale hands across the fading and narrow sheen of the window. Never see him! I saw him clearly enough then. I shall see this eloquent phantom as long as I live, and I shall see her, too, a tragic and familiar Shade, resembling in this gesture another one, tragic also, and bedecked with powerless charms, stretching bare brown arms over the glitter of the infernal stream, the stream of darkness. She said suddenly very low, 'He died as he lived.'

" 'His end,' said I, with dull anger stirring in me, 'was in every way worthy of his life.'

" 'And I was not with him,' she murmured. My anger subsided before a feeling of infinite pity.

" 'Everything that could be done—' I mumbled.

" 'Ah, but I believed in him more than anyone on earth—more than his own mother, more than—himself. He needed me! Me! I would have treasured every sigh, every word, every sign, every glance.'

"I felt like a chill grip on my chest. 'Don't,' I said, in a muffled voice.

" 'Forgive me. I—I—have mourned so long in silence—in silence. . . . You were with him—to the last? I think of his loneliness. Nobody near to understand him as I would have understood. Perhaps no one to hear. . . .'

" 'To the very end,' I said, shakily. 'I heard his very last words. . . .' I stopped in a fright.

" 'Repeat them,' she murmured in a heartbroken tone. 'I want—I want—something—something—to—to live with.'

"I was on the point of crying at her, 'Don't you hear them?' The dusk was repeating them in a persistent whisper all around us, in a whisper that seemed to swell menacingly like the first whisper of a rising wind. 'The horror! the horror!'

" 'His last word—to live with,' she insisted. 'Don't you understand I loved him—I loved him—I loved him!'

"I pulled myself together and spoke slowly.

" 'The last word he pronounced was—your name.'

"I heard a light sigh and then my heart stood still, stopped dead short by an exulting and terrible cry, by the cry of inconceivable triumph and of unspeakable pain. 'I knew it—I was sure!' . . . She knew. She was sure. I heard her weeping; she had hidden her face in her hands. It seemed to me that the house would collapse before I could escape, that the heavens would fall upon my head. But nothing happened. The heavens do not fall for such a trifle. Would they have fallen, I wonder, if I had rendered Kurtz that justice which was his due? Hadn't he said he wanted only justice? But I couldn't. I could not tell her. It would have been too dark—too dark altogether. . . ."

Marlow ceased, and sat apart, indistinct and silent, in the pose of a meditating Buddha. Nobody moved for a time. "We have lost the first of the ebb," said the director, suddenly. I raised my head. The offing was barred by a black bank of clouds, and the tranquil waterway leading to the uttermost ends of the earth flowed somber under an overcast sky—seemed to lead into the heart of an immense darkness.

End of the Game

Julio Cortázar

Letitia, Holanda and I used to play by the Argentine Central tracks during the hot weather, hoping that Mama and Aunt Ruth would go up to their siesta so that we could get out past the white gate. After washing the dishes, Mama and Aunt Ruth were always tired, especially when Holanda and I were drying, because it was then that there were arguments, spoons on the floor, secret words that only we understood, and in general, an atmosphere in which the smell of grease, José's yowling, and the dimness of the kitchen would end up in an incredible fight and the subsequent commotion. Holanda specialized in rigging this sort of brawl, for example, letting an already clean glass slip into the pan of dirty water, or casually dropping a remark to the effect that the Loza house had two maids to do all the work. I had other systems: I liked to suggest to Aunt Ruth that she was going to get an allergy rash on her hands if she kept scrubbing the pots instead of doing the cups and plates once in a while, which were exactly what Mama liked to wash, and over which they would confront one another soundlessly in a war of advantage to get the easy item. The heroic expedient, in case the bits of advice and the drawn-out family recollections began to bore us, was to upset some boiling water on the cat's back. Now that's a big lie about a scalded cat, it really is, except that you have to take the reference to cold water literally; because José never backed away from hot water, almost insinuating himself under it, poor animal, when we spilled a half-cup of it somewhere around 220°F., or less, a good deal less, probably, because his hair never fell out. The whole point was to get Troy burning, and in the confusion, crowned by a splendid G-flat from Aunt Ruth and Mama's sprint for the whipstick, Holanda and I would take no time at all to get lost in the long porch, toward the empty rooms off the back, where Letitia would be waiting for us, reading Ponson de Terrail, or some other equally inexplicable book.

Normally, Mama chased us a good part of the way, but her desire to bust in our skulls evaporated soon enough, and finally (we had barred the door and were begging for mercy in emotion-filled and very theatrical voices), she got tired and went off, repeating the same sentence: "Those ruffians'll end up on the street."

Where we ended up was by the Argentine Central tracks, when the house had settled down and was silent, and we saw the cat stretched out under the lemon tree to take its siesta also, a rest buzzing with fragrances and wasps. We'd open the white gate slowly, and when we shut it again with a slam like a blast of wind, it was a freedom which took us by the hands, seized the whole of our bodies and tumbled us out. Then we ran, trying to get the speed to scramble up the low embankment of the right-of-way, and there spread out upon the world, we silently surveyed our kingdom.

Our kingdom was this: a long curve of the tracks ended its bend just opposite the back section of the house. There was just the gravel incline, the crossties, and the double line of track; some dumb sparse grass among the rubble where mica, quartz and feldspar—the components of granite—sparkled like real diamonds in the two o'clock afternoon sun. When we stooped down to touch the rails (not wasting time because it would have been dangerous to spend much time there, not so much from the trains as for fear of being seen from the house), the heat off the stone roadbed flushed our faces, and facing into the wind from the river there was a damp heat against our cheeks and ears. We liked to bend our legs and squat down, rise, squat again, move from one kind of hot zone to the other, watching each other's faces to measure the perspiration—a minute or two later we would be sopping with it. And we were always quiet, looking down the track into the distance, or at the river on the other side, that stretch of coffee-and-cream river.

After this first inspection of the kingdom, we'd scramble down the bank and flop in the meager shadow of the willows next the wall enclosing the house where the white gate was. This was the capital city of the kingdom, the wilderness city and the headquarters of our game. Letitia was the first to start the game; she was the luckiest and the most privileged of the three of us. Letitia didn't have to dry dishes or make the beds, she could laze away the day reading or pasting up pictures, and at night they let her stay up later if she asked to, not counting having a room to herself, special hot broth when she wanted it, and all kinds of other advantages. Little by little she had taken more and more advantage of these privileges, and had been presiding over the game since the summer before, I think really she was presiding over the whole kingdom; in any case she was quicker at saying things, and Holanda and I accepted them without protest, happy almost. It's likely that Mama's long lectures on how we ought to behave toward Letitia had had their effect, or simply that we loved her enough and it didn't bother us that she was boss. A pity that she didn't have the looks for the boss, she was the shortest of the three of us and very skinny. Holanda was skinny, and I never weighed over 110, but Letitia was scragglier than we were, and even worse, that kind of skinniness you can see from a distance in the neck and ears. Maybe it was the stiffness of her back that made her look so thin, for instance she could hardly move her head from side to side, she was like a folded-up ironing board, one of those kind they had in the Loza house, with a cover of white material. Like an ironing board with the wide part up, leaning closed against the wall. And she led us.

The best satisfaction was to imagine that someday Mama or Aunt Ruth would find out about the game. If they managed to find out about the game there would be an unbelievable mess. The G-flat and fainting fits, incredible protests of devotion and sacrifice ill-rewarded, and a string of words threatening the more celebrated punishments, closing the bid with a dire prediction of our fates, which consisted of the three of us ending up on the street. This final prediction always left us somewhat perplexed, because to end up in the street always seemed fairly normal to us.

First Letitia had us draw lots. We used to use pebbles hidden in the hand, count to twenty-one, any way at all. If we used the count-to-twenty-one system, we would pretend two or three more girls and include them in the counting to prevent cheating. If one of them came out 21, we dropped her from the group and started drawing again, until one of us won. Then Holanda and I lifted the stone and we got out the ornament-box. Suppose Holanda had won, Letitia and I chose the ornaments. The game took two forms: Statues and Attitudes. Attitudes did not require ornaments but an awful lot of expressiveness, for Envy you could show your teeth, make fists and hold them in a position so as to seem cringing. For Charity the ideal was an angelic face, eyes turned up to the sky, while the hands offered something—a rag, a ball, a branch of willow—to a poor invisible orphan. Shame and Fear were easy to do; Spite and Jealousy required a more conscientious study. The Statues were determined, almost all of them, by the choice of ornaments, and here absolute liberty reigned. So that a statue would come out of it, one had to think carefully of every detail in the costume. It was a rule of the game that the one chosen could not take part in the selection; the two remaining argued out the business at hand and then fitted the ornaments on. The winner had to invent her statue taking into account what they'd dressed her in, and in this way the game was much more complicated and exciting because sometimes there were counterplots, and the victim would find herself rigged out in adornments which were completely hopeless; so it was up to her to be quick then in composing a good statue. Usually when the game called for Attitudes, the winner came up pretty well outfitted, but there were times when the Statues were horrible failures.

Well, the story I'm telling, lord knows when it began, but things changed the day the first note fell from the train. Naturally the Attitudes and Statues were not for our own consumption, we'd have gotten bored immediately. The rules were that the winner had to station herself at the foot of the embankment, leaving the shade of the willow trees, and wait for the train from Tigre that passed at 2:08. At that height above Palermo the trains went by pretty fast and we weren't bashful doing the Statue or the Attitude. We hardly saw the people in the train windows, but with time, we got a bit more expert, and we knew that some of the passengers were expecting to see us. One man with white hair and tortoise-shell glasses used to stick his head out of the window and wave at the Statue or the Attitude with a handkerchief. Boys sitting on the steps of the coaches on their way back from school shouted things as the train went by, but some of them remained serious and watching us. In actual fact, the Statue or the Attitude saw nothing at all, because she had to concentrate so hard on holding herself stock-still, but the other two under the willows would analyze in excruciating detail the great success produced, or the audience indifference. It was a Wednesday when the note dropped as the second coach went by. It fell very near Holanda (she did Malicious Gossip that day) and ricocheted toward me. The small piece of paper was tightly folded up and had been shoved through a metal nut. In a man's handwriting, and pretty bad too, it said: "The Statues very pretty. I ride in the third window of the second coach. Ariel B." For all the trouble of stuffing it through the nut and tossing it, it seemed to us a little dry, but it delighted us. We chose lots to see who would keep it, and I won. The next day nobody wanted to play because we all wanted to see what Ariel B. was like, but we were afraid he would misinterpret our interruption, so finally we chose lots and Letitia won. Holanda and I were very happy because Letitia did Statues very well, poor thing. The paralysis wasn't noticeable when she was still, and she was capable of gestures of enormous nobility. With Attitudes she always chose Generosity, Piety, Sacrifice and Renunciation. With Statues she tried for the style of the Venus in the parlor which Aunt Ruth called the Venus de Nilo. For that reason we chose ornaments especially so that Ariel would be very impressed. We hung a piece of green velvet on her like a tunic, and a crown of willow on her hair. As we were wearing short sleeves, the Greek effect was terrific. Letitia practiced a little in the shade, and we decided that we'd show ourselves also and wave at Ariel, discreetly, but very friendly.

Letitia was magnificent, when the train came she didn't budge a finger. Since she couldn't turn her head, she threw it backward, bringing her arms against her body almost as though she were missing them; except for the green tunic, it was like looking at the Venus de Nilo. In the third window we saw a boy with blond curly hair and light eyes, who smiled brightly when he saw that Holanda and I were waving at him. The train was gone in a second, but it was 4:30 and we were still discussing whether he was wearing a dark suit, a red tie, and if he were really nice or a creep. On Thursday I did an Attitude, Dejection, and we got another note which read: "The three of you I like very much. Ariel." Now he stuck his head and one arm out the window and laughed and waved at us. We figured him to be eighteen (we were sure he was no older than sixteen), and we decided that he was coming back every day from some English school, we couldn't stand the idea of any of the regular peanut factories. You could see that Ariel was super.

As it happened, Holanda had the terrific luck to win three days running. She surpassed herself, doing the attitudes Reproach and Robbery, and a very difficult Statue of The Ballerina, balancing on one foot from the time the train hit the curve. The next day I won, and the day after that too; when I was doing Horror, a note from Ariel almost caught me on the nose; at first we didn't understand it: "The prettiest is the laziest." Letitia was the last to understand it; we saw that she blushed and went off by herself, and Holanda and I looked at each other, just a little furious. The first judicial opinion it occurred to us to hand down was that Ariel was an idiot, but we couldn't tell Letitia that, poor angel, with the disadvantage she had to put up with. She said nothing, but it seemed to be understood that the paper was hers, and she kept it. We were sort of quiet going back to the house that day, and didn't get together that night. Letitia was very happy at the supper table, her eyes shining, and Mama looked at Aunt Ruth a couple of times as evidence of her own high spirits. In those days they were trying out a new strengthening treatment for Letitia, and considering how she looked, it was miraculous how well she was feeling.

Before we went to sleep, Holanda and I talked about the business. The note from Ariel didn't bother us so much, thrown from a train going its own way, that's how it is, but it seemed to us that Letitia from her privileged position was taking too much advantage of us. She knew we weren't going to say anything to her, and in a household where there's someone with some physical defect and a lot of pride, everyone pretends to ignore it starting with the one who's sick, or better yet, they pretend they don't know that the other one knows. But you don't have to exaggerate it either, and the way Letitia was acting at the table, or the way she kept the note, was just too much. That night I went back to having nightmares about trains, it was morning and I was walking on enormous railroad beaches covered with rails filled with switches, seeing in the distance the red glows of locomotives approaching, anxiously trying to calculate if the train was going to pass to my left and threatened at the same time by the arrival of an express back of me or—what was even worse—that one of the trains would switch off onto one of the sidings and run directly over me. But I forgot it by morning because Letitia was all full of aches and we had to help her get dressed. It seemed to us that she was a little sorry for the business yesterday and we were very nice to her, telling her that's what happens with walking too much and that maybe it would be better for her to stay in her room reading. She said nothing but came to the table for breakfast, and when Mama asked, she said she was fine and her back hardly hurt at all. She stated it firmly and looked at us.

That afternoon I won, but at that moment, I don't know what came over me, I told Letitia that I'd give her my place, naturally without telling her why. That this guy clearly preferred her and would look at her until his eyes fell out. The game drew to Statues, and we selected simple items so as not to complicate life, and she invented a sort of Chinese Princess, with a shy air, looking at the ground, and the hands placed together as Chinese princesses are wont to do. When the train passed, Holanda was lying on her back under the willows, but I watched and saw that Ariel had eyes only for Letitia. He kept looking at her until the train disappeared around the curve, and Letitia stood there motionless and didn't know that he had just looked at her that way. But when it came to resting under the trees again, we saw that she knew all right, and that she'd have been pleased to keep the costume on all afternoon and all night.

Wednesday we drew between Holanda and me, because Letitia said it was only fair she be left out. Holanda won, darn her luck, but Ariel's letter fell next to me. When I picked it up I had the impulse to give it to Letitia who didn't say a word, but I thought, then, that neither was it a matter of catering to everybody's wishes, and I opened it slowly. Ariel announced that the next day he was going to get off at the nearby station and that he would come by the embankment to chat for a while. It was all terribly written, but the final phrase was handsomely put: "Warmest regards to the three Statues." The signature looked like a scrawl though we remarked on its personality.

While we were taking the ornaments off Holanda, Letitia looked at me once or twice. I'd read them the message and no one had made any comments, which was very upsetting because finally, at last, Ariel was going to come and one had to think about this new development and come to some decision. If they found out about it at the house, or if by accident one of the Loza girls, those envious little runts, came to spy on us, there was going to be one incredible mess. Furthermore, it was extremely unlike us to remain silent over a thing like this; we hardly looked at one another, putting the ornaments away and going back through the white gate to the house.

Aunt Ruth asked Holanda and me to wash the cat, and she took Letitia off for the evening treatment and finally we could get our feelings off our chests. It seemed super that Ariel was going to come, we'd never had a friend like that, our cousin Tito we didn't count, a dumbbell who cut out paper dolls and believed in first communion. We were extremely nervous in our expectation and José, poor angel, got the short end of it. Holanda was the braver of the two and brought up the subject of Letitia. I didn't know what to think, on the one hand it seemed ghastly to me that Ariel should find out, but also it was only fair that things clear themselves up, no one had to out and out put herself on the line for someone else. What I really would have wanted was that Letitia not suffer; she had enough to put up with and now the new treatment and all those things.

That night Mama was amazed to see us so quiet and said what a miracle, and had the cat got our tongues, then looked at Aunt Ruth and both of them thought for sure we'd been raising hell of some kind and were conscience-stricken. Letitia ate very little and said that she hurt and would they let her go to her room to read Rocambole. Though she didn't much want to, Holanda gave her a hand, and I sat down and started some knitting, something I do only when I'm nervous. Twice I thought to go down to Letitia's room, I couldn't figure out what the two of them were doing there alone, but then Holanda came back with a mysterious air of importance and sat next to me not saying a word until Mama and Aunt Ruth cleared the table. "She doesn't want to go tomorrow. She wrote a letter and said that if he asks a lot of questions we should give it to him." Half-opening the pocket of her blouse she showed me the lilac-tinted envelope. Then they called us in to dry the dishes, and that night we fell asleep almost immediately, exhausted by all the high-pitched emotion and from washing José.

The next day it was my turn to do the marketing and I didn't see Letitia all morning, she stayed in her room. Before they called us to lunch I went in for a moment and found her sitting at the window with a pile of pillows and a new Rocambole novel. You could see she felt terrible, but she started to laugh and told me about a bee that couldn't find its way out and about a funny dream she had had. I said it was a pity she wasn't coming out to the willows, but I found it difficult to put it nicely. "If you want, we can explain to Ariel that you feel upset," I suggested, but she said no and shut up like a clam. I insisted for a little while, really, that she should come, and finally got terribly gushy and told her she shouldn't be afraid, giving as an example that true affection knows no barriers and other fat ideas we'd gotten from *The Treasure of Youth*, but it got harder and harder to say anything to her because she was looking out the window and looked as if she were going to cry. Finally I left, saying that Mama needed me. Lunch lasted for days, and Holanda got a slap from Aunt Ruth for having spattered some tomato sauce from the spaghetti onto the tablecloth. I don't even remember doing the dishes, right away we were out under the willows hugging one another, very happy, and not jealous of one another in the slightest. Holanda explained to me everything we had to say about our studies so that Ariel would be impressed, because high school students despised girls who'd only been through grade school and studied just home ec and knew how to do raised needlework. When the train went past at 2:08, Ariel waved his arms enthusiastically, and we waved a welcome to him with our embossed handkerchiefs. Some twenty minutes later we saw him arrive by the embankment; he was taller than we had thought and dressed all in grey.

I don't even remember what we talked about at first; he was somewhat shy in spite of having come and the notes and everything, and said a lot of considerate things. Almost immediately he praised our Statues and Attitudes and asked our names, and why had the third one not come. Holanda explained that Letitia had not been able to come, and he said that that was a pity and that he thought Letitia was an exquisite name. Then he told us stuff about the Industrial High School, it was not the English school, unhappily, and wanted to know if we would show him the ornaments. Holanda lifted the stone and we let him see the things. He seemed to be very interested in them, and at different times he would take one of the ornaments and say, "Letitia wore this one day," or "This was for the Oriental statue," what he meant was the Chinese Princess. We sat in the shade under a willow and he was happy but distracted, and you could see that he was only being polite. Holanda looked at me two or three times when the conversation lapsed into silence, and that made both of us feel awful, made us want to get out of it, or wish that Ariel had never come at all. He asked again if Letitia were ill and Holanda looked at me and I thought she was going to tell him, but instead she answered that Letitia had not been able to come. Ariel drew geometric figures in the dust with a stick and occasionally looked at the white gate and we knew what he was thinking, and because of that Holanda was right to pull out the lilac envelope and hand it up to him, and he stood there surprised with the envelope in his hand; then he blushed while we explained to him that Letitia had sent it to him, and he put the letter in an inside jacket pocket, not wanting to read it in front of us. Almost immediately he said that it had been a great pleasure for him and that he was delighted to have come, but his hand was soft and unpleasant in a way it'd have been better for the interview to end right away, although later we could only think of his grey eyes and the sad way he had of smiling. We also agreed on how he had said goodbye: "Until always," a form we'd never heard at home and which seemed to us so godlike and poetic. We told all this to Letitia who was waiting for us under the lemon tree in the patio, and I would have liked to have asked her what she had said in the letter, but I don't know what it was because she'd sealed the envelope before giving it to Holanda, so I didn't say anything about that and only told her what Ariel was like and how many times he'd asked for her. This was not at all an easy thing to do because it was a nice thing and a terrible thing at the same time; we noticed that Letitia was feeling very happy and at the same time she was almost crying, and we found ourselves saying that Aunt Ruth wanted us now and we left her looking at the wasps in the lemon tree.

When we were going to sleep that night, Holanda said to me, "The game's finished from tomorrow on, you'll see." But she was wrong though not by much, and the next day Letitia gave us the regular signal when dessert came around. We went out to wash the dishes somewhat astonished, and a bit sore, because that was sheer sauciness on Letitia's part and not the right thing to do. She was waiting for us at the gate, and we almost died of fright when we got to the willows for she brought out of her pocket Mama's pearl collar and all her rings, even Aunt Ruth's big one with the ruby. If the Loza girls were spying on us and saw us with the jewels, sure as anything Mama would learn about it right away and kill us, the nasty little creeps. But Letitia wasn't scared and said if anything happened she was the only one responsible. "I would like you to leave it to me today," she added without looking at us. We got the ornaments out right away, all of a sudden we wanted to be very kind to Letitia and give her all the pleasure, although at the bottom of everything we were still feeling a little spiteful. The game came out Statues, and we chose lovely things that would go well with the jewels, lots of peacock feathers to set in the hair, and a fur that from a distance looked like silver fox, and a pink veil that she put on like a turban. We saw that she was thinking, trying the Statue out, but without moving, and when the train appeared on the curve she placed herself at the foot of the incline with all the jewels sparkling in the sun. She lifted her arms as if she were going to do an Attitude instead of a Statue, her hands pointed at the sky with her head thrown back (the only direction she could, poor thing) and bent her body backwards so far it scared us. To us it seemed terrific, the most regal statue she'd ever done; then we saw Ariel looking at her, hung halfway out the window he looked just at her, turning his head and looking at her without seeing us, until the train carried him out of sight all at once. I don't know why, the two of us started running at the same time to catch Letitia who was standing there, still with her eyes closed and enormous tears all down her face. She pushed us back, not angrily, but we helped her stuff the jewels in her pocket, and she went back to the house alone while we put the ornaments away in their box for the last time. We knew almost what was going to happen, but just the same we went out to the willows the next day, just the two of us, after Aunt Ruth imposed absolute silence so as not to disturb Letitia who hurt and who wanted to sleep. When the train came by, it was no surprise to see the third window empty, and while we were grinning at one another, somewhere between relief and being furious, we imagined Ariel riding on the other side of the coach, not moving in his seat, looking off toward the river with his grey eyes.

That Evening Sun

William Faulkner

Monday is no different from any other weekday in Jefferson now. The streets are paved now, and the telephone and electric companies are cutting down more and more of the shade trees—the water oaks, the maples and locusts and elms—to make room for iron poles bearing clusters of bloated and ghostly and bloodless grapes, and we have a city laundry which makes the rounds on Monday morning, gathering the bundles of clothes into bright-colored, specially-made motor cars: the soiled wearing of a whole week now flees apparitionlike behind alert and irritable electric horns, with a long diminishing noise of rubber and asphalt like tearing silk, and even the Negro women who still take in white people's washing after the old custom, fetch and deliver it in automobiles.

But fifteen years ago, on Monday morning the quiet, dusty, shady streets would be full of Negro women with, balanced on their steady, turbaned heads, bundles of clothes tied up in sheets, almost as large as cotton bales, carried so without touch of hand between the kitchen door of the white house and the blackened washpot beside a cabin door in Negro Hollow.

Nancy would set her bundle on the top of her head, then upon the bundle in turn she would set the black straw sailor hat which she wore winter and summer. She was tall, with a high, sad face sunken a little where her teeth were missing. Sometimes we would go a part of the way down the lane and across the pasture with her, to watch the balanced bundle and the hat that never bobbed nor wavered, even when she walked down into the ditch and up the other side and stooped through the fence. She would go down on her hands and knees and crawl through the gap, her head rigid, uptilted, the bundle steady as a rock or a balloon, and rise to her feet again and go on.

Sometimes the husbands of the washing women would fetch and deliver the clothes, but Jesus never did that for Nancy, even before father told him to stay away from our house, even when Dilsey was sick and Nancy would come to cook for us.

And then about half the time we'd have to go down the lane to Nancy's cabin and tell her to come on and cook breakfast. We would stop at the ditch, because father told us to not have anything to do with Jesus—he was a short black man, with a razor scar down his face—and we would throw rocks at Nancy's house until she came to the door, leaning her head around it without any clothes on.

"What yawl mean, chunking my house?" Nancy said. "What you little devils mean?"

"Father says for you to come on and get breakfast," Caddy said. "Father says it's over a half an hour now, and you've got to come this minute."

"I aint studying no breakfast," Nancy said. "I going to get my sleep out."

"I bet you're drunk," Jason said. "Father says you're drunk. Are you drunk, Nancy?"

"Who says I is?" Nancy said. "I got to get my sleep out. I aint studying no breakfast."

So after a while we quit chunking the cabin and went back home. When she finally came, it was too late for me to go to school. So we thought it was whisky until that day they arrested her again and they were taking her to jail and they passed Mr Stovall. He was the cashier in the bank and a deacon in the Baptist church, and Nancy began to say:

"When you going to pay me, white man? When you going to pay me, white man? It's been three times now since you paid me a cent—" Mr Stovall knocked her down, but she kept on saying, "When you going to pay me, white man? It's been three times now since—" until Mr Stovall kicked her in the mouth with his heel and the marshal caught Mr Stovall back, and Nancy lying in the street, laughing. She turned her head and spat out some blood and teeth and said, "It's been three times now since he paid me a cent."

That was how she lost her teeth, and all that day they told about Nancy and Mr Stovall, and all that night the ones that passed the jail could hear Nancy singing and yelling. They could see her hands holding to the window bars, and a lot of them stopped along the fence, listening to her and to the jailer trying to make her stop. She didn't shut up until almost daylight, when the jailer began to hear a bumping and scraping upstairs and he went up there and found Nancy hanging from the window bar. He said that it was cocaine and not whisky, because no nigger would try to commit suicide unless he was full of cocaine, because a nigger full of cocaine wasn't a nigger any longer.

The jailer cut her down and revived her; then he beat her, whipped her. She had hung herself with her dress. She had fixed it all right, but when they arrested her she didn't have on anything except a dress and so she didn't have anything to tie her hands with and she couldn't make her hands let go of the window ledge. So the jailer heard the noise and ran up there and found Nancy hanging from the window, stark naked, her belly already swelling out a little, like a little balloon.

When Dilsey was sick in her cabin and Nancy was cooking for us, we could see her apron swelling out; that was before father told Jesus to stay away from the house. Jesus was in the kitchen, sitting behind the stove, with his razor scar on his black face like a piece of dirty string. He said it was a watermelon that Nancy had under her dress.

"It never come off of your vine, though," Nancy said.

"Off of what vine?" Caddy said.

"I can cut down the vine it did come off of," Jesus said.

"What makes you want to talk like that before these chillen?" Nancy said. "Whyn't you go on to work? You done et. You want Mr Jason to catch you hanging around his kitchen, talking that way before these chillen?"

"Talking what way?" Caddy said. "What vine?"

"I cant hang around white man's kitchen," Jesus said. "But white man can hang around mine. White man can come in my house, but I cant stop him. When white man want to come in my house, I aint got no house. I cant stop him, but he cant kick me outen it. He cant do that."

Dilsey was still sick in her cabin. Father told Jesus to stay off our place. Dilsey was still sick. It was a long time. We were in the library after supper.

"Isn't Nancy through in the kitchen yet?" mother said. "It seems to me that she has had plenty of time to have finished the dishes."

"Let Quentin go and see," father said. "Go and see if Nancy is through, Quentin. Tell her she can go on home."

I went to the kitchen. Nancy was through. The dishes were put away and the fire was out. Nancy was sitting in a chair, close to the cold stove. She looked at me.

"Mother wants to know if you are through," I said.

"Yes," Nancy said. She looked at me. "I done finished." She looked at me.

"What is it?" I said. "What is it?"

"I aint nothing but a nigger," Nancy said. "It aint none of my fault."

She looked at me, sitting in the chair before the cold stove, the sailor hat on her head. I went back to the library. It was the cold stove and all, when you think of a kitchen being warm and busy and cheerful. And with a cold stove and the dishes all put away, and nobody wanting to eat at that hour.

"Is she through?" mother said.

"Yessum," I said.

"What is she doing?" mother said.

"She's not doing anything. She's through."

"I'll go and see," father said.

"Maybe she's waiting for Jesus to come and take her home," Caddy said.

"Jesus is gone," I said. Nancy told us how one morning she woke up and Jesus was gone.

"He quit me," Nancy said. "Done gone to Memphis, I reckon. Dodging them city *po*-lice for a while, I reckon."

"And a good riddance," father said. "I hope he stays there."

"Nancy's scaired of the dark," Jason said.

"So are you," Caddy said.

"I'm not," Jason said.

"Scairy cat," Caddy said.

"I'm not," Jason said.

"You, Candace!" mother said. Father came back.

"I am going to walk down the lane with Nancy," he said. "She says that Jesus is back."

"Has she seen him?" mother said.

"No. Some Negro sent her word that he was back in town. I wont be long."

"You'll leave me alone, to take Nancy home?" mother said. "Is her safety more precious to you than mine?"

"I wont be long," father said.

"You'll leave these children unprotected, with that Negro about?"

"I'm going too," Caddy said. "Let me go, father."

"What would he do with them, if he were unfortunate enough to have them?" father said.

"I want to go, too," Jason said.

"Jason!" mother said. She was speaking to father. You could tell that by the way she said the name. Like she believed that all day father had been trying to think of doing the thing she wouldn't like the most, and that she knew all the time that after a while he would think of it. I stayed quiet, because father and I both knew that mother would want him to make me stay with her if she just thought of it in time. So father didn't look at me. I was the oldest. I was nine and Caddy was seven and Jason was five.

"Nonsense," father said. "We wont be long."

Nancy had her hat on. We came to the lane. "Jesus always been good to me," Nancy said. "Whenever he had two dollars, one of them was mine." We walked in the lane. "If I can just get through the lane," Nancy said, "I be all right then."

The lane was always dark. "This is where Jason got scared on Hallowe'en," Caddy said.

"I didn't," Jason said.

"Cant Aunt Rachel do anything with him?" father said. Aunt Rachel was old. She lived in a cabin beyond Nancy's, by herself. She had white hair and she smoked a pipe in the door, all day long; she didn't work any more. They said she was Jesus' mother. Sometimes she said she was and sometimes she said she wasn't any kin to Jesus.

"Yes, you did," Caddy said. "You were scairder than Frony. You were scairder than T. P. even. Scairder than niggers."

"Cant nobody do nothing with him," Nancy said. "He say I done woke up the devil in him and aint but one thing going to lay it down again."

"Well, he's gone now," father said. "There's nothing for you to be afraid of now. And if you'd just let white men alone."

"Let what white men alone?" Caddy said. "How let them alone?"

"He aint gone nowhere," Nancy said. "I can feel him. I can feel him now, in this lane. He hearing us talk, every word, hid somewhere, waiting. I aint seen him, and I aint going to see him again but once more, with that razor in his mouth. That razor on that string down his back, inside his shirt. And then I aint going to be even surprised."

"I wasn't scaired," Jason said.

"If you'd behave yourself, you'd have kept out of this," father said. "But it's all right now. He's probably in St. Louis now. Probably got another wife by now and forgot all about you."

"If he has, I better not find out about it," Nancy said. "I'd stand there right over them, and every time he wropped her, I'd cut that arm off. I'd cut his head off and I'd slit her belly and I'd shove—"

"Hush," father said.

"Slit whose belly, Nancy?" Caddy said.

"I wasn't scaired," Jason said. "I'd walk right down this lane by myself."

"Yah," Caddy said. "You wouldn't dare to put your foot down in it if we were not here too."

II

Dilsey was still sick, so we took Nancy home every night until mother said, "How much longer is this going on? I to be left alone in this big house while you take home a frightened Negro?"

We fixed a pallet in the kitchen for Nancy. One night we waked up, hearing the sound. It was not singing and it was not crying, coming up the dark stairs. There was a light in mother's room and we heard father going down the hall, down the back stairs, and Caddy and I went into the hall. The floor was cold. Our toes curled away from it while we listened to the sound. It was like singing and it wasn't like singing, like the sounds that Negroes make.

Then it stopped and we heard father going down the back stairs, and we went to the head of the stairs. Then the sound began again, in the stairway, not loud, and we could see Nancy's eyes halfway up the stairs, against the wall. They looked like cat's eyes do, like a big cat against the wall, watching us. When we came down the steps to where she was, she quit making the sound again, and we stood there until father came back up from the kitchen, with his pistol in his hand. He went back down with Nancy and they came back with Nancy's pallet.

We spread the pallet in our room. After the light in mother's room went off, we could see Nancy's eyes again. "Nancy," Caddy whispered, "are you asleep, Nancy?"

Nancy whispered something. It was oh or no, I dont know which. Like nobody had made it, like it came from nowhere and went nowhere, until it was like Nancy was not there at all; that I had looked so hard at her eyes on the stairs that they had got printed on my eyeballs, like the sun does when you have closed your eyes and there is no sun. "Jesus," Nancy whispered. "Jesus."

"Was it Jesus?" Caddy said. "Did he try to come into the kitchen?"

"Jesus," Nancy said. Like this: Jeeeeeeeeeeeeeeeesus, until the sound went out, like a match or a candle does.

"It's the other Jesus she means," I said.

"Can you see us, Nancy?" Caddy whispered. "Can you see our eyes too?"

"I aint nothing but a nigger," Nancy said. "God knows. God knows."

"What did you see down there in the kitchen?" Caddy whispered. "What tried to get in?"

"God knows," Nancy said. We could see her eyes. "God knows."

Dilsey got well. She cooked dinner. "You'd better stay in bed a day or two longer," father said.

"What for?" Dilsey said. "If I had been a day later, this place would be to rack and ruin. Get on out of here now, and let me get my kitchen straight again."

Dilsey cooked supper too. And that night, just before dark, Nancy came into the kitchen.

"How do you know he's back?" Dilsey said. "You aint seen him."

"Jesus is a nigger," Jason said.

"I can feel him," Nancy said. "I can feel him laying yonder in the ditch."

"Tonight?" Dilsey said. "Is he there tonight?"

"Dilsey's a nigger too," Jason said.

"You try to eat something," Dilsey said.

"I dont want nothing," Nancy said.

"I aint a nigger," Jason said.

"Drink some coffee," Dilsey said. She poured a cup of coffee for Nancy. "Do you know he's out there tonight? How come you know it's tonight?"

"I know," Nancy said. "He's there, waiting. I know. I done lived with him too long. I know what he is fixing to do fore he know it himself."

"Drink some coffee," Dilsey said. Nancy held the cup to her mouth and blew into the cup. Her mouth pursed out like a spreading adder's, like a rubber mouth, like she had blown all the color out of her lips with blowing the coffee.

"I aint a nigger," Jason said. "Are you a nigger, Nancy?"

"I hellborn, child," Nancy said. "I wont be nothing soon. I going back where I come from soon."

III

She began to drink the coffee. While she was drinking, holding the cup in both hands, she began to make the sound again. She made the sound into the cup and the coffee sploshed out onto her hands and her dress. Her eyes looked at us and she sat there, her elbows on her knees, holding the cup in both hands, looking at us across the wet cup, making the sound. "Look at Nancy," Jason said. "Nancy cant cook for us now. Dilsey's got well now."

"You hush up," Dilsey said. Nancy held the cup in both hands, looking at us, making the sound, like there were two of them: one looking at us and the other making the sound. "Whyn't you let Mr Jason telefoam the marshal?" Dilsey said. Nancy stopped then, holding the cup in her long brown hands. She tried to drink some coffee again, but it sploshed out of the cup, onto her hands and her dress, and she put the cup down. Jason watched her.

"I cant swallow it," Nancy said. "I swallows but it wont go down me."

"You go down to the cabin," Dilsey said. "Frony will fix you a pallet and I'll be there soon."

"Wont no nigger stop him," Nancy said.

"I aint a nigger," Jason said. "Am I, Dilsey?"

"I reckon not," Dilsey said. She looked at Nancy. "I dont reckon so. What you going to do, then?"

Nancy looked at us. Her eyes went fast, like she was afraid there wasn't time to look, without hardly moving at all. She looked at us, at all three of us at one time. "You member that night I stayed in yawls' room?" she said. She told about how we waked up early the next morning, and played. We had to play quiet, on her pallet, until father woke up and it was time to get breakfast. "Go and ask your maw to let me stay here tonight," Nancy said. "I wont need no pallet. We can play some more."

Caddy asked mother. Jason went too. "I cant have Negroes sleeping in the bedrooms," mother said. Jason cried. He cried until mother said he couldn't have any dessert for three days if he didn't stop. Then Jason said he would stop if Dilsey would make a chocolate cake. Father was there.

"Why dont you do something about it?" mother said. "What do we have officers for?"

"Why is Nancy afraid of Jesus?" Caddy said. "Are you afraid of father, mother?"

"What could the officers do?" father said. "If Nancy hasn't seen him, how could the officers find him?"

"Then why is she afraid?" mother said.

"She says he is there. She says she knows he is there tonight."

"Yet we pay taxes," mother said. "I must wait here alone in this big house while you take a Negro woman home."

"You know that I am not lying outside with a razor," father said.

"I'll stop if Dilsey will make a chocolate cake," Jason said. Mother told us to go out and father said he didn't know if Jason would get a chocolate cake or not, but he knew what Jason was going to get in about a minute. We went back to the kitchen and told Nancy.

"Father said for you to go home and lock the door and you'll be all right," Caddy said. "All right from what, Nancy? Is Jesus mad at you?" Nancy was holding the coffee cup in her hands again, her elbows on her knees and her hands holding the cup between her knees. She was looking into the cup. "What have you done that made Jesus mad?" Caddy said. Nancy let the cup go. It didn't break on the floor, but the coffee spilled out, and Nancy sat there with her hands still making the shape of the cup. She began to make the sound again, not loud. Not singing and not unsinging. We watched her.

"Here," Dilsey said. "You quit that, now. You get aholt of yourself. You wait here. I going to get Versh to walk home with you." Dilsey went out.

We looked at Nancy. Her shoulders kept shaking, but she quit making the sound. We watched her. "What's Jesus going to do to you?" Caddy said. "He went away."

Nancy looked at us. "We had fun that night I stayed in yawls' room, didn't we?"

"I didn't," Jason said. "I didn't have any fun."

"You were asleep in mother's room," Caddy said. "You were not there."

"Let's go down to my house and have some more fun," Nancy said.

"Mother wont let us," I said. "It's too late now."

"Dont bother her," Nancy said. "We can tell her in the morning. She wont mind."

"She wouldn't let us," I said.

"Dont ask her now," Nancy said. "Dont bother her now."

"She didn't say we couldn't go," Caddy said.

"We didn't ask," I said.

"If you go, I'll tell," Jason said.

"We'll have fun," Nancy said. "They wont mind, just to my house. I been working for yawl a long time. They won't mind."

"I'm not afraid to go," Caddy said. "Jason is the one that's afraid. He'll tell."

"I'm not," Jason said.

"Yes, you are," Caddy said. "You'll tell."

"I wont tell," Jason said. "I'm not afraid."

"Jason aint afraid to go with me," Nancy said. "Is you, Jason?"

"Jason is going to tell," Caddy said. The lane was dark. We passed the pasture gate. "I bet if something was to jump out from behind that gate, Jason would holler."

"I wouldn't," Jason said. We walked down the lane. Nancy was talking loud.

"What are you talking so loud for, Nancy?" Caddy said.

"Who; me?" Nancy said. "Listen at Quentin and Caddy and Jason saying I'm talking loud."

"You talk like there was five of us here," Caddy said. "You talk like father was here too."

"Who; me talking loud, Mr Jason?" Nancy said.

"Nancy called Jason 'Mister,' " Caddy said.

"Listen how Caddy and Quentin and Jason talk," Nancy said.

"We're not talking loud," Caddy said. "You're the one that's talking like father—"

"Hush," Nancy said; "hush, Mr Jason."

"Nancy called Jason 'Mister' aguh—"

"Hush," Nancy said. She was talking loud when we crossed the ditch and stooped through the fence where she used to stoop through with the clothes on her head. Then we came to her house. We were going fast then. She opened the door. The smell of the house was like the lamp and the smell of Nancy was like the wick, like they were waiting for one another to begin to smell. She lit the lamp and closed the door and put the bar up. Then she quit talking loud, looking at us.

"What're we going to do?" Caddy said.

"What do yawl want to do?" Nancy said.

"You said we would have some fun," Caddy said.

There was something about Nancy's house; something you could smell besides Nancy and the house. Jason smelled it, even. "I dont want to stay here," he said. "I want to go home."

"Go home, then," Caddy said.

"I dont want to go by myself," Jason said.

"We're going to have some fun," Nancy said.

"How?" Caddy said.

Nancy stood by the door. She was looking at us, only it was like she had emptied her eyes, like she had quit using them. "What do you want to do?" she said.

"Tell us a story," Caddy said.

"Can you tell a story?"

"Yes," Nancy said.

"Tell it," Caddy said. We looked at Nancy. "You dont know any stories."

"Yes," Nancy said. "Yes, I do."

She came and sat in a chair before the hearth. There was a little fire there. Nancy built it up, when it was already hot inside. She built a good blaze. She told a story. She talked like her eyes looked, like her eyes watching us and her voice talking to us did not belong to her. Like she was living somewhere else, waiting somewhere else. She was outside the cabin. Her voice was inside and the shape of her, the Nancy that could stoop under a barbed wire fence with a bundle of clothes balanced on her head as though without weight, like a balloon, was there. But that was all. "And so this here queen come walking up to the ditch, where that bad man was hiding. She was walking up to the ditch, and she say, 'If I can just get past this here ditch,' was what she say . . ."

"What ditch?" Caddy said. "A ditch like that one out there? Why did a queen want to go into a ditch?"

"To get to her house," Nancy said. She looked at us. "She had to cross the ditch to get into her house quick and bar the door."

"Why did she want to go home and bar the door?" Caddy said.

IV

Nancy looked at us. She quit talking. She looked at us. Jason's legs stuck straight out of his pants where he sat on Nancy's lap. "I dont think that's a good story," he said. "I want to go home."

"Maybe we had better," Caddy said. She got up from the floor. "I bet they are looking for us right now." She went toward the door.

"No," Nancy said. "Dont open it." She got up quick and passed Caddy. She didn't touch the door, the wooden bar.

"Why not?" Caddy said.

"Come back to the lamp," Nancy said. "We'll have fun. You dont have to go."

"We ought to go," Caddy said. "Unless we have a lot of fun." She and Nancy came back to the fire, the lamp.

"I want to go home," Jason said. "I'm going to tell."

"I know another story," Nancy said. She stood close to the lamp. She looked at Caddy, like when your eyes look up at a stick balanced on your nose. She had to look down to see Caddy, but her eyes looked like that, like when you are balancing a stick.

"I wont listen to it," Jason said. "I'll bang on the floor."

"It's a good one," Nancy said. "It's better than the other one."

"What's it about?" Caddy said. Nancy was standing by the lamp. Her hand was on the lamp, against the light, long and brown.

"Your hand is on that hot globe," Caddy said. "Dont it feel hot to your hand?"

Nancy looked at her hand on the lamp chimney. She took her hand away, slow. She stood there, looking at Caddy, wringing her long hand as though it were tied to her wrist with a string.

"Let's do something else," Caddy said.

"I want to go home," Jason said.

"I got some popcorn," Nancy said. She looked at Caddy and then at Jason and then at me and then at Caddy again. "I got some popcorn."

"I dont like popcorn," Jason said. "I'd rather have candy."

Nancy looked at Jason. "You can hold the popper." She was still wringing her hand; it was long and limp and brown.

"All right," Jason said. "I'll stay a while if I can do that. Caddy cant hold it. I'll want to go home again if Caddy holds the popper."

Nancy built up the fire. "Look at Nancy putting her hands in the fire," Caddy said. "What's the matter with you, Nancy?"

"I got popcorn," Nancy said. "I got some." She took the popper from under the bed. It was broken. Jason began to cry.

"Now we cant have any popcorn," he said.

"We ought to go home, anyway," Caddy said. "Come on, Quentin."

"Wait," Nancy said; "wait. I can fix it. Dont you want to help me fix it?"

"I dont think I want any," Caddy said. "It's too late now."

"You help me, Jason," Nancy said. "Dont you want to help me?"

"No," Jason said. "I want to go home."

"Hush," Nancy said; "hush. Watch. Watch me. I can fix it so Jason can hold it and pop the corn." She got a piece of wire and fixed the popper.

"It wont hold good," Caddy said.

"Yes, it will," Nancy said. "Yawl watch. Yawl help me shell some corn."

The popcorn was under the bed too. We shelled it into the popper and Nancy helped Jason hold the popper over the fire.

"It's not popping," Jason said. "I want to go home."

"You wait," Nancy said. "It'll begin to pop. We'll have fun then." She was sitting close to the fire. The lamp was turned up so high it was beginning to smoke.

"Why dont you turn it down some?" I said.

"It's all right," Nancy said. "I'll clean it. Yawl wait. The popcorn will start in a minute."

"I dont believe it's going to start," Caddy said. "We ought to start home, anyway. They'll be worried."

"No," Nancy said. "It's going to pop. Dilsey will tell um yawl with me. I been working for yawl long time. They won't mind if yawl at my house. You wait, now. It'll start popping any minute now."

Then Jason got some smoke in his eyes and he began to cry. He dropped the popper into the fire. Nancy got a wet rag and wiped Jason's face, but he didn't stop crying.

"Hush," she said. "Hush." But he didn't hush. Caddy took the popper out of the fire.

"It's burned up," she said. "You'll have to get some more popcorn, Nancy."

"Did you put all of it in?" Nancy said.

"Yes," Caddy said. Nancy looked at Caddy. Then she took the popper and opened it and poured the cinders into her apron and began to sort the grains, her hands long and brown, and we watching her.

"Haven't you got any more?" Caddy said.

"Yes," Nancy said; "yes. Look. This here aint burnt. All we need to do is—"

"I want to go home," Jason said. "I'm going to tell."

"Hush," Caddy said. We all listened. Nancy's head was already turned toward the barred door, her eyes filled with red lamplight. "Somebody is coming," Caddy said.

Then Nancy began to make that sound again, not loud, sitting there above the fire, her long hands dangling between her knees; all of a sudden water began to come out on her face in big drops, running down her face, carrying in each one a little turning ball of firelight like a spark until it dropped off her chin. "She's not crying," I said.

"I aint crying," Nancy said. Her eyes were closed. "I aint crying. Who is it?"

"I dont know," Caddy said. She went to the door and looked out. "We've got to go now," she said. "Here comes father."

"I'm going to tell," Jason said. "Yawl made me come."

The water still ran down Nancy's face. She turned in her chair. "Listen. Tell him. Tell him we going to have fun. Tell him I take good care of yawl until in the morning. Tell him to let me come home with yawl and sleep on the floor. Tell him I wont need no pallet. We'll have fun. You member last time how we had so much fun?"

"I didn't have fun," Jason said. "You hurt me. You put smoke in my eyes. I'm going to tell."

V

Father came in. He looked at us. Nancy did not get up.

"Tell him," she said.

"Caddy made us come down here," Jason said. "I didn't want to."

Father came to the fire. Nancy looked up at him. "Cant you go to Aunt Rachel's and stay?" he said. Nancy looked up at father, her hands between her knees. "He's not here," father said. "I would have seen him. There's not a soul in sight."

"He in the ditch," Nancy said. "He waiting in the ditch yonder."

"Nonsense," father said. He looked at Nancy. "Do you know he's there?"

"I got the sign," Nancy said.

"What sign?"

"I got it. It was on the table when I come in. It was a hogbone, with blood meat still on it, laying by the lamp. He out there. When yawl walk out that door, I gone."

"Gone where, Nancy?" Caddy said.

"I'm not a tattletale," Jason said.

"Nonsense," father said.

"He out there," Nancy said. "He looking through that window this minute, waiting for yawl to go. Then I gone."

"Nonsense," father said. "Lock up your house and we'll take you on to Aunt Rachel's."

" 'Twont do no good," Nancy said. She didn't look at father now, but he looked down at her, at her long, limp, moving hands. "Putting it off wont do no good."

"Then what do you want to do?" father said.

"I dont know," Nancy said. "I cant do nothing. Just put it off. And that dont do no good. I reckon it belong to me. I reckon what I going to get aint no more than mine."

"Get what?" Caddy said. "What's yours?"

"Nothing," father said. "You all must get to bed."

"Caddy made me come," Jason said.

"Go on to Aunt Rachel's," father said.

"It wont do no good," Nancy said. She sat before the fire, her elbows on her knees, her long hands between her knees. "When even your own kitchen wouldn't do no good. When even if I was sleeping on the floor in the room with your chillen, and the next morning there I am, and blood—"

"Hush," father said. "Lock the door and put out the lamp and go to bed."

"I scared of the dark," Nancy said. "I scared for it to happen in the dark."

"You mean you're going to sit right here with the lamp lighted?" father said. Then Nancy began to make the sound again, sitting before the fire, her long hands between her knees. "Ah, damnation," father said. "Come along, chillen. It's past bedtime."

"When yawl go home, I gone," Nancy said. She talked quieter now, and her face looked quiet, like her hands. "Anyway, I got my coffin money saved up with Mr Lovelady." Mr Lovelady was a short, dirty man who collected the Negro insurance, coming around to the cabins or the kitchens every Saturday morning, to collect fifteen cents. He and his wife lived at the hotel. One morning his wife committed suicide. They had a child, a little girl. He and the child went away. After a week or two he came back alone. We would see him going along the lanes and the back streets on Saturday mornings.

"Nonsense," father said. "You'll be the first thing I'll see in the kitchen tomorrow morning."

"You'll see what you'll see, I reckon," Nancy said. "But it will take the Lord to say what that will be."

VI

We left her sitting before the fire.

"Come and put the bar up," father said. But she didn't move. She didn't look at us again, sitting quietly there between the lamp and the fire. From some distance down the lane we could look back and see her through the open door.

"What, father?" Caddy said. "What's going to happen?"

"Nothing," father said. Jason was on father's back, so Jason was the tallest of all of us. We went down into the ditch. I looked at it, quiet. I couldn't see much where the moonlight and the shadows tangled.

"If Jesus is hid here, he can see us, cant he?" Caddy said.

"He's not there," father said. "He went away a long time ago."

"You made me come," Jason said, high; against the sky it looked like father had two heads, a little one and a big one. "I didn't want to."

We went up out of the ditch. We could still see Nancy's house and the open door, but we couldn't see Nancy now, sitting before the fire with the door open, because she was tired. "I just done got tired," she said. "I just a nigger. It aint no fault of mine."

But we could hear her, because she began just after we came up out of the ditch, the sound that was not singing and not unsinging. "Who will do our washing now, father?" I said.

"I'm not a nigger," Jason said, high and close above father's head.

"You're worse," Caddy said, "you are a tattletale. If something was to jump out, you'd be scairder than a nigger."

"I wouldn't," Jason said.

"You'd cry," Caddy said.

"Caddy," father said.

"I wouldn't!" Jason said.

"Scairy cat," Caddy said.

"Candace!" father said.

All You Faceless Voyagers

Ivan Gold

It has always seemed to me that people who hate me must be suffering from some strange form of lunacy.

Sei Shonagon

Methinks, quoth Sancho, a Man can't be in great Affliction when he can turn his Brain to the making of Verses.

Cervantes

The world may kill you. All around them things were happening to the purpose. Camus was seventy-two hours from the finish in a fast car and a week removed from official interment in the *Times Literary Supplement,* a generally favorable comparison with the author of *Howards End.* In Cologne the same day an eighty-year-old Jew was threatened with sainthood through the mails upside down on the cross, and admitted to anxiety from behind bolted doors to a sympathetic press. In California, a still-young man having a resemblance to

Manolete entered the stretch after twelve years amidst law books, reporters, and piped Guy Lombardo, awaiting painless death for certain crimes against the social body, and much troubled the governor, the State Department very briefly, and the overseas press. The only thing to fear besides fear itself was the lunatic and the fast car and the ostrich's substitute for bravery. On a one-funneled boat built in 1910 called *Jorge Segundo* the second-class cabin smelled intensely of socks, which was irritating but the price the traveler paid for not paying the price, because potentially they were first-class people. Not that there lacked, all the same, legitimate cause for complaint: on the trip out from Barcelona to Palma second class had been a private two-berth cabin with a sink with two taps and delicious sea-borne intimacy with his unwed Swedish lady in a papal country, but between Ibiza and Alicante second-class passage was separate, dismal compartments with similarly-sexed strangers. (All he asked from *La Compañía Transbaleárica* was predictability, not the best of everything.) The girl shared the filthy basin and the fetid air with three women and a male child who slept on the floor and cried from eleven until two, after which the girl slept soundly until the *guardia* woke her at three. After seeing her cabin he thought himself lucky, for the smell of socks was one man's smell, leaving all that acreage with two bunks unoccupied. The others, alas, would come: a young MD and a fat, gallused older man who wished to sleep. But for the moment he was alone and hopeful with the one other who lay in his underwear facing the wall. He shoved his crippled Olivetti (accidentally oxidized with champagne in their hotel room in Palma de Majorca on Christmas Eve) beneath the bed and placed his disintegrating blue plastic zippered suitcase next to the brown one which stood by the washstand, and sat on his lower berth to wait for the girl. Across and above the man raised up and turned. He was youngish and slight, with a ferret's face and bright red hair and large brown liquid eyes of terrifying eagerness.

"Anglais?"

"No. . . . norteamericano."

"Bon. J'aime les américains."

"Es Usted francés?"

"No. I am citizen of the world."

Now he dropped to the floor in his stockinged feet and leaned over and touched his arm.

"I speak English *y alemán.* I am citizen of the world. *Vous êtes journaliste?"*

"No, tourist. *Soy turista."*

"Ah. I too am tourist. I am citizen of the world."

Well that was a fine thing to be in the narrow straits of our times, but he was the sort of person who did not like to be touched. But the girl stuck her glorious Nordic head past the curtain into the cabin, saving him from discomfort or rudeness, he would never know. He excused himself from the intense, fulsome friendliness with good reason, he thought (the midnight sun of Ingalill), and they went above and held hands around the crowded circumference of the deck and poked into the deck passengers' room, which was rows of wooden chairs facing a blank wall like a cinema in which nothing ever played, and into the third-class sleeping quarters, a dim stinking community cave over the groaning engines which looked as bad as any of the troop or slave ships he had ever read about or remembered. So they had a compensating drink in the first-class bar, which he would have sworn a moment before they could not afford. They watched the suave newscaster on TV's only station cast the news in a manner no head of state or first-class traveler could object to—border skirmishes in unpronounceable places, distant, impossible tragedies. (But of the rush among university students in Barcelona, where this couple had met, on Fidel Castro beards, a pretty tame rebellion, no mention.) By the time they left the lounge the island of Ibiza was well behind, but they could see the lights, and in the clear, starry night she fancied she made out the lighthouse, and their hotel, and the clock on the church on the mountain. Happiness, regret for its loss, mingled and rose from her like a child's perfume, moving him to quick tears of love for her little girl's wonder and joy. The best lay ahead, the best was behind. Fatigue and the wind drove them below at last, from the best moment since the trip began, or since they met, from the kind of moment that in his ignorance he would have ceased to treasure if they came more often, and Alicante was a new world ahead in the dawn they might witness if they went to bed now. So at twenty past ten he slapped her rump in farewell outside the contiguous, segregated cabins.

His own room was dark. In the light from the corridor he gloomily spotted a valise on the bed above him and one more on the bed across, but their owners were no longer in the cabin. The citizen seemed safely lost beneath his blankets, asleep in the darkness, the curtain around his bed undrawn. With luck, he would drift into sleep himself before the newcomers returned. From his jacket he removed his passport and wallet and crammed them into the pockets of his trousers. He took off the jacket and folded it onto a shelf beside the bed. He felt beneath the bed and touched the typewriter, then slipped off his shoes and socks. He pulled the denim curtain around the narrow bed and stretched out above the blankets. Then he noticed the breeze, and that the smell had gone. He peered out. The cabin's porthole, above the citizen's bed, had been opened halfway. The breeze was warm and gentle. He turned for brief moments, luring sleep, teased it awhile, let it flow through him and drag him down—but the keys began to jingle and the talk began. The talk was in French, distinct and loud. A bunk squealed and he looked out through a chink in the curtains, barely moving his head, and saw the redhead sit up and stare through the porthole; suddenly throw the covers back and swing his legs over the side of the bed. He was fully dressed. The citizen looked toward him, toward his eyes, and he slitted his eyes. Slowly, slightly, he turned his head, and when he opened his eyes again he could see nothing but the inside of the *camarote*. He heard the citizen sit noisily on the lower bunk and put on his shoes, still talking, and move toward the door, and switch on the lights, but he sensed more than saw the glare; for the denim curtain held back the light.

—Pardon . . . I need light. . . . It flooded him, and for reply, blocking out that eager sudden face, he flung his arm across his eyes. *Bueno.* The curtain fell to, he heard splashing at the basin and the click of the lights and Good night, and again the unspoilt darkness.

He lay still. He had to go to the toilet. He put on his shoes and groped down the narrow passageway to the cabinet. Returning, he saw a sailor stagger through the hall, outside his cabin, outside Ingalill's cabin, out of control, spewing vomit on the walls and floor, moving away from the toilet, a sorry seasick sailor on the calmest of star-studded nights. The sick man reached the end of the corridor, and disappeared up the stairway. A further reason to dive into sleep, before the smell wafted through the cloth curtain which served instead of door into his cabin, and he hurried into the cabin as if sleep waited in his bed, but not for long.

But he was already too late. Sleep had flown. Five minutes later the fat man entered, stripped quietly in the dark, removed his suitcase, and grunted into the bunk above. The younger man arrived an instant later, and the fat man switched on the light. The younger man thanked him. They talked quietly. There seem to be no facilities for hanging one's clothes, the younger man said, but that was the least of it, the fat man said; this was positively the oldest and worst ship the monopoly allowed on the line. The younger man was not stopping in Alicante but was going on to Madrid, and the fat man said that according to the papers it had recently snowed in Madrid. The younger man (but they were only voices now—he would not see the doctor to know him in a professional or merely embodied capacity until five in the morning, and the fat man at eight, waiting to disembark, staring at him puffy and joyless like a shorn Santa Claus, much behind in sleep), the doctor, crawled into the lower berth across from his own, and the fat man switched off the light, and curtains swished above and to the right and he was alone once more in the dark with the faceless travelers and his wholly triumphant wakefulness. Really, though, it did not matter—he would try to sleep, he would lie there until sleep came as it would have to come before the dawn, and he would wind up sleeping two or three hours, but it did not matter: the day ahead would be warm and fine and they would find a hotel with a hot shower and leave their bags behind and eat better than they could afford to in the new city to hold off fatigue and then they would go to the beach and he would sleep for a few hours in the sun. In the corridor were sounds of gaiety, but seven cabins faced off the passageway, and it was reasonable to hope that the sounds would pass him by. It was reasonable because citizens of the world who jingle their keys and talk to themselves and poke their heads into your bed while you try to sleep are difficult to believe in after one exposure; it was reasonable because if these acts really took place they were perpetrated by a madman; and how many madmen could be traveling (in his cabin) between Ibiza and the mainland on the first day of the new year in the second class? Yet when the sounds burst into the cabin, he was not really surprised. Beyond his cocoon the light blazed again, and silently, stealthily, he placed his arm on his forehead, almost covering his eyes. He stared at the dark, wild voices that issued from the space between the sink and the door, and he pictured the cipher above, nonplused at the row inches from his head, wondering whether to wait out the tumult or take action and end it—for certainly, in the wide Latin World, there must be people braver and more given to active indignation than he. But from neither above nor across came any sound to acknowledge or discourage the joyful argument. High-school French brought him piecemeal to the heart of the matter: the citizen had befriended and rescued a stranger from third class or worse, and was begging him to spend the night in the cabin. —There is plenty of room, see, don't be an idiot. Things were moved, suitcases were moved from the area between the sink and the wall. —My pillow and both my blankets are yours. I demand you stay. Try not to be a lunatic. The demurrers, the grateful, less frantic but louder, drunker refusals were laced with profuse, impersonal apologies. Excuse me, all of you, pardon this mad, drunken, ill-considered debate between friends, forgive the senseless shouting that deprives you of sleep, and all at once, *alors, bon,* a new wonderful silence came to the cabin. The voices trailed down the hall. From above now safely issued an imprecation, a fat man's groan, a remark on the absence of luck and the healing powers of sleep, a click, and the cabin became a crypt, hymn to silent darkness. By comparison. The engine throbbed and the light filtered in from the hall and (it sounded like) loose metal balls rolled and clattered in the walls and it did not matter anyway—sleep was a myth, and he had to go to the toilet. He sat up and rubbed his eyes. His plastic suitcase lay on the red-haired fellow's bed, a nice blue piece in its time, its metal skeleton poking through its ruined sides, its zipper cranky now, precariously placed atop the man's own. The citizen's pillow and blankets were on the floor. Now *that* was the limit, tampering with private property, and he snatched up his suitcase and shoved it under his bed. Then he slipped into his shoes and went to the toilet. He was gone about two or three minutes. On his return someone moved about the cabin. He saw poorly without his glasses, which were tucked safely in his jacket pocket on the shelf next to his bed, and he mumbled a greeting to the man bound for Madrid, realizing his mistake even before the narrow, eager face pushed into his, and the conspiratorial hand gripped his arm: "*Écoute . . .*" Wordlessly, roughly, he disengaged himself, pain and disgust clear on his face in the flickering light, slipped quickly out of his shoes and took possession of his bed. "*Pardon,*" the citizen said (what had he done? stepped on the body below?), thudding into the upper berth, dropping his suitcase to the floor. For some seconds there was the silence of the engines and the silence of the metal objects clacking in the walls. Then the noise began, the earlier impossible sounds insanely magnified: the keys he jangled were bells, the voice in which he spoke was meant for thousands; now too he discovered a musicality, a pernicious, perfect whistling through Spanish love songs, and now too he opened, and gazed out, and slammed shut and re-opened the porthole.

The fat man groaned, an equivocal sound which could have been made in his sleep. He could no more be asleep than the redhead himself. Hearing the guarded protest from above, he wondered if it were more or less hypocritical than his own paralyzed pondering on the possibility of changing cabins—which he would not act upon for fear of inciting the citizen and the difficulty in explaining matters to the people in charge if he had known where on this disorganized tub to find them—he decided no, the groan was not more hypocritical; he therefore fixed on an arbitrary, undefined breaking point (five thousand bilingual words? six or seven well-whistled airs? within these limits the citizen could tire; madmen sleep) reaching which he would spring from the bed and say listen here, you, it's time to write 30 to this antisocial crap, or he would say nothing but pick up his Olivetti and his bag and seek refuge through the reeking corridor in another cabin. So he lay still in his cradle while the old ship nosed toward the mainland, creasing the flannels and the drip-dry shirt, figuratively counting the words.

The citizen's remarks were in the main unkind. Ibizencos were a narrow, bitter people. Alicante was a joke of a town. Spain was in sad condition and a franco, a new franco, was worth twelve pesetas, no more. Twelve pesetas make a franc. *Franco vale doce pesetas.* His French was fluent, Spanish nearly so. His whistling was almost professional. What he saw when he looked from the porthole might have been beautiful. Most interesting of all to contemplate was the distress of the others, the cautious groaner, the Madrid-bound sufferer in silence. Forewarned is forearmed. They had had no notion they would spend the endless night with a screwloose citizen of the world.

But when the man fell silent, and remained silent, he was nothing if not grateful. He looked at his watch in the dimness and read twelve-fifteen. It was not as late as he thought. To sleep from one to seven, no more, would render unnecessary his elaborate phony compromise —hot bath, huge meal, nap in the sun—six hours' uninterrupted sleep was all he asked of God and bedlam and his body. Yawning silently he turned to the wall.

"No bueno."

It was almost a whisper. The sounds of moving about, dropping to the floor, were strangely muffled, as if in consideration for people asleep. Even the light clicked on gently, and since he could not now see the light (his face to the wall) he refused to acknowledge any of it, the sounds or the light or the wild beating of his heart.

Above him the curtains screeched apart. —Sir, I would like to talk with you. . . .

—No, no, please, I want to sleep, the fat man cried. I have to sleep.

"Ah. Pardon. Mil pardons."

The curtain clattered shut, and the tap ran. The water, on full blast, smashed into the basin. Slowly, soundlessly, he turned over onto his back. The water ran. Slowly, silently he brought his eye to the crack between the curtains at the instant the curtain dissolved and left him face to face with his tormentor.

"De Gaulle is excellent leader, do you not think, *journaliste?*"

"Yes. Yes."

"Listen to me carefully. . . . I have much information of de Gaulle."

"I am not interested. *No me interesa.* Why don't you go to bed and let other people do the same?" and again, with an arm, blocked his eyes. The curtain remained open. The piercing whistle rode over the splashing sounds. He opened his eyes. The citizen stood at the basin, combing his hair. The citizen stared into the mirror above the washstand and the bright, eager eyes met his own, he knew, although without his glasses he could not really see. The torrent ceased. The whistling stopped. The redhead brought his face up close to the mirror and gripped his hair.

"I speak English! Americans hypocrites! Filthy American *journaliste* hypocrites!" More came in a garbled German and rapid French he was content not to understand. He pulled the curtain to, but the halves did not meet, and he saw the citizen approach his bed and kneel by his bed, still talking. He did not move. There was a scraping sound, and his suitcase suddenly appeared in the middle of the floor of the cabin. The redhead straightened and shut the light.

"*Bon. Bon. Me voy. Adiós. Buenas noches.*" But he fumbled and poked some more in the dark in corners of the cabin. "*Adiós.*" In each hand he held a piece of luggage, this much was clear through the myopic fuzz as the man walked through the curtain into the corridor.

He groped for his glasses, could not find them, leaped from the bed, and stuck his head out the door. The citizen neared the stairway at the end of the corridor. He could not see what he held in his hands. His blue suitcase was there all right, he tripped over it when he went to squint down the hall, but the typewriter! He dropped to his knees and reached frantically under the bed, hand, arm, shoulder, and he touched it, shoved back against the wall by his own blue case when he rescued it from the stranger's bed and pushed it beneath his own. He looked around him in the dark, to share his relief. There were no signs of life in the other *camarotes.* He could not blame them. The man below had not been molested. The man above had been permitted to sleep. Two large suitcases stood by the washstand. It appeared the red-haired man had stolen nothing; picked up his own luggage and abandoned the cabin. Perhaps he had gone above to watch the stars. Perhaps he had gone into steerage to join his friend. What was the difference? The lunatic was gone, bag and baggage, into the unlikely world from which he came.

He was tired enough to sleep, but it took a little time. Footsteps outside, alerting him, turned out to be en route to the toilet. Stealthy noises were mostly in his mind. At last his body took charge, that fallible arbiter, and the next waking thing he remembered he would always remember.

He dreamt a grimmer, fitter ending to the small fraud in the harbor. As it had happened, they strolled slowly along the seafront, pausing to admire the scuttling sea things, invisible to most people, she had discovered in nooks and crannies in the palings of the wharves, halting longer to consider, not for the first time, the upright corpse of the cat, levitated midway in five feet of water in the corner of the harbor, astonishment in its wide, gleaming eyes, about to spring, continuing on in the balmy December morning past the sailboats and yachts and fishing smacks until they reached the wharf where the ancient, awkward rowboats were. She spotted a boy dozing in a sailboat at the end of the pier, no one else in sight, and they went over and woke him gently. The price was ten pesetas an hour. They rowed straight across the calm and clear blue stretch, shallow as a lagoon in some places, to the beach they had bicycled to the day before, then along the bank out past the lighthouse jetty to where the water darkened and rippled and roughened, becoming without transition the open sea. He bounced bravely into the black, choppy waves for a couple of yards before they both became frightened, turned with difficulty and worked the cumbersome boat back into the abrupt safety of the shallows. They shifted seats and she rowed them home. The boy was gone when they returned. Across the road was a fisherman's shack she wanted him to look into. Ten pesetas would buy four *coñacs* along the Vara del Rey, but he peered into the shack and found three old men playing cards. "*Buenos días . . .*" he began; they mumbled perfunctorily and looked away. Explanation was pointless. He shrugged, grabbed the girl's hand, and led her back toward the hotel, three times glancing stiffly over his shoulder. The cat eyed him balefully when they turned the corner. The girl hummed to herself. No one pursued.

This time the cat struck, and the furious, screaming boy closed the distance behind. As he turned to face him and pay him the girl disappeared, and the cat tore away his glasses, so he could not see the face clearly, even from three feet away. He could, however, see his hair, the flaming red of the citizen's, brilliant enough to alert the dreaming blind. From the dreamy funk came cracks of bone on bone, nothing he could hope to see any more or feel, either; the fists landed with blurred speed and painless shock out of the nightmare one wakes out of more often than into, but next he was seated in the dried vomit (at three a.m.) of the drunken Spanish sailor and scrambling backwards on his hands, away from the crimson center that pursued him on a treadmill, never more than a yard away; he stood again, moving backwards, and he dreamed for the first time in his life in Spanish (to prolong this colossal conceit), he heard himself referred to as the son of a whore, which was absurd, and about the time of the next crunching blow in the face he became aware of the butterscotch sound, the syrupy moan of naked terror, which had begun before this moment and would continue after it although he knew it was himself making it and though he would have liked to stop, and he was down in the slime again scuttling backwards on hands and bare heels and standing again, and here came speechifying murder, talking steadily into the pleading howl, a yard away as usual, and moaning, he struck a blow. It must have been a glancing left, because later, on the knuckles of the little and ring fingers of that hand were the brave half-moon cuts which were all he would salvage from New Year's Day, 1960, except his property and his life. It felt pretty good to hang one on Death, and with his own weapon too. But he was down again, and this time he knew why: somebody alert and alive had hit him in the face. Somebody had smashed him on the ears and mouth and eyes with a mace and blind and terrified or not he could see there was no help forthcoming from the cabins off the corridor. The curtains were being pulled tighter around the *camarotes* from here until the end of time.

"*Bien. Basta.* Good-by."

He saw the citizen turn, and go, but he moved backwards on his heels and hands another six feet before he stood and staggered to the stairway. Reprieved! He carried his noise with him into the second-class dining room. It was less than involuntary now, it was more than merely terror, it was louder now, the deliberate prolongation of the fruits of waking nightmare resolving into a cry for help: *Listen to this inhuman sound you sacked-out people, help me, or poorly protected as you are you'll get the same;* they were women, prone on the floor and benches and tables of the dining room, preferring this to sitting up all night in the screenless cinema of the third class, but the steward they had tipped for the privilege sat dozing at a table and he made for the white jacket and held back the sound and gasped out words: "*Hay un loco abajo, un hombre loco,*" and the steward said —All right, calm yourself, we'll go and see. But the *mayordomo* appeared from his cabin, shaking off the caul of sleep, a giant, already half dressed, who regarded him briefly and started down the stairway—the steward behind on the narrow stairs and he behind the steward. The corridor was deserted, but he sensed activity behind the curtains now; a curtain lifted just off the stairway and an old man emerged, a second steward, superfluous people both in the usual course of events on the *Jorge Segundo* in the second class because there had been no dinner and there would be no breakfast—but there they both stood in their dirty white jackets, and there coming down the empty corridor toward the foot of the stairs was the citizen of the world and he carried a blue suitcase.

The *mayordomo* stopped his progress by standing at his ease in the corridor. —This is your friend? he asked. He nodded dumbly. —Where are you going? the *mayordomo* said, and the citizen said —Above, man, above, and the *mayordomo* said —We will go with you. —No, the old steward said to him, clutching his arm, you stay here with me. Suddenly there were people, a half-dozen jamming the corridor, regarding with interest and horror the foreigner with the battered face assaying calm in bare feet and vomit-stained trousers and losing blood onto his chest from a hidden place under his chin. O, the blood, a woman said. Until that moment he had not even seen it. He regarded it with disbelief, for it came fast, dyeing the nylon as if generated by the cloth itself, and he had no idea where it came from, and he felt no incommoding pain. But the old steward brought a stool into the corridor and gripped his shoulders and sat him down, and tipped his head back and mopped his throat with a wet towel. —The doctor is coming, the old steward said. I do this as a temporary measure.

"Are you English?" a sailor said. "I speak English."

"Do you have a cigarette?"

"No. I don't smoke."

Neither the steward nor the onlookers had any tobacco. "I will find a cigarette," the sailor said.

Slowly, the corridor cleared. One or two lingered, ultracurious or insomniac. They sought information, but he was not helpful. The steward was bathing his wound. The sailor was looking for a cigarette. It was no longer urgent that the world, awake or sleeping, draw a moral from his accident.

"He has my suitcase."

"Mande?"

"El loco tiene mi maleta," he said, *containing clothing which is replaceable and notes for a novel of uncertain value. The worst that will happen he will throw it overboard from some logic of his madness. I knew a man once had his Ph.D. thesis stolen on a train to Milan. I do not appear to be crippled.*

The steward did not understand. The sailor returned with an Ideal, 5¢ for a pack of eighteen. "The madman has my suitcase," he said slowly.

"Ah? I will report this to the *mayordomo,"* the sailor said. "I go upstairs at once."

He sat there (a carton of L&M in his valise) with the yellow cigarette that would not draw, the old steward hovering concerned and useless with the towel, promising the arrival of the ship's doctor imminently, which was taking a lot upon himself because the ship had no doctor, and after a while the *mayordomo* came hugely down the stairs carrying his suitcase.

"Es la suya?"

"Si."

—You will kindly open it.

He tried, but someone, less kindly, had tried before; the zipper was torn, the clasp was jammed.

—If it is yours, you have the key.

—There is no key. I lost the key three years ago.

—There is no key?

—No.

—Then it may be opened easily.

—Someone has broken the clasp. Why must I open it?

—He says you have stolen his shoes.

The *mayordomo* looked at him shrewdly. He sat on a stool in the gangway dripping blood from his chin, his eye beginning to puff and darken, the blows already struck under and on both sides of the jaw which would make it seem for the next three weeks that his inner ears were tied to his cheeks so that chewing at all at first and then chewing with any degree of interest or speed would bring on a jerk of impossible pain much out of proportion to whatever he might have hoped for in the way of enjoyment. He was also barefoot. He could see, glancing at the *mayordomo,* that all this worked in his favor.

—I was asleep. I did not steal his shoes. He is a madman.

The *mayordomo* smiled. —There is probably some truth in that. He is upstairs now with the *guardia civil* discoursing on the stairs.

—I can't get the case open.

—Let it go for now.

The citizen descended the stairway, jaunty, eyes eager and fire-bright. He was smoking a cigarette. Behind him were two civil guards. The old steward hovered protectively. The English-speaking sailor looked interested. The young steward came down behind the *guardias.* As he moved by the stool the citizen made a pass under his chin with the cigarette, slowly and experimentally, as a child holds a match to a wingless fly. Now for many nights afterward he would lie stark awake in the Barcelona flat starting at sounds and perspiring and puzzling the mystery of sleep, for racking his memory he could not antedate his presence in the corridor, his helpless mortal presence in the corridor, as the true beginning; he could conjecture that the man struck the first, most damaging blow while he was in bed and he sprang up and out of the cabin automatically, in the interests of self-preservation, or he could hypothesize that the man shook him gently with the gentleness of the grave, said Come, come, and he went, but all he could re-create for certain was horror. (Someday, maybe, he would hire a hypnotist.) But at the moment he was no wingless fly, there was not all that difference between them, and he shot off the stool pulse pounding in his wound and was restrained by the stewards, the citizen already past him when he rose and wrong to move at all, he realized, given his station in life.

—What takes place now? the *mayordomo* said, smiling at the *guardia civil,* the one with the face of a horse, who replied,

—He has something of great importance to show us in the cabin.

—Well, good, the *mayordomo* said, I will join you in a moment.

He heard the citizen's booming voice. He turned to the sailor.

"Could you do me a favor. . . ."

"What do you like?"

"My things are in my cabin. Could you bring them here? *Una chaqueta, zapatos, una máquina de escribir.*"

"At once."

The old steward, who had followed the *mayordomo* to the cabin, returned alone, his sunken mouth stretched wide.

—You should have seen it. The *mayordomo* delivered a blow. . . .

—You didn't stop the blood, he said. I would like to see the doctor.

—Still the blood! Do not worry. He will be here any moment. I will bring a fresh dressing. The steward disappeared into his cabin, to the left of the stairway, emerging with a freshly moistened towel.

He held the towel against the wound which would be cleaned and clipped together in Alicante later that morning by a government doctor with little ado. Six days later the stitches would be removed by a government doctor in Barcelona. Chewing would remain difficult, he would be summoned to the Maritime Office and questioned on the nature and extent of his injury, in order to determine, by some medieval magic, the length of the citizen's incarceration, and he would be advised by the American Consulate not to sue. That would end it. He accepted the steward's pottering attention out of politeness and because the towel might do something toward stanching the blood.

—The scream was monstrous, the old steward said.

The women, the sailor, and the two stewards remained in the corridor.

—It woke us all up, one of the women said.

—When I heard the scream I thought it was over, the old steward said. I did not even move from my bed. Once between Las Canarias and Cadiz there was a similar scream and a throat had been cut while its owner slept much in the same way as here. It is a terrible scream. Only one thought, the Italian word *finito,* ran through my mind.

—The bleeding has stopped, he said.

He was about to catch a last glimpse of the citizen. The procession moved down the corridor, but his back was to it. The steward faced it. The old man almost lifted him from the stool and pushed him into his own cabin. The old man quickly pulled the curtain, but not all the way. Down the hall they came, the *mayordomo,* the horse-faced *guardia civil,* the citizen, a second guard. The citizen was the citizen of a world the size of a pingpong ball, but his voice was unbroken, still unwinding. His nose was crushed bloody pulp, all over his face, and around his waist and throat were ropes of incongruous thickness, to drop an anchor by, which the second *guardia civil* held and manipulated, and stopped the citizen's progress at the foot of the stairway.

—Remove your trousers.

—The filthy Madrid fascists who misunderstand de Gaulle . . .

His head jerked backward.

—You will take off your trousers.

The redhead bent and with much effort, and briefly silent, removed his trousers. He worked them laboriously over his shoes, exposing white drawers and thin white legs, straightened and saw him peering from between the hastily drawn curtains. "Hypocrite!" he yelled, and began to curse, in Spanish and French, as the guard behind prodded him up the stairway. The old steward did all but bring the back of his hand to his mouth. He pulled the curtain completely shut and he said —Do not listen. Pay no heed. Refuse to hear him. Do not remember, as the sounds died out up the stairway.

He parted the curtains. The young steward smiled at him.

—Who is he?

—A lunatic.

—Is he French or Spanish?

—He is too crazy to be Spanish. They think he is Algerian, but he threw his luggage into the sea with his identification inside. Nobody knows.

—He threw his own bags overboard?

—So it appears. Do you not think you should go back to bed?

—I'm not tired. Could you bring some *coñac?* The young steward looked helplessly at the old steward, who shook his head. —The pantry is closed. It is impossible to get brandy now. Perhaps in the morning . . . If you had seen the blow the *mayordomo* inflicted. . . .

"*Fuck* the blow," he said. —Where is the doctor? My suit is ruined. My watch is destroyed.

—All will be taken care of when we dock, the young steward said. Don't upset yourself. The Company will take you at once to the hospital and clean your suit and pay for your watch. Now you should try to sleep.

—I'll sit upstairs awhile.

He put on his shoes and socks, he picked up his suitcase and his typewriter and jacket and went upstairs. On the floor and on benches and tables the classless people wrestled with sleep. He was fairly quiet. He fought the suitcase open on a vacant table and extracted a pack of cigarettes. The young steward came up and joined him. They puffed for a time in semi-darkness. There began the sharp, steady throbbing in his ear.

—You were asleep? the young steward said.

He nodded.

—He is definitely insane. You are very lucky. He used only his keys.

—Keys?

—He held them protruding between the fingers of his fist, as (the young man shook his head) he illustrated for the *mayordomo.*

He derived comfort from this information more useful still in weeks to come, flailing up from sleep with the yell on his lips beside the poor girl in the double bed, staring twice at redheads on crowded sunlit streets, heartsick peering through the aperture when the porter rang each day at noon to bring the mail. No wonder. Not merely shocked from sleep by a madman, but a madman armed; that keys were not lethal was the measure of his luck (throat not cut, loins not slashed); that they did greater damage than bare fists was demonstrated by the long jagged scar on his jaw.

—You speak Spanish?

He turned to the civil guard. —Some.

—It is necessary to ask some questions.

His nationality, his marital status, the date of his entry into Spain, his future plans, his occupation, his address, the nature of his quarrel with the citizen, the extent of their acquaintance, all came into question. He said that he had never seen the man before he entered the cabin; there had been no words between them; he had been asleep when the attack occurred; previously the man had kept all other occupants of the cabin awake by whistling and talking and switching on the light and playing with his keys. He mentioned also the citizen's dispute with his French friend. He did not mention the citizen's opinion of Americans nor did he dwell on his own refusal (a reasonable, sensible refusal: a man preferred sleep to intercourse with the unwashed insane) to treat the citizen kindly. Yet that worried him now; he was at fault; you owed the nearest lunatic, on many counts, a measure of civility.

—You're traveling alone?

—My fiancée is with me.

—And where is she?

—Below, asleep.

—The girl is also North American?

—She is Swedish.

—It will be necessary to ask her some questions.

—She is asleep. She has nothing to do with this.

—Where does she sleep?

—In the cabin next to mine.

—Which bed?

—The upper, near the door. There is no need to wake her.

The guard disappeared below.

—Is there no coffee either? he asked the young steward.

—Not until six. What time is it now?

—My watch is broken.

—They do not open the pantry until six. I am very sorry.

He looked sorry. He looked sorrier at six, when there could be nothing until seven, and at seven, when the pantry would not be open until seven-thirty, and at seven-twenty-five he disappeared, as two dozen second-class passengers grumbled for coffee. He returned with three cups of coffee shortly before eight. One of these (since the others had begun to disembark) he drank himself, and the two remaining went to him and Ingalill.

—Why must he question my fiancée?

—He is the law. He questions everybody.

She came up the stairs finally, blinking, disheveled, saw him seated there in his spattered shirt with his battered face, and she began to cry. When he saw her last she effused a child's pure joy that enhanced her loveliness, and now she was a kid lorn and scared, no relation to the child before. Poor thing. An entire kindergarten, joyful and terrified.

He soothed her; he knew how bad he looked. He'd seen in a mirror in the old steward's cabin. The bumps swelled on his cheek and forehead, the eye had begun to close, the wound beneath the chin still bled, but he was recognizable, she'd get used to it. It hurt his ears to talk, so he gave it up, and stroked her hand.

"I wasn't asleep when he came in," she said. "He put on the light and looked in all the wrong beds first. He ordered me to dress and come outside. As soon as he came in the door I knew something terrible had happened to you. Those horrible yells. I knew they were you."

"Let's forget the yells."

"He asked a thousand questions, but he wouldn't say what was wrong. I thought you were dead. When I started up here I thought you were dead."

"He didn't have to wake you."

"It's better that he did."

"I feel so bad," she said after a while. "So rotten and empty."

"Try to sleep for an hour or two. There's no point in your staying here."

"Your shirt . . . all that blood . . ."

He looked down at his shirt. "I'll change it." He opened the suitcase and took out a red, short-sleeved sport shirt, a gift earlier in the year from his younger sister on his twenty-seventh birthday. It was much too loud, and he wore it only at the beach. "I'll put this on."

"Why did he hit you?"

"I told you, no reason. He's out of his mind."

The *mayordomo* came up the stairs and paused at the entrance to his cabin.

—When it commenced, you were asleep?

—Yes.

—A rough awakening. He smiled. —But you now may sleep in earnest. Your friend is secure in another part of the ship. He's unlikely to bother you.

"You broke his nose, you fat prick."

"Buenas noches," said the *mayordomo.*

"Buenas noches," said the young steward.

She sat with him a while, querulous and numb. Finally he got her to leave. The young steward slept again with his head on his arms and the women slept on the floor and benches and he was alone now with the chimeras: the chimeras had red hair and had burst their ropes. They bounded up the stairway, crashed through the heavy doors leading from the deck, they were every creak and footstep on a ship soldered with creaks and footsteps. At last he picked up his suitcase and typewriter and struggled down the stairs back into his cabin. He lay there for fifteen minutes between the fat man's snores and the light from the passage, waiting for the citizen to dive through the curtain. Had there been a door to lock he might even have slept. He returned upstairs with his baggage and sat at the table. Soon a thin, dark man entered from below, nodded, and sat at the table.

—You were unable to sleep just now?

—What?

—I occupy the bed across from yours. Just now I heard you come in, and leave.

—I was attacked in the cabin not long ago. Perhaps you heard the noise. But then, you and the other are heavy sleepers.

—I saw the fight in the corridor.

—Fight?

—I saw you and the other. I thought it was a drunken quarrel, like the earlier one.

—That was not me earlier. That was someone else. I was asleep. I was attacked in bed.

—As I have heard. Are you badly hurt?

—I don't know.

—May I see? I am a doctor.

He tilted his head back and the doctor gently fingered the wound.

—It is not bad. It is not good, but not bad.

—There's a sharp pain in my ears.

—Can you hear?

—Yes.

—It is not serious.

—How did the fight begin?

—I don't know. I heard the sounds, got up, and saw you in the corridor.

The doctor remained a while longer, sympathetic, but shedding no light. At last the doctor excused himself. He passed the girl on the stairway.

"I can't sleep," she said. "I'd rather sit here with you."

"What time is it?"

"Half-past five. Two and a half more hours."

"If there was only something to drink . . ."

They missed the dawn. Morning came, passengers woke, dressed, gathered in the lounge to wait for the coffee that never came. He was the object of many stares, which he ignored. He was lucky to have the girl to seem to occupy him. The old steward told the story tirelessly, highlighting the eerie moans and the magnitude of the *mayordomo*'s blow.

"You look like you've been in a traffic accident," she said.

"Feel like it."

"You look very tough."

"I am. I should be dead now. Once, between the Canaries and Cadiz, he cut a man's throat."

"Who?"

"The madman on the boat. He makes every run."

"What?"

"You're losing your tan, Ingalill. Alicante will do you good."

"I'm afraid to stay in Alicante. I think we should go on to Valencia, or straight back to Barcelona."

"We'll stay awhile."

—How are you feeling? the guard said.

—As I look.

—You will not disembark with the rest. You will come first briefly to the vestibule to sign a complaint.

—May I finish my coffee?

—Of course. You are not a prisoner.

They were in Alicante. The morning sun poured into the harbor. Gray-green mountains rose behind the city. The *Jorge Segundo* must have radioed ahead, for scores of police and heavily armed *guardia civil* milled around at dockside. That was clever, he thought, *un franco vale* fifteen *pesetas, por lo menos;* they would certainly contain one wild man with that army.

A porter boarded the ship, advertising a third-class hotel. He sent the girl with the porter. Talking with the police and seeing the doctor might take some time. He took the name and address of the hotel and handed his typewriter to Ingalill. She followed the porter off the boat. He went to the captain's office in the stern, the area thickest with police.

The chief of police, a large, gentle man, presented him with a document which he signed after a quick, fruitless attempt to read. He stood against the wall in the vestibule. To his right was the captain's office, where he could see the captain conferring with a gaudily dressed civil guard. From behind the curtain to his left issued unregenerate comments on the Iberian scene.

"Arriba España, viva España," said the familiar voice, Up Spain. *"Franco! Franco! Franco! Vive de Gaulle."* C——, c——, and l—— are components of the *guardia civil.* There was much of astrologic interest, and some whistling. He did not sound like a man with a broken nose. The two *guardia* who had, luckily, made the crossing, had been replaced by two others outside the cabin. The new pair exchanged smiles. He nodded, when one of them brought a circling finger to his three-cornered hat, indicating the state of the citizen's faculties. He had confronted the citizen for the last time in his waking life, and he did not wish it otherwise. But he wished he were invisible. Not to gloat, in order to believe. Hearing was believing, the presence of the police, his raw, tautening face, the moan that still sounded in his ears was believing, but he wanted to see, to inspect the trussed redhead one more time.

The citizen began to shout obscenely. One of the guards sadly shook his head, unslung his rifle, and entered the cabin. *"Hola!"* the citizen said. Hello and good night. There was no more noise. The guard stepped back into the vestibule. He smiled sheepishly. —He is asleep now, he said, *"El duerme bien."*

A tap, a nap. In handling the criminal insane one meets the need for applied brutality. This is the murderous world now. It pays to befriend the law, as well as the madman. Smile often and be a good listener. Stay clear of politics. He was sick and tired, he wanted to see a doctor and go to the hotel. He accosted the chief of police.

—Do you need me here?

—No . . . no. How long will you be in Alicante?

—A day or two.

—Where will you be staying?

—Here. He produced the card he had taken from the porter.

—Good. I want nothing more from you. But you will have to speak briefly with the Civil Guard.

—Your passport, a tall, gray, uniformed man said, waggling his fingers. The *guardia* did not look at him. He fumbled in his jacket and trouser pockets for his passport.

—Come, your passport!

He produced it at last, and the man laboriously copied the information it held.

—The names of your parents.

—Charles Seth and Eve Lillian.

—You will write those here. How long have you known the man inside?

—I never saw him before the boat.

—That is not what he says.

—He is a madman.

—That is your opinion. He says you quarreled over a girl.

—There was no quarrel. I was asleep and he attacked me.

—That is not what he says.

—He is mad, the chief of police said. It is obvious.

—He is perhaps not so mad as he seems. He says he knows your sister.

His sister was nineteen now, a sophomore at Smith.

—It is a lie.

—So you say. We will find out, you can be sure. Go now.

—I'm waiting for the doctor. They said I would be taken to a doctor.

—Then wait for the doctor. Do as you please.

This led him to believe that there would be no doctor, let alone dry-cleaning or repair for the watch, but he waited for twenty minutes, standing on the deck apart from the thronging officials and ignoring stone-faced the workers and merchants who boarded the ship and stared at him frankly and curiously (although he had but recently revalued courtesy). A doctor came at last, to inspect the citizen. He emerged from the cabin and pronounced the citizen in good health. He held his breath, expecting the citizen to reappear, but he did not. When the doctor moved by him, down the gangplank, he decided to make his own way to a hospital. But the chief of police stopped the doctor, talked to him briefly, and the doctor turned and beckoned and led him to a taxi. A third man, a dock official, joined them. He had once been an ordinary seaman and traveled all over the world, he said, but particularly enjoyed New York. An old man with a smoker's cough, the doctor sat up front with the driver, smoking and saying nothing. He seemed bored. It was as the victim suspected; the citizen made every run, the doctor met every boat.

When they arrived at his office, the doctor clipped two metal prongs into his chin and covered them with gauze, free of charge. The dock official treated him to coffee in a nearby café. He ordered a croissant, he was very hungry, but he could not chew it. A short, dark man entered the café whom the dock official knew. One side of the man's face was completely hidden by bandages. The officer recounted the shipboard mishap to his friend. Where he lacked information, or seriously erred, the victim filled in. Told this way, the story had its lighter side, but the short man listened quietly with rising indignation.

—I would have killed him had he done it to me.

—I was asleep, he defended himself.

—That is the point. If he had woken me that way I would have killed him.

He shrugged. He put it down to hyperbole, the Latin temperament. But afterward, when he considered, it was the only line to take. He would murder the citizen the next time they met.

The Light of the World

Ernest Hemingway

When he saw us come in the door the bartender looked up and then reached over and put the glass covers on the two free-lunch bowls.

"Give me a beer," I said. He drew it, cut the top off with the spatula and then held the glass in his hand. I put the nickel on the wood and he slid the beer toward me.

"What's yours?" he said to Tom.

"Beer."

He drew that beer and cut it off and when he saw the money he pushed the beer across to Tom.

"What's the matter?" Tom asked.

The bartender didn't answer him. He just looked over our heads and said, "What's yours?" to a man who'd come in.

"Rye," the man said. The bartender put out the bottle and glass and a glass of water.

Tom reached over and took the glass off the free-lunch bowl. It was a bowl of pickled pigs' feet and there was a wooden thing that worked like a scissors, with two wooden forks at the end to pick them up with.

"No," said the bartender and put the glass cover back on the bowl. Tom held the wooden scissors fork in his hand. "Put it back," said the bartender.

"You know where," said Tom.

The bartender reached a hand forward under the bar, watching us both. I put fifty cents on the wood and he straightened up.

"What was yours?" he said.

"Beer," I said, and before he drew the beer he uncovered both the bowls.

"Your goddam pigs' feet stink," Tom said, and spit what he had in his mouth on the floor. The bartender didn't say anything. The man who had drunk the rye paid and went out without looking back.

"You stink yourself," the bartender said. "All you punks stink."

"He says we're punks," Tommy said to me.

"Listen," I said. "Let's get out."

"You punks clear the hell out of here," the bartender said.

"I said we were going out," I said. "It wasn't your idea."

"We'll be back," Tommy said.

"No you won't," the bartender told him.

"Tell me how wrong he is," Tom turned to me.

"Come on," I said.

Outside it was good and dark.

"What the hell kind of place is this?" Tommy said.

"I don't know," I said. "Let's go down to the station."

We'd come in that town at one end and we were going out the other. It smelled of hides and tan bark and the big piles of sawdust. It was getting dark as we came in, and now that it was dark it was cold and the puddles of water in the road were freezing at the edges.

Down at the station there were five whores waiting for the train to come in, and six white men and four Indians. It was crowded and hot from the stove and full of stale smoke. As we came in nobody was talking and the ticket window was down.

"Shut the door, can't you!" somebody said.

I looked to see who said it. It was one of the white men. He wore stagged trousers and lumbermen's rubbers and a mackinaw shirt like the others, but he had no cap and his face was white and his hands were white and thin.

"Aren't you going to shut it?"

"Sure," I said, and shut it.

"Thank you," he said. One of the other men snickered.

"Ever interfere with a cook?" he said to me.

"No."

"You can interfere with this one," he looked at the cook. "He likes it."

The cook looked away from him holding his lips tight together.

"He puts lemon juice on his hands," the man said. "He wouldn't get them in dishwater for anything. Look how white they are."

One of the whores laughed out loud. She was the biggest whore I ever saw in my life and the biggest woman. And she had on one of those silk dresses that change colors. There were two other whores that were nearly as big but the big one must have weighed three hundred and fifty pounds. You couldn't believe she was real when you looked at her. All three had those changeable silk dresses. They sat side by side on the bench. They were huge. The other two were just ordinary looking whores, peroxide blondes.

"Look at his hands," the man said and nodded his head at the cook. The whore laughed again and shook all over.

The cook turned and said to her quickly, "You big disgusting mountain of flesh."

She just kept on laughing and shaking.

"Oh, my Christ," she said. She had a nice voice. "Oh, my sweet Christ."

The two other whores, the big ones, acted very quiet and placid as though they didn't have much sense, but they were big, nearly as big as the biggest one. They'd have both gone well over two hundred and fifty pounds. The other two were dignified.

Of the men, besides the cook and the one who talked, there were two other lumberjacks, one that listened, interested but bashful, and the other that seemed getting ready to say something, and two Swedes. Two Indians were sitting down at the end of the bench and one standing up against the wall.

The man who was getting ready to say something spoke to me very low, "Must be like getting on top of a hay mow."

I laughed and said it to Tommy.

"I swear to Christ I've never been anywhere like this," he said. "Look at the three of them." Then the cook spoke up.

"How old are you boys?"

"I'm ninety-six and he's sixty-nine," Tommy said.

"Ho! Ho! Ho!" the big whore shook with laughing. She had a really pretty voice. The other whores didn't smile.

"Oh, can't you be decent?" the cook said. "I asked just to be friendly."

"We're seventeen and nineteen," I said.

"What's the matter with you?" Tommy turned to me.

"That's all right."

"You can call me Alice," the big whore said and then she began to shake again.

"Is that your name?" Tommy asked.

"Sure," she said. "Alice. Isn't it?" she turned to the man who sat by the cook.

"Alice. That's right."

"That's the sort of name you'd have," the cook said.

"It's my real name," Alice said.

"What's the other girls' names?" Tom asked.

"Hazel and Ethel," Alice said. Hazel and Ethel smiled. They weren't very bright.

"What's your name?" I said to one of the blondes.

"Frances," she said.

"Frances what?"

"Frances Wilson. What's it to you?"

"What's yours?" I asked the other one.

"Oh, don't be fresh," she said.

"He just wants us all to be friends," the man who talked said. "Don't you want to be friends?"

"No," the peroxide one said. "Not with you."

"She's just a spitfire," the man said. "A regular little spitfire."

The one blonde looked at the other and shook her head.

"Goddamned mossbacks," she said.

Alice commenced to laugh again and to shake all over.

"There's nothing funny," the cook said. "You all laugh but there's nothing funny. You two young lads; where are you bound for?"

"Where are you going yourself?" Tom asked him.

"I want to go to Cadillac," the cook said. "Have you ever been there? My sister lives there."

"He's a sister himself," the man in the stagged trousers said.

"Can't you stop that sort of thing?" the cook asked. "Can't we speak decently?"

"Cadillac is where Steve Ketchel came from and where Ad Wolgast is from," the shy man said.

"Steve Ketchel," one of the blondes said in a high voice as though the name had pulled a trigger in her. "His own father shot and killed him. Yes, by Christ, his own father. There aren't any more men like Steve Ketchel."

"Wasn't his name Stanley Ketchel?" asked the cook.

"Oh, shut up," said the blonde. "What do you know about Steve? Stanley. He was no Stanley. Steve Ketchel was the finest and most beautiful man that ever lived. I never saw a man as clean and as white and as beautiful as Steve Ketchel. There never was a man like that. He moved just like a tiger and he was the finest, free-est spender that ever lived."

"Did you know him?" one of the men asked.

"Did I know him? Did I know him? Did I love him? You ask me that? I knew him like you know nobody in the world and I loved him like you love God. He was the greatest, finest, whitest, most beautiful man that ever lived, Steve Ketchel, and his own father shot him down like a dog."

"Were you out on the coast with him?"

"No. I knew him before that. He was the only man I ever loved."

Every one was respectful to the peroxide blonde, who said all this in a high stagey way, but Alice was beginning to shake again. I felt it sitting by her.

"You should have married him," the cook said.

"I wouldn't hurt his career," the peroxide blonde said. "I wouldn't be a drawback to him. A wife wasn't what he needed. Oh, my God, what a man he was."

"That was a fine way to look at it," the cook said. "Didn't Jack Johnson knock him out though?"

"It was a trick," Peroxide said. "That big dinge took him by surprise. He'd just knocked Jack Johnson down, the big black bastard. That nigger beat him by a fluke."

The ticket window went up and the three Indians went over to it.

"Steve knocked him down," Peroxide said. "He turned to smile at me."

"I thought you said you weren't on the coast," someone said.

"I went out just for that fight. Steve turned to smile at me and that black son of a bitch from hell jumped up and hit him by surprise. Steve could lick a hundred like that black bastard."

"He was a great fighter," the lumberjack said.

"I hope to God he was," Peroxide said. "I hope to God they don't have fighters like that now. He was like a god, he was. So white and clean and beautiful and smooth and fast and like a tiger or like lightning."

"I saw him in the moving pictures of the fight," Tom said. We were all very moved. Alice was shaking all over and I looked and saw she was crying. The Indians had gone outside on the platform.

"He was more than any husband could ever be," Peroxide said. "We were married in the eyes of God and I belong to him right now and always will and all of me is his. I don't care about my body. They can take my body. My soul belongs to Steve Ketchel. By God, he was a man."

Everybody felt terribly. It was sad and embarrassing. Then Alice, who was still shaking, spoke, "You're a dirty liar," she said in that low voice. "You never layed Steve Ketchel in your life and you know it."

"How can you say that?" Peroxide said proudly.

"I say it because it's true," Alice said. "I'm the only one here that ever knew Steve Ketchel and I come from Mancelona and I knew him there and it's true and you know it's true and God can strike me dead if it isn't true."

"He can strike me too," Peroxide said.

"This is true, true, true, and you know it. Not just made up and I know exactly what he said to me."

"What did he say?" Peroxide asked, complacently.

Alice was crying so she could hardly speak from shaking so. "He said, 'You're a lovely piece, Alice.' That's exactly what he said."

"It's a lie," Peroxide said.

"It's true," Alice said. "That's truly what he said."

"It's a lie," Peroxide said proudly.

"No, it's true, true, true, to Jesus and Mary true."

"Steve couldn't have said that. It wasn't the way he talked," Peroxide said happily.

"It's true," said Alice in her nice voice. "And it doesn't make any difference to me whether you believe it or not." She wasn't crying any more and she was calm.

"It would be impossible for Steve to have said that," Peroxide declared.

"He said it," Alice said and smiled. "And I remember when he said it and I *was* a lovely piece then exactly as he said, and right now I'm a better piece than you, you dried up old hot-water bottle."

"You can't insult me," said Peroxide. "You big mountain of pus. I have my memories."

"No," Alice said in that sweet lovely voice, "you haven't got any real memories except having your tubes out and when you started C. and M. Everything else you just read in the papers. I'm clean and you know it and men like me, even though I'm big, and you know it, and I never lie and you know it."

"Leave me with my memories," Peroxide said. "With my true, wonderful memories."

Alice looked at her and then at us and her face lost that hurt look and she smiled and she had about the prettiest face I ever saw. She had a pretty face and a nice smooth skin and a lovely voice and she was nice all right and really friendly. But my God she was big. She was as big as three women. Tom saw me looking at her and he said, "Come on. Let's go."

"Good-bye," said Alice. She certainly had a nice voice.
"Good-bye," I said.
"Which way are you boys going?" asked the cook.
"The other way from you," Tom told him.

The Last Leaf

O. Henry

In a little district west of Washington Square the streets have run crazy and broken themselves into small strips called "places." These "places" make strange angles and curves. One street crosses itself a time or two. An artist once discovered a valuable possibility in this street. Suppose a collector with a bill for paints, paper and canvas should, in traversing this route, suddenly meet himself coming back, without a cent having been paid on account!

So, to quaint old Greenwich Village the art people soon came prowling, hunting for north windows and eighteenth-century gables and Dutch attics and low rents. Then they imported some pewter mugs and a chafing dish or two from Sixth Avenue, and became a "colony."

At the top of a squatty, three-story brick Sue and Johnsy had their studio. "Johnsy" was familiar for Joanna. One was from Maine; the other from California. They had met at the *table d'hôte* of an Eighth Street "Delmonico's," and found their tastes in art, chicory salad and bishop sleeves so congenial that the joint studio resulted.

That was in May. In November a cold, unseen stranger, whom the doctors called Pneumonia, stalked about the colony, touching one here and there with his icy fingers. Over on the east side this ravager strode boldly, smiting his victims by scores, but his feet trod slowly through the maze of the narrow and moss-grown "places."

Mr. Pneumonia was not what you would call a chivalric old gentleman. A mite of a little woman with blood thinned by California zephyrs was hardly fair game for the red-fisted, short-breathed old duffer. But Johnsy he smote; and she lay, scarcely moving, on her painted iron bedstead, looking through the small Dutch window-panes at the blank side of the next brick house.

One morning the busy doctor invited Sue into the hallway with a shaggy, gray eyebrow.

"She has one chance in—let us say, ten," he said, as he shook down the mercury in his clinical thermometer. "And that chance is for her to want to live. This way people have of lining-up on the side of the undertaker makes the entire pharmacopoeia look silly. Your little lady has made up her mind that she's not going to get well. Has she anything on her mind?"

"She—she wanted to paint the Bay of Naples some day," said Sue.

"Paint?—bosh! Has she anything on her mind worth thinking about twice—a man, for instance?"

"A man?" said Sue, with a jew's-harp twang in her voice. "Is a man worth—but, no, doctor; there is nothing of the kind."

"Well, it is the weakness, then," said the doctor. "I will do all that science, so far as it may filter through my efforts, can accomplish. But whenever my patient begins to count the carriages in her funeral procession I subtract 50 percent from the curative power of medicines. If you will get her to ask one question about the new winter styles in cloak sleeves I will promise you a one-in-five chance for her, instead of one in ten."

After the doctor had gone Sue went into the workroom and cried a Japanese napkin to a pulp. Then she swaggered into Johnsy's room with her drawing board, whistling ragtime.

Johnsy lay, scarcely making a ripple under the bedclothes, with her face toward the window. Sue stopped whistling, thinking she was asleep.

She arranged her board and began a pen-and-ink drawing to illustrate a magazine story. Young artists must pave their way to Art by drawing pictures for magazine stories that young authors write to pave their way to Literature.

As Sue was sketching a pair of elegant horseshow riding trousers and a monocle on the figure of the hero, an Idaho cowboy, she heard a low sound, several times repeated. She went quickly to the bedside.

Johnsy's eyes were open wide. She was looking out the window and counting—counting backward.

"Twelve," she said, and a little later "eleven"; and then "ten," and "nine"; and then "eight" and "seven," almost together.

Sue looked solicitously out of the window. What was there to count? There was only a bare, dreary yard to be seen, and the blank side of the brick house twenty feet away. An old, old ivy vine, gnarled and decayed at the roots, climbed half way up the brick wall. The cold breath of autumn had stricken its leaves from the vine until its skeleton branches clung, almost bare, to the crumbling bricks.

"What is it, dear?" asked Sue.

"Six," said Johnsy, in almost a whisper. "They're falling faster now. Three days ago there were almost a hundred. It made my head ache to count them. But now it's easy. There goes another one. There are only five left now."

"Five what, dear? Tell your Sudie."

"Leaves. On the ivy vine. When the last one falls I must go, too. I've known that for three days. Didn't the doctor tell you?"

"Oh, I never heard of such nonsense," complained Sue, with magnificent scorn. "What have old ivy leaves to do with your getting well? And you used to love that vine, so, you naughty girl. Don't be a goosey. Why, the doctor told me this morning that your chances for getting well real soon were—let's see exactly what he said—he said the chances were ten to one! Why, that's almost as good a chance as we have in New York when we ride on the street cars or walk past a new building. Try to take some broth now, and let Sudie go back to her drawing, so she can sell the editor man with it, and buy port wine for her sick child, and pork chops for her greedy self."

"You needn't get any more wine," said Johnsy, keeping her eyes fixed out the window. "There goes another. No, I don't want any broth. That leaves just four. I want to see the last one fall before it gets dark. Then I'll go, too."

"Johnsy, dear," said Sue, bending over her, "will you promise me to keep your eyes closed, and not look out the window until I am done working? I must hand those drawings in by tomorrow. I need the light, or I would draw the shade down."

"Couldn't you draw in the other room?" asked Johnsy, coldly.

"I'd rather be here by you," said Sue. "Besides, I don't want you to keep looking at those silly ivy leaves."

"Tell me as soon as you have finished," said Johnsy, closing her eyes, and lying white and still as a fallen statue, "because I want to see the last one fall. I'm tired of waiting. I'm tired of thinking. I want to turn loose my hold on everything, and go sailing down, down, just like one of those poor, tired leaves."

"Try to sleep," said Sue. "I must call Behrman up to be my model for the old hermit miner. I'll not be gone a minute. Don't try to move 'til I come back."

Old Behrman was a painter who lived on the ground floor beneath them. He was past sixty and had a Michael Angelo's Moses beard curling down from the head of a satyr along the body of an imp. Behrman was a failure in art. Forty years he had wielded the brush without getting near enough to touch the hem of his Mistress's robe. He had been always about to paint a masterpiece, but had never yet begun it. For several years he had painted nothing except now and then a daub in the line of commerce or advertising. He earned a little by serving as a model to those young artists in the colony who could not pay the price of a professional. He drank gin to excess, and still talked of his coming masterpiece. For the rest he was a fierce little old man, who scoffed terribly at softness in any one, and who regarded himself as especial mastiff-in-waiting to protect the two young artists in the studio above.

Sue found Behrman smelling strongly of juniper berries in his dimly lighted den below. In one corner was a blank canvas on an easel that had been waiting there for twenty-five years to receive the first line of the masterpiece. She told him of Johnsy's fancy, and how she feared she would, indeed, light and fragile as a leaf herself, float away, when her slight hold upon the world grew weaker.

Old Behrman, with his red eyes plainly streaming, shouted his contempt and derision for such idiotic imaginings.

"Vass!" he cried. "Is dere people in de world mit der foolishness to die because leafs dey drop off from a confounded vine? I haf not heard of such a thing. No, I will not bose as a model for your fool hermit-dunderhead. Vy do you allow dot silly pusiness to come in der brain of her? Ach, dot poor leetle Miss Yohnsy."

"She is very ill and weak," said Sue, "and the fever has left her mind morbid and full of strange fancies. Very well, Mr. Behrman, if you do not care to pose for me, you needn't. But I think you are a horrid old—old flibbertigibbet."

"You are just like a woman!" yelled Behrman. "Who said I will not bose? Go on. I come mit you. For half an hour I haf peen trying to say dot I am ready to bose. Gott! dis is not any blace in which one so goot as Miss Yohnsy shall lie sick. Some day I vill baint a masterpiece, and ve shall all go away. Gott! yes."

Johnsy was sleeping when they went upstairs. Sue pulled the shade down to the window-sill, and motioned Behrman into the other room. In there they peered out the window fearfully at the ivy vine. Then they looked at each other for a moment without speaking. A persistent, cold rain was falling, mingled with snow. Behrman, in his old blue shirt, took his seat as the hermit miner on an upturned kettle for a rock.

When Sue awoke from an hour's sleep the next morning she found Johnsy with dull, wide-open eyes staring at the drawn green shade.

"Pull it up; I want to see," she ordered, in a whisper.

Wearily Sue obeyed.

But, lo! after the beating rain and fierce gusts of wind that had endured through the livelong night, there yet stood out against the brick wall one ivy leaf. It was the last on the vine. Still dark green near its stem, but with its serrated edges tinted with the yellow of dissolution and decay, it hung bravely from a branch some twenty feet above the ground.

"It is the last one," said Johnsy. "I thought it would surely fall during the night. I heard the wind. It will fall today, and I shall die at the same time."

"Dear, dear!" said Sue, leaning her worn face down to the pillow, "think of me, if you won't think of yourself. What would I do?"

But Johnsy did not answer. The lonesomest thing in all the world is a soul when it is making ready to go on its mysterious, far journey. The fancy seemed to possess her more strongly as one by one the ties that bound her to friendship and to earth were loosed.

The day wore away, and even through the twilight they could see the lone ivy leaf clinging to its stem against the wall. And then, with the coming of the night the north wind was again loosed, while the rain still beat against the windows and pattered down from the low Dutch eaves.

When it was light enough Johnsy, the merciless, commanded that the shade be raised.

The ivy leaf was still there.

Johnsy lay for a long time looking at it. And then she called to Sue, who was stirring her chicken broth over the gas stove.

"I've been a bad girl, Sudie," said Johnsy. "Something has made that last leaf stay there to show me how wicked I was. It is a sin to want to die. You may bring me a little broth now, and some milk with a little port in it, and—no; bring me a hand-mirror first, and then pack some pillows about me, and I will sit up and watch you cook."

An hour later she said:

"Sudie, some day I hope to paint the Bay of Naples."

The doctor came in the afternoon, and Sue had an excuse to go into the hallway as he left.

"Even chances," said the doctor, taking Sue's thin, shaking hand in his. "With good nursing you'll win. And now I must see another case I have downstairs. Behrman, his name is—some kind of an artist, I believe. Pneumonia, too. He is an old, weak man, and the attack is acute. There is no hope for him; but he goes to the hospital today to be made more comfortable."

The next day the doctor said to Sue: "She's out of danger. You've won. Nutrition and care now—that's all."

And that afternoon Sue came to the bed where Johnsy lay, contentedly knitting a very blue and very useless woollen shoulder scarf, and put one arm around her, pillows and all.

"I have something to tell you, white mouse," she said. "Mr. Behrman died of pneumonia today in the hospital. He was ill only two days. The janitor found him on the morning of the first day in his room downstairs helpless with pain. His shoes and clothing were wet through and icy cold. They couldn't imagine where he had been on such a dreadful night. And then they found a lantern, still lighted, and a ladder that had been dragged from its place, and some scattered brushes, and a palette with green and yellow colors mixed on it, and —look out the window, dear, at the last ivy leaf on the wall. Didn't you wonder why it never fluttered or moved when the wind blew? Ah, darling, it's Behrman's masterpiece—he painted it there the night that the last leaf fell."

A Bundle of Letters

Henry James

I

September 5th, 1879

From Miss Miranda Hope, *in Paris, to* Mrs Abraham C. Hope, *at Bangor, Maine*

My Dear Mother,

I have kept you posted as far as Tuesday week last, and, although my letter will not have reached you yet, I will begin another, before my news accumulates too much. I am glad you show my letters round in the family, for I like them all to know what I am doing, and I can't write to every one, though I try to answer all reasonable expectations. But there are a great many unreasonable ones, as I suppose you know—not yours, dear mother, for I am bound to say that you never required of me more than was natural. You see you are reaping your reward: I write to you before I write to any one else.

There is one thing, I hope—that you don't show any of my letters to William Platt. If he wants to see any of my letters, he knows the right way to go to work. I wouldn't have him see one of these letters, written for circulation in the family, for anything in the world. If he wants one for himself, he has got to write to me first. Let him write to me first, and then I will see about answering him. You can show him this if you like; but if you show him anything more, I will never write to you again.

I told you in my last about my farewell to England, my crossing the channel, and my first impressions of Paris. I have thought a great deal about that lovely England since I left it, and all the famous historic scenes I visited; but I have come to the conclusion that it is not a country in which I should care to reside. The position of woman does not seem to me at all satisfactory, and that is a point, you know, on which I feel very strongly. It seems to me that in England they play a very faded-out part, and those with whom I conversed had a kind of depressed and humiliated tone; a little dull, tame look, as if they were used to being snubbed and bullied, which made me want to give them a good shaking. There are a great many people—and a great many things, too—over here that I should like to perform that operation upon. I should like to shake the starch out of some of them, and the dust out of the others. I know fifty girls in Bangor that come much more up to my notion of the stand a truly noble woman should take, than those young ladies in England. But they had a most lovely way of speaking (in England), and the men are *remarkably handsome.* (You can show this to William Platt, if you like.)

I gave you my first impressions of Paris, which quite came up to my expectations, much as I had heard and read about it. The objects of interest are extremely numerous, and the climate is remarkably cheerful and sunny. I should say the position of woman here was considerably higher, though by no means coming up to the American standard. The manners of the people are in some respects extremely peculiar, and I feel at last that I am indeed in *foreign parts.* It is, however, a truly elegant city (very superior to New York), and I have spent a great deal of time in visiting the various monuments and palaces. I won't give you an account of all my wanderings, though I have been most indefatigable; for I am keeping, as I told you before, a most *exhaustive* journal, which I will allow you the *privilege* of reading on my return to Bangor. I am getting on remarkably well, and I must say I am sometimes surprised at my universal good fortune. It only shows what a little energy and common-sense will accomplish. I have discovered none of these objections to a young lady travelling in Europe by herself, of which we heard so much before I left, and I don't expect I ever shall, for I certainly don't mean to look for them. I know what I want and I always manage to get it.

I have received a great deal of politeness—some of it really most pressing, and I have experienced no drawbacks whatever. I have made a great many pleasant acquaintances in travelling round (both ladies and gentlemen), and had a great many most interesting talks. I have collected a great deal of information, for which I refer you to my journal. I assure you my journal is going to be a splendid thing. I do just exactly as I do in Bangor, and I find I do perfectly right; and at any rate, I don't care if I don't. I didn't come to Europe to lead a merely conventional life; I could do that at Bangor. You know I never *would* do it at Bangor, so it isn't likely I am going to make myself miserable over here. So long as I accomplish what I desire, and make my money hold out, I shall regard the thing as a success. Sometimes I feel rather lonely, especially in the evening; but I generally manage to interest myself in something or in some one. In the evening I usually read up about the objects of interest I have visited during the day, or I post up my journal. Sometimes I go to the theatre; or else I play the piano in the public parlour. The public parlour at the hotel isn't much; but the piano is better than that fearful old thing at the Sebago House. Sometimes I go downstairs and talk to the lady who keeps the books —a French lady, who is remarkably polite. She is very pretty, and always wears a black dress, with the most beautiful fit; she speaks a little English; she tells me she had to learn it in order to converse with the Americans who come in such numbers to this hotel. She has given me a great deal of information about the position of woman in France, and much of it is very encouraging. But she has told me at the same time some things that I should not like to write to you (I am hesitating even about putting them into my journal), especially if my letters are to be handed round in the family. I assure you they appear to talk about things here that we never think of mentioning at Bangor, or even of thinking about. She seems to think she can tell me everything, because I told her I was travelling for general culture. Well, I *do* want to know so much that it seems sometimes as if I wanted to know everything; and yet there are some things that I think I don't want to know. But, as a general thing, everything is intensely interesting; I don't mean only everything that this French lady tells me, but everything I see and hear for myself. I feel really as if I should gain all I desire.

I meet a great many Americans, who, as a general thing, I must say, are not as polite to me as the people over here. The people over here—especially the gentlemen—are much more what I should call *attentive.* I don't know whether Americans are more *sincere;* I haven't yet made up my mind about that. The only drawback I experience is when Americans sometimes express surprise that I should be travelling round alone; so you see it doesn't come from Europeans. I always have my answer ready: "For general culture, to acquire the languages, and to see Europe for myself;" and that generally seems to satisfy them. Dear mother, my money holds out very well, and it *is* real interesting.

II

September 16th

From the Same to the Same

Since I last wrote to you I have left that hotel, and come to live in a French family. It's a kind of boarding-house combined with a kind of school; only it's not like an American boarding-house, nor like an American school either. There are four or five people here that have come to learn the language—not to take lessons, but to have an opportunity for conversation. I was very glad to come to such a place, for I had begun to realise that I was not making much progress with the French. It seemed to me that I should feel ashamed to have spent two months in Paris, and not to have acquired more insight into the language. I had always heard so much of French conversation, and I found I was having no more opportunity to practise it than if I had remained at Bangor. In fact, I used to hear a great deal more at Bangor, from those French Canadians that came down to cut the ice, than I saw I should ever hear at that hotel. The lady that kept the books seemed to want so much to talk to me in English (for the sake of practice, too, I suppose), that I couldn't bear to let her know I didn't like it. The chambermaid was Irish, and all the waiters were German, so that I never heard a word of French spoken. I suppose you might hear a great deal in the shops; only, as I don't buy anything—I prefer to spend my money for purposes of culture—I don't have that advantage.

I have been thinking some of taking a teacher, but I am well acquainted with the grammar already, and teachers always keep you bothering over the verbs. I was a good deal troubled, for I felt as if I didn't want to go away without having, at least, got a general idea of French conversation. The theatre gives you a good deal of insight, and, as I told you in my last, I go a good deal to places of amusement. I find no difficulty whatever in going to such places alone, and am always treated with the politeness which, as I told you before, I encounter everywhere. I see plenty of other ladies alone (mostly French), and they generally seem to be enjoying themselves as much as I. But, at the theatre, every one talks so fast that I can scarcely make out what they say; and, besides, there are a great many vulgar expressions which it is unnecessary to learn. But it was the theatre, nevertheless, that put me on the track. The very next day after I wrote to you last,

I went to the Palais Royal, which is one of the principal theatres in Paris. It is very small, but it is very celebrated, and in my guide-book it is marked with *two stars*, which is a sign of importance attached only to *first-class* objects of interest. But after I had been there half an hour I found I couldn't understand a single word of the play, they gabbled it off so fast, and they made use of such peculiar expressions. I felt a good deal disappointed and troubled—I was afraid I shouldn't gain all I had come for. But while I was thinking it over—thinking what I *should* do—I heard two gentlemen talking behind me. It was between the acts, and I couldn't help listening to what they said. They were talking English, but I guess they were Americans.

"Well," said one of them, "it all depends on what you are after. I'm after French; that's what I'm after."

"Well," said the other, "I'm after Art."

"Well," said the first, "I'm after Art too; but I'm after French most."

Then, dear mother, I am sorry to say the second one swore a little. He said, "Oh, damn French!"

"No, I won't damn French," said his friend. "I'll acquire it—that's what I'll do with it. I'll go right into a family."

"What family'll you go into?"

"Into some French family. That's the only way to do—to go to some place where you can talk. If you're after Art, you want to stick to the galleries; you want to go right through the Louvre, room by room; you want to take a room a day, or something of that sort. But, if you want to acquire French, the thing is to look out for a family. There are lots of French families here that take you to board and teach you. My second cousin—that young lady I told you about—she got in with a crowd like that, and they booked her right up in three months. They just took her right in and they talked to her. That's what they do to you; they set you right down and they talk *at* you. You've got to understand them; you can't help yourself. That family my cousin was with has moved away somewhere, or I should try and get in with them. They were very smart people, that family; after she left, my cousin corresponded with them in French. But I mean to find some other crowd, if it takes a lot of trouble!"

I listened to all this with great interest, and when he spoke about his cousin I was on the point of turning around to ask him the address of the family that she was with; but the next moment he said they had moved away; so I sat still. The other gentleman, however, didn't seem to be affected in the same way as I was.

"Well," he said, "you may follow up that if you like; I mean to follow up the pictures. I don't believe there is ever going to be any considerable demand in the United States for French; but I can promise you that in about ten years there'll be a big demand for Art! And it won't be temporary either."

That remark may be very true, but I don't care anything about the demand; I want to know French for its own sake. I don't want to think I have been all this while without having gained an insight. . . . The very next day, I asked the lady who kept the books at the hotel whether she knew of any family that could take me to board and give me the benefit of their conversation. She instantly threw up her hands, with several little shrill cries (in their French way, you know), and told me that her dearest friend kept a regular place of that kind. If she had known I was looking out for such a place she would have told me before; she had not spoken of it herself, because she didn't wish to injure the hotel by being the cause of my going away. She told me this was a charming family, who had often received American ladies (and others as well) who wished to follow up the language, and she was sure I should be delighted with them. So she gave me their address, and offered to go with me to introduce me. But I was in such a hurry that I went off by myself, and I had no trouble in finding these good people. They were delighted to receive me, and I was very much pleased with what I saw of them. They seemed to have plenty of conversation, and there will be no trouble about that.

I came here to stay about three days ago, and by this time I have seen a great deal of them. The price of board struck me as rather high; but I must remember that a quantity of conversation is thrown in. I have a very pretty little room—without any carpet, but with seven mirrors, two clocks, and five curtains. I was rather disappointed after I arrived to find that there are several other Americans here for the same purpose as myself. At least there are three Americans and two English people; and also a German gentleman. I am afraid, therefore, our conversation will be rather mixed, but I have not yet time to judge. I try to talk with Madame de Maisonrouge all I can (she is the lady of the house, and the *real* family consists only of herself and her two daughters). They are all most elegant, interesting women, and I am sure we shall become intimate friends. I will write you more about them in my next. Tell William Platt I don't care what he does.

III

September 21st

From Miss Violet Ray, *in Paris, to* Miss Agnes Rich, *in New York*

We had hardly got here when father received a telegram saying he would have to come right back to New York. It was for something about his business—I don't know exactly what; you know I never understand those things, never want to. We had just got settled at the hotel, in some charming rooms, and mother and I, as you may imagine, were greatly annoyed. Father is extremely fussy, as you know, and his first idea, as soon as he found he should have to go back, was that we should go back with him. He declared he would never leave us in Paris alone, and that we must return and come out again. I don't know what he thought would happen to us; I suppose he thought we should be too extravagant. It's father's theory that we are always running up bills, whereas a little observation would show him that we wear the same old *rags* FOR MONTHS. But father has no observation; he has nothing but theories. Mother and I, however, have, fortunately, a great deal of *practice,* and we succeeded in making him understand that we wouldn't budge from Paris, and that we would rather be chopped into small pieces than cross that dreadful ocean again. So, at last, he decided to go back alone, and to leave us here for three months. But, to show you how fussy he is, he refused to let us stay at the hotel, and insisted that we should go into a *family.* I don't know what put such an idea into his head, unless it was some advertisement that he saw in one of the American papers that are published here.

There are families here who receive American and English people to live with them, under the pretence of teaching them French. You may imagine what people they are—I mean the families themselves. But the Americans who choose this peculiar manner of seeing Paris must be actually just as bad. Mother and I were horrified, and declared that *main force* should not remove us from the hotel. But father has a way of arriving at his ends which is more efficient than violence. He worries and fusses; he "nags," as we used to say at school; and, when mother and I are quite worn out, his triumph is assured. Mother is usually worn out more easily than I, and she ends by siding with father; so that, at last, when they combine their forces against poor little me, I have to succumb. You should have heard the way father went on about this "family" plan; he talked to every one he saw about it; he used to go round to the banker's and talk to the people there—the people in the post-office; he used to try and exchange ideas about it with the waiters at the hotel. He said it would be more safe, more respectable, more economical; that I should perfect my French; that mother would learn how a French household is conducted; that he should feel more easy, and five hundred reasons more. They were none of them good, but that made no difference. It's all humbug, his talking about economy, when every one knows that business in America has completely recovered, that the prostration is all over, and that *immense fortunes* are being made. We have been economising for the last five years, and I supposed we came abroad to reap the benefits of it.

As for my French, it is quite as perfect as I want it to be. (I assure you I am often surprised at my own fluency, and, when I get a little more practice in the genders and the idioms, I shall do very well in this respect.) To make a long story short, however, father carried his point, as usual; mother basely deserted me at the last moment, and, after holding out alone for three days, I told them to do with me what they pleased! Father lost three steamers in succession by remaining in Paris to argue with me. You know he is like the schoolmaster in Goldsmith's "Deserted Village"—"e'en though vanquished, he would argue still." He and mother went to look at some seventeen families (they had got the addresses somewhere), while I retired to my sofa, and would have nothing to do with it. At last they made arrangements, and I was transported to the establishment from which I now write you. I write you from the bosom of a Parisian ménage—from the depths of a second-rate boarding-house.

Father only left Paris after he had seen us what he calls comfortably settled here, and had informed Madame de Maisonrouge (the mistress of the establishment—the head of the "family") that he wished my French pronunciation especially attended to. The pronunciation, as it happens, is just what I am most at home in; if he had said my genders or my idioms there would have been some sense. But poor father had no tact, and this defect is especially marked since he has been in Europe. He will be absent, however, for three months, and mother and I shall breathe more freely; the situation will be less intense. I must confess that we breathe more freely than I expected, in this place, where we have been for about a week. I was sure, before we came, that it would prove to be an establishment of the *lowest description;* but I must say that, in this respect, I am agreeably disappointed. The French are so clever that they know even how to manage a place of this kind. Of course it is very disagreeable to live with strangers, but as, after all, if I were not staying with Madame de Maisonrouge I should not be living in the Faubourg St.-Germain, I don't know that from the point of view of exclusiveness it is any great loss to be here.

Our rooms are very prettily arranged, and the table is remarkably good. Mamma thinks the whole thing—the place and the people, the manners and customs—very amusing; but mamma is very easily amused. As for me, you know, all that I ask is to be let alone, and not to have people's society *forced upon me.* I have never wanted for society of my own choosing, and, so long as I retain possession of my faculties, I don't suppose I ever shall. As I said, however, the place is very well managed, and I succeed in doing as I please, which, you know, is my most cherished pursuit. Madame de Maisonrouge has a great deal of tact—much more than poor father. She is what they call here a *belle femme,* which means that she is a tall, ugly woman, with style. She dresses very well, and has a great deal of talk; but, though she is a very good imitation of a lady, I never see her behind the dinner-table, in the evening, smiling and bowing, as the people come in, and looking all the while at the dishes and the servants, without thinking of a *dame de comptoir* blooming in a corner of a shop or a restaurant. I am sure that, in spite of her fine name, she was once a *dame de comptoir.* I am also sure that, in spite of her smiles and the pretty things she says to every one, she hates us all, and would like to murder us. She is a hard, clever Frenchwoman, who would like to amuse herself and enjoy her Paris, and she must be bored to death at passing all her time in the midst of stupid English people who mumble broken French at her. Some day she will poison the soup or the *vin rouge;* but I hope that will not be until after mother and I shall have left her. She has two daughters, who, except that one is decidedly pretty, are meagre imitations of herself.

The "family," for the rest, consists altogether of our beloved compatriots, and of still more beloved Englanders. There is an Englishman here, with his sister, and they seem to be rather nice people. He is remarkably handsome, but excessively affected and patronising, especially to us Americans; and I hope to have a chance of biting his head off before long. The sister is very pretty, and, apparently, very nice; but, in costume, she is Britannia incarnate. There is a very pleasant little Frenchman—when they are nice they are charming—and a German doctor, a big, blond man, who looks like a great white bull; and two Americans, besides mother and me. One of them is a young man from Boston,—an aesthetic young man, who talks about its being "a real Corot day," etc., and a young woman—a girl, a female, I don't know what to call her—from Vermont, or Minnesota, or some such place. This young woman is the most extraordinary specimen of artless Yankeeism that I ever encountered; she is really too horrible, I have been three times to Clémentine about your underskirt, etc.

IV

September 25th

From Louis Leverett, *in Paris, to* Harvard Trement, *in Boston*

My Dear Harvard,

I have carried out my plan, of which I gave you a hint in my last, and I only regret that I should not have done it before. It is human nature, after all, that is the most interesting thing in the world, and it only reveals itself to the truly earnest seeker. There is a want of earnestness in that life of hotels and railroad trains, which so many of our countrymen are content to lead in this strange Old World, and I was distressed to find how far I, myself, had been led along the dusty, beaten track. I had, however, constantly wanted to turn aside into more unfrequented ways; to plunge beneath the surface and see what I should discover. But the opportunity had always been missing; somehow, I never meet those opportunities that we hear about and read about—the things that happen to people in novels and biographies. And yet I am always on the watch to take advantage of any opening that may present itself; I am always looking out for experiences, for sensations—I might almost say for adventures.

The great thing is to *live,* you know—to feel, to be conscious of one's possibilities; not to pass through life mechanically and insensibly, like a letter through the post-office. There are times, my dear Harvard, when I feel as if I were really capable of everything—*capable de tout,* as they say here—of the greatest excesses as well as the greatest heroism. Oh, to be able to say that one has lived—*qu'on a vécu,* as they say here—that idea exercises an indefinable attraction for me. You will, perhaps, reply, it is easy to say it; but the thing is to make people believe you! And, then, I don't want any second-hand, spurious sensations; I want the knowledge that leaves a trace—that leaves strange scars and stains and reveries behind it! But I am afraid I shock you, perhaps even frighten you.

If you repeat my remarks to any of the West Cedar Street circle, be sure you tone them down as your discretion will suggest. For yourself, you will know that I have always had an intense desire to see something of *real French life.* You are acquainted with my great sympathy with the French; with my natural tendency to enter into the French way of looking at life. I sympathise with the artistic temperament; I remember you used sometimes to hint to me that you thought my own temperament too artistic. I don't think that in Boston there is any real sympathy with the artistic temperament; we tend to make everything a matter of right and wrong. And in Boston one can't *live —on ne peut pas vivre,* as they say here. I don't mean one can't reside —for a great many people manage that; but one can't live, aesthetically—I may almost venture to say, sensuously. This is why I have always been so much drawn to the French, who are so aesthetic, so sensuous. I am so sorry that Théophile Gautier has passed away; I should have liked so much to go and see him, and tell him all that I owe him. He was living when I was here before; but, you know, at that time I was travelling with the Johnsons, who are not aesthetic, and who used to make me feel rather ashamed of my artistic temperament. If I had gone to see the great apostle of beauty, I should have had to go clandestinely—*en cachette,* as they say here; and that is not my nature; I like to do everything frankly, freely, *naïvement, au grand jour.* That is the great thing—to be free, to be frank, to be *naïf.* Doesn't Matthew Arnold say that somewhere—or is it Swinburne, or Pater?

When I was with the Johnsons everything was superficial; and, as regards life, everything was brought down to the question of right and wrong. They were too didactic; art should never be didactic; and what is life but an art? Pater has said that so well, somewhere. With the Johnsons I am afraid I lost many opportunities; the tone was gray and cottony, I might almost say woolly. But now, as I tell you, I have determined to take right hold for myself; to look right into European life, and judge it without Johnsonian prejudices. I have taken up my residence in a French family, in a real Parisian house. You see I have the courage of my opinions; I don't shrink from carrying out my theory that the great thing is to *live.*

You know I have always been intensely interested in Balzac, who never shrank from the reality, and whose almost *lurid* pictures of Parisian life have often haunted me in my wanderings through the old wicked-looking streets on the other side of the river. I am only sorry that my new friends—my French family—do not live in the old city—*au coeur du vieux Paris,* as they say here. They live only in the Boulevard Haussman, which is less picturesque; but in spite of this they have a great deal of the Balzac tone. Madame de Maisonrouge belongs to one of the oldest and proudest families in France; but she has had reverses which have compelled her to open an establishment in which a limited number of travellers, who are weary of the beaten track, who have the sense of local colour—she explains it herself, she expresses it so well—in short, to open a sort of boarding-house. I don't see why I should not, after all, use that expression, for it is the correlative of the term *pension bourgeoise,* employed by Balzac in the *Père Goriot.* Do you remember the *pension bourgeoise* of Madame Vauquer *née* de Conflans? But this establishment is not at all like that: and indeed it is not at all *bourgeois;* there is something distinguished, something aristocratic, about it. The Pension Vauquer was dark, brown, sordid, *graisseuse;* but this is in quite a different tone, with high, clear, lightly-draped windows, tender, subtle, almost morbid, colours, and furniture in elegant, studied, reed-like lines. Madame de Maisonrouge reminds me of Madame Hulot—do you remember "la belle Madame Hulot?" —in *Les Parents Pauvres.* She has a great charm; a little artificial, a little fatigued, with a little suggestion of hidden things in her life; but I have always been sensitive to the charm of fatigue, of duplicity.

I am rather disappointed, I confess, in the society I find here; it is not so local, so characteristic, as I could have desired. Indeed, to tell the truth, it is not local at all; but, on the other hand, it is cosmopolitan, and there is a great advantage in that. We are French, we are English, we are American, we are German: and, I believe, there are some Russians and Hungarians expected. I am much interested in the study of national types; in comparing, contrasting, seizing the strong points, the weak points, the point of view of each. It is interesting to shift one's point of view—to enter into strange, exotic ways of looking at life.

The American types here are not, I am sorry to say, so interesting as they might be, and, excepting myself, are exclusively feminine. We are *thin,* my dear Harvard; we are pale, we are sharp. There is something meagre about us; our line is wanting in roundness, our composition in richness. We lack temperament; we don't know how to live; *nous ne savons pas vivre,* as they say here. The American temperament is represented (putting myself aside, and I often think that my temperament is not at all American) by a young girl and her mother, and another young girl without her mother—without her mother or any attendant or appendage whatever. These young girls are rather curious types; they have a certain interest, they have a certain grace, but they are disappointing too; they don't go far; they don't keep all they promise; they don't satisfy the imagination. They are cold, slim, sexless; the physique is not generous, not abundant; it is only the drapery, the skirts and furbelows (that is, I mean in the young lady who has her mother) that are abundant. They are very different: one of them all elegance, all expensiveness, with an air of high fashion, from New York; the other a plain, pure, clear-eyed, straight-waisted, straight-stepping maiden from the heart of New England. And yet they are very much alike too—more alike than they would care to think themselves; for they eye each other with cold, mistrustful, deprecating looks. They are both specimens of the emancipated young American girl—practical, positive, passionless, subtle, and knowing, as you please, either too much or too little. And yet, as I say, they have a certain stamp, a certain grace; I like to talk with them, to study them.

The fair New Yorker is, sometimes, very amusing; she asks me if every one in Boston talks like me—if every one is as "intellectual" as your poor correspondent. She is for ever throwing Boston up at me; I can't get rid of Boston. The other one rubs it into me too; but in a different way; she seems to feel about it as a good Mahommedan feels toward Mecca, and regards it as a kind of focus of light for the whole human race. Poor little Boston, what nonsense is talked in thy name! But this New England maiden is, in her way, a strange type: she is travelling all over Europe alone—"to see it," she says, "for herself." For herself! What can that stiff, slim self of hers do with such sights, such visions! She looks at everything, goes everywhere, passes her way, with her clear, quiet eyes wide open; skirting the edge of obscene abysses without suspecting them; pushing through brambles without tearing her robe; exciting, without knowing it, the most injurious suspicions; and always holding her course, passionless, stainless, fearless, charmless! It is a little figure in which, after all, if you can get the right point of view, there is something rather striking.

By way of contrast, there is a lovely English girl, with eyes as shy as violets, and a voice as sweet! She has a sweet Gainsborough head, and a great Gainsborough hat, with a mighty plume in front of it, which makes a shadow over her quiet English eyes. Then she has a sage-green robe, "mystic, wonderful," all embroidered with subtle devices and flowers, and birds of tender tint; very straight and tight in front, and adorned behind, along the spine, with large, strange, iridescent buttons. The revival of taste, of the sense of beauty, in England, interests me deeply; what is there in a simple row of spinal buttons to make one dream—to *donner à rêver,* as they say here? I think that a great aesthetic renascence is at hand, and that a great light will be kindled in England, for all the world to see. There are spirits there that I should like to commune with; I think they would understand me.

This gracious English maiden, with her clinging robes, her amulets and girdles, with something quaint and angular in her step, her carriage, something mediaeval and Gothic in the details of her person and dress, this lovely Evelyn Vane (isn't it a beautiful name?) is deeply, delightfully picturesque. She is much a woman—*elle est bien femme,* as they say here; simpler, softer, rounder, richer than the young girls I spoke of just now. Not much talk—a great, sweet silence. Then the violet eye—the very eye itself seems to blush; the great shadowy hat, making the brow so quiet; the strange, clinging, clutching, pictured raiment! As I say, it is a very gracious, tender type. She has her brother with her, who is a beautiful, fair-haired, gray-eyed young Englishman. He is purely objective; and he, too, is very plastic.

V

September 26th

From Miranda Hope *to her* Mother

You must not be frightened at not hearing from me oftener; it is not because I am in any trouble, but because I am getting on so well. If I were in any trouble I don't think I should write to you; I should just keep quiet and see it through myself. But that is not the case at present; and, if I don't write to you, it is because I am so deeply interested over here that I don't seem to find time. It was a real providence that brought me to this house, where, in spite of all obstacles, I am able to do much good work. I wonder how I find the time for all I do; but when I think that I have only got a year in Europe, I feel as if I wouldn't sacrifice a single hour.

The obstacles I refer to are the disadvantages I have in learning French, there being so many persons around me speaking English, and that, as you may say, in the very bosom of a French family. It seems as if you heard English everywhere; but I certainly didn't expect to find it in a place like this. I am not discouraged, however, and I talk French all I can, even with the other English boarders. Then I have a lesson every day from Miss Maisonrouge (the elder daughter of the lady of the house), and French conversation every evening in the *salon,* from eight to eleven, with Madame herself, and some friends of hers that often come in. Her cousin, Mr Verdier, a young French gentleman, is fortunately staying with her, and I make a point of talking with him as much as possible. I have *extra private lessons* from him, and I often go out to walk with him. Some night, soon, he is to accompany me to the opera. We have also a most interesting plan of visiting all the galleries in Paris together. Like most of the French, he converses with great fluency, and I feel as if I should really gain from him. He is remarkably handsome, and extremely polite—paying a great many compliments, which, I am afraid, are not always *sincere.* When I return to Bangor I will tell you some of the things he has said to me. I think you will consider them extremely curious, and very beautiful *in their way.*

The conversation in the parlour (from eight to eleven) is often remarkably brilliant, and I often wish that you, or some of the Bangor folks, could be there to enjoy it. Even though you couldn't understand it I think you would like to hear the way they go on; they seem to express so much. I sometimes think that at Bangor they don't express enough (but it seems as if over there, there was less to express). It seems as if, at Bangor, there were things that folks never *tried* to say; but here, I have learned from studying French that you have no idea what you *can* say, before you try. At Bangor they seem to give it up beforehand; they don't make any effort. (I don't say this in the least for William Platt, *in particular.*)

I am sure I don't know what they will think of me when I get back. It seems as if, over here, I had learned to come out with everything. I suppose they will think I am not sincere; but isn't it more sincere to come out with things than to conceal them? I have become very good friends with every one in the house—that is (you see, I *am* sincere), with *almost* every one. It is the most interesting circle I ever was in. There's a girl here, an American, that I don't like so much as the rest; but that is only because she won't let me. I should like to like her, ever so much, because she is most lovely and most attractive; but she doesn't seem to want to know me or to like me. She comes from New York, and she is remarkably pretty, with beautiful eyes and the most delicate features; she is also remarkably elegant—in this respect would bear comparison with any one I have seen over here. But it seems as if she didn't want to recognise me, or associate with me; as if she wanted to make a difference between us. It is like people they call "haughty" in books. I have never seen any one like that before—any one that wanted to make a difference; and at first I was right down interested, she seemed to me so like a proud young lady in a novel. I kept saying to myself all day, "haughty, haughty," and I wished she would keep on so. But she did keep on; she kept on too long; and then I began to feel hurt. I couldn't think what I have done, and I can't think yet. It's as if she had got some idea about me, or had heard someone say something. If some girls should behave like that I shouldn't make any account of it; but this one is so refined, and looks as if she might be so interesting if I once got to know her, that I think about it a good deal. I am bound to find out what her reason is—for of course she has got some reason; I am right down curious to know.

I went up to her to ask her the day before yesterday; I thought that was the best way. I told her I wanted to know her better, and would like to come and see her in her room—they tell me she has got a lovely room—and that if she had heard anything against me, perhaps she would tell me when I came. But she was more distant than ever, and she just turned it off; said that she had never heard me mentioned, and that her room was too small to receive visitors. I suppose she spoke the truth, but I am sure she has got some reason, all the same. She has got some idea, and I am bound to find out before I go, if I have to ask everybody in the house. I *am* right down curious. I wonder if she doesn't think me refined—or if she had ever heard anything against Bangor? I can't think it is that. Don't you remember when Clara Barnard went to visit in New York, three years ago, how much attention she received? And you know Clara *is* Bangor, to the soles of her shoes. Ask William Platt—so long as he isn't a native—if he doesn't consider Clara Barnard refined.

Apropos, as they say here, of refinement, there is another American in the house—a gentleman from Boston—who is just crowded with it. His name is Mr Louis Leverett (such a beautiful name, I think), and he is about thirty years old. He is rather small, and he looks pretty sick; he suffers from some affection of the liver. But his conversation is remarkably interesting, and I delight to listen to him—he has such beautiful ideas. I feel as if it were hardly right, not being in French; but, fortunately, he uses a great many French expressions. It's in a different style from the conversation of Mr Verdier—not so complimentary, but more intellectual. He is intensely fond of pictures, and has given me a great many ideas about them which I should never have gained without him; I shouldn't have known where to look for such ideas. He thinks everything of pictures; he thinks we don't make near enough of them. They seem to make a good deal of them here; but I couldn't help telling him the other day that in Bangor I really don't think we do.

If I had any money to spend I would buy some and take them back, to hang up. Mr Leverett says it would do them good—not the pictures, but the Bangor folks. He thinks everything of the French, too, and says we don't make nearly enough of *them.* I couldn't help telling him the other day that at any rate they make enough of themselves. But it is very interesting to hear him go on about the French, and it is so much gain to me, so long as that is what I came for. I talk to him as much as I dare about Boston, but I do feel as if this were right down wrong—a stolen pleasure.

I can get all the Boston culture I want when I go back, if I carry out my plan, my happy vision, of going there to reside. I ought to direct all my efforts to European culture now, and keep Boston to finish off. But it seems as if I couldn't help taking a peep now and then, in advance—with a Bostonian. I don't know when I may meet one again; but if there are many others like Mr Leverett there, I shall be certain not to want when I carry out my dream. He is just as full of culture as he can live. But it seems strange how many different sorts there are.

There are two of the English who I suppose are very cultivated too; but it doesn't seem as if I could enter into theirs so easily, though I try all I can. I do love their way of speaking, and sometimes I feel almost as if it would be right to give up trying to learn French, and just try to learn to speak our own tongue as these English speak it. It isn't the things they say so much, though these are often rather curious, but it is in the way they pronounce, and the sweetness of their voice. It seems as if they must *try* a good deal to talk like that; but these English that are here don't seem to try at all, either to speak or do anything else. They are a young lady and her brother. I believe they belong to some noble family. I have had a good deal of intercourse with them, because I have felt more free to talk to them than to the Americans—on account of the language. It seems as if in talking with them I was almost learning a new one.

I never supposed, when I left Bangor, that I was coming to Europe to learn *English*! If I do learn it, I don't think you will understand me when I get back, and I don't think you'll like it much. I should be a good deal criticised if I spoke like that at Bangor. However, I verily believe Bangor is the most critical place on earth; I have seen nothing like it over here. Tell them all I have come to the conclusion that they are *a great deal too fastidious*. But I was speaking about this English young lady and her brother. I wish I could put them before you. She is lovely to look at; she seems so modest and retiring. In spite of this, however, she dresses in a way that attracts great attention, as I couldn't help noticing when one day I went out to walk with her. She was ever so much looked at; but she didn't seem to notice it, until at last I couldn't help calling attention to it. Mr Leverett thinks everything of it; he calls it the "costume of the future." I should call it rather the costume of the past—you know the English have such an attachment to the past. I said this the other day to Madame de Maisonrouge—that Miss Vane dressed in the costume of the past. *De l'an passé, vous voulez dire?* said Madame, with her little French laugh (you can get William Platt to translate this, he used to tell me he knew so much French).

You know I told you, in writing some time ago, that I had tried to get some insight into the position of woman in England, and, being here with Miss Vane, it has seemed to me to be a good opportunity to get a little more. I have asked her a great deal about it; but she doesn't seem able to give me much information. The first time I asked her she told me the position of a lady depended upon the rank of her father, her eldest brother, her husband, etc. She told me her own position was very good, because her father was some relation—I forget what—to a lord. She thinks everything of this; and that proves to me that the position of woman in her country cannot be satisfactory; because, if it were, it wouldn't depend upon that of your relations, even your nearest. I don't know much about lords, and it does try my patience (though she is just as sweet as she can live) to hear her talk as if it were a matter of course that I should.

I feel as if it were right to ask her as often as I can if she doesn't consider every one equal; but she always says she doesn't, and she confesses that she doesn't think she is equal to "Lady Something-or-other," who is the wife of that relation of her father. I try and persuade her all I can that she is; but it seems as if she didn't want to be persuaded; and when I ask her if Lady So-and-so is of the same opinion (that Miss Vane isn't her equal), she looks so soft and pretty with her eyes, and says, "Of course she is!" When I tell her that this is right down bad for Lady So-and-so, it seems as if she wouldn't believe me, and the only answer she will make is that Lady So-and-so is "extremely nice." I don't believe she is nice at all; if she were nice, she wouldn't have such ideas as that. I tell Miss Vane that at Bangor we think such ideas vulgar; but then she looks as though she had never heard of Bangor. I often want to shake her, though she *is* so sweet. If she isn't angry with the people who make her feel that way, I am angry for her. I am angry with her brother, too, for she is evidently very much afraid of him, and this gives me some further insight into the subject. She thinks everything of her brother, and thinks it natural that she should be afraid of him, not only physically (for this *is* natural as he is enormously tall and strong, and has very big fists), but morally and intellectually. She seems unable, however, to take in any argument, and she makes me realise what I have often heard—that if you are timid nothing will reason you out of it.

Mr Vane, also (the brother), seems to have the same prejudices, and when I tell him, as I often think it right to do, that his sister is not his subordinate, even if she does think so, but his equal, and, perhaps in some respects his superior, and that if my brother, in Bangor, were to treat me as he treats this poor young girl, who has not spirit enough to see the question in its true light, there would be an indignation-meeting of the citizens, to protest against such an outrage to the sanctity of womanhood—when I tell him all this, at breakfast or dinner, he bursts out laughing so loud that all the plates clatter on the table.

But at such a time as this there is always one person who seems interested in what I say—a German gentleman, a professor, who sits next to me at dinner, and whom I must tell you more about another time. He is very learned, and has a great desire for information; he appreciates a great many of my remarks, and, after dinner, in the salon, he often comes to me to ask me questions about them. I have to think a little, sometimes, to know what I did say, or what I do think. He takes you right up where you left off, and he is almost as fond of discussing things as William Platt is. He is splendidly educated, in the German style, and he told me the other day that he was an "intellectual broom." Well, if he is, he sweeps clean; I told him that. After he has been talking to me I feel as if I hadn't got a speck of dust left in my mind anywhere. It's a most delightful feeling. He says he's an observer; and I am sure there is plenty over here to observe. But I have told you enough for to-day. I don't know how much longer I shall stay here; I am getting on so fast that it sometimes seems as if I shouldn't need all the time I have laid out. I suppose your cold weather has promptly begun, as usual; it sometimes makes me envy you. The fall weather here is very dull and damp, and I feel very much as if I should like to be braced up.

VI

Paris, September 30th

From Miss Evelyn Vane, *in Paris, to the* Lady Augusta Fleming, *at Brighton*

Dear Lady Augusta,

I am afraid I shall not be able to come to you on January 7th, as you kindly proposed at Homburg. I am so very, very sorry; it is a great disappointment to me. But I have just heard that it has been settled that mamma and the children are coming abroad for a part of the winter, and mamma wishes me to go with them to Hyères, where Georgina has been ordered for her lungs. She has not been at all well these three months, and now that the damp weather has begun she is very poorly indeed; so that last week papa decided to have a consultation, and he and mamma went with her up to town and saw some three or four doctors. They all of them ordered the south of France, but they didn't agree about the place; so that mamma herself decided for Hyères, because it is the most economical. I believe it is very dull, but I hope it will do Georgina good. I am afraid, however, that nothing will do her good until she consents to take more care of herself; I am afraid she is very wild and wilful, and mamma tells me that all this month it has taken papa's positive orders to make her stop in-doors. She is very cross (mamma writes me) about coming abroad, and doesn't seem at all to mind the expense that papa has been put to,—talks very ill-naturedly about losing the hunting, etc. She expected to begin to hunt in December, and wants to know whether anybody keeps hounds at Hyères. Fancy a girl wanting to follow the hounds when her lungs are so bad! But I dare say that when she gets there she will be glad enough to keep quiet, as they say that the heat is intense. It may cure Georgina, but I am sure it will make the rest of us very ill.

Mamma, however, is only going to bring Mary and Gus and Fred and Adelaide abroad with her; the others will remain at Kingscote until February (about the 3d), when they will go to Eastbourne for a month with Miss Turnover, the new governess, who has turned out such a very nice person. She is going to take Miss Travers, who has been with us so long, but who is only qualified for the younger children, to Hyères, and I believe some of the Kingscote servants. She has perfect confidence in Miss T.; it is only a pity she has such an odd name.

Mamma thought of asking her if she would mind taking another when she came; but papa thought she might object. Lady Battledown makes all her governesses take the same name; she gives £5 more a year for the purpose. I forget what it is she calls them; I think it's Johnson (which to me always suggests a lady's maid). Governesses shouldn't have too pretty a name; they shouldn't have a nicer name than the family.

I suppose you heard from the Desmonds that I did not go back to England with them. When it began to be talked about that Georgina should be taken abroad, mamma wrote to me that I had better stop in Paris for a month with Harold, so that she could pick me up on their way to Hyères. It saves the expense of my journey to Kingscote and back, and gives me the opportunity to "finish" a little, in French.

You know Harold came here six weeks ago, to get up his French for those dreadful examinations that he has to pass so soon. He came to live with some French people that take in young men (and others) for this purpose; it's a kind of coaching place, only kept by women. Mamma had heard it was very nice; so she wrote to me that I was to come and stop here with Harold. The Desmonds brought me and made the arrangement, or the bargain, or whatever you call it. Poor Harold was naturally not at all pleased; but he has been very kind, and has treated me like an angel. He is getting on beautifully with his French; for though I don't think the place is so good as papa supposed, yet Harold is so immensely clever that he can scarcely help learning. I am afraid I learn much less, but, fortunately, I have not to pass an examination—except if mamma takes it into her head to examine me. But she will have so much to think of with Georgina that I hope this won't occur to her. If it does, I shall be, as Harold says, in a dreadful funk.

This is not such a nice place for a girl as for a young man, and the Desmonds though it *exceedingly odd* that mamma should wish me to come here. As Mrs Desmond said, it is because she is so very unconventional. But you know Paris is so very amusing, and if only Harold remains good-natured about it, I shall be content to wait for the caravan (that's what he calls mamma and the children). The person who keeps the establishment, or whatever they call it, is rather odd, and *exceedingly foreign;* but she is wonderfully civil, and is perpetually sending to my door to see if I want anything. The servants are not at all like English servants, and come bursting in, the footman (they have only one) and the maids alike, at all sorts of hours, in the *most sudden way.* Then when one rings, it is half an hour before they come. All this is very uncomfortable, and I daresay it will be worse at Hyères. There, however, fortunately, we shall have our own people.

There are some very odd Americans here, who keep throwing

Harold into fits of laughter. One is a dreadful little man who is always sitting over the fire, and talking about the colour of the sky. I don't believe he ever saw the sky except through the window-pane. The other day he took hold of my frock (that green one you thought so nice at Homburg) and told me that it reminded him of the texture of the Devonshire turf. And then he talked for half an hour about the Devonshire turf, which I thought such a very extraordinary subject. Harold says he is mad. It is very strange to be living in this way, with people one doesn't know. I mean that one doesn't know as one knows them in England.

The other Americans (beside the madman) are two girls, about my own age, one of whom is rather nice. She has a mother; but the mother is always sitting in her bed-room, which seems so very odd. I should like mamma to ask them to Kingscote, but I am afraid mamma wouldn't like the mother, who is rather vulgar. The other girl is rather vulgar too, and is travelling about quite alone. I think she is a kind of schoolmistress; but the other girl (I mean the nicer one, with the mother) tells me she is more respectable than she seems. She has, however, the most extraordinary opinions—wishes to do away with the aristocracy, thinks it wrong that Arthur should have Kingscote when papa dies, etc. I don't see what it signifies to her that poor Arthur should come into the property, which will be so delightful—except for papa dying. But Harold says she is mad. He chaffs her tremendously about her radicalism, and he is so immensely clever that she can't answer him, though she is rather clever, too.

There is also a Frenchman, a nephew, or cousin, or something, of the person of the house, who is extremely nasty; and a German professor, or doctor, who eats with his knife and is a great bore. I am so very sorry about giving up my visit. I am afraid you will never ask me again.

VII

September 28th

From Léon Verdier *in Paris, to* Prosper Gobain, *at Lille*

My Dear Prosper,

It is a long time since I have given you of my news, and I don't know what puts it into my head to-night to recall myself to your affectionate memory. I suppose it is that when we are happy the mind reverts instinctively to those with whom formerly we shared our exaltations and depressions, and *je t'en ai trop dit, dans le bon temps, mon gros Prosper*, and you always listened to me too imperturbably, with your pipe in your mouth, your waistcoat unbuttoned, for me not to feel that I can count upon your sympathy to-day. *Nous en sommes nous flanquées, des confidences*—in those happy days when my first thought in seeing an adventure *poindre à l'horizon* was of the pleasure I should have in relating it to the great Prosper. As I tell thee, I am happy; decidedly, I am happy, and from this affirmation I fancy you can construct the rest. Shall I help thee a little? Take three adorable girls . . . three, my good Prosper—the mystic number—neither more nor less. Take them and place thy insatiable little Léon in the midst of them! Is the situation sufficiently indicated, and do you apprehend the motives of my felicity?

You expected, perhaps, I was going to tell you that I had made my fortune, or that the Uncle Blondeau had at last decided to return into the breast of nature, after having constituted me his universal legatee. But I needn't remind you that women are always for something in the happiness of him who writes to thee—for something in his happiness, and for a good deal more in his misery. But don't let me talk of misery now; time enough when it comes; *ces demoiselles* have gone to join the serried ranks of their amiable predecessors. Excuse me—I comprehend your impatience. I will tell you of whom *ces demoiselles* consist.

You have heard me speak of my *cousine* de Maisonrouge, that *grande belle femme,* who, after having married, *en secondes noces*—there had been, to tell the truth, some irregularity about her first union—a venerable relic of the old noblesse of Poitou, was left, by the death of her husband, complicated by the indulgence of expensive tastes on an income of 17,000 francs, on the pavement of Paris, with two little demons of daughters to bring up in the path of virtue. She managed to bring them up; my little cousins are rigidly virtuous. If you ask me how she managed it, I can't tell you; it's no business of mine, and, *a fortiori,* none of yours. She is now fifty years old (she confesses to thirty-seven), and her daughters, whom she has never been able to marry, are respectively twenty-seven and twenty-three (they confess to twenty and to seventeen). Three years ago she had the thrice-blessed idea of opening a sort of *pension* for the entertainment and instruction of the blundering barbarians who come to Paris in the hope of picking up a few stray particles of the language of Voltaire—or of Zola. The idea *lui a porté bonheur;* the shop does a very good business. Until within a few months ago it was carried on by my cousins alone; but lately the need of a few extensions and embellishments has caused itself to be felt. My cousin has undertaken them, regardless of expense; she has asked me to come and stay with her—board and lodging gratis—and keep an eye on the grammatical eccentricities of her *pensionnaires.* I am the extension, my good Prosper; I am the embellishment! I live for nothing, and I straighten up the accent of the prettiest English lips. The English lips are not all pretty, heaven knows, but enough of them are so to make it a gaining bargain for me.

Just now, as I told you, I am in daily conversation with three separate pairs. The owner of one of them has private lessons; she pays extra. My cousin doesn't give me a sou of the money; but I make bold nevertheless, to say that my trouble is remunerated. But I am well, very well, with the proprietors of the two other pairs. One of them is a little Anglaise, of about twenty—a little *figure de keepsake;* the most adorable miss that you ever, or at least that I ever, beheld. She is decorated all over with beads and bracelets and embroidered dandelions; but her principal decoration consists of the softest little gray eyes in the world, which rest upon you with a profundity of confidence—a confidence that I really feel some compunction in betraying. She has a tint as white as this sheet of paper, except just in the middle of each cheek, where it passes into the purest and most transparent, most liquid, carmine. Occasionally this rosy fluid overflows into the rest of her face—by which I mean that she blushes—as softly as the mark of your breath on the window-pane.

Like every Anglaise, she is rather pinched and prim in public; but it is very easy to see that when no one is looking *elle ne demande qu'à se laisser aller!* Whenever she wants it I am always there, and I have given her to understand that she can count upon me. I have every reason to believe that she appreciates the assurance, though I am bound in honesty to confess that with her the situation is a little less advanced than with the others. *Que voulez-vous?* The English are heavy, and the Anglaises move slowly, that's all. The movement, however, is perceptible, and once this fact is established I can let the pottage simmer. I can give her time to arrive, for I am over-well occupied with her *concurrentes. Celles-ci* don't keep me waiting, *par exemple!*

These young ladies are Americans, and you know that it is the national character to move fast. "All right—go ahead!" (I am learning a great deal of English, or, rather, a great deal of American.) They go ahead at a rate that sometimes makes it difficult for me to keep up. One of them is prettier than the other; but this latter (the one that takes the private lessons) is really *une fille prodigieuse. Ah, par exemple, elle brûle ses vaisseux celle-la!* She threw herself into my arms the very first day, and I almost owed her a grudge for having deprived me of that pleasure of gradation, of carrying the defences, one by one, which is almost as great as that of entering the place.

Would you believe that at the end of exactly twelve minutes she gave me a rendezvous? It is true it was in the Galerie d'Apollon, at the

Louvre; but that was respectable for a beginning, and since then we have had them by the dozen; I have ceased to keep the account. *Non, c'est une fille qui me dépasse.*

The little one (she has a mother somewhere, out of sight, shut up in a closet or a trunk) is a good deal prettier, and, perhaps, on that account *elle y met plus de façons.* She doesn't knock about Paris with me by the hour; she contents herself with long interviews in the *petit salon,* with the curtains half-drawn, beginning at about three o'clock, when every one is *à la promenade.* She is admirable, this little one; a little too thin, the bones rather accentuated, but the detail, on the whole, most satisfactory. And you can say anything to her. She takes the trouble to appear not to understand, but her conduct, half an hour afterwards, reassures you completely—oh, completely!

However, it is the tall one, the one of the private lessons, that is the most remarkable. These private lessons, my good Prosper, are the most brilliant invention of the age, and a real stroke of genius on the part of Miss Miranda! They also take place in the *petit salon,* but with the doors tightly closed, and with explicit directions to every one in the house that we are not to be disturbed. And we are not, my good Prosper; we are not! Not a sound, not a shadow, interrupts our felicity. My *cousine* is really admirable; the shop deserves to succeed. Miss Miranda is tall and rather flat; she is too pale; she hasn't the adorable *rougeurs* of the little Anglaise. But she has bright, keen, inquisitive eyes, superb teeth, a nose modelled by a sculptor, and a way of holding up her head and looking every one in the face, which is the most finished piece of impertinence I ever beheld. She is making the *tour du monde,* entirely alone, without even a soubrette to carry the ensign, for the purpose of seeing for herself *à quoi s'en tenir sur les hommes et les choses*—on *les hommes* particularly. *Dis donc,* Prosper, it must be a *drôle de pays* over there, where young persons animated by this ardent curiosity are manufactured! If we should turn the tables, some day, thou and I, and go over and see it for ourselves. It is as well that we should go and find them *chez elles,* as that they should come out here after us. *Dis donc, mon gros Prosper. . . .*

VIII

From Dr Rudolf Staub, *in Paris, to* Dr Julius Hirsch, *at Göttingen*

My Dear Brother in Science,

I resume my hasty notes, of which I sent you the first instalment some weeks ago. I mentioned then that I intended to leave my hotel, not finding it sufficiently local and national. It was kept by a Pomeranian, and the waiters, without exception, were from the Fatherland. I fancied myself at Berlin, Unter den Linden, and I reflected that, having taken the serious step of visiting the headquarters of the Gallic genius, I should try and project myself, as much as possible, into the circumstances which are in part the consequence and in part the cause of its irrepressible activity. It seemed to me that there could be no well-grounded knowledge without this preliminary operation of placing myself in relations, as slightly as possible modified by elements proceeding from a different combination of causes, with the spontaneous home-life of the country.

I accordingly engaged a room in the house of a lady of pure French extraction and education, who supplements the shortcomings of an income insufficient to the ever-growing demands of the Parisian system of sense-gratification, by providing food and lodging for a limited number of distinguished strangers. I should have preferred to have my room alone in the house, and to take my meals in a brewery, of very good appearance, which I speedily discovered in the same street; but this arrangement, though very lucidly proposed by myself, was not acceptable to the mistress of the establishment (a woman with a mathematical head), and I have consoled myself for the extra expense by fixing my thoughts upon the opportunity that conformity to the customs of the house gives me of studying the table-manners of my companions, and of observing the French nature at a peculiarly physiological moment, the moment when the satisfaction of the *taste,* which is the governing quality in its composition, produces a kind of exhalation, an intellectual transpiration, which, though light and perhaps invisible to a superficial spectator, is nevertheless appreciable by a properly adjusted instrument.

I have adjusted my instrument very satisfactorily (I mean the one I carry in my good, square German head), and I am not afraid of losing a single drop of this valuable fluid, as it condenses itself upon the plate of my observation. A prepared surface is what I need, and I have prepared my surface.

Unfortunately here, also, I find the individual native in the minority. There are only four French persons in the house—the individuals concerned in its management, three of whom are women, and one a man. This preponderance of the feminine element is, however, in itself characteristic, as I need not remind you what an abnormally-developed part this sex has played in French history. The remaining figure is apparently that of a man, but I hesitate to classify him so superficially. He appears to me less human than simian, and whenever I hear him talk I seem to myself to have paused in the street to listen to the shrill clatter of a hand-organ, to which the gambols of a hairy *homunculus* form an accompaniment.

I mentioned to you before that my expectation of rough usage, in consequence of my German nationality, had proved completely unfounded. No one seems to know or to care what my nationality is, and I am treated, on the contrary, with the civility which is the portion of every traveller who pays the bill without scanning the items too narrowly. This, I confess, has been something of a surprise to me, and I have not yet made up my mind as to the fundamental cause of the anomaly. My determination to take up my abode in a French interior was largely dictated by the supposition that I should be substantially disagreeable to its inmates. I wished to observe the different forms taken by the irritation that I should naturally produce; for it is under the influence of irritation that the French character most completely expresses itself. My presence, however, does not appear to operate as a stimulus, and in this respect I am materially disappointed. They treat me as they treat every one else; whereas, in order to be treated differently, I was resigned in advance to be treated worse. I have not, as I say, fully explained to myself this logical contradiction; but this is the explanation to which I tend. The French are so exclusively occupied with the idea of themselves, that in spite of the very definite image the German personality presented to them by the war of 1870, they have at present no distinct apprehension of its existence. They are not very sure that there are any Germans; they have already forgotten the convincing proofs of the fact that were presented to them nine years ago. A German was something disagreeable, which they determined to keep out of their conception of things. I therefore think that we are wrong to govern ourselves upon the hypothesis of the *revanche;* the French nature is too shallow for that large and powerful plant to bloom in it.

The English-speaking specimens, too, I have not been willing to neglect the opportunity to examine; and among these I have paid special attention to the American varieties, of which I find here several singular examples. The two most remarkable are a young man who presents all the characteristics of a period of national decadence; reminding me strongly of some diminutive Hellenised Roman of the third century. He is an illustration of the period of culture in which the faculty of appreciation has obtained such a preponderance over that of production that the latter sinks into a kind of rank sterility, and the mental condition becomes analogous to that of a malarious bog. I learn from him that there is an immense number of Americans exactly resembling him, and that the city of Boston, indeed, is almost exclusively composed of them. (He communicated this fact very proudly, as if it were greatly to the credit of his native country; little perceiving the truly sinister impression it made upon me.)

What strikes one in it is that it is a phenomenon to the best of my knowledge—and you know what my knowledge is—unprecedented and unique in the history of mankind; the arrival of a nation at an ultimate stage of evolution without having passed through the mediate one; the passage of the fruit, in other words, from crudity to rottenness, without the interposition of a period of useful (and ornamental) ripeness. With the Americans, indeed, the crudity and the rottenness are identical and simultaneous; it is impossible to say, as in the conversation of this deplorable young man, which is one and which is the other; they are inextricably mingled. I prefer the talk of the French *homunculus;* it is at least more amusing.

It is interesting in this manner to perceive, so largely developed, the germs of extinction in the so-called powerful Anglo-Saxon family. I find them in almost as recognisable a form in a young woman from the State of Maine, in the province of New England, with whom I have had a good deal of conversation. She differs somewhat from the young man I just mentioned, in that the faculty of production, of action, is, in her, less inanimate; she has more of the freshness and vigour that we suppose to belong to a young civilisation. But unfortunately she produces nothing but evil, and her tastes and habits are similarly those of a Roman lady of the lower Empire. She makes no secret of them, and has, in fact, elaborated a complete system of licentious behaviour. As the opportunities she finds in her own country do not satisfy her, she has come to Europe "to try," as she says, "for herself." It is the doctrine of universal experience professed with a cynicism that is really most extraordinary, and which, presenting itself in a young woman of considerable education, appears to me to be the judgment of a society.

Another observation which pushes me to the same induction—that of the premature vitiations of the American population—is the attitude of the Americans whom I have before me with regard to each other. There is another young lady here, who is less abnormally developed than the one I have just described, but who yet bears the stamp of this peculiar combination of incompleteness and effeteness. These three persons look with the greatest mistrust and aversion upon each other; and each has repeatedly taken me apart and assured me, secretly, that he or she only is the real, the genuine, the typical American. A type that has lost itself before it has been fixed—what can you look for from this?

Add to this that there are two young Englanders in the house, who hate all the Americans in a lump, making between them none of the distinctions and favourable comparisons which they insist upon, and you will, I think, hold me warranted in believing that, between precipitate decay and internecine enmities, the English-speaking family is destined to consume itself, and that with its decline the prospect of general pervasiveness, to which I alluded above, will brighten for the deep-lunged children of the Fatherland!

IX

October 22nd

Miranda Hope *to her* Mother

Dear Mother,

I am off in a day or two to visit some new country; I haven't yet decided which. I have satisfied myself with regard to France, and obtained a good knowledge of the language. I have enjoyed my visit to Madame de Maisonrouge deeply, and feel as if I were leaving a circle of real friends. Everything has gone on beautifully up to the end, and every one has been as kind and attentive as if I were their own sister, especially Mr Verdier, the French gentleman, from whom I have gained more than I ever expected (in six weeks), and with whom I have promised to *correspond.* So you can imagine me dashing off the most correct French letters; and, if you don't believe it, I will keep the rough draft to show you when I go back.

The German gentleman is also more interesting, the more you know him; it seems sometimes as if I could fairly drink in his ideas. I have found out why the young lady from New York doesn't like me! It is because I said one day at dinner that I *admired* to go to the Louvre. Well, when I first came, it seemed as if I *did* admire everything!

Tell William Platt his letter has come. I knew he would have to write, and I was bound I would make him! I haven't decided what country I will visit yet; it seems as if there were so many to choose from. But I shall take care to pick out a good one, and to meet plenty of fresh experiences.

Dearest mother, my money holds out, and it *is* most interesting!

Clay

James Joyce

The matron had given her leave to go out as soon as the women's tea was over and Maria looked forward to her evening out. The kitchen was spick and span: the cook said you could see yourself in the big copper boilers. The fire was nice and bright and on one of the side-tables were four very big barmbracks. These barmbracks seemed uncut; but if you went closer you would see that they had been cut into long thick even slices and were ready to be handed round at tea. Maria had cut them herself.

Maria was a very, very small person indeed but she had a very long nose and a very long chin. She talked a little through her nose, always soothingly: *Yes, my dear,* and *No, my dear.* She was always sent for when the women quarrelled over their tubs and always succeeded in making peace. One day the matron had said to her:

—Maria, you are a veritable peace-maker!

And the sub-matron and two of the Board ladies had heard the compliment. And Ginger Mooney was always saying what she wouldn't do to the dummy who had charge of the irons if it wasn't for Maria. Everyone was so fond of Maria.

The women would have their tea at six o'clock and she would be able to get away before seven. From Ballsbridge to the Pillar, twenty minutes; from the Pillar to Drumcondra, twenty minutes; and twenty minutes to buy the things. She would be there before eight. She took out her purse with the silver clasps and read again the words *A Present from Belfast.* She was very fond of that purse because Joe had brought it to her five years before when he and Alphy had gone to Belfast on a Whit-Monday trip. In the purse were two half-crowns and some coppers. She would have five shillings clear after paying tram fare. What a nice evening they would have, all the children singing! Only she hoped that Joe wouldn't come in drunk. He was so different when he took any drink.

Often he had wanted her to go and live with them; but she would have felt herself in the way (though Joe's wife was ever so nice with her) and she had become accustomed to the life of the laundry. Joe was a good fellow. She had nursed him and Alphy too; and Joe used often say:

—Mamma is mamma but Maria is my proper mother.

After the break-up at home the boys had got her that position in the *Dublin by Lamplight* laundry, and she liked it. She used to have such a bad opinion of Protestants but now she thought they were very nice people, a little quiet and serious, but still very nice people to live with. Then she had her plants in the conservatory and she liked looking after them. She had lovely ferns and wax-plants and, whenever anyone came to visit her, she always gave the visitor one or two slips from her conservatory. There was one thing she didn't like and that was the tracts on the walls; but the matron was such a nice person to deal with, so genteel.

When the cook told her everything was ready she went into the women's room and began to pull the big bell. In a few minutes the women began to come in by twos and threes, wiping their steaming hands in their petticoats and pulling down the sleeves of their blouses over their red steaming arms. They settled down before their huge mugs which the cook and the dummy filled up with hot tea, already mixed with milk and sugar in huge tin cans. Maria superintended the distribution of the barmbrack and saw that every woman got her four slices. There was a great deal of laughing and joking during the meal. Lizzie Fleming said Maria was sure to get the ring and, though Fleming had said that for so many Hallow Eves, Maria had to laugh and say she didn't want any ring or man either; and when she laughed her grey-green eyes sparkled with disappointed shyness and the tip of her nose nearly met the tip of her chin. Then Ginger Mooney lifted up her mug of tea and proposed Maria's health while all the other women clattered with their mugs on the table, and said she was sorry she hadn't a sup of porter to drink it in. And Maria laughed again till the tip of her nose nearly met the tip of her chin and till her minute body nearly shook itself asunder because she knew that Mooney meant well though, of course, she had the notions of a common woman.

But wasn't Maria glad when the women had finished their tea and the cook and the dummy had begun to clear away the tea-things! She went into her little bedroom and, remembering that the next morning was a mass morning, changed the hand of the alarm from seven to six. Then she took off her working skirt and her house-boots and laid her best skirt out on the bed and her tiny dress-boots beside the foot of the bed. She changed her blouse too and, as she stood before the mirror, she thought of how she used to dress for mass on Sunday morning when she was a young girl; and she looked with quaint affection at the diminutive body which she had so often adorned. In spite of its years she found it a nice tidy little body.

When she got outside the streets were shining with rain and she was glad of her old brown raincloak. The tram was full and she had to sit on the little stool at the end of the car, facing all the people, with her toes barely touching the floor. She arranged in her mind all she was going to do and thought how much better it was to be independent and to have your own money in your pocket. She hoped they would have a nice evening. She was sure they would but she could not help thinking what a pity it was Alphy and Joe were not speaking. They were always falling out now but when they were boys together they used to be the best of friends: but such was life.

She got out of her tram at the Pillar and ferreted her way quickly among the crowds. She went into Downes's cake-shop but the shop was so full of people that it was a long time before she could get herself attended to. She bought a dozen of mixed penny cakes, and at last came out of the shop laden with a big bag. Then she thought what else would she buy: she wanted to buy something really nice. They would be sure to have plenty of apples and nuts. It was hard to know what to buy and all she could think of was cake. She decided to buy some plumcake but Downes's plumcake had not enough almond icing on top of it so she went over to a shop in Henry Street. Here she was a long time in suiting herself and the stylish young lady behind the counter, who was evidently a little annoyed by her, asked her was it wedding-cake she wanted to buy. That made Maria blush and smile at the young lady; but the young lady took it all very seriously and finally cut a thick slice of plumcake, parcelled it up and said:

—Two-and-four, please.

She thought she would have to stand in the Drumcondra tram because none of the young men seemed to notice her but an elderly gentleman made room for her. He was a stout gentleman and he wore a brown hard hat; he had a square red face and a greyish moustache. Maria thought he was a colonel-looking gentleman and she reflected how much more polite he was than the young men who simply stared straight before them. The gentleman began to chat with her about Hallow Eve and the rainy weather. He supposed the bag was full of good things for the little ones and said it was only right that the youngsters should enjoy themselves while they were young. Maria agreed with him and favoured him with demure nods and hems. He was very nice with her, and when she was getting out at the Canal Bridge she thanked him and bowed, and he bowed to her and raised his hat and smiled agreeably; and while she was going up along the terrace, bending her tiny head under the rain, she thought how easy it was to know a gentleman even when he has a drop taken.

Everybody said: *O, here's Maria!* when she came to Joe's house. Joe was there, having come home from business, and all the children had their Sunday dresses on. There were two big girls in from next door and games were going on. Maria gave the bag of cakes to the eldest boy, Alphy, to divide and Mrs Donnelly said it was too good of her to bring such a big bag of cakes and made all the children say:

—Thanks, Maria.

But Maria said she had brought something special for papa and mamma, something they would be sure to like, and she began to look for her plumcake. She tried in Downes's bag and then in the pockets of her raincloak and then on the hallstand but nowhere could she find it. Then she asked all the children had any of them eaten it—by mistake, of course—but the children all said no and looked as if they did not like to eat cakes if they were to be accused of stealing. Everybody had a solution for the mystery and Mrs Donnelly said it was plain that Maria had left it behind her in the tram. Maria, remembering how confused the gentleman with the greyish moustache had made her, coloured with shame and vexation and disappointment. At the thought of the failure of her little surprise and of the two and fourpence she had thrown away for nothing she nearly cried outright.

But Joe said it didn't matter and made her sit down by the fire. He was very nice with her. He told her all that went on in his office, repeating for her a smart answer which he had made to the manager. Maria did not understand why Joe laughed so much over the answer he had made but she said that the manager must have been a very overbearing person to deal with. Joe said he wasn't so bad when you knew how to take him, that he was a decent sort so long as you didn't rub him the wrong way. Mrs Donnelly played the piano for the children and they danced and sang. Then the two next-door girls handed round the nuts. Nobody could find the nutcrackers and Joe was nearly getting cross over it and asked how did they expect Maria to crack nuts without a nutcracker. But Maria said she didn't like nuts and that they weren't to bother about her. Then Joe asked would she take a bottle of stout and Mrs Donnelly said there was port wine too in the house if she would prefer that. Maria said she would rather they didn't ask her to take anything: but Joe insisted.

So Maria let him have his way and they sat by the fire talking over old times and Maria thought she would put in a good word for Alphy. But Joe cried that God might strike him stone dead if ever he spoke a word to his brother again and Maria said she was sorry she had mentioned the matter. Mrs Donnelly told her husband it was a great shame for him to speak that way of his own flesh and blood but Joe said that Alphy was no brother of his and there was nearly being a row on the head of it. But Joe said he would not lose his temper on account of the night it was and asked his wife to open some more stout. The two next-door girls had arranged some Hallow Eve games and soon everything was merry again. Maria was delighted to see the children so merry and Joe and his wife in such good spirits. The next-door girls put some saucers on the table and then led the children up to the table, blindfold. One got the prayer-book and the other three got the water; and when one of the next-door girls got the ring Mrs Donnelly shook her finger at the blushing girl as much as to say: *O, I know all about it!* They insisted then on blindfolding Maria and leading her up to the table to see what she would get; and, while they were putting on the bandage, Maria laughed and laughed again till the tip of her nose nearly met the tip of her chin.

They led her up to the table amid laughing and joking and she put her hand out in the air as she was told to do. She moved her hand about here and there in the air and descended on one of the saucers. She felt a soft wet substance with her fingers and was surprised that nobody spoke or took off her bandage. There was a pause for a few seconds; and then a great deal of scuffling and whispering. Somebody said something about the garden, and at last Mrs Donnelly said something very cross to one of the next-door girls and told her to throw it out at once: that was no play. Maria understood that it was wrong that time and so she had to do it over again: and this time she got the prayer-book.

After that Mrs Donnelly played Miss McCloud's Reel for the children and Joe made Maria take a glass of wine. Soon they were all quite merry again and Mrs Donnelly said Maria would enter a convent before the year was out because she had got the prayer-book. Maria had never seen Joe so nice to her as he was that night, so full of pleasant talk and reminiscences. She said they were all very good to her.

At last the children grew tired and sleepy and Joe asked Maria would she not sing some little song before she went, one of the old songs. Mrs Donnelly said *Do, please, Maria!* and so Maria had to get up and stand beside the piano. Mrs Donnelly bade the children be quiet and listen to Maria's song. Then she played the prelude and said *Now, Maria!* and Maria, blushing very much, began to sing in a tiny quavering voice. She sang *I Dreamt that I Dwelt,* and when she came to the second verse she sang again:

I dreamt that I dwelt in marble halls
  With vassals and serfs at my side,
And of all who assembled within those walls
  That I was the hope and the pride.
I had riches too great to count; could boast
  Of a high ancestral name,
But I also dreamt, which pleased me most,
  That you loved me still the same.

But no one tried to show her her mistake; and when she had ended her song Joe was very much moved. He said that there was no time like the long ago and no music for him like poor old Balfe, whatever other people might say; and his eyes filled up so much with tears that he could not find what he was looking for and in the end he had to ask his wife to tell him where the corkscrew was.

A Hunger Artist

Franz Kafka

During these last decades the interest in professional fasting has markedly diminished. It used to pay very well to stage such great performances under one's own management, but today that is quite impossible. We live in a different world now. At one time the whole town took a lively interest in the hunger artist; from day to day of his fast the excitement mounted; everybody wanted to see him at least once a day; there were people who bought season tickets for the last few days and sat from morning till night in front of his small barred cage; even in the nighttime there were visiting hours, when the whole effect was heightened by torch flares; on fine days the cage was set out in the open air, and then it was the children's special treat to see the hunger artist; for their elders he was often just a joke that happened to be in fashion, but the children stood open-mouthed, holding each other's hands for greater security, marveling at him as he sat there pallid in black tights, with his ribs sticking out so prominently, not even on a seat but down among straw on the ground, sometimes giving a courteous nod, answering questions with a constrained smile, or perhaps stretching an arm through the bars so that one might feel how thin it was, and then again withdrawing deep into himself, paying no attention to anyone or anything, not even to the all-important striking of the clock that was the only piece of furniture in his cage, but merely staring into vacancy with half-shut eyes, now and then taking a sip from a tiny glass of water to moisten his lips.

Besides casual onlookers there were also relays of permanent watchers selected by the public, usually butchers, strangely enough, and it was their task to watch the hunger artist day and night, three of them at a time, in case he should have some secret recourse to nourishment. This was nothing but a formality, instituted to reassure the masses, for the initiates knew well enough that during his fast the artist would never in any circumstances, not even under forcible compulsion, swallow the smallest morsel of food; the honor of his profession forbade it. Not every watcher, of course, was capable of understanding this, there were often groups of night watchers who were very lax in carrying out their duties and deliberately huddled together in a retired corner to play cards with great absorption, obviously intending to give the hunger artist the chance of a little refreshment, which they supposed he could draw from some private hoard. Nothing annoyed the artist more than such watchers; they made him miserable; they made his fast seem unendurable; sometimes he mastered his feebleness sufficiently to sing during their watch for as long as he could keep going, to show them how unjust their suspicions were. But that was of little use; they only wondered at his cleverness in being able to fill his mouth even while singing. Much more to his taste were the watchers who sat close up to the bars, who were not content with the dim night lighting of the hall but focused him in the full glare of the electric pocket torch given them by the impresario. The harsh light did not trouble him at all, in any case he could never sleep properly, and he could always drowse a little, whatever the light, at any hour, even when the hall was thronged with noisy onlookers. He was quite happy at the prospect of spending a sleepless night with such watchers; he was ready to exchange jokes with them, to tell them stories out of his nomadic life, anything at all to keep them awake and demonstrate to them again that he had no eatables in his cage and that he was fasting as not one of them could fast. But his happiest moment was when the morning came and an enormous breakfast was brought them, at his expense, on which they flung themselves with the keen appetite of healthy men after a weary night of wakefulness. Of course there were people who argued that this breakfast was an unfair attempt to bribe the watchers, but that was going rather too far, and when they were invited to take on a night's vigil without a breakfast, merely for the sake of the cause, they made themselves scarce, although they stuck stubbornly to their suspicions.

Such suspicions, anyhow, were a necessary accompaniment to the profession of fasting. No one could possibly watch the hunger artist continuously, day and night, and so no one could produce first-hand evidence that the fast had really been rigorous and continuous; only the artist himself could know that, he was therefore bound to be the sole completely satisfied spectator of his own fast. Yet for other reasons he was never satisfied; it was not perhaps mere fasting that had brought him to such skeleton thinness that many people had regretfully to keep away from his exhibitions, because the sight of him was too much for them, perhaps it was dissatisfaction with himself that had worn him down. For he alone knew, what no other initiate knew, how easy it was to fast. It was the easiest thing in the world. He made no secret of this, yet people did not believe him, at the best they set him down as modest, most of them, however, thought he was out for publicity or else was some kind of cheat who found it easy to fast because he had discovered a way of making it easy, and then had the impudence to admit the fact, more or less. He had to put up with all that, and in the course of time had got used to it, but his inner dissatisfaction always rankled, and never yet, after any term of fasting—this must be granted to his credit—had he left the cage of his own free will. The longest period of fasting was fixed by his impresario at forty days, beyond that term he was not allowed to go, not even in great cities, and there was good reason for it, too. Experience had proved that for about forty days the interest of the public could be stimulated by a steadily increasing pressure of advertisement, but after that the town began to lose interest, sympathetic support began notably to fall off; there were of course local variations as between one town and another or one country and another, but as a general rule forty days marked the limit. So on the fortieth day the flower-bedecked cage was opened, enthusiastic spectators filled the hall, a military band played, two doctors entered the cage to measure the results of the fast, which were announced through a megaphone, and finally two young ladies appeared, blissful at having been selected for the honor, to help the hunger artist down the few steps leading to a small table on which was spread a carefully chosen invalid repast. And at this very moment the artist always turned stubborn. True, he would entrust his bony arms to the outstretched helping hands of the ladies bending over him, but stand up he would not. Why stop fasting at this particular moment, after forty days of it? He had held out for a long time, an illimitably long time; why stop now, when he was in his best fasting form, or rather, not yet quite in his best fasting form? Why should he be cheated of the fame he would get for fasting longer, for being not only the record hunger artist of all time, which presumably he was already, but for beating his own record by a performance beyond human imagination, since he felt that there were no limits to his capacity for fasting? His public pretended to admire him so much, why should it have so little patience with him; if he could endure fasting longer, why shouldn't the public endure it? Besides, he was tired, he was comfortable sitting in the straw, and now he was supposed to lift himself to his full height and go down to a meal the very thought of which gave him a nausea that only the presence of the ladies kept him from betraying, and even that with an effort. And he looked up into the eyes of the ladies who were apparently so friendly and in reality so cruel, and shook his head, which felt too heavy on its strengthless neck. But then there happened yet again what always happened. The impresario came forward, without a word—for the band made speech impossible—lifted his arms in the air above the artist, as if inviting Heaven to look down upon its creature here in the straw, this suffering martyr, which indeed he was, although in quite another sense; grasped him round the emaciated waist, with exaggerated caution, so that the frail condition he was in might be appreciated; and committed him to the care of the blenching ladies, not without secretly giving him a shaking so that his legs and body tottered and swayed. The artist now submitted completely; his head lolled on his breast as if it had landed there by chance; his body was hollowed out; his legs in a spasm of self-preservation clung close to each other at the knees, yet scraped on the ground as if it were not really solid ground, as if they were only trying to find solid ground; and the whole weight of his body, a featherweight after all, relapsed onto one of the ladies, who, looking round for help and panting a little—this post of honor was not at all what she had expected it to be—first stretched her neck as far as she could to keep her face at least free from contact with the artist, then finding this impossible, and her more fortunate companion not coming to her aid but merely holding extended on her own trembling hand the little bunch of knucklebones that was the artist's, to the great delight of the spectators burst into tears and had to be replaced by an attendant who had long been stationed in readiness. Then came the food, a little of which the impresario managed to get between the artist's lips, while he sat in a kind of half-fainting trance, to the accompaniment of cheerful patter designed to distract the public's attention from the artist's condition; after that, a toast was drunk to the public, supposedly prompted by a whisper from the artist in the impresario's ear; the band confirmed it with a mighty flourish, the spectators melted away, and no one had any cause to be dissatisfied with the proceedings, no one except the hunger artist himself, he only, as always.

So he lived for many years, with small regular intervals of recuperation, in visible glory, honored by the world, yet in spite of that troubled in spirit, and all the more troubled because no one would take his trouble seriously. What comfort could he possibly need? What more could he possibly wish for? And if some good-natured person, feeling sorry for him, tried to console him by pointing out that his melancholy was probably caused by fasting, it could happen, especially when he had been fasting for some time, that he reacted with an outburst of fury and to the general alarm began to shake the bars of his cage like a wild animal. Yet the impresario had a way of punishing these outbreaks which he rather enjoyed putting into operation. He would apologize publicly for the artist's behavior, which was only to be excused, he admitted, because of the irritability caused by fasting; a condition hardly to be understood by well-fed people; then by natural transition he went on to mention the artist's equally incomprehensible boast that he could fast for much longer than he was doing; he praised the high ambition, the good will, the great self-denial undoubtedly implicit in such a statement; and then quite simply countered it by bringing out photographs, which were also on sale to the public, showing the artist on the fortieth day of a fast lying in bed almost dead from exhaustion. This perversion of the truth, familiar to the artist though it was, always unnerved him afresh and proved too much for him. What was a consequence of the premature ending of his fast was here presented as the cause of it! To fight against this lack of understanding, against a whole world of non-understanding, was impossible. Time and again in good faith he stood by the bars listening to the impresario, but as soon as the photographs appeared he always let go and sank with a groan back on to his straw, and the reassured public could once more come close and gaze at him.

A few years later when the witnesses of such scenes called them to mind, they often failed to understand themselves at all. For meanwhile the aforementioned change in public interest had set in; it seemed to happen almost overnight; there may have been profound causes for it, but who was going to bother about that; at any rate the pampered hunger artist suddenly found himself deserted one fine day by the amusement seekers, who went streaming past him to other more favored attractions. For the last time the impresario hurried him over half Europe to discover whether the old interest might still survive here and there; all in vain; everywhere, as if by secret agreement, a positive revulsion from professional fasting was in evidence. Of course it could not really have sprung up so suddenly as all that, and many premonitory symptoms which had not been sufficiently remarked or suppressed during the rush and glitter of success now came retrospectively to mind, but it was now too late to take any countermeasures. Fasting would surely come into fashion again at some future date, yet that was no comfort for those living in the present. What, then, was the hunger artist to do? He had been applauded by thousands in his time and could hardly come down to showing himself in a street booth at village fairs, and as for adopting another profession, he was not only too old for that but too fanatically devoted to fasting. So he took leave of the impresario, his partner in an unparalleled career, and hired himself to a large circus; in order to spare his own feelings he avoided reading the conditions of his contract.

A large circus with its enormous traffic in replacing and recruiting men, animals and apparatus can always find a use for people at any time, even for a hunger artist, provided of course that he does not ask too much, and in this particular case anyhow it was not only the artist who was taken on but his famous and long-known name as well, indeed considering the peculiar nature of his performance, which was not impaired by advancing age, it could not be objected that here was an artist past his prime, no longer at the height of his professional skill, seeking a refuge in some quiet corner of a circus, on the contrary, the hunger artist averred that he could fast as well as ever, which was entirely credible, he even alleged that if he were allowed to fast as he liked, and this was at once promised him without more ado, he could astound the world by establishing a record never yet achieved, a statement which certainly provoked a smile among the other professionals, since it left out of account the change in public opinion, which the hunger artist in his zeal conveniently forgot.

He had not, however, actually lost his sense of the real situation and took it as a matter of course that he and his cage should be stationed, not in the middle of the ring as a main attraction, but outside, near the animal cages, on a site that was after all easily accessible. Large and gaily painted placards made a frame for the cage and announced what was to be seen inside it. When the public came thronging out in the intervals to see the animals, they could hardly avoid passing the hunger artist's cage and stopping there for a moment, perhaps they might even have stayed longer had not those pressing behind them in the narrow gangway, who did not understand why they should be held up on their way towards the excitements of the menagerie, made it impossible for anyone to stand gazing quietly for any length of time. And that was the reason why the hunger artist, who had of course been looking forward to these visiting hours as the main achievement of his life, began instead to shrink from them. At first he could hardly wait for the intervals; it was exhilarating to watch the crowds come streaming his way, until only too soon—not even the most obstinate self-deception, clung to almost consciously, could hold out against the fact—the conviction was borne in upon him that these people, most of them, to judge from their actions, again and again, without exception, were all on their way to the menagerie. And the first sight of them from the distance remained the best. For when they reached his cage he was at once deafened by the storm of shouting and abuse that arose from the two contending factions, which renewed themselves continuously, of those who wanted to stop and stare at him—he soon began to dislike them more than the others—not out of real interest but only out of obstinate self-assertiveness, and those who wanted to go straight on to the animals. When the first great rush was past, the stragglers came along, and these, whom nothing could have prevented from stopping to look at him as long as they had breath, raced past with long strides, hardly even glancing at him, in their haste to get to the menagerie in time. And all too rarely did it happen that he had a stroke of luck, when some father of a family fetched up before him with his children, pointed a finger at the hunger artist and explained at length what the phenomenon meant, telling stories of earlier years when he himself had watched similar but much more thrilling performances, and the children, still rather uncomprehending, since neither inside nor outside school had they been sufficiently prepared for this lesson—what did they care about fasting?—yet showed by the brightness of their intent eyes that new and better times might be coming. Perhaps, said the hunger artist to himself many a time, things would be a little better if his cage were set not quite so near the menagerie. That made it too easy for people to make their choice, to say nothing of what he suffered from the stench of the menagerie, the animals' restlessness by night, the carrying past of raw lumps of flesh for the beasts of prey, the roaring at feeding times, which depressed him continually. But he did not dare to lodge a complaint with the management; after all, he had the animals to thank for the troops of people who passed his cage, among whom there might always be one here and there to take an interest in him, and who could tell where they might seclude him if he called attention to his existence and thereby to the fact that, strictly speaking, he was only an impediment on the way to the menagerie.

A small impediment, to be sure, one that grew steadily less. People grew familiar with the strange idea that they could be expected, in times like these, to take an interest in a hunger artist, and with this familiarity the verdict went out against him. He might fast as much as he could, and he did so; but nothing could save him now, people passed him by. Just try to explain to anyone the art of fasting! Anyone who has no feeling for it cannot be made to understand it. The fine placards grew dirty and illegible, they were torn down; the little notice board telling the number of fast days achieved, which at first was changed carefully every day, had long stayed at the same figure, for after the first few weeks even this small task seemed pointless to the staff; and so the artist simply fasted on and on, as he had once dreamed of doing, and it was no trouble to him, just as he had always foretold, but no one counted the days, no one, not even the artist himself, knew what records he was already breaking, and his heart grew heavy. And when once in a time some leisurely passer-by stopped, made merry over the old figure on the board and spoke of swindling, that was in its way the stupidest lie ever invented by indifference and inborn malice, since it was not the hunger artist who was cheating, he was working honestly, but the world was cheating him of his reward.

Many more days went by, however, and that too came to an end. An overseer's eye fell on the cage one day and he asked the attendants why this perfectly good stage should be left standing there unused with dirty straw inside it; nobody knew, until one man, helped out by the notice board, remembered about the hunger artist. They poked into the straw with sticks and found him in it. "Are you still fasting?" asked the overseer, "when on earth do you mean to stop?" "Forgive me, everybody," whispered the hunger artist; only the overseer, who had his ear to the bars, understood him. "Of course," said the overseer, and tapped his forehead with a finger to let the attendants know what state the man was in, "we forgive you." "I always wanted you to admire my fasting," said the hunger artist. "We do admire it," said the overseer, affably. "But you shouldn't admire it," said the hunger artist. "Well then we don't admire it," said the overseer, "but why shouldn't we admire it?" "Because I have to fast, I can't help it," said the hunger artist. "What a fellow you are," said the overseer, "and why can't you help it?" "Because," said the hunger artist, lifting his head a little and speaking, with his lips pursed, as if for a kiss, right into the overseer's ear, so that no syllable might be lost, "because I couldn't find the food I liked. If I had found it, believe me, I should have made no fuss and stuffed myself like you or anyone else." These were his last words, but in his dimming eyes remained the firm though no longer proud persuasion that he was still continuing to fast.

"Well, clear this out now!" said the overseer, and they buried the hunger artist, straw and all. Into the cage they put a young panther. Even the most insensitive felt it refreshing to see this wild creature leaping around the cage that had so long been dreary. The panther was all right. The food he liked was brought him without hesitation by the attendants; he seemed not even to miss his freedom; his noble body, furnished almost to the bursting point with all that it needed, seemed to carry freedom around with it too; somewhere in his jaws it seemed to lurk; and the joy of life streamed with such ardent passion from his throat that for the onlookers it was not easy to stand the shock of it. But they braced themselves, crowded round the cage, and did not want ever to move away.

Tickets, Please

D. H. Lawrence

There is in the Midlands a single-line tramway system which boldly leaves the county town and plunges off into the black, industrial country-side, up hill and down dale, through the long ugly villages of workmen's houses, over canals and railways, past churches perched high and nobly over the smoke and shadows, through stark, grimy cold little market-places, tilting away in a rush past cinemas and shops down to the hollow where the collieries are, then up again, past a little rural church, under the ash trees, on in a rush to the terminus, the last little ugly place of industry, the cold little town that shivers on the edge of the wild, gloomy country beyond. There the green and creamy coloured tram-car seems to pause and purr with curious satisfaction. But in a few minutes—the clock on the turret of the Co-operative Wholesale Society's shops gives the time—away it starts once more on the adventure. Again there are the reckless swoops downhill, bouncing the loops: again the chilly wait in the hill-top market-place: again the breathless slithering round the precipitous drop under the church:

again the patient halts at the loops, waiting for the outcoming car: so on and on, for two long hours, till at last the city looms beyond the fat gas-works, the narrow factories draw near, we are in the sordid streets of the great town, once more we sidle to a standstill at our terminus, abashed by the great crimson and cream-coloured city cars, but still perky, jaunty, somewhat dare-devil, green as a jaunty sprig of parsley out of a black colliery garden.

To ride on these cars is always an adventure. Since we are in war-time, the drivers are men unfit for active service: cripples and hunchbacks. So they have the spirit of the devil in them. The ride becomes a steeplechase. Hurray! we have leapt in a clear jump over the canal bridge—now for the four-lane corner. With a shriek and a trail of sparks we are clear again. To be sure, a tram often leaps the rails—but what matter! It sits in a ditch till other trams come to haul it out. It is quite common for a car, packed with one solid mass of living people, to come to a dead halt in the midst of unbroken blackness, the heart of nowhere on a dark night, and for the driver and the girl conductor to call: "All get off—car's on fire!" Instead, however, of rushing out in a panic, the passengers stolidly reply: "Get on—get on! We're not coming out. We're stopping where we are. Push on, George." So till flames actually appear.

The reason for this reluctance to dismount is that the nights are howlingly cold, black, and windswept, and a car is a haven of refuge. From village to village the miners travel, for a change of cinema, of girl, of pub. The trams are desperately packed. Who is going to risk himself in the black gulf outside, to wait perhaps an hour for another tram, then to see the forlorn notice 'Depot Only,' because there is something wrong! Or to greet a unit of three bright cars all so tight with people that they sail past with a howl of derision. Trams that pass in the night.

This, the most dangerous tram-service in England, as the authorities themselves declare, with pride, is entirely conducted by girls, and driven by rash young men, a little crippled, or by delicate young men, who creep forward in terror. The girls are fearless young hussies. In their ugly blue uniform, skirts up to their knees, shapeless old peaked caps on their heads, they have all the *sang-froid* of an old non-commissioned officer. With a tram packed with howling colliers, roaring hymns downstairs and a sort of antiphony of obscenities upstairs, the lasses are perfectly at their ease. They pounce on the youths who try to evade their ticket-machine. They push off the men at the end of their distance. They are not going to be done in the eye—not they. They fear nobody—and everybody fears them.

"Hello, Annie!"

"Hello, Ted!"

"Oh, mind my corn, Miss Stone. It's my belief you've got a heart of stone, for you've trod on it again."

"You should keep it in your pocket," replies Miss Stone, and she goes sturdily upstairs in her high boots.

"Tickets, please."

She is peremptory, suspicious, and ready to hit first. She can hold her own against ten thousand. The step of that tram-car is her Thermopylae.

Therefore, there is a certain wild romance aboard these cars—and in the sturdy bosom of Annie herself. The time for soft romance is in the morning, between ten o'clock and one, when things are rather slack: that is, except market-day and Saturday. Thus Annie has time to look about her. Then she often hops off her car and into a shop where she has spied something, while the driver chats in the main road. There is very good feeling between the girls and the drivers. Are they not companions in peril, shipments aboard this careering vessel of a tram-car, for ever rocking on the waves of a stormy land.

Then, also, during the easy hours, the inspectors are most in evidence. For some reason, everybody employed in this tram-service is young: there are no grey heads. It would not do. Therefore the inspectors are of the right age, and one, the chief, is also good-looking. See him stand on a wet, gloomy morning, in his long oilskin, his peaked cap well down over his eyes, waiting to board a car. His face ruddy, his small brown moustache is weathered, he has a faint impudent smile. Fairly tall and agile, even in his waterproof, he springs aboard a car and greets Annie.

"Hello, Annie! Keeping the wet out?"

"Trying to."

There are only two people in the car. Inspecting is soon over. Then for a long and impudent chat on the foot-board, a good, easy, twelve-mile chat.

The inspector's name is John Thomas Raynor—always called John Thomas, except sometimes, in malice, Coddy. His face sets in fury when he is addressed, from a distance, with this abbreviation. There is considerable scandal about John Thomas in half a dozen villages. He flirts with the girl conductors in the morning, and walks out with them in the dark night, when they leave their tram-car at the depôt. Of course, the girls quit the service frequently. Then he flirts and walks out with the newcomer: always providing she is sufficiently attractive, and that she will consent to walk. It is remarkable, however, that most of the girls are quite comely, they are all young, and this roving life aboard the car gives them a sailor's dash and recklessness. What matter how they behave when the ship is in port? To-morrow they will be aboard again.

Annie, however, was something of a Tartar, and her sharp tongue had kept John Thomas at arm's length for many months. Perhaps, therefore, she liked him all the more: for he always came up smiling, with impudence. She watched him vanquish one girl, then another. She could tell by the movement of his mouth and eyes, when he flirted with her in the morning, that he had been walking out with this lass, or the other, the night before. A fine cock-of-the-walk he was. She could sum him up pretty well.

In this subtle antagonism they knew each other like old friends, they were as shrewd with one another almost as man and wife. But Annie had always kept him sufficiently at arm's length. Besides, she had a boy of her own.

The Statutes fair, however, came in November, at Bestwood. It happened that Annie had the Monday night off. It was a drizzling ugly night, yet she dressed herself up and went to the fair-ground. She was alone, but she expected soon to find a pal of some sort.

The roundabouts were veering round and grinding out their music, the side-shows were making as much commotion as possible. In the coconut shies there were no coconuts, but artificial war-time substitutes, which the lads declared were fastened into the irons. There was a sad decline in brilliance and luxury. None the less, the ground was muddy as ever, there was the same crush, the press of faces lighted up by the flares and the electric lights, the same smell of naphtha and a few potatoes, and of electricity.

Who should be the first to greet Miss Annie on the show-ground but John Thomas. He had a black overcoat buttoned up to his chin, and a tweed cap pulled down over his brows, his face between was ruddy and smiling and handy as ever. She knew so well the way his mouth moved.

She was very glad to have a "boy." To be at the Statutes without a fellow was no fun. Instantly, like the gallant he was, he took her on the Dragons, grim-toothed, roundabout switchbacks. It was not nearly so exciting as a tram-car actually. But, then, to be seated in a shaking, green dragon, uplifted above the sea of bubble faces, careering in a rickety fashion in the lower heavens, whilst John Thomas leaned over her, his cigarette in his mouth, was after all the right style. She was a plump, quick, alive little creature. So she was quite excited and happy.

John Thomas made her stay on for the next round. And therefore she could hardly for shame repulse him when he put his arm round her and drew her a little nearer to him, in a very warm and cuddly manner. Besides he was fairly discreet, he kept his movement as hidden as possible. She looked down, and saw that his red, clean hand was out of sight of the crowd. And they knew each other so well. So they warmed up to the fair.

After the dragons they went on the horses. John Thomas paid each time, so she could but be complaisant. He, of course, sat astride on the outer horse—named "Black Bess"—and she sat sideways, towards him, on the inner horse—named "Wildfire." But of course John Thomas was not going to sit discreetly on "Black Bess," holding the brass bar. Round they spun and heaved, in the light. And round he swung on his wooden steed, flinging one leg across her mount, and perilously tipping up and down, across the space, half lying back, laughing at her. He was perfectly happy; she was afraid her hat was on one side, but she was excited.

He threw quoits on a table, and won for her two large, pale blue hat-pins. And then, hearing the noise of the cinemas, announcing another performance, they climbed the boards and went in.

Of course, during these performances pitch darkness falls from time to time, when the machine goes wrong. Then there is a wild whooping, and a loud smacking of simulated kisses. In these moments John Thomas drew Annie towards him. After all, he had a wonderfully warm, cosy way of holding a girl with his arm, he seemed to make such a nice fit. And, after all, it was pleasant to be so held: so very comforting and cosy and nice. He leaned over her and she felt his breath on her hair; she knew he wanted to kiss her on the lips. And, after all, he was so warm and she fitted in to him so softly. After all, she wanted him to touch her lips.

But the light sprang up; she also started electrically, and put her hat straight. He left his arm lying nonchalantly behind her. Well, it was fun, it was exciting to be at the Statutes with John Thomas.

When the cinema was over they went for a walk across the dark, damp fields. He had all the arts of love-making. He was especially good at holding a girl, when he sat with her on a stile in the black, drizzling darkness. He seemed to be holding her in space, against his own warmth and gratification. And his kisses were soft and slow and searching.

So Annie walked out with John Thomas, though she kept her own boy dangling in the distance. Some of the tram-girls chose to be huffy. But there, you must take things as you find them, in this life.

There was no mistake about it, Annie liked John Thomas a good deal. She felt so rich and warm in herself whenever he was near. And John Thomas really liked Annie, more than usual. The soft, melting way in which she could flow into a fellow, as if she melted into his very bones, was something rare and good. He fully appreciated this.

But with a developing acquaintance there began a developing intimacy. Annie wanted to consider him a person, a man: she wanted to take an intelligent interest in him, and to have an intelligent response. She did not want a mere nocturnal presence, which was what he was so far. And she prided herself that he could not leave her.

Here she made a mistake. John Thomas intended to remain a nocturnal presence; he had no idea of becoming an all-round individual to her. When she started to take an intelligent interest in him and his life and his character, he sheered off. He hated intelligent interest. And he knew that the only way to stop it was to avoid it. The possessive female was aroused in Annie. So he left her.

It is no use saying she was not surprised. She was at first startled, thrown out of her count. For she had been so *very* sure of holding him. For a while she was staggered, and everything became uncertain to her. Then she wept with fury, indignation, desolation, and misery. Then she had a spasm of despair. And then, when he came, still impudently, on to her car, still familiar, but letting her see by the movement of his head that he had gone away to somebody else for the time being, and was enjoying pastures new, then she determined to have her own back.

She had a very shrewd idea what girls John Thomas had taken out. She went to Nora Purdy. Nora was a tall, rather pale, but well-built girl, with beautiful yellow hair. She was rather secretive.

"Hey!" said Annie, accosting her; then softly: "Who's John Thomas on with now?"

"I don't know," said Nora.

"Why, tha does," said Annie, ironically lapsing into dialect. "Tha knows as well as I do."

"Well, I do, then," said Nora. "It isn't me, so don't bother."

"It's Cissy Meakin, isn't it?"

"It is, for all I know."

"Hasn't he got a face on him!" said Annie. "I don't half like his cheek. I could knock him off the foot-board when he comes round at me."

"He'll get dropped on one of these days," said Nora.

"Ay, he will, when somebody makes up their mind to drop it on him. I should like to see him taken down a peg or two, shouldn't you?"

"I shouldn't mind," said Nora.

"You've got quite as much cause to as I have," said Annie. "But we'll drop on him one of these days, my girl. What? Don't you want to?"

"I don't mind," said Nora.

But as a matter of fact, Nora was much more vindictive than Annie.

One by one Annie went the round of the old flames. It so happened that Cissy Meakin left the tramway service in quite a short time. Her mother made her leave. Then John Thomas was on the *qui vive.* He cast his eyes over his old flock. And his eyes lighted on Annie. He thought she would be safe now. Besides, he liked her.

She arranged to walk home with him on Sunday night. It so happened that her car would be in the depôt at half-past nine: the last car would come in at 10:15. So John Thomas was to wait for her there.

At the depôt the girls had a little waiting-room of their own. It was quite rough, but cosy, with a fire and an oven and a mirror, and table and wooden chairs. The half-dozen girls who knew John Thomas only too well had arranged to take service this Sunday afternoon. So, as the cars began to come in, early, the girls dropped into the waiting-room. And instead of hurrying off home, they sat around the fire and had a cup of tea. Outside was the darkness and lawlessness of war-time.

John Thomas came on the car after Annie, at about a quarter to ten. He poked his head easily into the girls' waiting-room.

"Prayer-meeting?" he asked.

"Ay," said Laura Sharp. "Ladies only."

"That's me!" said John Thomas. It was one of his favourite exclamations.

"Shut the door, boy," said Muriel Baggaley.

"Oh, which side of me?" said John Thomas.

"Which tha likes," said Polly Birkin.

He had come in and closed the door behind him. The girls moved in their circle, to make a place for him near the fire. He took off his great-coat and pushed back his hat.

"Who handles the teapot?" he said.

Nora Purdy silently poured him out a cup of tea.

"Want a bit o' my bread and drippin'?" said Muriel Baggaley to him.

"Ay, give us a bit."

And he began to eat his piece of bread.

"There's no place like home, girls," he said.

They all looked at him as he uttered this piece of impudence. He seemed to be sunning himself in the presence of so many damsels.

"Especially if you're not afraid to go home in the dark," said Laura Sharp.

"Me! By myself I am."

They sat till they heard the last tram come in. In a few minutes Emma Houselay entered.

"Come on, my old duck!" cried Polly Birkin.

"It *is* perishing," said Emma, holding her fingers to the fire.

"But—I'm afraid to, go home in, the dark," sang Laura Sharp, the tune having got into her mind.

"Who're you going with to-night, John Thomas?" asked Muriel Baggaley coolly.

"To-night?" said John Thomas. "Oh, I'm going home by myself to-night—all on my lonely-o."

"That's me!" said Nora Purdy, using his own ejaculation.

The girls laughed shrilly.

"Me as well, Nora," said John Thomas.

"Don't know what you mean," said Laura.

"Yes, I'm toddling," said he, rising and reaching for his overcoat.

"Nay," said Polly. "We're all here waiting for you."

"We've got to be up in good time in the morning," he said, in the benevolent official manner.

They all laughed.

"Nay," said Muriel. "Don't leave us all lonely, John Thomas. Take one!"

"I'll take the lot, if you like," he responded gallantly.

"That you won't, either," said Muriel. "Two's company; seven's too much of a good thing."

"Nay—take one," said Laura. "Fair and square, all above board and say which."

"Ay," cried Annie, speaking for the first time. "Pick, John Thomas; let's hear thee."

"Nay," he said. "I'm going home quiet to-night. Feeling good, for once."

"Whereabouts?" said Annie. "Take a good 'un, then. But tha's got to take one of us!"

"Nay, how can I take one," he said, laughing uneasily. "I don't want to make enemies."

"You'd only make *one*," said Annie.

"The chosen *one*," added Laura.

"Oh, my! Who said girls!" exclaimed John Thomas, again turning, as if to escape. "Well—good-night."

"Nay, you've got to make your pick," said Muriel. "Turn your face to the wall, and say which one touches you. Go on—we shall only just touch your back—one of us. Go on—turn your face to the wall, and don't look, and say which one touches you."

He was uneasy, mistrusting them. Yet he had not the courage to break away. They pushed him to a wall and stood him there with his face to it. Behind his back they all grimaced, tittering. He looked so comical. He looked around uneasily.

"Go on!" he cried.

"You're looking—you're looking!" they shouted.

He turned his head away. And suddenly, with a movement like a swift cat, Annie went forward and fetched him a box on the side of the head that sent his cap flying and himself staggering. He started round.

But at Annie's signal they all flew at him, slapping him, pinching him, pulling his hair, though more in fun than in spite or anger. He, however, saw red. His blue eyes flamed with strange fear as well as fury, and he butted through the girls to the door. It was locked. He wrenched at it. Roused, alert, the girls stood round and looked at him. He faced them, at bay. At that moment they were rather horrifying to him, as they stood in their short uniforms. He was distinctly afraid.

"Come on, John Thomas! Come on! Choose!" said Annie.

"What are you after? Open the door," he said.

"We shan't—not till you've chosen!" said Muriel.

"Chosen what?" he said.

"Chosen the one you're going to marry," she replied.

He hesitated a moment.

"Open the blasted door," he said, "and get back to your senses." He spoke with official authority.

"You've got to choose!" cried the girls.

"Come on!" cried Annie, looking him in the eye. "Come on! Come on!"

He went forward, rather vaguely. She had taken off her belt, and swinging it, she fetched him a sharp blow over the head with the buckle end. He sprang and seized her. But immediately the other girls rushed upon him, pulling and tearing and beating him. Their blood was now thoroughly up. He was their sport now. They were going to have their own back, out of him. Strange, wild creatures, they hung on him and rushed at him to bear him down. His tunic was torn right up the back, Nora had hold at the back of his collar, and was actually strangling him. Luckily the button burst. He struggled in a wild frenzy of fury and terror, almost mad terror. His tunic was simply torn off his back, his shirt-sleeves were torn away, his arms were naked. The girls rushed at him, clenched their hands on him and pulled at him: or they rushed at him and pushed him, butted him with all their might: or they struck him wild blows. He ducked and cringed and struck sideways. They became more intense.

At last he was down. They rushed on him, kneeling on him. He had neither breath nor strength to move. His face was bleeding with a long scratch, his brow was bruised.

Annie knelt on him, the other girls knelt and hung on to him. Their faces were flushed, their hair wild, their eyes were all glittering strangely. He lay at last quite still, with face averted, as an animal lies when it is defeated and at the mercy of the captor. Sometimes his eye glanced back at the wild faces of the girls. His breast rose heavily, his wrists were torn.

"Now, then, my fellow!" gasped Annie at length. "Now then—now ——"

At the sound of her terrifying, cold triumph, he suddenly started to struggle as an animal might, but the girls threw themselves upon him with unnatural strength and power, forcing him down.

"Yes—now, then!" gasped Annie at length.

And there was a dead silence, in which the thud of heart-beating was to be heard. It was a suspense of pure silence in every soul.

"Now you know where you are," said Annie.

The sight of his white, bare arm maddened the girls. He lay in a kind of trance of fear and antagonism. They felt themselves filled with supernatural strength.

Suddenly Polly started to laugh—to giggle wildly—helplessly—and Emma and Muriel joined in. But Annie and Nora and Laura remained the same, tense, watchful, with gleaming eyes. He winced away from these eyes.

"Yes," said Annie, in a curious low tone, secret and deadly. "Yes! You've got it now. You know what you've done, don't you? You know what you've done."

He made no sound nor sign, but lay with bright, averted eyes, and averted, bleeding face.

"You ought to be *killed,* that's what you ought," said Annie, tensely. "You ought to be *killed!*" And there was a terrifying lust in her voice.

Polly was ceasing to laugh, and giving long-drawn Oh-h-hs and sighs as she came to herself.

"He's got to choose," she said vaguely.

"Oh, yes, he has," said Laura, with vindictive decision.

"Do you hear—do you hear?" said Annie. And with a sharp movement, that made him wince, she turned his face to her.

"Do you hear?" she repeated, shaking him.

But he was quite dumb. She fetched him a sharp slap on the face. He started, and his eyes widened. Then his face darkened with defiance, after all.

"Do you hear?" she repeated.

He only looked at her with hostile eyes.

"Speak!" she said, putting her face devilishly near his.

"What?" he said, almost overcome.

"You've got to *choose!*" she cried, as if it were some terrible menace, and as if it hurt her that she could not exact more.

"What?" he said, in fear.

"Choose your girl, Coddy. You've got to choose her now. And you'll get your neck broken if you play any more of your tricks, my boy. You're settled now."

There was a pause. Again he averted his face. He was cunning in his overthrow. He did not give in to them really—no, not if they tore him to bits.

"All right, then," he said, "I choose Annie." His voice was strange and full of malice. Annie let go of him as if he had been a hot coal.

"He's chosen Annie!" said the girls in chorus.

"Me!" cried Annie. She was still kneeling, but away from him. He was still lying prostrate, with averted face. The girls grouped uneasily around.

"Me!" repeated Annie, with a terrible bitter accent.

Then she got up, drawing away from him with strange disgust and bitterness.

"I wouldn't touch him," she said.

But her face quivered with a kind of agony, she seemed as if she would fall. The other girls turned aside. He remained lying on the floor, with his torn clothes and bleeding, averted face.

"Oh, if he's chosen——" said Polly.

"I don't want him—he can choose again," said Annie, with the same rather bitter hopelessness.

"Get up," said Polly, lifting his shoulder. "Get up."

He rose slowly, a strange, ragged, dazed creature. The girls eyed him from a distance, curiously, furtively, dangerously.

"Who wants him?" cried Laura, roughly.

"Nobody," they answered, with contempt. Yet each one of them waited for him to look at her, hoped he would look at her. All except Annie, and something was broken in her.

He, however, kept his face closed and averted from them all. There was a silence of the end. He picked up the torn pieces of his tunic, without knowing what to do with them. The girls stood about uneasily, flushed, panting, tidying their hair and their dress unconsciously, and watching him. He looked at none of them. He espied his cap in a corner, and went and picked it up. He put it on his head, and one of the girls burst into a shrill, hysteric laugh at the sight he presented. He, however, took no heed, but went straight to where his overcoat hung on a peg. The girls moved away from contact with him as if he had been an electric wire. He put on his coat and buttoned it down. Then he rolled his tunic-rags into a bundle, and stood before the locked door, dumbly.

"Open the door, somebody," said Laura.

"Annie's got the key," said one.

Annie silently offered the key to the girls. Nora unlocked the door.

"Tit for tat, old man," she said. "Show yourself a man, and don't bear a grudge."

But without a word or sign he had opened the door and gone, his face closed, his head dropped.

"That'll learn him," said Laura.

"Coddy!" said Nora.

"Shut up, for God's sake!" cried Annie fiercely, as if in torture.

"Well, I'm about ready to go, Polly. Look sharp!" said Muriel.

The girls were all anxious to be off. They were tidying themselves hurriedly, with mute, stupefied faces.

The Man Who Studied Yoga

Norman Mailer

I

I would introduce myself if it were not useless. The name I had last night will not be the same as the name I have tonight. For the moment, then, let me say that I am thinking of Sam Slovoda. Obligatorily, I study him, Sam Slovoda who is neither ordinary nor extraordinary, who is not young nor yet old, not tall nor short. He is sleeping, and it is fit to describe him now, for like most humans he prefers sleeping to not sleeping. He is a mild pleasant-looking man who has just turned forty. If the crown of his head reveals a little bald spot, he has nourished in compensation the vanity of a mustache. He has generally when he is awake an agreeable manner, at least with strangers; he appears friendly, tolerant, and genial. The fact is that like most of us, he is full of envy, full of spite, a gossip, a man who is pleased to find others are as unhappy as he, and yet—this is the worst to be said—he is a decent man. He is better than most. He would prefer to see a more equitable world, he scorns prejudice and privilege, he tries to hurt no one, he wishes to be liked. I will go even further. He has one serious virtue—he is not fond of himself, he wishes he were better. He would like to free himself of envy, of the annoying necessity to talk about his friends, he would like to love people more; specifically, he would like to love his wife more, and to love his two daughters without the tormenting if nonetheless irremediable vexation that they closet his life in the dusty web of domestic responsibilities and drudging for money.

How often he tells himself with contempt that he has the cruelty of a kind weak man.

May I state that I do not dislike Sam Slovoda; it is just that I am disappointed in him. He has tried too many things and never with a whole heart. He has wanted to be a serious novelist and now merely indulges the ambition; he wished to be of consequence in the world, and has ended, temporarily perhaps, as an overworked writer of continuity for comic magazines; when he was young he tried to be a bohemian and instead acquired a wife and family. Of his appetite for a variety of new experience I may say that it is matched only by his fear of new people and novel situations.

I will give an instance. Yesterday, Sam was walking along the street and a bum approached him for money. Sam did not see the man until too late; lost in some inconsequential thought, he looked up only in time to see a huge wretch of a fellow with a red twisted face and an outstretched hand. Sam is like so many; each time a derelict asks for a dime, he feels a coward if he pays the money, and is ashamed of himself if he doesn't. This once, Sam happened to think, I will not be bullied, and hurried past. But the bum was not to be lost so easily. "Have a heart, Jack," he called after in a whisky voice, "I need a drink bad." Sam stopped, Sam began to laugh. "Just so it isn't for coffee, here's a quarter," he said; and he laughed, and the bum laughed. "You're a man's man," the bum said. Sam went away pleased with himself, thinking about such things as the community which existed between all people. It was cheap of Sam. He should know better. He should know he was merely relieved the situation had turned out so well. Although he thinks he is sorry for bums, Sam really hates them. Who knows what violence they can offer?

At this time, there is a powerful interest in Sam's life, but many would ridicule it. He is in the process of being psychoanalyzed. Myself, I do not jeer. It has created the most unusual situation between Sam and me. I could go into details but they are perhaps premature. It would be better to watch Sam awaken.

His wife, Eleanor, has been up for an hour, and she has shut the window and neglected to turn off the radiator. The room is stifling. Sam groans in a stupor which is neither sleep nor refreshment, opens one eye, yawns, groans again, and lies twisted, strangled and trussed in pajamas which are too large for him. How painful it is for him to rise. Last night there was a party, and this morning, Sunday morning, he is awakening with a hangover. Invariably, he is depressed in the morning, and it is no different today. He finds himself in the flat and familiar dispirit of nearly all days.

It is snowing outside. Sam finally lurches to the window, and opens it for air. With the oxygen of a winter morning clearing his brain, he looks down six stories into the giant quadrangle of the Queens housing development in which he lives, staring morosely at the inch of slush which covers the monotonous artificial park that separates his apartment building from an identical structure not two hundred feet away. The walks are black where the snow has melted, and in the children's playground, all but deserted, one swing oscillates back and forth, pushed by an irritable little boy who plays by himself among the empty benches, swaddled in galoshes, muffler, and overcoat. The snow falls sluggishly, a wet snow which probably will turn to rain. The little boy in the playground gives one last disgusted shove to the swing and trudges away gloomily, his overshoes leaving a small animal track behind him. Back of Sam, in the four-room apartment he knows like a blind man, there is only the sound of Eleanor making breakfast.

Well, thinks Sam, depression in the morning is a stage of his analysis, Dr. Sergius has said.

This is the way Sam often phrases his thoughts. It is not altogether his fault. Most of the people he knows think that way and talk that way, and Sam is not the strongest of men. His language is doomed to the fashion of the moment. I have heard him remark mildly, almost apologetically, about his daughters: "My relation with them still suffers because I haven't worked through all my feminine identifications." The saddest thing is that the sentence has meaning to Sam even if it will not have meaning to you. A great many ruminations, discoveries, and memories contribute their connotation to Sam. It has the significance of a cherished line of poetry to him.

Although Eleanor is not being analyzed, she talks in a similar way. I have heard her remark in company, "Oh, you know Sam, he not only thinks I'm his mother, he blames me for being born." Like most women, Eleanor can be depended upon to employ the idiom of her husband.

What amuses me is that Sam is critical of the way others speak. At the party last night he was talking to a Hollywood writer, a young man with a great deal of energy and enthusiasm. The young man spoke something like this: "You see, boychick, I can spike any script with yaks, but the thing I can't do is heartbreak. My wife says she's gonna give me heartbreak. The trouble is I've had a real solid-type life. I mean I've had my ups and downs like all of humanity, but there's never been a shriek in my life. I don't know how to write shrieks."

On the trip home, Sam had said to Eleanor, "It was disgraceful. A writer should have some respect for language."

Eleanor answered with a burlesque of Sam's indignation. "Listen, I'm a real artist-type. Culture is for comic-strip writers."

Generally, I find Eleanor attractive. In the ten years they have been married she has grown plump, and her dark hair which once was long is now cropped in a mannish cut of the prevailing mode. But, this is quibbling. She still possesses her best quality, a healthy exuberance which glows in her dark eyes and beams in her smile. She has beautiful teeth. She seems aware of her body and pleased with it. Sam tells himself he would do well to realize how much he needs her. Since he has been in analysis he has come to discover that he remains with Eleanor for more essential reasons than mere responsibility. Even if there were no children, he would probably cleave to her.

Unhappily, it is more complicated than that. She is always—to use their phrase—competing with him. At those times when I do not like Eleanor, I am irritated by her lack of honesty. She is too sharp-tongued, and she does not often give Sam what he needs most, a steady flow of uncritical encouragement to counteract the harshness with which he views himself. Like so many who are articulate on the subject, Eleanor will tell you that she resents being a woman. As Sam is disappointed in life, so is Eleanor. She feels Sam has cheated her from a proper development of her potentialities and talent, even as Sam feels cheated. I call her dishonest because she is not so ready as Sam to put the blame on herself.

Sam, of course, can say all this himself. It is just that he experiences it in a somewhat different way. Like most men who have been married for ten years, Eleanor is not quite real to him. Last night at the party, there were perhaps half a dozen people whom he met for the first time, and he talked animatedly with them, sensing their reactions, feeling their responses, aware of the life in them, as they were aware of the life in him. Eleanor, however, exists in his nerves. She is a rather vague embodiment, he thinks of her as "she" most of the time, someone to conceal things from. Invariably, he feels uneasy with her. It is too bad. No matter how inevitable, I am always sorry when love melts into that pomade of affection, resentment, boredom and occasional compassion which is the best we may expect of a man and woman who have lived together a long time. So often, it is worse, so often no more than hatred.

They are eating breakfast now, and Eleanor is chatting about the party. She is pretending to be jealous about a young girl in a strapless evening gown, and indeed, she does not have to pretend altogether. Sam, with liquor inside him, had been leaning over the girl; obviously he had coveted her. Yet, this morning, when Eleanor begins to talk about her, Sam tries to be puzzled.

"Which girl was it now?" he asks a second time.

"Oh, you know, the hysteric," Eleanor says, "the one who was parading her bazooms in your face." Eleanor has ways of impressing certain notions upon Sam. "She's Charlie's new girl."

"I didn't know that," Sam mutters. "He didn't seem to be near her all evening."

Eleanor spread marmalade over her toast and takes a bite with evident enjoyment. "Apparently, they're all involved. Charles was funny about it. He said he's come to the conclusion that the great affairs of history are between hysterical women and detached men."

"Charles hates women," Sam says smugly. "If you notice, almost everything he says about them is a discharge of aggression." Sam has the best of reasons for not liking Charles. It takes more than ordinary character for a middle-aged husband to approve of a friend who moves easily from woman to woman.

"At least Charles discharges his aggression," Eleanor remarks.

"He's almost a classic example of the Don Juan complex. You notice how masochistic his women are?"

"I know a man or two who's just as masochistic."

Sam sips his coffee. "What made you say the girl was an hysteric?"

Eleanor shrugs. "She's an actress. And I could see she was a tease."

"You can't jump to conclusions," Sam lectures. "I had the impression she was a compulsive. Don't forget you've got to distinguish between the outer defenses, and the more deeply rooted conflicts."

I must confess that this conversation bores me. As a sample it is representative of the way Sam and Eleanor talk to each other. In Sam's defense I can say nothing; he has always been too partial to jargon.

I am often struck by how eager we are to reveal all sorts of supposedly ugly secrets about ourselves. We can explain the hatred we feel for our parents, we are rather pleased with the perversions to which we are prone. We seem determinedly proud to be superior to ourselves. No motive is too terrible for our inspection. Let someone hint, however, that we have bad table manners and we fly into a rage. Sam will agree to anything you may say about him, provided it is sufficiently serious—he will be the first to agree he has fantasies of murdering his wife. But tell him that he is afraid of waiters, or imply to Eleanor that she is a nag, and they will be quite annoyed.

Sam has noticed this himself. There are times when he can hear the jargon in his voice, and it offends him. Yet, he seems powerless to change his habits.

An example: He is sitting in an armchair now, brooding upon his breakfast, while Eleanor does the dishes. The two daughters are not home; they have gone to visit their grandmother for the week-end. Sam had encouraged the visit. He had looked forward to the liberty Eleanor and himself would enjoy. For the past few weeks the children had seemed to make the most impossible demands upon his attention. Yet now they are gone and he misses them, he even misses their noise. Sam, however, cannot accept the notion that many people are dissatisfied with the present, and either dream of the past or anticipate the future. Sam must call this "ambivalence over possessions." Once he even felt obliged to ask his analyst, Dr. Sergius, if ambivalence over possessions did not characterize him almost perfectly, and Sergius whom I always picture with the flat precision of a coin's head—bald skull and horn-rimmed glasses—answered in his German accent, "But, my dear Mr. Slovoda, as I have told you, it would make me happiest if you did not include in your reading, these psychoanalytical text-works."

At such rebukes, Sam can only wince. It is so right, he tells himself, he is exactly the sort of ambitious fool who uses big words when small ones would do.

II

While Sam sits in the armchair, gray winter light is entering the windows, snow falls outside. He sits alone in a modern seat, staring at the gray, green, and beige décor of their living room. Eleanor was a painter before they were married, and she has arranged this room. It is very pleasant, but like many husbands, Sam resents it, resents the reproductions of modern painters upon the wall, the slender coffee table, a free-form poised like a spider on wire legs, its feet set onto a straw rug. In the corner, most odious of all, is the playmate of his children, a hippopotamus of a television-radio-and-phonograph cabinet with the blind monstrous snout of the video tube.

Eleanor has set the Sunday paper near his hand. Soon, Sam intends to go to work. For a year, he has been giving a day once or twice a month to a bit of thought and a little writing on a novel he hopes to begin sometime. Last night, he told himself he would work today. But he has little enthusiasm now. He is tired, he is too depressed. Writing for the comic strips seems to exhaust his imagination.

Sam reads the paper as if he were peeling an enormous banana. Flap after flap of newsprint is stripped away and cast upon the straw rug until only the Magazine Section is left. Sam glances through it with restless irritability. A biography of a political figure runs its flatulent prose into the giant crossword puzzle at the back. An account of a picturesque corner of the city becomes lost in statistics and exhortations on juvenile delinquency, finally to emerge with photographs about the new style of living which desert architecture provides. Sam looks at a wall of windows in rotogravure with a yucca tree framing the pool.

There is an article about a workingman. His wife and his family are described, his apartment, his salary and his budget. Sam reads a description of what the worker has every evening for dinner, and how he spends each night of the week. The essay makes its point; the typical American workingman must watch his pennies, but he is nonetheless secure and serene. He would not exchange his life for another.

Sam is indignant. A year ago he had written a similar article in an attempt to earn some extra money. Subtly, or so he thought, he had suggested that the average workingman was raddled with insecurity. Naturally, the article had been rejected.

Sam throws the Magazine Section away. Moments of such anger torment him frequently. Despite himself, Sam is enraged at editorial dishonesty, at the smooth strifeless world which such articles present. How angry he is—how angry and how helpless. "It is the actions of men and not their sentiments which make history," he thinks to himself, and smiles wryly. In his living room he would go out to tilt the windmills of a vast, powerful, and hypocritical society; in his week of work he labors in an editorial cubicle to create spaceships, violent death, women with golden tresses and wanton breasts, men who act with their fists and speak with patriotic slogans.

I know what Sam feels. As he sits in the armchair, the Sunday papers are strewn around him, carrying their war news, their murders, their parleys, their entertainments, mummery of a real world which no one can grasp. It is terribly frustrating. One does not know where to begin.

Today, Sam considers himself half a fool for having been a radical. There is no longer much consolation in the thought that the majority of men who succeed in a corrupt and acquisitive society are themselves obligatorily corrupt, and one's failure is therefore the price of one's idealism. Sam cannot recapture the pleasurable bitterness which resides in the notion that one has suffered for one's principles. Sergius is too hard on him for that.

They have done a lot of work on the subject. Sergius feels that Sam's concern with world affairs has always been spurious. For example, they have uncovered in analysis that Sam wrote his article about the worker in such a way as to make certain it would be refused. Sam, after all, hates editors; to have such a piece accepted would mean he is no better than they, that he is a mediocrity. So long as he fails he is not obliged to measure himself. Sam, therefore, is being unrealistic. He rejects the world with his intellect, and this enables him not to face the more direct realities of his present life.

Sam will argue with Sergius but it is very difficult. He will say, "Perhaps you sneer at radicals because it is more comfortable to ignore such ideas. Once you became interested it might introduce certain unpleasant changes in your life."

"Why," says Sergius, "do you feel it is so necessary to assume that I am a bourgeois interested only in my comfort?"

"How can I discuss these things," says Sam, "if you insist that my opinions are the expression of neurotic needs, and your opinions are merely dispassionate medical advice?"

"You are so anxious to defeat me in an argument," Sergius will reply. "Would you admit it is painful to relinquish the sense of importance which intellectual discussion provides you?"

I believe Sergius has his effect. Sam often has thoughts these days which would have been repellent to him years ago. For instance, at the moment, Sam is thinking it might be better to live the life of a worker, a simple life, to be completely absorbed with such necessities as food and money. Then one could believe that to be happy it was necessary only to have more money, more goods, less worries. It would be nice, Sam thinks wistfully, to believe that the source of one's unhappiness comes not from oneself, but from the fault of the boss, or the world, or bad luck.

Sam has these casual daydreams frequently. He likes to think about other lives he might have led, and he envies the most astonishing variety of occupations. It is easy enough to see why he should wish for the life of an executive with the power and sense of command it may offer, but virtually from the same impulse Sam will wish himself a bohemian living in an unheated loft, his life a catch-as-catch-can from day to day. Once, after reading an article, Sam even wished himself a priest. For about ten minutes it seemed beautiful to him to surrender his life to God. Such fancies are common, I know. It is just that I, far better than Sam, know how serious he really is, how fanciful, how elaborate, his imagination can be.

The phone is ringing. Sam can hear Eleanor shouting at him to answer. He picks up the receiver with a start. It is Marvin Rossman who is an old friend, and Marvin has an unusual request. They talk for several minutes, and Sam squirms a little in his seat. As he is about to hang up, he laughs. "Why, no, Marvin, it gives me a sense of adventure," he says.

Eleanor has come into the room toward the end of this conversation. "What is it all about?" she asks.

Sam is obviously a bit agitated. Whenever he attempts to be most casual, Eleanor can well suspect him. "It seems," he says slowly, "that Marvin has acquired a pornographic movie."

"From whom?" Eleanor asks.

"He said something about an old boy friend of Louise's."

Eleanor laughs. "I can't imagine Louise having an old boy friend with a dirty movie."

"Well, people are full of surprises," Sam says mildly.

"Look, here," says Eleanor suddenly. "Why did he call us?"

"It was about our projector."

"They want to use it?" Eleanor asks.

"That's right." Sam hesitates. "I invited them over."

"Did it ever occur to you I might want to spend my Sunday some other way?" Eleanor asks crossly.

"We're not doing anything," Sam mumbles. Like most men, he feels obliged to act quite nonchalantly about pornography. "I'll tell you, I am sort of curious about the film. I've never seen one, you know."

"Try anything once, is that it?"

"Something of the sort." Sam is trying to conceal his excitement. The truth is that in common with most of us, he is fascinated by pornography. It is a minor preoccupation, but more from lack of opportunity than anything else. Once or twice, Sam has bought the sets of nude photographs which are sold in marginal bookstores, and with guilty excitement has hidden them in the apartment.

"Oh, this is silly," Eleanor says. "You were going to work today."

"I'm just not in the mood."

"I'll have to feed them," Eleanor complains. "Do we have enough liquor?"

"We can get beer." Sam pauses. "Alan Sperber and his wife are coming too."

"Sam, you're a child."

"Look, Eleanor," says Sam, controlling his voice, "if it's too much trouble, I can take the projector over there."

"I ought to make you do that."

"Am I such an idiot that I must consult you before I invite friends to the house?"

Eleanor has the intuition that Sam, if he allowed himself, could well drown in pornography. She is quite annoyed at him, but she would never dream of allowing Sam to take the projector over to Marvin Rossman's where he could view the movie without her—that seems indefinably dangerous. Besides she would like to see it, too. The mother in Eleanor is certain it cannot hurt her.

"All right, Sam," she says, "but you are a child."

More exactly, an adolescent, Sam decides. Ever since Marvin phoned, Sam has felt the nervous glee of an adolescent locking himself in the bathroom. Anal fixation, Sam thinks automatically.

While Eleanor goes down to buy beer and cold cuts in a delicatessen, Sam gets out the projector and begins to clean it. He is far from methodical in this. He knows the machine is all right, he has shown movies of Eleanor and his daughters only a few weeks ago, but from the moment Eleanor left the apartment, Sam has been consumed by an anxiety that the projection bulb is burned out. Once he has examined it, he begins to fret about the motor. He wonders if it needs oiling, he blunders through a drawer of household tools looking for an oilcan. It is ridiculous. Sam knows that what he is trying to keep out of his mind are the reactions Sergius will have. Sergius will want to "work through" all of Sam's reasons for seeing the movie. Well, Sam tells himself, he knows in advance what will be discovered: detachment, not wanting to accept Eleanor as a sexual partner, evasion of responsibility, etc. etc. The devil with Sergius. Sam has never seen a dirty movie, and he certainly wants to.

He feels obliged to laugh at himself. He could not be more nervous, he knows, if he were about to make love to a woman he had never touched before. It is really disgraceful.

When Eleanor comes back, Sam hovers about her. He is uncomfortable with her silence. "I suppose they'll be here soon," Sam says.

"Probably."

Sam does not know if he is angry at Eleanor or apprehensive that she is angry at him. Much to his surprise he catches her by the waist and hears himself saying, "You know, maybe tonight when they're gone . . . I mean, we do have the apartment, to ourselves." Eleanor moves neither toward him nor away from him. "Darling, it's not because of the movie," Sam goes on, "I swear. Don't you think maybe we could . . ."

"Maybe," says Eleanor.

III

The company has arrived, and it may be well to say a word or two about them. Marvin Rossman who has brought the film is a dentist, although it might be more accurate to describe him as a frustrated doctor. Rossman is full of statistics and items of odd information about the malpractice of physicians, and he will tell these things in his habitually gloomy voice, a voice so slow, so sad, that it almost conceals the humor of his remarks. Or, perhaps, that is what creates his humor. In his spare time, he is a sculptor, and if Eleanor may be trusted, he is not without talent. I often picture him working in the studio loft he has rented, his tall bony frame the image of dejection. He will pat a piece of clay to the armature, he will rub it sadly with his thumb, he will shrug, he does not believe that anything of merit could come from him. When he talked to Sam over the phone, he was pessimistic about the film they were to see. "It can't be any good," he said in his melancholy voice. "I know it'll be a disappointment." Like Sam, he has a mustache, but Rossman's will droop at the corners.

Alan Sperber who has come with Rossman is the subject of some curiosity for the Slovodas. He is not precisely womanish; in fact, he is a large plump man, but his voice is too soft, his manners too precise. He is genial, yet he is finicky; waspish, yet bland; he is fond of telling long rather affected stories, he is always prepared with a new one, but to general conversation he contributes little. As a lawyer, he seems miscast. One cannot imagine him inspiring a client to confidence. He is the sort of heavy florid man who seems boyish at forty, and the bow ties and gray flannel suits he wears do not make him appear more mature.

Roslyn Sperber, his wife, used to be a schoolteacher, and she is a quiet nervous woman who talks a great deal when she is drunk. She is normally quite pleasant, and has only one habit which is annoying to any degree. It is a little flaw, but social life is not unlike marriage in that habit determines far more than vice or virtue. This mannerism which has become so offensive to the friends of the Sperbers is Roslyn's social pretension. Perhaps I should say intellectual pretension. She entertains people as if she were conducting a salon, and in her birdlike voice is forever forcing her guests to accept still another intellectual canapé. "You must hear Sam's view of the world market," she will say, or "Has Louise told you her statistics on divorce?" It is quite pathetic for she is so eager to please. I have seen her eyes fill with tears at a sharp word from Alan.

Marvin Rossman's wife, Louise, is a touch grim and definite in her opinions. She is a social welfare worker, and will declare herself with force whenever conversation impinges on those matters where she is expert. She is quite opposed to psychoanalysis, and will say without quarter, "It's all very well for people in the upper-middle area"—she is referring to the upper middle class—"but, it takes more than a couch to solve the problems of . . ." and she will list narcotics, juvenile delinquency, psychosis, relief distribution, slum housing, and other descriptions of our period. She recites these categories with an odd anticipation. One would guess she was ordering a meal.

Sam is fond of Marvin but he cannot abide Louise. "You'd think she discovered poverty," he will complain to Eleanor.

The Slovodas do feel superior to the Rossmans and the Sperbers. If pressed, they could not offer the most convincing explanation why. I suppose what it comes down to is that Sam and Eleanor do not think of themselves as really belonging to a class, and they feel that the Sperbers and Rossmans are petit-bourgeois. I find it hard to explain their attitude. Their company feels as much discomfort and will apologize as often as the Slovodas for the money they have, and the money they hope to earn. They are all of them equally concerned with progressive education and the methods of raising children to be well adjusted—indeed, they are discussing that now—they consider themselves relatively free of sexual taboo, or put more properly, Sam and Eleanor are no less possessive than the others. The Slovodas' culture is not more profound; I should be hard put to say that Sam is more widely read, more seriously informed, than Marvin or Alan, or for that matter, Louise. Probably, it comes to this: Sam, in his heart, thinks himself a rebel, and there are few rebels who do not claim an original mind. Eleanor has been a bohemian and considers herself more sophisticated than her friends who merely went to college and got married. Louise Rossman could express it most soundly. "Artists, writers, and people of the creative layer have in their occupational ideology the belief that they are classless."

One thing I might remark about the company. They are all being the most unconscionable hypocrites. They have rushed across half the city of New York to see a pornographic film, and they are not at all interested in each other at the moment. The women are giggling like tickled children at remarks which cannot possibly be so funny. Yet, they are all determined to talk for a respectable period of time. No less, it must be serious talk. Roslyn has said once, "I feel so funny at the thought of seeing such a movie," and the others have passed her statement by.

At the moment, Sam is talking about value. I might note that Sam loves conversation and thrives when he can expound an idea.

"What are our values today?" he asks. "It's really fantastic when you stop to think of it. Take any bright talented kid who's getting out of college now."

"My kid brother, for example," Marvin interposes morosely. He passes his bony hand over his sad mustache, and somehow the remark has become amusing, much as if Marvin had said, "Oh, yes, you have reminded me of the trials, the worries, and the cares which my fabulous younger brother heaps upon me."

"All right, take him," Sam says. "What does he want to be?"

"He doesn't want to be anything," says Marvin.

"That's my point," Sam says excitedly. "Rather than work at certain occupations, the best of these kids would rather do nothing at all."

"Alan has a cousin," Roslyn says, "who swears he'll wash dishes before he becomes a businessman."

"I wish that were true," Eleanor interrupts. "It seems to me everybody is conforming more and more these days."

They argue about this. Sam and Eleanor claim the country is suffering from hysteria; Alan Sperber disagrees and says it's merely a reflection of the headlines; Louise says no adequate criteria exist to measure hysteria; Marvin says he doesn't know anything at all.

"More solid liberal gains are being made in this period," says Alan, "than you would believe. Consider the Negro—"

"Is the Negro any less maladjusted?" Eleanor shouts with passion.

Sam maneuvers the conversation back to his thesis. "The values of the young today, and by the young I mean the cream of the kids, the ones with ideas, are a reaction of indifference to the culture crisis. It really is despair. All they know is what they don't want to do."

"That is easier," Alan says genially.

"It's not altogether unhealthy," Sam says. "It's a corrective for smugness and the false value of the past, but it has created new false value." He thinks it worth emphasizing. "False value seems always to beget further false value."

"Define your terms," says Louise, the scientist.

"No, look," Sam says, "there's no revolt, there's no acceptance. Kids today don't want to get married, and—"

Eleanor interrupts. "Why should a girl rush to get married? She loses all chance for developing herself."

Sam shrugs. They are all talking at once. "Kids don't want to get married," he repeats, "and they don't want not to get married. They merely drift."

"It's a problem we'll all have to face with our own kids in ten years," Alan says, "although I think you make too much of it, Sam."

"My daughter," Marvin states. "She's embarrassed I'm a dentist. Even more embarrassed than I am." They laugh.

Sam tells a story about his youngest, Carol Ann. It seems he had a fight with her, and she went to her room. Sam followed, he called through the door.

"No answer," Sam says. "I called her again, 'Carol Ann.' I was a little worried you understand, because she seemed so upset, so I said to her, 'Carol Ann, you know I love you.' What do you think she answered?"

"What?" asks Roslyn.

"She said, 'Daddie, why are you so anxious?' "

They all laugh again. There are murmurs about what a clever thing it was to say. In the silence which follows, Roslyn leans forward and says quickly in her high voice, "You must get Alan to tell you his wonderful story about the man who studied yogi."

"Yoga," Alan corrects. "It's too long to tell."

The company prevails on him.

"Well," says Alan, in his genial courtroom voice, "it concerns a friend of mine named Cassius O'Shaugnessy."

"You don't mean Jerry O'Shaugnessy, do you?" asks Sam.

Alan does not know Jerry O'Shaugnessy. "No, no, this is Cassius O'Shaugnessy," he says. "He's really quite an extraordinary fellow." Alan sits plumply in his chair, fingering his bow tie. They are all used to his stories, which are told in a formal style and exhibit the attempt to recapture a certain note of urbanity, wit, and *élan* which Alan has probably copied from someone else. Sam and Eleanor respect his ability to tell these stories, but they resent the fact that he talks *at* them.

"You'd think we were a jury of his inferiors," Eleanor has said. "I hate being talked down to." What she resents is Alan's quiet implication that his antecedents, his social position, in total his life outside the room is superior to the life within. Eleanor now takes the promise from Alan's story by remarking, "Yes, and let's see the movie when Alan has finished."

"Ssh," Roslyn says.

"Cassius was at college a good while before me," says Alan, "but I knew him while I was an undergraduate. He would drop in and visit from time to time. An absolutely extraordinary fellow. The most amazing career. You see, he's done about everything."

"I love the way Alan tells it," Roslyn pipes nervously.

"Cassius was in France with Dos Passos and Cummings, he was even arrested with e.e. After the war, he was one of the founders of the Dadaist school, and for a while I understand he was Fitzgerald's guide to the gold of the Côte D'Azur. He knew everybody, he did everything. Do you realize that before the twenties had ended, Cassius had managed his father's business and then entered a monastery? It is said he influenced T. S. Eliot."

"Today, we'd call Cassius a psychopath," Marvin observes.

"Cassius called himself a great dilettante," Alan answers, "although perhaps the nineteenth-century Russian conception of the great sinner would be more appropriate. What do you say if I tell you this was only the beginning of his career?"

"What's the point?" Louise asks.

"Not yet," says Alan, holding up a hand. His manner seems to say that if his audience cannot appreciate the story, he does not feel obliged to continue. "Cassius studied Marx in the monastery. He broke his vows, quit the Church, and became a Communist. All through the thirties he was a figure in the Party, going to Moscow, involved in all the Party struggles. He left only during the Moscow trials."

Alan's manner while he relates such stories is somewhat effeminate. He talks with little caresses of his hand, he mentions names and places with a lingering ease as if to suggest that his audience and he are aware, above all, of nuance. The story as Alan tells it is drawn overlong. Suffice it that the man about whom he is talking, Cassius O'Shaugnessy, becomes a Trotskyist, becomes an anarchist, is a pacifist during the second World War, and suffers it from a prison cell.

"I may say," Alan goes on, "that I worked for his defense, and was successful in getting him acquitted. Imagine my dolor when I learned that he had turned his back on his anarchist friends and was living with gangsters."

"This is weird," Eleanor says.

"Weird, it is," Alan agrees. "Cassius got into some scrape, and disappeared. What could you do with him? I learned only recently that he had gone to India and was studying yoga. In fact, I learned it from Cassius himself. I asked him of his experiences at Brahna-puth-thar, and he told me the following story."

Now Alan's voice alters, he assumes the part of Cassius and speaks in a tone weary of experience, wise and sad in its knowledge. " 'I was sitting on my haunches contemplating my navel,' Cassius said to me, 'when of a sudden I discovered my navel under a different aspect. It seemed to me that if I were to give a counter-clockwise twist, my navel would unscrew.' "

Alan looks up, he surveys his audience which is now rapt and uneasy, not certain as yet whether a joke is to come. Alan's thumb and forefinger pluck at the middle of his ample belly, his feet are crossed upon the carpet in symbolic suggestion of Cassius upon his haunches.

" 'Taking a deep breath, I turned, and the abysses of Vishtarni loomed beneath. My navel had begun to unscrew. I knew I was about to accept the reward of three years of contemplation. So,' said Cassius, 'I turned again, and my navel unscrewed a little more. I turned and I turned,' " Alan's fingers now revolving upon his belly, " 'and after a period I knew that with one more turn my navel would unscrew itself forever. At the edge of revelation, I took one sweet breath, and turned my navel free.' "

Alan looks up at his audience.

" 'Damn,' said Cassius, 'if my ass didn't fall off.' "

IV

The story has left the audience in an exasperated mood. It has been a most untypical story for Alan to tell, a little out of place, not offensive exactly, but irritating and inconsequential. Sam is the only one to laugh with more than bewildered courtesy, and his mirth seems excessive to everyone but Alan, and of course, Roslyn, who feels as if she has been the producer. I suppose what it reduces to, is a lack of taste. Perhaps that is why Alan is not the lawyer one would expect. He does not have that appreciation—as necessary in his trade as for an actor—of what is desired at any moment, of that which will encourage as opposed to that which does not encourage a stimulating but smooth progression of logic and sentiment. Only a fool would tell so long a story when everyone is awaiting the movie.

Now, they are preparing. The men shift armchairs to correspond with the couch, the projector is set up, the screen is unfolded. Sam attempts to talk while he is threading the film, but no one listens. They seem to realize suddenly that a frightful demand has been placed upon them. One does not study pornography in a living room with a beer glass in one's hand, and friends at the elbow. It is the most unsatisfactory of compromises; one can draw neither the benefits of solitary contemplation nor of social exchange. There is, at bottom, the same exasperated fright which one experiences in turning the shower tap and receiving cold water when the flesh has been prepared for heat. Perhaps that is why they are laughing so much now that the movie is begun.

A title, *The Evil Act,* twitches on the screen, shot with scars, holes, and the dust lines of age. A man and woman are sitting on a couch, they are having coffee. They chat. What they say is conveyed by printed words upon an ornately flowered card, interjected between glimpses of their casual gestures, a cup to the mouth, a smile, a cigarette being lit. The man's name, it seems, is Frankie Idell; he is talking to his wife, Magnolia. Frankie is dark, he is sinister, he confides in Magnolia, his dark counterpart, with a grimace of his brows, black from make-up pencil.

This is what the titles read:

FRANKIE: She will be here soon.
MAGNOLIA: This time the little vixen will not escape.
FRANKIE: No, my dear, this time we are prepared.
(He looks at his watch.)
FRANKIE: Listen, she knocks!

There is a shot of a tall blond woman knocking on the door. She is probably over thirty, but by her short dress and ribboned hat it is suggested that she is a girl of fifteen.

FRANKIE: Come in, Eleanor.

As may be expected, the audience laughs hysterically at this. It is so wonderful a coincidence. "How I remember Frankie," says Eleanor Slovoda, and Roslyn Sperber is the only one not amused. In the midst of the others' laughter, she says in a worried tone, obviously adrift upon her own concerns, "Do you think we'll have to stop the film in the middle to let the bulb cool off?" The others hoot, they giggle, they are weak from the combination of their own remarks and the action of the plot.

Frankie and Magnolia have sat down on either side of the heroine, Eleanor. A moment passes. Suddenly, stiffly, they attack. Magnolia from her side kisses Eleanor, and Frankie commits an indecent caress.

ELEANOR: How dare you? Stop!
MAGNOLIA: Scream, my little one. It will do you no good. The walls are soundproofed.
FRANKIE: We've fixed a way to make you come across.
ELEANOR: This is hideous. I am hitherto undefiled. Do not touch me!

The captions fade away. A new title takes their place. It says, *But There Is No Escape From The Determined Pair.* On the fade-in, we discover Eleanor in the most distressing situation. Her hands are tied to loops running from the ceiling, and she can only writhe in helpless perturbation before the deliberate and progressive advances of Frankie and Magnolia. Slowly they humiliate her, with relish they probe her.

The audience laughs no longer. A hush has come upon them. Eyes unblinking they devour the images upon Sam Slovoda's screen.

Eleanor is without clothing. As the last piece is pulled away, Frankie and Magnolia circle about her in a grotesque of pantomime, a leering of lips, limbs in a distortion of desire. Eleanor faints. Adroitly, Magnolia cuts her bonds. We see Frankie carrying her inert body.

Now, Eleanor is trussed to a bed, and the husband and wife are tormenting her with feathers. Bodies curl upon the bed in postures so complicated, in combinations so advanced, that the audience leans forward, Sperbers, Rossmans, and Slovodas, as if tempted to embrace the moving images. The hands trace abstract circles upon the screen, passes and recoveries upon a white background so illumined that hollows and swells, limb to belly and mouth to undescribables, tip of a nipple, orb of a navel, swim in giant magnification, flow and slide in a lurching yawing fall, blotting out the camera eye.

A little murmur, all unconscious, passes from their lips. The audience sways, each now finally lost in himself, communing hungrily with shadows, violated or violating, fantasy triumphant.

At picture's end, Eleanor the virgin whore is released from the bed. She kisses Frankie, she kisses Magnolia. "You dears," she says, "let's do it again." The projector lamp burns empty light, the machine keeps turning, the tag of film goes *slap-tap, slap-tap, slap-tap, slap-tap, slap-tap, sla-ta.*

"Sam, turn it off," says Eleanor.

But when the room lights are on, they cannot look at one another. "Can we see it again?" someone mutters. So, again, Eleanor knocks on the door, is tied, defiled, ravished, and made rapturous. They watch it soberly now, the room hot with the heat of their bodies, the darkness a balm for orgiastic vision. To the Deer Park, Sam is thinking, to the Deer Park of Louis XV were brought the most beautiful maidens of France, and there they stayed, dressed in fabulous silks, perfumed and wigged, the mole drawn upon their cheek, ladies of pleasure awaiting the pleasure of the king. So Louis had stripped an empire, bankrupt a treasury, prepared a deluge, while in his garden on summer evenings the maidens performed their pageants, eighteenth-century tableaux of the evil act, beauteous instruments of one man's desire, lewd translation of a king's power. That century men sought wealth so they might use its fruits; this epoch men lusted for power in order to amass more power, a compounding of power into pyramids of abstraction whose yield are cannon and wire enclosure, pillars of statistics to the men who are the kings of this century and do no more in power's leisure time than go to church, claim to love their wives, and eat vegetables.

Is it possible, Sam wonders, that each of them here, two Rossmans, two Sperbers, two Slovodas, will cast off their clothes when the movie is done and perform the orgy which tickles at the heart of their desire? They will not, he knows, they will make jokes when the projector is put away, they will gorge the plate of delicatessen Eleanor provides, and swallow more beer, he among them. He will be the first to make jokes.

Sam is right. The movie has made him extraordinarily alive to the limits of them all. While they sit with red faces, eyes bugged, glutting sandwiches of ham, salami, and tongue, he begins the teasing.

"Roslyn," he calls out, "is the bulb cooled off yet?"

She cannot answer him. She chokes on beer, her face glazes, she is helpless with self-protecting laughter.

"Why are you so anxious, Daddie?" Eleanor says quickly.

They begin to discuss the film. As intelligent people they must dominate it. Someone wonders about the actors in the piece, and discussion begins afresh. "I fail to see," says Louise, "why they should be hard to classify. Pornography is a job to the criminal and prostitute element."

"No, you won't find an ordinary prostitute doing this," Sam insists. "It requires a particular kind of personality."

"They have to be exhibitionists," says Eleanor.

"It's all economic," Louise maintains.

"I wonder what those girls felt?" Roslyn asks. "I feel sorry for them."

"I'd like to be the cameraman," says Alan.

"I'd like to be Frankie," says Marvin sadly.

There is a limit to how long such a conversation may continue. The jokes lapse into silence. They are all busy eating. When they begin to talk again, it is of other things. Each dollop of food sops the agitation which the movie has spilled. They gossip about the party the night before, they discuss which single men were interested in which women, who got drunk, who got sick, who said the wrong thing, who went home with someone else's date. When this is exhausted, one of them mentions a play the others have not seen. Soon they are talking about books, a concert, a one-man show by an artist who is a friend. Dependably, conversation will voyage its orbit. While the men talk of politics, the women are discussing fashions, progressive schools, and recipes they have attempted. Sam is uncomfortable with the division; he knows Eleanor will resent it, he knows she will complain later of the insularity of men and the basic contempt they feel for women's intelligence.

"But you collaborated," Sam will argue. "No one forced you to be with the women."

"Was I to leave them alone?" Eleanor will answer.

"Well, why do the women always have to go off by themselves?"

"Because the men aren't interested in what we have to say."

Sam sighs. He has been talking with interest, but really he is bored. These are nice pleasant people, he thinks, but they are ordinary people, exactly the sort he has spent so many years with, making little jokes, little gossip, living little everyday events, a close circle where everyone mothers the other by his presence. The womb of middle-class life, Sam decides heavily. He is in a bad mood indeed. Everything is laden with dissatisfaction.

Alan has joined the women. He delights in preparing odd dishes when friends visit the Sperbers, and he is describing to Eleanor how he makes blueberry pancakes. Marvin draws closer to Sam.

"I wanted to tell you," he says, "Alan's story reminded me. I saw Jerry O'Shaugnessy the other day."

"Where was he?"

Marvin is hesitant. "It was a shock, Sam. He's on the Bowery. I guess he's become a wino."

"He always drank a lot," says Sam.

"Yeah." Marvin cracks his bony knuckles. "What a stinking time this is, Sam."

"It's probably like the years after 1905 in Russia," Sam says.

"No revolutionary party will come out of this."

"No," Sam says, "nothing will come."

He is thinking of Jerry O'Shaugnessy. What did he look like? what did he say? Sam asks Marvin, and clucks his tongue at the dispiriting answer. It is a shock to him. He draws closer to Marvin, he feels a bond. They have, after all, been through some years together. In the thirties they have been in the Communist Party, they have quit together, they are both weary of politics today, still radicals out of habit, but without enthusiasm and without a cause. "Jerry was a hero to me," Sam says.

"To all of us," says Marvin.

The fabulous Jerry O'Shaugnessy, thinks Sam. In the old days, in the Party, they had made a legend of him. All of them with their middle-class origins and their desire to know a worker-hero.

I may say that I was never as fond of Jerry O'Shaugnessy as was Sam. I thought him a showman and too pleased with himself. Sam, however, with his timidity, his desire to travel, to have adventure and know many women, was obliged to adore O'Shaugnessy. At least he was enraptured with his career.

Poor Jerry who ends as a bum. He has been everything else. He has been a trapper in Alaska, a chauffeur for gangsters, an officer in the Foreign Legion, a labor organizer. His nose was broken, there were scars on his chin. When he would talk about his years at sea or his experiences in Spain, the stenographers and garment workers, the radio writers and unemployed actors would listen to his speeches as if he were the prophet of new romance, and their blood would be charged with the magic of revolutionary vision. A man with tremendous charm. In those days it had been easy to confuse his love for himself with his love for all underprivileged workingmen.

"I thought he was still in the Party," Sam says.

"No," says Marvin, "I remember they kicked him out a couple of years ago. He was supposed to have piddled some funds, that's what they say."

"I wish he'd taken the treasury," Sam remarks bitterly. "The Party used him for years."

Marvin shrugs. "They used each other." His mustache droops. "Let me tell you about Sonderson. You know he's still in the Party. The most progressive dentist in New York." They laugh.

While Marvin tells the story, Sam is thinking of other things. Since he has quit Party work, he has studied a great deal. He can tell you about prison camps and the secret police, political murders, the Moscow trials, the exploitation of Soviet labor, the privileges of the bureaucracy; it is all painful to him. He is straddled between the loss of a country he has never seen, and his repudiation of the country in which he lives. "Doesn't the Party seem a horror now?" he bursts out.

Marvin nods. They are trying to comprehend the distance between Party members they have known, people by turn pathetic, likable, or annoying—people not unlike themselves—and in contrast the immensity of historic logic which deploys along statistics of the dead.

"It's all schizoid," Sam says. "Modern life is schizoid."

Marvin agrees. They have agreed on this many times, bored with the petulance of their small voices, yet needing the comfort of such complaints. Marvin asks Sam if he has given up his novel, and Sam says, "Temporarily." He cannot find a form, he explains. He does not want to write a realistic novel, because reality is no longer realistic. "I don't know what it is," says Sam. "To tell you the truth, I think I'm kidding myself. I'll never finish this book. I just like to entertain the idea I'll do something good some day." They sit there in friendly depression. Conversation has cooled. Alan and the women are no longer talking.

"Marvin," asks Louise, "what time is it?"

They are ready to go. Sam must say directly what he had hoped to approach by suggestion. "I was wondering," he whispers to Rossman, "would you mind if I held onto the film for a day or two?"

Marvin looks at him. "Oh, why of course, Sam," he says in his morose voice. "I know how it is." He pats Sam on the shoulder as if, symbolically, to convey the exchange of ownership. They are fellow conspirators.

"If you ever want to borrow the projector," Sam suggests.

"Nah," says Marvin, "I don't know that it would make much difference."

It has been, when all is said, a most annoying day. As Sam and Eleanor tidy the apartment, emptying ash trays and washing the few dishes, they are fond neither of themselves nor each other. "What a waste today has been," Eleanor remarks, and Sam can only agree. He has done no writing, he has not been outdoors, and still it is late in the evening, and he has talked too much, eaten too much, is nervous from the movie they have seen. He knows that he will watch it again with Eleanor before they go to sleep; she has given her assent to that. But as is so often the case with Sam these days, he cannot await their embrace with any sure anticipation. Eleanor may be in the mood or Eleanor may not; there is no way he can control the issue. It is depressing; Sam knows that he circles about Eleanor at such times with the guilty maneuvers of a sad hound. Resent her as he must, be furious with himself as he will, there is not very much he can do about it. Often, after they have made love, they will lie beside each other in silence, each offended, each certain the other is to blame. At such times, memory tickles them with a cruel feather. Not always has it been like this. When they were first married, and indeed for the six months they lived together before marriage, everything was quite different. Their affair was very exciting to them; each told the other with some hyperbole but no real mistruth that no one in the past had ever been comparable as lover.

I suppose I am a romantic. I always feel that this is the best time in people's lives. There is, after all, so little we accomplish, and that short period when we are beloved and triumph as lovers is sweet with power. Rarely are we concerned then with our lack of importance; we are too important. In Sam's case, disillusion means even more. Like so many young men, he entertained the secret conceit that he was an extraordinary lover. One cannot really believe this without supporting at the same time the equally secret conviction that one is fundamentally inept. It is—no matter what Sergius would say—a more dramatic and therefore more attractive view of oneself than the sober notion which Sam now accepts with grudging wisdom, that the man as lover is dependent upon the bounty of the woman. As I say, he accepts the notion, it is one of the lineaments of maturity but there is a part of him which, no matter how harried by analysis, cannot relinquish the antagonism he feels that Eleanor has respected his private talent so poorly, and has not allowed him to confer its benefits upon more women. I mock Sam, but he would mock himself on this. It hardly matters; mockery cannot accomplish everything, and Sam seethes with that most private and tender pain: even worse than being unattractive to the world is to be unattractive to one's mate; or, what is the same and describes Sam's case more accurately, never to know in advance when he shall be undesirable to Eleanor.

I make perhaps too much of the subject, but that is only because it is so important to Sam. Relations between Eleanor and him are not really that bad—I know other couples who have much less or nothing at all. But comparisons are poor comfort to Sam; his standards are so high. So are Eleanor's. I am convinced the most unfortunate people are those who would make an art of love. It sours other effort. Of all artists, they are certainly the most wretched.

Shall I furnish a model? Sam and Eleanor are on the couch and the projector, adjusted to its slowest speed, is retracing the elaborate pantomime of the three principals. If one could allow these shadows a life . . . but indeed such life has been given them. Sam and Eleanor are no more than an itch, a smart, a threshold of satisfaction; the important share of themselves has steeped itself in Frankie-, Magnolia-, and Eleanor-of-the-film. Indeed the variations are beyond telling. It is the most outrageous orgy performed by five ghosts.

Self-critical Sam! He makes love in front of a movie, and one cannot say that it is unsatisfactory any more than one can say it is pleasant. It is dirty, downright porno dirty, it is a lewd slop-brush slapped through the middle of domestic exasperations and breakfast eggs. It is so dirty that only half of Sam—he is quite divisible into fractions—can be exercised at all. The part that is his brain worries along like a cuckolded burgher. He is taking the pulse of his anxiety. Will he last long enough to satisfy Eleanor? Will the children come back tonight? He cannot help it. In the midst of the circus, he is suddenly convinced the children will walk through the door. "Why are you so anxious, Daddie?"

So it goes. Sam the lover is conscious of exertion. One moment he is Frankie Idell, destroyer of virgins—take that! you whore!—the next, body moving, hands caressing, he is no more than some lines from a psychoanalytical text. He is thinking about the sensitivity of his scrotum. He has read that this is a portent of femininity in a male. How strong is his latent homosexuality worries Sam, thrusting stiffly, warm sweat running cold. Does he identify with Eleanor-of-the-film?

Technically, the climax is satisfactory. They lie together in the dark, the film ended, the projector humming its lonely revolutions in the quiet room. Sam gets up to turn it off; he comes back and kisses Eleanor upon the mouth. Apparently, she has enjoyed herself more than he; she is tender and fondles the tip of his nose.

"You know, Sam," she says from her space beside him, "I think I saw this picture before."

"When?"

"Oh, you know when. That time."

Sam thinks dully that women are always most loving when they can reminisce about infidelity.

"That time!" he repeats.

"I think so."

Racing forward from memory like the approaching star which begins as a point on the mind and swells to explode the eyeball with its odious image, Sam remembers, and is weak in the dark. It is ten years, eleven perhaps, before they were married, yet after they were lovers. Eleanor has told him, but she has always been vague about details. There had been two men it seemed, and another girl, and all had been drunk. They had seen movie after movie. With reluctant fascination, Sam can conceive the rest. How it had pained him, how excited him. It is years now since he has remembered, but he remembers. In the darkness he wonders at the unreasonableness of jealous pain. That night was impossible to imagine any longer—therefore it is more real; Eleanor his plump wife who presses a pigeon's shape against her housecoat, forgotten heroine of black orgies. It had been meaningless, Eleanor claimed; it was Sam she loved, and the other had been no more than a fancy of which she wished to rid herself. Would it be the same today, thinks Sam, or had Eleanor been loved by Frankie, by Frankie of the other movies, by Frankie of the two men she never saw again on that night so long ago?

The pleasure I get from this pain, Sam thinks furiously.

It is not altogether perverse. If Eleanor causes him pain, it means after all that she is alive for him. I have often observed that the reality of a person depends upon his ability to hurt us; Eleanor as the vague accusing embodiment of the wife is different, altogether different, from Eleanor who lies warmly in Sam's bed, an attractive Eleanor who may wound his flesh. Thus, brother to the pleasure of pain, is the sweeter pleasure which follows pain. Sam, tired, lies in Eleanor's arms, and they talk with the cozy trade words of old professionals, agreeing that they will not make love again before a movie, that it was exciting but also not without detachment, that all in all it has been good but not quite right, that she had loved this action he had done, and was uncertain about another. It is their old familiar critique, a sign that they are intimate and well disposed. They do not talk about the act when it has failed to fire; then they go silently to sleep. But now, Eleanor's enjoyment having mollified Sam's sense of no enjoyment, they talk with the apologetics and encomiums of familiar mates. Eleanor falls asleep, and Sam falls almost asleep, curling next to her warm body, his hand over her round belly with the satisfaction of a sculptor. He is drowsy, and he thinks drowsily that these few moments of creature-pleasure, this brief compassion he can feel for the body that trusts itself to sleep beside him, his comfort in its warmth, is perhaps all the meaning he may ask for his life. That out of disappointment, frustration, and the passage of dreary years come these few moments when he is close to her, and their years together possess a connotation more rewarding than the sum of all which has gone into them.

But then he thinks of the novel he wants to write, and he is wide-awake again. Like the sleeping pill which fails to work and leaves one warped in an exaggeration of the ills which sought the drug, Sam passes through the promise of sex-emptied sleep, and is left with nervous loins, swollen jealousy of an act ten years dead, and sweating irritable resentment of the woman's body which hinders his limbs. He has wasted the day, he tells himself, he has wasted the day as he has wasted so many days of his life, and tomorrow in the office he will be no more than his ten fingers typing plot and words for Bramba the Venusian and Lee-Lee Deeds, Hollywood Star, while that huge work with which he has cheated himself, holding it before him as a covenant of his worth, that enormous novel which would lift him at a bound from the impasse in which he stifles, whose dozens of characters would develop a vision of life in bountiful complexity, lies foundered, rotting on a beach of purposeless effort. Notes here, pages there, it sprawls through a formless wreck of incidental ideas and half-episodes, utterly without shape. He has not even a hero for it.

One could not have a hero today, Sam thinks, a man of action and contemplation, capable of sin, large enough for good, a man immense. There is only a modern hero damned by no more than the ugliness of wishes whose satisfaction he will never know. One needs a man who could walk the stage, someone who—no matter who, not himself. Someone, Sam thinks, who reasonably could not exist.

The novelist, thinks Sam, perspiring beneath blankets, must live in paranoia and seek to be one with the world; he must be terrified of experience and hungry for it; he must think himself nothing and believe he is superior to all. The feminine in his nature cries for proof he is a man; he dreams of power and is without capacity to gain it; he loves himself above all and therefore despises all that he is.

He is that, thinks Sam, he is part of the perfect prescription, and yet he is not a novelist. He lacks energy and belief. It is left for him to write an article some day about the temperament of the ideal novelist.

In the darkness, memories rise, yeast-swells of apprehension. Out of bohemian days so long ago, comes the friend of Eleanor, a girl who had been sick and was committed to an institution. They visited her, Sam and Eleanor, they took the suburban train and sat on the lawn of the asylum grounds while patients circled about intoning a private litany, or shuddering in boob-blundering fright from an insect that crossed their skin. The friend had been silent. She had smiled, she had answered their questions with the fewest words, and had returned again to her study of sunlight and blue sky. As they were about to leave, the girl had taken Sam aside. "They violate me," she said in a whisper. "Every night when the doors are locked, they come to my room and they make the movie. I am the heroine and am subjected to all variety of sexual viciousness. Tell them to leave me alone so I may enter the convent." And while she talked, in a horror of her body, one arm scrubbed the other. Poor tortured friend. They had seen her again, and she babbled, her face had coarsened into an idiot leer.

Sam sweats. There is so little he knows, and so much to know. Youth of the depression with its economic terms, what can he know of madness or religion? They are both so alien to him. He is the mongrel, Sam thinks, brought up without religion from a mother half Protestant and half Catholic, and a father half Catholic and half Jew. He is the quarter-Jew, and yet he is a Jew, or so he feels himself, knowing nothing of Gospel, tabernacle, or Mass, the Jew through accident, through state of mind. What . . . whatever did he know of penance? self-sacrifice? mortification of the flesh? the love of his fellow man? Am I concerned with my relation to God? ponders Sam, and smiles sourly in the darkness. No, that has never concerned him, he thinks, not for better nor for worse. "They are making the movie," says the girl into the ear of memory, "and so I cannot enter the convent."

How hideous was the mental hospital. A concentration camp, decides Sam. Perhaps it would be the world some day, or was that only his projection of feelings of hopelessness? "Do not try to solve the problems of the world," he hears from Sergius, and pounds a lumpy pillow.

However could he organize his novel? What form to give it? It is so complex. Too loose, thinks Sam, too scattered. Will he ever fall asleep? Wearily, limbs tense, his stomach too keen, he plays again the game of putting himself to sleep. "I do not feel my toes," Sam says to himself, "my toes are dead, my calves are asleep, my calves are sleeping . . ."

In the middle from wakefulness to slumber, in the torpor which floats beneath blankets, I give an idea to Sam. "Destroy time, and chaos may be ordered," I say to him.

"Destroy time, and chaos may be ordered," he repeats after me, and in desperation to seek his coma, mutters back, "I do not feel my nose, my nose is numb, my eyes are heavy, my eyes are heavy."

So Sam enters the universe of sleep, a man who seeks to live in such a way as to avoid pain, and succeeds merely in avoiding pleasure. What a dreary compromise is life!

Bartleby the Scrivener

A Story of Wall Street

Herman Melville

I am a rather elderly man. The nature of my avocations, for the last thirty years, has brought me into more than ordinary contact with what would seem an interesting and somewhat singular set of men, of whom, as yet, nothing, that I know of, has ever been written—I mean, the law-copyists, or scriveners. I have known very many of them, professionally and privately, and, if I pleased, could relate divers histories, at which good-natured gentlemen might smile, and sentimental souls might weep. But I waive the biographies of all other scriveners, for a few passages in the life of Bartleby, who was a scrivener, the strangest I ever saw, or heard of. While, of other law-copyists, I might write the complete life, of Bartleby nothing of that sort can be done. I believe that no materials exist for a full and satisfactory biography of this man. It is an irreparable loss to literature. Bartleby was one of those beings of whom nothing is ascertainable, except from the original sources, and, in his case, those are very small. What my own astonished eyes saw of Bartleby, *that* is all I know of him, except, indeed, one vague report, which will appear in the sequel.

Ere introducing the scrivener, as he first appeared to me, it is fit I make some mention of myself, my *employés,* my business, my chambers, and general surroundings; because some such description is indispensable to an adequate understanding of the chief character about to be presented. Imprimis: I am a man who, from his youth upwards, has been filled with a profound conviction that the easiest way of life is the best. Hence, though I belong to a profession proverbially energetic and nervous, even to turbulence, at times, yet nothing of that sort have I ever suffered to invade my peace. I am one of those unambitious lawyers who never addresses a jury, or in any way draws down public applause; but, in the cool tranquillity of a snug retreat, do a snug business among rich men's bonds, and mortgages, and title-deeds. All who know me, consider me an eminently *safe* man. The late John Jacob Astor, a personage little given to poetic enthusiasm, had no hesitation in pronouncing my first grand point to be prudence; my next, method. I do not speak it in vanity, but simply record the fact, that I was not unemployed in my profession by the late John Jacob Astor; a name which, I admit, I love to repeat; for it hath a rounded and orbicular sound to it, and rings like unto bullion. I will freely add, that I was not insensible to the late John Jacob Astor's good opinion.

Some time prior to the period at which this little history begins, my avocations had been largely increased. The good old office, now extinct in the State of New York, of a Master in Chancery, had been conferred upon me. It was not a very arduous office, but very pleasantly remunerative. I seldom lose my temper; much more seldom indulge in dangerous indignation at wrongs and outrages; but, I must be permitted to be rash here, and declare, that I consider the sudden and violent abrogation of the office of Master in Chancery, by the new Constitution, as a —— premature act; inasmuch as I had counted upon a life-lease of the profits, whereas I only received those of a few short years. But this is by the way.

My chambers were up stairs, at No. — Wall Street. At one end, they looked upon the white wall of the interior of a spacious sky-light shaft, penetrating the building from top to bottom.

This view might have been considered rather tame than otherwise, deficient in what landscape painters call "life." But, if so, the view from the other end of my chambers offered, at least, a contrast, if nothing more. In that direction, my windows commanded an unobstructed view of a lofty brick wall, black by age and everlasting shade; which wall required no spy-glass to bring out its lurking beauties, but, for the benefit of all near-sighted spectators, was pushed up to within ten feet of my window panes. Owing to the great height of the surrounding buildings, and my chambers being on the second floor, the interval between this wall and mine not a little resembled a huge square cistern.

At the period just preceding the advent of Bartleby, I had two persons as copyists in my employment, and a promising lad as an office-boy. First, Turkey; second, Nippers; third, Ginger Nut. These may seem names, the like of which are not usually found in the Directory. In truth, they were nicknames, mutually conferred upon each other by my three clerks, and were deemed expressive of their respective persons or characters. Turkey was a short, pursy Englishman, of about my own age—that is, somewhere not far from sixty. In the morning, one might say, his face was of a fine florid hue, but after twelve o'clock, meridian—his dinner hour—it blazed like a grate full of Christmas coals; and continued blazing—but, as it were, with a gradual wane—till six o'clock P.M., or thereabouts; after which, I saw no more of the proprietor of the face, which, gaining its meridian with the sun, seemed to set with it, to rise, culminate, and decline the following day, with the like regularity and undiminished glory. There are many singular coincidences I have known in the course of my life, not the least among which was the fact, that, exactly when Turkey displayed his fullest beams from his red and radiant countenance, just then, too, at that critical moment, began the daily period when I considered his business capacities as seriously disturbed for the remainder of the twenty-four hours. Not that he was absolutely idle, or averse to business, then; far from it. The difficulty was, he was apt to be altogether too energetic. There was a strange, inflamed, flurried, flighty recklessness of activity about him. He would be incautious in dipping his pen into his inkstand. All his blots upon my documents were dropped there after twelve o'clock meridian. Indeed, not only would he be reckless, and sadly given to making blots in the afternoon, but, some days, he went further, and was rather noisy. At such times, too, his face flamed with augmented blazonry, as if cannel coal had been heaped on anthracite. He made an unpleasant racket with his chair; spilled his sand-box; in mending his pens, impatiently split them all to pieces, and threw them on the floor in a sudden passion; stood up, and leaned over his table, boxing his papers about in a most indecorous manner, very sad to behold in an elderly man like him. Nevertheless, as he was in many ways a most valuable person to me, and all the time before twelve o'clock meridian, was the quickest, steadiest creature, too, accomplishing a great deal of work in a style not easily to be matched—for these reasons, I was willing to overlook his eccentricities, though, indeed, occasionally, I remonstrated with him. I did this very gently, however, because, though the civilest, nay, the blandest and most reverential of men in the morning, yet, in the afternoon, he was disposed, upon provocation, to be slightly rash with his tongue—in fact, insolent. Now, valuing his morning services as I did, and resolved not to lose them—yet, at the same time, made uncomfortable by his inflamed ways after twelve o'clock—and being a man of peace, unwilling by my admonitions to call forth unseemly retorts from him, I took upon me, one Saturday noon (he was always worse on Saturdays) to hint to him, very kindly, that, perhaps, now that he was growing old, it might be well to abridge his labors; in short, he need not come to my chambers after twelve o'clock, but, dinner over, had best go home to his lodgings, and rest himself till tea-time. But no; he insisted upon his afternoon devotions. His countenance became intolerably fervid, as he oratorically assured me—gesticulating with a long ruler at the other end of the room—that if his services in the morning were useful, how indispensable, then, in the afternoon?

"With submission, sir," said Turkey, on this occasion, "I consider myself your right-hand man. In the morning I but marshal and deploy my columns; but in the afternoon I put myself at their head, and gallantly charge the foe, thus"—and he made a violent thrust with the ruler.

"But the blots, Turkey," intimated I.

"True; but, with submission, sir, behold these hairs! I am getting old. Surely, sir, a blot or two of a warm afternoon is not to be severely urged against gray hairs. Old age—even if it blot the page—is honorable. With submission, sir, we *both* are getting old."

This appeal to my fellow-feeling was hardly to be resisted. At all events, I saw that go he would not. So, I made up my mind to let him stay, resolving, nevertheless, to see to it that, during the afternoon, he had to do with my less important papers.

Nippers, the second on my list, was a whiskered, sallow, and, upon the whole, rather piratical-looking young man, of about five and twenty. I always deemed him the victim of two evil powers—ambition and indigestion. The ambition was evinced by a certain impatience of the duties of a mere copyist, an unwarrantable usurpation of strictly professional affairs, such as the original drawing up of legal documents. The indigestion seemed betokened in an occasional nervous testiness and grinning irritability, causing the teeth to audibly grind together over mistakes committed in copying; unnecessary maledictions, hissed, rather than spoken, in the heat of business; and especially by a continual discontent with the height of the table where he worked. Though of a very ingenious, mechanical turn, Nippers could never get this table to suit him. He put chips under it, blocks of various sorts, bits of pasteboard, and at last went so far as to attempt an exquisite adjustment, by final pieces of folded blotting-paper. But no invention would answer. If, for the sake of easing his back, he brought the table lid at a sharp angle well up towards his chin, and wrote there like a man using the steep roof of a Dutch house for his desk, then he declared that it stopped the circulation in his arms. If now he lowered the table to his waistbands, and stooped over it in writing, then there was a sore aching in his back. In short, the truth of the matter was, Nippers knew not what he wanted. Or, if he wanted anything, it was to be rid of a scrivener's table altogether. Among the manifestations of his diseased ambition was a fondness he had for receiving visits from certain ambiguous-looking fellows in seedy coats, whom he called his clients. Indeed, I was aware that not only was he, at times, considerable of a ward-politician, but he occasionally did a little business at the Justices' courts, and was not unknown on the steps of the Tombs. I have good reason to believe, however, that one individual who called upon him at my chambers, and who, with a grand air, he insisted was his client, was no other than a dun, and the alleged title-deed, a bill. But, with all his failings, and the annoyances he caused me, Nippers, like his compatriot Turkey, was a very useful man to me; wrote a neat, swift hand; and, when he chose, was not deficient in a gentlemanly sort of deportment. Added to this, he always dressed in a gentlemanly sort of way; and so, incidentally, reflected credit upon my chambers. Whereas, with respect to Turkey, I had much ado to keep him from being a reproach to me. His clothes were apt to look oily, and smell of eating-houses. He wore his pantaloons very loose and baggy in summer. His coats were execrable; his hat not to be handled. But while the hat was a thing of indifference to me, inasmuch as his natural civility and deference, as a dependent Englishman, always led him to doff it the moment he entered the room, yet his coat was another matter. Concerning his coats, I reasoned with him; but with no effect. The truth was, I suppose, that a man with so small an income could not afford to sport such a lustrous face and a lustrous coat at one and the same time. As Nippers once observed, Turkey's money went chiefly for red ink. One winter day, I presented Turkey with a highly respectable-looking coat of my own—a padded gray coat, of a most comfortable warmth, and which buttoned straight up from the knee to the neck. I thought Turkey would appreciate the favor, and abate his rashness and obstreperousness of afternoons. But no; I verily believe that buttoning himself up in so downy and blanket-like a coat had a pernicious effect upon him—upon the same principle that too much oats are bad for horses. In fact, precisely as a rash, restive horse is said to feel his oats, so Turkey felt his coat. It made him insolent. He was a man whom prosperity harmed.

Though, concerning the self-indulgent habits of Turkey, I had my own private surmises, yet, touching Nippers, I was well persuaded that, whatever might be his faults in other respects, he was, at least, a temperate young man. But, indeed, nature herself seemed to have been his vintner, and, at his birth, charged him so thoroughly with an irritable, brandy-like disposition, that all subsequent potations were needless. When I consider how, amid the stillness of my chambers, Nippers would sometimes impatiently rise from his seat, and stooping over his table, spread his arms wide apart, seize the whole desk, and move it, and jerk it, with a grim, grinding motion on the floor, as if the table were a perverse voluntary agent and vexing him, I plainly perceive that, for Nippers, brandy-and-water were altogether superfluous.

It was fortunate for me that, owing to its peculiar cause—indigestion—the irritability and consequent nervousness of Nippers were mainly observable in the morning, while in the afternoon he was comparatively mild. So that, Turkey's paraxysms only coming on about twelve o'clock, I never had to do with their eccentricities at one time. Their fits relieved each other, like guards. When Nippers's was on, Turkey's was off; and *vice versa.* This was a good natural arrangement, under the circumstances.

Ginger Nut, the third on my list, was a lad, some twelve years old. His father was a car-man, ambitious of seeing his son on the bench instead of a cart, before he died. So he sent him to my office, as student at law, errand-boy, cleaner and sweeper, at the rate of one dollar a week. He had a little desk to himself; but he did not use it much. Upon inspection, the drawer exhibited a great array of the shells of various sorts of nuts. Indeed, to this quick-witted youth, the whole noble science of the law was contained in a nutshell. Not the least among the employments of Ginger Nut, as well as one which he discharged with the most alacrity, was his duty as cake and apple purveyor for Turkey and Nippers. Copying law-papers being proverbially a dry, husky sort of business, my two scriveners were fain to moisten their mouths very often with Spitzenbergs, to be had at the numerous stalls nigh the Custom House and Post Office. Also, they sent Ginger Nut very frequently for that peculiar cake—small, flat, round, and very spicy—after which he had been named by them. Of a cold morning, when business was but dull, Turkey would gobble up scores of these cakes, as if they were mere wafers—indeed, they sell them at the rate of six or eight for a penny—the scrape of his pen blending with the crunching of the crisp particles in his mouth. Rashest of all the fiery afternoon blunders and flurried rashnesses of Turkey, was his once moistening a ginger-cake between his lips, and clapping it on to a mortgage, for a seal. I came within an ace of dismissing him then. But he mollified me by making an oriental bow, and saying—

"With submission, sir, it was generous of me to find you in stationery on my own account."

Now my original business—that of a conveyancer and title hunter, and drawer-up of recondite documents of all sorts—was considerably increased by receiving the master's office. There was now great work for scriveners. Not only must I push the clerks already with me, but I must have additional help.

In answer to my advertisement, a motionless young man one morning stood upon my office threshold, the door being open, for it was summer. I can see that figure now—pallidly neat, pitiably respectable, incurably forlorn! It was Bartleby.

After a few words touching his qualifications, I engaged him, glad to have among my corps of copyists a man of so singularly sedate an aspect, which I thought might operate beneficially upon the flighty temper of Turkey, and the fiery one of Nippers.

I should have stated before that ground glass folding-doors divided my premises into two parts, one of which was occupied by my scriveners, the other by myself. According to my humor, I threw open these doors, or closed them. I resolved to assign Bartleby a corner by the folding-doors, but on my side of them, so as to have this quiet man within easy call, in case any trifling thing was to be done. I placed his desk close up to a small side-window in that part of the room, a window which originally had afforded a lateral view of certain grimy backyards and bricks, but which, owing to subsequent erections, commanded at present no view at all, though it gave some light. Within three feet of the panes was a wall, and the light came down from far above, between two lofty buildings, as from a very small opening in a dome. Still further to a satisfactory arrangement, I procured a high green folding screen, which might entirely isolate Bartleby from my sight, though not remove him from my voice. And thus, in a manner, privacy and society were conjoined.

At first, Bartleby did an extraordinary quantity of writing. As if long famishing for something to copy, he seemed to gorge himself on my documents. There was no pause for digestion. He ran a day and night line, copying by sun-light and by candle-light. I should have been quite delighted with his application, had he been cheerfully industrious. But he wrote on silently, palely, mechanically.

It is, of course, an indispensable part of a scrivener's business to verify the accuracy of his copy, word by word. Where there are two or more scriveners in an office, they assist each other in this examination, one reading from the copy, the other holding the original. It is a very dull, wearisome, and lethargic affair. I can readily imagine that, to some sanguine temperaments, it would be altogether intolerable. For example, I cannot credit that the mettlesome poet, Byron, would have contentedly sat down with Bartleby to examine a law document of, say five hundred pages, closely written in a crimpy hand.

Now and then, in the haste of business, it had been my habit to assist in comparing some brief document myself, calling Turkey or Nippers for this purpose. One object I had, in placing Bartleby so handy to me behind the screen, was to avail myself of his services on such trivial occasions. It was on the third day, I think, of his being with me, and before any necessity had arisen for having his own writing examined, that, being much hurried to complete a small affair I had in hand, I abruptly called to Bartleby. In my haste and natural expectancy of instant compliance, I sat with my head bent over the original on my desk, and my right hand sideways, and somewhat nervously extended with the copy, so that, immediately upon emerging from his retreat, Bartleby might snatch it and proceed to business without the least delay.

In this very attitude did I sit when I called to him, rapidly stating what it was I wanted him to do—namely, to examine a small paper with me. Imagine my surprise, nay, my consternation, when, without moving from his privacy, Bartleby, in a singularly mild, firm voice, replied, "I would prefer not to."

I sat awhile in perfect silence, rallying my stunned faculties. Immediately it occurred to me that my ears had deceived me, or Bartleby had entirely misunderstood my meaning. I repeated my request in the clearest tone I could assume; but in quite as clear a one came the previous reply, "I would prefer not to."

"Prefer not to," echoed I, rising in high excitement, and crossing the room with a stride. "What do you mean? Are you moon-struck? I want you to help me compare this sheet here—take it," and I thrust it towards him.

"I would prefer not to," said he.

I looked at him steadfastly. His face was leanly composed; his gray eye dimly calm. Not a wrinkle of agitation rippled him. Had there been the least uneasiness, anger, impatience, or impertinence in his manner; in other words, had there been any thing ordinarily human about him, doubtless I should have violently dismissed him from the premises. But as it was, I should have as soon thought of turning my pale plaster-of-paris bust of Cicero out of doors. I stood gazing at him awhile, as he went on with his own writing, and then reseated myself at my desk. This is very strange, thought I. What had one best do? But my business hurried me. I concluded to forget the matter for the present, reserving it for my future leisure. So calling Nippers from the other room, the paper was speedily examined.

A few days after this, Bartleby concluded four lengthy documents, being quadruplicates of a week's testimony taken before me in my High Court of Chancery. It became necessary to examine them. It was an important suit, and great accuracy was imperative. Having all things arranged, I called Turkey, Nippers, and Ginger Nut from the next room, meaning to place the four copies in the hands of my four clerks, while I should read from the original. Accordingly, Turkey, Nippers, and Ginger Nut had taken their seats in a row, each with his document in his hand, when I called to Bartleby to join this interesting group.

"Bartleby! quick, I am waiting."

I heard a slow scrape of his chair legs on the uncarpeted floor, and soon he appeared standing at the entrance of his hermitage.

"What is wanted?" said he, mildly.

"The copies, the copies," said I, hurriedly. "We are going to examine them. There—" and I held towards him the fourth quadruplicate.

"I would prefer not to," he said, and gently disappeared behind the screen.

For a few moments I was turned into a pillar of salt, standing at the head of my seated column of clerks. Recovering myself, I advanced towards the screen, and demanded the reason for such extraordinary conduct.

"*Why* do you refuse?"

"I would prefer not to."

With any other man I should have flown outright into a dreadful passion, scorned all further words, and thrust him ignominiously from my presence. But there was something about Bartleby that not only strangely disarmed me, but in a wonderful manner, touched and disconcerted me. I began to reason with him.

"These are your own copies we are about to examine. It is labor saving to you, because one examination will answer for your four papers. It is common usage. Every copyist is bound to help examine his copy. Is it not so? Will you not speak? Answer!"

"I prefer not to," he replied in a flutelike tone. It seemed to me that, while I had been addressing him, he carefully revolved every statement that I made; fully comprehended the meaning; could not gainsay the irresistible conclusion; but, at the same time, some paramount consideration prevailed with him to reply as he did.

"You are decided, then, not to comply with my request—a request made according to common usage and common sense?"

He briefly gave me to understand, that on that point my judgment was sound. Yes: his decision was irreversible.

It is not seldom the case that, when a man is browbeaten in some unprecedented and violently unreasonable way, he begins to stagger in his own plainest faith. He begins, as it were, vaguely to surmise that, wonderful as it may be, all the justice and all the reason is on the other side. Accordingly, if any disinterested persons are present, he turns to them for some reinforcement of his own faltering mind.

"Turkey," said I, "what do you think of this? Am I not right?"

"With submission, sir," said Turkey, in his blandest tone, "I think that you are."

"Nippers," said I, "what do *you* think of it?"

"I think I should kick him out of the office."

(The reader, of nice perceptions, will here perceive that, it being morning, Turkey's answer is couched in polite and tranquil terms, but Nippers replies in ill-tempered ones. Or, to repeat a previous sentence, Nippers's ugly mood was on duty, and Turkey's off.)

"Ginger Nut," said I, willing to enlist the smallest suffrage in my behalf, "what do *you* think of it?"

"I think, sir, he's a little *luny*," replied Ginger Nut, with a grin.

"You hear what they say," said I, turning towards the screen, "come forth and do your duty."

But he vouchsafed no reply. I pondered a moment in sore perplexity. But once more business hurried me. I determined again to postpone the consideration of this dilemma to my future leisure. With a little trouble we made out to examine the papers without Bartleby, though at every page or two Turkey deferentially dropped his opinion, that this proceeding was quite out of the common; while Nippers, twitching in his chair with a dyspeptic nervousness, ground out, between his set teeth, occasional hissing maledictions against the stubborn oaf behind the screen. And for his (Nippers's) part, this was the first and the last time he would do another man's business without pay.

Meanwhile Bartleby sat in his hermitage, oblivious to everything but his own peculiar business there.

Some days passed, the scrivener being employed upon another lengthy work. His late remarkable conduct led me to regard his ways narrowly. I observed that he never went to dinner; indeed, that he never went anywhere. As yet I had never, of my personal knowledge, known him to be outside of my office. He was a perpetual sentry in the corner. At about eleven o'clock though, in the morning, I noticed that Ginger Nut would advance toward the opening in Bartleby's screen, as if silently beckoned thither by a gesture invisible to me where I sat. The boy would then leave the office, jingling a few pence, and reappear with a handful of ginger-nuts, which he delivered in the hermitage, receiving two of the cakes for his trouble.

He lives, then, on ginger-nuts, thought I; never eats a dinner, properly speaking; he must be a vegetarian, then; but no; he never eats even vegetables; he eats nothing but ginger-nuts. My mind then ran on in reveries concerning the probable effects upon the human constitution of living entirely on ginger-nuts. Ginger-nuts are so called, because they contain ginger as one of their peculiar constituents, and the final flavoring one. Now, what was ginger? A hot, spicy thing. Was Bartleby hot and spicy? Not at all. Ginger, then, had no effect upon Bartleby. Probably he preferred it should have none.

Nothing so aggravates an earnest person as a passive resistance. If the individual so resisted be of a not inhumane temper, and the resisting one perfectly harmless in his passivity, then, in the better moods of the former, he will endeavor charitably to construe to his imagination what proves impossible to be solved by his judgment. Even so, for the most part, I regarded Bartleby and his ways. Poor fellow! thought I, he means no mischief; it is plain he intends no insolence; his aspect sufficiently evinces that his eccentricities are involuntary. He is useful to me. I can get along with him. If I turn him away, the chances are he will fall in with some less-indulgent employer, and then he will be rudely treated, and perhaps driven forth miserably to starve. Yes. Here I can cheaply purchase a delicious self-approval. To befriend Bartleby; to humor him in his strange willfulness, will cost me little or nothing, while I lay up in my soul what will eventually prove a sweet morsel for my conscience. But this mood was not invariable with me. The passiveness of Bartleby sometimes irritated me. I felt strangely goaded on to encounter him in new opposition—to elicit some angry spark from him answerable to my own. But, indeed, I might as well have essayed to strike fire with my knuckles against a bit of Windsor soap. But one afternoon the evil impulse in me mastered me, and the following little scene ensued:

"Bartleby," said I, "when those papers are all copied, I will compare them with you."

"I would prefer not to."

"How? Surely you do not mean to persist in that mulish vagary?"

No answer.

I threw open the folding-doors near by, and, turning upon Turkey and Nippers, exclaimed:

"Bartleby a second time says, he won't examine his papers. What do you think of it, Turkey?"

It was afternoon, be it remembered. Turkey sat glowing like a brass boiler; his bald head steaming; his hands reeling among his blotted papers.

"Think of it?" roared Turkey; "I think I'll just step behind his screen, and black his eyes for him!"

So saying, Turkey rose to his feet and threw his arms into a pugilistic position. He was hurrying away to make good his promise, when I detained him, alarmed at the effect of incautiously rousing Turkey's combativeness after dinner.

"Sit down, Turkey," said I, "and hear what Nippers has to say. What do you think of it, Nippers? Would I not be justified in immediately dismissing Bartleby?"

"Excuse me, that is for you to decide, sir. I think his conduct quite unusual, and, indeed, unjust, as regards Turkey and myself. But it may only be a passing whim."

"Ah," exclaimed I, "you have strangely changed your mind, then —you speak very gently of him now."

"All beer," cried Turkey; "gentleness is effects of beer—Nippers and I dined together to-day. You see how gentle *I* am, sir. Shall I go and black his eyes?"

"You refer to Bartleby, I suppose. No, not to-day, Turkey," I replied; "pray, put up your fists."

I closed the doors, and again advanced towards Bartleby. I felt additional incentives tempting me to my fate. I burned to be rebelled against again. I remembered that Bartleby never left the office.

"Bartleby," said I, "Ginger Nut is away; just step around to the Post Office, won't you? (it was but a three minutes' walk), and see if there is anything for me."

"I would prefer not to."

"You *will* not?"

"I *prefer* not."

I staggered to my desk, and sat there in a deep study. My blind inveteracy returned. Was there any other thing in which I could procure myself to be ignominiously repulsed by this lean, penniless wight?—my hired clerk? What added thing is there, perfectly reasonable, that he will be sure to refuse to do?

"Bartleby!"

No answer.

"Bartleby," in a louder tone.

No answer.

"Bartleby," I roared.

Like a very ghost, aggreably to the laws of magical invocation, at the third summons, he appeared at the entrance of his hermitage.

"Go to the next room, and tell Nippers to come to me."

"I prefer not to," he respectfully and slowly said, and mildly disappeared.

"Very good, Bartleby," said I, in a quiet sort of serenely-severe, self-possessed tone, intimating the unalterable purpose of some terrible retribution very close at hand. At the moment I half intended something of the kind. But upon the whole, as it was drawing towards my dinner-hour, I thought it best to put on my hat and walk home for the day, suffering much from perplexity and distress of mind.

Shall I acknowledge it? The conclusion of this whole business was, that it soon became a fixed fact of my chambers, that a pale young scrivener, by the name of Bartleby, had a desk there; that he copied for me at the usual rate of four cents a folio (one hundred words); but he was permanently exempt from examining the work done by him, that duty being transferred to Turkey and Nippers, out of compliment, doubtless, to their superior acuteness; moreover, said Bartleby was never, on any account, to be dispatched on the most trivial errand of any sort; and that even if entreated to take upon him such a matter, it was generally understood that he would "prefer not to"—in other words, that he would refuse point-blank.

As days passed on, I became considerably reconciled to Bartleby. His steadiness, his freedom from all dissipation, his incessant industry (except when he chose to throw himself into a standing revery behind his screen), his great stillness, his unalterableness of demeanor under all circumstances, made him a valuable acquisition. One prime thing was this—*he was always there*—first in the morning, continually through the day, and the last at night. I had a singular confidence in his honesty. I felt my most precious papers perfectly safe in his hands. Sometimes, to be sure, I could not, for the very soul of me, avoid falling into sudden spasmodic passions with him. For it was exceeding difficult to bear in mind all the time those strange peculiarities, privileges, and unheard of exemptions, forming the tacit stipulations on Bartleby's part under which he remained in my office. Now and then, in the eagerness of dispatching pressing business, I would inadvertently summon Bartleby, in a short, rapid tone, to put his finger, say, on the incipient tie of a bit of red tape with which I was about compressing some papers. Of course, from behind the screen the usual answer, "I prefer not to," was sure to come; and then, how could a human creature, with the common infirmities of our nature, refrain from bitterly exclaiming upon such perverseness—such unreasonableness. However, every added repulse of this sort which I received only tended to lessen the probability of my repeating the inadvertence.

Here it must be said, that according to the custom of most legal gentlemen occupying chambers in densely-populated law buildings, there were several keys to my door. One was kept by a woman residing in the attic, which person weekly scrubbed and daily swept and dusted my apartments. Another was kept by Turkey for convenience sake. The third I sometimes carried in my own pocket. The fourth I knew not who had.

Now, one Sunday morning I happened to go to Trinity Church, to hear a celebrated preacher, and finding myself rather early on the ground I thought I would walk around to my chambers for a while. Luckily I had my key with me; but upon applying it to the lock, I found it resisted by something inserted from the inside. Quite surprised, I called out; when to my consternation a key was turned from within; and thrusting his lean visage at me, and holding the door ajar, the apparition of Bartleby appeared, in his shirt sleeves, and otherwise in a strangely tattered *déshabillé,* saying quietly that he was sorry, but he was deeply engaged just then, and—preferred not admitting me at present. In a brief word or two, he moreover added, that perhaps I had better walk around the block two or three times, and by that time he would probably have concluded his affairs.

Now, the utterly unsurmised appearance of Bartleby, tenanting my law-chambers of a Sunday morning, with his cadaverously gentlemanly *nonchalance,* yet withal firm and self-possessed, had such a strange effect upon me, that incontinently I slunk away from my own door, and did as desired. But not without sundry twinges of impotent rebellion against the mild effrontery of this unaccountable scrivener. Indeed, it was his wonderful mildness chiefly, which not only disarmed me, but unmanned me as it were. For I consider that one, for the time, is somehow unmanned when he tranquilly permits his hired clerk to dictate to him, and order him away from his own premises. Furthermore, I was full of uneasiness as to what Bartleby could possibly be doing in my office in his shirt sleeves, and in an otherwise dismantled condition of a Sunday morning. Was anything amiss going on? Nay, that was out of the question. It was not to be thought of for a moment that Bartleby was an immoral person. But what could he be doing there?—copying? Nay again, whatever might be his eccentricities, Bartleby was an eminently decorous person. He would be the last man to sit down to his desk in any state approaching to nudity. Besides, it was Sunday; and there was something about Bartleby that forbade the supposition that he would by any secular occupation violate the proprieties of the day.

Nevertheless, my mind was not pacified; and full of a restless curiosity, at last I returned to the door. Without hindrance I inserted my key, opened it, and entered. Bartleby was not to be seen. I looked round anxiously, peeped behind his screen; but it was very plain that he was gone. Upon more closely examining the place, I surmised that for an indefinite period Bartleby must have eaten, dressed, and slept in my office, and that, too, without plate, mirror, or bed. The cushioned seat of a rickety old sofa in one corner bore the faint impress of a lean, reclining form. Rolled away under his desk, I found a blanket; under the empty grate, a blacking box and brush; on a chair, a tin basin, with soap and a ragged towel; in a newspaper a few crumbs of ginger-nuts and a morsel of cheese. Yes, thought I, it is evident enough that Bartleby has been making his home here, keeping bachelor's hall all by himself. Immediately then the thought came sweeping across me, what miserable friendlessness and loneliness are here revealed! His poverty is great; but his solitude, how horrible! Think of it. Of a Sunday, Wall Street is deserted as Petra; and every night of every day it is an emptiness. This building, too, which of weekdays hums with industry and life, at nightfall echoes with sheer vacancy, and all through Sunday is forlorn. And here Bartleby makes his home; sole spectator of a solitude which he has seen all populous—a sort of innocent and transformed Marius brooding among the ruins of Carthage!

For the first time in my life a feeling of over-powering stinging melancholy seized me. Before, I had never experienced aught but a not unpleasing sadness. The bond of a common humanity now drew me irresistibly to gloom. A fraternal melancholy! For both I and Bartleby were sons of Adam. I remembered the bright silks and sparkling faces I had seen that day, in gala trim, swan-like sailing down the Mississippi of Broadway; and I contrasted them with the pallid copyist, and thought to myself, Ah, happiness courts the light, so we deem the world is gay; but misery hides aloof, so we deem that misery there is none. These sad fancyings—chimeras, doubtless, of a sick and silly brain—led on to other and more special thoughts, concerning the eccentricities of Bartleby. Presentiments of strange discoveries hovered round me. The scrivener's pale form appeared to me laid out, among uncaring strangers, in its shivering winding sheet.

Suddenly I was attracted by Bartleby's closed desk, the key in open sight left in the lock.

I mean no mischief, seek the gratification of no heartless curiosity, thought I; besides, the desk is mine, and its contents, too, so I will make bold to look within. Everything was methodically arranged, the papers smoothly placed. The pigeon holes were deep, and removing the files of documents, I groped into their recesses. Presently I felt something there, and dragged it out. It was an old bandanna handkerchief, heavy and knotted. I opened it, and saw it was a savings's bank.

I now recalled all the quiet mysteries which I had noted in the man. I remembered that he never spoke but to answer; that, though at intervals he had considerable time to himself, yet I had never seen him reading—no, not even a newspaper; that for long periods he would stand looking out, at his pale window behind the screen, upon the dead brick wall; I was quite sure he never visited any refectory or eating house; while his pale face clearly indicated that he never drank beer like Turkey, or tea and coffee even, like other men; that he never went anywhere in particular that I could learn; never went out for a walk, unless, indeed, that was the case at present; that he had declined telling who he was, or whence he came, or whether he had any relatives in the world; that though so thin and pale, he never complained of ill health. And more than all, I remembered a certain unconscious air of pallid—how shall I call it?—of pallid haughtiness, say, or rather an austere reserve about him, which had positively awed me into my tame compliance with his eccentricities, when I had feared to ask him to do the slightest incidental thing for me, even though I might know, from his long-continued motionlessness, that behind his screen he must be standing in one of those dead-wall reveries of his.

Revolving all these things, and coupling them with the recently discovered fact, that he made my office his constant abiding place and home, and not forgetful of his morbid moodiness; revolving all these things, a prudential feeling began to steal over me. My first emotions had been those of pure melancholy and sincerest pity; but just in proportion as the forlornness of Bartleby grew and grew to my imagination, did that same melancholy merge into fear, that pity into repulsion. So true it is, and so terrible, too, that up to a certain point the thought or sight of misery enlists our best affections; but, in certain special cases, beyond that point it does not. They err who would assert that invariably this is owing to the inherent selfishness of the human heart. It rather proceeds from a certain hopelessness of remedying excessive and organic ill. To a sensitive being, pity is not seldom pain. And when at last it is perceived that such pity cannot lead to effectual succor, common sense bids the soul be rid of it. What I saw that morning persuaded me that the scrivener was the victim of innate and incurable disorder. I might give alms to his body; but his body did not pain him; it was his soul that suffered, and his soul I could not reach.

I did not accomplish the purpose of going to Trinity Church that morning. Somehow, the things I had seen disqualified me for the time from church-going. I walked homeward, thinking what I would do with Bartleby. Finally, I resolved upon this—I would put certain calm questions to him the next morning, touching his history, etc., and if he declined to answer them openly and unreservedly (and I supposed he would prefer not), then to give him a twenty dollar bill over and above whatever I might owe him, and tell him his services were no longer required; but that if in any other way I could assist him, I would be happy to do so, especially if he desired to return to his native place, wherever that might be, I would willingly help to defray the expenses. Moreover, if, after reaching home, he found himself at any time in want of aid, a letter from him would be sure of a reply.

The next morning came.

"Bartleby," said I, gently calling to him behind his screen.

No reply.

"Bartleby," said I, in a still gentler tone, "come here; I am not going to ask you to do anything you would prefer not to do—I simply wish to speak to you."

Upon this he noiselessly slid into view.

"Will you tell me, Bartleby, where you were born?"

"I would prefer not to."

"Will you tell me *anything* about yourself?"

"I would prefer not to."

"But what reasonable objection can you have to speak to me? I feel friendly towards you."

He did not look at me while I spoke, but kept his glance fixed upon my bust of Cicero, which, as I then sat, was directly behind me, some six inches above my head.

"What is your answer, Bartleby," said I, after waiting a considerable time for a reply, during which his countenance remained immovable, only there was the faintest conceivable tremor of the white attenuated mouth.

"At present I prefer to give no answer," he said, and retired into his hermitage.

It was rather weak in me I confess, but his manner, on this occasion, nettled me. Not only did there seem to lurk in it a certain calm disdain, but his perverseness seemed ungrateful, considering the undeniable good usage and indulgence he had received from me.

Again I sat ruminating what I should do. Mortified as I was at his behavior, and resolved as I had been to dismiss him when I entered my office, nevertheless I strangely felt something superstitious knocking at my heart, and forbidding me to carry out my purpose, and denouncing me for a villain if I dared to breathe one bitter word against this forlornest of mankind. At last, familiarly drawing my chair behind his screen, I sat down and said: "Bartleby, never mind, then, about revealing your history; but let me entreat you, as a friend, to comply as far as may be with the usages of this office. Say now, you will help to examine papers to-morrow or next day: in short, say now, that in a day or two you will begin to be a little reasonable:—say so, Bartleby."

"At present I would prefer not to be a little reasonable," was his mildly cadaverous reply.

Just then the folding-doors opened, and Nippers approached. He seemed suffering from an unusually bad night's rest, induced by severer indigestion than common. He overheard those final words of Bartleby.

"*Prefer not,* eh?" gritted Nippers—"I'd *prefer* him, if I were you, sir," addressing me—"I'd *prefer* him; I'd give him preferences, the stubborn mule! What is it, sir, pray, that he *prefers* not to do now?"

Bartleby moved not a limb.

"Mr. Nippers," said I, "I'd prefer that you would withdraw for the present."

Somehow, of late, I had got into the way of involuntarily using this word "prefer" upon all sorts of not exactly suitable occasions. And I trembled to think that my contact with the scrivener had already and seriously affected me in a mental way. And what further and deeper aberration might it not yet produce? This apprehension had not been without efficacy in determining me to summary measures.

As Nippers, looking very sour and sulky, was departing, Turkey blandly and deferentially approached.

"With submission, sir," said he, "yesterday I was thinking about Bartleby here, and I think that if he would but prefer to take a quart of good ale every day, it would do much towards mending him, and enabling him to assist in examining his papers."

"So you have got the word, too," said I, slightly excited.

"With submission, what word, sir," asked Turkey, respectfully crowding himself into the contracted space behind the screen, and by so doing, making me jostle the scrivener. "What word, sir?"

"I would prefer to be left alone here," said Bartleby, as if offended at being mobbed in his privacy.

"*That's* the word, Turkey," said I—"*that's* it."

"Oh, *prefer?* oh yes—queer word. I never use it myself. But, sir, as I was saying, if he would but prefer—"

"Turkey," interrupted I, "you will please withdraw."

"Oh certainly, sir, if you prefer that I should."

As he opened the folding-door to retire, Nippers at his desk caught a glimpse of me, and asked whether I would prefer to have a certain paper copied on blue paper or white. He did not in the least roguishly accent the word prefer. It was plain that it involuntarily rolled from his tongue. I thought to myself, surely I must get rid of a demented man, who already has in some degree turned the tongues, if not the heads of myself and clerks. But I thought it prudent not to break the dismission at once.

The next day I noticed that Bartleby did nothing but stand at his window in his dead-wall revery. Upon asking him why he did not write, he said that he decided upon doing no more writing.

"Why, how now? what next?" exclaimed I, "do no more writing?"

"No more."

"And what is the reason?"

"Do you not see the reason for yourself," he indifferently replied.

I looked steadfastly at him, and perceived that his eyes looked dull and glazed. Instantly it occurred to me, that his unexampled diligence in copying by his dim window for the first few weeks of his stay with me might have temporarily impaired his vision.

I was touched. I said something in condolence with him. I hinted that of course he did wisely in abstaining from writing for a while; and urged him to embrace that opportunity of taking wholesome exercise in the open air. This, however, he did not do. A few days after this, my other clerks being absent, and being in a great hurry to dispatch certain letters by the mail, I thought that, having nothing else earthly to do, Bartleby would surely be less inflexible than usual, and carry these letters to the post-office. But he blankly declined. So, much to my inconvenience, I went myself.

Still added days went by. Whether Bartleby's eyes improved or not, I could not say. To all appearance I thought they did. But when I asked him if they did, he vouchsafed no answer. At all events, he would do no copying. At last, in reply to my urgings, he informed me that he had permanently given up copying.

"What!" exclaimed I; "suppose your eyes should get entirely well —better than ever before—would you not copy then?"

"I have given up copying," he answered, and slid aside.

He remained as ever, a fixture in my chamber. Nay—if that were possible—he became still more of a fixture than before. What was to be done? He would do nothing in the office; why should he stay there? In plain fact, he had now become a millstone to me, not only useless as a necklace, but afflictive to bear. Yet I was sorry for him. I speak less than truth when I say that, on his own account, he occasioned me uneasiness. If he would but have named a single relative or friend, I would instantly have written, and urged their taking the poor fellow away to some convenient retreat. But he seemed alone, absolutely alone in the universe. A bit of wreck in the mid Atlantic. At length, necessities connected with my business tyrannized over all other considerations. Decently as I could, I told Bartleby that in six days time he must unconditionally leave the office. I warned him to take measures, in the interval, for procuring some other abode. I offered to assist him in his endeavor, if he himself would but take the first step towards a removal. "And when you finally quit me, Bartleby," added I, "I shall see that you go not away entirely unprovided. Six days from this hour, remember."

At the expiration of that period, I peeped behind the screen, and lo! Bartleby was there.

I buttoned up my coat, balanced myself; advanced slowly towards him, touched his shoulder, and said, "The time has come; you must quit this place; I am sorry for you; here is money; but you must go."

"I would prefer not," he replied, with his back still towards me.

"You *must.*"

He remained silent.

Now I had an unbounded confidence in this man's common honesty. He had frequently restored to me sixpences and shillings carelessly dropped upon the floor, for I am apt to be very reckless in such shirt-button affairs. The proceeding, then, which followed will not be deemed extraordinary.

"Bartleby," said I, "I owe you twelve dollars on account; here are thirty-two; the odd twenty are yours—Will you take it?" and I handed the bills towards him.

But he made no motion.

"I will leave them here, then," putting them under a weight on the table. Then taking my hat and cane and going to the door, I tranquilly turned and added—"After you have removed your things from these offices, Bartleby, you will of course lock the door—since every one is now gone for the day but you—and if you please, slip your key underneath the mat, so that I may have it in the morning. I shall not see you again; so good-by to you. If, hereafter, in your new place of abode, I can be of any service to you, do not fail to advise me by letter. Good-by, Bartleby, and fare you well."

But he answered not a word; like the last column of some ruined temple, he remained standing mute and solitary in the middle of the otherwise deserted room.

As I walked home in a pensive mood, my vanity got the better of my pity. I could not but highly plume myself on my masterly management in getting rid of Bartleby. Masterly I call it, and such it must appear to any dispassionate thinker. The beauty of my procedure seemed to consist in its perfect quietness. There was no vulgar bullying, no bravado of any sort, no choleric hectoring, and striding to and fro across the apartment, jerking out vehement commands for Bartleby to bundle himself off with his beggarly traps. Nothing of the kind. Without loudly bidding Bartleby depart—as an inferior genius might have done—I *assumed* the ground that depart he must; and upon that assumption built all I had to say. The more I thought over my procedure, the more I was charmed with it. Nevertheless, next morning, upon awakening, I had my doubts—I had somehow slept off the fumes of vanity. One of the coolest and wisest hours a man has, is just after he awakes in the morning. My procedure seemed as sagacious as ever—but only in theory. How it would prove in practice—there was the rub. It was truly a beautiful thought to have assumed Bartleby's departure; but, after all, that assumption was simply my own, and none of Bartleby's. The great point was, not whether I had assumed that he would quit me, but whether he would prefer so to do. He was more a man of preferences than assumptions.

After breakfast, I walked down town, arguing the probabilities *pro* and *con*. One moment I thought it would prove a miserable failure, and Bartleby would be found all alive at my office as usual; the next moment it seemed certain that I should find his chair empty. And so I kept veering about. At the corner of Broadway and Canal Street, I saw quite an excited group of people standing in earnest conversation.

"I'll take odds he doesn't," said a voice as I passed.

"Doesn't go?—done!" said I; "put up your money."

I was instinctively putting my hand in my pocket to produce my own, when I remembered that this was an election day. The words I had overheard bore no reference to Bartleby, but to the success or non-success of some candidate for the mayoralty. In my intent frame of mind, I had, as it were, imagined that all Broadway shared in my excitement, and were debating the same question with me. I passed on, very thankful that the uproar of the street screened my momentary absent-mindedness.

As I had intended, I was earlier than usual at my office door. I stood listening for a moment. All was still. He must be gone. I tried the knob. The door was locked. Yes, my procedure had worked to a charm; he indeed must be vanished. Yet a certain melancholy mixed with this: I was almost sorry for my brilliant success. I was fumbling under the door mat for the key, which Bartleby was to have left there for me, when accidentally my knee knocked against a panel, producing a summoning sound, and in response a voice came to me from within—"Not yet; I am occupied."

It was Bartleby.

I was thunderstruck. For an instant I stood like the man who, pipe in mouth, was killed one cloudless afternoon long ago in Virginia, by summer lightning; at his own warm open window he was killed, and remained leaning out there upon the dreamy afternoon, till some one touched him, when he fell.

"Not gone!" I murmured at last. But again obeying that wondrous ascendancy which the inscrutable scrivener had over me, and from which ascendancy, for all my chafing, I could not completely escape, I slowly went down stairs and out into the street, and while walking round the block, considered what I should next do in this unheard-of perplexity. Turn the man out by an actual thrusting I could not; to drive him away by calling him hard names would not do; calling in the police was an unpleasant idea; and yet, permit him to enjoy his cadaverous triumph over me—this, too, I could not think of. What was to be done? or, if nothing could be done, was there anything further that I could *assume* in the matter? Yes, as before I had prospectively assumed that Bartleby would depart, so now I might retrospectively assume that departed he was. In the legitimate carrying out of this assumption, I might enter my office in a great hurry, and pretending not to see Bartleby at all, walk straight against him as if he were air. Such a proceeding would in a singular degree have the appearance of a home-thrust. It was hardly possible that Bartleby could withstand such an application of the doctrine of assumptions. But upon second thoughts the success of the plan seemed rather dubious. I resolved to argue the matter over with him again.

"Bartleby," said I, entering the office, with a quietly severe expression, "I am seriously displeased. I am pained, Bartleby. I had thought better of you. I had imagined you of such a gentlemanly organization, that in any delicate dilemma a slight hint would suffice—in short, an assumption. But it appears I am deceived. Why," I added, unaffectedly starting, "you have not even touched that money yet," pointing to it, just where I had left it the evening previous.

He answered nothing.

"Will you, or will you not, quit me?" I now demanded in a sudden passion, advancing close to him.

"I would prefer *not* to quit you," he replied, gently emphasizing the *not*.

"What earthly right have you to stay here? Do you pay any rent? Do you pay my taxes? Or is this property yours?"

He answered nothing.

"Are you ready to go on and write now? Are your eyes recovered? Could you copy a small paper for me this morning? or help examine a few lines? or step round to the post-office? In a word, will you do anything at all, to give a coloring to your refusal to depart the premises?"

He silently retired into his hermitage.

I was now in such a state of nervous resentment that I thought it but prudent to check myself at present from further demonstrations. Bartleby and I were alone. I remembered the tragedy of the unfortunate Adams and the still more unfortunate Colt in the solitary office of the latter; and how poor Colt, being dreadfully incensed by Adams, and imprudently permitted himself to get wildly excited, was at unawares hurried into his fatal act—an act which certainly no man could possibly deplore more than the actor himself. Often it had occurred to me in my ponderings upon the subject, that had that altercation taken place in the public street, or at a private residence, it would not have terminated as it did. It was the circumstance of being alone in a solitary office, upstairs, of a building entirely unhallowed by humanizing domestic associations—an uncarpeted office, doubtless, of a dusty, haggard sort of appearance—this it must have been, which greatly helped to enhance the irritable desperation of the hapless Colt.

But when this old Adam of resentment rose in me and tempted me concerning Bartleby, I grappled him and threw him. How? Why, simply by recalling the divine injunction: "A new commandment give I unto you, that ye love one another." Yes, this it was that saved me. Aside from higher considerations, charity often operates as a vastly wise and prudent principle—a great safeguard to its possessor. Men have committed murder for jealousy's sake, and anger's sake, and hatred's sake, and selfishness' sake, and spiritual pride's sake; but no man, that ever I heard of, ever committed a diabolical murder for sweet charity's sake. Mere self-interest, then, if no better motive can be enlisted, should, especially with high-tempered men, prompt all beings to charity and philanthropy. At any rate, upon the occasion in question, I strove to drown my exasperated feelings towards the scrivener by benevolently construing his conduct. Poor fellow, poor fellow! thought I, he don't mean anything; and besides, he has seen hard times, and ought to be indulged.

I endeavored, also, immediately to occupy myself, and at the same time to comfort my despondency. I tried to fancy, that in the course of the morning, at such time as might prove agreeable to him, Bartleby, of his own free accord, would emerge from his hermitage and take up some decided line of march in the direction of the door. But no. Half-past twelve o'clock came; Turkey began to glow in the face, overturn his inkstand, and become generally obstreperous; Nippers abated down into quietude and courtesy; Ginger Nut munched his noon apple; and Bartleby remained standing at his window in one of his profoundest dead-wall reveries. Will it be credited? Ought I to acknowledge it? That afternoon I left the office without saying one further word to him.

Some days now passed, during which, at leisure intervals I looked a little into "Edwards on the Will," and "Priestley on Necessity." Under the circumstances, those books induced a salutary feeling. Gradually I slid into the persuasion that these troubles of mine, touching the scrivener, had been all predestinated from eternity, and Bartleby was billeted upon me for some mysterious purpose of an allwise Providence, which it was not for a mere mortal like me to fathom. Yes, Bartleby, stay there behind your screen, thought I; I shall persecute you no more; you are harmless and noiseless as any of these old chairs; in short, I never feel so private as when I know you are here. At last I see it, I feel it; I penetrate to the predestinated purpose of my life.

I am content. Others may have loftier parts to enact; but my mission in this world, Bartleby, is to furnish you with office-room for such period as you may see fit to remain.

I believe that this wise and blessed frame of mind would have continued with me, had it not been for the unsolicited and uncharitable remarks obtruded upon me by my professional friends who visited the rooms. But thus it often is, that the constant friction of illiberal minds wears out at last the best resolves of the more generous. Though to be sure, when I reflected upon it, it was not strange that people entering my office should be struck by the peculiar aspect of the unaccountable Bartleby, and so be tempted to throw out some sinister observations concerning him. Sometimes an attorney, having business with me, and calling at my office, and finding no one but the scrivener there, would undertake to obtain some sort of precise information from him touching my whereabouts; but without heeding his idle talk, Bartleby would remain standing immovable in the middle of the room. So after contemplating him in that position for a time, the attorney would depart, no wiser than he came.

Also, when a reference was going on, and the room full of lawyers and witnesses, and business driving fast, some deeply-occupied legal gentleman present, seeing Bartleby wholly unemployed, would request him to run round to his (the legal gentleman's) office and fetch some papers for him. Thereupon, Bartleby would tranquilly decline, and yet remain idle as before. Then the lawyer would give a great stare, and turn to me. And what could I say? At last I was made aware that all through the circle of my professional acquaintance, a whisper of wonder was running round, having reference to the strange creature I kept at my office. This worried me very much. And as the idea came upon me of his possibly turning out a long-lived man, and keep occupying my chambers, and denying my authority; and perplexing my visitors; and scandalizing my professional reputation; and casting a general gloom over the premises; keeping soul and body together to the last upon his savings (for doubtless he spent but half a dime a day), and in the end perhaps outlive me, and claim possession of my office by right of his perpetual occupancy: as all these dark anticipations crowded upon me more and more, and my friends continually intruded their relentless remarks upon the apparition in my room; a great change was wrought in me. I resolved to gather all my faculties together, and forever rid me of this intolerable incubus.

Ere revolving any complicated project, however, adapted to this end, I first simply suggested to Bartleby the propriety of his permanent departure. In a calm and serious tone, I commended the idea to his careful and mature consideration. But, having taken three days to meditate upon it, he apprised me, that his original determination remained the same; in short, that he still preferred to abide with me.

What shall I do? I now said to myself, buttoning up my coat to the last button. What shall I do? what ought I to do? what does my conscience say I *should* do with this man, or, rather, ghost. Rid myself of him, I must; go, he shall. But how? You will not thrust him, the poor, pale, passive mortal—you will not thrust such a helpless creature out of your door? you will not dishonor yourself by such cruelty? No, I will not, I cannot do that. Rather would I let him live and die here, and then mason up his remains in the wall. What, then, will you do? For all your coaxing, he will not budge. Bribes he leaves under your own paperweight on your table; in short, it is quite plain that he prefers to cling to you.

Then something severe, something unusual must be done. What! surely you will not have him collared by a constable, and commit his innocent pallor to the common jail? And upon what ground could you procure such a thing to be done?—a vagrant, is he? What! he a vagrant, a wanderer, who refuses to budge? It is because he will *not* be a vagrant, then, that you seek to count him *as* a vagrant. That is too absurd. No visible means of support: there I have him. Wrong again: for indubitably he *does* support himself, and that is the only unanswerable proof that any man can show of his possessing the means so to do. No more, then. Since he will not quit me, I must quit him. I will change my offices; I will move elsewhere, and give him fair notice, that if I find him on my new premises I will then proceed against him as a common trespasser.

Acting accordingly, next day I thus addressed him: "I find these chambers too far from the City Hall; the air is unwholesome. In a word, I propose to remove my offices next week, and shall no longer require your services. I tell you this now, in order that you may seek another place."

He made no reply; and nothing more was said.

On the appointed day I engaged carts and men, proceeded to my chambers, and, having but little furniture, everything was removed in a few hours. Throughout, the scrivener remained standing behind the screen, which I directed to be removed the last thing. It was withdrawn; and, being folded up like a huge folio, left him the motionless occupant of a naked room. I stood in the entry watching him a moment, while something from within me upbraided me.

I re-entered, with my hand in my pocket—and—and my heart in my mouth.

"Good-by, Bartleby; I am going—good-by, and God some way bless you; and take that," slipping something in his hand. But it dropped upon the floor, and then—strange to say—I tore myself from him whom I had so longed to be rid of.

Established in my new quarters, for a day or two I kept the door locked, and started at every footfall in the passages. When I returned to my rooms, after any little absence, I would pause at the threshold for an instant, and attentively listen, ere applying my key. But these fears were needless. Bartleby never came nigh me.

I thought all was going well, when a perturbed-looking stranger visited me, inquiring whether I was the person who had recently occupied rooms at No. — Wall Street.

Full of forebodings, I replied that I was.

"Then, sir," said the stranger, who proved a lawyer, "you are responsible for the man you left there. He refuses to do any copying; he refuses to do anything; he says he prefers not to; and he refuses to quit the premises."

"I am very sorry, sir," said I, with assumed tranquillity, but an inward tremor, "but, really, the man you allude to is nothing to me—he is no relation or apprentice of mine, that you should hold me responsible for him."

"In mercy's name, who is he?"

"I certainly cannot inform you. I know nothing about him. Formerly I employed him as a copyist; but he has done nothing for me now for some time past."

"I shall settle him, then—good morning, sir."

Several days passed, and I heard nothing more; and, though I often felt a charitable prompting to call at the place and see poor Bartleby, yet a certain squeamishness, of I know not what, withheld me.

All is over with him, by this time, thought I, at last, when, through another week, no further intelligence reached me. But, coming to my room the day after, I found several persons waiting at my door in a high state of nervous excitement.

"That's the man—here he comes," cried the foremost one, whom I recognized as the lawyer who had previously called upon me alone.

"You must take him away, sir, at once," cried a portly person among them, advancing upon me, and whom I knew to be the landlord of No. — Wall Street. "These gentlemen, my tenants, cannot stand it any longer; Mr. B——," pointing to the lawyer, "has turned him out of his room, and he now persists in haunting the building generally, sitting upon the banisters of the stairs by day, and sleeping in the entry by night. Everybody is concerned; clients are leaving the offices; some fears are entertained of a mob; something you must do, and that without delay."

Aghast at this torrent, I fell back before it, and would fain have locked myself in my new quarters. In vain I persisted that Bartleby was nothing to me—no more than to any one else. In vain—I was the last person known to have anything to do with him, and they held me to the terrible account. Fearful, then, of being exposed in the papers (as one person present obscurely threatened), I considered the matter, and, at length, said, that if the lawyer would give me a confidential interview with the scrivener, in his (the lawyer's) own room, I would, that afternoon, strive my best to rid them of the nuisance they complained of.

Going up stairs to my old haunt, there was Bartleby silently sitting upon the banister at the landing.

"What are you doing here, Bartleby?" said I.

"Sitting upon the banister," he mildly replied.

I motioned him into the lawyer's room, who then left us.

"Bartleby," said I, "are you aware that you are the cause of great tribulation to me, by persisting in occupying the entry after being dismissed from the office?"

No answer.

"Now one of two things must take place. Either you must do something, or something must be done to you. Now what sort of business would you like to engage in? Would you like to re-engage in copying for some one?"

"No; I would prefer not to make any change."

"Would you like a clerkship in a dry-goods store?"

"There is too much confinement about that. No, I would not like a clerkship; but I am not particular."

"Too much confinement," I cried, "why you keep yourself confined all the time!"

"I would prefer not to take a clerkship," he rejoined, as if to settle that little item at once.

"How would a bar-tender's business suit you? There is no trying of the eye-sight in that."

"I would not like it at all; though, as I said before, I am not particular."

His unwonted wordiness inspirited me. I returned to the charge.

"Well, then, would you like to travel through the country collecting bills for the merchants? That would improve your health."

"No, I would prefer to be doing something else."

"How, then, would going as a companion to Europe, to entertain some young gentleman with your conversation—how would that suit you?"

"Not at all. It does not strike me that there is anything definite about that. I like to be stationary. But I am not particular."

"Stationary you shall be, then," I cried, now losing all patience, and, for the first time in all my exasperating connection with him, fairly flying into a passion. "If you do not go away from these premises before night, I shall feel bound—indeed, I *am* bound—to—to—to quit the premises myself!" I rather absurdly concluded, knowing not with what possible threat to try to frighten his immobility into compliance. Despairing of all further efforts, I was precipitately leaving him, when a final thought occurred to me—one which had not been wholly unindulged before.

"Bartleby," said I, in the kindest tone I could assume under such exciting circumstances, "will you go home with me now—not to my office, but my dwelling—and remain there till we can conclude upon some convenient arrangement for you at our leisure? Come, let us start now, right away."

"No: at present I would prefer not to make any change at all."

I answered nothing; but, effectually dodging every one by the suddenness and rapidity of my flight, rushed from the building, ran up Wall Street towards Broadway, and, jumping into the first omnibus, was soon removed from pursuit. As soon as tranquillity returned, I distinctly perceived that I had now done all that I possibly could, both in respect to the demands of the landlord and his tenants, and with regard to my own desire and sense of duty, to benefit Bartleby, and shield him from rude persecution. I now strove to be entirely care-free and quiescent; and my conscience justified me in the attempt; though, indeed, it was not so successful as I could have wished. So fearful was I of being again hunted out by the incensed landlord and his exasperated tenants, that, surrendering my business to Nippers, for a few days, I drove about the upper part of the town and through the suburbs, in my rockaway; crossed over to Jersey City and Hoboken, and paid fugitive visits to Manhattanville and Astoria. In fact, I almost lived in my rockaway for the time.

When again I entered my office, lo, a note from the landlord lay upon the desk. I opened it with trembling hands. It informed me that the writer had sent to the police, and had Bartleby removed to the Tombs as a vagrant. Moreover, since I knew more about him than any one else, he wished me to appear at that place, and make a suitable statement of the facts. These tidings had a conflicting effect upon me. At first I was indignant; but, at last, almost approved. The landlord's energetic, summary disposition, had led him to adopt a procedure which I do not think I would have decided upon myself; and yet, as a last resort, under such peculiar circumstances, it seemed the only plan.

As I afterwards learned, the poor scrivener, when told that he must be conducted to the Tombs, offered not the slightest obstacle, but, in his pale, unmoving way, silently acquiesced.

Some of the compassionate and curious bystanders joined the party; and headed by one of the constables arm in arm with Bartleby, the silent procession filed its way through all the noise, and heat, and joy of the roaring thoroughfares at noon.

The same day I received the note, I went to the Tombs, or, to speak more properly, the Halls of Justice. Seeking the right officer, I stated the purpose of my call, and was informed that the individual I described was, indeed, within. I then assured the functionary that Bartleby was a perfectly honest man, and greatly to be compassionated, however unaccountably eccentric. I narrated all I knew, and closed by suggesting the idea of letting him remain in as indulgent confinement as possible, till something less harsh might be done—though, indeed, I hardly knew what. At all events, if nothing else could be decided upon, the alms-house must receive him. I then begged to have an interview.

Being under no disgraceful charge, and quite serene and harmless in all his ways, they had permitted him freely to wander about the prison, and, especially, in the inclosed grass-platted yards thereof. And so I found him there, standing all alone in the quietest of the yards, his face towards a high wall, while all around, from the narrow slits of the jail windows, I thought I saw peering out upon him the eyes of murderers and thieves.

"Bartleby!"

"I know you," he said, without looking round—"and I want nothing to say to you."

"It was not I that brought you here, Bartleby," said I, keenly pained at his implied suspicion. "And to you, this should not be so vile a place. Nothing reproachful attaches to you by being here. And see, it is not so sad a place as one might think. Look, there is the sky, and here is the grass."

"I know where I am," he replied, but would say nothing more, and so I left him.

As I entered the corridor again, a broad meat-like man, in an apron, accosted me, and, jerking his thumb over his shoulder, said—"Is that your friend?"

"Yes."

"Does he want to starve? If he does, let him live on the prison fare, that's all."

"Who are you?" asked I, not knowing what to make of such an unofficially speaking person in such a place.

"I am the grub-man. Such gentlemen as have friends here, hire me to provide them with something good to eat."

"Is this so?" said I, turning to the turnkey.

He said it was.

"Well, then," said I, slipping some silver into the grub-man's hands (for so they called him), "I want you to give particular attention to my friend there; let him have the best dinner you can get. And you must be as polite to him as possible."

"Introduce me, will you?" said the grub-man, looking at me with an expression which seemed to say he was all impatience for an opportunity to give a specimen of his breeding.

Thinking it would prove of benefit to the scrivener, I acquiesced; and, asking the grub-man his name, went up with him to Bartleby.

"Bartleby, this is a friend; you will find him very useful to you."

"Your sarvant, sir, your sarvant," said the grub-man, making a low salutation behind his apron. "Hope you find it pleasant here, sir; nice grounds—cool apartments—hope you'll stay with us sometime—try to make it agreeable. What will you have for dinner to-day?"

"I prefer not to dine to-day," said Bartleby, turning away. "It would disagree with me; I am unused to dinners." So saying, he slowly moved to the other side of the inclosure, and took up a position fronting the dead-wall.

"How's this?" said the grub-man, addressing me with a stare of astonishment. "He's odd, ain't he?"

"I think he is a little deranged," said I, sadly.

"Deranged? deranged is it? Well, now, upon my word, I thought that friend of yourn was a gentleman forger; they are always pale and genteel-like, them forgers. I can't help pity 'em—can't help it, sir. Did you know Monroe Edwards?" he added, touchingly, and paused. Then, laying his hand piteously on my shoulder, sighed, "he died of consumption at Sing-Sing. So you weren't acquainted with Monroe?"

"No, I was never socially acquainted with any forgers. But I cannot stop longer. Look to my friend yonder. You will not lose by it. I will see you again."

Some few days after this, I again obtained admission to the Tombs, and went through the corridors in quest of Bartleby; but without finding him.

"I saw him coming from his cell not long ago," said a turnkey, "may be he's gone to loiter in the yards."

So I went in that direction.

"Are you looking for the silent man?" said another turnkey, passing me. "Yonder he lies—sleeping in the yard there. 'Tis not twenty minutes since I saw him lie down."

The yard was entirely quiet. It was not accessible to the common prisoners. The surrounding walls, of amazing thickness, kept off all sounds behind them. The Egyptian character of the masonry weighed upon me with its gloom. But a soft imprisoned turf grew under foot. The heart of the eternal pyramids, it seemed, wherein, by some strange magic, through the clefts, grass-seed, dropped by birds, had sprung.

Strangely huddled at the base of the wall, his knees drawn up, and lying on his side, his head touching the cold stones, I saw the wasted Bartleby. But nothing stirred. I paused; then went close up to him; stooped over, and saw that his dim eyes were open; otherwise he seemed profoundly sleeping. Something prompted me to touch him. I felt his hand, when a tingling shiver ran up my arm and down my spine to my feet.

The round face of the grub-man peered upon me now. "His dinner is ready. Won't he dine to-day, either? Or does he live without dining?"

"Lives without dining," said I, and closed the eyes.

"Eh!—He's asleep, ain't he?"

"With kings and counselors," murmured I.

There would seem little need for proceeding further in this history. Imagination will readily supply the meagre recital of poor Bartleby's interment. But, ere parting with the reader, let me say, that if this little narrative has sufficiently interested him, to awaken curiosity as to who Bartleby was, and what manner of life he led prior to the present narrator's making his acquaintance, I can only reply, that in such curiosity I fully share, but am wholly unable to gratify it. Yet here I hardly know whether I should divulge one little item of rumor, which came to my ear a few months after the scrivener's decease. Upon what basis it rested, I could never ascertain; and hence, how true it is I cannot now tell. But, inasmuch as this vague report has not been without a certain suggestive interest to me, however said, it may prove the same with some others; and so I will briefly mention it. The report was this: that Bartleby had been a subordinate clerk in the Dead Letter Office at Washington, from which he had been suddenly removed by a change in the administration. When I think over this rumor, hardly can I express the emotions which seize me. Dead letters! does it not sound like dead men? Conceive a man by nature and misfortune prone to a pallid hopelessness, can any business seem more fitted to heighten it than that of continually handling these dead letters, and assorting them for the flames? For by the cart-load they are annually burned. Sometimes from out the folded paper the pale clerk takes a ring—the finger it was meant for, perhaps, moulders in the grave; a bank-note sent in swiftest charity—he whom it would relieve, nor eats nor hungers any more; pardon for those who died despairing; hope for those who died unhoping; good tidings for those who died stifled by unrelieved calamities. On errands of life, these letters speed to death.

Ah, Bartleby! Ah, humanity!

Four Summers

Joyce Carol Oates

It is some kind of special day. "Where's Sissie?" Ma says. Her face gets sharp, she is frightened. When I run around her chair she laughs and hugs me. She is pretty when she laughs. Her hair is long and pretty.

We are sitting at the best table of all, out near the water. The sun is warm and the air smells nice. Daddy is coming back from the building with some glasses of beer held in his arms. He makes a grunting noise when he sits down.

"Is the lake deep?" I ask them.

They don't hear me, they're talking. A woman and a man are sitting with us. The man marched in the parade we saw just a while ago; he is a volunteer fireman and is wearing a uniform. Now his shirt is pulled open because it is hot. I can see the dark curly hair way up by his throat.

A man in a soldier's uniform comes over to us. They are all friends, but I can't remember him. We used to live around here, Ma told me, and then we moved away. The men are laughing. The man in the uniform leans back against the railing, laughing, and I am afraid it will break and he will fall into the water.

"Can we go out in a boat? Dad?" says Jerry.

He and Frank keep running back and forth. I don't want to go with them, I want to stay by Ma. She smells nice. Frank's face is dirty with sweat. "Dad," he says, whining, "can't we go out in a boat? Them kids are going out."

A big lake is behind the building and the open part where we are sitting. Some people are rowing on it. This tavern is noisy and everyone is laughing; it is too noisy for Dad to think about what Frank said.

"Harry," says Ma, "the kids want a boatride. Why don't you leave off drinking and take them?"

"What?" says Dad.

He looks up from laughing with the men. His face is damp with sweat and he is happy. "Yeah, sure, in a few minutes. Go over there and play and I'll take you out in a few minutes."

The boys run out back by the rowboats, and I run after them. I have a bag of potato chips.

An old man with a white hat pulled down over his forehead is sitting by the boats, smoking. "You kids be careful," he says.

Frank is leaning over and looking at one of the boats. "This here is the best one," he says.

"Why's this one got water in it?" says Jerry.

"You kids watch out. Where's your father?" the man says.

"He's gonna take us for a ride," says Frank.

"Where is he?"

The boys run along, looking at the boats that are tied up. They don't bother with me. The boats are all painted dark green, but the paint is peeling off some of them in little pieces. There is water inside some of them. We watch two people come in, a man and a woman. The woman is giggling. She has on a pink dress and she leans over to touch one finger in the water. "What's all this filthy stuff by the shore?" she says. There is some scum in the water. It is colored a light brown, and there are little seeds and twigs and leaves in it.

The man helps the woman out of the boat. They laugh together. Around their rowboat little waves are still moving; they make a churning noise that I like.

"Where's Dad?" Frank says.

"He ain't coming," says Jerry.

They are tossing pebbles out into the water. Frank throws his sideways, twisting his body. He is ten and very big. "I bet he ain't coming," Jerry says, wiping his nose with the back of his hand.

After a while we go back to the table. Behind the table is the white railing, and then the water, and then the bank curves out so that the weeping willow trees droop over the water. More men in uniforms, from the parade, are walking by.

"Dad," says Frank, "can't we go out? Can't we? There's a real nice boat there—"

"For Christ's sake, get them off me," Dad says. He is angry with Ma. "Why don't you take them out?"

"Honey, I can't row."

"Should we take out a boat, us two?" the other woman says. She has very short wet-looking hair. It is curled in tiny little curls close to her head and is very bright. "We'll show them, Lenore. Come on, let's give your kids a ride. Show these guys how strong we are."

"That's all you need, to sink a boat," her husband says.

They all laugh.

The table is filled with brown beer bottles and wrappers of things. I can feel how happy they all are together, drawn together by the round table. I lean against Ma's warm leg and she pats me without looking down. She lunges forward and I can tell even before she says something that she is going to be loud.

"You guys're just jealous! Afraid we'll meet some soldiers!" she says.

"Can't we go out, Dad? Please?" Frank says. "We won't fight . . ."

"Go and play over there. What're those kids doing—over there?" Dad says, frowning. His face is damp and loose, the way it is sometimes when he drinks. "In a little while, okay? Ask your mother."

"She can't do it," Frank says.

"They're just jealous," Ma says to the other woman, giggling. "They're afraid we might meet somebody somewhere."

"Just who's gonna meet this one here?" the other man says, nodding with his head at his wife.

Frank and Jerry walk away. I stay by Ma. My eyes burn and I want to sleep, but they won't be leaving for a long time. It is still daylight. When we go home from places like this it is always dark and getting chilly and the grass by our house is wet.

"Duane Dorsey's in jail," Dad says. "You guys heard about that?"

"Duane? Yeah, really?"

"It was in the newspaper. His mother-in-law or somebody called the police, he was breaking windows in her house."

"That Duane was always a nut!"

"Is he out now, or what?"

"I don't know, I don't see him these days. We had a fight," Dad says.

The woman with the short hair looks at me. "She's a real cute little thing," she says, stretching her mouth. "She drink beer, Lenore?"

"I don't know."

"Want some of mine?"

She leans toward me and holds the glass by my mouth. I can smell the beer and the warm stale smell of perfume. There are pink lipstick smudges on the glass.

"Hey, what the hell are you doing?" her husband says.

When he talks rough like that I remember him: we were with him once before.

"Are you swearing at me?" the woman says.

"Leave off the kid, you want to make her a drunk like yourself?"

"It don't hurt, one little sip . . ."

"It's okay," Ma says. She puts her arm around my shoulders and pulls me closer to the table.

"Let's play cards. Who wants to?" Dad says.

"Sissie wants a little sip, don't you?" the woman says. She is smiling at me and I can see that her teeth are darkish, not nice like Ma's.

"Sure, go ahead," says Ma.

"I said leave off that, Sue, for Christ's sake," the man says. He jerks the table. He is a big man with a thick neck; he is bigger than Dad. His eyebrows are blond, lighter than his hair, and are thick and tufted. Dad is staring at something out on the lake without seeing it. "Harry, look, my goddam wife is trying to make your kid drink beer."

"Who's getting hurt?" Ma says angrily.

Pa looks at me all at once and smiles. "Do you want it, baby?"

I have to say yes. The woman grins and holds the glass down to me, and it clicks against my teeth. They laugh. I stop swallowing right away because it is ugly, and some of the beer drips down on me. "Honey, you're so clumsy," Ma says, wiping me with a napkin.

"She's a real cute girl," the woman says, sitting back in her chair. "I wish I had a nice little girl like that."

"Lay off of that," says her husband.

"Hey, did you bring any cards?" Dad says to the soldier.

"They got some inside."

"Look, I'm sick of cards," Ma says.

"Yeah, why don't we all go for a boatride?" says the woman. "Be real nice, something new. Every time we get together we play cards. How's about a boatride?"

"It better be a big boat, with you in it," her husband says. He is pleased when everyone laughs, even the woman. The soldier lights a cigarette and laughs. "How come your cousin here's so skinny and you're so fat?"

"She isn't fat," says Ma. "What the hell do you want? Look at yourself."

"Yes, the best days of my life are behind me," the man says. He wipes his face and then presses a beer bottle against it. "Harry, you're lucky you moved out. It's all going downhill, back in the neighborhood."

"You should talk, you let our house look like hell," the woman says. Her face is blotched now, some parts pale and some red. "Harry don't sit out in his back yard all weekend, drinking. He gets something done."

"Harry's younger than me."

Ma reaches over and touches Dad's arm. "Harry, why don't you take the kids out? Before it gets dark."

Dad lifts his glass and finishes his beer. "Who else wants more?" he says.

"I'll get them, you went last time," the soldier says.

"Get a chair for yourself," says Dad. "We can play poker."

"I don't want to play poker, I want to play rummy," the woman says.

"At church this morning Father Reilly was real mad," says Ma. "He said some kids or somebody was out in the cemetery and left some beer bottles. Isn't that awful?"

"Duane Dorsey used to do worse than that," the man says, winking.

"Hey, who's that over there?"

"You mean that fat guy?"

"Isn't that the guy at the lumberyard that owes all that money?"

Dad turns around. His chair wobbles and he almost falls; he is angry.

"This goddam place is too crowded," he says.

"This is a real nice place," the woman says. She is taking something out of her purse. "I always liked it, didn't you, Lenore?"

"Sue and me used to come here a lot," says Ma. "And not just with you two, either."

"Yeah, we're real jealous," the man says.

"You should be," says the woman.

The soldier comes back. Now I can see that he is really a boy. He runs to the table with the beer before he drops anything. He laughs.

"Jimmy, your ma wouldn't like to see you drinking!" the woman says happily.

"Well, she ain't here."

"Are they still living out in the country?" Ma says to the woman.

"Sure. No electricity, no running water, no bathroom—same old thing. What can you do with people like that?"

"She always talks about going back to the old country," the soldier says. "Thinks she can save up money and go back."

"Poor old bastards don't know there was a war," Dad says. He looks as if something tasted bad in his mouth. "My old man died thinking he could go back in a year or two. Stupid old bastards!"

"Your father was real nice . . ." Ma says.

"Yeah, real nice," says Dad. "Better off dead."

Everybody is quiet.

"June Dieter's mother's got the same thing," the woman says in a low voice to Ma. "She's had it a year now and don't weigh a hundred pounds—you remember how big she used to be."

"She was big, all right," Ma says.

"Remember how she ran after June and slapped her? We were there—some guys were driving us home."

"Yeah. So she's got it too."

"Hey," says Dad, "why don't you get a chair, Jimmy? Sit down here."

The soldier looks around. His face is raw in spots, broken out. But his eyes are nice. He never looks at me.

"Get a chair from that table," Dad says.

"Those people might want it."

"Hell, just take it. Nobody's sitting on it."

"They might—"

Dad reaches around and yanks the chair over. The people look at him but don't say anything. Dad is breathing hard. "Here, sit here," he says. The soldier sits down.

Frank and Jerry come back. They stand by Dad, watching him. "Can we go out now?" Frank says.

"What?"

"Out for a boatride."

"What? No, next week. Do it next week. We're going to play cards."

"You said—"

"Shut up, we'll do it next week." Dad looks up and shades his eyes. "The lake don't look right, anyway."

"Lots of people are out there—"

"I said shut up."

"Honey," Ma whispers, "let him alone. Go and play by yourselves."

"Can we sit in the car?"

"Okay, but don't honk the horn."

"Ma, can't we go for a ride?"

"Go and play by yourselves, stop bothering us," she says. "Hey, will you take Sissie?"

They look at me. They don't like me, I can see it, but they take me with them. We run through the crowd and somebody spills a drink—he yells at us. "Oops, got to watch it!" Frank giggles.

We run along the walk by the boat. A woman in a yellow dress is carrying a baby. She looks at us like she doesn't like us.

Down at the far end some kids are standing together.

"Hey, lookit that," Frank says.

A blackbird is caught in the scum, by one of the boats. It can't fly up. One of the kids, a long-legged girl in a dirty dress, is poking at it with a stick.

The bird's wings keep fluttering but it can't get out. If it could get free it would fly and be safe, but the scum holds it down.

One of the kids throws a stone at it. "Stupid old goddam bird," somebody says. Frank throws a stone. They are all throwing stones. The bird doesn't know enough to turn away. Its feathers are all wet and dirty. One of the stones hits the bird's head.

"Take that!" Frank says, throwing a rock. The water splashes up and some of the girls scream.

I watch them throwing stones. I am standing at the side. If the bird dies then everything can die, I think. Inside the tavern there is music from the jukebox.

We are at the boathouse tavern again. It is a mild day, a Sunday afternoon. Dad is talking with some men; Jerry and I are waiting by the boats. Mommy is at home with the new baby. Frank went off with some friends of his, to a stock car race. There are some people here, sitting out at the tables, but they don't notice us.

"Why doesn't he hurry up?" Jerry says.

Jerry is twelve now. He has pimples on his forehead and chin.

He pushes one of the rowboats with his foot. He is wearing sneakers that are dirty. I wish I could get in that boat and sit down, but I am afraid. A boy not much older than Jerry is squatting on the boardwalk, smoking. You can tell he is in charge of the boats.

"Daddy, come on. Come on," Jerry says, whining. Daddy can't hear him.

I have mosquito bites on my arms and legs. There are mosquitoes and flies around here; the flies crawl around the sticky mess left on tables. A car over in the parking lot has its radio on loud. You can hear the music all this way. "He's coming," I tell Jerry, so he won't be mad. Jerry is like Dad, the way his eyes look.

"Oh, that fat guy keeps talking to him," Jerry says.

The fat man is one of the bartenders; he has on a dirty white apron. All these men are familiar. We have been seeing them for years. He punches Dad's arm, up by the shoulder, and Dad pushes him. They are laughing, though. Nobody is mad.

"I'd sooner let a nigger—" the bartender says. We can't hear anything more, but the men laugh again.

"All he does is drink," Jerry says. "I hate him."

At school, up on the sixth-grade floor, Jerry got in trouble last month. The principal slapped him. I am afraid to look at Jerry when he's mad.

"I hate him, I wish he'd die," Jerry says.

Dad is trying to come to us, but every time he takes a step backward and gets ready to turn, one of the men says something. There are three men beside him. Their stomachs are big, but Dad's isn't. He is wearing dark pants and a white shirt; his tie is in the car. He wears a tie to church, then takes it off. He has his shirtsleeves rolled up and you can see how strong his arms must be.

Two women cross over from the parking lot. They are wearing high-heeled shoes and hats and bright dresses—orange and yellow—and when they walk past, the men look at them. They go into the tavern. The men laugh about something. The way they laugh makes my eyes focus on something away from them—a bird flying in the sky—and it is hard for me to look anywhere else. I feel as if I'm falling asleep.

"Here he comes," Jerry says.

Dad walks over to us, with his big steps. He is smiling and carrying a bottle of beer. "Hey, kid," he says to the boy squatting on the walk, "how's about a boat?"

"This one is the best," Jerry says.

"The best, huh? Great." Dad grins at us. "Okay, Sissie, let's get you in. Be careful now." He picks me up even though I am too heavy for it, and sets me in the boat. It hurts a little where he held me, under the arms, but I don't care.

Jerry climbs in. Dad steps in and something happens—he almost slips, but he catches himself. With the wet oar he pushes us off from the boardwalk.

Dad can row fast. The sunlight is gleaming on the water. I sit very still, facing him, afraid to move. The boat goes fast, and Dad is leaning back and forth and pulling on the oars, breathing hard, doing everything fast like he always does. He is always in a hurry to get things done. He has set the bottle of beer down by his leg, pressed against the side of the boat so it won't fall.

"There's the guys we saw go out, before," Jerry says. Coming around the island is a boat with three boys in it, older than Jerry. "They went on the island. Can we go there too?"

"Sure," says Dad. His eyes squint in the sun. He is suntanned, and there are freckles on his forehead. I am sitting close to him, facing him, and it surprises me what he looks like—he is like a stranger, with his eyes narrowed. The water beneath the boat makes me feel funny. It keeps us up now, but if I fell over the side I would sink and drown.

"Nice out here, huh?" Dad says. He is breathing hard.

"We should go over that way, to get on the island," Jerry says.

"This goddam oar has splinters in it," Dad says. He hooks the oar up and lets us glide. He reaches down to get the bottle of beer. Though the lake and some trees and the buildings back on shore are in front of me, what makes me look at it is my father's throat, the way it bobs when he swallows. He wipes his forehead. "Want to row, Sissie?" he says.

"Can I?"

"Let me do it," says Jerry.

"Naw, I was just kidding," Dad says.

"I can do it. It ain't hard."

"Stay where you are," Dad says.

He starts rowing again, faster. Why does he go so fast? His face is getting red, the way it does at home when he has trouble with Frank. He clears his throat and spits over the side; I don't like to see that but I can't help but watch. The other boat glides past us, heading for shore. The boys don't look over at us.

Jerry and I look to see if anyone else is on the island, but no one is. The island is very small. You can see around it.

"Are you going to land on it, Dad?" Jerry says.

"Sure, okay." Dad's face is flushed and looks angry.

The boat scrapes bottom and bumps. "Jump out and pull it in," Dad says. Jerry jumps out. His shoes and socks are wet now, but Dad doesn't notice. The boat bumps; it hurts me. I am afraid. But then we're up on the land and Dad is out and lifting me. "Nice ride, sugar?" he says.

Jerry and I run around the island. It is different from what we thought, but we don't know why. There are some trees on it, some wild grass, and then bare caked mud that goes down to the water. The water looks dark and deep on the other side, but when we get there it's shallow. Lily pads grow there; everything is thick and tangled. Jerry wades in the water and gets his pants legs wet. "There might be money in the water," he says.

Some napkins and beer cans are nearby. There is part of a hotdog bun, with flies buzzing around it.

When we go back by Dad, we see him squatting over the water

doing something. His back jerks. Then I see that he is being sick. He is throwing up in the water and making a noise like coughing.

Jerry turns around right away and runs back. I follow him, afraid. On the other side we can look back at the boathouse and wish we were there.

Marian and Betty went to the show, but I couldn't. She made me come along here with them. "And cut out that snippy face," Ma said, to let me know she's watching. I have to help her take care of Linda—poor fat Linda, with her runny nose! So here we are inside the tavern. There's too much smoke, I hate smoke. Dad is smoking a cigar. I won't drink any more root beer, it's flat, and I'm sick of potato chips. Inside me there is something that wants to run away, that hates them. How loud they are, my parents! My mother spilled something on the front of her dress, but does she notice? And my Aunt Lucy and Uncle Joe, they're here. Try to avoid them. Lucy has false teeth that makes everyone stare at her. I know that everyone is staring at us. I could hide my head in my arms and turn away, I'm so tired and my legs hurt from sunburn and I can't stand them any more.

"So did you ever hear from them? That letter you wrote?" Ma says to Lucy.

"I'm still waiting. Somebody said you got to have connections to get on the show. But I don't believe it. That Howie Masterson that's the m. c., he's a real nice guy. I can tell."

"It's all crap," Dad says. "You women believe anything."

"I don't believe it," I say.

"Phony as hell," says my uncle.

"You do too believe it, Sissie," says my mother. "Sissie thinks he's cute. I know she does."

"I hate that guy," I tell her, but she and my aunt are laughing. "I said I hate him! He's greasy."

"All that stuff is phony as hell," says my Uncle Joe. He is tired all the time, and right now he sits with his head bowed. I hate his bald head with the little fringe of gray hair on it. At least my father is still handsome. His jaws sag and there are lines in his neck—edged with dirt, I can see, embarrassed—and his stomach is bulging a little against the table, but still he is a handsome man. In a place like this, women look at him. What's he see in *her?* they think. My mother had her hair cut too short last time; she looks queer. There is a photograph taken of her when she was young, standing by someone's motorcycle, with her hair long. In the photograph she was pretty, almost beautiful, but I don't believe it. Not really. I can't believe it, and I hate her. Her forehead gathers itself up in little wrinkles whenever she glances down at Linda, as if she can't remember who Linda is.

"Well, nobody wanted you, kid," she once said to Linda. Linda was a baby then, one year old. Ma was furious, standing in the kitchen where she was washing the floor, screaming: "Nobody wanted you, it was a goddam accident! A accident!" That surprised me so I didn't know what to think, and I didn't know if I hated Ma or not; but I kept it all a secret . . . only my girl friends know, and I won't tell the priest either. Nobody can make me tell. I narrow my eyes and watch my mother leaning forward to say something—it's like she's going to toss something out on the table—and think that maybe she isn't my mother, after all, and she isn't that pretty girl in the photograph, but someone else.

"A woman was on the show last night that lost two kids in a fire. Her house burned down," my aunt says loudly. "And she answered the questions right off and got a lot of money and the audience went wild. You could see she was a real lady. I love that guy, Howie Masterson. He's real sweet."

"He's a bastard," Dad says.

"Harry, what the hell? You never even seen him," Ma says.

"I sure as hell never did. Got better things to do at night." Dad turns to my uncle and his voice changes. "I'm on the night shift, now."

"Yeah, I hate that, I . . ."

"I can sleep during the day. What's the difference?"

"I hate those night shifts."

"What's there to do during the day?" Dad says flatly. His eyes scan us at the table as if he doesn't see anything, then they seem to fall off me and go behind me, looking at nothing.

"Not much," says my uncle, and I can see his white scalp beneath his hair. Both men are silent.

Dad pours beer into his glass and spills some of it. I wish I could look away. I love him, I think, but I hate to be here. Where would I rather be? With Marian and Betty at the movies, or in my room, lying on the bed and staring at the photographs of movie stars on my walls—those beautiful people that never say anything—while out in the kitchen my mother is waiting for my father to come home, so they can continue their quarrel. It never stops, that quarrel. Sometimes they laugh together, kid around, they kiss. Then the quarrel starts up again in a few minutes.

"Ma, can I go outside and wait in the car?" I say. "Linda's asleep."

"What's so hot about the car?" she says, looking at me.

"I'm tired. My sunburn hurts."

Linda is sleeping in Ma's lap, with her mouth open and drooling on the front of her dress. "Okay, go on," Ma says. "But we're not going to hurry just for you." When she has drunk too much there is a struggle in her between being angry and being affectionate; she fights both of them, as if standing with her legs apart and her hands on her hips, bracing a strong wind.

When I cross through the crowded tavern I'm conscious of people looking at me. My hair lost its curl because it was so humid today, my legs are too thin, my figure is flat and not nice like Marian's—I want to hide somewhere, hide my face from them. I hate this noisy place and these people. Even the music is ugly because it belongs to them. Then, when I'm outside, the music gets faint right away and it doesn't sound so bad. It's cooler out here. No one is around. Out back, the old rowboats are tied up. Nobody's on the lake. There's no moon, the sky is overcast, it was raining earlier.

When I turn around, a man is standing by the door watching me.

"What're you doing?" he says.

"Nothing."

He has dark hair and a tanned face, I think, but everything is confused because the light from the door is pinkish—there's a neon sign there. My heart starts to pound. The man leans forward to stare at me. "Oh, I thought you were somebody else," he says.

I want to show him I'm not afraid. "Yeah, really? Who did you think I was?" When we ride on the schoolbus we smile out the windows at strange men, just for fun. We do that all the time. I'm not afraid of any of them.

"You're not her," he says.

Some people come out the door and he has to step out of their way. I say to him, "Maybe you seen me around here before. We come here pretty often."

"Who do you come with?" He is smiling as if he thinks I'm funny. "Anybody I know?"

"That's my business."

It's a game. I'm not afraid. When I think of my mother and father inside, something makes me want to step closer to this man—why should I be afraid? I could be wild like some of the other girls. Nothing surprises me.

We keep on talking. At first I can tell he wants me to come inside the tavern with him, but then he forgets about it; he keeps talking. I don't know what we say, but we talk in drawling voices, smiling at each other but in a secret knowing way, as if each one of us knew more than the other. My cheeks start to burn. I could be wild like Betty is sometimes—like some of the other girls. Why not? Once before I talked with a man like this, on the bus. We were both sitting in the back. I wasn't afraid. This man and I keep talking and we talk about nothing, he wants to know how old I am, but it makes my heart pound so hard that I want to touch my chest to calm it. We are walking along the old boardwalk and I say: "Somebody took me out rowing once, here."

"Is that so?" he says. "You want me to take you out?"

He has a hard, handsome face. I like that face. Why is he alone? When he smiles I know he's laughing at me, and this makes me stand taller, walk with my shoulders raised.

"Hey, are you with somebody inside there?" he says.

"I left them."

"Have a fight?"

"A fight, yes."

He looks at me quickly. "How old are you, anyway?"

"That's none of your business."

"Girls your age are all alike."

"We're not all alike!" I arch my back and look at him in a way I must have learned somewhere—where?—with my lips not smiling but ready to smile, and my eyes narrowed. One leg is turned as if I'm ready to jump away from him. He sees all this. He smiles.

"Say, you're real cute."

We're walking over by the parking lot now. He touches my arm. Right away my heart trips, but I say nothing, I keep walking. High above us the tree branches are moving in the wind. It's cold for June. It's late—after eleven. The man is wearing a jacket, but I have on a sleeveless dress and there are goose pimples on my arms.

"Cold, huh?" he says.

He takes hold of my shoulders and leans toward me. This is to show me he's no kid, he's grown-up, this is how they do things; when he kisses me his grip on my shoulders gets tighter. "I better go back," I say to him. My voice is queer.

"What?" he says.

I am wearing a face like one of those faces pinned up in my room, and what if I lose it? This is not my face. I try to turn away from him.

He kisses me again. His breath smells like beer, maybe, it's like my father's breath, and my mind is empty; I can't think what to do. Why am I here? My legs feel numb, my fingers are cold. The man rubs my arms and says, "You should have a sweater or something . . ."

He is waiting for me to say something, to keep on the way I was before. But I have forgotten how to do it. Before, I was Marian or one of the older girls; now I am just myself. I am fourteen. I think of Linda sleeping in my mother's lap, and something frightens me.

"Hey, what's wrong?" the man says.

He sees I'm afraid but pretends he doesn't. He comes to me again and embraces me, his mouth presses against my neck and shoulder, I feel as if I'm suffocating. "My car's over here," he says, trying to catch his breath. I can't move. Something dazzling and icy rises up in me, an awful fear, but I can't move and can't say anything. He is touching me with his hands. His mouth is soft but wants too much from me. I think: What is he doing? Do they all do this? Do I have to have it done to me too?

"You cut that out," I tell him.

He steps away. His chest is heaving and his eyes look like a dog's eyes, surprised and betrayed. The last thing I see of him is those eyes, before I turn and run back to the tavern.

Jesse says, "Let's stop at this place. I been here a few times before."

It's the "Lakeside Bar." That big old building with the grubby siding, and a big pink neon sign in front, and the cinder driveway that's so bumpy. Yes, everything the same. But different, too—smaller, dirtier. There is a custard stand nearby with a glaring orange roof, and people are crowded around it. That's new. I haven't been here for years.

"I feel like a beer," he says.

He smiles at me and caresses my arm. He treats me as if I were something that might break; in my cheap-linen maternity dress I feel ugly and heavy. My flesh is so soft and thick that nothing could hurt it.

"Sure, honey. Pa used to stop in here too."

We cross through the parking lot to the tavern. Wild grass grows along the sidewalk and in the cracks of the sidewalk. Why is this place so ugly to me? I feel as if a hand were pressing against my chest, shutting off my breath. Is there some secret here? Why am I afraid?

I catch sight of myself in a dusty window as we pass. My hair is long, down to my shoulders. I am pretty, but my secret is that I am pretty like everyone is. My husband loves me for this but doesn't know it. I have a pink mouth and plucked darkened eyebrows and soft bangs over my forehead; I know everything, I have no need to learn from anyone else now. I am one of those girls younger girls study closely, to learn from. On buses, in five-and-tens, thirteen-year-old girls must look at me solemnly, learning, memorizing.

"Pretty Sissie!" my mother likes to say when we visit, though I told her how I hate that name. She is proud of me for being pretty, but thinks I'm too thin. "You'll fill out nice, after the baby," she says. Herself, she is fat and veins have begun to darken on her legs; she scuffs around the house in bedroom slippers. Who is my mother? When I think of her I can't think of anything—do I love her or hate her, or is there nothing there?

Jesse forgets and walks ahead of me, I have to walk fast to catch up. I'm wearing pastel blue high heels—that must be because I am proud of my legs. I have little else. Then he remembers and turns to put out his hand for me, smiling to show he is sorry. Jesse is the kind of young man thirteen-year-old girls stare at, secretly; he is not a man, not old enough, but not a boy either. He is a year older than I am, twenty. When I met him he was wearing a navy uniform and he was with a girl friend of mine.

Just a few people sitting outside at the tables. They're afraid of rain—the sky doesn't look good. And how bumpy the ground is here, bare spots and little holes and patches of crabgrass, and everywhere napkins and junk. Too many flies, outside. Has this place changed hands? The screens at the windows don't fit right; you can see why flies get inside. Jesse opens the door for me and I go in. All bars smell alike. There is a damp, dark odor of beer and something indefinable—spilled soft drinks, pretzels getting stale? This bar is just like any other. Before we were married we went to places like this, Jesse and me and other couples. We had to spend a certain amount of time doing things like that—and going to movies, playing miniature golf, bowling, dancing, swimming—then we got married, now we're going to have a baby. I think of the baby all the time, because my life will be changed then; everything will be different. Four months from now. I should be frightened, but a calm laziness has come over me. It was so easy for my mother . . . But it will be different with me because my life will be changed by it, and nothing ever changed my mother. You couldn't change her! Why should I think? Why should I be afraid? My body is filled with love for this baby, and I will never be the same again.

We sit down at a table near the bar. Jesse is in a good mood. My father would have liked him, I think; when he laughs Jesse reminds me of him. Why is a certain kind of simple, healthy, honest man always destined to lose everything? Their souls are as clean and smooth as the muscular line of their arms. At night I hold Jesse, thinking of my father and what happened to him—all that drinking, then the accident at the factory—and I pray that Jesse will be different. I hope that his quick, open, loud way of talking is just a disguise, that really he is someone else—slower and calculating. That kind of man grows old without jerks and spasms. Why did I marry Jesse, then?

Someone at the bar turns around, and it's a man I think I know —I have known. Yes. That man outside, the man I met outside. I stare at him, my heart pounding, and he doesn't see me. He is dark, his hair is neatly combed but is thinner than before; he is wearing a cheap gray suit. But is it the same man? He is standing with a friend and looking around, as if he doesn't like what he sees. He is tired, too. He has grown years older.

Our eyes meet. He glances away. He doesn't remember—that frightened girl he held in his arms.

I am tempted to put my hand on Jesse's arm and tell him about that man, but how can I? Jesse is talking about trading in our car for a new one . . . I can't move, my mind seems to be coming to a stop. Is that the man I kissed, or someone else? A feeling of angry loss comes over me. Why should I lose everything? Everything? Is it the same man, and would he remember? My heart bothers me, it's stupid to be like this: here I sit, powdered and sweet, a girl safely married, pregnant and secured to the earth, with my husband beside me. He still loves me. Our love keeps on. Like my parents' love, it will subside someday, but nothing surprises me because I have learned everything.

The man turns away, talking to his friend. They are weary, tired of something. He isn't married yet, I think, and that pleases me. Good. But why are these men always tired? Is it the jobs they hold, the kind of men who stop in at this tavern? Why do they flash their teeth when they smile, but stop smiling so quickly? Why do their children cringe from them sometimes—an innocent upraised arm a frightening thing? Why do they grow old so quickly, sitting at kitchen tables with bottles of beer? They are everywhere, in every house. All the houses in this neighborhood and all neighborhoods around here. Jesse is young, but the outline of what he will be is already in his face; do you think I can't see it? Their lives are like hands dealt out to them in their innumerable card games. You pick up the sticky cards, and there it is: there it is. Can't change anything, all you can do is switch some cards around, stick one in here, one over here . . . pretend there is some sense, a secret scheme.

The man at the bar tosses some coins down and turns to go. I want to cry out to him, "Wait, wait!" But I cannot. I sit helplessly and watch him leave. Is it the same man? If he leaves I will be caught here, what can I do? I can almost hear my mother's shrill laughter, coming in from outside, and some drawling remark of my father's—lifting for a moment above the music. Those little explosions of laughter, the slap of someone's hand on the damp table, in anger, the clink of bottles accidentally touching—and there, there, my drunken aunt's voice, what is she saying? I am terrified at being left with them. I watch the man at the door and think that I could have loved him. I know it.

He has left, he and his friend. He is nothing to me, but suddenly I feel tears in my eyes. What's wrong with me? I hate everything that springs upon me and seems to draw itself down and oppress me in a way I could never explain to anyone . . . I am crying because I am pregnant but not with that man's child. It could have been his child, I could have gone with him to his car; but I did nothing, I ran away, I was afraid, and now I'm sitting here with Jesse, who is picking the label off his beer bottle with his thick squarish fingernails. I did nothing. I was afraid. Now he has left me here and what can I do?

I let my hand fall onto my stomach to remind myself that I am in love: with this baby, with Jesse, with everything. I am in love with our house and our life and the future and even this moment—right now—that I am struggling to live through.

Revelation

Flannery O'Connor

The doctor's waiting room, which was very small, was almost full when the Turpins entered and Mrs. Turpin, who was very large, made it look even smaller by her presence. She stood looming at the head of the magazine table set in the center of it, a living demonstration that the room was inadequate and ridiculous. Her little bright black eyes took in all the patients as she sized up the seating situation. There was one vacant chair and a place on the sofa occupied by a blond child in a dirty blue romper who should have been told to move over and make room for the lady. He was five or six, but Mrs. Turpin saw at once that no one was going to tell him to move over. He was slumped down in the seat, his arms idle at his sides and his eyes idle in his head; his nose ran unchecked.

Mrs. Turpin put a firm hand on Claud's shoulder and said in a voice that included anyone who wanted to listen, "Claud, you sit in that chair there," and gave him a push down into the vacant one. Claud was florid and bald and sturdy, somewhat shorter than Mrs. Turpin, but he sat down as if he were accustomed to doing what she told him to.

Mrs. Turpin remained standing. The only man in the room besides Claud was a lean stringy old fellow with a rusty hand spread out on each knee, whose eyes were closed as if he were asleep or dead or pretending to be so as not to get up and offer her his seat. Her gaze settled agreeably on a well-dressed grey-haired lady whose eyes met hers and whose expression said: if that child belonged to me, he would have some manners and move over—there's plenty of room there for you and him too.

Claud looked up with a sigh and made as if to rise.

"Sit down," Mrs. Turpin said. "You know you're not supposed to stand on that leg. He has an ulcer on his leg," she explained.

Claud lifted his foot onto the magazine table and rolled his trouser leg up to reveal a purple swelling on a plump marble-white calf.

"My!" the pleasant lady said. "How did you do that?"

"A cow kicked him," Mrs. Turpin said.

"Goodness!" said the lady.

Claud rolled his trouser leg down.

"Maybe the little boy would move over," the lady suggested, but the child did not stir.

"Somebody will be leaving in a minute," Mrs. Turpin said. She could not understand why a doctor—with as much money as they made charging five dollars a day to just stick their head in the hospital door and look at you—couldn't afford a decent-sized waiting room. This one was hardly bigger than a garage. The table was cluttered with limp-looking magazines and at one end of it there was a big green glass ash tray full of cigaret butts and cotton wads with little blood spots on them. If she had had anything to do with the running of the place, that would have been emptied every so often. There were no chairs against the wall at the head of the room. It had a rectangular-shaped panel in it that permitted a view of the office where the nurse came and went and the secretary listened to the radio. A plastic fern in a gold pot sat in the opening and trailed its fronds down almost to the floor. The radio was softly playing gospel music.

Just then the inner door opened and a nurse with the highest stack of yellow hair Mrs. Turpin had ever seen put her face in the crack and called for the next patient. The woman sitting beside Claud grasped the two arms of her chair and hoisted herself up; she pulled her dress free from her legs and lumbered through the door where the nurse had disappeared.

Mrs. Turpin eased into the vacant chair, which held her tight as a corset. "I wish I could reduce," she said, and rolled her eyes and gave a comic sigh.

"Oh, *you* aren't fat," the stylish lady said.

"Ooooo I am too," Mrs. Turpin said. "Claud he eats all he wants to and never weighs over one hundred and seventy-five pounds, but me I just look at something good to eat and I gain some weight," and her stomach and shoulders shook with laughter. "You can eat all you want to, can't you, Claud?" she asked, turning to him.

Claud only grinned.

"Well, as long as you have such a good disposition," the stylish lady said, "I don't think it makes a bit of difference what size you are. You just can't beat a good disposition."

Next to her was a fat girl of eighteen or nineteen, scowling into a thick blue book which Mrs. Turpin saw was entitled *Human Development.* The girl raised her head and directed her scowl at Mrs. Turpin as if she did not like her looks. She appeared annoyed that anyone should speak while she tried to read. The poor girl's face was blue with acne and Mrs. Turpin thought how pitiful it was to have a face like that at that age. She gave the girl a friendly smile but the girl only scowled the harder. Mrs. Turpin herself was fat but she had always had good skin, and, though she was forty-seven years old, there was not a wrinkle in her face except around her eyes from laughing too much.

Next to the ugly girl was the child, still in exactly the same position, and next to him was a thin leathery old woman in a cotton print dress. She and Claud had three sacks of chicken feed in their pump house that was in the same print. She had seen from the first that the child belonged with the old woman. She could tell by the way they sat —kind of vacant and white-trashy, as if they would sit there until Doomsday if nobody called and told them to get up. And at right angles but next to the well-dressed pleasant lady was a lank-faced woman who was certainly the child's mother. She had on a yellow sweat shirt and wine-colored slacks, both gritty-looking, and the rims of her lips were stained with snuff. Her dirty yellow hair was tied behind with a little piece of red paper ribbon. Worse than niggers any day, Mrs. Turpin thought.

The gospel hymn playing was, "When I looked up and He looked down," and Mrs. Turpin, who knew it, supplied the last line mentally, "And wona these days I know I'll we-eara crown."

Without appearing to, Mrs. Turpin always noticed people's feet. The well-dressed lady had on red and grey suede shoes to match her dress. Mrs. Turpin had on her good black patent leather pumps. The ugly girl had on Girl Scout shoes and heavy socks. The old woman had on tennis shoes and the white-trashy mother had on what appeared to be bedroom slippers, black straw with gold braid threaded through them—exactly what you would have expected her to have on.

Sometimes at night when she couldn't go to sleep, Mrs. Turpin would occupy herself with the question of who she would have chosen to be if she couldn't have been herself. If Jesus had said to her before he made her, "There's only two places available for you. You can either be a nigger or white-trash," what would she have said? "Please, Jesus, please," she would have said, "just let me wait until there's another place available," and he would have said, "No, you have to go right now and I have only those two places so make up your mind." She would have wiggled and squirmed and begged and pleaded but it would have been no use and finally she would have said, "All right, make me a nigger then—but that don't mean a trashy one." And he would have made her a neat clean respectable Negro woman, herself but black.

Next to the child's mother was a red-headed youngish woman, reading one of the magazines and working a piece of chewing gum, hell for leather, as Claud would say. Mrs. Turpin could not see the woman's feet. She was not white-trash, just common. Sometimes Mrs. Turpin occupied herself at night naming the classes of people. On the bottom of the heap were most colored people, not the kind she would have been if she had been one, but most of them; then next to them—not above, just away from—were the white-trash; then above them were the home-owners, and above them the home-and-land owners, to which she and Claud belonged. Above she and Claud were people with a lot of money and much bigger houses and much more land. But here the complexity of it would begin to bear in on her, for some of the people with a lot of money were common and ought to be below she and Claud and some of the people who had good blood had lost their money and had to rent and then there were colored people who owned their homes and land as well. There was a colored dentist in town who had two red Lincolns and a swimming pool and a farm with registered white-face cattle on it. Usually by the time she had fallen asleep all the classes of people were moiling and roiling around in her head, and she would dream they were all crammed in together in a box car, being ridden off to be put in a gas oven.

"That's a beautiful clock," she said and nodded to her right. It was a big wall clock, the face encased in a brass sunburst.

"Yes, it's very pretty," the stylish lady said agreeably. "And right on the dot too," she added, glancing at her watch.

The ugly girl beside her cast an eye upward at the clock, smirked, then looked directly at Mrs. Turpin and smirked again. Then she returned her eyes to her book. She was obviously the lady's daughter because, although they didn't look anything alike as to disposition, they both had the same shape of face and the same blue eyes. On the lady they sparkled pleasantly but in the girl's seared face they appeared alternately to smolder and to blaze.

What if Jesus had said, "All right, you can be white-trash or a nigger or ugly"!

Mrs. Turpin felt an awful pity for the girl, though she thought it was one thing to be ugly and another to act ugly.

The woman with the snuff-stained lips turned around in her chair and looked up at the clock. Then she turned back and appeared to look a little to the side of Mrs. Turpin. There was a cast in one of her eyes. "You want to know wher you can get you one of themther clocks?" she asked in a loud voice.

"No, I already have a nice clock," Mrs. Turpin said. Once somebody like her got a leg in the conversation, she would be all over it.

"You can get you one with green stamps," the woman said. "That's most likely wher he got hisn. Save you up enough, you can get you most anythang. I got me some joo'ry."

Ought to have got you a wash rag and some soap, Mrs. Turpin thought.

"I get contour sheets with mine," the pleasant lady said.

The daughter slammed her book shut. She looked straight in front of her, directly through Mrs. Turpin and on through the yellow curtain and the plate glass window which made the wall behind her. The girl's eyes seemed lit all of a sudden with a peculiar light, an unnatural light like night road signs give. Mrs. Turpin turned her head to see if there was anything going on outside that she should see, but she could not see anything. Figures passing cast only a pale shadow through the curtain. There was no reason the girl should single her out for her ugly looks.

"Miss Finley," the nurse said, cracking the door. The gum-chewing woman got up and passed in front of her and Claud and went into the office. She had on red high-heeled shoes.

Directly across the table, the ugly girl's eyes were fixed on Mrs. Turpin as if she had some very special reason for disliking her.

"This is wonderful weather, isn't it?" the girl's mother said.

"It's good weather for cotton if you can get the niggers to pick it," Mrs. Turpin said, "but niggers don't want to pick cotton any more. You can't get the white folks to pick it and now you can't get the niggers —because they got to be right up there with the white folks."

"They gonna *try* anyways," the white-trash woman said, leaning forward.

"Do you have one of those cotton-picking machines?" the pleasant lady asked.

"No," Mrs. Turpin said, "they leave half the cotton in the field. We don't have much cotton anyway. If you want to make it farming now, you have to have a little of everything. We got a couple of acres of cotton and a few hogs and chickens and just enough white-face that Claud can look after them himself."

"One thang I don't want," the white-trash woman said, wiping her mouth with the back of her hand. "Hogs. Nasty stinking things, a-gruntin and a-rootin all over the place."

Mrs. Turpin gave her the merest edge of her attention. "Our hogs are not dirty and they don't stink," she said. "They're cleaner than some children I've seen. Their feet never touch the ground. We have a pig-parlor—that's where you raise them on concrete," she explained to the pleasant lady, "and Claud scoots them down with the hose every afternoon and washes off the floor." Cleaner by far than that child right there, she thought. Poor nasty little thing. He had not moved except to put the thumb of his dirty hand into his mouth.

The woman turned her face away from Mrs. Turpin. "I know I wouldn't scoot down no hog with no hose," she said to the wall.

You wouldn't have no hog to scoot down, Mrs. Turpin said to herself.

"A-gruntin and a-rootin and a-groanin," the woman muttered.

"We got a little of everything," Mrs. Turpin said to the pleasant lady. "It's no use in having more than you can handle yourself with help like it is. We found enough niggers to pick our cotton this year but Claud he has to go after them and take them home again in the evening. They can't walk that half a mile. No they can't. I tell you," she said and laughed merrily, "I sure am tired of buttering up niggers, but you got to love em if you want em to work for you. When they come in the morning, I run out and say, 'Hi yawl this morning?' and when Claud drives them off to the field I just wave to beat the band and they just wave back." And she waved her hand rapidly to illustrate.

"Like you read out of the same book," the lady said, showing she understood perfectly.

"Child, yes," Mrs. Turpin said. "And when they come in from the field, I run out with a bucket of icewater. That's the way it's going to be from now on," she said. "You may as well face it."

"One thang I know," the white-trash woman said. "Two thangs I ain't going to do: love no niggers or scoot down no hog with no hose." And she let out a bark of contempt.

The look that Mrs. Turpin and the pleasant lady exchanged indicated they both understood that you had to *have* certain things before you could *know* certain things. But every time Mrs. Turpin exchanged a look with the lady, she was aware that the ugly girl's peculiar eyes were still on her, and she had trouble bringing her attention back to the conversation.

"When you got something," she said, "you got to look after it." And when you ain't got a thing but breath and britches, she added to herself, you can afford to come to town every morning and just sit on the Court House coping and spit.

A grotesque revolving shadow passed across the curtain behind her and was thrown palely on the opposite wall. Then a bicycle clattered down against the outside of the building. The door opened and a colored boy glided in with a tray from the drug store. It had two large red and white paper cups on it with tops on them. He was a tall, very black boy in discolored white pants and a green nylon shirt. He was chewing gum slowly, as if to music. He set the tray down in the office opening next to the fern and stuck his head through to look for the secretary. She was not in there. He rested his arms on the ledge and waited, his narrow bottom stuck out, swaying slowly to the left and right. He raised a hand over his head and scratched the base of his skull.

"You see that button there, boy?" Mrs. Turpin said. "You can punch that and she'll come. She's probably in the back somewhere."

"Is thas right?" the boy said agreeably, as if he had never seen the button before. He leaned to the right and put his finger on it. "She sometime out," he said and twisted around to face his audience, his elbows behind him on the counter. The nurse appeared and he twisted back again. She handed him a dollar and he rooted in his pocket and made the change and counted it out to her. She gave him fifteen cents for a tip and he went out with the empty tray. The heavy door swung to slowly and closed at length with the sound of suction. For a moment no one spoke.

"They ought to send all them niggers back to Africa," the white-trash woman said. "That's wher they come from in the first place."

"Oh, I couldn't do without my good colored friends," the pleasant lady said.

"There's a heap of things worse than a nigger," Mrs. Turpin agreed. "It's all kinds of them just like it's all kinds of us."

"Yes, and it takes all kinds to make the world go round," the lady said in her musical voice.

As she said it, the raw-complexioned girl snapped her teeth together. Her lower lip turned downwards and inside out, revealing the pale pink inside of her mouth. After a second it rolled back up. It was the ugliest face Mrs. Turpin had ever seen anyone make and for a moment she was certain that the girl had made it at her. She was looking at her as if she had known and disliked her all her life—all of Mrs. Turpin's life, it seemed too, not just all the girl's life. Why, girl, I don't even know you, Mrs. Turpin said silently.

She forced her attention back to the discussion. "It wouldn't be practical to send them back to Africa," she said. "They wouldn't want to go. They got it too good here."

"Wouldn't be what they wanted—if I had anythang to do with it," the woman said.

"It wouldn't be a way in the world you could get all the niggers back over there," Mrs. Turpin said. "They'd be hiding out and lying down and turning sick on you and wailing and hollering and raring and pitching. It wouldn't be a way in the world to get them over there."

"They got over here," the trashy woman said. "Get back like they got over."

"It wasn't so many of them then," Mrs. Turpin explained.

The woman looked at Mrs. Turpin as if here was an idiot indeed but Mrs. Turpin was not bothered by the look, considering where it came from.

"Nooo," she said, "they're going to stay here where they can go to New York and marry white folks and improve their color. That's what they all want to do, every one of them, improve their color."

"You know what comes of that, don't you?" Claud asked.

"No, Claud, what?" Mrs. Turpin said.

Claud's eyes twinkled. "White-faced niggers," he said with never a smile.

Everybody in the office laughed except the white-trash and the ugly girl. The girl gripped the book in her lap with white fingers. The trashy woman looked around her from face to face as if she thought they were all idiots. The old woman in the feed sack dress continued to gaze expressionless across the floor at the high-top shoes of the man opposite her, the one who had been pretending to be asleep when the Turpins came in. He was laughing heartily, his hands still spread out on his knees. The child had fallen to the side and was lying now almost face down in the old woman's lap.

While they recovered from their laughter, the nasal chorus on the radio kept the room from silence.

"You go to blank blank
And I'll go to mine
But we'll all blank along
To-geth-ther,
And all along the blank

We'll hep eachother out
Smile-ling in any kind of
Weath-ther!"

Mrs. Turpin didn't catch every word but she caught enough to agree with the spirit of the song and it turned her thoughts sober. To help anybody out that needed it was her philosophy of life. She never spared herself when she found somebody in need, whether they were white or black, trash or decent. And of all she had to be thankful for, she was most thankful that this was so. If Jesus had said, "You can be high society and have all the money you want and be thin and svelte-like, but you can't be a good woman with it," she would have had to say, "Well don't make me that then. Make me a good woman and it don't matter what else, how fat or how ugly or how poor!" Her heart rose. He had not made her a nigger or white-trash or ugly! He had made her herself and given her a little of everything. Jesus, thank you! she said. Thank you thank you thank you! Whenever she counted her blessings she felt as buoyant as if she weighed one hundred and twenty-five pounds instead of one hundred and eighty.

"What's wrong with your little boy?" the pleasant lady asked the white-trashy woman.

"He has a ulcer," the woman said proudly. "He ain't give me a minute's peace since he was born. Him and her are just alike," she said, nodding at the old woman, who was running her leathery fingers through the child's pale hair. "Look like I can't get nothing down them two but Co'Cola and candy."

That's all you try to get down em, Mrs. Turpin said to herself. Too lazy to light the fire. There was nothing you could tell her about people like them that she didn't know already. And it was not just that they didn't have anything. Because if you gave them everything, in two weeks it would all be broken or filthy or they would have chopped it up for lightwood. She knew all this from her own experience. Help them you must, but help them you couldn't.

All at once the ugly girl turned her lips inside out again. Her eyes were fixed like two drills on Mrs. Turpin. This time there was no mistaking that there was something urgent behind them.

Girl, Mrs. Turpin exclaimed silently, I haven't done a thing to you! The girl might be confusing her with somebody else. There was no need to sit by and let herself be intimidated. "You must be in college," she said boldly, looking directly at the girl. "I see you reading a book there."

The girl continued to stare and pointedly did not answer.

Her mother blushed at this rudeness. "The lady asked you a question, Mary Grace," she said under her breath.

"I have ears," Mary Grace said.

The poor mother blushed again. "Mary Grace goes to Wellesley College," she explained. She twisted one of the buttons on her dress. "In Massachusetts," she added with a grimace. "And in the summer she just keeps right on studying. Just reads all the time, a real book worm. She's done real well at Wellesley; she's taking English and Math and History and Psychology and Social Studies," she rattled on, "and I think it's too much. I think she ought to get out and have fun."

The girl looked as if she would like to hurl them all through the plate glass window.

"Way up north," Mrs. Turpin murmured and thought, well, it hasn't done much for her manners.

"I'd almost rather to have him sick," the white-trash woman said, wrenching the attention back to herself. "He's so mean when he ain't. Look like some children just take natural to meanness. It's some gets bad when they get sick but he was the opposite. Took sick and turned good. He don't give me no trouble now. It's me waitin to see the doctor," she said.

If I was going to send anybody back to Africa, Mrs. Turpin thought, it would be your kind, woman. "Yes, indeed," she said aloud, but looking up at the ceiling, "it's a heap of things worse than a nigger." And dirtier than a hog, she added to herself.

"I think people with bad dispositions are more to be pitied than anyone on earth," the pleasant lady said in a voice that was decidedly thin.

"I thank the Lord he has blessed me with a good one," Mrs. Turpin said. "The day has never dawned that I couldn't find something to laugh at."

"Not since she married me anyways," Claud said with a comical straight face.

Everybody laughed except the girl and the white-trash.

Mrs. Turpin's stomach shook. "He's such a caution," she said, "that I can't help but laugh at him."

The girl made a loud ugly noise through her teeth.

Her mother's mouth grew thin and tight. "I think the worst thing in the world," she said, "is an ungrateful person. To have everything and not appreciate it. I know a girl," she said, "who has parents who would give her anything, a little brother who loves her dearly, who is getting a good education, who wears the best clothes, but who can never say a kind word to anyone, who never smiles, who just criticizes and complains all day long."

"Is she too old to paddle?" Claud asked.

The girl's face was almost purple.

"Yes," the lady said, "I'm afraid there's nothing to do but leave her to her folly. Some day she'll wake up and it'll be too late."

"It never hurt anyone to smile," Mrs. Turpin said. "It just makes you feel better all over."

"Of course," the lady said sadly, "but there are just some people you can't tell anything to. They can't take criticism."

"If it's one thing I am," Mrs. Turpin said with feeling, "it's grateful. When I think who all I could have been besides myself and what all I got, a little of everything, and a good disposition besides, I just feel like shouting, 'Thank you, Jesus, for making everything the way it is!' It could have been different!" For one thing, somebody else could have got Claud. At the thought of this, she was flooded with gratitude and a terrible pang of joy ran through her. "Oh thank you, Jesus, Jesus, thank you!" she cried aloud.

The book struck her directly over her left eye. It struck almost at the same instant that she realized the girl was about to hurl it. Before she could utter a sound, the raw face came crashing across the table toward her, howling. The girl's fingers sank like clamps into the soft flesh of her neck. She heard the mother cry out and Claud shout, "Whoa!" There was an instant when she was certain that she was about to be in an earthquake.

All at once her vision narrowed and she saw everything as if it were happening in a small room far away, or as if she were looking at it through the wrong end of a telescope. Claud's face crumpled and fell out of sight. The nurse ran in, then out, then in again. Then the gangling figure of the doctor rushed out of the inner door. Magazines flew this way and that as the table turned over. The girl fell with a thud and Mrs. Turpin's vision suddenly reversed itself and she saw everything large instead of small. The eyes of the white-trashy woman were staring hugely at the floor. There the girl, held down on one side by the nurse and on the other by her mother, was wrenching and turning in their grasp. The doctor was kneeling astride her, trying to hold her arm down. He managed after a second to sink a long needle into it.

Mrs. Turpin felt entirely hollow except for her heart which swung from side to side as if it were agitated in a great empty drum of flesh.

"Somebody that's not busy call for the ambulance," the doctor said in the off-hand voice young doctors adopt for terrible occasions.

Mrs. Turpin could not have moved a finger. The old man who had been sitting next to her skipped nimbly into the office and made the call, for the secretary still seemed to be gone.

"Claud!" Mrs. Turpin called.

He was not in his chair. She knew she must jump up and find him but she felt like some one trying to catch a train in a dream, when everything moves in slow motion and the faster you try to run the slower you go.

"Here I am," a suffocated voice, very unlike Claud's, said.

He was doubled up in the corner on the floor, pale as paper, holding his leg. She wanted to get up and go to him but she could not move. Instead, her gaze was drawn slowly downward to the churning face on the floor, which she could see over the doctor's shoulder.

The girl's eyes stopped rolling and focused on her. They seemed a much lighter blue than before, as if a door that had been tightly closed behind them was now open to admit light and air.

Mrs. Turpin's head cleared and her power of motion returned. She leaned forward until she was looking directly into the fierce brilliant eyes. There was no doubt in her mind that the girl did know her, knew her in some intense and personal way, beyond time and place and condition. "What you got to say to me?" she asked hoarsely and held her breath, waiting, as for a revelation.

The girl raised her head. Her gaze locked with Mrs. Turpin's. "Go back to hell where you came from, you old wart hog," she whispered. Her voice was low but clear. Her eyes burned for a moment as if she saw with pleasure that her message had struck its target.

Mrs. Turpin sank back in her chair.

After a moment the girl's eyes closed and she turned her head wearily to the side.

The doctor rose and handed the nurse the empty syringe. He leaned over and put both hands for a moment on the mother's shoulders, which were shaking. She was sitting on the floor, her lips pressed together, holding Mary Grace's hand in her lap. The girl's fingers were gripped like a baby's around her thumb. "Go on to the hospital," he said. "I'll call and make the arrangements."

"Now let's see that neck," he said in a jovial voice to Mrs. Turpin. He began to inspect her neck with his first two fingers. Two little moon-shaped lines like pink fish bones were indented over her windpipe. There was the beginning of an angry red swelling above her eye. His fingers passed over this also.

"Lea' me be," she said thickly and shook him off. "See about Claud. She kicked him."

"I'll see about him in a minute," he said and felt her pulse. He was a thin grey-haired man, given to pleasantries. "Go home and have yourself a vacation the rest of the day," he said and patted her on the shoulder.

Quit your pattin me, Mrs. Turpin growled to herself.

"And put an ice pack over that eye," he said. Then he went and squatted down beside Claud and looked at his leg. After a moment he pulled him up and Claud limped after him into the office.

Until the ambulance came, the only sounds in the room were the tremulous moans of the girl's mother, who continued to sit on the floor. The white-trash woman did not take her eyes off the girl. Mrs. Turpin looked straight ahead at nothing. Presently the ambulance drew up, a long dark shadow, behind the curtain. The attendants came in and set the stretcher down beside the girl and lifted her expertly onto it and carried her out. The nurse helped the mother gather up her things. The shadow of the ambulance moved silently away and the nurse came back in the office.

"That ther girl is going to be a lunatic, ain't she?" the white-trash woman asked the nurse, but the nurse kept on to the back and never answered her.

"Yes, she's going to be a lunatic," the white-trash woman said to the rest of them.

"Po' critter," the old woman murmured. The child's face was still in her lap. His eyes looked idly out over her knees. He had not moved during the disturbance except to draw one leg up under him.

"I thank Gawd," the white-trash woman said fervently, "I ain't a lunatic."

Claud came limping out and the Turpins went home.

As their pick-up truck turned into their own dirt road and made the crest of the hill, Mrs. Turpin gripped the window ledge and looked out suspiciously. The land sloped gracefully down through a field dotted with lavender weeds and at the start of the rise their small yellow frame house, with its little flower beds spread out around it like a fancy apron, sat primly in its accustomed place between two giant hickory trees. She would not have been startled to see a burnt wound between two blackened chimneys.

Neither of them felt like eating so they put on their house clothes and lowered the shade in the bedroom and lay down, Claud with his leg on a pillow and herself with a damp washcloth over her eye. The instant she was flat on her back, the image of a razor-backed hog with warts on its face and horns coming out behind its ears snorted into her head. She moaned, a low quiet moan.

"I am not," she said tearfully, "a wart hog. From hell." But the denial had no force. The girl's eyes and her words, even the tone of her voice, low but clear, directed only to her, brooked no repudiation. She had been singled out for the message, though there was trash in the room to whom it might justly have been applied. The full force of this fact struck her only now. There was a woman there who was neglecting her own child but she had been overlooked. The message had been given to Ruby Turpin, a respectable, hard-working, church-going woman. The tears dried. Her eyes began to burn instead with wrath.

She rose on her elbow and the washcloth fell into her hand. Claud was lying on his back, snoring. She wanted to tell him what the girl had said. At the same time, she did not wish to put the image of herself as a wart hog from hell into his mind.

"Hey, Claud," she muttered and pushed his shoulder.

Claud opened one pale baby blue eye.

She looked into it warily. He did not think about anything. He just went his way.

"Wha, whasit?" he said and closed the eye again.

"Nothing," she said. "Does your leg pain you?"

"Hurts like hell," Claud said.

"It'll quit terreckly," she said and lay back down. In a moment Claud was snoring again. For the rest of the afternoon they lay there. Claud slept. She scowled at the ceiling. Occasionally she raised her fist and made a small stabbing motion over her chest as if she was defending her innocence to invisible guests who were like the comforters of Job, reasonable-seeming but wrong.

About five-thirty Claud stirred. "Got to go after those niggers," he sighed, not moving.

She was looking straight up as if there were unintelligible handwriting on the ceiling. The protuberance over her eye had turned a greenish-blue. "Listen here," she said.

"What?"

"Kiss me."

Claud leaned over and kissed her loudly on the mouth. He pinched her side and their hands interlocked. Her expression of ferocious concentration did not change. Claud got up, groaning and growling, and limped off. She continued to study the ceiling.

She did not get up until she heard the pick-up truck coming back with the Negroes. Then she rose and thrust her feet in her brown oxfords, which she did not bother to lace, and stumped out onto the back porch and got her red plastic bucket. She emptied a tray of ice cubes into it and filled it half full of water and went out into the back yard. Every afternoon after Claud brought the hands in, one of the boys helped him put out hay and the rest waited in the back of the truck until he was ready to take them home. The truck was parked in the shade under one of the hickory trees.

"Hi yawl this evening?" Mrs. Turpin asked grimly, appearing with the bucket and the dipper. There were three women and a boy in the truck.

"Us doin nicely," the oldest woman said. "Hi you doin?" and her gaze stuck immediately on the dark lump on Mrs. Turpin's forehead. "You done fell down, ain't you?" she asked in a solicitous voice. The old woman was dark and almost toothless. She had on an old felt hat of Claud's set back on her head. The other two women were younger and lighter and they both had new bright green sun hats. One of them had hers on her head; the other had taken hers off and the boy was grinning beneath it.

Mrs. Turpin set the bucket down on the floor of the truck. "Yawl hep yourselves," she said. She looked around to make sure Claud had gone. "No. I didn't fall down," she said, folding her arms. "It was something worse than that."

"Ain't nothing bad happen to you!" the old woman said. She said it as if they all knew that Mrs. Turpin was protected in some special way by Divine Providence. "You just had you a little fall."

"We were in town at the doctor's office for where the cow kicked Mr. Turpin," Mrs. Turpin said in a flat tone that indicated they could leave off their foolishness. "And there was this girl there. A big fat girl with her face all broke out. I could look at that girl and tell she was peculiar but I couldn't tell how. And me and her mamma were just talking and going along and all of a sudden WHAM! She throws this big book she was reading at me and . . ."

"Naw!" the old woman cried out.

"And then she jumps over the table and commences to choke me."

"Naw!" they all exclaimed, "naw!"

"Hi come she do that?" the old woman asked. "What ail her?"

Mrs. Turpin only glared in front of her.

"Somethin ail her," the old woman said.

"They carried her off in an ambulance," Mrs. Turpin continued, "but before she went she was rolling on the floor and they were trying to hold her down to give her a shot and she said something to me." She paused. "You know what she said to me?"

"What she say?" they asked.

"She said," Mrs. Turpin began, and stopped, her face very dark and heavy. The sun was getting whiter and whiter, blanching the sky overhead so that the leaves of the hickory tree were black in the face of it. She could not bring forth the words. "Something real ugly," she muttered.

"She sho shouldn't said nothin ugly to you," the old woman said. "You so sweet. You the sweetest lady I know."

"She pretty too," the one with the hat on said.

"And stout," the other one said. "I never knowed no sweeter white lady."

"That's the truth befo' Jesus," the old woman said. "Amen! You des as sweet and pretty as you can be."

Mrs. Turpin knew just exactly how much Negro flattery was worth and it added to her rage. "She said," she began again and finished this time with a fierce rush of breath, "that I was an old wart hog from hell."

There was an astounded silence.

"Where she at?" the youngest woman cried in a piercing voice. "Lemme see her. I'll kill her!"

"I'll kill her with you!" the other one cried.

"She b'long in the sylum," the old woman said emphatically. "You the sweetest white lady I know."

"She pretty too," the other two said. "Stout as she can be and sweet. Jesus satisfied with her!"

"Deed he is," the old woman declared.

Idiots! Mrs. Turpin growled to herself. You could never say anything intelligent to a nigger. You could talk at them but not with them. "Yawl ain't drunk your water," she said shortly. "Leave the bucket in the truck when you're finished with it. I got more to do than just stand around and pass the time of day," and she moved off and into the house.

She stood for a moment in the middle of the kitchen. The dark protuberance over her eye looked like a miniature tornado cloud which might any moment sweep across the horizon of her brow. Her lower lip protruded dangerously. She squared her massive shoulders. Then she marched into the front of the house and out the side door and started down the road to the pig parlor. She had the look of a woman going single-handed, weaponless, into battle.

The sun was a deep yellow now like a harvest moon and was riding westward very fast over the far tree line as if it meant to reach the hogs before she did. The road was rutted and she kicked several good-sized stones out of her path as she strode along. The pig parlor was on a little knoll at the end of a lane that ran off from the side of the barn. It was a square of concrete as large as a small room, with a board fence about four feet high around it. The concrete floor sloped slightly so that the hog wash could drain off into a trench where it was carried to the field for fertilizer. Claud was standing on the outside, on the edge of the concrete, hanging onto the top board, hosing down the floor inside. The hose was connected to the faucet of a water trough nearby.

Mrs. Turpin climbed up beside him and glowered down at the hogs inside. There were seven long-snouted bristly shoats in it—tan with liver-colored spots—and an old sow a few weeks off from farrowing. She was lying on her side grunting. The shoats were running about shaking themselves like idiot children, their little slit pig eyes searching the floor for anything left. She had read that pigs were the most intelligent animal. She doubted it. They were supposed to be smarter than dogs. There had even been a pig astronaut. He had performed his assignment perfectly but died of a heart attack afterwards because they left him in his electric suit, sitting upright throughout his examination when naturally a hog should be on all fours.

A-gruntin and a-rootin and a-groanin.

"Gimme that hose," she said, yanking it away from Claud. "Go on and carry them niggers home and then get off that leg."

"You look like you might have swallowed a mad dog," Claud observed, but he got down and limped off. He paid no attention to her humors.

Until he was out of earshot, Mrs. Turpin stood on the side of the pen, holding the hose and pointing the stream of water at the hind quarters of any shoat that looked as if it might try to lie down. When he had had time to get over the hill, she turned her head slightly and her wrathful eyes scanned the path. He was nowhere in sight. She turned back again and seemed to gather herself up. Her shoulders rose and she drew in her breath.

"What do you send me a message like that for?" she said in a low fierce voice, barely above a whisper but with the force of a shout in its concentrated fury. "How am I a hog and me both? How am I saved and from hell too?" Her free fist was knotted and with the other she gripped the hose, blindly pointing the stream of water in and out of the eye of the old sow whose outraged squeal she did not hear.

The pig parlor commanded a view of the back pasture where their twenty beef cows were gathered around the hay-bales Claud and the boy had put out. The freshly cut pasture sloped down to the highway. Across it was their cotton field and beyond that a dark green dusty wood which they owned as well. The sun was behind the wood, very red, looking over the paling of trees like a farmer inspecting his own hogs.

"Why me?" she rumbled. "It's no trash around here, black or white, that I haven't given to. And break my back to the bone every day working. And do for the church."

She appeared to be the right size woman to command the arena before her. "How am I a hog?" she demanded. "Exactly how am I like them?" and she jabbed the stream of water at the shoats. "There was plenty of trash there. It didn't have to be me.

"If you like trash better, go get yourself some trash then," she railed. "You could have made me trash. Or a nigger. If trash is what you wanted why didn't you make me trash?" She shook her fist with the hose in it and a watery snake appeared momentarily in the air. "I could quit working and take it easy and be filthy," she growled. "Lounge about the sidewalks all day drinking root beer. Dip snuff and spit in every puddle and have it all over my face. I could be nasty.

"Or you could have made me a nigger. It's too late for me to be a nigger," she said with deep sarcasm, "but I could act like one. Lay down in the middle of the road and stop traffic. Roll on the ground."

In the deepening light everything was taking on a mysterious hue. The pasture was growing a peculiar glassy green and the streak of highway had turned lavender. She braced herself for a final assault and this time her voice rolled out over the pasture. "Go on," she yelled, "call me a hog! Call me a hog again. From hell. Call me a wart hog from hell. Put that bottom rail on top. There'll still be a top and bottom!"

A garbled echo returned to her.

A final surge of fury shook her and she roared, "Who do you think you are?"

The color of everything, field and crimson sky, burned for a moment with a transparent intensity. The question carried over the pasture and across the highway and the cotton field and returned to her clearly like an answer from beyond the wood.

She opened her mouth but no sound came out of it.

A tiny truck, Claud's, appeared on the highway, heading rapidly out of sight. Its gears scraped thinly. It looked like a child's toy. At any moment a bigger truck might smash into it and scatter Claud's and the niggers' brains all over the road.

Mrs. Turpin stood there, her gaze fixed on the highway, all her muscles rigid, until in five or six minutes the truck reappeared, returning. She waited until it had had time to turn into their own road. Then like a monumental statue coming to life, she bent her head slowly and gazed, as if through the very heart of mystery, down into the pig parlor at the hogs. They had settled all in one corner around the old sow who was grunting softly. A red glow suffused them. They appeared to pant with a secret life.

Until the sun slipped finally behind the tree line, Mrs. Turpin remained there with her gaze bent to them as if she were absorbing some abysmal life-giving knowledge. At last she lifted her head. There was only a purple streak in the sky, cutting through a field of crimson and leading, like an extension of the highway, into the descending dusk. She raised her hands from the side of the pen in a gesture hieratic and profound. A visionary light settled in her eyes. She saw the streak as a vast swinging bridge extending upward from the earth through a field of living fire. Upon it a vast horde of souls were rumbling toward heaven. There were whole companies of white-trash, clean for the first time in their lives, and bands of black niggers in white robes, and battalions of freaks and lunatics shouting and clapping and leaping like frogs. And bringing up the end of the procession was a tribe of people whom she recognized at once as those who, like herself and Claud, had always had a little of everything and the God-given wit to use it right. She leaned forward to observe them closer. They were marching behind the others with great dignity, accountable as they had always been for good order and common sense and respectable behavior. They alone were on key. Yet she could see by their shocked and altered faces that even their virtues were being burned away. She lowered her hands and gripped the rail of the hog pen, her eyes small but fixed unblinkingly on what lay ahead. In a moment the vision faded but she remained where she was, immobile.

At length she got down and turned off the faucet and made her slow way on the darkening path to the house. In the woods around her the invisible cricket choruses had struck up, but what she heard were the voices of the souls climbing upward into the starry field and shouting hallelujah.

Flowering Judas

Katherine Anne Porter

Braggioni sits heaped upon the edge of a straight-backed chair much too small for him, and sings to Laura in a furry, mournful voice. Laura has begun to find reasons for avoiding her own house until the latest possible moment, for Braggioni is there almost every night. No matter how late she is, he will be sitting there with a surly, waiting expression, pulling at his kinky yellow hair, thumbing the strings of his guitar, snarling a tune under his breath. Lupe the Indian maid meets Laura at the door, and says with a flicker of a glance towards the upper room, "He waits."

Laura wishes to lie down, she is tired of her hairpins and the feel of her long tight sleeves, but she says to him, "Have you a new song for me this evening?" If he says yes, she asks him to sing it. If he says no, she remembers his favorite one, and asks him to sing it again. Lupe brings her a cup of chocolate and a plate of rice, and Laura eats at the small table under the lamp, first inviting Braggioni, whose answer is always the same: "I have eaten, and besides, chocolate thickens the voice."

Laura says, "Sing, then," and Braggioni heaves himself into song. He scratches the guitar familiarly as though it were a pet animal, and sings passionately off key, taking the high notes in a prolonged painful squeal. Laura, who haunts the markets listening to the ballad singers, and stops every day to hear the blind boy playing his reed-flute in Sixteenth of September Street, listens to Braggioni with pitiless courtesy, because she dares not smile at his miserable performance. Nobody dares to smile at him. Braggioni is cruel to everyone, with a kind of specialized insolence, but he is so vain of his talents, and so sensitive to slights, it would require a cruelty and vanity greater than his own to lay a finger on the vast cureless wound of his self-esteem. It would require courage, too, for it is dangerous to offend him, and nobody has this courage.

Braggioni loves himself with such tenderness and amplitude and eternal charity that his followers—for he is a leader of men, a skilled revolutionist, and his skin has been punctured in honorable warfare —warm themselves in the reflected glow, and say to each other: "He has a real nobility, a love of humanity raised above mere personal affections." The excess of this self-love has flowed out, inconveniently for her, over Laura, who, with so many others, owes her comfortable situation and her salary to him. When he is in a very good humor, he tells her, "I am tempted to forgive you for being a *gringa. Gringita!*" and Laura, burning, imagines herself leaning forward suddenly, and with a sound back-handed slap wiping the suety smile from his face. If he notices her eyes at these moments he gives no sign.

She knows what Braggioni would offer her, and she must resist tenaciously without appearing to resist, and if she could avoid it she would not admit even to herself the slow drift of his intention. During these long evenings which have spoiled a long month for her, she sits in her deep chair with an open book on her knees, resting her eyes on the consoling rigidity of the printed page when the sight and sound of Braggioni singing threaten to identify themselves with all her remembered afflictions and to add their weight to her uneasy premonitions of the future. The gluttonous bulk of Braggioni has become a symbol of her many disillusions, for a revolutionist should be lean, animated by heroic faith, a vessel of abstract virtues. This is nonsense, she knows it now and is ashamed of it. Revolution must have leaders, and leadership is a career for energetic men. She is, her comrades tell her, full of romantic error, for what she defines as cynicism in them is merely "a developed sense of reality." She is almost too willing to say, "I am wrong, I suppose I don't really understand the principles," and afterward she makes a secret truce with herself, determined not to surrender her will to such expedient logic. But she cannot help feeling that she has been betrayed irreparably by the disunion between her way of living and her feeling of what life should be, and at times she is almost contented to rest in this sense of grievance as a private store of consolation. Sometimes she wishes to run away, but she stays. Now she longs to fly out of this room, down the narrow stairs, and into the street where the houses lean together like conspirators under a single mottled lamp, and leave Braggioni singing to himself.

Instead she looks at Braggioni, frankly and clearly, like a good child who understands the rules of behavior. Her knees cling together under sound blue serge, and her round white collar is not purposely nun-like. She wears the uniform of an idea, and has renounced vanities. She was born Roman Catholic, and in spite of her fear of being seen by someone who might make a scandal of it, she slips now and again into some crumbling little church, kneels on the chilly stone, and says a Hail Mary on the gold rosary she bought in Tehuantepec. It is no good and she ends by examining the altar with its tinsel flowers and ragged brocades, and feels tender about the battered doll-shape of some male saint whose white, lace-trimmed drawers hang limply around his ankles below the hieratic dignity of his velvet robe. She has encased herself in a set of principles derived from her early training, leaving no detail of gesture or of personal taste untouched, and for this reason she will not wear lace made on machines. This is her private heresy, for in her special group the machine is sacred, and will be the salvation of the workers. She loves fine lace, and there is a tiny edge of fluted cobweb on this collar, which is one of twenty precisely alike, folded in blue tissue paper in the upper drawer of her clothes chest.

Braggioni catches her glance solidly as if he had been waiting for it, leans forward, balancing his paunch between his spread knees, and sings with tremendous emphasis, weighing his words. He has, the song relates, no father and no mother, nor even a friend to console him; lonely as a wave of the sea he comes and goes, lonely as a wave. His mouth opens round and yearns sideways, his balloon cheeks grow oily with the labor of song. He bulges marvelously in his expensive garments. Over his lavender collar, crushed upon a purple necktie, held by a diamond hoop: over his ammunition belt of tooled leather worked in silver, buckled cruelly around his gasping middle: over the tops of his glossy yellow shoes Braggioni swells with ominous ripeness, his mauve silk hose stretched taut, his ankles bound with the stout leather thongs of his shoes.

When he stretches his eyelids at Laura she notes again that his eyes are the true tawny yellow cat's eyes. He is rich, not in money, he tells her, but in power, and this power brings with it the blameless ownership of things, and the right to indulge his love of small luxuries.

"I have a taste for the elegant refinements," he said once, flourishing a yellow silk handkerchief before her nose. "Smell that? It is Jockey Club, imported from New York." Nonetheless he is wounded by life. He will say so presently. "It is true everything turns to dust in the hand, to gall on the tongue." He sighs and his leather belt creaks like a saddle girth. "I am disappointed in everything as it comes. Everything." He shakes his head. "You, poor thing, you will be disappointed too. You are born for it. We are more alike than you realize in some things. Wait and see. Some day you will remember what I have told you, you will know that Braggioni was your friend."

Laura feels a slow chill, a purely physical sense of danger, a warning in her blood that violence, mutilation, a shocking death, wait for her with lessening patience. She has translated this fear into something homely, immediate, and sometimes hesitates before crossing the street. "My personal fate is nothing, except as the testimony of a mental attitude," she reminds herself, quoting from some forgotten philosophic primer, and is sensible enough to add, "Anyhow, I shall not be killed by an automobile if I can help it."

"It may be true I am as corrupt, in another way, as Braggioni," she thinks in spite of herself, "as callous, as incomplete," and if this is so, any kind of death seems preferable. Still she sits quietly, she does not run. Where could she go? Uninvited she has promised herself to this place; she can no longer imagine herself as living in another country, and there is no pleasure in remembering her life before she came here.

Precisely what is the nature of this devotion, its true motives, and what are its obligations? Laura cannot say. She spends part of her days in Xochimilco, near by, teaching Indian children to say in English, "The cat is on the mat." When she appears in the classroom they crowd about her with smiles on their wise, innocent, clay-colored faces, crying, "Good morning, my titcher!" in immaculate voices, and they make of her desk a fresh garden of flowers every day.

During her leisure she goes to union meetings and listens to busy important voices quarreling over tactics, methods, internal politics. She visits the prisoners of her own political faith in their cells, where they entertain themselves with counting cockroaches, repenting of their indiscretions, composing their memoirs, writing out manifestoes and plans for their comrades who are still walking about free, hands in pockets, sniffing fresh air. Laura brings them food and cigarettes and a little money, and she brings messages disguised in equivocal phrases from the men outside who dare not set foot in the prison for fear of disappearing into the cells kept empty for them. If the prisoners confuse night and day, and complain, "Dear little Laura, time doesn't pass in this infernal hole, and I won't know when it is time to sleep unless I have a reminder," she brings them their favorite narcotics, and says in a tone that does not wound them with pity, "Tonight will really be night for you," and though her Spanish amuses them, they find her comforting, useful. If they lose patience and all faith, and curse the slowness of their friends in coming to their rescue with money and influence, they trust her not to repeat everything, and if she inquires, "Where do you think we can find money, or influence?" they are certain to answer, "Well, there is Braggioni, why doesn't he do something?"

She smuggles letters from headquarters to men hiding from firing squads in back streets in mildewed houses, where they sit in tumbled beds and talk bitterly as if all Mexico were at their heels, when Laura knows positively they might appear at the band concert in the Alameda on Sunday morning, and no one would notice them. But Braggioni says, "Let them sweat a little. The next time they may be careful. It is very restful to have them out of the way for a while." She is not afraid to knock on any door in any street after midnight, and enter in the darkness, and say to one of these men who is really in danger: "They will be looking for you—seriously—tomorrow morning after six. Here is some money from Vicente. Go to Vera Cruz and wait."

She borrows money from the Roumanian agitator to give to his bitter enemy the Polish agitator. The favor of Braggioni is their disputed territory, and Braggioni holds the balance nicely, for he can use them both. The Polish agitator talks love to her over café tables, hoping to exploit what he believes is her secret sentimental preference for him, and he gives her misinformation which he begs her to repeat as the solemn truth to certain persons. The Roumanian is more adroit. He is generous with his money in all good causes, and lies to her with an air of ingenuous candor, as if he were her good friend and confidant. She never repeats anything they may say. Braggioni never asks questions. He has other ways to discover all that he wishes to know about them.

Nobody touches her, but all praise her gray eyes, and the soft, round under lip which promises gayety, yet is always grave, nearly always firmly closed: and they cannot understand why she is in Mexico. She walks back and forth on her errands, with puzzled eyebrows, carrying her little folder of drawings and music and school papers. No dancer dances more beautifully than Laura walks, and she inspires some amusing, unexpected ardors, which cause little gossip, because nothing comes of them. A young captain who had been a soldier in Zapata's army attempted, during a horseback ride near Cuernavaca, to express his desire for her with the noble simplicity befitting a rude folk-hero: but gently, because he was gentle. This gentleness was his defeat, for when he alighted, and removed her foot from the stirrup, and essayed to draw her down into his arms, her horse, ordinarily a tame one, shied fiercely, reared and plunged away. The young hero's horse careered blindly after his stable-mate, and the hero did not return to the hotel until rather late that evening. At breakfast he came to her table in full charro dress, gray buckskin jacket and trousers with strings of silver buttons down the leg, and he was in a humorous, careless mood. "May I sit with you?" and "You are a wonderful rider. I was terrified that you might be thrown and dragged. I should never have forgiven myself. But I cannot admire you enough for your riding!"

"I learned to ride in Arizona," said Laura.

"If you will ride with me again this morning, I promise you a horse that will not shy with you," he said. But Laura remembered that she must return to Mexico City at noon.

Next morning the children made a celebration and spent their playtime writing on the blackboard, "We lov ar ticher," and with tinted chalks they drew wreaths of flowers around the words. The young hero wrote her a letter: "I am a very foolish, wasteful, impulsive man. I should have first said I love you, and then you would not have run away. But you shall see me again." Laura thought, "I must send him a box of colored crayons," but she was trying to forgive herself for having spurred her horse at the wrong moment.

A brown, shock-haired youth came and stood in her patio one night and sang like a lost soul for two hours, but Laura could think of nothing to do about it. The moonlight spread a wash of gauzy silver over the clear spaces of the garden, and the shadows were cobalt blue. The scarlet blossoms of the Judas tree were dull purple, and the names of the colors repeated themselves automatically in her mind, while she watched not the boy, but his shadow, fallen like a dark garment across the fountain rim, trailing in the water. Lupe came silently and whispered expert counsel in her ear: "If you will throw him one little flower, he will sing another song or two and go away." Laura threw the flower, and he sang a last song and went away with the flower tucked in the band of his hat. Lupe said, "He is one of the organizers of the Typographers Union, and before that he sold corridos in the Merced market, and before that, he came from Guanajuato, where I was born. I would not trust any man, but I trust least those from Guanajuato."

She did not tell Laura that he would be back again the next night, and the next, nor that he would follow her at a certain fixed distance around the Merced market, through the Zócolo, up Francisco I. Madero Avenue, and so along the Paseo de la Reforma to Chapultepec Park, and into the Philosopher's Footpath, still with that flower withering in his hat, and an indivisible attention in his eyes.

Now Laura is accustomed to him, it means nothing except that he is nineteen years old and is observing a convention with all propriety, as though it were founded on a law of nature, which in the end it might well prove to be. He is beginning to write poems which he prints on a wooden press, and he leaves them stuck like handbills in her door. She is pleasantly disturbed by the abstract, unhurried watchfulness of his black eyes which will in time turn easily towards another object. She tells herself that throwing the flower was a mistake, for she is twenty-two years old and knows better; but she refuses to regret it, and persuades herself that her negation of all external events as they occur is a sign that she is gradually perfecting herself in the stoicism she strives to cultivate against that disaster she fears, though she cannot name it.

She is not at home in the world. Every day she teaches children who remain strangers to her, though she loves their tender round hands and their charming opportunist savagery. She knocks at unfamiliar doors not knowing whether a friend or a stranger shall answer, and even if a known face emerges from the sour gloom of that unknown interior, still it is the face of a stranger. No matter what this stranger says to her, nor what her message to him, the very cells of her flesh reject knowledge and kinship in one monotonous word. No. No. No. She draws her strength from this one holy talismanic word which does not suffer her to be led into evil. Denying everything, she may walk anywhere in safety, she looks at everything without amazement.

No, repeats this firm unchanging voice of her blood; and she looks at Braggioni without amazement. He is a great man, he wishes to impress this simple girl who covers her great round breasts with thick dark cloth, and who hides long, invaluably beautiful legs under a heavy skirt. She is almost thin except for the incomprehensible fullness of her breasts, like a nursing mother's, and Braggioni, who considers himself a judge of women, speculates again on the puzzle of her notorious virginity, and takes the liberty of speech which she permits without a sign of modesty, indeed, without any sort of sign, which is disconcerting.

"You think you are so cold, *gringita!* Wait and see. You will surprise yourself some day! May I be there to advise you!" He stretches his eyelids at her, and his ill-humored cat's eyes waver in a separate glance for the two points of light marking the opposite ends of a smoothly drawn path between the swollen curve of her breasts. He is not put off by that blue serge, nor by her resolutely fixed gaze. There is all the time in the world. His cheeks are bellying with the wind of song. "O girl with the dark eyes," he sings, and reconsiders. "But yours are not dark. I can change all that. O girl with the green eyes, you have stolen my heart away!" then his mind wanders to the song, and Laura feels the weight of his attention being shifted elsewhere. Singing thus, he seems harmless, he is quite harmless, there is nothing to do but sit patiently and say "No," when the moment comes. She draws a full breath, and her mind wanders also, but not far. She dares not wander too far.

Not for nothing has Braggioni taken pains to be a good revolutionist and a professional lover of humanity. He will never die of it. He has the malice, the cleverness, the wickedness, the sharpness of wit, the hardness of heart, stipulated for loving the world profitably. *He will never die of it.* He will live to see himself kicked out from his feeding trough by other hungry world-saviors. Traditionally he must sing in spite of his life which drives him to bloodshed, he tells Laura, for his father was a Tuscany peasant who drifted to Yucatan and married a Maya woman: a woman of race, an aristocrat. They gave him the love and knowledge of music, thus: and under the rip of his thumbnail, the strings of the instrument complain like exposed nerves.

Once he was called Delgadito by all the girls and married women who ran after him; he was so scrawny all his bones showed under his thin cotton clothing, and he could squeeze his emptiness to the very backbone with his two hands. He was a poet and the revolution was only a dream then; too many women loved him and sapped away his youth, and he could never find enough to eat anywhere, anywhere! Now he is a leader of men, crafty men who whisper in his ear, hungry men who wait for hours outside his office for a word with him, emaciated men with wild faces who waylay him at the street gate with a timid, "Comrade, let me tell you . . ." and they blow the foul breath from their empty stomachs in his face.

He is always sympathetic. He gives them handfuls of small coins from his own pocket, he promises them work, there will be demonstrations, they must join the unions and attend the meetings, above all they must be on the watch for spies. They are closer to him than his own brothers, without them he can do nothing—until tomorrow, comrade!

Until tomorrow. "They are stupid, they are lazy, they are treacherous, they would cut my throat for nothing," he says to Laura. He has good food and abundant drink, he hires an automobile and drives in the Paseo on Sunday morning, and enjoys plenty of sleep in a soft bed beside a wife who dares not disturb him; and he sits pampering his bones in easy billows of fat, singing to Laura, who knows and thinks these things about him. When he was fifteen, he tried to drown himself because he loved a girl, his first love, and she laughed at him. "A thousand women have paid for that," and his tight little mouth turns down at the corners. Now he perfumes his hair with Jockey Club, and confides to Laura: "One woman is really as good as another for me, in the dark. I prefer them all."

His wife organizes unions among the girls in the cigarette factories, and walks in picket lines, and even speaks at meetings in the evening. But she cannot be brought to acknowledge the benefits of true liberty. "I tell her I must have my freedom, net. She does not understand my point of view." Laura has heard this many times. Braggioni scratches the guitar and meditates. "She is an instinctively virtuous woman, pure gold, no doubt of that. If she were not, I should lock her up, and she knows it."

His wife, who works so hard for the good of the factory girls, employs part of her leisure lying on the floor weeping because there are so many women in the world, and only one husband for her, and she never knows where nor when to look for him. He told her: "Unless you can learn to cry when I am not here, I must go away for good." That day he went away and took a room at the Hotel Madrid.

It is this month of separation for the sake of higher principles that has been spoiled not only for Mrs. Braggioni, whose sense of reality is beyond criticism, but for Laura, who feels herself bogged in a nightmare. Tonight Laura envies Mrs. Braggioni, who is alone, and free to weep as much as she pleases about a concrete wrong. Laura has just come from a visit to the prison, and she is waiting for tomorrow with a bitter anxiety as if tomorrow may not come, but time may be caught immovably in this hour, with herself transfixed, Braggioni singing on forever, and Eugenio's body not yet discovered by the guard.

Braggioni says: "Are you going to sleep?" Almost before she can shake her head, he begins telling her about the May-day disturbances coming on in Morelia, for the Catholics hold a festival in honor of the Blessed Virgin, and the Socialists celebrate their martyrs on that day. "There will be two independent processions, starting from either end of town, and they will march until they meet, and the rest depends . . ." He asks her to oil and load his pistols. Standing up, he unbuckles his ammunition belt, and spreads it laden across her knees. Laura sits with the shells slipping through the cleaning cloth dipped in oil, and he says again he cannot understand why she works so hard for the revolutionary idea unless she loves some man who is in it. "Are you not in love with someone?" "No," says Laura. "And no one is in love with you?" "No." "Then it is your own fault. No woman need go begging. Why, what is the matter with you? The legless beggar woman in the Alameda has a perfectly faithful lover. Did you know that?"

Laura peers down the pistol barrel and says nothing, but a long, slow faintness rises and subsides in her; Braggioni curves his swollen fingers around the throat of the guitar and softly smothers the music out of it, and when she hears him again he seems to have forgotten her, and is speaking in the hypnotic voice he uses when talking in small rooms to a listening, close-gathered crowd. Some day this world, now seemingly so composed and eternal, to the edges of every sea shall be merely a tangle of gaping trenches, of crashing walls and broken bodies. Everything must be torn from its accustomed place where it has rotted for centuries, hurled skyward and distributed, cast down again clean as rain, without separate identity. Nothing shall survive that the stiffened hands of poverty have created for the rich and no one shall be left alive except the elect spirits destined to procreate a new world cleansed of cruelty and injustice, ruled by benevolent anarchy: "Pistols are good, I love them, cannon are even better, but in the end I pin my faith to good dynamite," he concludes, and strokes the pistol lying in her hands. "Once I dreamed of destroying this city, in case it offered resistance to General Ortíz, but it fell into his hands like an overripe pear."

He is made restless by his own words, rises and stands waiting. Laura holds up the belt to him: "Put that on, and go kill somebody in Morelia, and you will be happier," she says softly. The presence of death in the room makes her bold. "Today, I found Eugenio going into a stupor. He refused to allow me to call the prison doctor. He had taken all the tablets I brought him yesterday. He said he took them because he was bored."

"He is a fool, and his death is his own business," says Braggioni, fastening his belt carefully.

"I told him if he had waited only a little while longer, you would have got him set free," says Laura. "He said he did not want to wait."

"He is a fool and we are well rid of him," says Braggioni, reaching for his hat.

He goes away. Laura knows his mood has changed, she will not see him any more for a while. He will send word when he needs her to go on errands into strange streets, to speak to the strange faces that will appear, like clay masks with the power of human speech, to mutter their thanks to Braggioni for his help. Now she is free, and she thinks, I must run while there is time. But she does not go.

Braggioni enters his own house where for a month his wife has spent many hours every night weeping and tangling her hair upon her pillow. She is weeping now, and she weeps more at the sight of him, the cause of all her sorrows. He looks about the room. Nothing is changed, the smells are good and familiar, he is well acquainted with the woman who comes toward him with no reproach except grief on her face. He says to her tenderly: "You are so good, please don't cry any more, you dear good creature." She says, "Are you tired, my angel? Sit here and I will wash your feet." She brings a bowl of water, and kneeling, unlaces his shoes, and when from her knees she raises her sad eyes under her blackened lids, he is sorry for everything, and bursts into tears. "Ah, yes, I am hungry, I am tired, let us eat something together," he says, between sobs. His wife leans her head on his arm and says, "Forgive me!" and this time he is refreshed by the solemn, endless rain of her tears.

Laura takes off her serge dress and puts on a white linen nightgown and goes to bed. She turns her head a little to one side, and lying still, reminds herself that it is time to sleep. Numbers tick in her brain like little clocks, soundless doors close of themselves around her. If you would sleep, you must not remember anything, the children will say tomorrow, good morning, my teacher, the poor prisoners who come every day bringing flowers to their jailor. 1–2–3–4–5—it is monstrous to confuse love with revolution, night with day, life with death—ah, Eugenio!

The tolling of the midnight bell is a signal, but what does it mean? Get up, Laura, and follow me: come out of your sleep, out of your bed, out of this strange house. What are you doing in this house? Without a word, without fear she rose and reached for Eugenio's hand, but he eluded her with a sharp, sly smile and drifted away. This is not all, you shall see—Murderer, he said, follow me, I will show you a new country, but it is far away and we must hurry. No, said Laura, not unless you take my hand, no; and she clung first to the stair rail, and then to the topmost branch of the Judas tree that bent down slowly and set her upon the earth, and then to the rocky ledge of a cliff, and then to the jagged wave of a sea that was not water but a desert of crumbling stone. Where are you taking me, she asked in wonder but without fear. To death, and it is a long way off, and we must hurry, said Eugenio. No, said Laura, not unless you take my hand. Then eat these flowers, poor prisoner, said Eugenio in a voice of pity, take and eat: and from the Judas tree he stripped the warm bleeding flowers, and held them to her lips. She saw that his hand was fleshless, a cluster of small white petrified branches, and his eye sockets were without light, but she ate the flowers greedily for they satisfied both hunger and thirst. Murderer! said Eugenio, and Cannibal! This is my body and my blood. Laura cried No! and at the sound of her own voice, she awoke trembling, and was afraid to sleep again.

Supperburger

Jonathan Strong

To have a town house in town, in the center of things, has been one of my desires, like the red brick town houses with black trim and iron balconies on the street that curves down the hill to the river. I think it would be nice to sit in a dark red Victorian chair in the afternoons, reading, looking at the balconies across the street as they catch the sunlight on their ironwork and the red of the bricks deepens. In fact that is how it is now, that is where I am sitting, but the house is not mine. I am on the second floor, in the living room. The first floor has a dining room in front and a kitchen in back. I caught sight of a bowl of peaches on the dining table when I was let in and sent directly upstairs. The back room on the second floor seems to be a study, or perhaps a music room. Arthur Supperburger owns the house, and he is a composer. I am just a boy, or a kid, as I like to say. Boy sounds round and soft, but kid is a little more straight up and down, a little harder, perhaps a little less likely to grow old. It includes an attitude, a free way of knowing people, a sense of unattachment. If I am a kid, I can come here for supper a couple of times, for a few weeks, and then go off for a while. It would be my privilege. If I am a boy, I have to report, I have to let them know what I am doing so they can watch over me. When I grow up, and I do not think I will have to for a while because people still mistake me for fifteen and I am already eighteen and I imagine it will go on like that for some time and perhaps when I am twenty-six they will think I am twenty, but when I do grow up I will have to come to supper only if I am prepared to make something of it, to keep being friends with the people who ask me, to bear the responsibilities and maybe ask them to supper sometimes. The thought of it scares me because most people end up liking me much more than I like them, and all I can do is get up and leave and not be seen for a while and perhaps pretend not to see them if I pass them on the street. The street is the trouble, I suppose, the one that curves down the hill to the river. I pass many people there, especially now that I am out of school and see people who only come out during the day as well as the people I used to meet in the evenings. That means I meet a lot of ladies, the sort who live by themselves in old town houses. They all know each other and get together at the concerts on Friday afternoons and maybe other times, like at their reading clubs. I have come to like the concerts a lot because I go almost every Friday with one of the ladies or another. I meet most of them walking their dogs. I say something about the dog, and they say something about my hat or my boots, and then when they find out I am a nice kid and know how to talk to ladies they ask me for tea. So that way I get to know a lot of them during the day. My friends from school get out about four, and I run into them at the doughnut shop, and we sit around. It gets boring, but I like to catch up on what they are doing. Most of my friends are a year younger, so they are still in school. They usually go home in the evenings, and I am pretty much on my own after six, though I do have some friends my age on the hill. First I stop by my room, just a small one without any bathroom which I pay for by the week, and I change my clothes. During the day I usually wear my suede cowboy boots because they do not look as tough for the ladies. At night I wear the black ones, and I put on my faded jeans. I spend a lot of money on colored shirts, and I try to wear a different one every night. Then I have my old suede jacket and of course my hat, which is what the ladies usually like most even though I cannot wear it to the concerts. Then I go out to see who is around. That is when I meet men or at least older kids, kids from college. I do not usually like kids from college because, even though they are very nice to me and ask me to go places, they get across the idea that they think they are better than I am. But sometimes I do not mind them. I met Supperburger in the evening. I knew who he was because they played one of his compositions at a concert I went to and he had taken a bow. He walked past me and did not seem to notice me, but on an impulse I turned and ran up to him and asked if he was not Arthur Supperburger even though I knew he was. Then I told him I had heard his Symphony No. I, but he did not say anything except that he hoped I liked it. Then he walked on. I am used to talking to people on the street, and I am able to tell what they are thinking. Most people would think this composer fellow was simply not interested in talking to a kid, but I can tell when someone is a snob and when he wishes inside he could talk. I was pretty sure Supperburger wished he knew how to talk to me but was so embarrassed and surprised that he wanted to avoid the situation. I could tell because I noticed his eyes catch sight of the way my bright yellow shirt was unbuttoned a few buttons so my dark red T-shirt would show. The light was good then. We were standing by one of the gas lamps they have to make the street look more Victorian. He only looked for a second, but usually if a person looks only a little it means he likes me. I think it is strange how most people do not try to look good. If everyone did, it would be more interesting. I decided to see Supperburger again, though I did not run after him. That would make him even more uneasy, so I left him and went to look in a phone book for his address. The next night I stood across the street from his house, looking up at the window I am sitting inside now. I usually change my shirt, as I said, but I thought I would wear the same one again that night, so he would remember. He came out early in the evening and noticed me. Supperburger is a nice-looking man, but he is in his forties and could have been my father. His hair is sandy gray, and he is rather tall. Once I tried to imagine him as a kid, but I do not think he was one for long. It is September now, when I am sitting inside his house and most of my friends are back in school, so I am thinking of him with September colors in his face and hair, but it was early August when I met him, and I had a feeling he was remembering an August many years before. I am good at telling people's feelings, and I think I may talk to him about it tonight. Anyway, that night he came out of his town house and saw me standing across the street. While I had been waiting there I had seen the maid cleaning up in the dining room, and I had seen Supperburger standing at one of the living room windows with a woman beside him, looking out. I wondered if it was his wife or maybe his sister. But he came out alone, with a trench coat on because it was cool. He saw me immediately, and he must have recognized me because I was under a lamp, but he did a funny turn and went the opposite way up the street. I have been through this sort of thing before, but it can still seem funny to me. If people would be less afraid of looking at each other, they would enjoy each other more. Just as

Supperburger went off up the street a girl named Charles walked by. I know her from hanging around the doughnut shop. I think Charles is her last name. She likes me a lot, but she is a sad one because she is sort of dumpy and does not try to do much with her face. She laughed because she saw me standing under the lamp, and then she played at being a whore picking me up, but I just stood smiling. Then she got mad because I did not say much to her. She said she wanted to go to a party and no one would take her and of course I would not either, she said. She did most of the talking. Then she got a little sad and said how cute I looked and she did not care what I thought of her as long as she could look at me. I feel sorry for her, most of the time, but I cannot think of the right things to say so I just keep quiet, and I know that hurts her. But soon she was on her way that night, off to the party by herself. There are a lot of parties on the hill in the summer. When she was gone I was about to track down Supperburger when I saw him coming down the street. He must have assumed I had gone and was returning to make his walk down the hill. When he saw me it was too late to turn around again, so he walked briskly by as if he had planned his roundabout route. I stepped right out and asked for the time, and he almost flinched, but he told me, and then I knew I had been right all along because he asked if I was not the boy who had told him yesterday about hearing his symphony. I smiled and got in stride with him, and we walked down to the river together. I introduced myself as Patrick Polo, which is my full name. He asked me what I did, and I said I was an art student, which is not really true though I do have two drawing classes a week. Then he asked if I was bored and lonely here, and that surprised me. I have met a lot of people on the street and never known them to ask something as personal as that right away. I was glad he had asked it, so I decided to tell him the truth, which I usually avoid on the subject of boredom and loneliness, and I said yes. From then on I felt I was friends with Supperburger.

Sitting by the window here and looking around the room I like to imagine the house is mine, or maybe my father's. Of course I would rearrange it exactly my way, but the feeling would be mostly the same. I like the bookshelves being full. The shelf right next to me has books by men I have never heard of: Dowson, Swinburne, Henley, but of course I have heard of Kipling and there is a big set of his books, and I know about Wilde. Rossetti sounds like he would be Italian, but he is not because I took one volume out. I am Italian, or at least I am on one side. The other side is mostly Irish which must be where I get my blond hair. I just took down one of the Swinburnes, and one poem called "The Triumph of Time" is all underlined in red, by Supperburger I suppose. I like it, but it is sad.

> Before our lives divide forever,
>   While time is with us and hands are free
> (Time, swift to fasten and swift to sever
>   Hand from hand, as we stand by the sea),
> I will say no word that a man might say
> Whose whole life's love goes down in a day;
>   For this could never have been, and never—
> Though the gods and the years relent—shall be.

I used to write poems in school, but I have not since I left. I went to the best high school in the city, even though I did not live near it, because I was good in school. My father sent the extra money because it cost a little, but then he decided he would not send me any for college. I do not mind because, as I said, I usually do not like college kids. I am supposed to have a job, actually, but my father does send me some money and I get a lot of free meals, so I will not have to work for a while. He does not live in this part of the city and never comes here, so he does not know what I am doing. He would not like it if he found out about my life here, but he does not really care, and it is not his business anymore anyway. He came to my graduation last June, but he had to stay inconspicuous, he said. He is the Italian side. That is where I get a name like Polo, though it is no relation to Marco Polo as far as I know. My nickname is Pony, but I did not tell Supperburger who calls me Patrick. Some people call me Polo Pony and some just call me Pony, like Charles. Some of the older kids on the hill call me Polo in a sort of tough way. My mother, being Irish by ancestry, calls me Pat, but she is the only one who does. She lives in this part of the city, though not too near, and so I go have suppers with her occasionally. Personally I like being called Pony though I have often thought of introducing myself as Rick instead, just to see what it would be like having someone call me Rick. Anyway, it is Patrick with Supperburger. I imagine he is composing now. This is the fifth time he has asked me for supper, and I usually come early because I do not mind waiting in this room. Up above the Kiplings is a shelf of music books, mostly operas I have never heard of, like *Lakmé* and *L'Africaine,* and then *The Tales of Hoffmann* which I think I have heard of. I have never seen an opera, but Mrs. Supperburger said they would take me. It was his wife, it turned out, who was standing at the window with him that night. I was surprised. I would not have thought so, but you never know about people for certain. She usually does not say much, which is the opposite of Charles and also of most of the ladies I meet in the afternoons. She just makes tea and sits behind the tea table which is always very pretty, with china and linen napkins and silverware and usually tomato sandwiches, though once it was cinnamon toast. Then at the dining table she makes sure I have enough without forcing it on me like my mother does. Mrs. Supperburger's name is Ruth, and one night, when I was in the hall putting on my suede jacket and my hat and Supperburger had not come downstairs yet, she came up to me and said very sweetly that I should call her Aunt Ruth if I liked. It surprised me because I did not think she would ever say something as openly as that. So I call her Aunt Ruth, even though I think of her as Mrs. Supperburger, just as I think of him as Mr. Supperburger or just Supperburger as his name was on the program. Mrs. Supperburger is the sweetest woman I have met, and most of the ladies on the hill are sweet in one way or another. But she is gentle besides and a little sad, without pitying herself like so many ladies around here do. When she carries in the tray with the tea it looks very natural and pretty. I drew her like that in one of my classes. She is a dignified sort of woman, not short or dumpy at all. Her hair is almost gray, but she seems pretty young still. Her clothes are usually soft colors and flowery, which is nice on her. She never really laughs, but she is always smiling. In a few minutes she will be coming in here, and then Supperburger will come out of his study. He and his wife look good together because he is strong enough to make her feel taken care of but not too strong, not to overpower her. I wonder if he is a great composer. I am no judge, and I know the ladies on Friday afternoons are no judges. They all applauded politely because he is a local celebrity of sorts, but the music was strange. It is hard for me to describe it because I know nothing about music and cannot even sing, though I can dance rock and roll pretty well. I often go to the Banjo Room which is where they have live rock and roll bands. But I did like his piece. In fact it was not like any other piece I have heard, and I think it is beautiful when someone can do something like no one else has. The same goes for dressing. When I got my hat my mother did not like it because none of the other kids wore a hat like that. My mother is very scared that I might be different. There was one part of the symphony I can still remember, though not exactly how it sounded. It was quiet, and two trumpets started playing melodies to each other—most of the time not fitting together very well and sort of twisting around, but that made the parts that did fit seem all the more lovely. Then one got farther and farther away, and I imagined one sailing boat slowly drifting out to sea and me standing on the land calling to it as it became more and more cloudy with mist.

I can hear Mrs. Supperburger coming upstairs with the tea.

P: Hi, Aunt Ruth.
MRS. S: Good afternoon, Patrick. Matty said she let you in about half an hour ago. I hope you haven't been bored.
P: No, I was looking at the books.
MRS. S: What is it? Oh, Swinburne. That's one of Arthur's favorites. I wonder how you happened to pick that. No one reads him anymore.
P: It was on the shelf right here. It's a little sad, but I like it.
MRS. S: It seems so old-fashioned to me when I read it. I remember when I was a girl being told by my grandmother that Swinburne was not the sort of thing a girl should read. Imagine that now.
P: It didn't seem old-fashioned to me, really.
MRS. S: Where's that one poem? "Laus Veneris." It was so shocking. My poor grandmother. There it is: ". . . for her neck, kissed over close, wears yet a purple speck wherein the pained blood falters and goes out."

It is funny to hear Mrs. Supperburger talking about things like that. Of course I know about them, hickeys the kids call them. That is why I wear turtlenecks a lot, so they will not show if I am going home for supper. It is especially hard in the summer when I am on the beach a lot not to be embarrassed by them. Mrs. Supperburger seems a little nervous. She is talking more than usual.

MRS. S: "Lips that cling hard till the kissed face has grown of one same fire and color with their own." It's so silly. Arthur loves it.
P: Aunt Ruth, you seem a little nervous today.
MRS. S: You're so funny, Patrick, the way you come right out and say things. Well, I'll tell you the reason. It's our anniversary, our twenty-fifth. Arthur and I were married on the twenty-first of September, nineteen-forty-one.
P: I really oughtn't to come to supper on your anniversary.
MRS. S: Why not?
P: I mean you probably would rather be alone.
MRS. S: Not at all. Arthur wanted you to come especially. It's a sort of party. Our nephew Louis is coming down from school. He's in the East now for college. Do you want cinnamon toast?
P: Yes, please.

Now Mrs. Supperburger is getting silent again. She is leafing through the Swinburne with a sweet smile. I am drinking the tea and picking out the most buttery cinnamon toast. I am afraid their nephew Louis is going to be one of those college kids, especially if he is not from around here. I wonder if he is ever called Louie. I usually do not like people who are always called by their full name. If the three of them start talking about intellectual things I might get bored. I like intellectual things, but people usually talk about them as if they were things everyone knew about already. Some of the college kids come into the doughnut shop and talk about things like Kierkegaard as if they invented it. If you want to say something I think you should say it on your own and not go quoting people. That is one nice thing about the ladies on Friday afternoons, they never quote anything. I suppose it is because they never read except at their reading clubs where one of them reads and the others are supposed to listen but do not. I went once, and it was very boring. Supperburger reads a lot, but I have never heard him quote. Everything he says comes from his own head. I wish he would come in. I get feeling awkward when I am alone with Mrs. Supperburger very long. She is looking a little wistful, reading one of the pages in Swinburne. Her eyes are even a little wet. If she cries I will not know what to say. It is just like with Charles, although Charles is a self-pitier. I am afraid of saying nothing. The sunlight is coming in the windows at quite a slant now. All the dust on the round table by the couch shows.

MRS. S: Do you like the way I keep the house, Patrick?
P: You know it's my favorite house on the hill, Aunt Ruth, and I've been in most of them.

I said that with a laugh. I am beginning to feel very funny. I have never heard her say these sorts of things.

MRS. S: I wasn't sure about having everything so Victorian at first. Arthur wanted it, so we did. I've kept it just as he liked all these years.

She is talking as though she was one of the old ladies. But she is only forty-five, I think. I might say she is almost being a little self-pitying.

MRS. S: Does it seem old-fashioned, Patrick? Arthur says the reaction against Victorian things is over and they are coming back in fashion. I think he's right. The way you dress. That hat's out of Dickens. And your boots, not the cowboy ones but the others. You're like a street urchin. Do you suppose there will be street urchins again, like gypsies?
P: There always have been, I imagine.
MRS. S: I never noticed them till now. They're all over the hill. Kids like you all decked out in bright colors. Every afternoon they're swarming up and down. I see them dancing in the windows. In the summer they're down by the river singing with their guitars. It's hats and boots, I think, and lots of hair and colors. When I was your age, in the thirties, everyone was so much more drab.

P: There are lots of kids these days.
MRS. S: I never saw them for so many years. All so lovely.

I like the word lovely. I know kids do not usually say words like that. Old ladies use it a lot. I wonder if Mrs. Supperburger is turning into an old lady. That means Supperburger is old too, though men usually do not get old as soon. They die sooner though. That is why there are a lot of old ladies living by themselves on the hill. I often think I will give it all up when I find I cannot keep my stomach flat anymore. I wonder if I will have much hair on my stomach. A lot of blond people do not, but then Italians do. I think Supperburger has German ancestry. He used to be blond, and he does not have much hair on his stomach. The knob on the music room door just turned. He has finished composing, I guess, and he is coming in.

S: Good afternoon, Patrick. Ruth, Patrick, I have finished my Ninth Symphony.

Now it is after dinner, and we are sitting around the table with coffee cups and peaches and special fruit-peeling knives to peel them. The announcement about the Ninth Symphony was very exciting and got us all celebrating. Mrs. Supperburger carried out the tea and came back with a bottle of champagne, and we all made toasts. That was when Louis came up, shown in by Matty, the maid. Supperburger welcomed him in a fatherly sort of way and introduced me as Patrick Polo, but I cannot remember what he said Louis's last name was. Supperburger is very good at making people feel easy and at home right away. Maybe it is because he is a little shy himself but not so shy as not to know what to say or not to keep saying things when everyone else is awkwardly pausing. It is a good thing because Louis does not seem to say much. So far he has only said hello and a few other things like yes and no and that he likes college a lot. In a way it is nice to hear a college kid not talk so much. Mrs. Supperburger told Louis right away about the symphony and gave him a glass of champagne, though I noticed he did not drink it all. Then Supperburger said how it was a four-way celebration, not just because there were four people but because firstly it was the anniversary, secondly it was the day he finished the Ninth Symphony, thirdly it was Louis's first visit, and fourthly it was the first time Louis and I had met. That last thing was a little awkward. I felt funny because it is hard to be told you are going to be great friends with someone, but I did not mind because Louis is very nice. He has absolutely black hair, so he must be from Mrs. Supperburger's side which would also explain the last name I did not remember. He is about my size, medium, and has just as long hair coming down to his eyebrows. The funny thing is that while I have dark brown eyes, which is strange for a blond kid, he has shiny blue eyes, which is what I ought to have and he ought to have mine. Anyway, they look nice, and I was also glad he was not wearing the sorts of things college kids usually wear, like Madras, but just a regular colored shirt with a T-shirt and jeans, except his were white jeans instead of blue. After Supperburger caused an awkward moment with his fourth reason, he quickly added that there was a fifth reason to make this day special but that was a secret. So we all wondered about that, looking forward to some surprise, and then I asked Louis if they ever call him Louie and he said no, so I said I would and told him he could call me Rick for short. I have always wanted to do that. The bad thing is that when Matty was serving lamb chops she said, "Pony, do you want two?" because she hears the kids calling me Pony when she waits for her bus outside the doughnut shop. So then Louie thought that was funny. In fact it was the only time he really relaxed, and he started calling me Pony. I think the champagne has calmed Mrs. Supperburger down. She had three glasses, which is more than the rest of us put together. She talked a lot during the meal, in a relaxed and pleasant way, telling us how she and Supperburger had met at the beginning of the summer in 1941 at a beach on the ocean. He was just out of college, where he had studied art it turns out and not composing, and he had a little cottage on the beach because he had decided to try to write music. That was when he started the symphony I heard. She said they had played it in honor of their twenty-fifth anniversary. It sounds as though she had a beautiful time on the beach that summer, and they had decided to get married in the fall. She had to spend the month of August with her family on some cruise, and when she came back he had just finished the second movement. I remembered that was the one with the trumpets. She said he wrote the third movement as a sort of wedding march, and they were married on the first day of fall. I started wondering what the last two movements were supposed to be. Maybe the fourth was their wedding night. The fifth was short and came to a very funny end, and I could not imagine what it was. Anyway, it was nice to hear Mrs. Supperburger remembering things so happily. Maybe I will want to get married someday after all if it can still be so nice after twenty-five years. My parents never see each other anymore, though they are supposed to be married still because we are Catholics. I am not really a Catholic myself. I know one girl on the hill who drinks a lot and sort of sleeps around. She goes to two confessionals. In one she says she ate meat on Friday or something small like that, and in the other she says that she lied once! I do not go at all anymore. I would not have time to get it all in, and I do not think it matters anyway. Of course my mother assumes I go, and whenever I do see my father he says something about going to church which is funny coming from him. I do not think the Supperburgers ever go to church. Mrs. Supperburger talked all through the main course, and now that it is dessert she is still talking but is getting a little vague. It reminds me of the night she asked me to call her Aunt Ruth. She was fuzzy and vague then too. Louie is not saying anything, though he keeps looking at me. Supperburger seems to be collecting his thoughts, just like me. I really like Mrs. Supperburger better when she keeps quiet and sweet.

> Mrs. S: I really don't know why we have to have a maid, Arthur. I used to do most of it myself. It seems wrong for Matty to devote her life to keeping someone else's house and making someone else's food. Everyone should be doing his best to keep his own house. It's hard enough keeping your own things straight. Keeping a house should be private, not like a business. But no one tells us these things, and we go on thinking we should have a maid. A woman has to spend her waking hours making the house comfortable, but that's the way it's meant to be. A woman's supposed to. That is what she wants. The balance is slipping. There aren't the lines between husband and wife anymore. These career women! My grandmother may have said Swinburne was not for little girls, but she knew what a little girl was, by God, and I don't anymore. Louis, you're smart. You're at college. Do people know the difference anymore? I don't think there is one now. These children on the hill, they're roaming around all evening. They don't know the difference.
>
> S: I don't mean to interrupt the sociological discussion, but there is something I want to show Patrick upstairs. Louis, Ruth, you'll excuse us?

That came as a relief, though it seems a little cold of him, just when Mrs. Supperburger is getting nervous again. As we leave she starts to talk about family things with Louie, aunts and uncles and people on her side, and Matty is clearing off the table.

I stopped on the second floor because Supperburger told me to run in and get the Swinburnes. I am a little uneasy about being alone upstairs with him again. But maybe it is just the secret fifth reason for the champagne he wants to talk to me about. He is already on the third floor, in the front bedroom. It is a comfortable room and looks like a man's room. All of Mrs. Supperburger's things are in the back bedroom, and I think she sleeps in there sometimes too. He is in the big leather chair under the painting of a boat. I give him the Swinburnes and sit down on the edge of the bed. I think someday I may end up looking like Supperburger, except for his gray eyes. Of course he is taller and his teeth are all perfectly straight, but his coloring is like mine and he also looks younger than he is. He wears very dignified clothes, usually gray or sandy colored suits, but they do not make him look old or stuffy. In fact they set off how young he is inside them. He is built pretty well. His face is strong too, and though his skin is sort of rough, his gray eyes make him seem sweet-natured.

S: This is the day I have to say good-bye to you, Patrick.
P: What? Can't I come here anymore?
S: Were you planning to, really?
P: I wasn't planning not to.
S: You'll be going soon anyway. I know. So I would rather have it be good-bye on a recognized basis. Don't you think?
P: But you're not going anywhere?
S: No, but people come and go, don't they? You're coming and going most of the time and will be for a number of years. Eighteen, and you look younger. That makes a difference on the hill. You'll be at it for another ten years. Maybe . . .
P: Don't you want me to come back?
S: Yes, Patrick. You can come whenever you want. I am just saying good-bye now.

I am feeling scared, but I do not think I am showing it.

S: Patrick, how do you plan to keep from loneliness, in your life?
P: Well, everyone has to face that, don't they? I'll find other people who are lonely.
S: For supper, now and then?
P: No, I know I'll grow out of that. I'll want to settle down more.
S: But there will always be new people, up and down the street all day and in the evening.
P: Do you think you're a great composer?
S: No.
P: But a good one?
S: No.
P: But I never heard anything like your symphony. I think it is beautiful when someone does something different.
S: My music has been just like the other music being written today.
P: I never heard anything like it.
S: But you haven't been to many concerts, have you?
P: I've been to all three so far this year.
S: Well, I just follow the current style, rearrange it a little from someone else.
P: But you never quote! I have never heard you quote. You always say things of your own.
S: With you, Patrick, I don't need to quote. You have only seen me with

you, or taking a bow from the audience, applauded by the little ladies.
P: I've seen you with Louie. He goes to college.
S: Do you like Louis?
P: Yes. He's very quiet.
S: Patrick, in saying good-bye, please forget the first night you came. All right?
P: All right.
S: Until you know someone, you do not know what you should do, or what they expect you to do, or what they want you to do, or even what you really want to do yourself. You were right then.
P: All right.
S: So you like my music. I hope you will like my Ninth Symphony. I had Matty put two packages in the hall, one for you and one for Louis. They are manuscripts of the Ninth. It is dedicated to both of you. The manuscripts won't mean much, just a lot of notes, but one is for you. Make sure Louis gets his.
P: Thank you. Mr. Supperburger . . .
S: Maybe they will perform it soon on a Friday.
P: I'll be there.
S: I know.
P: Mr. Supperburger, is it at all like the second movement of your Symphony No. I?

He suddenly stood up, so quickly, almost with a leap. His eyes are watery, and I have never seen a look like his now, in his gray eyes.

S: Patrick, you understand people very well.
P: I meet a lot.
S: You have seen something there. You have seen a connection. Of course, it's just nonsense. My meanings indulge my own feelings, that's all. The music is still there, meaningless. A lot of notes, no objectivity, no architecture, just copy and my indulgences. But anyway, you have seen something there. You hope the Ninth will be like that second movement?
P: I liked that part best.

Now he is sitting down again, under the painting, and his eyes are really tearful. I am surprised at myself because I do not feel funny about moving over and putting my arm on his shoulder and trying to make him feel better, though I do not keep it there long. After a while he looks up and starts to tell me a story.

S: You noticed the painting? I did it twenty-five years ago. You heard my wife talking about our summer together and how she left with her family in August. On the fifth of August, I was relaxing from my symphony by painting a motor yacht anchored out beyond the sand bar. A dark-haired boy came walking along the beach. He liked the painting, which so far was very brightly colored and not as misty as it has turned out, and he said it was his father's boat. Furthermore, his family was on shore then and had given him the yacht to use by himself for a month. His name was Fred, but I have forgotten his last name. Well, to put it shortly, I went with him, and we sailed freely, up and down the coast, in the cockpit with the wind blowing, drifting in the sun a lot, out of sight of land, for the rest of the month. Then on a misty night, on the pier at the resort town where his parents stayed, they rejoined the ship. And I went ashore. I stood on the pier as servants carried trunks and boxes aboard. Fred helped. He was eighteen. Imagine the freedom of a boy at eighteen, already competent enough to sail off into the Atlantic alone, or not really alone, but his parents thought he was. He knew all about that boat, everything there was. His parents, two of their elegant friends, and his little brother, and a maid, they all went on board, and finally Fred, after saying good-bye. I never saw him after that, just a boy standing on the deck of his father's yacht, blowing a trumpet maybe as my musical indulgence told it, while the boat became more and more cloudy with mist and I blew one back to him.

Now my eyes are watery too, and that is strange for me. I hear the door opening and quickly get back all the way on the bed and wipe my eyes, but Supperburger does not change his attitude at all. It is his wife, and she is holding a cocktail glass which she puts on the dresser. Now everything is wrong. I am beginning to feel so uneasy with these older people. I want to go talk to Louie.

S: I was showing Patrick my painting.
Mrs. S: Oh, but he's been in here before.
S: I told him the story about it.
Mrs. S: What did you make of that, Patrick?

She is sounding like my mother does sometimes, sort of menacing. I cannot talk. My mouth is trembling. I think she knows about everything. She takes a sip of her drink, and now she does not look as angry, just worried instead and very sweet.

Mrs. S: Patrick, think what you are supposed to be. I'm a nice woman. I was watched over when I was little, but when I grew up I found I was able to take the world as it is. I'm willing to accept things. But where's love? What will happen to you? Arthur reads Swinburne. Well, that's fine. But that's sex. Where's love? That's beauty and color, and sound—music, you see, sensual things, dancing, colors and hair, that boat. That couldn't stay, Patrick, do you see? Because that depended on two people being exactly the same and wanting the same, and staying the same. They can't. And you'll walk up and down the street, Patrick. You're only eighteen. You have to draw, to do something, not just be beautiful, not just draw beautifully, but draw strongly. If you had a family—who can teach you this?

I am too scared. In a moment I am going to have to get up and leave, run out of here.

The front room on the fourth floor is a guest room. Louie is unpacking his things because he will be staying over the weekend. I did not know this was his room, but I am glad to be here. He says, "Hello, Pony," when I come in, but then he does not know what else to say and keeps busy with his unpacking. I do not want to talk anyway. I sit down on the bed. He is looking at me again. Suddenly I am starting to cry and he is beside me saying things will be all right.

Now it is later, and very dark. We hear someone in the hall. It is both Mr. and Mrs. Supperburger, and they have coats on. They say it is a lovely night and to come up on the roof and watch the stars. Being kids we do not need our coats, because it is really not that cool yet. Fall is just beginning. The stairs are in the hall closet and twist around until you come out on a big flat roof. It is higher than the others on the block, and there are two chairs and some flowerpots. I am scared of heights, and there is not much of a rail around the edge. But the sky is beautiful, absolutely black with every star showing. And you can see all the rooftops on this side of the hill and look down the street to the river which is gray and flat in the distance. The gas lamps and the lights in rooms and houses are shining. Most windows are open, and I can hear rock and roll coming from every direction, up the hill and down it. Someone is playing "Good Lovin' " by the Young Rascals, which is my favorite song. I wish I was wearing my hat and my boots right now. I feel a little like the king of the hill. There is Louie, shivering a little. Even now he has not said much. I wonder what he will be like to know. This may be one of the last party nights before it gets cold. Charles is probably looking for someone to take her to one. It is only ten o'clock. I do not think Louie is much of a partygoer. Maybe that is better. Parties get boring.

Mrs. S: The sky is lovely late at night.
P: It's only ten.
Mrs. S: It's almost the time of year for Orion. I wish he was out on a night like this. That would be a glorious sight.
S: Do you know *The Tales of Hoffmann,* Louis?
L: Yes. I love it.
S: Stella was his one perfect love, told through his stories.
Mrs. S: What are you talking about, Arthur?
S: Patrick knows. The stories I have told myself in my nine symphonies! And told no one else. Nine symphonies. If I could have written one great fugue, one tiny two-part invention even, worthy of a great composer, but —nine symphonies. I pore over the scores in the afternoons, and they eat

me away. Nine manuscripts are out in the world, two for this last one. The manuscript for the First went down on a battleship, in the war. But as music? They were entirely in the fashion. If I could have written in the nineteenth century, I could have done it better. Today's styles don't suit my feelings. But what can you do? Revamp Massenet? Raff? At least, most people don't know that I'm copying, yet. My ladies applaud. But my wife knows. She always knew, and she loves me still. She keeps my name, Supperburger. That's a very silly name, but everyone gets used to it and forgets how silly it is.

He is standing by the edge. I think he wants to sail out, over it, to fall down to the gray circle around the gas lamp in front of the house. I am scared of heights. Luckily Mrs. Supperburger has his hand.

S: They're eating me away, my nine symphonies. I can't spend my time poring over them anymore. Soon they'll lose themselves in libraries.

We are all looking up at the sky. When you look up you forget about the roof. You might be at sea or on a beach, except for all the music and the sound of cars, but I forget about them. We are standing quietly for a long time. Louie looks cold. I had almost forgotten about him while Supperburger was talking, so I give him a smile now. Supperburger is still standing by the edge. He starts to talk again, to himself, but out loud. I notice he is holding one of the Swinburnes.

S: If I had not been turned away the first time, if it had held on, and changed as one . . .

We are all listening, but it is hard to understand him, Supperburger.

S: This is the day I have to say good-bye. People are afraid of being the same. It's too threatening. But to be different, truly, is very hard too. We should all try to be truly different and alone, someday. If you have written a symphony, you may still be just a child. The greatest, with me, could never have been.

He is standing on the edge, holding Swinburne out, over the street. In this starlight, from behind, he looks almost like a boy. In this month I have not known him at all. He is very far from me. The book falls.

Mrs. S: Arthur!

She is pulling him back from the edge, he is in her arms, he says to her, "My only love."

Now it is very late. We have been walking and telling each other things for hours. He is easy to talk to now. We said good night to the Supperburgers and to Matty, then we ran into Charles on the street but we got rid of her pretty easily. I think most of the parties are over now, and everyone is in bed on the hill, except us, walking down the street, under the gas lamps, to the river. I may soon get tired of this street. I have never had anyone my age as interesting to talk to as Louie. Maybe I can get a job at his college, in the kitchen or something. I could live there and try writing poems again. Or take drawing classes. All sorts of plans are going through my head. If I only had more money. I will have to work, that is only fair. I am eighteen. The funny thing is I do not really know Louie. Maybe he will like me more than I like him. I have to learn to get used to people. Maybe I will become completely different. If life really is stretching out, and I am only eighteen, it is a long time.

A Memory

Eudora Welty

One summer morning when I was a child I lay on the sand after swimming in the small lake in the park. The sun beat down—it was almost noon. The water shone like steel, motionless except for the feathery curl behind a distant swimmer. From my position I was looking at a rectangle brightly lit, actually glaring at me, with sun, sand, water, a little pavilion, a few solitary people in fixed attitudes, and around it all a border of dark rounded oak trees, like the engraved thunderclouds surrounding illustrations in the Bible. Ever since I had begun taking painting lessons, I had made small frames with my fingers, to look out at everything.

Since this was a weekday morning, the only persons who were at liberty to be in the park were either children, who had nothing to occupy them, or those older people whose lives are obscure, irregular, and consciously of no worth to anything: this I put down as my observation at that time. I was at an age when I formed a judgment upon every person and every event which came under my eye, although I was easily frightened. When a person, or a happening, seemed to me not in keeping with my opinion, or even my hope or expectation, I was terrified by a vision of abandonment and wildness which tore my heart with a kind of sorrow. My father and mother, who believed that I saw nothing in the world which was not strictly coaxed into place like a vine on our garden trellis to be presented to my eyes, would have been badly concerned if they had guessed how frequently the weak and inferior and strangely turned examples of what was to come showed themselves to me.

I do not know even now what it was that I was waiting to see; but in those days I was convinced that I almost saw it at every turn. To watch everything about me I regarded grimly and possessively as a *need.* All through this summer I had lain on the sand beside the small lake, with my hands squared over my eyes, finger tips touching, looking out by this device to see everything: which appeared as a kind of projection. It did not matter to me what I looked at; from any observation I would conclude that a secret of life had been nearly revealed to me—for I was obsessed with notions about concealment, and from the smallest gesture of a stranger I would wrest what was to me a communication or a presentiment.

This state of exaltation was heightened, or even brought about, by the fact that I was in love then for the first time: I had identified love at once. The truth is that never since has any passion I have felt remained so hopelessly unexpressed within me or appeared so grotesquely altered in the outward world. It is strange that sometimes, even now, I remember unadulteratedly a certain morning when I touched my friend's wrist (as if by accident, and he pretended not to notice) as we passed on the stairs in school. I must add, and this is not so strange, that the child was not actually my friend. We had never exchanged a word or even a nod of recognition; but it was possible during that entire year for me to think endlessly on this minute and brief encounter which we endured on the stairs, until it would swell with a sudden and overwhelming beauty, like a rose forced into premature bloom for a great occasion.

My love had somehow made me doubly austere in my observations of what went on about me. Through some intensity I had come almost into a dual life, as observer and dreamer. I felt a necessity for absolute conformity to my ideas in any happening I witnessed. As a result, all day long in school I sat perpetually alert, fearing for the untoward to happen. The dreariness and regularity of the school day were a protection for me, but I remember with exact clarity the day in Latin class when the boy I loved (whom I watched constantly) bent suddenly over and brought his handkerchief to his face. I saw red—vermilion—blood flow over the handkerchief and his square-shaped hand; his nose had begun to bleed. I remember the very moment: several of the older girls laughed at the confusion and distraction; the boy rushed from the room; the teacher spoke sharply in warning. But this small happening which had closed in upon my friend was a tremendous shock to me; it was unforeseen, but at the same time dreaded; I recognized it, and suddenly I leaned heavily on my arm and fainted. Does this explain why, ever since that day, I have been unable to bear the sight of blood?

I never knew where this boy lived, or who his parents were. This occasioned during the year of my love a constant uneasiness in me. It was unbearable to think that his house might be slovenly and unpainted, hidden by tall trees, that his mother and father might be shabby—dishonest—crippled—dead. I speculated endlessly on the dangers of his home. Sometimes I imagined that his house might catch on fire in the night and that he might die. When he would walk into the schoolroom the next morning, a look of unconcern and even stupidity on his face would dissipate my dream; but my fears were increased through his unconsciousness of them, for I felt a mystery deeper than danger which hung about him. I watched everything that he did, trying to learn and translate and verify. I could reproduce for you now the clumsy weave, the exact shade of faded blue in his sweater. I remember how he used to swing his foot as he sat at his desk—softly, barely not touching the floor. Even now it does not seem trivial.

As I lay on the beach that sunny morning, I was thinking of my friend and remembering in a retarded, dilated, timeless fashion the incident of my hand brushing his wrist. It made a very long story. But like a needle going in and out among my thoughts were the children running on the sand, the upthrust oak trees growing over the clean pointed roof of the white pavilion, and the slowly changing attitudes of the grown-up people who had avoided the city and were lying prone and laughing on the water's edge. I still would not care to say which was more real—the dream I could make blossom at will, or the sight of the bathers. I am presenting them, you see, only as simultaneous.

I did not notice how the bathers got there, so close to me. Perhaps I actually fell asleep, and they came out then. Sprawled close to where I was lying, at any rate, appeared a group of loud, squirming, ill-assorted people who seemed thrown together only by the most confused accident, and who seemed driven by foolish intent to insult each other, all of which they enjoyed with a hilarity which astonished my heart. There were a man, two women, two young boys. They were brown and roughened, but not foreigners; when I was a child such people were called "common." They wore old and faded bathing suits which did not hide either the energy or the fatigue of their bodies, but showed it exactly.

The boys must have been brothers, because they both had very white straight hair, which shone like thistles in the red sunlight. The older boy was greatly overgrown—he protruded from his costume at every turn. His cheeks were ballooned outward and hid his eyes, but it was easy for me to follow his darting, sly glances as he ran clumsily around the others, inflicting pinches, kicks, and idiotic sounds upon them. The smaller boy was thin and defiant; his white bangs were plastered down where he had thrown himself time after time headfirst into the lake when the older child chased him to persecute him.

Lying in leglike confusion together were the rest of the group, the man and the two women. The man seemed completely given over to the heat and glare of the sun; his relaxed eyes sometimes squinted with faint amusement over the brilliant water and the hot sand. His arms were flabby and at rest. He lay turned on his side, now and then scooping sand in a loose pile about the legs of the older woman.

She herself stared fixedly at his slow, undeliberate movements, and held her body perfectly still. She was unnaturally white and fatly aware, in a bathing suit which had no relation to the shape of her body. Fat hung upon her upper arms like an arrested earthslide on a hill. With the first motion she might make, I was afraid that she would slide down upon herself into a terrifying heap. Her breasts hung heavy and widening like pears into her bathing suit. Her legs lay prone one on the other like shadowed bulwarks, uneven and deserted, upon which, from the man's hand, the sand piled higher like the teasing threat of oblivion. A slow, repetitious sound I had been hearing for a long time unconsciously, I identified as a continuous laugh which came through the motionless open pouched mouth of the woman.

The younger girl, who was lying at the man's feet, was curled tensely upon herself. She wore a bright green bathing suit like a bottle from which she might, I felt, burst in a rage of churning smoke. I could feel the genie-like rage in her narrowed figure as she seemed both to crawl and to lie still, watching the man heap the sand in his careless way about the larger legs of the older woman. The two little boys were running in wobbly ellipses about the others, pinching them indiscriminately and pitching sand into the man's roughened hair as though they were not afraid of him. The woman continued to laugh, almost as she would hum an annoying song. I saw that they were all resigned to each other's daring and ugliness.

There had been no words spoken among these people, but I began to comprehend a progression, a circle of answers, which they were flinging toward one another in their own way, in the confusion of vulgarity and hatred which twined among them all like a wreath of steam rising from the wet sand. I saw the man lift his hand filled with crumbling sand, shaking it as the woman laughed, and pour it down inside her bathing suit between her bulbous descending breasts. There it hung, brown and shapeless, making them all laugh. Even the angry girl laughed, with an insistent hilarity which flung her to her feet and tossed her about the beach, her stiff, cramped legs jumping and tottering. The little boys pointed and howled. The man smiled, the way panting dogs seem to be smiling, and gazed about carelessly at them all and out over the water. He even looked at me, and included me. Looking back, stunned, I wished that they all were dead.

But at that moment the girl in the green bathing suit suddenly whirled all the way around. She reached rigid arms toward the screaming children and joined them in a senseless chase. The small boy dashed headfirst into the water, and the larger boy churned his overgrown body through the blue air onto a little bench, which I had not even known was there! Jeeringly he called to the others, who laughed as he jumped, heavy and ridiculous, over the back of the bench and tumbled exaggeratedly in the sand below. The fat woman leaned over the man to smirk, and the child pointed at her, screaming. The girl in green then came running toward the bench as though she would destroy it, and with a fierceness which took my breath away, she dragged herself through the air and jumped over the bench. But no one seemed to notice, except the smaller boy, who flew out of the water to dig his fingers into her side, in mixed congratulation and derision; she pushed him angrily down into the sand.

I closed my eyes upon them and their struggles but I could see them still, large and almost metallic, with painted smiles, in the sun. I lay there with my eyes pressed shut, listening to their moans and their frantic squeals. It seemed to me that I could hear also the thud and the fat impact of all their ugly bodies upon one another. I tried to withdraw to my most inner dream, that of touching the wrist of the boy I loved on the stair; I felt the shudder of my wish shaking the darkness like leaves where I had closed my eyes; I felt the heavy weight of sweetness which always accompanied this memory; but the memory itself did not come to me.

I lay there, opening and closing my eyes. The brilliance and then the blackness were like some alternate experiences of night and day. The sweetness of my love seemed to bring the dark and to swing me gently in its suspended wind; I sank into familiarity; but the story of my love, the long narrative of the incident on the stairs, had vanished. I did not know, any longer, the meaning of my happiness; it held me unexplained.

Once when I looked up, the fat woman was standing opposite the smiling man. She bent over and in a condescending way pulled down the front of her bathing suit, turning it outward, so that the lumps of mashed and folded sand came emptying out. I felt a peak of horror, as though her breasts themselves had turned to sand, as though they were of no importance at all and she did not care.

When finally I emerged again from the protection of my dream, the undefined austerity of my love, I opened my eyes onto the blur of an empty beach. The group of strangers had gone. Still I lay there, feeling victimized by the sight of the unfinished bulwark where they had piled and shaped the wet sand around their bodies, which changed the appearance of the beach like the ravages of a storm. I looked away, and for the object which met my eye, the small worn white pavilion, I felt pity suddenly overtake me, and I burst into tears.

That was my last morning on the beach. I remember continuing to lie there, squaring my vision with my hands, trying to think ahead to the time of my return to school in winter. I could imagine the boy I loved walking into a classroom, where I would watch him with this hour on the beach accompanying my recovered dream and added to my love. I could even foresee the way he would stare back, speechless and innocent, a medium-sized boy with blond hair, his unconscious eyes looking beyond me and out the window, solitary and unprotected.

The Boiler Room

Rudolph Wurlitzer

I'm locked up in the Castle. The Castle is the army stockade on Governors Island. The Staten Island ferry passes by Governors Island, and you can see the Castle and the golf course and the red brick buildings. It looks like a country club. I suppose the Castle is the oldest building on the island. There's a plaque on the wall, but I make a point not to look at it. Outside, the Castle might look like a Civil War fort, but inside it's just another jail. They say that when Rocky Graziano was locked up here he tried to swim to Brooklyn, and there are stories of other guys trying to make it. But I won't try. I've declared bankruptcy. I never think about wanting anything. I do what they tell me, and I keep my mouth shut so they don't give me too much harassment. I pull details during the day: cleaning latrines, mowing the lawn, clipping the hedges, KP in the officer and NCO clubs. The days go by. I'm not sure what month it is. Until my trial comes up I won't connect with anything too strongly. Any way they go I'm going to lose. If they decide I'm just another nut, I'll probably believe them. And if they say I'm just another criminal, I'll probably accept that too. The only time for me to look at anything straight is when it doesn't matter. And so on Sunday afternoons, when nothing matters at all, I use my footlocker for a desk and put it all down on paper.

I made it through basic all right. I was in good shape because I had just come from a summer of minor league baseball. When they learned I was a ballplayer they made me a squad leader. Jocks, policemen, longshoremen—they have it made in basic. I don't look like a leader or, at first, even much of a ballplayer because I'm short and wear glasses. But all anyone has to do is see me in action to know what I can do. I'm fast—I'm known as "Roadrunner" Schuller—and I hustle. I can't hit too good, but I get on base. And I can catch anything.

But lying on my bunk after chow or sometimes late at night when I couldn't sleep, I would get very low. More than half the men my age don't get called up. Most of my friends beat it when they pretended they were queer or they took coffee beans or some kind of dope before they went up for their physical. I come from that kind of a neighborhood. I not only was slow enough to get caught, but I didn't even sneak in on the six months deal. For a ballplayer, two years in the army just about finishes you. The front office forgets your name. If you miss a season, they don't know you, unless, of course, you're a bonus baby or a star. Every spring they have to see your sweaty and eager face or you don't exist. My only hope was to play ball for an army team, stay in shape, play winter ball in Latin America when I got out, and report to spring training for one last shot.

But I goofed. One week before the end of basic, I came back after an overnight pass, and passed out on my bunk, a flask half-full of Old Crow on my stomach. The first sergeant picked that night to come into the barracks. He saw the flask, I called him some kind of a name, and the next morning I was standing tall before Captain Gonzales, the company commander. Captain Gonzales asked me if I was some kind of a playboy. I said yes, I thought I was a playboy, definitely, and then something slipped further inside me, and I started lying all over the place.

I heard myself asking if it was in my rights to make a phone call. I said I wanted to ask for advice from someone who knew the score. Captain Gonzales asked me very politely just who I was going to call. I said I thought I would call Washington. I've never been to Washington except on my high school senior class trip, and I don't even know the Secretary of State's name. (I had it in my mind that I was going to ring up the Secretary of State.) There was this silence, and then Captain Gonzales—he was only half believing me—said I could go ahead and use the phone if I called collect but that I shouldn't take this thing too seriously, as all I would get would be, at the maximum, a summary court-martial.

I picked up the phone. I sort of stroked the phone, and for a few seconds I really believed that I knew the Secretary of State and that I was going to bang a few heads around the company. But then I put the phone back and just stood tall. Captain Gonzales didn't waste any time giving me a summary court, confining me to the company area, and docking me two thirds of my next month's pay. He promised to ship me off the entire post. And he lived up to his word. After basic I was shipped to Camp Drum.

In the winter, Camp Drum might just as well be in Iceland as in New York State. It's near the St. Lawrence River about thirty miles from Canada and ten miles from Watertown. As you get farther north, the train gets slower and colder. I changed trains at Syracuse at 3 A.M., and from then on I saw only one other passenger, and he was asleep with a newspaper over his head. I sang songs to myself and drank almost a pint of bourbon. I was feeling plenty sorry for myself. When I got to Watertown I sat in the station for five hours. I just sat there and stared at my duffel bag and waited until I sobered up. Finally I called the post, and they sent a jeep for me.

When I reported to the orderly room the first sergeant said to sit down until he thought of something. Then he went on reading a paper-backed book. I must have sat there for half an hour before he looked up from his book. There was something weird about the way he looked at me. He didn't quite focus. It was like he had forgotten that he was a sergeant. Later on I got used to that look because everyone at Camp Drum had it.

"There's no need for anyone to sweat anything around here," he said. "In the summer the National Guard and the ready reserve use the camp for two-week training periods, and then we work our tails off, but in the winter there's only a skeleton crew to guard the place and do paper work for the summer. It's a boneyard. I suppose we could put you on permanent KP or use you to shovel snow. I don't know, son. We already got too many personnel; about seventy-five enlisted men and ten officers: What did you do in civilian life?"

"I was a ballplayer."

He went on to tell me about his career, from American Legion to semipro ball to when he played for the Sixth Army team in the South Pacific. He couldn't stop talking baseball. He was a good-field-no-hit second baseman who had never banged more than a double in his entire life. Finally he said that seeing as how I was a ballplayer, he could find work for me in the message center.

The detachment—it wasn't even a company—was grouped together right at the edge of the post. In back of us there stretched one hundred and eight thousand acres of flat fields, empty barracks, and various training areas. The trees were bent from the north wind. That wind would scream around the barracks, picking up snow and whipping it at us like frozen hairs as we stood in morning formation or waited in the chow line. You became used to living with two colors: brown and white. The barracks and other buildings were brown and your clothes were brown and even the food looked brown. Everything else was white, and around the company area the snow didn't stay white very long until it turned brown. The barracks were old and creaky. We didn't have a dayroom or a place to write letters or play pool or ping-pong. There was no beer hall, and the PX was a little shelf of toilet articles that they opened up twice a week in the administration building. The only place to go was the NCO club, which was open to everyone. The NCO club had red and green lights over the entrance, a jukebox, and a white zinc-covered bar.

Every three weeks the NCO club was shipped a pornographic movie from the air force base fifty miles away. The movies were traded among the four or five military camps around northern New York State. I only took in one show because it would get a little too weird sitting there in the dark and listening to the groans and whistles and strange shifting movements. It made things worse. You could never make it with a girl in Watertown unless you were willing to put in a lot of time. You also had to be lucky and something of a con man. They had all been warned about soldiers and weren't about to get knocked up by some PFC out for a good time. It was a lot easier not to tease myself. I was hung up enough as it was. Watertown was a nice enough town—I don't mean to put it down—but I never spent too much time there. Once in a while on a weekend I would hitch-hike in for a movie or to shoot a little pool, but that was about it.

As soon as I was assigned my bunk and had put up my calendar, I started checking off the days. I had six hundred and fifty-five days to go. At Camp Drum everyone was hung up about time. For two weeks I didn't say anything to anybody. I didn't know the name of the guy in the next bunk. I just sat around and thought about how it would be when I got out. I kept seeing myself working as a clerk in my brother's toy store. My hands started to shake, and I had trouble putting the mail in the right slots. I couldn't concentrate on the sports page. I even threw up in the mornings when I got out of bed.

Then I goofed again. I almost killed a guy. There was this fat cook, Geruzzi, who must have weighed two hundred and seventy-five pounds, easy. He was everybody's buddy. He was like a guy who will talk big in practice and say all the words and make all the tricky moves, but when it comes to game time he'll freeze. (Maybe that's why he got to me so much. I was frozen solid myself.) Geruzzi had black curly hair that ran wild all over his head and tiny eyes that never stopped moving around. He was scared of everyone. There was this one thing he would do that did me in. Every morning when the lights went on he would be the first one up. His bunk was at the far end of the barracks, away from mine. He would stand there for a moment, patting his belly, which hung out over his underpants. Then he would give an insane yell, stick his finger into his belly button like he was gripping a bowling ball, and start running down the hall. At the end of the hall he would release this imaginary bowling ball like he was trying to roll a strike toward the orderly room. I had the cot at the end of the hall, near the door, and Geruzzi would come to a halt six inches away from my face, his belly shaking like a mound of jello. Then he would step outside, in the cold, and yell in a high squeaky voice: "I want to thank you world! Hey, baby! Hello Camp Drum! Hello First Sergeant!" Then he would slam the door and salute and march into the latrine. It cracked everybody up.

I didn't say anything, but it kept building up inside me. I tried to shut him out. I kept my head under the covers until he finished his act. But the more I tried to shut him out the more I thought about him. One morning I leaped out of bed and pushed him up against the wall. I said that if he ever waved his belly in my face again I would punch him. And then I couldn't control myself and I belted him one anyway. He sat down on my bunk and looked at the floor, saying over and over again that I had broken his nose. I started throwing everything I could lay my hands on at him: boots, pillows, helmets, duffel bags. A part of me kept hoping that someone would stop me, but everyone just stood around laughing. Finally I was tackled and sat upon while someone went for the first sergeant.

They confined me to company quarters for a month and put me on two hours extra duty shoveling snow every evening. It didn't matter. I had nowhere to go and nothing to do. I was even glad to move around. But the whole thing scared me, and I kept even more to myself.

It was then, sometime in the middle of January, that I met Pannel.

I would go to the mess hall when everyone else was finished so that I could sit by myself. This one evening I must have come in early because the mess hall was still crowded. I picked out a table where only one other person was sitting. I had seen Pannel before, but I had never spoken to him. I knew he was the mimeograph operator and that he had a little room in back of the personnel section. He delivered mimeographed forms to the message center. There weren't many forms in the winter, so he didn't come in often.

Pannel was a spade, very tall and thin, with an emaciated, sunk-in face. I was never able to look at any one point in his face, the way you do with most guys. The other thing about him was that he was extremely neat. He always wore pressed fatigues, highly starched, although no one else in Camp Drum bothered to. He would pull his pants very high up on his waist. I've seen ballplayers do that; I guess being a highpockets makes them feel tighter and more compact.

"How's the mimeograph machine?" I asked. For some reason I felt I could talk to Pannel.

"Man, I don't work that machine," he said. "I seduce it. I'm the best mimeograph operator you'll ever see. I want to tell you."

He laughed.

Between bites I watched Pannel. You couldn't help but watch him. I've seen spades eat before, the way they use sauces and spices, but I never saw anyone do to his food what Pannel did. There was liver, and Pannel cut up the liver into small pieces and mixed it in with his rice and peas. He covered the whole mess with salt and pepper. Then he put ketchup and mustard on top of the salt and pepper and finished the whole thing off with big dabs of Louisiana Hot Sauce. Then he mixed it all up again.

He started to watch me watch him.

"Did you run track?" I asked. He looked like a track man. You could tell he had real thin ankles without even looking at them. He looked brittle. There was something startled about him, like he was just about to take off.

"Too much work," he said slowly. "I used to run the four-forty, and it did me in. I had to quit. Work don't exactly agree with me."

"I ran in high school. I did the hundred in nine-nine." I only felt comfortable when I was talking sports. "I ran the half-mile too, but then it got in the way of baseball. I don't like to let anything get in the way of playing ball."

Pannel didn't answer. He ate very fast, and when he finished, he left.

I saw Pannel three nights later when I pulled fire guard. The fire guard's job was to keep the furnaces going in the three barracks and in the orderly room and in the officers' quarters down the road. There was a big furnace in each boiler room for the heat, and then there was a smaller one for the hot water. I never minded pulling fire guard. I would bank the coal up real high so that there was an edge of blue flame in the back. I liked to keep the fires in extra fine shape. Some nights I would get to really piling it on. "Burn the bastards up," I'd say to the flames. I would wander from boiler room to boiler room all night with coal dust all over me. I could taste it, and it would get matted in my hair. They gave the fire guard the morning off to sleep. That was the best time, taking a hot shower and going to bed when everyone else was getting up.

I met Pannel in one of the boiler rooms. He was sitting up against the wall. There was a small portable phonograph next to him, but there wasn't any record on it. He had his eyes closed. When he opened them he didn't seem glad to see me.

"This is my spot," he said. "I'll keep your fires going."

He shut his eyes.

I made my rounds, and then I came back to Pannel's boiler room. I knew I was pressing him, but I needed to talk. Maybe I wanted to talk to him because he seemed so far away, as if it was safe to talk to him. I don't know. He had some kind of record on.

I sat down.

When the record stopped I started right in bitching about the army. I didn't even look at Pannel. I was gone. I went on about how I was through as far as playing ball went and how the army had screwed me up and about how my hands shook in the mornings. I told him about how I almost killed Geruzzi. I even said I wouldn't be too sad if they sent me out to fight somewhere, just for a while. Maybe three months. I could sort of live off the experience until I got straight. All the time I was bitching I got the feeling Pannel wasn't listening, that he didn't give a damn what I said. Which is not to say he wasn't polite. That strange smile never left his face. After a while I ran out of words.

Pannel had a weird way of sitting. He kneeled on both knees even though the floor was cement. He always took off his boots in the boiler room. He would sit very straight, giving you this impression of being very quiet. Sometimes he would breathe deeply and slowly, not so you could really notice, but more like he was using his whole body, starting the breath from his heels.

We sat there a long time. The silence began to make me uncomfortable. I began to think that I had better leave and that I had no real business being out there. I began to think that Pannel might even be some kind of a maniac.

"Why don't you say something?" I said.

He just looked at me.

"Don't pull that crap on me," I said. I was damn near crying. But as I stood up to go, Pannel started to speak. He didn't look at me. He looked at the floor.

"I'm having a good time," he said. "The army is a good time. It's very worthwhile. Out here I don't want to hear that the army isn't a good time."

I stayed where I was. It was better than walking out there in the cold between boiler rooms.

"I don't come to conclusions," he said. "You know what I mean? I don't ask nothing of nobody. I'm just here. You count the days, right?"

"Five hundred and ninety-two to go."

"I gave the whole thing up. I don't ever think about the time. When they came to get me, I canceled myself out. I don't bother to figure anything. They take care of that. There are lots of cats far out and lost, doing all kinds of misdemeanors, but not me. I gave up."

"That's right," I said. I wasn't really listening to him. I was looking at the open mouth of the furnace and the blue flames dancing over the coal.

"I come out here and drop my net way down and pull it up," Pannel went on. "I just let anything flop out that wants to."

I got it into my head that Pannel was putting me down in some way. I stood up and picked up my shovel. I didn't need anybody to tell me where I was at.

I walked out and checked my other fires. It was very cold, and my boots crunched on the dry snow. I was standing in front of the orderly room, and the stars were jumping and flashing around like silver bursts of rifle fire. I went back to Pannel's boiler room, but he was gone.

After that I went out every night to the boiler room. For over a week Pannel didn't talk to me. But it was warm in the boiler room, and it was better than sitting in the barracks. I sat there and listened to his records. The only time he would talk would be to say the titles very softly as he put a record on. Titles like Moose the Mooche, Frantic Fancies, and Scrapple From the Apple.

When we did start to talk to each other we talked sports. Pannel didn't like baseball too much, but he was good on the fights and on basketball and football. We went through a lot of fights we had seen. We talked about Marciano and Louis and Johannson and Patterson. We both had been fans of Jersey Joe Walcott's, even though he dumped that fight with Marciano. We preferred middleweights and lightweights, guys like Willie Pep and Jake La Motta, Sugar Ray Robinson and Kid Gavilan. We were terrific on football, especially pro football, and we would give out with our all-star lineups. I would say something like: "You got to have Y. A. Tittle as your quarterback. I'll back him with Bobby Layne."

And Pannel would say, "No, man. Tittle, now he's mean, but he don't hold *nothing* when it comes to Otto Graham. You ever see Otto Graham on a good day when Mac Speedie was his end? I mean, you got to take him. And Lujack, what about Lujack? And then Van Brocklin could throw. And we haven't even *talked* about Unitas yet."

"Who you got for halfbacks?" I'd say.

"You got to give me Doak Walker. Grange and them old guys I didn't see, but I remember Buddy Young when he was with the Yanks, and jack, he was fast, and I know it sounds insane, but I'll take Lenny Moore because for a halfback he can do anything, and then he just moves beautiful."

It got to be very important to go out to the boiler room every night. Pannel and I didn't see each other during the day. On the weekends Pannel wouldn't see me or anyone else because he said that he had to have at least two days alone. But during the week I went out to the boiler room like I imagine some people go to church or to a cathouse.

It calmed me down. It kept me together. We got so that we never talked about ourselves, only sports; and sometimes we didn't say anything at all; we would just sit and listen to the same records over and over. In Watertown I bought an old green felt covering that had been on a pool table. We put the phonograph and the records on it. We got into our own way of talking so much that eventually we just settled on basketball. We could talk basketball better than any two people I've ever heard. After we spent a few nights on our all-star teams, we started to play out some games. Pannel's favorite team was the Boston Celtics. I would have liked to go with the New York Knickerbockers, New York being my hometown, but they never could hold the Celts, so I had to go with the Los Angeles Lakers. After a while, though, we kind of mixed in our favorite players from the other teams, so it was more like two all-star lineups.

"Robertson puts the ball into play," I'd say, bringing my club downcourt. "He passes over to Guy Rodgers. Rodgers starts a weave, fakes a jump shot—he's *fast,* that Rodgers—passes it in to the big boy, Wilt the Stilt Chamberlain. Chamberlain is tied up by Bellamy. Out to Arizin. Arizin jumps, shoots— Good."

"Here comes Cousy," Pannel would say. "Look at how he works the ball. Either hand. He doesn't look. Over to Baylor. Baylor brings it hippity-hop over mid-court. In to Reed. Reed tries to drive down the middle but can't get his shot. Out to Barnett. Barnett dribbles in to the key, fakes once, twice with his head, falls back, delays, and there's a long, soft jumper. Off the rim and out. But Nate Thurmond is up there for the tap. Two points. One! Two!"

Sometimes Pannel would get cute and pull off a steal. I'd be putting the ball into play, and he would break in:

"K.C. Jones comes out of *no*where and scoops the ball away from Gola, and now it's the fast break and down the floor they come. It's two on one. Jones over to Cousy, Cousy back to Jones, and now it's the Couse with a behind-the-back dribble. He fakes right, goes left, and the ball is up and *in!* Beautiful!"

Most of our games would go into overtime. Once in a while there'd be trades and talk of fixes, and some of the players would get in fights, like the night Pannel was tired and wanted to go to bed, so he had Jungle Jim Loscutoff slug Robertson. We had to call the game off because the fans got out of control.

We got so good at talking basketball that we even started to invent players and different shots. We'd invent their whole history, where they played high school ball, how they did in college, and what happened to them in the pros. We had this one player, Alston MacKintosh, from Oleander College in Nebraska, who could hit nine out of ten from the foul line with his back to the basket. He was a real hot dog, but when we had him move up to the pros he couldn't take the pressure. He eventually blew up in a game with the Detroit Pistons when he threw the ball into the stands every time he got the ball. He had to be sent down to the Eastern League.

After a few hours in the boiler room, we would sometimes walk up to the NCO club and have a beer. It was a night in late February, after we had played a few games, when something happened that changed everything between us. We were standing in front of the NCO club. I was demonstrating how Warren Spahn pitched with the big windup, bringing my right leg around and following through the way Spahn does. I was using chunks of ice to throw at a mound across the road.

We were a little drunk. I asked Pannel why it was that spades never hit much from the outside. I was just talking, not really thinking about what I was saying, when Pannel suddenly became very serious. He said he never knew that spades could never hit from the outside. We discussed Guy Rodgers and Hal Greer and a few other backcourt men and how they hardly ever seemed to hit from the outside. I remembered old Sweetwater Clifton and how he used to try a two-hand set all the time when he was with the Knicks and how he never scored with it. Pannel said no one used long set shots anymore and that it didn't matter. He said that it wasn't true anyway. Then he sighed and said how nice it was that he was no longer a spade. I didn't know what to say so I imitated Warren Spahn again.

"You take any side of the question," Pannel said, although I didn't know what the question was, "and I'll agree with you."

He went on to talk about politics and urban problems and minority groups and other things that I didn't know about and that made no sense to me. He talked about slaves and about how some of them had been more free than he was ever going to be. They had boiler rooms, he said, that they could go to without thinking about it. He went on like that, and I couldn't listen to him. I had hardly ever heard Pannel talk that way. It depressed me. I thought we had decided not to bullshit. I wanted to go inside and have a beer, but I thought I should hear him out.

"You got to be a strange cat to do your own stuff these days," he said, "and Roadrunner, I'm not strange enough. If I was really doing my own thing I wouldn't be coming on with you like this. No, man, listen, when I get out I'll be hustling and talking my ass off and trying to be equal and different at the same time, which is about the stupidest thing a man can do. I know I will. But don't call me a spade. Right now I'm not a spade. And you're not a ballplayer."

Pannel turned and walked down the road. After that night it was never the same with him.

When Pannel was quiet now, he would make me nervous. I began to talk when I didn't really want to. I kept talking to him because I had gotten dependent on doing that, and besides, there wasn't anything else to do. He didn't seem to make a connection with me anymore. We stopped talking sports. Sometimes he would laugh, and the laugh would seem to come from nowhere, and I would never know what he was laughing at. Those laughs would last a long time, and they always made me feel self-conscious. I would try and laugh back, but because I didn't know what was happening, my throat would get stuck. We drank more. We'd get a carton of beer from the NCO club and take it back to the boiler room. Or we wouldn't bother and just get loaded up there.

Pannel didn't want to be alone anymore on the weekends, so he would come into the barracks and drag me away from a card game. We would go into the boiler room and drink and listen to music. I started to hate that music. But there was still something in the place, because I couldn't stop from going out there. But one night I couldn't take it anymore. I blew up. I stood up and yelled at him:

"Goddamnit, be a nigger, be a soldier, be a maniac, but be *something.*"

I started to shake. I wanted to kill him, to snuff him out. I swear to God.

Pannel looked at me. He was cold. It was like when I first met him.

"The thing that's important," he said, "is to get to that point where it doesn't matter whether someone understands you. Where you never have to call on anyone. When you can wait and not expect anything one way or the other . . . But it's very icy there."

He got up and left.

I put on a record. When the record was over, I took the phonograph and the records back to the barracks and went to sleep. I didn't know how to think about anything.

The next morning Pannel missed roll call. He was reported AWOL. It didn't cause much of a stir. Going AWOL was no unusual act in Camp Drum, and no one had ever really noticed Pannel. He just wasn't there. The next day everyone forgot about it.

Everyone, that is, but me. At first I told myself that it was his problem. He would have said that himself. But I couldn't help wondering where he had gone. He only had five weeks to go before he would have processed out. Now if they caught him he would be in for a long time. But I don't think they'll catch him, because I don't think he's the type to go home. Pannel won't leave any tracks. It's strange, but I don't even know where his home is. He never talked about it. I assumed he was from New York because he talked about jazz so much and he seemed to know some musicians. But for all I know he might have been from North Dakota. If he had only said something to me about going. Even if he had just joked about it and told me a lie. If he had only said: "Roadrunner, I got me a beautiful cabin up in the Canadian woods. You ought to see it. I thought about it, and it's all set up. I have two thousand records and a lovely chick who just happens to have *lots* of money." That would have been enough for me. But the bastard, I thought. He didn't leave me with anything, except, maybe, his phonograph and records, which I kept. But I never used that phonograph once.

It was like I had been caught in a room without knowing how to get out. I tried the window, but it was too high. I tried the chimney, but it was too narrow. I got the feeling all I had to do was turn around and I would see the door had been open all the time—but I couldn't turn around. I was stuck.

It wasn't that I hated the army. I didn't hate anything, and I didn't like anything. If I could have spent some time in a gym I would have been all right. I would have been around some action, something I didn't have to think about. Something was wrong. My mind was going too fast, as if it was out of control. I didn't know how to put on the brakes. Before, I always had some little guy inside me, like a coach, telling me what I should do and what I shouldn't do. It was like he had disappeared or just quit. The more I shouted around trying to find him the worse it got. I would go out behind the barracks and walk across a field lined with pine trees. I would throw chunks of snow at the trees. Once I shouted. It didn't help. I went out to the boiler room. I tried to breathe deeply and feel completely still. I sat there for a long time. But nothing happened.

I drank my way into April. After a while just getting through the winter seemed enough and coming into April was like taking a hook slide from way out and just managing to touch the base with your finger. The weather got warmer and the snow disappeared. Two companies arrived from Fort Devens. We had inspections again and G.I. parties. I was busted to private for not having my name tags sewed on. I complained and started counting the days left, now five hundred and eighteen. The camp filled up. I played a little softball on the weekends. I even started to talk to the men in my barracks. Everyone has a bad winter now and then. And me, who wasn't smart enough to go to college or be an officer or just duck the whole thing, why should I have to figure out why one winter is good and another one bad? They do all that for you. So I sat back and tried to ride it out, and I was doing fine until Sergeant Harrison Mountain showed up in the beginning of May.

Sergeant Mountain was sent up from army headquarters to start the post newspaper. If you saw him from across the company area, you might think he was a general, or if you were closer and saw his stripes, you would figure him for one of the last of the old-time sergeants. He was very classy. People pointed out his resemblance to MacArthur, but I preferred to see him as an old Western scout, the kind you see in the comics and movies, pale-blue eyes, very straight and cool, ready to ride into hostile Indian territory without looking back. He had hair the color of steel wool and a white mustache that bent slightly at the corners. That mustache was better than Errol Flynn's. (I learned later that he wore a toupee; you could see it shift a little when the weather was warm and the top of his head sweated.) All of Mountain's uniforms were tailor-made, and he wore the combat infantry badge and three lines of ribbons. Pannel would have checked him out because Mountain's face was very hard to read. Pannel was always checking out faces. He said you could tell what most guys were doing just by looking at their faces. He was looking for the face where nothing showed. A lot seemed to show in Mountain's face, but there was finally some tight thing he did with all the lines around his mouth that kept it from you.

Mountain liked the message center. He would sniff and poke around the mailboxes and read all the return addresses on the officers' mail. He kept careful note of all leaves and three-day passes. There wasn't much else for him to do. He was supposed to set up a place for the new Public Information Office and recruit a newspaper staff, but he had done that kind of thing so often he could do it in half a day, and he had conned four weeks for himself.

Mountain was old, he had killed men, he might have raped women. And he treated me like a private, which I liked. I didn't have to think about Mountain. Everything was laid out by regulations. I made myself fit into his style. I became a kind of aide to him, although that was mostly in my mind because Mountain rarely talked to me. But I soldiered. I shined my brass and shoes, and I stood tall. I was putting him on, I guess. But I didn't want to think anymore. I wanted to rest . . . I guess what I'm trying to say is that I told him a lie. I waited about a week, just to feel him out, and then I told him I used to be a sports reporter on the New York *Post.* I wanted to work on the newspaper. Mountain was my way out of the message center. He had authority. He seemed to know exactly what he was doing. I made him my man. I got the job.

We set up the PIO office together.

But I don't want to talk about the newspaper, or about the PIO section, or about the summer, or about Camp Drum. All that doesn't matter. I want to talk about the way it ended. I want to put it down because I don't understand it.

When the camp filled with reserves and National Guard troops, we worked. Even Mountain went out to the field to cover stories. On weekends we often had three or four governors inspecting their troops, and we had to cover them.

One afternoon in the beginning of July, I took a jeep and went out to the field to get a story on an artillery company. It was a forty-minute drive to the range. The road was rutted by tanks. It was hot. Tired and out-of-shape platoons marched slowly along the side of the road. When I heard the howitzers, I pulled the jeep off the road. I had plenty of time.

I lay down. The ground was sandy, with a few scattered pine trees and tufts of grass. The only sound was howitzers going off at three-minute intervals. They were 105's. It was always unreal for me to drive out to the range and listen to big weapons going off. I never believed them. I never felt part of the game. That wasn't so unusual, there weren't many guys who felt part of the game, but I felt frozen, a little scared. The howitzers made me think about how much I hated noise. Any noise. I needed to play ball. If I could have just gotten to a ball park, anywhere, to work it out. I began to talk basketball to myself: "Robertson dribbles over the center court. He passes it on to Embry. Embry is tied up by Bellamy. Out to Twyman. He throws up a left-handed hook . . . Good. The Royals lead thirty-two to twenty-eight."

I spoke louder, trying to drown out the 105's. "Here comes Jerry West over to Komives. Komives loses the ball! Richie Guerin and Kevin Loughery on the fast break. It's in to Loughery, and he makes a beautiful driving lay-up and gets fouled in the process. A possible three-point play."

It didn't help to talk basketball. It never helped anymore. I got up and drove out to where they were firing. I interviewed a few privates, getting their hometown addresses, what they did in civilian life, that kind of thing, when I saw near the last howitzer in line, Mountain. It was really Mountain. I could spot him anywhere. There were three or four men around him, and they were coming up the line of howitzers. The men on the howitzers saluted as they walked past. Mountain would answer their salutes. When they got closer I saw the stars on Mountain's shirt. I walked away, behind a tree, and stood with a group of men drinking coffee.

"Who's that?" I asked, motioning toward Mountain.

"Some inspecting general. I never seen him before."

I walked forward. I went right up to the group. I didn't feel anxious. I don't know why. I didn't feel much of anything. Mountain looked at me distractedly, as if he had never seen me before. I saluted.

"Are you from PIO, soldier?" he asked.

"Yes, sir," I said.

"I want you to drive me back to camp. Something happened to my driver. Go back to your jeep and wait for me."

I went back to the jeep. Mountain was doing the whole shot. A brigadier general. I didn't laugh. It was real enough. But it wasn't fair, I thought. It wasn't fair to me that Mountain was a maniac. I didn't know how long he had been doing this. I didn't know why. But I couldn't handle it. To do something about it I would have had to be clear on a whole lot of things. And everything was muddy, very muddy. I couldn't report him. I wasn't afraid of him. It was something in myself that held me there, some kind of exuberance that I kept pushing down. Like on opening day of the season when you're so turned on you feel like throwing the ball into the stands.

Mountain came up to the jeep with the company commander, a brisk New York businessman, delighted to be in the army for two weeks.

"A fine company," Mountain said. "I am impressed, Captain. They have good spirit. They have a sense of order."

"Thank you, sir," the captain said. "I'm proud of them . . . yes, they're a great bunch of men. Are you sure you won't let us drive you in, sir?"

"It's perfectly all right this way," Mountain said. They saluted, and Mountain got in next to me. He was wearing a pistol. I drove off very fast.

"What's your name, soldier?" Mountain asked.

"Come off it, Sarge," I said. "You can play your game. I don't care. I'll just drive you back to the post, and you can do what you want. I won't squeal."

"We're not going back to the post. We're going to the nearest PX, and then we're coming back to the training areas. There are more troops to inspect."

"Not me," I said.

Mountain pulled out his pistol from the holster and shot it into the air.

"You have to understand, Schuller," he said, "there is something to do." He looked very tired and old. His voice suddenly wavered. "Look, Schuller, it isn't going to work. We're not going to take over the post. We're going to go out and look at the troops."

"Yes, sir," I said.

I drove to the nearest PX. Mountain was smart in choosing a brigadier general. There were lots of them wandering around. Anything with more than one star would be conspicuous. No one would notice him if he stayed out in training areas with the reserves. At the PX I stopped, and he got out and went in. I thought of driving off. I should have driven off. I know that. He came out a few seconds later. Without saying anything, he pinned two gold bars on my collar. I was Second Lieutenant Schuller. We drove off to inspect the troops.

When we got to the training areas he directed me up another road like the one I had come out on. After twenty minutes we passed a company bivouacked among some pine trees.

"Pull up," Mountain said.

We walked slowly up to the tents. It was about four in the afternoon. The company must have still been out in the field. No one was around. A mess truck was parked off to one side, and some KP's were setting up trays and food containers for the evening meal.

A lieutenant ran up and saluted.

"Lieutenant Maugham reporting, sir. Company K."

Mountain looked past the lieutenant's left ear.

"We've come to see if your company is up to par, Lieutenant. It's important that each and every one of your men is up to par. Tell me the name of your platoon sergeants."

The lieutenant stiffened. He was very young, probably just out of college. He pressed a swagger stick nervously against his side.

"There's Spalding in the third platoon, sir," he said finally. "Then there's my platoon, the fourth platoon, that would be Sergeant Randall. Tony Randall. Then there's Orback in the third. The first has, let's see, the first platoon has, it must have—"

He stood staring at us.

"This is not good, Lieutenant," Mountain said gravely, a little sadly. "This is not good at all."

"Yes, sir," the lieutenant said.

"No," Mountain repeated, "this is not good at all. We'll have to wait for your company commander. Bring us some chairs, and we'll sit under these trees." He waved toward a group of scrub oak trees at the end of the row of tents. The lieutenant hurried off. He came back carrying two canvas chairs.

"We won't need you, Lieutenant," Mountain said, waving him away.

We sat without speaking. One of the KP's dropped a stack of metal trays. A jeep went by on the road. I clung to each sound. Mountain stared off beyond the tents. I wasn't sure what he was thinking, even if he was thinking at all. I just sat there.

The sun began to move down through the trees in back of us. The light grew softer. The end of the day is always bad for me. I felt it in my throat, like something was stuck that I couldn't swallow. Mountain didn't move or shift in his chair when the troops were heard down the road. They were counting cadence, shouting it out the way troops do in their first few weeks of basic. They weren't army voices. The voices weren't weary or disgusted enough. They didn't tell you they had been through a boring, stupid day. They told you they were happy to be outdoors, happy to be doing a man's work, happy to be away from home. The platoons marched in and formed into company formation. Lieutenant Maugham saluted the company commander. The company commander looked over at us. Then he walked briskly over.

He saluted. "Major Tucker reporting, sir."

Mountain stared at him. The major was young and efficient. He didn't mind being looked over. He had an educated voice with a slight English accent.

"We've been inspecting troops all day," Mountain said after a long pause. His voice had become slower and more deliberate. "I won't inspect your company. What I've seen so far has looked good enough. A certain lack of military bearing in one of the younger officers but otherwise perfectly sufficient. I am even rather impressed by the way you set yourself up here, putting yourself under camouflage from air attack."

"Thank you, sir," Major Tucker said. "We have reason to be proud of K Company."

"We're tired," Mountain said stiffly, "extremely tired. I wonder if it would be too much to ask if we could share your evening meal tonight?"

"Delighted, General," Major Tucker said. He wasn't at all disturbed by having a general around. He never looked at me. "Dinner will be ready in half an hour. We expect pork and green vegetables. Our cook is a chef at one of Philadelphia's better restaurants."

We followed the major over to his tent. Three wooden tables with white tablecloths had been set up outside.

"This is comfortable," Mountain said, sitting down. "It's always encouraging to run across people who know how to live well in the field."

"To tell you the truth, General, I've picked up a few tricks on safari. When you've been hunting big game all day the evening is a precious time, a time to relax, have a drink, and enjoy good conversation. My officers and I have a little ritual we go through after a day's training. Two drinks before eating. These two weeks of training are precious to us. We try and get the most out of them. I don't suppose you've been on safari, General?"

"I spent three years in the Pacific hunting human beings."

"I see. Did you by chance know my father? The late Colonel Tucker? He served with General Wingate."

"I don't recall the name," Mountain said. "Wingate was never a great favorite of mine. Where did you say you served?"

"I beg your pardon, sir?" Major Tucker said politely.

"In the war, for god's sake, Major. In the war."

"I'm afraid I was a bit too young for the Second World War, but I was fortunate enough to get in on Korea."

"That kind of luck is uninteresting," Mountain said. "Damned uninteresting."

"Indeed," the major said. He stood up. "What would you care to drink, sir?"

"Bourbon on the rocks."

"And you, Lieutenant?"

"The same, thank you, sir." Those were the first words I had spoken. They were hollow and forced. As the major mixed drinks from a small portable bar, the rest of the company officers, two second lieutenants, came up and stood stiffly at attention.

"At ease, gentlemen," Mountain said. "For Christ's sake, sit down."

The company was lining up behind the chow trucks. They were quiet and orderly, the word having spread that the CO was eating with a general. I was afraid now but in a strange way. I was full of violence. I needed a woman badly. I tried staring at a point somewhat to the left of the major's head. Mountain had shoved off; he was on his own trip. All I could do was sit back and ride it out. I felt light-headed, my mouth dry, almost parched. If anyone had said anything to me out of the ordinary I would have been unable to reply. I concentrated on trying to hold on. Mountain was talking about the South Pacific.

"I had the great honor to be on Corregidor before it fell," he was saying. "Damned lucky I was friends with the engineers. They thought I was some kind of a fighting fool, they did. A regular god. Decent bunch, those engineers. Always ate well with the engineers. They would work like niggers when they had to, but when they were off they knew how to enjoy themselves. The Japs would be bombing hell out of us, and we would be sitting in a tunnel as comfortable as a bunch of retired sergeants, eating salmon and drinking white wine. They had stolen delicacies from a submerged Filipino yacht. MacArthur was there. We were always worried about MacArthur because he never paid the slightest attention to the bombings."

"I've often thought about Corregidor," Major Tucker said. "It was an interesting operation, tactics-wise."

"Don't you believe it," Mountain said sharply. "Don't you believe it when some old fogy stands up and says, 'War is a detestable thing.' The bastard is always a rear-line general embarrassed because he's not in it. You can bet on that. Of course, there were those who had bad wars. Terrible wars. But I had a good war; not a great one, you understand, but a damned satisfying one."

"I think I can see your point," Major Tucker said.

Dinner was served.

"I studied the morale of the British troops in Malaya in forty-one," Major Tucker said, trying to fill in the silence. "What was interesting was why the British didn't hold out longer."

"I don't want to hear about morale," Mountain said. "British troops are not the point about morale."

"Well, sir," the major continued calmly, "consider the problem. Malaya was a country that had been asleep for over two hundred years. But that wasn't the real reason the country collapsed. Nor was it that the climate was impossible. The troops simply hadn't been trained. Their equipment was too heavy and awkward for jungle fighting. But most of all, they had no hardness, no fighting spirit. They were too civilized. They weren't fanatic enough."

"Rubbish," Mountain said. "You either had a good war or you didn't."

"I don't understand, sir," said a lieutenant.

"I'm not interested in what lieutenants have to say or what they understand," Mountain said. "Or majors for that matter. None of you knows what it's like to stick a bayonet into someone's belly."

"I beg your pardon, sir," the lieutenant said. "I spent two years in Korea."

"Korea was a monstrosity," Mountain said. "No one was ever there. I won't hear any more about Korea."

I forced myself to take a bite of food.

"Consider the complete destruction of the Japanese Twenty-eighth Army," Major Tucker said hopefully. "They were caught and surrounded in Burma. It was a fantastic engagement. They were completely destroyed by the Seventeenth and Nineteenth Indian Divisions!"

"Captain, I am not interested in what happened to the Twenty-eighth Japanese Army," Mountain said. "I don't want to consider anything. I am only interested in what happens to one man. I want to know what one man feels like when, half-alive, he has a ring chopped off his finger by an enemy soldier. I am interested in the mind of the battle-fatigued soldier bending over a native woman. I am interested in what it feels like to see a man burn alive from a flamethrower. You are in the ice age of military thought, Captain. There is no more power of maneuver."

Mountain choked a little on his food. He wiped his mouth with the back of his hand and unloosened his shirt from his belt.

"I want to know what one man does when faced with fear," he continued, rising from his chair. "Does he relieve himself in his pants or does he fight?"

"Are you all right, sir?" Major Tucker asked.

Mountain took out his pistol and pointed it at the major's forehead.

"I want to know what one man thinks before the trigger is pulled, Captain."

One of the lieutenants started to stand up.

"Don't do that," I heard myself say.

The lieutenant sank back in his chair.

"Mountain," I said, "you'd better put it away. There's not much point in killing these guys."

"Not much point, you say," Mountain said quietly, sitting down. "There is no point at all."

He stared at the ground, the pistol hanging loosely from his fingertips. A lieutenant stood up and slipped quietly away.

"I would tell you a story, but I don't feel like it," Mountain said, placing the pistol on the table. "I just don't feel like it. You can all go to hell."

There was nothing to do. The major talked about something. A kind of delaying action. I don't remember. We sat quietly, waiting. Mountain looked at his plate. He took a small bite out of his pork chop, lifted it up to his mouth, hesitated, and then dropped the fork down on the plate. Then he stood up and pointed the pistol at the side of his head and pulled the trigger. A good deal of his head got on the table and a little of it on my pants. There wasn't any more to it than that. Everyone was stunned, of course, but it wasn't long before they swung into action. Someone pointed an M-1 at me. In a little while the MP's came and took me away.

The next day they sent me down to Governors Island. They didn't really believe what I told them. It doesn't matter. All I can do now is wait for them to decide something, which for them, I guess, isn't such a hard thing to do.